Two classic novels by Joan Hohl, one of today's most beloved romance authors . . .

WHILE THE FIRE RAGES

As ambitious as she was beautiful, Jo Lawrence ran the Renninger Corporation's multimillion-dollar hotel business with skill and ease. But when her boss died and his moody brother took charge, Jo's busy world was turned upside down. Jo knew she was falling in love with Brett Renninger from the start, but Brett's odd behavior and short temper made her wonder if their relationship could survive the transition from the boardroom to the bedroom.

THE GAME IS PLAYED

Still smarting from the pain of a disastrous relationship, Dr. Helen Cassidy buried herself in the work she loved, convinced that another man could only bring her more pain. But one man—charming, relentless Marshall Kirk—was determined to prove her wrong.

THE BEST OF JOAN HOHL

WRITING AS AMII LORIN

WHILE THE FIRE RAGES
—AND—
THE GAME IS PLAYED

LEISURE BOOKS　NEW YORK CITY

A LEISURE BOOK®

September 1989

Published by

Dorchester Publishing Co., Inc.
276 Fifth Avenue
New York, NY 10001

WHILE THE FIRE RAGES Copyright©MCMLXXXIV by Joan Hohl
THE GAME IS PLAYED Copyright©MCMLXXXI by Amii Lorin

Printed in the United States of America.

WHILE THE FIRE RAGES

For Vivian Stephens,
who started it all for me,
with deep respect, appreciation, and gratitude.

CHAPTER ONE

Brett Renninger stood at the wide window staring at the wind-tossed, grayish-green sea. The Atlantic flung its waves with uncaring force against the shoreline bordering Ocean City, New Jersey. The wide window covered most of the wall in what was now an office but had been the living room of Brett's brother Wolf's apartment. The personal quarters he kept in one of many Renninger hotels.

Wolf.

Brett sighed, deeply, soundlessly. It was over three weeks now, three long, tension-filled weeks. He had been the logical choice to take over, but even had he not been, he'd have volunteered. Of course, he had not had to volunteer—he'd been summarily drafted.

Had anyone asked him if he could metaphorically fill Wolf's shoes one week, one day, ten minutes before the call came, Brett would have answered promptly, emphatically: No way!

That phone call. Brett's lips twisted. The memory of it was vividly clear and fresh. Perhaps it always would be.

As his hands had been employed with a bottle and a corkscrew

11

when the phone rang in his Atlanta apartment, he had nodded his assent when the lovely young thing sitting close to him on the long, velvet couch asked sweetly, "Would you like me to answer that, Brett, honey?"

Brett could even remember the assessing glance he'd swept over the curvacious blonde as she rose languidly, experience again the curl of desire he'd felt watching her glide across the plush carpeting to where the phone rested on his desk. He'd returned his attention to the business in hand as the blonde murmured a husky hello, only to slice a frowning glance at the slim gold watch on his wrist when she said softly, "Brett, honey, it's a Mrs. Renninger. Your mother?"

He had returned to Atlanta late that afternoon, after a three-week-long trip to New Mexico to iron out the final details concerning the company's plans for the erection of a tri-complex condominium unit. In the seconds required to set aside the bottle and walk to his desk, he'd chided himself for ever entertaining the belief that his mother would wait until he was in his office the following morning for her regulation briefing on his trip. Not on the outcome, of course, for that was—at least in his mother's mind—a foregone conclusion. Thus he'd deliberately laced his tone with rueful amusement and dispensed with the usual greeting.

"Yes, sir?" he'd drawled insolently, fully expecting to hear his mother's appreciative chuckle ripple along the line from Miami. The tightly controlled tone of his mother's voice washed the amusement from his face.

"Wolf has been injured in an accident, Brett. He's in a hospital in Boston."

Brett could still feel the shock of his mother's opening statement, could hear the echo of his own exclaimed, "What?"

"Micki called me less then ten minutes ago," she'd supplied tensely. "I have no details, as the child was practically incoherent but"—the choking pause that followed instilled cold fear in

12

Brett—"I—she—Brett, she said the doctors aren't sure if they can save him."

Standing at the window, staring sightlessly at the roiling sea, Brett shivered with the memory of the never-before-heard stark terror in his mother's voice. In truth, the emotion that had momentarily gripped him had come damned close to a like terror.

His big brother, Wolf?

Thankfully, the need for action had sent the destructive emotion into retreat almost immediately.

"I'll leave at once, Mother," he'd begun with forced calm.

"I'm going with you, I've called Eric," she said, referring to her third son. "He's having the Lear readied. We'll be in Atlanta within two hours."

"I'll be waiting."

Never would he forget that early-morning flight north: his mother's colorless face—for the very first time revealing every one of its sixty-five years; Eric's handsomeness, strangely enhanced by his rigidly controlled expression; his own thoughts of Wolf. Wolf—the hero of his boyhood, the—

The rustle of papers from behind him scattered the memory. Turning slowly, Brett ran a contemplative gaze over the gleaming dark head bent over Wolf's large, rectangular desk.

The super-efficient assistant. Brett's assessment was not complimentary. Lids narrowing over eyes chilled to a steely gray by his thoughts, he inventoried the woman's exterior.

Even seated, her height was obvious. Somewhere between five feet nine and ten, he estimated—correctly. Slender—almost too slender, her fine bone structure lending an appearance of fragility.

Brett had to suppress a snort of disdain. A confection spun of pure steel, he condemned scathingly, his glance raking her delicate facial features, the pink-tinged ivory skin that covered them, the beautifully sculpted lips that hid perfect white teeth.

13

Thick, long hair in a rich, dark brown adorned her classically shaped head. Brett knew that when, eventually, she raised her eyes from her work, she would gaze at him from gold-flecked hazel eyes surrounded by lashes as dark and full as her hair, and so long as to appear artificial.

Brett had committed the vitals to memory: JoAnne Lawrence; age twenty-eight; unmarried; degree in business management, a certificate in hotel management. She had gone to work for the Renninger Corporation on completion of training, first as an assistant manager, then manager of a Renninger hotel in Pittsburg, Pennsylvania. Three years earlier she had been hired as the assistant to the assistant to the East Coast manager of Renninger Corporation—Madam President's firstborn, Wolfgang. She had secured the coveted position of first assistant fifteen months before when Wolf's righthand man, wanting a change, asked for and was granted a transfer to the newly open Hawaii region.

His face free of expression, Brett stared at the shining crown of her head. Oh, yes, he knew quite a bit about Ms. JoAnne Lawrence—usually referred to as Jo. He had made it his business to know. Neither idle curiosity nor personal interest had motivated his research. His interest in her had been aroused in a hotel lounge in Boston late one night nearly three weeks ago by the stricken face and anguished voice of his sister-in-law, Wolf's wife, Micki.

"He was with a woman, Brett," Micki had blurted suddenly. "Probably his assistant, Jo."

At first, Brett had given little credence to her outburst. The waiting, nerve-shattering days following Wolf's accident had left them all on edge. Micki was distraught and very close to exhaustion. Hurting for her, feeling protective, he had tried to soothe what he thought were her irrational fears.

"Honey, if this Jo whoever is his assistant, his being with her would be the normal order of business."

14

"Not if he was trying to conceal it, and from all indications, he was."

"What indications?" Brett had deliberately injected a chiding note into his tone.

"I know how you feel about Wolf, Brett, but, please, don't patronize me." Micki had blinked furiously against the tears shimmering in her eyes.

Brett was very fond of Micki. In fact, he rather envied Wolf. His brothers, at least, had been extremely lucky in their chosen life mates. Seeing Micki so near the breaking point alarmed him.

"I'm sorry." Reaching across the dimly lighted table, he'd clasped her hand with his. "Okay. Tell me what these indications are."

"I had a commiserating call from a friend at home today," she'd begun haltingly. "She'd read of Wolf's accident in the paper. I was thanking her for her concern when she interrupted with 'and to think I saw you only hours before it happened. I called to you but you were already in the car. But, of course, Wolf told you he saw me'—I was stunned."

"And that's it?" he'd asked incredulously.

"No." Micki shook her head impatiently. "I was confused. I told my friend Wolf hadn't mentioned seeing her. Then I asked her where she'd seen him. She said right in front of the hotel, *this* hotel. She added that Wolf seemed distracted and in a hurry, and that he hadn't even acknowledged her greeting."

"But, honey, I fail to see any indication of a clandestine meeting in that!" Brett, fully aware of Micki's utter weariness, had tried to reason with her. "It sounds to me like the work of a malicious woman whose nose had been put out of joint because a man, an *important* man, did not give her the recognition she probably thinks she deserves."

Micki had been shaking her head in denial before he'd finished his rationalization. "No, Brett, not this woman. She is one of our best friends. In fact, I'm sure you know her. Cindy Grant? She and her husband, Benny, are the cub's godparents."

15

Now, as he had three weeks ago, Brett smiled gently at the reference to Wolf's son, dubbed "the cub." Now the smile was as fleeting as it had been that night.

"Okay, there was no malicious intent on Cindy's part." He'd sighed. "But I still cannot believe you think this sketchy information enough evidence to bear out a conviction. *If* the woman in the car was his assistant, she had every right to be there."

"Oh, it was her." Micki's bitter tone had been a shock simply because Brett had never heard the like of it from her before. "I checked. She was registered." Her lips twisted. "Her room was on the floor above his."

Considering what she'd been through the preceding days, Brett had stifled his growing impatience. "Honey, she's his assistant. There's nothing at all unusual ab—"

"No. Not as a rule," she'd interrupted harshly. "She travels with him quite often. And, like a fool, I'd believed quite innocently."

Brett had felt heartsick at the pain in her voice, the anguish in her usually so-bright blue eyes. He knew only too well what she was going through. Perhaps that was why she'd confided in him and not Eric. She'd sought a fellow sufferer. Still, unconvinced, he'd objected.

"Micki, there is no proof."

"Wolf told me, before he left, that she would not be going with him." Micki's response had had the measured sound of a death knell. "He offered the information. I had not asked. I think I have a very good case, Brett," she'd gone on in a whisper, her voice reedy with weariness. "By the way, her name is Jo Lawrence. She's beautiful."

Beautiful?
Hardly.
At that moment it seemed the vibrations from Brett's intense stare penetrated the concentration Jo Lawrence was applying to her work. Lifting her head, she met his stare with thought-

clouded hazel eyes, one perfectly shaped, dark brow arching questioningly.

"Is something wrong, Mr. Renninger?"

Everything's wrong, Ms. Lawrence.

"No." The tiny frown that briefly marred her smooth brow told him his attempted smile had been cynical. "I was just thinking."

"I see."

Her eyes drifted to the window to gaze out at the wind-ruffled, white-capped waves. Sitting up straight, she raised a slim hand to massage the back of her neck.

Beautiful?

In sudden decision, Brett strode to the door, taking his tweed jacket from the back of a chair as he passed it.

"I'm going to run out to the house." he said, referring to the home Wolf and Micki owned a short distance away. He tossed the toneless statement over his shoulder without looking at her again. "If you need me for anything, call me—or put it on hold till I get back." He was very careful not to slam the door behind him.

The silver Porsche 928S gleamed dully in the watery, late-afternoon sunlight. As Brett pushed through the wide, double-glass entrance doors, his eyes caressed the sleek lines of the powerful machine, parked in the no-parking section in the motel forecourt. He'd made sure the car was driven up from Atlanta for him as soon as possible and was happy now that it was at his disposal. It didn't really matter where he parked the car since, as the motel was closed for the season, the large lot was empty.

Standing beside the car, the wind sweeping back his gold-streaked, ash-blond hair, Brett breathed in deeply, filling his lungs with the crisp, sea-scented air. A raucous, mournful cry drew his attention, and, tilting his head back, he followed the gliding flight pattern of a lone sea gull. The bird's solitary passage struck a responsive chord in him.

For what seemed a very long time now, he'd known a like, if

17

earthbound, solitude. Even when in the company of others—others, in his case, being female—his soul had emitted a silent, lonely cry.

"Damn all women."

Even as he muttered the oath Brett knew he didn't mean it. There were women and then there were women. Most assuredly he would never damn Micki or his brother Eric's lovely lady-wife. But there were others, like his former playmate—in no way had she ever been a real *wife* to him—and the woman whose presence he'd escaped moments ago.

What in blazing hell were you thinking of?

The admonition was not self-directed. In his mind he flung the question at possibly the one and only man he'd hesitate in verbalizing it to: his brother, the formidable Wolfgang.

Damn you, Wolf, you had it all! Brett, folding his long length behind the wheel, mentally chastized the idol who had suddenly developed feet of clay. You had Micki, and two beautiful children, and the good life, and you risked it all—and for what?

Brett shook his head in wonder as he inserted the key into the ignition. With his inner eye he envisioned the object of his censure: whole, that slashing grin softening the chiseled planes of his face, his eyes glittering silver, the formally lone Wolf.

Do you love her, big brother? Or were you merely playing king stud?

Twisting the key with unnecessary force, Brett growled, "Get it in gear!" He was not referring to the car, which had quickly purred to life without a complaint.

Driving along the nearly deserted streets instilled in Brett a vaguely eerie sensation. It was as if the warning had gone out to evacuate and everybody had heard it but him.

Brett smiled at the whimsical thought. Actually, he rather liked the desolate look of the summer resort town in mid-October. He did not like the oddly abandoned look of his brother's large white-brick ranch house.

Separating the proper key from the others on his gold ring,

Brett loped along the flagstone walk to the wide door. Before he had a chance to put the key to use the door was opened by Wolf's housekeeper.

"Well, hello, Mrs. Jorgeson." Brett's smile was easy; he liked *this* woman. "I didn't expect to see you here today."

"Good afternoon, Mr. Renninger." Gertrude Jorgeson's return smile revealed a mutual regard. "I'm putting up the last of the tomatoes."

"In what way?" Brett's frown conveyed his ignorance of the hows and whys of putting up anything.

"Into sauce and stewed tomatoes." Gertrude smiled through eyes grown wise from sixty-one years of observing life. "Your brother and your sister-in-law love stewed tomatoes."

"I see." Brett's tone was noncommittal. He personally hated stewed tomatoes. "Well, I won't get in your way. I'll be in Wolf's study."

"All right, sir." Gertrude smiled again. "Would you like a cup of coffee?"

"No. Thank you." Brett grinned. "I think I'll help myself to the Scotch."

"As you like." The small, well-rounded woman turned back toward the kitchen. "Call me if there is anything I can help you with."

In the study, Brett went directly to the liquor cabinet set into one wall between well-stocked bookshelves. After measuring a good two inches of the expensive whisky into a short, squat glass, he splashed in a token amount of seltzer water, then, sipping at the liquid appreciatively, he glanced around the comfortable room.

The earth-tone colors, the functional yet luxurious furnishings, the oversized desk, stamped the room as Wolf's domain. However, there were small signs indicating the domain had been invaded.

A smile softened Brett's finely molded lips as his eyes paused on a large, brazenly red fire engine parked neatly in one corner.

He had witnessed his nephew tearing through the house on the riding toy with the same panache Wolf displayed behind the wheel of his equally brazen red Ferrari.

His thought banished the soft smile. The Ferrari was gone, totally demolished in the accident. It was several seconds before a twinge of pain in his jaw brought Brett out of his reverie to the realization of his tightly clenched teeth.

Damn, it was only a car! A car can be replaced. He would gladly write out his own personal check for a half dozen Ferraris if only Wolf . . .

Literally shaking himself out of his introspection, Brett moved purposefully to the desk. It had grown completely dark beyond the window behind him before he pushed the padded leather covered chair back and stood up.

The plot sickens.

Raking long, bony fingers through thick strands of slightly wavy hair, he grimaced sourly at the innocent-looking envelope on the desktop. The tightness in his stomach bore out his appraisal of the play unfolding in his mind.

Raising eyes gone steely gray with anger, Brett ran his gaze slowly around the room, seeing everything, seeing nothing, the document neatly folded inside the long, buff-colored envelope imprinted on his inner vision.

Does she love him?

Damn it! Whether or not Jo Lawrence was in love with Wolf should not be his uppermost consideration! Micki was the one who would suffer from this. *If* she found out.

Lids narrowing over eyes now icy with calculation, he sliced his gaze back to the desk. He had discovered the damned thing inside the locked top drawer of the desk, which, as he was in possession of Wolf's keyring, he'd opened without the slightest compunction.

As expected, he'd found everything pertaining to the company in perfect order. It was that one long envelope that had shaken him.

It was his job to make sure Micki did not find out.

"Damn!"

His very long, deceptively lean looking frame taut with frustration and anger, Brett snatched the empty whisky glass and walked out of the room with his habitual long stride.

Well trained to neatness by a caring mother, he rinsed the glass under steaming hot water and placed it in the draining rack beside the sink, his mind examining the ways in which to handle this new, unsavory development.

I ought to strangle the bitch.

Impractical, but effective. A wry smile shadowed his perfectly shaped lips as he strode back into his brother's study, his eyes, cold as the North Atlantic, fastening on the cause of his anger.

Crossing to the desk, he extended a hand to pluck the envelope up, then, turning abruptly, he walked out of the room. After activating the computerized alarm system to secure the house for the night, he left the house and loped to the low sports car shimmering like liquid silver in the moonlight.

The weightless document lay heavy in Brett's breast pocket as he backed the vehicle out of the driveway. Instead of making the turn that would take him back to the center of town, he spun the leather-covered wheel and headed toward the bay.

Now, in early evening, the streets were even more deserted than they'd been when he left the motel. The uncanny sensation of being the only living being in a dark, abandoned ghost town was even more pronounced.

Parking at the base of a street that dead-ended at the bay, Brett uncoiled his considerable length from behind the wheel and strolled to stand on the wide, oily-looking wood pilings.

The moonlight struck a glittering path across the ever-shifting water, dancing in time to the muted swish as wavelets wound themselves around the spindly legs supporting long, narrow docking piers. Empty now, the berthing slips had a forsaken look that would vanish with the return of spring and the water craft of all sizes, both motorized and those with the tall masts.

21

To the lone man, standing with hands thrust deep into the pockets of hand-tailored slacks, the scene was more conducive to contemplation than depression.

Because of the frantic mental state his sister-in-law had been in, Brett had found it relatively easy to convince Micki of Wolf's fidelity.

Without shame or misgiving, he had lied through his teeth.

The memory was strong, fanning the anger seething in him to a full, outraged blaze.

"I must know," Micki had whispered brokenly. "Brett, please, you must find out if it's true."

Suspicion aroused is not guilt proven. Brett would have preferred living with the doubt.

"To what purpose now, honey?" he'd soothed, attempting to dissuade her, knowing too well the hell in facing the truth. "You've been through so much, and you've got to get through a lot more. Why put yourself through the agony of—"

"You don't understand," she'd interrupted fiercely, grasping his hand tightly. "I don't want to know for myself." Her lids dropped over eyes sparkling like blue jewels from their glaze of tears, and she swallowed with obvious difficulty. "I'd just as soon *not* know, but you have got to go to New York and find out if it's true."

"You're right, I don't understand," Brett exploded, if softly. "If you would rather not know, then why . . . ?"

"For *him!*" Again she'd not let him finish. "I think—I thought I knew him, and the man I thought I knew would not enter lightly into infidelity. He must love her very much."

Brett had actually felt the pain that had scored her face. In that instant the rage had been born deep inside him.

"Go to New York, Brett." Micki's eyes pleaded as effectively as her quivering voice. "And, if you find it's true, bring her back with you."

"What!" Mindful of the other patrons scattered around the

dimly lighted lounge, Brett had managed to keep his tone low, but it was all the more intense for the incredulity lacing it.

"If"—a spasm fleetingly distorted her lovely features and she bit her lips before correcting herself harshly—"*when* he comes around, he will need the strength of the woman he loves."

Her slender hand grasping his tightened, oval nails digging into his palm. Brett felt the pain, not in his hand but in his heart. The rage spread fiery fingers into his mind with her next impassioned words.

"I hate it, Brett. I hate the very thought of it." Two tears escaped their blinking bounds to slide slowly down her cheeks. "But I want him to live. Oh, dear God, I want him to live, and I will use anyone, suffer *anything*, if it will help him." Staring directly into his eyes, she'd begged, "Don't think of me, Brett, think of him. Go to New York."

Of course he'd given in to her. How could he not? The affection and respect he'd felt for her from the beginning blossomed into pure filial love. He would do anything, perform any task she charged him with.

After escorting her to her room, he had gone to his own long enough to pick up a few things. One of those things was the phone, over which he informed his mother of his intentions—but not his motives. Another of those things was Wolf's briefcase, which he'd taken possession of on arrival but not as yet opened.

During the short flight from Boston to New York, he'd perused the contents of Wolf's case. Most of the papers inside were directly related to the reason Wolf had gone to Boston in the first place—that of the feasibility of renovating a rather run-down, old hotel into modern condominiums and the company's acquisition of same if the resultant figures proved out that feasibility.

One slim folder stood out glaringly in its difference.

The data confined between the covers of the cream-colored folder had come from the personnel manager directly to Wolf. One quick glance over the four sheets of pristine white paper and

Brett had a crawling suspicion he was closer to knowing the answer to Micki's question.

During the cab ride from Kennedy to Wolf's spacious apartment with its panoramic view of Central Park, Brett came very close to hating the formerly adored one.

It had been a long day. In truth, it had been three very long days, each one riddled with fear as Brett, his mother, Eric, and Micki, so brave, so vulnerable, waited, waited, waited.

Brett had been tired, and disillusioned, and bitter, yet, before dropping onto Wolf's over-oversized bed, he had more thoroughly studied the four sheets of paper. Each paper contained a detailed account of the professional performance of four company employees—three men and one woman.

The information had been gathered, at Wolf's request, for the purpose of choosing a replacement for a retiring senior executive of the East Coast branch of Renninger Corporation.

The lone female under consideration for the coveted position was JoAnne Lawrence.

Brett's last thought before falling asleep had been: I just might throw up.

The following morning, feeling charged with restless energy after days spent in the confines of hospital waiting rooms and corridors, Brett politely declined the apartment doorman's respectful offer of a cab.

Had he wanted to ride, there would have been no need to do it in the back of a world-famous—infamous?—New York City cab. All that would have been required were a few words spoken into a telephone and a limousine, plush, comfortable, fitted out to the nines, would have been waiting at the curb for him. When the occasion warranted, Brett was not averse to using his name, position, power, or wealth. This particular morning, Mr. Renninger chose to walk.

His brother's briefcase firmly in hand, he strode off, appearing, at least to the casual glance, much like hundreds of other young executives en route to the city's amalgam of offices. The more discerning eye would have noted the supple leather of handmade shoes, the fine material of perfectly tailored, vested, chocolate-brown suit, the real silk of muted shrimp-toned shirt. The discerning female eye would appreciate the long, well-knit torso, the thick crop of sun-streaked, loose waves caressing a beautifully sculpted head, features so sharply etched as to appear austere in their masculine beauty, lips that promised heaven in their pleasure, hell in their disfavor. At the moment the tightness of those lips proclaimed extreme disfavor with someone.

Brett's strides ate up the sidewalk. Seeming so self-absorbed as to be aware of nothing around him, he was, in fact, fully conscious of everything within the radius of his near-perfect vision. Eyes dull steel, flat in contemplation of what may lay at destination's end, he strode on, his mind alive with his sister-in-law's charge:

"Go to New York, Brett, and, if you find it's true, bring her back with you."

Now, as he approached the tall glass-and-steel building that housed the offices of East Coast Region—Renninger Corporation, his mind repeated the same silent reply as the night before.

No way in hell!

Stepping out of the elevator at the twenty-third floor, Brett walked briskly down the carpeted hall to the office of the personnel manager. When he walked out of the office, fifteen minutes later, the retiring senior executive's replacement had been chosen. The choice was not a female.

From personnel, Brett took the elevator up three more floors. His body taut with purpose, he strode to a solid, unmarked door, twisted the handle, and, eyes narrowing with intent, stepped inside.

"May I help you?"

The query was directed at him from a frowning young woman seated behind the latest model in typewriters. Her confused expression made a demand: Who the devil are you? And how did you get up here unannounced?

A sardonic smile teased Brett's tightly compressed mouth. It *had* been a long time since his last foray into New York.

"Is Ms. Lawrence in?" Brett asked quietly, the smile tugging harder at his lips as he observed the confusion deepen in the young woman's eyes. Her expressive face telegraphed her mental self-questioning: Should I know this man? Is he someone important?

"Yes, sir." The secretary nodded. "But she is very busy. She left orders not to be disturbed."

"She'll see me." His cool, deliberately arrogant tone brought out the excellent secretarial school training instilled in the young woman who, at any other time, Brett would have found more than passably attractive.

"Really?" she replied with matching coolness. "I doubt it. She *is* very busy."

This pretty ball of fluff was actually giving him the brushoff! So much for one's self-image of intimidating authority!

Play time's over, honey.

"Press the little switch down on your intercom," he instructed patiently, "and inform *your* boss that *her* boss is waiting."

"Her boss?" The girl's brows drew together. "I don't understand."

Brett sighed. Of course she didn't understand. How could she? Hanging on to his patience, he smiled benignly.

"Tell Ms. Lawrence Brett Renninger wishes to see her."

"Oh my God!" The woman's eyes swallowed half her face.

"Exactly."

Wide brown eyes staring at him beseechingly, the girl's trembling fingers groped for the intercom. Before she could press the correct button, a door three feet to her right was thrust open and a melodious but impatient voice demanded:

"Reni! Who are you socializing with? I need that report you're working on."

"Ms. Lawrence, I . . . I . . . he . . ."

The attempted explanation died on her lips as JoAnne Lawrence followed her voice into the room.

At first sight of her something that had died inside Brett made its first faint stirrings toward resurrection.

Beautiful?

Brett was hard put not to laugh aloud. As a descriptive adjective, beautiful, in regards to the tall woman glaring at him, seemed woefully inadequate.

"Who are you? And what are you doing in here?"

Brett had been thankful for her imperious tone; it reminded him of exactly who this woman was.

"Oh, Ms. Lawrence," Reni squeaked fearfully, "he's . . . he's . . ."

"Reni! Will you please finish that report!" JoAnne's eyes sliced a quelling glance to Reni, then shot back to him. "Answer me!"

"With pleasure." Brett felt a curl of satisfaction when her impossibly long lashes flickered at his too-smooth, too-soft tone. Experiencing a sensation quite like joy, he let her have it with both barrels.

"Brett Renninger," he introduced himself silkily, feeling the curl of satisfaction spreading at the stillness that gripped her. "And I am here in the capacity of your employer for the duration."

In retrospect, Brett had to admit her aplomb was magnificient. There was a split second of appalled hesitation, then she stepped toward him gracefully, slim right hand extended.

"I'm sorry, sir," she apologized in a soft, clear voice.

A cool breeze skipped across the water, ruffling its inky-dark surface. Brett shivered inside the insufficient protection of the tweed sport coat. Chilled out of his reverie, he moved his shoulders in a tension-relieving shrug, a vague hollowness inside bringing awareness of how long it had been since he'd eaten.

At least he attributed the empty feeling to hunger.

Turning abruptly, he frowned as his ear caught the faint

27

crackle of the envelope nestled inside his breast pocket. The hole in his middle grew to a mini chasm.

Cold all over, Brett strode to the low-slung car, repressing a shudder as he slid behind the wheel. Punishing the ignition once again for his own conflicting emotions, he slammed his palm against the gear stick and backed the car the length of the street.

It had been so ridiculously easy to reassure Micki of Wolf's fidelity.

Cruising along the deserted street, a grimace broke the tight line of Brett's lips. He had simply relayed almost verbatim JoAnne's—rehearsed?—response to his interrogation in her office that morning.

Yes, she had been with Wolf in Boston.

No, the original arrangements had not been for her to accompany him.

Wolf had called her late in the afternoon the day after his arrival in Boston.

"I don't like the setup." JoAnne had quoted Wolf. "I think they believe they're dealing with a lightweight here. They should know better. But then, so should I. I failed to run a routine check. Get research on it now. I want a full report by tomorrow noon, hand delivered, by you."

Yes, she had delivered the report to him the following afternoon. They had gone over it together during dinner.

Yes, he had booked a room for her at the hotel but, as she had scheduled a meeting with his staff for the following morning, he drove her to the airport sometime around eleven that night. She had flown back to New York on the same company plane that had carried her to Boston.

Yes, he must have been on the way back to the hotel when the accident occurred.

Micki had gratefully, tearfully swallowed it whole; hook, line, and sinker.

Brett was a different type of fish. Keeping his own council, he had decided to search out the true depth of JoAnne's seemingly still waters.

Depth indeed!

Brett's entire body felt icy except for that one rectangular spot on his chest. The envelope crackled again as he mounted the steps in the silent motel.

I really ought to strangle the bitch.

Unlocking the apartment door, he strode angrily inside and stopped dead. Assuming she'd have gone to her own room by now, he had not expected to find her waiting for him. Brett voiced the first thought that came to his mind.

"Trouble?"

"No." Her sleek, dark hair moved sharply in the negative. "I just now decided to call it a day." An odd, sad smile brushed her soft, moist lips. "Possibly because I also just realized I haven't eaten since breakfast."

Brett shelved the idea of strangling her; very likely because he knew, subconsciously, that if he touched her, the strangling would come after he'd done a lot of other things to her first.

Instead, he took her out to dinner.

CHAPTER TWO

Absently unaware of the sensuousness of her actions, Jo toyed with her tulip-shaped wineglass, the fingers of her left hand caressing the stem with long, evocative strokes, the tip of her right forefinger slowly circling the rim.

Oblivious to the gray gaze following her finger play, she sighed with the unwilling realization that for the last several hours her thought pattern had mirrored the movement of her fingertips—round and round.

Why does he dislike me so?

After three weeks of regular repetition, the question was a familiar, if painful, refrain. She had repeatedly scoured her mind for reasons for his antipathy, and she came up blank time after time. Other than that first regretful morning in her office, she had scrupulously shown him all due respect. Surely the man had more intelligence than to carry a grudge for so slight an infraction! He *had* barged unannounced into her office! Her reaction to his sudden appearance had been completely normal.

Yet, since that first morning, uncomfortable waves of tension simmered between them whenever they were in the same room together, regardless of the number of feet that measured the distance between them.

It was more than unnerving; it was disheartening, because her initial reaction to him had been very positive, deeply favorable. In effect, Jo didn't even have to *be* in the same room with him to reexperience her initial reaction; all she had to do was *think* of him and tiny little physical devils began a game of touch and run with her libido. It was enough to make a fully mature, intelligent, reasonably level-headed woman weep with longing!

Though Jo was unconscious of the yearning sigh that whispered through her lips, Brett, very obviously, was not.

"Tired?"

Blinking herself out of the fruitless introspection, Jo donned a mask of nonchalance before raising her eyes to his.

"Yes." Her reply was blunt for two reasons; first, it was nothing but the plain truth; second, his taunting tone had instilled a chill. Was it her imagination, or did he continually use that exact tone with her for some reason she was too dim to decipher? Keeping a rigid harness on her own tongue—which did itch to lash a bit—she added tonelessly, "It's been a long three weeks."

For some obscure reason her statement seemed to anger him. Jo's carefully constructed mask slipped to reveal bafflement when Brett stiffened abruptly.

"I imagine it has been," he drawled icily. "Time has a tendency to drag when you're missing someone."

Jo's bafflement retreated at the advance of sheer incredulity. What the deuce was he talking about? Missing someone? Whoever could he . . . good grief, he couldn't possibly be referring to Gary? How had he even heard of that ill-fated involvement? Though she wasn't aware of any gossip about her breakup with Gary Devlin, there was always the chance he had heard through the company grapevine. This man would surely demand to know all there was to know about an assistant he had no voice in choosing. All there was to know officially, and unofficially. But why would he think she was missing Gary? It was almost a year and a half since . . .

"If you're ready to leave?"

Brett's cold query put an end to her conjecturing. Employing fierce determination to keep her eyebrows from joining in a frown, Jo let a cool nod suffice for an answer. Inside, she seethed to tell him to go take a flying leap into the bay. Who the hell was he to think he could speak so condescendingly to her!

Inside the sports car, Jo sat rigidly erect, staring out the windshield all the way back to the motel.

Did he *have* to smell so damned good? Jo blessed the darkness that concealed the rush of heat to her face at the unexpected thought.

Slowly, very carefully, she inhaled, drawing the mingled scent of pure male and expensive aftershave into her senses.

I wonder what he tastes like? The heat in her cheeks intensified at the reflection. Jo shifted against the supple leather covering the bucket seat, becoming more uncomfortable from the heat uncoiling inside than the warmth singeing her outermost layer of skin.

Eyes forced ruthlessly forward, she forbade her sight the pleasure of examining his breath-robbing, austerely handsome face, the contemplation of the possible ecstasy his beautiful mouth could wreak on hers.

What does he look like stripped to the buff? That consideration cut her breath off in her throat.

I am going totally mad!

Thankfully, at that moment Brett drove the car onto the motel parking lot and her musings were shifted to the edge of consciousness. The ensuing opening and closing of car doors were the only sounds that broke the silence from the time they left the car until they came to an awkward halt at the door to her room.

For one pulse-shattering, brief instant, Jo fancifully imagined she saw a flame leap in the remote grayness of the eyes studying

32

her face. Then, with a brusquely muttered good night, he spun and strode to the door of Wolf's former lair.

Stepping quickly into the pitch-black room, Jo closed and locked the door, then sagged back against its solid support. After gulping in numerous deep, calming breaths, she pushed her limp body erect, her hand groping for the wall switch.

For one infinitesimal moment there she had actually thought he might kiss her. What would she have done if he had? Jo frowned as she mentally ticked off her possible responses. Would she have chastized him in a scathing, acidic tone? Or, would she, perhaps, have laughed it off as of little meaning? Or, would she, much less likely, have allowed her palm to meet his cheek with resounding force?

Who are you trying to kid? she asked herself wearily. After three weeks of wondering, hoping, longing, you know exactly how you would have responded: You would have wrapped yourself around him like a wet bath towel!

The thought conjured the image and an anticipatory shiver feathered her skin, raising tiny goose bumps on her arms and thighs. Her physical response to the mere idea of being crushed to Brett's hard, lean body no longer had the power to shock her, although it certainly had the first time it had occurred.

Performing the routine before-bed ritual of cleansing her skin and brushing her teeth, Jo's thoughts backtracked to the first time she'd felt that hot-cold reaction to him.

It had certainly not happened that first morning, when he'd presented himself to her. She'd been much too flustered and embarrassed then to notice much of anything other than the fact that the Renninger brothers bore very little resemblance, physically or in personality.

Actually, he'd been in her office a very short time, during which he'd fired questions at her in a taut, angry tone that she'd later attributed to anxiety over Wolf's accident.

Somewhat proud of herself for the appearance of composure she'd maintained, she had answered his questions clearly and concisely. It was when it became obvious that he was about to make an abrupt departure that Jo, voicing a query of her own, received the impression of his dislike of her. Confused, wondering why he should dislike her when he didn't even know her, she had nevertheless repeated her question when he hesitated over answering.

"How *is* Wolf doing?"

"He is still on the critical list," he'd finally, begrudgingly answered, confusing her all the more by his apparent unwillingness to discuss his brother's condition. "I'm leaving now to fly back to Boston," he'd gone on coldly, long fingers curling around the doorknob, giving the impression he couldn't get out fast enough. "If there are any questions"—he'd paused, tone hardening—"pertaining to business, call the hotel and leave a message. I'll get back to you."

Stunned by both his tone and his attitude, frowning in perplexity, Jo had mutely watched as he opened the door then closed it again before turning to pin her with an icy, narrow-eyed stare.

"By the way," he'd almost purred, "I've tapped Bob Harley for the executive slot opening soon." The silky satisfaction in his voice went through her like the sound of a nail being scraped the length of a blackboard. "Sorry about that."

With a twist of his lips that was more a sneer than a smile, he strode from her office, leaving her staring after him in total bewilderment.

Four days later he was back.

Those four days had been rather trying for Jo—what with holding down the fort, so to speak, and worrying about Wolf, she'd been getting a teensy bit short-tempered.

In truth, Jo almost adored Wolfgang Renninger. In her admittedly prejudiced opinion he was kind, considerate, oftimes droll, and a dynamic businessman. Her liking for him had been spontaneous, her respect endless. Strangely, she had never felt even the mildest tug of physical attraction toward him. Wolf was employer, friend, and, during a few weak moments Jo had experienced, confidant.

Brett was a whole new ball game.

Added to the business responsibilities she'd shouldered—she'd be damned if she'd call and leave *messages* for *him*—and her concern for Wolf, Jo had further strained her nerves by repeatedly reviewing that scene in the office.

Why had Brett been so very tense, so very hostile?

Why had he seemed so smugly satisfied about informing her of Bob Harley's promotion? In Jo's opinion Bob was the logical choice for the job!

Why did he dislike her?

It was the last of the constantly revolving trio of questions that bothered her most of all, simply because, she assured herself, she had done nothing to warrant his disdain.

She had had no prior warning of his imminent return. Arriving at the office before her secretary that Tuesday morning, she had no sooner pulled her chair to her desk when the phone rang, the blinking button on the white instrument indicating an inner office line. Her response had been as it always was.

"Jo Lawrence."

"I want to see you, now, in Wolf's . . . my . . . office."

That was it. No time wasted on mundane pleasantries such as good morning, merely, in effect, get in here.

Staring at the receiver in her hand, Jo had rationalized the sudden burst of adrenaline rushing through her as her body gearing for a verbal confrontation, *not* in expectancy of the sight of him.

HA!

With all her assumed coolness intact, she had walked briskly into Wolf's . . . Brett's . . . office, taken one look at him, and, metaphorically at least, begun melting.

It simply was not fair for one man to look that damn good! The image this man projected did not sneak up on one; to the contrary, his persona immediately ensnared, jolting emotions, tangling thoughts, luring the unwary to further investigate his seeming quintessence.

After four days of grappling with the fact of his apparent disdain, Jo was nothing if not wary. Lashes lowered over hazel eyes too bright with feminine interest, she viewed the splendor of his male form.

He stood so very straight, his bearing almost military, and so very tall, taller even than Wolf's six feet. His thick, silky-looking, fair hair was cut short at the sides and back. The hint of a wave in the sweep in front was an invitation to eager, feminine fingers. The shortness of his hair revealed the perfect sculpting of his head, his wide brow, straight nose, high cheekbones, and firm jawline lending an overall effect of a mastersculptor's finest work of art. The very spare but sinewy flesh that covered his long frame enhanced the illusion of an elite warrior of a bygone era.

That magnificent human form should never be adorned in anything more than the merest wisp of draping over the hips.

The thought conjured the image. Her composure threatened by her own reflective imaginings, Jo had blurted the first unrelated subject her scrambled mind was successful in latching onto.

"Wolf?"

Jo was much too busy being amazed at the picture of aloof composure her cool tone had drawn for him to notice the glittery sheen that came into his eyes.

"He'll live."

Her amazement did not extend to missing the frost that rimmed his voice, but she ignored it in the relief that swept through her entire being; not until that moment had she allowed herself to face the very real possibility that Wolf might actually die. Her sigh was more eloquent of her feelings than any amount of words could have been.

The glitter in the gray eyes intensified, embuing a molten steel quality. If his expression of cold hauteur was assumed to intimidate, it worked admirably.

"But," he finally continued with icy deliberation, "if you are eagerly looking forward to seeing me dispatched back to Atlanta before long, forget it. Wolf will be a long time in mending."

"His injuries were extensive?" With an unconsciously beguiling sweep of her incredibly thick long lashes, Jo forced herself to meet his direct stare, praying he could not hear the *ba-bump* kick her heart telegraphed.

"Yes." Brett's clipped reply indicated he would not elaborate, thus it surprised Jo when he did. "The point of impact was at the door on the left." At Jo's horror-widened eyes, he nodded once, sharply. "Quite." His lips twisted briefly, as if in memory of a painful sight. "There is hardly an inch on Wolf's left side that is not contused, lacerated, or fractured; not to mention concussed. When I left him this morning he resembled a mummy more than a man." The cloudy haze that had momentarily dulled his eyes dissipated. Once again he staked her with that glittering stare. "As stated, the mending will take a long time." His lids narrowed menacingly, causing a twist of alarm in Jo's midsection. "Had that drunken bastard who ran into Wolf's car not have died in his self-created hell, I'd have sent him there with my own hands."

Jo did not doubt his word for a second. In that instant, Brett looked frighteningly capable of perpetrating a man's demise without weaponry. Appalled by the quiet fierceness of him, feeling herself pale under the steely rapier points flashing from his eyes, Jo slowly collapsed onto the tweed-covered chair to the side of his desk.

Pray God I never incite this man's wrath! Holding her breath, fighting to control the series of shudders quaking through her, Jo gripped the slender arms of the chair, unmindful of her whitening knuckles.

"Okay. Business as usual."

Smothering a gasp, Jo started at his abrupt change in tone and facial expression. Oh, he still looked haughty, but the mien of murderous intent had vanished. Taking command of Wolf's high-backed chair, Brett drew it to the large pine desk, then, settling back comfortably, he arched one pale, aristocratic brow at her.

"Any more questions?"

Jo ground her teeth at his patronizing tone, cautioning herself against incurring his wrath before their interview was over. She truly did not care to leave his office the victim of his displeasure. The very idea of the scene injected steel into her backbone—very cool steel that manifested itself in her voice.

"Yes . . . sir. Several." The tiny but telling pause over the term of respect was noted by a flicker in his attentive expression. Undaunted by a slight tightening at the edges of his lips, Jo led off with query one.

"Does the prognosis call for complete recovery?"

"At this point, yes."

"How long will he be confined to the hospital?"

"The word this morning was at least three, possibly four, weeks."

Four weeks! Jo swallowed her dismay at the thought of having to work side by side with this man for the better part of a month.

"May I see him?" She was further dismayed by the pleading note threading her voice.

"No."

Jo's eyes widened at his icily emphatic denial. What possible reason could he have for refusing her visitation rights to her boss? Or did he believe himself above the need for reasons? Her loss of control was evidenced by the angry outcry.

"But why?"

"The idea, *Ms.* Lawrence, is recuperation. You represent something altogether different."

Anger drowned in a flood of confusion. Had Brett really sneered that last assertion? Could he consider her role of assistant so unimportant as to be sneered at? Jo figuratively shook the consideration away. She knew he employed several assistants himself; he could not help but be aware of the responsibilities entailed. But then, damn it, why *had* he sneered at her?

38

Jetting her mind free of the quagmire of her own thoughts, Jo faced him boldly.

"You will be . . . filling in . . . for him the entire three or four weeks?"

"In every way required."

For some unfathomable reason, Jo was grateful for the ignorance she felt at not understanding the cause of his sardonic tone and matching smile. Thankfully, she was given no time to ponder either.

"Actually, I will very probably be in residence in this office a great deal longer than three or four weeks."

"But you just said—"

"I *said,*" Brett interrupted smoothly, "Wolf will be hospitalized for that length of time. Plans have already been made for him to complete his recuperation at our mother's horse farm in Florida."

Jo opened her mouth to ask the obvious. Brett anticipated her.

"Anywhere from four to six months."

Uh-huh. You bet. Why not?

Rapid fire, the seemingly unrelated terms sprang pell-mell into Jo's thoroughly rattled brain. I am not really hearing what I think I'm hearing, she assured herself a trifle wildly. He did not actually raise the possibility of six months—did he? I'll kill myself!

Had she been, at that moment, presented with a mirror, Jo would have been shocked. Inside, she felt somewhat like a quivering mass of mush. Outwardly she appeared unruffled and unaffected by the news she'd received.

Transmitting an order to her hands to release their death grip on the innocent chair arms, she laced her tension-numbed fingers together demurely in her lap. Between evenly spaced breaths, she managed to calmly ask the question whose answer would see her retained or deposed.

"You will be bringing Richard Colby to New York?"

Over the previous three years, Jo had heard much, all of it

good, of Richard Colby, redoubtable right arm to the head of the mid-Atlantic Coast region. Her assumption that Brett would want his right arm with him now was natural, if unsettling.

"Not likely." Brett's disclaimer startled Jo; had she really detected a hint of amusement in his tone? His dry smile answered her silent question. "Richard hates New York." Brett's voice was every bit as dry as his smile and held a very deliberate drawl. "He hates the pace. He hates the weather. And, more than the preceding, he hates the hard, Yank-ee twang."

Oh help!

Staring at him in bemusement, Jo felt the melting process begin all over again. His soft, drawling tone turned her rigidly stiff spine to the consistency of soft wax. Glory, but he is beautiful! His face is beautiful. His body is beautiful. His voice is beautiful. He is probably magnificently beautiful in bed as well.

Lost in her own suddenly erotic imaginings, Jo was sublimely unaware of the seconds sliding into minutes. What she *was* suddenly aware of was a longing to experience the magnificence of his beautiful body.

"Ms. Lawrence?"

Jo blinked herself back to reality. Though Brett's voice had lost the long drawl, its softness enticed a shivering response through the entire length of her body.

"Have I wakened you?" Brett's taunt was a mild reprimand for her inattentiveness.

Yes, damn you! Jo silently acknowledged the taunt for a much more earthy reason. You've awakened me inside, where I live, and I don't particularly like it, especially since it's so very obvious *you* don't particularly like me.

"No, sir." Jo's independent spirit cringed at the self-satisfied smile he flaunted in reaction to her unhesitating use of the respectful term.

"I'm relieved." His tone was a blatant denial of his assertion. "I'm certain that having a woman as lovely as you fall asleep while I'm speaking would do irreparable damage to my ego."

How very droll. How very sophisticated. How very deceitful. Positive her eyes were flashing her mental accusations at him, Jo lowered her lashes in concealment.

"Is your ego so very delicate?" she ventured softly, hating the surge of excitement that pulsed through her veins. What would it be like, she asked herself, to possess the power to damage this man's ego? You'll never know, her self answered with discouraging swiftness.

"No." Brett's reply was equally swift, equally discouraging, and amused in the bargain. "I'd say my ego is about as delicate as an enraged Brahma bull."

Well, now that I've been firmly put in my place, where do we go from here? Jo wondered bleakly. Apparently Brett's train of thought was running along the same track, only he knew the name of the next station was: Business first, always.

"Now." He sat forward in his chair and placed his palms flat on the desk. "If there are no further questions?"

Feeling anything but the highly efficient assistant she knew herself to be, Jo shook her head mutely.

Sliding between the cold sheets on the unfamiliar motel room bed, Jo sighed with the realization of the number of times she'd shaken her head mutely over the previous three weeks.

God! Had it really only been three weeks? It seemed like years, decades, a millennium! And every second of it filled to bursting with *him*.

Jo had no idea why it had happened. She had no idea how it had happened. She only knew most assuredly that it *had* happened. Against all reason or sense of self-protection, she was stupidly, hopelessly, mushily in love with Brett Renninger.

Balling the covers into a comforting bunch under her chin, Jo rolled onto her side, drawing her knees up almost to her chest. Then she did something she would have been mortified to have Brett witness: She cried long into the night.

Habits formed, good or bad, are not easily set aside. With less than four hours sleep, and that not very restful, Jo woke at her usual early hour. Filled with periodic spells of weeping and tossing, the long night had produced little comfort. As Jo lay staring through the large, square window at a brilliant blue Indian summer sky, her tired mind held on to the two concretes it had formed while blackness painted the window.

For good or ill, and very probably forever, she loved Brett Renninger—that was concrete number one. Concrete number two was wrapped around the fact that, at all costs, she had to diligently work at preventing Brett form discovering concrete number one.

How this feat was to be accomplished when the mere thought of Brett's existence on the earth was enough to activate the inner melting process, had been the major cause of Jo's sleeplessness. The thought had occurred of secrecy through distance. All she had to do to remove herself from temptation was resign her position as his assistant; she'd have as soon resigned her soul to purgatory.

As daylight seemed to have little effect in diverting her endlessly circling thoughts, Jo pushed back the covers, deciding she might as well face the morning—and her own haggard reflection in the mirror.

Thirty-five minutes later, securely hidden behind the magic of expertly applied cosmetics and a neatly tailored, pearl-gray suit with a complementing heather-blue blouse, Jo walked briskly into the apartment-cum-office and came to a disbelieving halt, incredulous at the sight her sweeping gaze encountered.

Attired for the work day in navy suit pants, matching vest, crisp white shirt, and a red-on-gray diagonally striped tie, Brett presented to her widened eyes the picture of domesticity as he turned to greet her from his position at the range in the compact kitchen.

"Good morning, JoAnne. Pull a stool up to the counter, breakfast is almost ready."

The counter was atop a room divider that separated the living-room area from the kitchen. Shelves lined with books, both hardcover and paper, faced the living room. On the kitchen side, three stools, fashioned of cane, with padded seats, filled the space under the Formica counter.

"Breakfast?"

Jo heard the blank confusion her voice conveyed to him and, hearing it, strove to correct the impression of early-morning dullness.

"You're cooking breakfast? For me?"

She had to repress a wince at the expression of boredom that flirted with his features. True, the voice now held alertness; it was the question that, being obvious, was therefore stupid.

"I could hardly fix breakfast for myself alone"—Brett assumed the exaggerated drawl—"and still call myself a Southern gentleman, now could I?"

I could hardly smack your too-superior-looking face, Jo retorted bitterly, if silently, and still call myself *any* kind of rational woman, could I? The temptation to put thought into action was so strong Jo curled her slender fingers into her palms and held them rigidly at her sides, her body tightening with her determination not to respond to his taunt.

Brett's expression of boredom gave way to amusement as his sharp-eyed gaze swept over Jo's stiffening form. For some reason she could not begin to understand, he seemed to derive great satisfaction from knowing he had the power to rattle her composure.

A derisive half smile curving his far too attractive mouth, Brett swung back to the compact stove to dish up bacon and eggs.

"As is obvious"—a jerk of his head indicated the two place settings, complete with small glasses of orange juice and tall glasses of iced water, on the countertop—"everything is ready." Two steaming plates in hand, he turned to her. "If you will seat yourself, Ms. Lawrence, I will serve." His smile grew openly mocking. "You will then be among a small, select group of

43

women who have the right to claim they have been waited upon by Brett Renninger."

What is he trying to do? Holding his glittering gray stare with assumed carelessness, Jo walked slowly into the small kitchen. And why is he trying to do it? The questions teased her mind repeatedly as she slid her trim, rounded bottom onto the thickly padded seat. Had she lost all perceptiveness entirely, or was his mockery self-directed?

The Brett Renninger? Mocking himself? Sure—with the first frost to paint the nether reaches of hell! Why mock himself when he had a much more likely target in the form of his unwanted, unwelcome, uncared-for assistant?

"My meager efforts do not appeal?"

The vocal nudge came from beside her, one stool removed. Blinking, Jo focused first on the bit of gray visible through narrowed lids, then, shifting her glance, to the golden toast, creamy scrambled eggs, and perfectly crisped bacon on her plate. When had he poured the coffee? This as her gaze was caught by the aromatic, dark brew in a cup near her right hand.

"No . . . I mean, yes, of course . . . I'm sorry, I . . . " Darn! Why wouldn't her mouth work this morning?

"How fascinating." The drawl was more pronounced now. "Are you always this articulate first thing in the morning?" Brett arched one beautifully shaped blond brow.

Why did I have to fall for this stiletto-tongued, twentieth-century Adonis? Jo wondered, staring helplessly into a pair of gray eyes that danced with amusement at her expense. She had amused Gary at the beginning too. Perhaps it's true—the psychological thesis claiming women keep seeking out the same type of man. A vision of another Adonis, one with tanned skin, blue eyes, and dark hair, formed in her mind.

"Ah ha! I've solved the mystery!" Jo blinked at the sharp click of Brett's snapping fingers. "You're a somnambulist and not really aware of being here at all."

"How fascinating." Jo managed a fair imitation of his drawl. "Are you always this brilliant first thing in the morning?"

"I'm always this brilliant, period," Brett retorted dryly.

"Modest too!" Jo simpered, oversweetly. Turning away with slow deliberation, she picked up her fork and stabbed at her eggs—prudently denying the urge to sink the long prongs elsewhere. Much too aware of his sudden stillness, she conveyed the utensil to her mouth, chewing consideringly before offering, sincerely, "Very good; creamy. Mine always come out too dry." She sampled the bacon. "Perfectly cooked." The coffee came under her serious consideration. "Nectar," she concluded after one delicious sip. "You could very easily spoil a working woman with a passion for breakfast."

"And you have such a passion?"

His quiet tone and steady regard should have warned her. It didn't. She walked right into it.

"Yes," she admitted, "I'm a so-so cook who's a breakfast freak."

"I always fix my own breakfast when I'm at home." Brett ran a cool gaze over her before returning to her face to pin her with gray eyes that suddenly flared to glittering brilliance. "I would gladly perform the service *for* you"—a tiny pause—"in exchange for an even more basic service *from* you."

Jo's forkful of eggs hung suspended in midair. Was she pushed? Or had she jumped? Jo was uncertain of what method had brought it about, but she felt sure she had finally gone over the edge. She must have, it was the only reasonable explanation for this sensation of free-falling through space. As if it could anchor her to the stool, Jo gripped the handle of the fork and scoured her mind for a suitably scathing put-down. She couldn't find any—which was just as well, for she felt positive she'd misinterpreted his remark.

"I beg your pardon?" She certainly hadn't had to force the note of confusion into her tone; Jo was thoroughly confused.

"Is that a no?"

Jo blinked herself free of his impaling stare. He was serious! Incredible as it seemed, Brett Renninger, in his own peculiar fashion, had actually invited her—*her!*—into his bed!

Too damned much!

The temptation to thankfully, humbly, submissively accept his oddly offered proposition was so strong Jo's teeth ached—understandably, as they were locked together in a death clamp. Her answer required every ounce of willpower she possessed.

"Yes."

"Yes, that is a no?" Brett drawled mockingly. "Or, yes, you'll buy the first meal of the day"—a smile flirted with his lips—"with the last act of the evening?"

Cancel all doubt.

She had not slipped over reason's edge.

She had not misinterpreted him.

She had not passed go.

She had not collected two hundred dollars.

She *had* been propositioned.

The only doubt remaining had to do with her ability to refuse him.

"Yes, that is a no." Had she actually replied in that oh-so-cool, touch-me-not tone? Had she actually declined, when she was on fire and he was the only extinguisher? Was she, in fact, completely out of her mind? Hadn't she wept and writhed through most of the previous night in an agony of need for his touch, his possession?

The questions trembled, rapid fire, through Jo's mind while she strove to maintain a modicum of composure. She wanted him—yes, but not like this! Not at the casually proposed offer of breakfast. Breakfast, for heaven's sake!

The rotten bastard! Jo shocked herself with the silent accusation. But she loved him, she excused herself. While he, *he* has the unmitigated gall to suggest he share my bed—for the paltry sum of filling my stomach!

Jo was forced to lower her fork to the table as a shudder shook

46

her slender frame. Brett obviously saw and misinterpreted her movement.

"Have I shocked your sensitive little soul?" he taunted softly. With a minimum of expanded energy, he slid from his stool to the one beside her. As he leaned still closer Jo felt his warm breath caress her ear. "I can guarantee satisfaction with both performances—in the kitchen and the bedroom."

Jo, teetering on the edge of capitulation, and desperate because of it, steeled herself against the entreaty in his soft tone. When the much yearned for male lips brushed her ear, she jerked away frantically.

"Stop it!" Jo did not have to fabricate the angry tone; she *was* angry! All of a sudden she was explosively angry. The only explanation for his behavior that made any kind of sense was that she'd betrayed herself, her true feelings, to him. Positive he was merely tormenting her for having the temerity to fall in love with a Renninger, Jo lashed out at him defensively. "No, *sir*, you have not shocked my sensitve little soul. I've been propositioned before." With cold deliberation, she injected a sneer onto her lips, venom into her tone. "And one does not take note of an amateur when one has been approached by an expert."

Jo hadn't the vaguest idea what she was saying, yet; whatever it was, it worked. Brett, his expression suddenly blank, went stiff all over. Moving slowly, he straightened, then stood up and carried his barely touched meal to the sink. The sound of the food being scraped into the disposal was loud and abrasive.

"An expert!" Brett's soft, considering statement was not aimed at her. Still, made fearful by his stillness as he stood beside the sink, she raised challenging eyes to his.

"An expert," he repeated even more softly. "Of course."

The challenge in Jo's eyes was replaced by bafflement. Something in his tone conveyed acceptance—of some truth or other. But what? *She* had no idea what she was even talking about; how could he?

47

"Brett?" Jo didn't have an inkling of what to say to him. All she knew was she had to break through his strange stillness.

"Never mind." Moving abruptly, Brett strode from the kitchen. "Let's get this work cleaned up so we can get out of here."

Following his example, Jo scraped her own plate, then stacked their dishes in the dishwasher. As she absently performed the light kitchen duty, Jo told herself she absolutely had to get more sleep. She was beginning to talk off the top of her head, which, in itself, was bad enough. But, it would appear, she was also beginning to believe Brett fully understood her gibberish, and that was scary.

CHAPTER THREE

You are without doubt the most blundering of blundering fools on the entire East Coast.

Brett was, again, taking up space in front of the wide window. It was now some two hours since he'd stormed—childishly, he admitted to himself ruefully—out of the kitchen.

What devil had possessed him, prompting him to issue such an idiotic proposition? He didn't even like the woman, let alone desire her!

So your mind says, now convince your body!

Like or dislike, the cold fact was that he desired her with an intensity the like of which he'd never experienced before, and he'd known some raging passions.

I probably should simply fire her and have done with it.

The tip of Brett's tongue slid along the edge of his bottom teeth, and his unseeing eyes stared at the sun-sparkled Atlantic whitecaps.

If not firing then, at the very least, making her life pure misery was in order.

Damn!

Moving restlessly, Brett shoved his itching hands deep into the slash pockets in his slacks, a wry, self-derisive smile curving his lips. He knew the itch in his palms was not caused by the need to inflict violence; the itch came from the need to caress her soft, pale skin.

God, he wanted her, wanted her as he'd never wanted another woman.

This is sick!

Brett's shoulders moved, as if trying to dislodge an unwelcome rider on his back. His purpose had been so clearcut at the beginning. What the hell had happened to confuse the issue? Not to mention him?

Even though it *had* been ridiculously easy to reassure his sister-in-law concerning his brother's fidelity, Brett's own newly aroused suspicions were not mollified.

In relating to Micki Jo's reasons for being in Boston on the day of Wolf's accident, Brett had injected a businesslike briskness into his tone. Couched in that manner, Jo's explanation sounded plausible. Micki had, gratefully, swallowed it whole. But, then, Micki had not been there to witness the face of fear Jo had worn regarding the accident. Nor had Micki been in the New York office several days later to see, firsthand, Jo's face whiten on hearing the full extent of Wolf's injuries.

Brett had been there. He had kept a sharp eye out for her slightest reaction to his news, only to find a sharp eye had not been necessary; Jo's dismay had been obvious.

Now, three weeks later, Brett realized it had been at the moment she'd displayed the most pain that he'd decided Micki's fears were based on fact and Jo was, indeed, Wolf's mistress.

Again Brett's tongue snaked across his teeth. It was also at that exact moment, he finally acknowledged, that he'd felt the first lick of physical desire for her.

That moment had occurred after his detailed account of Wolf's injuries. Jo had gone deathly pale, then had nearly fallen into the chair by Wolf's desk, hand groping at the chair arm for support. It was when she'd lowered her lashes in pain that he'd allowed his gaze to leave her face to roam freely over her slender body. It was then he'd suffered the first stirring of need for her.

The question of whether he wanted Jo because she *was,* or had been, Wolf's reared its nasty little head. Instantly, Brett assured himself that their past relationship had nothing to do with his present yearnings. Hard on the heels of that self-assurance came the fervent hope that he was not lying to himself.

Brett was well aware of the depth of feeling he held for his older brother. He had idolized Wolf for as long as he could remember, had always tried to emulate him. But to carry his hero worship to the point of wanting to possess Wolf's mistress was not only ludicrous, it was downright unhealthy.

The fact remained that Jo had belonged to Wolf; in his own mind Brett was now certain of that. He had uncovered just too damned many incriminating signs during the previous three weeks for their liaison to be strictly business. One of those signs now lay snugly in a long envelope inside his breast pocket, crackling faintly every time he moved. Brett had even had the fanciful idea that the blasted envelope was laughing at him every time it crackled.

You are sick!

The self-admonition was silently issued in an attempt to quell the strong urge gripping him to turn and feast his eyes on Jo's tall, delicately formed body.

Feast his eyes, hell! He wanted, longed,· ached to feast his mouth, tongue, hands, and body on top of hers.

Again his tongue flicked at his teeth, barely withdrawing in time to prevent being lacerated by his descending hard upper teeth. Will you knock it off? She belongs to him! His hard white molars clamped together in frustration and self-disgust.

She belongs to him.

Without conscious thought, Brett's spine straightened and his shoulders squared. Face it, chum, he advised himself reluctantly. When Wolf comes back, should he so choose, it will be to take over Jo as well as the region.

Hot rebellion, more fierce than he'd felt throughout his rebellious teenage years, seared Brett's emotions. In an effort at maintaining control, he breathed in, slowly, deeply repeating the same phrase over and over in his mind: You're out of line here, she is his.

His ploy at self-chastisement was a total failure, for the rebel in his mind chanted back: He can no longer have her, I will make her mine.

Back and forth, the battle raged between control and rebellion, rendering him temporarily motionless while both vied for supremacy. The deciding factor came not from within but from without.

"Brett, I'm sorry to bother you." Jo's voice was entirely free of facetiousness. She genuinely sounded sorry about having to intrude on his thoughts; she also sounded genuinely confused. "There's something here I don't quite understand."

His given name, coming voluntarily from her soft lips, whipped Brett around as if he were attached to a string she held tightly in her slim fingers. Brett breathed a sigh of relief on realizing Jo had not witnessed his humiliatingly swift snap to obedience. Gleaming head bent, Jo scowled in consternation at the folder in her hands.

"Concerning what?" Strolling slowly—to make up for his earlier quickness?—to the desk, Brett held out one hand for the source of her confusion.

"The Vermont project." Unaware of his outstretched hand, Jo pursed her lips at the printed words under her perusal. "I thought Wolf had decided to scrap the idea of yet another condominium complex aimed at the skiing set, but, from the info here, he must have continued the preliminary investigation on his own."

Halting at the side of the desk, Brett leaned toward her. For a fleeting half instant he hesitated, fighting the impulse to slide his hand under her chin, tilt her head up, and taste her pursing lips with his own. The effort required to bypass her head and pluck the folder from her hands was evidenced by the barely discernable tremor in his fingers.

Jo had the good sense to remain quiet while he studied the folder's contents. Gradually, the tension eased out of Brett as his eyes skimmed the neatly typed lines on each successive sheet of paper contained within the folder's cream-colored covers.

Yes. Yes. A tiny smile played over Brett's lips in appreciation of the thorough investigative job Wolf had done on the proposed project. Before he came to the final sheet, Brett fully agreed with his brother's conclusions. The location was good. Wolf's figures, if accurate—and Brett knew they would be—were well within reason for a complex of this size. The time for action was now if the groundwork was to be completed and excavation begun by late spring.

Behind the typed sheets were several handwritten pages. Brett's smile grew on recognition of Wolf's slashing, straight-line penmanship. In a bold hand, Wolf had outlined a comprehensive, detailed directive on exactly how the official prospectus should be blocked out.

Impressive bit of work, old son, Brett silently congratulated his elder sibling, then he mentally telegraphed a promise: You very obviously wanted this. I'm going to get it for you. It may not be much in exchange for your oh-so-exquisite plaything here, but thems the breaks, bro.

Raising his head, Brett focused his attention on the hazel-eyed plaything sitting very quietly, very patiently at Wolf's desk. Gazing into the amber-flecked depths, Brett reiterated what he'd known for a very long time. One could never fault Wolf's taste in women. It seemed his taste in assistants was faultless as well, for Jo Lawrence was every bit as efficient at her work as his own paragon, Richard Colby. And that was a compliment Brett had bestowed on no other.

"You're staring, Brett."

Jo's tone conveyed enlightenment, not censure. Smiling wryly,

Brett brought the cream covers together with a businesslike snap before handing the folder to her.

"Slide this into your briefcase," he ordered as he started to turn away from the desk.

"We're going to pursue it?"

"We're going to pursue it," he repeated, tilting his head back to her. "Can we wrap it up here soon?" he went on, deliberately stifling any attempt she might have made at questioning him further. "I'd like to be on the road by lunchtime, and I want to stop by the house on our way out."

"This apparently not-to-be-discussed report was the last of it." Jo held up the folder. "Are you positive you feel safe leaving it in my care?" Her tone betrayed her slightly out-of-joint, but adorable, nose.

"Simmer down, Ms. Assistant." Brett sighed. "We will discuss the thing, probably to your screaming point, after we're back in the city." Stepping back, he indicated she was free to leave the desk without fear of having to get too close to him. "Are you packed?"

"Yes."

"Good." Brett ran a quick glance over her and took another step back, advising himself not to tempt fate or his own swiftly dissolving control. "So am I. Let's get this place in order and get out of here."

Working together, the apartment was quickly restored to the neat condition they had found it to be in on their arrival two days previously. It was when Brett strode into the hall toward the bedroom to collect his suitcase that he felt the now-familiar tightening in his stomach muscles. The juices inside that particular organ began to roil much like the gray-green waves pounding against the shoreline.

Brett didn't see the waves, or the shoreline; he didn't even see the long wide window that took up most of one of the bedroom's walls. A grimace twisting his lips reflected his inner image. His eyes, a moody dark gray, were fastened on the oversized bed. The

54

figures his actively churning imagination projected onto that bed were the cause of sudden nausea.

Within the luxury of that rich man's couch, Wolf had consummated his marriage to Micki. Brett knew that. What he didn't know and what had tormented him throughout most of last night was whether Wolf had also consummated his liaison with Jo Lawrence there as well.

God damn!

Standing perfectly still, his long body rigid with tension, Brett was not even aware of the fingers of his right hand curling into his palm; was not conscious of the urge that sent that hand hurtling out to make painful contact with the solid wood that framed the doorway. Consciousness came with the tongue of fire that shot from his knuckles to the base of his skull.

Eyes mirroring disbelief, Brett stared at the abraded skin covering his fingers. Although the door frame had been the recipient of his lashing blow, Wolf's face had been his mental target.

Wolf?

As he stared at his still-balled hand Brett's expression changed from disbelief to incredulity. Good God! Was he cracking up completely? He had never ever felt anything but near adulation for Wolf. Now, because of a woman . . . a shudder rippled through him. With a concentrated effort Brett uncurled his fingers.

Brett felt the sickness roil again as against his will his gaze drifted back to the opulent bed. Did he want Jo because of *who* she was, or because of *what* she was to Wolf?

Moving with an unusual jerky swiftness, Brett clutched the handles of his supple leather case and swung out of the room. There were connotations here he didn't want to examine at the moment. Later, when he was back in New York, and alone, he'd pick his mental and emotional feelings to pieces.

Jo stood patiently waiting for him in the hall, her tall, sleek body an invitation, her cool, aloof expression a denial of same.

Nodding curtly for her to precede him, he scooped up her

cream-toned suitcase, thankful for the necessity of bending over and thereby concealing the evidence of the need growing even greater within.

Following her smoothly swaying, ultra-slim hips along the corridor and down the open stairs to the first level, Brett wondered what had happened to his hard-won, tightly reined control. He had not touched his wife, Sondra, once during the last six months of the farce they'd called their marriage. And his celibacy had been by choice, not by Sondra's rejection.

His eyes caressing the enticing symmetry of Jo's tush, Brett's lip lifted in a sneer in memory of Sondra's professed willingness to, in her own words, share her wealth.

"Brett?"

The voice was not the soft, languid drawl that had captivated him five years ago but the businesslike clip of a motivated woman who had worked her way up from assistant hotel manager to assistant everything. With a mental shake, Brett banished the memory of his former wife—at least temporarily.

A frown on her more-than-merely-beautiful face, Jo held the heavy glass door for his passage.

"You have the look of a man who has forgotten something," Jo murmured as he strode by her. "Have you?"

I wish to hell I could forget *everything*, Brett thought savagely. Most particularly you! He let a sharp movement of his head answer in the negative.

After a last-minute check on Wolf's house, during which Jo remained in the car—because of an aversion to entering the home Wolf shared with Micki? Brett wondered—he headed the sports car toward New York.

To Brett the drive seemed exceptionally long and rife with tension. Being confined in such a small area with a woman—upon whose bones he ached to bounce—was not exactly conducive to tranquil travel. The fact that said woman smelled intoxicating, not of perfume but of pure, sweet female tormented him to the brink of squirming in the bucket seat.

I've got to have her, and it's got to be soon. The stark realization followed the silent sigh that slipped the barrier of his lips as Brett joined his car in jockeying for position in the melee laughingly referred to as New York traffic.

Jo's apartment, located in a fashionable if not exclusive section of the city, was relatively easy to find. Drawing the car to a halt in front of the high-rise, Brett stepped out of the low car and smiled sardonically at the doorman who moved with alacrity to assist Jo in alighting.

With a word to the obsequious man to stand by the Porsche, Brett again suffered the discomfort of trailing the delicate figure he lusted after. Confinement in the elevator proved almost as unnerving as confinement in the Porsche. Finally, after a long trek along the hall on the ninth floor, Jo came to a halt before an unmarked door. She had her key in hand. A long, oddly shaped key, the sight of which glued Brett's teeth together. He recognized that key. Was he not in possession of one exactly like it? Was it not, at that very moment, inside his pocket, nestled among the other keys on Wolf's gold ring?

He did.

It was.

God damn.

The emotions that welled to congregate in Brett's throat burned with a bitter sting. Fury, disappointment, disgust merged into a choking mass. Yet, overall, frustration reigned, prompting him to snatch the key from Jo impatiently when she hesitated at inserting it into the lock.

A quick, vicious turn of the key and the door swung open. Stepping back, Brett frowned a silent order for Jo to enter her apartment, knowing he had to get her inside as quickly as possible and get himself out of there.

Jo murmured, "Thank you."

Brett murmured, "You're welcome."

Then, being very careful not to look at her, he placed her bag

57

next to the door and stepped back into the hall, one hand outstretched to her.

"I'll have the Vermont report," he clipped shortly. Jo's startled look made him add, more gently, "I want to study it tonight. Come to my office first thing tomorrow morning. We'll go over it together." Silently he urged: Come to my bed tonight and we'll forget it together.

The longing that swept through him shook Brett to the core. Hurry, damn you, he commanded silently, watching Jo fumble with the clasps on her attaché case. Hurry, because if you don't I'm going to step back inside, throw you down, and take you right there on that expensive hand-loomed rug my prowling brother paid for. The last thought brought with it a shaft of pain that blanketed Brett's mind with shocked disbelief.

Pain!

Automatically, Brett's fingers closed on the folder Jo extended to him.

Pain?

Automatically, Brett responded to Jo's baffled-sounding words of farewell. And automatically, Brett retraced his tracks to the elevator.

Why pain?

Examining the puzzling emotion, Brett absently slipped a twenty-dollar bill into the doorman's hand before slipping behind the wheel of the Porsche. The key to the puzzle eluded him as he fought his way through the late-afternoon traffic to Wolf's apartment, which *was* located in a posh section of the city.

Inside the elegantly decorated, bi-level suite, Brett abandoned his case inside the door and drew a straight line to Wolf's well-stocked bar.

"There should be no pain involved here. Except of the physical discomfort type."

Measuring two fingers of amber liquid into a short, squat glass, Brett wasn't even aware of speaking the assertion aloud.

After swallowing the aged Scotch neat, he was fully aware of being vocal.

"Damn," he muttered as the whisky burned a path to his stomach. "The idea was to quench the desire, Renninger. Not burn a hole in your guts." He added ice cubes and water to the second drink.

Sipping at the diluted whisky, Brett retreived his suitcase and climbed the free-standing staircase to the apartment's second level and the largest of the two guest bedrooms.

Standing dead center in the room decorated in muted tones of blue and pearl gray, Brett relaxed his fingers and let the case drop carelessly to the deeply piled carpet. He didn't even hear the muffled thud as the supple leather made contact with the wool fibers. His spine rigid, Brett fought against the urge tugging at him and lost.

Following the emotional dictate, Brett, cursing himself softly, spun around and strode from the room and along the short hallway to the master bedroom. Flinging the door open, he took one step inside then halted, his eyes riveted to the enormous bed—in which, Brett was sure, Wolf was undoubtably the master.

"Have you had her here, you bastard?"

The sound of his own voice was startling in its harshness. Still it persisted in erupting from his stiff lips.

"While that beautiful creature who bore your children went serenely, trustfully about the business of keeping your home for you in that classy pile of bricks beside the ocean, did you wantonly debase her, and yourself, on that damned island you call a bed, with *my* woman?"

The echo of his own words slamming back at his mind, Brett remained unmoving for a timeless moment, not seeing, not even breathing. Then, his eyes filling with something akin to horror, he slowly shook his head from side to side.

"No!" Brett's whispered denial came in cadence with his head motion. "No. I couldn't, I wouldn't do something as stupid as fall in love with her!"

Closing his eyes to blot out the offensive sight of Wolf's satin-sheeted playground, Brett's lips thinned in endurance of the shudder that rent the fabric of his soul. The body tremor caused a crackle in his breast pocket. In the silence of the room, the crackle had the muted ring of mocking laughter.

Raising his right hand, he slipped the long envelope from his pocket, then withdrew the legal document from it. A bitter smile twisting his lips, he opened his eyes and again focused on the huge bed.

"No, brother mine, soiling your own nest would definitely not be your style. You would ensconce her expensively, but apart."

The document Brett unfolded was the deed to the apartment he had so recently retreated from.

Retreat appeared to be Brett's order of the day, for now he backed away from his brother's sleeping quarters, quietly closing the door as he went.

If Brett had found it a struggle coming to grips with his unexpected, unwanted physical need for Wolf's partner in dalliance, that struggle was as nothing compared to facing the reality of a deeper emotional need.

Never a coward, Brett nevertheless decided that there were times when facing reality was better done with a few stiff belts. Striding out purposely, he went back downstairs to the bar and the comfort of twelve-year-old Scotch.

It was while sipping on his third glass of barely diluted whisky, his elongated frame perched tiredly on a leather-covered, thickly padded bar stool, that Brett finally conceded defeat to the indefinable emotion commonly called love.

God, he hated it.

No doubt about it, chum, he taunted himself wryly. This time your engine has completely jumped its tracks. One might be forgiven for falling hard for the wrong woman once. But twice? Brett shook his head sadly. You, sir, seemed to have developed a penchant for loose-limbed, loose-moraled, shockingly beautiful females. But at least the first one had not been staked out by another man—and that man the silver-eyed Wolf no less. Brett's soft, self-mocking laughter skipped the length of the short bar.

If she finds out, she will rip you apart.

So how do you go about keeping the very beautiful, very sexy, but, regrettably, also very intelligent Jo Lawrence from finding out?

Propping his elbow on the polished wood bar, Brett held his glass aloft and frowned at the amber contents, a self-derisive smile curving his lips.

You are not going to find an answer at the bottom of a bottle of Scotch, he advised himself judiciously. Finish your drink and go rustle up some food to soak up the booze.

The refrigator, kept well stocked by Wolf's part-time housekeeper, yielded the makings of a Reuben sandwich, which Brett prepared with the same ease as he had breakfast earlier that morning.

Deciding coffee would be the prudent drink to have with his meal, Brett brewed a full pot and polished off the sandwich in between deep bracing swallows, all the while resisting the surge of memories of his first disastrous foray into the baffling emotion called love.

As a rule Brett was successful at keeping all recollection of his time with Sondra at bay, but this evening, taut with anger, actually aching with physical frustration, and saturated with whisky, the self-imposed mental barrier refused to stay in place.

Sighing in defeat, his beautiful male lips curling in a sneer of self-mockery, Brett refilled his cup, stretched his long legs out under the table, and let the memories rip.

Sondra Mallone had taken Brett's breath away from the first moment he saw her, greeting passengers as they entered the 745 bound from Chicago to Atlanta. His first thought had been that she was overall gorgeous. Of average height, Sondra had a neat, trim body with delectable curves, a fantastic mane of fiery red hair, and a face that could, and often did, stop men in their tracks. Of course, there was no outward indication betraying the fact that she also possessed the morals of a back-alley feline. Completely bowled over by her, it was a long time later that Brett learned, the hard way, that Sondra would sleep with anything that wore pants—if the pockets in those pants were heavily lined with gold.

Sipping at the strong black brew, Brett allowed his mind freedom to wander down the pathway to yesterday, allowed his senses to experience the trauma of the time he'd spent with Sondra.

Now, from a five-year distance, Brett realized he'd been a prime target for any Sondra who happened along. He'd been more than tired. After six weeks of flying from Atlanta to Dallas to Honolulu to San Diego to Chicago, on orders from Madam President to "pull the outer reaches of the company together," he'd been bone weary. As he'd also been without female companionship the entire length of those six weeks, he'd been horny as hell.

Enter the gorgeous redhead!

With a snort of disdain, Brett jackknifed to his feet and began clearing the table. When the kitchen was again restored to its usual neatness, he walked slowly to his temporary bedroom, extinguishing lights as he went. After a quick visit to the connecting bathroom for a brief ablution, the plying of a toothbrush, and the natural draining off of some of the liquid he'd consumed, Brett stripped to the buff and crawled between blue-and-gray striped percale sheets, only then allowing his memory free run once more. This time, their time together replayed in his mind in detail.

Anger tightened his frame, simmered in his eyes as Brett strode along the boarding ramp to the plane.

Damned incompetents! If I performed my duties with the

laxity of some of these airline baggage handlers, I'd be tossed out on my ear, Madam President's son or not.

The recipients of Brett's ire were the faceless airline employees who had somehow managed to mislay his bags between San Diego and Chicago. The mishandling in itself was bad enough but, on his second day in the windy city, he had been informed that his bags had been sent on to Atlanta and were awaiting him there. Thus Brett had been forced into an unscheduled shopping expedition. Brett detested shopping in general and clothes shopping in particular; he had remained furious over the incident throughout his entire five-day stay in the city. Nothing, not the fact that his exhausting back-to-back twelve-hour day meetings had gone so smoothly or the congratulatory phone call from his mother, had soothed his abraded temper. That is, not until he'd caught a flash of flaming red hair as he approached the entrance to the plane.

God, she's fantastic!

Anger forgotten, Brett increased his gait, plunging ahead for a closer inspection of the passenger-greeting stewardess.

"Good afternoon, sir." Sondra flashed perfect white teeth. "Your seat is lo—"

"Do you have a layover in Atlanta?" Brett interrupted softly, insinuatingly, his thumb and forefinger dipping into his breast pocket.

"Yes, sir, but . . ."

"If you feel the need of companionship." He again cut her off, pressing his embossed business card into her hand. "Give me a call." Giving her no time to respond or attempt to hand his card back, Brett strode into the plane.

Later, while delivering a Rob Roy to him, Sondra slid his card into the small handkerchief pocket on his suit coat with a whispered, "If you care to wait, I'll meet you in the departure lounge after we land."

If he cared to? Brett was grateful for the attaché case resting on his thighs, concealing the evidence of how very much he cared to wait. For the previous two weeks his body had been sending him signals of its need for release of sexual tension. Suddenly his need was centered on the tantalizing redhead.

Upon landing in Atlanta, Brett positioned himself at the long window in the departure lounge, his impatience camouflaged with cool composure, prepared to endure hours of waiting if necessary. The necessity did not arise as within a relatively short amount of time Sondra joined him at his sentry post.

"You're free to leave already?" Brett made no attempt to hide his pleasure at the sight of her.

"Free for three full days." Sondra smiled back at him.

"Three days!" Brett repeated, unabashedly delighted at the prospect. "Is that the norm for a layover?"

"No," Sondra admitted blithely.

"Then how did you manage it?" Brett grinned in anticipation.

"Wheedling, coaxing, and practically promising my firstborn to the girl who was due this layover."

Securing her elbow with his long-fingered hand, Brett steered her from the lounge. "Then let's get out of here before she changes her mind."

Smiling conspiratorially at each other, they hurried out of the terminal and into a cab.

Before the end of their first twenty-four hours together, Brett was thoroughly besotted with Sondra. She was not only gorgeous; she was bright, vivacious, and witty.

By the end of their second twenty-four hours, Brett decided Sondra was everything he'd ever wanted in a woman. He was so besotted he was beyond realizing that Sondra made a career out of being everything *every* man ever wanted in a woman.

Sondra's vacation never did end. The flight from Chicago to Atlanta was her last. After one particularly satisfying bedroom romp during their third twenty-four hours, Brett, positive he'd at last found a soulmate, proposed to her. They were married one week later at his mother's horse farm in Florida.

Brett, though not a confirmed workaholic, ran a close second in the energy and diligence he afforded the company. Sondra was a lotus eater to the marrow of her bones. The moment his diamond-encrusted wedding ring firmly encircled her finger, she prevailed upon him to come and play with her.

In truth, Brett needed very little coaxing to abandon duty for the intoxicating delights to be explored on the playground of her luscious body. For almost two years he was little more than a figurehead in his Atlanta office. It was only later that Brett would give thanks for whatever guidance had prompted him to hire Richard Colby as his assistant. For Richard not only held down the fort competently, he covered Brett's tracks completely.

The good life began to pall as their second anniversary crept over the horizon. Unnaturally tired, jaded, bored with it all, Brett announced his intention of going back to work one hungover midmorning.

At first, Sondra pouted prettily and coaxed beguilingly. When those tactics had no effect on Brett's determination, she turned on the waterworks. It was when the tears failed to dissuade him that she revealed the first glimpse of her true colors.

"God damn you," Sondra screamed at him. "What the hell do you expect me to do while you play at being the big corporate executive? Join a club of silly damned women who talk of nothing but their brats and redecorating the houses their husbands keep them chained to?"

Startled speechless, Brett had stared at her, unwilling to believe what he was hearing. Shock followed amazement as the tirade Sondra flung at him came straight from the gutter.

Though wealthy from birth, Brett had not led a sheltered existence. He had been all over the world. It would have been polite to say some of the places he'd been in were a mite unsavory. Yet he'd never encountered a female with Sondra's command of filthy language.

His head pounding from the effects of months of too much Scotch, too many late nights, and total abandonment to the physical senses, Brett, calmly walking away from her in mid-spate, strode into the bathroom and threw up.

From that point the marriage that never really was deteriorated rapidly. The twelve months that followed were sheer hell for Brett. Sondra, no longer concerned about his opinion of her, flaunted her true personality. She was still bright, if bitingly so. She was still vivacious, if frantically so. She was still witty, if sarcastically so. She continually turned Brett's stomach.

As one month dragged into another, Brett spent longer and yet longer hours in the office, more and more days on the road. He was fully cognizant of the audacious, unfettered life style Sondra was pursuing. At the dawn of their third anniversary he no longer cared; at least he thought he didn't.

His own personal breaking point came less then a week before their third anniversary. Brett had been in Philadelphia the previous week supervising the final details of a twin hotel-condominium complex the company was planning to build there. Although he was tired, he felt good, for he had successfully ironed out all the knots and twists that accompany a project the size and cost of the one in Philadelphia.

His mood soured slightly on entering the lavish condo Sondra had insisted on being installed in. Brett loathed everything about the place.

Ignoring his surroundings with singleminded concentration, Brett cut a direct path to the bedroom, his one desire being a hot shower and clean, cool, lightweight clothing. At the doorway to the bedroom he came to a jarring halt.

It was the middle of the afternoon and Sondra was in bed. She was not alone. The fact that she was in the act of defiling both him and his bed with another man was bad enough. That the other man had been a friend of Brett's since their university days was like receiving a kick in the teeth.

The other man was a very elite member of the old guard, old-money aristocracy, a prominent banker, and loaded—in more ways than one.

At sight of the writhing, moaning couple, Brett's feeling of well-being drowned in the anger that erupted at his core and surged hotly through him.

At sight of the nearly empty champagne bottle and forgotten glasses on the nightstand by the bed, his anger reached the boiling point.

But it was the sight of the small sugar bowl half full of cocaine that ignited the furious explosion that propelled him into the room.

Though his blood was running hot, Brett's mind remained icy cold. Fully aware of his actions, Brett strode across the deeply piled white carpet. Grasping his former friend by arm and thigh, Brett lifted the smaller man and tossed him to the floor.

"What the . . . !" The squeak slurred from the other man's throat an instant before he found himself flying through space.

"Brett! Stop this at—" Sondra's shrill command died on her bruised lips at the face of cold hauteur Brett turned to her.

"Pig." The condemnation that iced Brett's scathing tone twisted Sondra's features into a mask of fear. "Pig's the only name that suits you. You're worse than a whore. Well, though it may sound trite"—now he sneered—"you made your bed. Now you can wallow in it." Not bothering to glance at the man just regaining consciousness, Brett whipped around and strode to the door.

"It'll cost you a bundle to get rid of me," Sondra shrieked after him.

Pausing in the doorway, Brett slowly turned to face her, his expression amused, his smile relieved.

"And worth every dollar of it."

It had required six months, *and* every dollar of that bundle, but Brett had reclaimed his self-respect and his freedom.

Now, eighteen freedom months later, Brett derided himself for once again finding himself a slave to his own emotions. Though he would not have thought it possible, he felt a crushing need for another, if totally different, type of woman.

They are really sisters under the skin, Brett warned himself wryly.

I really should strangle the bitch and have done with it.

But what I'm going to do is get the hell out of her vicinity for a while and cool off. Vermont, here I come.

His lips curving in self-derision, Brett flung his arms over his head and went to sleep.

CHAPTER FOUR

For Jo, besieged by a barrage of questions and memories, escape into unconsciousness was not difficult to achieve; it was impossible.

Wandering restlessly, purposelessly through the large, roomy apartment, her distracted gaze skimmed sightlessly over the material rewards of her work effort.

The apartment itself was a reflection of Jo's success in her chosen career. The fact that she did not actually own it yet, or that the monthly payments were staggering, was immaterial. Jo was confident of her ability to meet those monthly payments. At least she had been before Wolf's horrible accident and the subsequent arrival of the disapproving Brett.

The furnishings, a reflection of Jo's personality, had been selected carefully, at her leisure, with little regard for cost. As yet the furnishings and bits and pieces of enhancing decor were sparse. It was less than six months since she'd taken possession of the apartment. Besides, Jo felt no driving compulsion to have the decorating chore finished. She had savored the purchase of each and every piece.

As Jo's chosen style of decor leaned from classic to ultra

modern, her task was made doubly difficult simply because the selection was abundant and varied.

Except for the kitchen and the apartment's two bathrooms, all the walls were painted a stark white. The living room was given life by the occasional splashes of brilliant color: the scarlet velvet that draped the large window with its stunning view of the city's towers; the blazing orange-red in the large print depicting a breathtaking sunset over the Pacific Ocean; the glaring lipstick red of the toss pillows littering the long white corduroy sofa and matching club chairs, and, underfoot, the rectangular scatter rugs in unrelenting black and white.

No, not at all the more common homey warmth. Yet it worked, and beautifully; the room invited conversation and relaxation. On this night Jo found little relaxation. Drifting in an aimless circle, her fingers touching a large glass ashtray here, the smooth surface of ebony tables there, she felt nothing, and saw less. Though the cause of her confusion had departed some fifteen minutes ago, Jo was still trying to grasp what had transpired while he stood at her door.

Was she, she wondered, so very infatuated with Brett she was beginning to imagine things? The night before she had felt certain he was on the point of kissing her before he'd turned away abruptly. Just moments ago she had received the impression that he was fighting a similar urge. Yet in both instances he had left her flat, and not very pleasantly at that! Was she reading something into Brett's behavior that simply was not there?

Hazel eyes cloudy with introspection, Jo walked slowly to her bedroom, switching off lights automatically as she passed them. With a featherlike touch to the dimmer switch mounted on the white wall of her bedroom, different but equally resplendent colors sprang into view. Here the draperies were of antique satin in a shimmering teal blue. The wall-to-wall carpet picked up the illusive hint of green in the drapes. A riot of blues and greens slashed diagonally across the satin bedspread. An impressionistic painting done in bold shades of blue was the only relief on one white wall.

Kicking off her shoes, Jo padded to the closet and began to undress, unaware of the carpet's soft fibers massaging her soles. Drat the man, she thought irritably, what was he thinking, feeling? Her distraction was evidenced by the fact that, although she was standing before the opened closet door, she dropped her clothes carelessly onto the floor. Seconds later Jo stood frowning under a hot shower. Usually the jet spray had a soothing effect. Tonight it simply was not working; in fact, nothing seemed to work for her anymore! Sighing tiredly, Jo stepped out of the tub, dripping unconcernedly onto the fluffy peach bathmat. Patting herself dry, she ignored her own reflection—no mean trick as the walls were tiled entirely in mirrors. There was not a hint of stark white in this room. Except for the mirror walls everything in the room was in the same soft peach shade as the mat she now dripped upon, including the roll of tissue set into the wall. The combination of mirrors and soft peach imbued the room with an innocent eroticism. The effect was not at all accidental; Jo had very carefully planned every room in the apartment.

Hanging her sodden towel neatly on the glass bar mounted on the wall, Jo glanced up and found her gaze caught by the unhappy expression in the hazel eyes gazing back at her. Had Brett been on the point of making a move on her? Devoid of enlightenment, hazel eyes stared at her. If he had wanted to kiss her, why hadn't he acted on the urge? He knew she was free. She knew he was divorced. And what did a kiss mean, anyway?

Long lashes fluttered in a quick blink. You may attempt to fool any other person in the world, Jo Lawrence, she chided herself, but never, never try to con yourself. From any other man a kiss would not only have no meaning, it would be forcefully rejected; from Brett Renninger, it might very well mean the end of existence as you know it and the beginning of a whole new, incredibly exciting world.

Wearing nothing but a dreamy expression on her lovely face,

71

Jo drifted into the bedroom and slid between wickedly expensive satin sheets. The feel of satin against her naked skin ignited a fire deep inside the very core of her being. Closing her eyes, Jo moved sensuously, her body growing vibrantly alive from the caressing touch of the cool, smooth material, her mind imagining that touch belonging to Brett's long, slim hands. Heat radiated from her now fiery core to lick hungrily through her veins, and Jo's trembling thighs parted in silent invitation. The low whimper that whispered through her dry lips alerted Jo to the folly she was indulging in. Moaning in frustration, she rolled onto her stomach and forced herself to lay perfectly still.

"Oh, God, why Brett?" Jo's cry was muffled by the silky pillowcase. "Of all the men in the world, why inflict me with the one who feels nothing but disdain for me?"

Jo grew still at the sound of her own voice, the context of her outcry. Why did Brett hold her in contempt? There were few people who knew her personal history. Still, could it be possible Brett had heard her rather pathetic story from one of them? Had he heard of her miserable attempt at playing mistress and dismissed her as a failure as a woman? Because she had failed. Gary Devlin had made sure she'd been aware of exactly had badly she'd fared in the male-female stakes.

The heat was gone, replaced by the chill of memory. Jo definitely did not want to think about Gary. Jo never wanted to think about Gary again for as long as she lived. But, given a choice between burning in the hell of desire's fire and reliving the hell she'd endured with Gary, she thought it prudent to think about him. Thoughts of him should not only keep her cool, they would very likely freeze her soul.

Gary. Had she really considered the possibility of spending the rest of her life with him? Yes, Jo admitted. At the beginning she had actually wanted marriage. Thank heaven Gary had hedged, opting for a trial, live-together period. That trial period had lasted a very short time. Jo shivered with the memory. She had not been able to hold Gary's interest for one full year! And, if he was to be believed, she had practically emasculated him as well!

Did all women who had reached a measure of success in their careers have this trouble in their relationships with men? Were all men intimidated by even the most mildly successful women? Jo didn't know the answers, and she was too private a person to ask the opinion of other professional women she knew.

Cool now, in body and mind, Jo rolled onto her back and stared into the darkness of her room. If their time together had emasculated Gary, she couldn't define what it had done to her. But she knew she was now afraid of any deep involvement with a man, and the very thought of making a commitment gave her the shakes. It's unbelievable, she mused sadly, how much damage two people can inflict on each other in such a short span of time. And it had begun so sweetly too.

She had met Gary while shopping one bright, warm morning in April in, of all places, a stalled elevator. Everyone on the car had become nervous immediately, including Jo. Gary had not. His tall, muscular frame propped lazily against the car's wall, he had coolly advised them to relax.

"This is at least the third time this has happened to me in this very car." Gary, a dry smile curving his lips, had offered the information in an attempt to calm a rather hysterical matron. "We'll be moving again shortly."

Within seconds of his promise the mechanism clanked into motion, then glided to a smooth stop at the next floor. Inside those seconds, his laughing eyes had captured Jo's and he'd winked conspiratorially. Acting completely out of character, Jo had winked back. As she stepped from the car he caught her arm in a gentle grasp.

"Now that our crisis is over," he'd whispered dramatically, "how about joining me in a celebratory cup of coffee?"

Jo couldn't help herself, she'd laughed aloud. "What, exactly, would we be celebrating?"

73

"Why, our very survival, what else?" He blinked owlishly at her, making her aware of the summer-sky blue of his eyes.

Completely charmed by his boyish smile, his dark, clean-cut attractiveness, and his engaging manner, Jo, flinging caution to the winds, went with him for coffee. Six months later she gave in to his plea to allow him to move in with her.

Less than a week after Gary had lugged his belongings up the three flights of stairs to her cramped, one-bedroom flat, Jo knew the arrangement had been a mistake. He was carelessly sloppy with his clothes, she soon discovered, leaving them laying in rumpled heaps all over the place. To someone as neat as Jo, the mere sight of the piles of soiled clothing induced a shudder. But even that irritating habit might have been bearable if it had not been combined with Gary's absolute refusal to help with the everyday household chores, claiming he wouldn't be caught dead doing "women's" work. But, by far, Jo's biggest disillusionment came on their very first night together.

Jo had been to bed with Gary before he'd moved in with her, of course, but always at his apartment, which he shared with a young accountant. Their sexual activity had therefore been less than satisfactory due, Gary had assured her, to the fact that his flatmate might walk in on them at any given moment. Yet, for some reason Jo could not explain even to herself, she had held firm in her refusal to having him spend time in her bed. When her capitulation came Jo had been every bit as surprised as Gary was.

In the darkness of a much more luxurious bedroom, Jo groaned in sympathy for the inhibited woman she'd been a few years ago.

Growing up in a home where her parents never displayed affection for each other, in fact rarely even spoke to each other except when absolutely necessary, Jo, harboring a wariness for the male-female relationship, had singlemindedly pursued first her studies, then her career. An only child, she had received an abundance of love from her parents, but always in separate doses. Jo was not yet ten years old when she realized her parents silently hated each other. Why they hated each other remained a mystery to Jo to this day. They never told her, she never asked.

Being a witness to this silent hatred through her formative years had inflicted fears as well as scars on her psyche. For as long as Jo could remember, everyone told her she was her mother all over again. In one respect this pleased her, for her mother was very beautiful. But in another way it frightened her, for her mother very obviously could not relate to any man. As she grew older Jo realized intellectually that looking like her mother did not necessarily mean she was *like* her mother. Still, no matter how she tried to convince herself otherwise, the fear of her own inability to express love for a man, either verbally or physically, would not be banished.

During her college and hotel-management training years Jo had dated infrequently, and always disastrously. Positive she would make a shambles of the evening, she always did. In fact, she said no so often that by her third year in college she had acquired the nickname No No Jo. It was only after she'd been working for some months that she began a slow emergence from her shell of fear. In the hotel business Jo naturally came in contact with different and varied types of people. Quiet and observant by nature, she studied the hotel guests and her fellow employees closely, most particularly the inner action between men and women. Slowly, as she conducted her secret servey, she came to the conclusion that she was not all that different from anybody else.

When, to Jo's own delighted surprise, she was promoted to assistant to the assistant to the head of the East Coast region of the Renninger Corporation and had to move to New York City, she discovered a whole new world to contemplate. Dedicated to her subject, and also to fill the hours when she was not at work, Jo devoured all the magazines devoted to the modern woman and every article she came across that dealt with the current mores on sexuality.

Gradually the tight bud of her self blossomed into mature young womanhood. Feeling free for the first time in her life, Jo felt ready for an adult relationship with a man. Then she met Gary Devlin. By the time their affair was over Gary had just about annihiliated all of Jo's hard-won confidence.

In personality they were complete opposites. Gary was outgoing, gregarious, and made friends easily, with just about anybody. Jo was as susceptible to his charm as most other women were. He was also the walking prototype of the cliché "tall, dark, and handsome." It wasn't until after he moved in with her that Jo realized he was also vain, shallow, and extremely immature. That Gary was unspectacular in bed as well did not immediately become apparent to her. Having had only one painful, and abortive, sexual experience while in college, Jo really had no previous knowledge upon which she could base a comparison. Gary accused her of being, if not frigid, coldly unresponsive. Jo believed him, at least for a time.

The telling blow came when Jo was chosen for the coveted position of Wolfgang Renninger's assistant. Euphoric, soaring on a natural achievement high, Jo rushed home after work, burst into the apartment, and, flinging her arms around Gary, cried joyfully, "Guess what?"

As Jo had been rather withdrawn for several weeks, Gary eyed her warily, his expression suspicious.

"What?" he responded after a brief hesitation.

"I've been picked to replace James Mattern!" Jo bubbled, forgetting that, as Gary never had shown the slightest interest in her job, he hadn't the vaguest idea who James Mattern was.

"And that's good?"

"Good!" Jo exclaimed, laughing as he'd never seen her laugh before. "That's fantastic! At this moment, you see before you Mr. Wolfgang Renninger's new personal assistant!"

Gary was obviously unimpressed. His expression said "big deal" though he didn't voice the opinion. To her dismay Jo had learned over the eight months they had been together that, unless it was in some way connected with the world of sports, Gary's interest in business was nonexistent. But he was interested in money.

"Will it mean a raise in salary?"

"Of course, silly," Jo said teasingly. She named a figure, then waited expectantly for his whoop of delight. A chill washed all the joy out of her when he stepped back, his face stiff with outrage.

"But that's twice what I earn a year!" he exclaimed harshly. "Exactly what do you have to do for this Renninger?" Before she could shake herself out of her shock to answer, he added nastily, "Boy, is that poor jerk in for a surprise!"

Jo didn't need to ask what he meant. After weeks of his verbal digs about her ineptitude as a bed partner, she knew. Still she was hurt. She was also suddenly blazingly angry.

"Mr. Renninger's a married man!" she defended her employer.

"He's a man, isn't he?" Gary sneered. "And for the kind of money you just mentioned, he's going to expect one hell of a lot of assistance, and not only in the office either."

Jo wanted very badly to believe Gary was merely jealous of her boss, but she now knew better. Although it was painful and demeaning, she finally faced the truth. Gary did not love her. Gary loved Gary. Gary also loved the image he had of himself. That image could not bear the idea of a woman who was capable of earning twice his salary a year. Jo was not surprised when he spat a command at her.

"Tell him to jam his damn job."

"No," Jo said quietly but firmly.

Amazement gave his face a comical cast for an instant. Not in all the short time they'd been together had Jo so adamantly refused to do as he dictated. Then his expression turned ugly.

"Either you refuse this job or I move out of here." Gary flung the ultimatum at her in the tone of voice a child might use when

77

threatening a parent with: If you won't let me have another piece of candy, I'll run away from home forever.

Jo answered in much the same way a weary parent might. "Shall I help you pack?" The difference between Jo's query and that of a parent was, Jo meant it. She had met his ultimatum with one of her own. And like the child he so obviously was, Gary resorted to verbal abuse.

"God! Am I glad I didn't let you talk me into marriage."

That was the mildest of the insults he snarled at her during the three day's required for him to find another gullible woman to move in with. When, finally, he was gone for good, Jo went through a brief but stormy period of weeping. Anger had kept her tight-lipped and dry-eyed throughout Gary's invective while removing himself from her flat. Unfortunately his final barb came via the telephone while she was at work, in Mr. Renninger's office.

"Is your boss there?" he'd asked innocently.

"Yes." Although she'd felt a warning prickle, she walked right into his nasty-little-kid trap. "Why?"

"You can tell the old boy I hope he gets his money's worth from you, but that I really doubt that he will. Even middle-aged men expect a little heat and cooperation from their bed partners once in a while." His derisive laugh burned Jo's ears as he hung up his receiver.

When the call had come through for her Wolf had pushed his chair back from the desk and walked to the window overlooking the busy avenue twenty-six floors below, thoughtfully allowing her a measure of privacy. Replacing the receiver with trembling fingers, Jo raised her eyes to the tall man at the window. Even though her chest felt tight from the pain caused by Gary's parting insult, she had to smile. Old boy? Middle-aged? Wolf Renninger? Her sight blurred by welling tears, she perused the height of him, the breadth of him, the muscularly athletic build that put Gary's to shame. A low, choking sound, part sob, part laugh, drew Wolf's attention. At the shattered look on her face his brows arched questioningly before coming together in a frown.

"What's wrong, Jo?"

It was not the question but the concern in his voice that released the flood of tears. Gulpingly, at times incoherently, Jo blurted out the whole miserable story to him, omitting only Gary's assertion that she was a cold, unresponsive woman. Sobbing out her unhappiness, she was hardly aware of Wolf crossing the room to take her into his arms, but she was grateful for the strong comfort of his embrace and the soothing strokes of his hand on her hair. There was nothing at all personal in his touch, and Jo was grateful for that as well. After the storm had passed he continued to hold her protectively for several minutes.

The sudden realization of her cheek resting on his tear-dampened shirt brought Jo to her senses. Embarrassed by her outburst and the position she found herself in, she stirred restlessly against his chest. Wolf immediately released her and stepped back.

"I-I'm sorry, sir, I . . ." Jo, feeling her cheeks grow hot, bit her lip in consternation.

Wolf's incredible silver eyes were soft with sympathy. "You don't need to apologize, Jo," he said quietly. Glancing down at his damp shirt, he smiled gently. "It'll dry." Then his smile twisted into a grimace. "He's not worth one of your tears, you know."

"Yes, I do know but . . . Oh, Mr. Renninger, I feel like such a fool!"

"First off, you can drop the Mr. Renninger bit." When she made to protest, he raised his hand to place one long finger over her lips. "I was going to request you call me Wolf anyway." A teasing gleam entered his eyes. "Besides, after what we've just been through together, Ms. Lawrence and Mr. Renninger would seem a mite formal. Don't you think?"

Jo smiled back at him, if hesitatingly. "I suppose so," she acceded, sounding unconvinced.

"Don't 'suppose so,' know so," he chided. "I've always insisted on a first-name basis with my assistants. We work too closely together to have it otherwise." It was then that Jo learned that Wolf was not only kind but forthright: "I like you, Jo. I have since the first interview I gave you. You are bright and alert and ambitious, and I like that. But, like my wife, you have retained your femininity, and I like that too. Friends?"

Soon after Jo had begun working in the New York office she had heard, via the office grapevine, of how Wolf's wife, Micki, adored him. At that moment she understood why.

Wolf's brother Brett was something else entirely.

Brett.

Rolling onto her side, Jo groaned aloud in protest against the intrusive image of the object of her unwilling affections. After that shaming debacle with Gary, she had felt positive it would be a very, very long time before she'd find anything attractive in another man. Yet, here she was, a little more than a year later, sleepless, achy, and longing for the sight and touch of a man who very obviously did not like her.

But there had been those moments when she'd sensed desire in him, desire for her. Or was she seeing emotions in him that simply were not there? Why did he dislike her so?

"Oh, hell!"

With the exclamation Jo turned onto her side, pounding the pillow in an attempt to vent her frustration. She was weary of the questions that buzzed incessantly inside her head, tired of searching for answers that were not there. Clutching the pillow close to her body, she shut her eyes tightly, certain she was in for another sleepless night. Within seconds Jo was oblivious to the world. She slept long, and deeply, her rest unmarred by remembered dreams.

Feeling and looking better than she had in well over two weeks, Jo sailed into Brett's office the following morning mere moments after he'd issued a rough-voiced command for her to do so. His appearance betrayed his own restless night. Though he was dressed immaculately, as usual, his eyes had a flat, dull look, faint white lines of strain edged his compressed lips, and a pallor underlay the toast tan on his cheeks.

"I'm leaving for Vermont after lunch," he said bluntly the minute she'd closed the door behind her. "I have no idea how long I'll be gone. It may be days, it may be weeks. Can you handle things here in my absence?"

"I have before." Jo was sorry for the arrogant-sounding assertion the minute it was out of her mouth. Would he think her statement too confident? The way his lids narrowed convinced her that he did. But, damn it, Brett knew her capabilities by now, didn't he? Brett gave further proof of his tiredness by shrugging instead of snapping at her.

"I'm relieved," he muttered irritably, tossing the folder that contained Wolf's project across the desk to her. "Okay, let's get at this. There's a lot to cover and I'm pressed for time."

Several times during the following hour and half Jo had to fight back the urge to scream at him. Brett fired questions at her with the rapidity of a machine gun, merely grunting when she knew an answer, grating "why not?" when she didn't. Finally, after about his tenth "why not?" Jo's tenuous hold on her temper snapped.

"I don't know because your brother chose to keep this project to himself!" Feeling as though her back was to the wall, Jo lashed out at him. "You know I believed this project had been scrapped. You *know,* and yet you persist in badgering me with questions I can't possibly be expected to know the answers to. Don't play games with me, *Mr. Renninger!*"

For an instant the flatness fled from his eyes and they glittered like sunlight on gun metal, then the light was gone and Brett lowered his eyes to the slim gold watch on his wrist. "I have a luncheon appointment," he droned without inflection. "Take the folder back to your office and familiarize yourself with the contents. I'll stop by and pick it up before I leave for Vermont."

Raising his head he stared at her, his expression remote, his eyes again dull gray with disinterest. "You may go now."

Dismissed! She had been dismissed like a bothersome child! Jo had to bite her lip to keep from crying out in protest. Both chilled and subdued by his manner, Jo withdrew into herself before rising to her feet, her composure her only shield against Brett's attitude. "Yes, sir." Jo was amazed at the degree of coolness her tone conveyed, for inside she was anything but cool. Actually, she wanted to run back to her office and weep with frustration. Moving with calculated slowness, she walked out of his office, closed the door carefully, then, her composure slipping, ran along the hall to her own office.

You must have masochistic tendencies. Jo made the silent observation while sitting slumped in her high-backed desk chair. It was over an hour since she'd beat a hasty retreat from Brett's office. In that time she had done nothing but stare at the walnut paneling that covered the wall facing her desk. She had not found a single solution to her emotional condition on the beautifully grained wood. Why was she putting herself through all this? Hadn't she had enough pain with Gary? Why couldn't she simply dismiss Brett from her mind as ruthlessly as he'd dismissed her from his sight? The questions repeated themselves with boring insistency. The answer was always the same: I love him.

Love. What the emotion did to a woman should be against the law of both God and man! What unadulterated fools it makes of us, Jo decided sadly. Who needs it, anyway? she railed at herself. You do, her self mocked smugly. I'm losing my mind! Am I actually arguing . . . with myself? Tearing her gaze from the wall, Jo jumped to her feet and stalked to the oversized window behind her desk. Yes, I am actually arguing with myself. It seems that love does that to us too. It makes us irrational! Who but an irrational being would invite pain into her heart?

Staring at the minuscule pedestrian and vehicular traffic on the avenue far below, Jo sighed in exasperation. How many, she wondered, out of the millions that jammed this greatest of all cities, how many people have indulged in a like self-analysis? And how many have reached any concrete conclusions? Probably none. A wry smile twisted Jo's soft lips. Don't feel like the Lone Ranger, girl, the odds are that you have plenty of company. So why don't I feel reassured? The smile growing into a grimace, Jo turned and walked slowly back to her desk. Forget it. Forget *him,* she advised herself. Sliding onto her chair, Jo picked up the now-hated folder. As she opened the cover Brett strode into her office.

"Hard at it, I see," he observed complacently.

Jo didn't know whether to laugh or cry. She did neither. Instead, she held his strangely intent gaze steadily, silently challenging him to do or say anything clever or smart. Fortunately, perhaps for both of them, he read her mood correctly. His expression wary, he arched an attractive eyebrow at her.

"Any questions?"

At least a hundred, Jo thought. "None," she answered.

"Good." Turning abruptly, he walked to the door, then paused, his hand on the knob, in much the same way he had weeks before. "Oh, yes, he said softly, "I've made up a list of things to do while I'm gone." Sliding his left hand into his jacket pocket, he withdrew a sheet of paper. Even from across the room Jo could see the list was lengthy. Holding the paper between thumb and forefinger, Brett waved it languidly in the air. "You'll take care of everything"—the brow inched higher—"won't you?"

"Yes, of course," she replied quietly, fully expecting him to backtrack and hand the paper to her. Brett didn't move.

"Of course," he repeated in a near whisper, his tone dry.

He's going to make me go to him! The realization struck as a taunting smile feathered Brett's lips. Standing stock still, Brett's eyes transmitted an order for her to get up. Resentment burning like acid in her throat, Jo pushed her chair back and stood up. Suddenly she knew what this little charade was all about. With cool deliberation Brett was making it clear exactly who was the boss and who was the lackey. Would you like me to shine your shoes, sir? Jo had to compress her lips to keep from voicing the question. The mood he was in, he'd very likely say yes, she decided sourly as she crossed the carpet to him. Her restraint nearly snapped when he smiled in self-satisfaction.

"I've written down the phone number where I'll be staying," he murmured silkily. "If you have any problems, call me. Don't, I repeat, do not even consider calling Wolf. He is in no condition to be bothered with you." Slowly, as he was speaking, his tone went rock hard.

Thoroughly confused, Jo frowned. Why in the world would he think she'd call Wolf? Had he no confidence in her ability at all? Did he believe she'd run to his brother at the first little snag she encountered? More hurt than insulted, Jo snatched the paper out of his hand, her gaze skimming the list swiftly.

"I think I can handle it," she assured him. And anything else you can dream up, she tacked on silently.

"Do you think so?" His tone sent a chill rippling down her spine. Could the man read her mind? Releasing his grasp on the doorknob, Brett took the single step necessary to close the distance between them. "Do you really think so?" Slowly, his eyes holding hers, he lowered his head.

Jo did not have to fight to keep from stepping back; quite the contrary, she had to fight a sudden need to step into him. Holding herself tautly still, she watched his descending face, positive he'd turn away at the final moment. She was wrong. When his lips brushed hers her eyes widened in astonishment, then her long lashes fluttered and lowered. That whisper touch brushed her lips a second, then a third time. A ripple of pure delicious sensation shivered through her. Why, why was he teasing her with these almost kisses? And why didn't he touch her, embrace her, crush her to him?

Fully conscious of what she was doing, Jo parted her lips in silent invitation. Although he still made no move to bring his body into contact with hers, Brett accepted her invitation at once. Open hard male lips fused with Jo's, moving slowly to engulf and encompass. A soft half sigh, half moan rose in Jo's throat, only to be muffled by the intrusion of Brett's stiffened, searching tongue. Electrified, Jo stood, trembling violently, longing to feel her softness molded to his hard length, aching for the feel of his hands on her overheated skin. Still he did not touch her.

Jo felt rather than heard the groan that passed from Brett's throat to hers an instant before he deepened the kiss. Revealing raw hunger, his lips consumed while his tongue made a masculine demand for active participation from hers. Jo responded to his demand without hesitation, parrying each thrust, riposting in turn, savoring the sweet male taste of him. Now the murmur that issued from his throat had more the sound of growl than moan, a feral sound that spoke to something wild deep within Jo.

And wildly sweet was the sensation of her blood rushing through her veins, converging in her head, making her legs weak and her need strong, pounding out one cry in her mind: Touch me, touch me, touch me. Still Brett did not touch her.

Brett's plunging, scouring tongue was everywhere, learning everything about the moist interior of her mouth. Her mind spinning, her senses going crazy, desperately afraid she'd collapse at his feet any second, Jo's lips clung to his. Growing deeper, more possessive, more demanding by each instant, his kiss went on and on, reducing Jo to a receiver of the erotic messages Brett was transmitting through the medium of his mouth. Then, suddenly, he ended it. Drawing away with obvious reluctance, he lifted his head.

There was no power on earth, certainly not her shattered will, that could have prevented Jo from swaying when his anchoring lips were removed. Bereft, disoriented, she waited long seconds for the floor to stop shifting under her shaky three-inch heels before raising leaden eyelids. The gaze that met hers came very close to undoing her completely. Smokey gray with passion, Brett's eyes bored into hers, underlining the messages his lips had sent to her. He wanted her, very badly, but for some unfathomable reason of his own, he had exerted every ounce of control he possessed to keep from laying even one finger on her body. As if his eyes were an open book, it was all there for her to read. The only pages missing were the ones explaining why. Refusing her the opportunity to ask questions, Brett straightened to his full height and stepped back, his hand grasping the doorknob.

"You look very beautiful today," he said softly, throwing Jo into deeper confusion with the first compliment he'd ever given her. "That color is very becoming on you. You should wear it more often."

Then he was gone and Jo stood staring at the door he'd closed so very gently. Pulling herself together, if loosely, Jo backed up until the back of her thighs bumped her desk. Sinking onto the solid wood support, she released a long, heartfelt sigh. Well, if nothing else, one question had been erased from her mind. Gary had repeatedly accused her of being unable to physically respond to a male advance. Moments ago she had responded with every quivering particle of her being. Unashamedly she admitted to herself that, had Brett asked it of her, she'd have sunk to the floor for him without hesitation. In amazement, Jo realized that for the first time in her life she wanted, really wanted to experience a man's physical lovemaking. A tiny, sad smile feathered her lips fleetingly. How grand! Here she was, at age twenty-eight, prepared to offer everything of herself for the first time in her life and the donee of her largess flaunts his iron control in her face.

The thought was chilling, but had to be examined. Brett's involvement in their mouth embrace had been as total as her own, Jo was as sure of that as she was of leaves falling in autumn. But he had not touched her, had not taken advantage of the opportunity to assuage the hunger he'd revealed through his kiss. Why hadn't he? The answer was obvious, at least to Jo. She had spent most of the last three weeks with him. She had seen the expression of disdain and often contempt on his face when in her company; Brett hadn't made the slightest attempt to hide his feelings. For reasons known only to himself, Brett simply did not like her. So then, did a man . . . a man like Brett Renninger . . . make a lover of a woman he could not like personally? Jo asked herself. Not very likely, she concluded unhappily. And where does that leave me? She wondered. Absolutely nowhere.

But he does think I'm beautiful! Grasping at the thought for all she was worth, Jo glanced down at the dress she'd hastily chosen that morning. She had not known until she'd walked out of her apartment that the garment had been the perfect choice for a crisp fall day. The wool-blend material was in a vibrant burnt orange that rivaled nature's brilliant autumnal display. The dress was cut in simple, classic lines that did full justice to Jo's slim yet curvaceous figure. Jo's lips twitched wryly as she remembered the enormous price that had been discreetly printed on the little frock's tiny price tag. At the time of purchase Jo had gasped at the cost. Now she was glad she had given in to temptation and whipped out her credit card before she'd had time to change her mind!

The buzzer on the intercom on Jo's desk peeled the information that her secretary, Reni, was back from lunch and back to work. And, apparently, Jo decided as the number-one button on her phone began to blink, so am I.

Leaning to the end of her desk, Jo lifted the tan receiver and asked with a briskness she was light-years away from feeling, "Yes, Reni?"

"Mr. Renninger's on line one, Jo," Reni reported calmly.

For one second Jo was certain she could not manage a normal tone. Fourteen questions jumbled together into a solid mass in her head. One stood out in glaring clarity: Is he going to ask me to go with him?

"Yes, Mr. Renninger?" How in sweet heaven had she contrived that coolly professional note?

"Ms. Lawrence, I hope you can help me. I need some information and Brett's secretary tells me he's out of the office."

Eric Renninger! Why hadn't Reni told her the caller was Eric

Renninger? Closing her eyes against a sudden, ridiculous sting, Jo drew in a deep breath before answering softly, "Yes, your brother left less than an hour ago, Mr. Renninger. I'll be happy to help you, if I can. Exactly what do you need?"

While she was being her most businesslike self, a vision rose to play havoc with Jo's concentration. The vision had slate-gray contemptuous eyes, a harshly unyielding countenance, and a mouth designed to make thinking women weep.

Her eyes foraging over the desk in an effort to escape the taunting image, Jo's glance settled on the cream-colored folder. Perhaps he hadn't found it all that easy to control himself. The austere Brett Renninger had forgotten what he'd originally come into her office for!

CHAPTER FIVE

Purring like a sleek, well-fed cat, the Porsche hugged the highway that unwound like a ribbon into the magnificent mountains
of New England. Though now past the peak of brilliance, the
world-famous foliage blazed in the waning afternoon sunlight, a
spectacular free show for anyone with the eyes to see. Brett's
awareness of fall's breathtaking display of colors was at a shallow
surface level. His glance noted the panorama, his mind didn't
register the glory of it at all. The tiny, picturesque villages tucked
into the folds of Vermont's sun-kissed mountains went virtually
unnoticed by gray eyes bleak with introspection. Grappling with
his own conflicting emotions, he was immune to summer's fiery
exit.

Why, Brett berated himself scathingly, in the name of peace
of body if not mind, why didn't you take her right there in her
office? She was willing. Hell, she was more than willing, she was
eager! And you were damned near incinerated! The memory of
the blast furnace created by the simple method of placing his lips
to Jo's ignited a fresh burst of fire inside Brett's already overheated body. Lord! How many females had he kissed since he'd
discovered how exciting the fusing of two mouths could be some-

where around his fifteenth birthday? A lot more then he cared to remember. Yet never before had he experienced the instantaneous, electrified arousal Jo's sweet lips had sent crashing through him. Even now, hours later, every living cell in his body cried more, more, more.

You are very definitely losing your grip, chum!

Slicing a glance to the rearview mirror, Brett grimaced at the unnaturally pale visage momentarily reflected in the small rectangular of silvered glass. Without even trying, you win the "big stupe" award! There's a blotch on your psychological makeup. Only a true glutton for punishment would go panting after the wrong type of woman twice!

Yet, against all the rationale he could muster, Brett wanted to possess Jo Lawrence with an intensity that shook his so recently well-ordered existence. The emotional hold she was beginning to have on him had been the very element that had induced his exertion on his control. The knowledge of how perilously close he'd come to losing restraint still had his hands trembling as they gripped the steering wheel. With sardonic humor directed at himself, Brett relived his hasty departure from Jo's office.

His arms aching with the need to hold her against his hardened body, his *body* screaming with the need to invade hers, Brett had literally run after he'd closed the office door between them. Never before in his life had he been so sorely tempted to throw all caution, propriety, and plain common sense to the wind! The battle that had raged inside his most sexual of organs, the one he formally called his rational mind, had been of mammoth proportions. The fact that reason had won imbued an intellectual satisfaction that in no way appeased the physical hunger. Against all the arguments he could manufacture, he wanted her, all of her, last night, this afternoon, tonight, and, the most sobering, frightening thought of all, for every one of the forever days and nights to come.

Brett's fingers worked spasmodically on the wheel. Frowning at his reflexive response to the mere thought of touching Jo, he advised himself to stop the lustful window wishing and concentrate on the job of work that was growing closer with each passing mile. He had things to do, and people to see, and he needed a clear mind and steady hand to accomplish the task he'd set for himself. Now, more than ever, he was determined to at least get the ball rolling on this project Wolf wanted.

One of the people he had to see was a Casey Delheny, the architect Wolf had chosen for the multi-unit. That Brett had never heard of Delheny before was not at all unusual. He was kept doubly busy looking after his own bailiwick. He rarely ever poked his nose into either of his brother's domains. Besides, were he inclined in that direction, Wolf would probably tell him to butt out. Brett smiled at the realization that their mother would very likely back Wolf. Violet Renninger had worked diligently at raising strong, independent sons!

That morning Brett had had his secretary call the architect to arrange a conference meeting. She had reported back to him that Delheny had a full schedule for the next day but would be happy to join Brett for dinner at the restaurant in the motel where he'd reserved a room.

If the man was that busy he was probably an excellent architect, Brett decided as he neared his destination less than fifty miles from the New Hampshire state line. Not at all disgruntled at having to wait on Delheny's convenience, Brett planned on spending the day checking out the building site and surrounding terrain. Wolf had delineated the proposed project with his usual painstaking care. Though Brett fully expected to find everything exactly as Wolf had described, still, he had to see for himself.

The motel was one of a large chain, fairly new, and decorated to blend in with the locale in an elegant early American motif. Thinking the early Americans never had it so good, Brett found his own way to the large, comfortable room assigned to him. He was tired but, having eaten nothing since lunch, he was also hungry. After depositing his case on the luggage rack, he washed his hands, splashed cold water on his face, then strode out of the

91

room again in search of sustenance, preferably in the form of a two-inch thick steak with a side order of Scotch and Scotch.

On entering the motel lobby, Brett had noticed a sign advertising a restaurant lounge. Back in the lobby, he followed the direction marker on the sign to a dimly lit room. As he neared the lounge entrance the melodic sound of an expertly played piano assailed his ears, along with the slightly offkey blending of several voices. Over half the tables in the large room were occupied with quietly conversing patrons. Every one of the high stools around the piano held a would-be soloist. The combined strains of a Billy Joel hit of a few years back was not at all unpleasant.

Settling his elongated frame into a well-padded chair at a table in a far corner of the room, Brett smiled when a discordant note rose above the harmonizing voices. His smile broadened as, undaunted, the man who had hit the sour note continued, still slightly out of tune, till the end. And he joined in with his fellow patrons when they offered a round of applause for the impromptu rendition.

The atmosphere in the lounge encouraged relaxation and conviviality, and Brett felt the tensions of the day ease out of his taut body. With conscious determination he relegated the disturbing thoughts that had traveled north with him to the farthest corner of his mind. The ambiance of the lounge imbued a feeling of well-being. Brett convinced himself good food would fill the emptiness inside.

The menu presented to him by a soft-spoken waiter was limited but included an open steak sandwich that Brett promptly ordered, medium rare, with French fries and a small salad. He also ordered Scotch but, remembering his foolishness of the night before, requested both ice and water in it. He had consumed the steak and salad and was putting the finishing touches to his fries when a young woman entered the lounge, glanced around, then, straightening her shoulders, walked directly to his table.

"Mr. Renninger?" she asked with just the tiniest bit of hesitation.

"Yes." Brett eyed her interestedly but discreetly. Small, well rounded without being at all heavy, the woman was not actually pretty. Her looks were too strong to be defined as anything but striking. Her features were almost sharp. Her eyes were almost slanted. Her mouth was almost too full. Yet the combination was appealing. Hair as fair as Brett's own was styled into a shining cap that framed her face to advantage. His perusal completed in seconds, Brett smiled in welcome of the diversion she presented. "What can I do for you?"

"May I sit down?" Interpreting his smile correctly, the hesitation disappeared from her voice.

Was she trying to pick him up? The idea intrigued Brett. Besides, he was curious as to how she'd known his name. "Please do," he invited softly, rising to pull a chair away from the table for her. Brett didn't get the chance to question her identity for she launched into an explanation as he reseated himself.

"My name is Marsha Wenger," she said quietly. "Casey Delheny told me you were booked into this motel." When this statement drew one pale brow into an arch, she clarified. "I asked for you at the desk. The clerk told me you were in here."

"I see." Of course, he didn't, but, what the hell. He shrugged mentally. He wasn't going anywhere, and she *was* attractive. "May I order you a drink?"

"Yes, please." She paused, eyeing his empty glass. "That is, if you're having another."

Brett's smile was unknowingly sardonic. "Oh, I was planning to have several others."

"All right then, I'll have white wine." Although her smooth tone had not altered, it was obvious his smile had confused her for a tiny frown appeared momentarily between her perfectly arched blond eyebrows.

Satisfied with having thrown her slightly off balance, Brett's smile grew into a grin as he motioned to the waiter for a refill.

He remained quiet, scrutinizing her with what he knew was unnerving intentness until their drinks had been placed before them and the waiter had departed. Then, lifting his glass in a silent salute, he sipped appreciatively, lowered his glass, and queried softly, "I can't help but wonder why Delheny would tell you where I'd registered." His smile turned suggestive. "Unless Casey decided I'd appreciate a little entertainment and diversion."

Although Marsha seemed startled at Brett's use of the architect's last name, her surprise was forgotten with his final conclusion.

"Casey decided no such thing!" she declared heatedly. "I am *not* a pros— call girl, Mr. Renninger!" Drawing a calming breath, she went on more quietly. "Casey mentioned your name quite casually and I—"

"Casually, Ms. Wenger?" Brett interrupted silkily, then added thoughtfully, "I beg your pardon. Is it *Ms.* Wenger?"

"Yes, it is." Marsha sipped distractedly at her wine. "And I said casually because . . . oh Lord, I'm screwing this up, and I wanted so badly to make a good impression!"

Now that he had her thoroughly rattled, Brett relaxed completely. You are a chauvinist bastard, he accused himself unrepentently. Somewhere on the very fringes of his conscousness Brett knew he was, in a very convoluted way, trying to get at Jo through this stranger. Yet, unwilling to face the power his vulnerability placed in Jo's hands, he refused to give a second thought to his own lack of logic. At this moment he simply enjoyed that fact that he had unnerved *any* woman.

"Don't despair, Ms. . . . may I call you Marsha?" he inquired respectfully—much too respectfully.

"Yes, please do. I-I—" Marsha had obviously not missed the nuance of a drawl in his overly polite request. Her expression revealing that she was indeed despairing, she grasped her glass and drank thirstily.

Suddenly Brett tired of the roasting game. Relenting, a little, he prompted, "You were saying my name was mentioned causally?"

"Yes, well, not really casually." Marsha took a final gulp from her wine, then dove head first into an explanation. "We had lunch together yesterday, Casey and I. When I mentioned"—she winced over the word—"that I'd just mailed a résumé off to you, Casey told me you were due to arrive in Vermont sometime today." She wet her lips before continuing. "The name of this motel was not offered. I asked Casey point blank where you would be staying."

"Résumé?" Brett pounced on the one word.

Marsha winced again but answered at once. "Yes. Through a friend in New York I learned about the managerial position open in your offices. As I'd been considering relocating to New York City for some time now, I decided to apply for the job."

"Go on," Brett prodded.

"That's all!" She smiled apologetically. "At least it was until yesterday. When Casey said you were coming here I decided to seek a personal interview with you."

"Here? Now?" Brett's expression and tone wiped away the image his casual slacks and sport shirt projected, revealing the hard businessman that was never very far from the surface. "A bit unorthodox, wouldn't you say?"

Marsha had the grace to blush with embarrassment. But she espoused her cause just the same. "I know," she admitted boldly. "But I have always believed that the only way to get something is to go for it fearlessly. Up until now my method has always worked."

Brett laughed. He had to. The woman's honesty genuinely amused him. Settling more comfortably in his chair, he fixed her to hers with eyes sharp with interest. "Okay, Marsha Wenger, fire at will. Give me a verbal account of what is contained in your résumé."

Leaning forward tensely, Marsha began speaking in a tone devoid of inflection. Her recitation went on nonstop for a full twenty minutes. When she was finished she sat back and matched Brett stare for stare, her expression composed with the knowledge that her credentials were impressive.

In actual fact, Brett *was* impressed. He was also relieved. The open managerial position Marsha had referred to was the New England area manager's job, which had not been filled since he'd figuratively kicked Bob Harley upstairs, the day he'd gone to the New York offices at his sister-in-law's request. Brett had lost count of the exact number of people he had interviewed for the job during the last three weeks. Most of the applicants had been unqualified, some had been overqualified. Now, incongruous as it seemed, in a motel in Vermont, at a very late hour, Brett had found his new manager!

"You got it."

"I-I beg your pardon?" Marsha blinked in surprise. After his long silence, it was clear his sudden pronouncement had startled her.

"The job." Brett smiled. "It's yours. When can you start?"

Marsha straightened abruptly, as if she'd been pinched in a very delicate spot. "At once!" she squeaked, then hedged. "Or, that is, as soon as I can relocate to the city."

"All right." Brett nodded his acceptance. "If you'll drop all the pertinent information off here at the desk tomorrow, I'll call it in to the office and have personnel fill out the necessary forms."

Marsha opened her mouth to agree but before she could speak Brett added, "Are you employed now?"

"Yes."

"You'll want to work out notice." It was not a question. Brett's tone indicated she had better want to work out a decent notice.

"I gave my firm a month's notice three weeks ago." Marsha was not quite successful in hiding her annoyance.

It would seem quite a bit happened three weeks ago, Brett thought wryly. The thought reminded him of Wolf and his own temporary tenancy as head man in the New York office. The

96

thought also reminded him of Jo, and that coated his voice with irritation.

"You do realize, I assume, that I'm only filling in for my brother, and the status quo might change when he's back in command?" At the harsh sound of his voice Brett modified his question-statement. "Understand, he will take my recommendations under consideration, but the final decision is his."

"Yes, Casey outlined the current situation." Marsha smiled. "I was also led to understand that *if* you hired me, your brother would very likely retain me." Her smile widened, revealing small, straight white teeth. "Casey seems to know your brother quite well."

"Indeed?" Brett murmured coolly, wondering at both her smile and her opinion. How buddy-buddy had Wolf and this Delheny become? he mused. He did not voice the question to Marsha, preferring to judge the extent of the men's friendship for himself.

Marsha appeared to take Brett's coolness and preoccupation as a hint for her to leave for, after swallowing the last of her wine, she picked up her purse and pushed her chair away from the table. Her actions drew an alert, questioning glance from him.

"I've taken up enough of your time," she explained. "I'll leave you to enjoy the rest of the evening."

"Alone?" Brett's smile held sheer enticement. "Stay and join me for another drink," he invited softly. "We'll discuss your problem of relocation."

Brett found Marsha as easy to charm as most of the other women he'd come in contact with . . . excluding Jo Lawrence, that was. Again the flashing memory of Jo sent a spasm of annoyance through him. Damned woman! He'd wipe all consideration of her out of his mind, or kill himself in the effort! Giving Marsha his warmest smile, he underlined his desire to keep her company. "You will stay, won't you?"

"Well, yes." She laughed, a soft, melodic sound that was easy on Brett's ears. "If you like."

"I do," he assured her firmly, consigning all thoughts of a tall, willowy body, a breathtakingly beautiful face, and a pair of maddeningly arousing lips to the farthest reaches of hell. Brett was content to smile at Marsha encouragingly until their fresh drinks were served, *then* he encouraged her to talk. "Tell me exactly what has to be done to accomplish this move to the big city."

"First"—she held up a long, slim forefinger—"I must finish out my month's notice which, in actual days, amounts to seven. Then I'll have to face the distasteful task of going through my things to decide what I want to take with me and what I will store temporarily. My friend has offered me the use of her sofa until I can find a place of my own, so I can't take too much of my own stuff along." She paused to gaze contemplatively into her wine. When she again raised her eyes to him, they were cloudy with consternation. "I understand finding a decent apartment in the city is the next thing to impossible."

"But not completely impossible," Brett assured her bracingly. While she'd been speaking a germ of an idea had stirred to life in his mind. Now, playing for time to allow the germ quiet in which to sprout, he took a long moment to taste his drink, savoring its bite on his tongue. In his foolishness over one kiss, Brett felt sure he'd revealed far too much of his feelings to Jo. Here, sitting next to him, was a way to disabuse her of any notions she might have conceived about his emotional state. The consideration that he'd be using Marsha didn't bother him in the least. He would be helping her as well and he'd be careful she was in no way involved afterward. The decision made to proceed, Brett put his hastily formed plan into action.

"As a matter of fact, when I call the vitals into personnel tomorrow, I'll have my assistant scout out a place for you." His smile could only be described as intriguingly wicked. "Ms. Lawrence is highly competent. I'm sure she'll have no trouble at all in finding the perfect place for you."

"Oh, but I can't infringe on your assistant's time like that!" Marsha protested, if not too convincingly.

Now Brett's smiled came very close to nasty. "She'll love it," he promised. "Apartments are her 'thing.' "

Though she looked suddenly skeptical, Marsha grasped at the offer. "Well, if you're positive she won't mind?"

She won't be given a choice, Brett thought with relish. Aloud, he merely reassured her. "She'll adore the search," he murmured facetiously. Controlling a prod from the devil to laugh out loud, Brett spun out another strand to his deception web. "I will be in Vermont for at least two weeks. If you can clear up everything here by then, you can drive back to New York with me." His smile was now sugar coated. "You could add the saved air fare to the rent money." His grimace was sincere. "The cost of renting decent living quarters is astronomical."

"So I've heard, and so I'd be a fool to argue over your offer." She grinned. "Thank you."

With a twinge of guilt he didn't wish to recognize, Brett waved her thanks aside. They talked of other things then, the beauty of Vermont, the many and varied attractions it had to offer, not the least being the skiing, and Brett's purpose in being in the state in the first place.

"Casey did tell me about the project some time ago," Marsha said when Brett finished his very brief account. "But I guess I assumed the project would be dropped, at least until your brother was fully recovered from his injuries."

Sipping his drink, Brett reached the conclusion that this Casey Delheny talked too damn much for the Renningers' own good. Where in hell had Wolf found this blabbermouth? Carefully concealing his thoughts from Marsha, he watched her polish off her wine.

"Would you like another?"

"No, thank you." One well-manicured hand, complete with raspberry-colored lacquer, covered his when he went to signal for the waiter. "I must be going. My alarm clock rings at the same early hour every working day, no matter what time I stumble into bed."

"I'll be in touch with you as to exactly when I'll be leaving for New York," Brett promised.

"Oh, you'll probably be running into me all over the place while you're here." She grinned. "In a town this size, people have to work at not tripping over each other every other day or so." With a final grin and a wave of her hand, she strode lightly from the room.

Having risen when Marsha stood up to leave, Brett watched her retreating back in appreciation of her shaply form. Even in the soft light from the small lamp that burned scented oil that had flickered away steadily during their conversation, Brett had reevaluated his initial judgment of her age. When she'd entered the lounge, he had guessed her age at mid to late twenties. Now he felt sure she was within striking distance of his own thirty-five years. Twenty-five or thirty-five, he mused, Marsha Wenger is one very attractive woman; smart too.

Brett moved to sit down again, then, changing his mind, decided to call it a night. He paid the check the waiter promptly presented to him, added a tip that from the man's grin insured Brett would be remembered the next time he entered the lounge, and, fighting a yawn, sauntered from the room. Traversing the motel corridors from lounge to elevator, then from elevator to his room, he gave up fighting the tiredness pulling at him and yawned widely. It had been a long, tension-filled day. The hours Brett had escaped consciousness the night before had not counted more than three. He was beat to a fare-thee-well. And fare-thee-well was the case as Brett slipped into sleep mere minutes after slipping, buck naked, between the cool sheets.

Ten hours of uninterrupted sleep did wonders for Brett's mental condition. Waking with the bright October sun on his face around mid-morning, Brett stretched hugely before springing off the bed. He felt good, raring to go, but he also felt empty. By the time room service delivered the large breakfast he ordered, Brett

100

was shaved, showered, and dressed to go roaming the project's site in jeans, a soft cotton shirt, a finely knit cashmere pullover, and tan suede desert boots.

In no particular hurry whatever, Brett savored every sip of the tart, chilled grapefruit juice, every forkful of creamy scrambled eggs, every crunching bite of golden-toasted English muffin, and every satisfying swallow of rich, dark coffee. Replete with good food and ready to face the day, Brett pushed the tray aside and reached for the telephone. The digits he heard register numbered eleven. The voice that answered at the other end of the line had already been familiar to him at age ten. The voice belonged to his mother's housekeeper at the horse farm in Florida. Even now it seemed to Brett that Elania Calaveri had been in residence at the farm forever. When he responded to her hello, Brett's tone was warm with affection.

"Good morning, Elania. How are you today?"

"Still kicking." The reply was a stock one, reserved for the offspring of her employer. Brett's retort was also stock.

"Anyone I know?"

Elania's chuckle was as hearty at seventy-odd as it had been at forty-five. "Your brother if he don't start behaving himself. I swear, that man is the worst patient I've ever cared for."

Brett was fully aware of the fact that Elania Calaveri was the main reason Wolf had been transferred to the farm instead of his own home to recuperate. Having grown up in the streets of Sicily, Elania was one tough cookie. Nobody, not Wolf or even the hard-nosed businesswoman they all called Mother, gave Elania an argument. If Elania decided Wolf was going to recover completely, Wolf had damn well better do it, and without complaint! Smiling at the thought of the fire Wolf was under, Brett politely inquired if his brother was up to speaking on the phone.

"I wouldn't know why not." Elania gave a long-suffering sigh. "He's been up to driving me to distraction since before six this morning. Hold on till I prop the prowler up."

101

Brett's appreciative smile still lingered on his voice when he responded to Wolf's growled, "What's up, Brett?"

"Mind your own sex life," Brett shot back, laughing at Wolf's groaning response to his feeble attempt at humor.

"You have a sex-oriented mind, baby brother," Wolf accused grittily.

"Merely following in your size fourteen shoes, big brother," Brett chided laughingly. "May I inquire how you are today?"

"In comparison to what? The wreck of the *Andrea Doria*?" Wolf drawled dryly before, relenting, he allowed affection to color his tone. "How's it going, Brett?"

"Hey, big prowler! You're the one in the sight of Elania's formidable gun, not me!" Brett laughed. "Compared to the heavy weather you've got to ride out, my job's a piece of cake!" Brett's opaque terminology in reference to Wolf's injuries had been deliberate, simply because he knew an openly solicitous query would not be welcomed warmly.

"Yeah, I know, but don't tell the boss." Wolf's dry tone didn't quite succeed in masking his weariness. "If she finds out how easy I usually have it up there, she'll probably create a new region just to keep me out of trouble."

The tired huskiness in Wolf's voice shot instant concern through Brett yet, knowing his brother would not welcome a display of that concern, he decided to claim an appointment and end the conversation. "Look, lazybones, I'm going to have to hang up in a minute. I have to see a man about a house," he paraphrased an old saw. "But first, tell me how Micki and the kids are making out in Florida."

"Basking in the sunshine." Wolf's voice held a smile. "I'd let you talk to Mick but she's having her riding lesson at the moment." His soft chuckle hummed through the wire to draw a smile from Brett. "She's doing pretty good at it," Wolf added. "She's only tumbled twice."

Brett's smile disappeared. "Was she hurt?" he asked sharply.

"Micki! Hell no!" Wolf actually chortled. "That hoyden's got more bounce than half a dozen tennis balls. At the rate she's going, she'll put all the rest of us in the shade in no time."

Mingled with the relief Brett was feeling was a growing urgency to cease and desist for Wolf's voice was now definitely reedy. Before he could ease into saying good-bye, Wolf asked a question that jolted him upright in his chair.

"How is my best girl working out as your assistant?"

"JoAnne Lawrence?" Brett asked tightly, stupidly.

"Well, of course, Jo," Wolf chided. "Isn't she something?"

Oh, she's something, all right, Brett mentally sneered. "Yes, she's very efficient."

"Jo is more than merely efficient!" Wolf defended strongly, much *too* strongly, to Brett's way of thinking. "I'd say she could give your Richard Colby a run for his money any day of the week!"

Richard Colby's not wealthy enough to even gain Jo's notice, Brett retorted silently. "Perhaps so," he hedged. Then, simmering with renewed anger, and hating it, Brett rushed on, "Look, old son, I really do have to get cracking. If I don't get the chance to call you again, I'll see all of you sometime over the holidays. Give my love to Micki and the kids."

After he'd cradled the receiver, Brett reached for the large manila envelope that had been delivered to him with his breakfast tray. Gone was the feeling of well-being he'd wakened with. He felt tense, and angry, and all because Wolf had asked about an employee. Had the query been about any other employee, Brett would have considered it the natural interest of an excellent employer, which Wolf was. But the question had not been about any other employee, it had been about Jo, and that annoyed Brett unreasonably.

A quick perusal of the envelope's contents was all that Brett required to assure himself of Marsha Wenger's qualifications. Everything she'd claimed the night before was true. She seemed perfect for the vacant manager's position.

Holding the pertinent papers in one hand, Brett lifted the

receiver and made another long-distance call, this time to the New York offices. He spoke first to the personnel manager, setting the gears of Marsha's employment in motion. Then he asked to have the call switched to Jo's office. While waiting for the interoffice connection to be made, a slightly cruel smile of satisfaction curled his lips. Brett's anger intensified with the frisson of warmth the sound of Jo's voice sent rippling through him.

"Jo Lawrence," she answered, as she always did.

"I have a job for you," Brett said without preamble.

"Yes, sir?" she clipped alertly.

Against his will Brett thought about the previous day and how the soft lips that had just moved in answer felt molded to his own. He could see her, he could taste her, and it hurt like hell. Groaning silently, he pushed the memory aside. When he spoke the roughness of his voice reflected the effort he was exerting to maintain his anger.

"I have found someone to fill the New England manager's job. It's a woman. Her name is Marsha Wenger. She'll be needing an apartment. I want you to find her one." Ignoring her muffled gasp, Brett went on ruthlessly, "You have two weeks. I'll be bringing her back to the city when I return." He paused long seconds, then added silkily, "Are there any questions?"

Even long distance Brett could hear the slow, deep breath Jo quietly drew into her lungs. After releasing it just as slowly she said calmly, "Yes, one. What if I'm unable to find an apartment by then?"

Brett knew Jo was holding on to her temper with every fiber of her being. The knowledge pleased him greatly. Keep a lid on it, beautiful, he advised silently. You can't afford to blow your stack now. Your lover's in no condition to protect you. And if you explode at me, I'll teach you how to behave! The method of how he'd accomplish this teaching process tantalized Brett's senses a moment. Then he *came* to his senses.

"In the event you're unable to find a *suitable* place for Marsha," he said smoothly, "I suppose she'll have to bunk with you until one *is* found."

This time Jo didn't gasp. This time she choked. "Stay with me!"

"You heard it. So you'd better get to work." Very gently, Brett replaced the receiver. Now let's see how efficient the assistant-mistress really is, he thought savagely.

Contrarily, as he strode from the room, Brett found himself hoping Jo would prove her capabilities to him. Shaken by his vacillation, he brought himself up short. You fool, he raged, you're so hot for her you don't know what the hell you do want! Scratch that, he jeered, storming out of the motel. You know exactly what you want . . . her! Her mouth, her body, everything that *is* her!

Brett worked the worst of his agitation off striding to, around, and from the huge land area Wolf had purchased for the multi-unit condo complex. The site was close to the base of the overlapping mountains and near existing ski trails. Off to the left, appearing to hang on the side of the tallest mountain, an attractive lodge sat in regal solitude. From studying Wolf's report, Brett knew exactly how many people the lodge could cater to. The motels located farther down in the valley accommodated some of the overflow but, when the skiing season was at its peak, quite a few hopeful schussers had to be turned down when seeking rooms. Wolf had estimated that with the growing popularity in the winter sport, the number of disappointed skiers would double, if not triple. Wolf's plan was for a Renninger complex to take up the slack, and make a great deal of money in the bargain.

Being a true Renninger, Brett fully approved of his brother's plan. As he walked back to the motel, his mind raced with ideas. Gone was the constraining anger of the morning. He had work to do. A great deal of work. And the first thing on his agenda was an in-depth discussion with the architect, Casey Delheny.

It wasn't until he'd finished a late lunch and had returned to his room to get Wolf's report from his briefcase that Brett discovered he'd come away without it. As a general rule, forgetting things was not at all his style . . . no matter what the provocation! And Jo's sweet mouth had been some provocation! Disgusted with his unusual lack of thoroughness, Brett snatched up the receiver and made yet another long-distance call. Jo's voice hadn't changed in the four hours since he'd heard it; it still had the power to fire his blood.

"Jo Lawrence."

"Fancy that!" Brett exclaimed in his most drawling drawl.

"Yes, sir?" The patience of a saint weighted her tone.

"I forgot the report," he said flatly. *I forgot to make love to you,* he thought longingly. "I want you to shoot it up—"

"I shot it up to you yesterday afternoon," Jo interrupted very gently, very sweetly. "You should be receiving it soon." There was a telling pause, then she asked nicely, "Is there anything else, *sir*?"

Fresh-mouthed woman! The thought had no sooner entered his mind when Brett had to concede the truth of it. Jo's mouth had been delightfully fresh. Suddenly needing to jar her with a zinger, Brett purred, "Have you found Marsha an apartment yet?"

"Well, I'm considering one," she zinged back. "But there are a few details I want to check out before committing 'Marsha' to it."

So help me, the minute I'm back in New York, I will strangle that witch! Brett found it heavy going not to laugh. She was an amusingly beguiling witch, after all! "I'm glad to hear it," he growled in an effort to conceal the smile in his voice. "Maybe you just might be worth the enormous salary Wolf is paying you."

"Oh, Mr. Renninger, sir," Jo simpered. "Please believe me, I am worth every penny of it." Apparently she considered it her turn to hang up on him, for she did so, quite as gently as he had that morning.

Jo's parting assertion ate at Brett for the remainder of the afternoon. At one point, pacing the room in frustration, he caught himself thinking: She's nothing but a damned high-priced ... At that moment, shocked at the direction his thoughts were taking, Brett forced his attention back to the folder that had been delivered to his room less than half an hour after she'd hung up on him. Brett played at being the dedicated businessman for several hours before giving up the farce.

A brisk shower and clean clothes did little for his disposition. Deciding what he needed was a stiff drink, Brett went to the motel's elegant dinning room some twenty minutes early for his appointment. After lining the maitre d's palm with a respectable inducement, he was ushered to a table with a flourish. He was three quarters into his second whisky when he glanced up to observe the maitre d' escorting a breathtakingly lovely redhead across the room. Wondering who the knockout was, Brett ran his eyes over her tall, well-proportioned body appreciatively. When the smirking maitre d' came to a stop at his table, Brett rose to his feet, one brow arched in query.

"How do you do, Mr. Renninger?" the knockout said, extending a long, slim hand. "I'm Casey Delheny."

Not another one! The protest jumped unbidden into Brett's suddenly alert mind. Wolf *has* been busy since I visited him last!

Within fifteen minutes of accepting Brett's hand during their cordial greeting, Casey simply and neatly disabused him of his initial opinion. Oh, Brett was quick to realize that Casey was indeed in love! But not with Wolf Renninger. The man she talked about in glowing terms of admiration and respect was a Sean Delheny, her husband of eleven months.

Gradually, as they savored their expertly prepared Chateaubriand and steamed fresh vegetables, Brett learned that Casey not only truly liked Wolf but that he would forever hold a place of affection in her heart. Wolf had introduced Casey to Sean. Over dessert, still smiling faintly at the idea of Wolf in the role of matchmaker, he acquired the additional information that Sean was the contractor Wolf had chosen to build the multicomplex and that he would be joining them for drinks after dinner.

"But why didn't he join us for dinner as well?" Brett wondered aloud.

"Because the appointment had been made with me," Casey explained. "Sean didn't want to, in his words"—she smiled— "horn in."

"He felt left out?" Brett asked sharply, responding to the hint of censure in her tone. Casey's shrug was eloquent. "Believe me, had I known of Wolf's intention to contract Mr. Delheny, I would have included him in on our meeting, whether he was your husband or not. I didn't know."

"But I don't understand," Her slight head movement caused a rippling in her hair that made Brett think of undulating waves on fire. "Didn't Wolf mention Sean at all?"

Before Brett could answer, a tall, brawny man with hair the exact same shade of red as Casey's came to a stop at their table. Brett immediately knew who the man was by the way her eyes lit up. After the introductions were made and fresh drinks ordered, Brett gave Sean a thumbnail account of the conversation prior to his arrival, then he answered Casey's last question.

"I didn't speak to Wolf about my decision to go ahead with this project." This time Brett's shrug was eloquent. "Wolf very obviously wanted this complex. I intend to give it to him. But, as his condition precludes any involvement with business matters, I am proceeding with the report he'd drawn up." He glanced at Sean and shrugged again. "Your name is not in the report."

"But surely Ms. Lawrence knew of Wolf's intention to give the contract to Sean!" Casey exclaimed. "She's closer to Wolf than his own shadow."

Even as Brett assured Casey that Ms. Lawrence knew no more about the project than he did himself, his mind seethed with renewed anger. Exactly what, he fumed, had Casey inadvertently let slip with that last remark? Was she aware of the liaison between Wolf and Jo? For that matter, had everybody been aware of the affair but him?

The questions teased Brett's mind throughout the rest of the evening, hovering on the edge of his consciousness while he officially hired Sean as project contractor, discussed the pros and cons of the job ahead, and made plans to meet with the couple again the following day in Casey's office. After bidding the Delhenys' good night, Brett went to his room to spend most of the night tormenting himself with even more questions, questions that conjured visions, visions that drove his anger into fury. And, at regular intervals, he repeated one phrase as if in hopes of convincing himself of its truth.

Damn it to hell, I do not love her!

Surprisingly, after that one tension-filled night, Brett found little difficulty in sleeping. Perhaps it was due to the hours he spent pouring over architectural drawings with Casey. Perhaps it was due to the hours he spent tramping over the building site with Sean. Then again, perhaps it was due to the evening hours spent in getting to know Marsha Wenger.

Brett called Marsha to invite her out to dinner the very next day. Squashing a ridiculous feeling of being in some strange way unfaithful, he shoved all thoughts and considerations of Jo from his mind. Marsha proved to be a delightful companion, easy to talk to and easy to laugh with. When she invited him in for a nightcap after he'd escorted her to the door of her apartment, Brett accepted, knowing full well he was going to at least attempt to make love to her. The scene that ensued would have been ludicrous, had it not been so sad.

Marsha made it clear that she was willing, so willing that the nightcaps were forgotten the moment they closed the apartment door. She came into his arms before the sound of the door closing faded in the room. Her softly welcoming lips moved with hungry abandon in time with his, sapping his strength as they sipped his taste. Their move from just inside the door to the bedroom was made smoothly, effortlessly, as were their movements as they undressed each other. It was after they embraced on the bed that they grew awkward. It simply did not work, and the harder they tried, each convinced the failure was their own, the less it worked. Brett finally ended the farce.

"I'm sorry," he muttered, appalled at his lack of a potency he had always reveled in. Rolling onto his back, he stared at the ceiling fighting a clawing fear that didn't bear thinking about.

"It's not your fault," Marsha whispered wretchedly. "I thought, after all this time . . ."

The misery in her tone caught his sympathy, the context of her words caught his attention. "All this time? I don't understand."

"I very foolishly divorced my husband last year when I found out he had been with another woman." Turning her head, she faced him unashamedly with tears trickling down her face. "I say foolishly because I've since learned it was the first and only time he had ever strayed." She smiled sadly. "He did have reason to seek solace elsewhere. At the time I was so wrapped up in getting my career off the ground, I neglected to remember we had a partnership."

Brett frowned, not in the least enlightened or reassured. "But I still don't—"

"You are the first man I've been able to relax with since I left my husband over a year ago." Marsha sighed. "I thought that . . . maybe this time I could"—she actually blushed—"you know? I couldn't stop thinking of him, all the time you were . . . I love him." She blinked against a fresh onslaught of tears. "I really am sorry, Brett."

"Yes, so am I." Reaching out his hand, Brett brushed the tears from her cheeks. "Not only for you, but for myself as well." His smile was as sad as hers. "It was not entirely your fault." Brett had never confided his most personal thoughts to anybody, not even Sondra. Drawing a deep breath, he decided that now, perhaps more than ever, he needed a confidant. "You weren't the only one unable to stop thinking of another. She has never belonged to me. Maybe she never will." A long sigh whispered

110

through his lips. "But I love her. I shouldn't. I don't want to. But I do."

They spent the night together. Brett asked no questions, Marsha didn't either. They did not make love. Giving and receiving comfort simply by holding each other close, they finally slept, secure in a friendship forged during the sharing of despair.

Two weeks later, after spending nearly all his evenings with Marsha, Brett left Vermont for New York. Marsha went with him.

CHAPTER SIX

The cab jarred to a splashing halt at the curb. Irritated, frustrated, and soaking wet into the bargain, Jo thrust a bill at the driver. Not bothering to ask for a receipt this time, she pushed open the door and stepped out of the cab, being careful of the miniriver rushing along the gutter. The cabbie pulled away from the curb as Jo was trying to hang onto her handbag and open her umbrella at the same time. The resultant spray of cold water against the back of her legs elicted a muttered, very unladylike curse from her anger-tautened lips. The umbrella slipped from her chilled fingers, exposing her bare head to the cold late October downpour. Straightening her arm with a jerk, Jo dashed for the entrance doors of the tall office building.

Inside the warmth of the building, she paused to catch her breath. I must be totally out of my mind, Jo thought waspishly. No marginally intelligent person would run around like some kind of a nut looking at apartments in this weather! I wish Brett Renninger would go to . . . Atlanta! Sighing with the realization that she really wished no such thing, Jo sloshed her way to the bank of elevators that would whisk her to the twenty-sixth floor and the comfort of her office, a place she'd seen very little of during the previous two weeks, most of which had been cold and rainy.

"Good grief, Jo, you look like you've just been pulled from the river!" Reni greeted her with wide-eyed exclamation. "You also look half frozen!"

Slumping back against the door for a moment's respite, Jo attempted a reassuring smile. "I think it's safe to conclude that Indian summer is truly over," she offered dryly. "That rain feels like it could turn into sleet without halfway trying." A shiver shook her slender body. "Why didn't I simply go home and call it a day?" she wondered aloud.

"Because you're dedicated?" Reni asked teasingly.

"Or not too bright," Jo retorted, pushing away from the supporting panel. "Well, since I'm here, I may as well stay. I might even surprise everyone and actually get some work accomplished." Stiff fingers fumbling with the large buttons on her wine-color raincoat, Jo planted wet footprints on the beige carpeting as she walked to her own office. "But"—she paused to level an arched glance at Reni—"all has not been in vain."

"You've found a place for her!" Reni piped hopefully.

"Yes, I've found a place for 'her.'" Jo smiled in satisfaction. "I've paid the first month's rent, the last month's rent, and a security deposit." Her deepening smile softened the forbidding line of her lips. "Someone, either 'her' or our exalted leader, owes me a lot of money." God! I hope it's her and not him! Ever since Brett had literally ordered Jo to find an apartment for Marsha Wenger, she had been torturing herself with the possibility of a relationship between him and the woman he'd so quickly hired for the vacant manager's position. The very idea of Brett sleeping with the unknown woman during the last two weeks didn't bear thinking about. Yet Jo had thought of little else but that! She had read the data on the woman that Brett had mailed to personnel; the woman was indeed qualified! Jo prayed that Marsha Wenger's qualifications extended only to the position of area manager and not to the much higher position of Brett's current bed partner.

"Are you all right?"

Reni's worry-ridden voice brought Jo out of her disheartening speculation. Shivering again, Jo shook her head. "No, as a matter of fact, I'm not," she answered candidly. "I'm cold, and wet, and, as I missed lunch, starving." Shrugging out of the limp raincoat, Jo opened the door to her office. "Call the executive dining room and tell that ego-inflated chef I'd like an omelet and a gallon of hot tea."

Reni's giggle drew a grin from Jo. At one time or another, every person in the building had felt the lash of the sarcastic tongue of Hans Vogel, self-proclaimed chef extraordinary. Everyone that is except Wolf and Brett, the brothers Renninger. They'd have either fired him or decked him—possibly both!

Jo walked into her office, then walked out again moments later, a char-gray suit and a pale-blue blouse that had just been delivered at the office from the dry cleaners draped over one arm. As she sailed by Reni she smiled devilishly. "Don't tell anybody but, while I'm waiting for my lunch, I'm going to make use of the mahout's private bathroom. Maybe a hot shower will chase the shivers."

Jo returned to her office warm of body and dry of clothes, to find her tea and food covered and waiting for her. Ah! She sighed silently, sipping the hot brew. Being the assistant to the big man *did* have its compensations at times. But not always, she quickly reminded herself. There were other attendant duties that were downright onerous! Like running around in inclement weather finding the impossible find! This gal had better be good, she thought grimly, then cringed in contemplation of exactly what Marsha Wenger might be exceptionally good at.

Glancing unnecessarily at her desk calendar, Jo chewed a bite of the egg mixture thoughtfully. It was sixteen days since Brett had whirled into her office and then out again, leaving her shattered from one touchless kiss! During those two weeks she had

114

swung from longing for the sight of him, to the gleeful consideration of taking a contract out on him with a hit man. Of course, Jo hadn't the vaguest idea of how to go about hiring a hit man, but that in no way impaired her enjoyment of the idea! Where in the . . . whole of New England was the kiss-and-run devil? she asked her nearly empty plate reproachfully.

After the lunch tray had been removed Jo got to work—or, at least, she tried to work in between glances at her digital desk clock. Where was the dratted so and so, anyway? He'd said two weeks, it had been sixteen days. When was he coming back? The questions skipped in and out of Jo's mind at regular intervals as the clock pulsed its way toward five, the last one always being: Why should I care? After the way he'd treated her before he left, then spoken to her on the phone, she really should not care if she never laid eyes on him again! But she did care, so deeply it scared her senseless. How very Cinderellaish; falling in love with the boss! Jo scowled at the contract she was holding in one hand. And Brett was certainly no Prince Charming! Focusing on the legal jargon, she reread the words that had little more meaning this time than they had the previous three times she'd read them.

"How impressively industrious she is!" The loved, hated, dreaded, longed-for drawl crept to her from the office doorway. "Perhaps I should reward her with a raise." He paused, deliberately Jo felt sure. "Or could I devise a more ingenious form of compensation?"

Good saints preserve us! Was this man trying to drive her mad? At the sound of Brett's husky drawl, Jo's entire system had hummed with joy. Quickly glancing up, the hum had switched to a screech of fury. Brett was not even looking in her direction, but was instead gazing down at a small blonde who could be no other than the new manager, Marsha Wenger. Jo had to fight an urge to fling the contract at his damnably handsome face. Controlling herself with difficulty, Jo smiled prettily through her gritted teeth.

"Welcome back, sir," she said overly politely. Rising graceful-

115

ly, Jo nodded her head with queenly condescension at the petite blonde. "And this must be Marsha?" She arched one dark brow elegantly at Brett, receiving a frown that might have been fear-inspiring if she'd been in a frame of mind to be intimidated. As Jo wasn't in such a frame of mind, she countered his frown with a brightly inquiring expression.

"Yes." The way Brett bit off the word was a clear warning to Jo that she was skating on very thin ice. "Marsha Wenger, my brother's . . . ah . . . assistant, JoAnne Lawrence." Brett's smile drew a chilling line down Jo's spine. "Have you found an apartment for Marsha, Ms. Lawrence?"

Jo felt the double insult as sharply as if he'd slapped her face! Not only had he hesitated derogatorily over the title of assistant, but he'd refused her the courtesy of introducing Marsha to her in turn! Quelling a sudden, degrading need to cry, Jo lifted her head proudly.

"As a matter of fact, *sir,* I have," she answered in an extremely soft voice. "I think Ms. Wenger will find it eminently *suitable.*" Jo figuratively flung the last word at him.

"I knew you could do it." Brett's smile was positively feral. "I told Marsha you have a . . . thing . . . for apartments."

Jo was thoroughly confused, and not only by Brett's odd tone and equally odd phrasing. Marsha's expression of bemused compassion as she glanced from Jo to Brett and then back to Jo again had Jo wondering what the devil the woman could possibly be thinking. Had she missed something along Brett's hurtful conversation route? Or, Jo cringed inwardly, had she been the target of Brett's barbed tongue prior to their arrival at the office? The very thought coated Jo's response with acid.

"Well, my 'thing' worked." Picking up a long white envelope from the desk, Jo held it out to Brett, forcing him to cross the room to her. "You will find all the information in there." Carefully avoiding his touch, she placed it in his hand. "As you will see, there's a detailed account of money owed to me."

"Just give me a total and I'll write out a check for you," Brett

116

snapped, thereby practically admitting his intention of "keeping" Marsha.

The pain that stabbed through Jo was unbelievable in its intensity. Though Marsha opened her crimson-tinted lips, Jo beat her into speech.

"There is no hurry, sir. I'm in no danger of either starvation or eviction." Fleetingly, Jo wondered at the strange look of fury her assurance sent flashing over Brett's face, but she was too upset to probe for reasons. "Now, if there's nothing else pressing"—she glanced at the clock's digits as they moved to five fourteen—"I've got a blasting headache, and I'd like to go home." It was not a lie or an excuse. Within the last few minutes Jo's temples had begun to beat like a demented drummer! Along with the pain in her head was the sickening feeling that the omelet she had consumed earlier was not going to stay down!

Her discomfort must have been visible, for Brett's cold expression changed to instant concern. "Of course!" he agreed to her leaving at once. Then, confusing her even more, his tone softened into what sounded very like tenderness—although Jo felt sure she was mistaken, probably due to her headache. "Look," he urged, "sit down for a moment while I call for a car." When she would have protested, he added adamantly, "I won't have you running for a bus in this weather."

Jo had to choke back a peel of hysterical laughter. After running for days in rotten weather, Sir Fairhaired Knight belatedly blunders to the rescue! Her stomach lurched and Jo sat down with a plop. Oh, fantastic! she thought sickly. He finally comes home, and I feel decidedly ill! At that moment the room began rocking.

"Brett!" Jo heard Marsha's warning cry through a fog of dizziness. "I think Ms. Lawrence is really ill!"

When Jo woke, she was in her own nightgown, in her own bed, with only a cloudy recollection of how she had gotten into either one of them. Lying still, she probed her memory for enlightenment.

As the clouds dissipated, bits and pieces of the puzzle began falling into place. With sudden clarity, Jo remembered the expression of alarm on Brett's face when he'd turned from the phone at Marsha's cry of concern. Never could she recall seeing anyone move quite so quickly as he did when he whipped around the desk to where she was slumped in her chair.

"God! She looks terrible!" he'd exclaimed in an oddly hoarse tone. Then, even more oddly, he'd gently pressed his palm to her forehead. "Good Lord! Jo, you're burning up!" He'd turned aside then to Marsha, saying harshly, "I've got to get her home."

Jo squirmed uncomfortably at the memory of what had happened next. Brett, his face set in lines of determination, gently slid one arm beneath her legs and the other arm around her back, to lift her gently. Still, with all his care of her, the already spinning room tilted and Jo's roiling stomach revolted, making her ignominiously sick, all over the expensive carpet and Brett's handmade Italian loafers.

Writhing in remembrance, Jo heard her own reedy gasps of apology, could hear again Brett's murmured, "Don't, Jo. Don't worry about it! The dammed shoes are unimportant!" Clutching her tightly to his chest, he had issued clipped orders to Jo's secretary. "Tuck her coat around her, then get on the horn and have a cleaning crew sent up here. I'm taking her home." After the coat was wrapped securely in place, he strode to the door, tossing over his shoulder, "And get a doctor . . . the best." He rattled off Jo's home address as he crossed the outer office.

Now Jo had total recall of the dizzying ride down on the elevator and of Brett's arms tightening reassuringly as he strode out of the lift and across the lobby. She could feel again the sting of sleet mingled with cold rain on her flushed cheeks, could clearly hear Brett's muttered curse as he dashed for the protection of the limo. Now Jo's face burned with embarrassment instead of fever as her awakened memory replayed the scene enacted in this very room after their rather over-the-speed-limit run from the office building to her apartment. Although she had

118

been barely conscious by the time Brett carried her into the bedroom, Jo had struggled with him when he'd started to undress her. Concentrating fiercely, she attempted to reconstruct his exact wording of admonition.

"Damn it, Jo. Stop fighting me! You're ill, and you must rest, and you can't very well do it fully clothed." At this point her recall was not quite as total for he'd gritted his teeth, or something. At any rate, only snatches of what he'd muttered remained clear. "Obstinate woman . . . you'd think I was Jack the Ripper or . . . will you be still . . . Jo, please, I'm not so desperate for you I'd—"

Whoa! Hold it! Jo brought her thoughts to a jarring stop. Had Brett said "I'm not so desperate for you" or "I'm not so desperate for a woman"? Jo wanted to believe it was the former, though she was certain it was the latter. In any case, he had finally managed to remove all her clothes and slip a nightgown over her head, all the while displaying a patience Jo would not have believed him capable of.

Then came the doctor, very distinguished looking and extremely irritated at having been called out in such weather. Brett toppled him off his high horse with one scathingly unrepeatable pronouncement. Now, hours removed from the incident, Jo could smile at it all, but at the time she'd been appalled at his arrogant crudeness.

Thoroughly cowed, the good doctor had examined Jo expertly, then, in an affronted tone, told Brett that she had contacted a virus.

"She's to have nothing by mouth for twenty-four hours after the cessation of vomiting," he'd intoned self-importantly. "Then a very light diet for a day or two after that." Gazing down at her he'd frowned. "Her pulse is a little rapid. Has she been under a strain?"

To give the devil his due, Jo now admitted to herself that Brett had had the conscience to flush, if lightly.

"Perhaps," he'd answered tersely. "I'd have no way of know-

119

ing for certain, as I've just returned from a two-week business trip."

Both men jerked to attention when Jo choked. A business trip indeed! Funny business! Monkey business! Physical business! Jo's spasm of choking subsided as she ran out of old accusations. Her reaction to Brett's pious excuse gained her a calming hypodermic needle in the posterior. Jo had fallen asleep within minutes of receiving the injection.

How long had she slept? Twisting her head around to the small alarm clock on her nightstand, Jo discovered two things: the first that she had slept approximately four hours as it was now nearing eleven P.M., the second that her headache and queasiness were gone. She felt extremely tired but no longer sick. Sighing in relief, she snuggled down again then groaned when she rubbed a tender spot on her derriere. Within seconds the door to her room was quietly pushed open and Brett's tall frame was outlined in the doorway by a light in the hall behind him. When he saw she was awake, and alert, he smiled.

"You groaned, madame?" His smile widening, he sauntered into the room. "You must be feeling somewhat better," he opined, studying her closely. "You've lost all that gorgeous green color." Bending down, he touched her forehead lightly. "The fever's gone too. What you need now is rest." His fingers lingered, then slowly trailed down her temple and over her cheek.

Her breathing suddenly shallow, Jo had to grit her teeth against the urge to turn her head to seek his palm with her lips. She felt lightheaded again, only this time she knew her loss of equilibrium was not caused by a virus. Still his fingers lingered, stroking her cheek, her jawline. When one long forefinger sought the delicate line of her lips, Jo knew she had to say something to break the tension twisting through her. Raking her mind, she blurted the first thought that entered.

"How . . . how did you know I was awake?" she babbled breathlessly, then nearly fell apart altogether with the gentle smile that curved his lips. But her purpose was achieved for he

120

straightened slightly and lifted his hand to indicate a small, dimly lit box on the dresser.

"The intercom," Brett replied blandly. "I have the volume turned up as high as it will go. I could hear the slightest rustle every time you moved."

"But where did it come from?" Jo frowned. "I've never seen it before."

"I had Doug pick it up when I sent him to my apartment for some clothes." Straightening fully, he reached out to switch on the small lamp on the nighttable. Doug Jensen was Brett's driver, the same one who had helped her into the car that afternoon. Jo moved restlessly with the memory of how very sick she'd been in the car, this time all over the expensive upholstery.

"I'm sorry," she whispered contritely.

"Sorry?" Brett repeated blankly. "Sorry for what?"

"The carpet, your shoes, the car. I'll pay to have them cleaned."

"Forget it." His hand sliced the air dismissively. "They have been cleaned. The only thing I want you to concentrate on is getting well." Now his hand moved to his head, fingers raking through the blond strands distractedly. "Though you obviously did have at least a touch of a virus, the doctor seemed inclined to think your problem was more exhaustion than anything else." Gray eyes captured hers. "What have you been up to these last two weeks?"

What had *she* been up to? What had she been up to! He dared ask that? When *he* was the one who had assigned her the duty of finding *suitable* living quarters for Marsha Wenger? Jo was still feeling very tired, and very weak. Now she was beginning to feel very, very edgy.

"What have I been up to?" she grated. "Why, I've been sitting in my office with my feet propped up on my desk, manicuring my nails, talking on the phone to all my friends, and generally goofing off. Isn't that what one is supposed to do when the boss is away?" Jo paused to draw breath, then demanded heatedly,

"What the hell do you think I've been up to? I've been up to the end of my patience with running around in all kinds of weather, trying to scare up a decent apartment for your latest . . . manager."

"Jo!" Brett cautioned softly, "calm down. The doctor said you are not to—"

"Calm down! Ha!" Really agitated now, Jo jerked to a sitting position, unmindful of the skimpiness of her nightgown. "I'll calm down when you and your stupid questions get out of here! I'm tired and, now that I think about it, I haven't felt quite right for days. Still, with your demands in mind, I've chased all over this blasted city examining some very unsuitable flats." She grimaced. "I'm so weary of the very word *apartment*, I could scream. And I do wish you'd get out of mine." The angry spate had consumed all of her breath and most of her energy. Feeling shaky, Jo eased back against the pillow with a soft sigh, her heavy eyelids dropping.

It was quiet for long minutes, much too quiet. Jo knew that Brett had not moved from beside the bed. She couldn't hear him breathing, but she knew he was there. Lifting her eyelids to mere slits, she stared at him balefully.

"Are you still here?"

"Do you always ask the obvious?" he retorted. "I'm here and I'm going to stay here . . . through the night."

Brett's flat statement sent a spurt of renewed energy zinging through Jo and, still unaware of her nearly naked state, she shot upright. "You are not!" she denied wildly. "I don't want you here. I'll be perfectly fine. All I need is a good night's rest and I'll—"

"You will stay in that bed for at least three days," Brett's adamant voice cut through her protest sharply. "Maybe longer if you don't behave."

"You . . . you can't . . ." she began sputteringly, only to be cut off again.

"I not only can, I will," Brett promised. "So be a good girl and stop arguing." A tiny smile quirking the corner of his lips, he ran an encompassing glance over her from hair to waist. "You know what?" he mused rhetorically. "Even in a state of . . . ah . . . dishevelment, you look very delectable." The quirk spread to a devilish grin. "If you're feeling so feisty, how about a quick wrestling match?"

Jo knew Brett expected her to clutch the covers to her chin with a maidenly blush. She was furious, yet she could not control the bubble of laughter that vibrated her vocal chords. "How many falls?" she gasped. "Two or three?" Placing her balled hands on her waist, she deliberately expanded her chest by drawing in a deep breath. "The mood I'm in at this minute, I'll probably pin you in seconds!"

Brett's grin disappeared and his eyes narrowed. "The mood I'm suddenly in, I'd let you pin me," he said seriously. "In fact, I'd enjoy it immensely." He took one step closer to the bed, then halted, as if catching himself. "I think you had better go back to sleep now," he warned softly. "You need R and R, not A S A." Turning abruptly, he started for the door.

A S A? Blinking, Jo racked her mind, finally giving up as he reached for the door knob. "What *is* A S A?"

"Abundant sexual activity, of course." The devilish grin flashed again as he stepped through the doorway and quietly closed the door.

Jo slowly slid into a prone position. That son of a something! Would he always have the last word in a confrontation with her? She knew he'd merely been amusing himself with her, yet . . . yet, Jo sighed. Stop dreaming, she chided herself. So he kissed you once, so what? So he's been very kind through this sickness thing, so darn what? You mean nothing to him. You are an employee. And, of course, now there's Marsha the manager! Oh, damn!

When she woke the second time, the angle of the sunrays in her room told her it was midmorning. While stretching herself into full wakefulness, Jo discovered two things. First, she realized that she was very hungry. Second, she found that she ached all over. What you need, my girl, is a long, hot shower, she told herself firmly. Her firmness wavered a bit when she slid out of bed and stood up. Jo wavered too. Brett entered the room as she was inching her way to the bathroom.

"What in hell do you think you're doing!" he roared. "Get back in bed!"

Afraid she'd fall on her face if she so much as paused, Jo continued groping along the wall to the bathroom. "I feel grubby," she panted. "I'm going to have a shower."

"Forget it."

As shaky as she was feeling, Jo probably would have docilely, happily gone back to bed had he said anything else. "Forget it" definitely did not make it as a convincer, except to convince her to keep going—if it killed her! Jo kept moving with dogged determination. "I said I'm going to take a shower, and I meant it. Go away, Mr. Renninger."

"Be sensible, Jo. You can't even stand up straight. Go back to bed." Jo hadn't heard him move away from the doorway, but now he was right behind her. His hands on her shoulders were warm, and reassuring, and, thankfully, supporting. "Let me help you."

"Do what? Take a shower or get back into bed?" Jo could have bitten her tongue for the smart, too-fast retort. She felt his fingers flex spasmodically into her shoulders, then she felt his warm breath feather her cheek.

"Both," he whispered. "If you like. In fact, I'll even join you—in both—if you like."

The idea was appealing, too appealing. Jo shrugged to dislodge his hands and found herself sitting on the floor. She didn't know whether to laugh hysterically or cry hysterically. She did neither, she simply sat there, listening to Brett swear as he bent to help her up.

"You have got to be the most obstinate woman I have ever met!" Though his voice was harsh, his hands were extremely gentle. "How the devil you ever got around Wolf—" He broke off to stare at the tears welling up in her eyes. "What's the matter?" he demanded, his face a study in concern. "Did you hurt yourself?"

"No." Jo shook her head, then sniffed. "Only my pride. What a dumb thing to do."

"Surprise, surprise!" Brett grinned. "We finally agree on something."

"But I really must have a shower," Jo murmured in a very conciliatory tone. "I feel so yucky. Please, Brett." The art of practicing cajolery was new to Jo. Not knowing quite how to go about it, she unconsciously did the right thing. Lowering her incredibly long lashes slowly, she repeated, "Please."

Brett was not at all a novice to the art, nor was he immune. A slow smile gathering along his lips, he knelt beside her. "Yucky, humm?" he murmured close to her ear. "Sounds uncomfortable." Raising his hand, he combed his fingers through her long, tangled mass of dark hair. "Okay, Delila." His quiet voice held a hint of teasing laughter. "You've chained me to the pillar. You may have, not a shower, but a bath. On one condition."

Victory within her grasp, Jo decided to push her luck. "Why not a shower? It's so much faster," she coaxed. "And on what condition?" she added quickly, hoping to put him off stride. Jo suspected her ploy wouldn't work. She was right; it didn't. Brett merely laughed aloud at her.

"First things first, my greenhorn temptress." A thread of tenderness wove through his chiding tone. "Consider your present position." Brett's gaze swept her crumpled form. "You could not remain erect with a wall to lean on. How were you planning to manage a curtained shower stall?" One silky blond brow arched exaggeratedly. "Have I made my point?"

"Point taken," Jo mumbled ungraciously. "But—"

"You simply do not quit." Brett shook his head in mock despair. "On to point two. My condition is, while pleasant, at least for me"—here his tone hardened—"absolutely necessary. I will supervise your bath."

The silence that descended on Jo, and the room, was eardrum-cracking. To maintain that one could hear a pin drop would be to understate the case; one could possibly have heard a feather flutter to the floor. Unfortunately, for Brett, the silence was short-lived and shattered by a female screech.

"You will what!"

"There is certainly no lack of strength in the lungs here," Brett observed to the room in general. "You heard me, sweetie. No supervision, no bath . . . and no arguments. Got that?"

Jo did not require an interpreter of facial expressions to tell her Brett was not talking to hear the melodious sound of his own voice. He was dead serious and equally determined. As wishing he'd drop dead, period, was no solution to her immediate problem, Jo declined from voicing the observation. She was quiet a long time—a very long time—wrestling with the pros and cons of her boxed-in situation. Brett simply remained still, metaphorically playing out enough rope. She either bathed with an audience of one, or she crawled back into bed without even as much as cleaning her teeth. Yuck! Of course, being a product of an age with a fetish for cleanliness, Jo hanged herself.

"Oh, all right!" But she couldn't quite let it go at that. "If you're so damned desperate to play voyeur while a woman bathes, let's get it over with."

Brett did not become angry at her nasty barb. He cracked up with laughter. Flinging himself onto the carpet, he roared at the ceiling. "Oh, goody," he gasped between barks of laughter. "I've been waiting thirty years to leer at a woman in her bath. Now, that erratic, erotic pleasure is to be mine." As Jo glared at him, Brett whooped with delight. "And not only is this woman beautifully pale of skin from a recent illness"—he paused to compose himself then went on—"she is also a trifle sick in the head."

Her back ramrod straight, Jo stared down at Brett in solemn consideration. Set into lines of superior austerity, Brett's face was breathtaking in its classical perfection. His visage softened by warmth and genuine amusement, he stole Jo's heart along with her breath. Suddenly, for reasons Jo didn't want to examine too closely, she was eager to undress for this perfect example of the magnificent male in his prime. Still, wary of his motives concerning much more than a silly bath, Jo was determined not to reveal her eagerness.

"You do have a rather strange sense of humor, Mr. Renninger." Jo offered her opinion with a solemnity that mirrored her expression. "Still, I would guess the undraped female form holds no mystery for you . . . humm?"

Brett literally fell apart again. The seizure of mirth lasted for several minutes, during which Jo fought valiantly against the onslaught of reciprocal laughter. When, at last, Brett brought himself under control, he sat up facing her and grasped her face in his hands.

"You know what?" he asked seriously. "*You* have a rather strange talent for tapping a deep emotional response from me, be it anger, or amusement, or . . . whatever." Jo would have liked to question the whatever part, but he added, frowning in thought, "I don't think I've laughed that spontaneously in at least twenty years." The corners of his mouth twitched with that funny quirk Jo was beginning to realize was all his own. "You may be a little weird"—he allowed the quirk to grow into a smile—"but you're a kinda nice weird." With that, he lowered his smiling lips to hers.

Turning her head, Jo robbed him of his target. "Brett, no!" She fought the insistent tug of his hands. "I haven't brushed my teeth!"

Brett's hands sprang away from her face as another paroxysm of laughter shuddered through him. "Okay, I give up!" Springing to his feet, he stared down at her, his chest actually rumbling with the effects of his amusement. "I'll run your bath for you. I'll even prop you up while you do your thing with a toothbrush. Then I'll wait right here, outside the door, while you perform your ablution ritual." He started for the bathroom, then paused to slice a sharp-eyed glance at her. "You know, I think you may damn well be worth every penny Wolf is paying you."

There was an underlying note in his voice that caused a chill in Jo's bones. Up until Brett's last statement, sexual tension had been drawing her nerves to a vibrating tautness. And riding the back of that tension was the faint spark of hope that Brett had revised his original opinion of her. With his sudden withdrawal the tension snapped and the tiny spark of hope was doused. What was it about her that turned him off? Jo asked herself as she sat, miserable and uncaring of her disheveled appearance. Listening to the rush of water into the bathtub, she stared into nothingness and scoured her mind for answers.

The physical attraction was not one-sided, Jo knew that. Brett felt the tug of sexual awareness every bit as strongly as she did. That single kiss they'd shared had revealed the depths of the physical desire Brett felt for her. Would he, she wondered tormentedly, have given in to his need a moment ago if she had not stopped him? As usual, when Jo began searching for answers to questions about the element of constraint between Brett and her, all she found were more questions. Circles, circles, circles. Whenever she contemplated Brett Renninger, her mind took on the characteristics of a carrousel.

"Have you passed out with your eyes open?" Brett's drawling query fragmented Jo's bemusement.

Oh, why couldn't she hate him? Or, at the very least, dislike him as he so obviously disliked her? Shaking her head more at herself than in a silent reply to him, Jo was unaware of the appealing picture she made with her mass of hair a riot around her head and shoulders and her slim, long-limbed body covered with the sheerest of nightgowns. All she was aware of was the suddenness of Brett's impatience with her.

"Well?" he snapped. "Are you going to sit there for the rest of the morning? Your water's getting cool."

As if she were a child, or a total incompetent, Brett assisted

Jo into the bathroom. His hands impersonal of touch, but firm of grip, clasped her about the waist while she brushed her teeth and cleansed her face. Then he left her, his dubious expression a silent question of her ability to get into, then out of the tub without doing injury to herself. Quelling the urge to scream in frustration, Jo stepped into the warm water, a soft "oh" of delight whispering through her lips.

Brett had not only filled the tub to less than an inch from the rim, he had sprinkled her scented bath crystals into the water. Sighing with pleasure, Jo slid down into the fragrant silkiness. The soothing warmth lapping her chin, she closed her eyes in contentment and promptly dozed off.

"What am I going to do with you?" Jo's eyes flew wide at the sound of exasperation in Brett's voice. He was standing beside the tub, hands on his hips, actually scowling at her. "The idea was to become clean, not dead." Snatching a fluffy peach bath sheet from a glass towel bar, he held it out in invitation. "Let's go, water baby, bath time's over."

"You promised to wait outside!" Jo exclaimed accusingly.

"I waited outside," he grated. "Twenty minutes, to be exact. That water has got to be cold by now." He shook the towel lightly, impatiently. "Out." It was not a request but a definite order.

It was at that moment that Jo realized she was covered by nothing more than clear liquid. The fact that Brett had seen everything there was to see of her the afternoon before had little impact on her now. Feeling herself flush, and hating it, Jo launched a verbal attack.

"*You* get out!" she snapped. "I am perfectly capable of getting out of the tub all by myself." With deliberate insolence she swept his lean length with hazel eyes sparkling with anger. "If you don't move quickly," she threatened softly, "I swear I'll splash water all over your elegant suit." And elegant it was too, all three pieces of expertly tailored wool blend in a rich dark brown that

129

contrasted beautifully with his pale-gold hair. Brett's response to her threat not only startled Jo, it shocked her.

"Screw the suit! I have dozens of suits. I have only one of you." His eyes narrowed in warning. "If you do not stand up and step out of that damned tub in five seconds," he enunciated clearly through gritted teeth, "I swear *I* will haul you out of there bodily. And I won't concern myself about what I touch, or how roughly I touch it."

Her head lifted in defiance, her eyes challanging him, daring him, Jo rose from the water slowly and stepped delicately onto the peach carpet. Then, her head back, her bearing regal, she stood before him in nature's covering of blushing ivory-toned skin.

Except for his eyes, Brett didn't move. For several seconds he didn't even breathe. Starting with Jo's now-sodden, tangled hair, his glinting gray gaze inched the length of her body to the tips of her water-wrinkled toes. When his eyes slowly returned to hers, he stared into their depths as if he were trying to search out the deepest secrets of her soul. The intensity of his gaze stopped the breath in Jo's throat and liquefied all the strength in her body.

"God! You are beautiful!" Brett's hushed, reverent tone drained all defiance, all resistance from her. "Your hair is beautiful." Slowly, holding the towel aloft, he moved to her. "Your skin is beautiful." Flipping the huge terry sheet behind her, he wrapped her in its voluminous folds. "Your eyes are beautiful." Sliding his arms around her, he drew her to him. "And your mouth." His arms tightened to crush her to him. His voice lowered to a murmured groan. "God, your mouth!"

The mouth that Brett groaned over trembled in reaction to a sudden, searing need racing wildly through Jo's body. She was afraid, afraid of her own ineptitude, her own inadequacy, but she was also powerless against the force that urged her to arch her neck and raise her lips to him in silent offering. Brett pounced on her offering with the vengeance of an angry deity. With a guttural growl her lips were taken inside his mouth to be devoured, nibbled on, and then gently laved by his searching tongue.

Giving in completely to the rioting sensations storming her body, Jo worked her arms free of the confining towel and coiled them around his neck, driving her fingers into the silken strands of his hair. The heat rising inside her found a measure of release as she obeyed his silent command to part her lips, wider and yet wider. All rational thought suspended, Jo's mouth consumed while being consumed. When Brett's stiffened tongue pierced into the moist warmth, Jo drew a moan from him by curling her own tongue around his. This time Brett placed no restraint upon his hands. His impatient mutter filled her mouth, and then the towel was torn from her body and tossed aside.

His hands moving restlessly over her back, Brett slid his lips from hers. Biting little kisses sensitized her skin from the corner of her mouth to the delicately curved edge of her ear. With a maddeningly slow, erotic rhythm the tip of his tongue dipped in and out of her ear. When his evocative play forced a groan from Jo's dry throat, Brett's hands moved down to cup her rounded bottom to pull her up and into the burgeoning hardness of his body.

"Will you part your thighs for me as quickly as you parted your lips, water baby?" he coaxed softly into her ear. Lost to everything but the need to have him fill every particle of her being, Jo complied to his coaxing with a whimper of surrender. The whimper turned to a gasp as Brett thrust his body against hers. Even fully clothed, Brett's arousal imprinted itself on her forcefully. Releasing his grasp on her, he brought his hands up to cradle her face. His eyes glinting like new steel in bright sunlight, he stared down at her.

"I must have you," he said clearly, fiercely. "Against all reason . . . and my better judgment, I *will* have you. In all probability we will both regret it afterward but, while the fire rages, I will feed my appetite for you on it."

131

A cold finger of unease poked warningly through the fog of passion clouding Jo's mind. There was something wrong here, something in the harsh tone of Brett's voice, and the rigid set of his features, something that looked frighteningly like disgust, both for her and himself. Not understanding this new element of fear he'd injected into their intimacy, Jo attempted a protest.

"Brett, no . . ."

"No?" he snarled, obviously misinterpreting her protest as a refusal. Grasping her by the shoulders, Brett spun her around, roughly pulling her back to his chest, imprisoning her easily by clamping his hands over her breasts. "Look at yourself," he ordered tersely. In a room of mirrors, there was no possible way to avoid looking at herself. Jo recognized the incongruity of the picture reflected back at her, she stark naked, Brett fully clothed. But that incongruity was not the point Brett was trying to make, as he very quickly proved.

"How dare you tell *me* no?" he demanded. "Just look at yourself. Your lips are wet and parted in anticipation, your eyes are dark with desire, and your entire body is quivering with sexual hunger." Watching her examine herself, Brett spread his fingers with cool deliberation. Immediately her hardened nipples thrust through the opening. Moving his hands slowly, he stroked the tips of Jo's breasts with his index fingers. When Jo could not deny the aching moan that whispered through her lips, Brett lowered his head to place his lips to her ear. "Now tell me no." As if to reinforce his point, he rotated his hips enticingly against her derriere. "If you still dare."

Jo's rational thinking process dissolved as Brett continued to stroke and manipulate her tingling nipples. Following the dictates of a passion flaring out of control, she arched her spine to press her aching breasts into his hands and twisted her head around, seeking his mouth with her avid lips. Grunting in satisfaction, Brett released his hold on her breasts to sweep her up into his arms. His mouth clinging to hers, he carried her into the bedroom. As he came to a stop beside her bed, Brett lifted his head, then froze when his glance brushed the nighttable. Cursing softly, vehemently, he set her reluctantly on her feet. Thoroughly confused, Jo stared at him in disbelief.

"Brett, what . . . "

"Gertrude will be here in approximately fifteen minutes," he cut her off harshly, still staring at the table and the small alarm on it.

"Gertrude?" Jo repeated blankly, then, because she only knew one Gertrude: "Gertrude Jorgeson? Wolf's housekeeper?"

"Yes. *Wolf's* housekeeper."

The sudden, inexplicable anger in his tone and stiffened body as he turned away from her created an empty, bereft feeling inside Jo. What had she done to anger him? Surely her response had been evidence enough of how badly she wanted him? Fighting a creeping sense of failure, Jo bit down hard on her lower lip as she watched him stride to the double dresser against one wall, pull open a drawer, then, without bothering about being selective, plunge a hand in. Grasping the first garment he touched, Brett withdrew it and flung it at her with a tersely snapped "Cover yourself."

Jo could not have been more shocked had Brett slapped her, hard, across the face. Blinking furiously against the sudden sting of tears, she pulled the filmy mid-thigh-length nightie over her head. By the time she'd tugged the short gown into place, Jo's hurt had given way to anger.

"What is Gertrude Jorgeson coming here for?" The cold, grating sound of her voice surprised Jo, and spun Brett around to face her.

"She's going to look after you for a few days." Brett's voice was as cold and grating as hers had been. What, Jo cried inside, had happened to all the passion of moments ago?

"I don't need anyone to look after me!" she exclaimed hotly. "I'm perfectly all right."

Cool eyes swept her from head to toe. "You are *not* all right. People who are all right do not throw up and then faint. Nor do

133

they fall to the floor the way you did a little while ago." Now Brett's eyes hardened in determination. "You will not return to the office until Monday."

"But this is only Tuesday, Brett!"

"Not before Monday," he repeated firmly. "And that is a direct order."

"But—"

"I said that's an order," he roared. "Now, get into that damn bed and stay there. Gertrude will be here shortly." Shooting his wrist from his cuff, he glanced at his watch. "It's just as well I remembered Gertrude's imminent arrival before undressing," he drawled—insultingly, Jo thought. "It's almost noon and I have an appointment at one." Shrugging his shoulders as if their abortive lovemaking was of little importance, Brett turned and walked from the room.

Still standing beside the bed, her eyes wide from the impact of his parting observation, Jo crossed her arms around her middle and hugged herself tightly in an effort to contain the pain clawing at her insides.

CHAPTER SEVEN

Monday morning Brett sat in his office, his gaze riveted to the digital clock on his desk. When the numbers read nine oh five, he thought, I'll give it five more minutes, then I'll call and order her to come to me. The small rectangle that contained the digits blurred as the phrase "come to me" echoed in his mind. Brett had not seen Jo since he'd walked out of her bedroom the previous Tuesday noontime. Now what he wanted, what he really wanted more than anything else in the world, was for Jo to come to him without the order to do so ever being issued. Brett knew, deep down in his bones, that what he wanted and what he'd get were two entirely different things. After the way he'd left her, he knew there was no way Jo would come anywhere near him without being summarily ordered.

His gaze still fixed on the dark wood-encased clock, Brett absently slid his hand across the desk to a pack of cigarettes lying to one side. Shaking a cigarette from the pack, he placed it between his lips and lighted it with a bright red disposable lighter. His fingers toying with the lighter, flicking it on and off repeatedly, Brett drew the acrid smoke deeply into his lungs, sighing with pleasure as he exhaled.

135

In the quiet room the clicking sound of the on-off play of his thumb drew his attention and his gaze shifted to his hand. His eyes bleak, Brett drew on the cigarette again, savoring the bite of tobacco on his tongue. Wisps of whitish-gray smoke swirling from his nostrils, Brett smiled in wry self-derision as he again brought the filter tip to his lips.

Brett had quit smoking, cold turkey, four months after his divorce from Sondra had become final. He had quit because the realization had struck suddenly one grim, hung-over morning that he had slowly increased his habit to three packs a day. The realization had been sobering in more ways than one. Since that morning fourteen months ago, Brett's consumption of alcohol had been curtailed drastically and he had not had as much as one drag of a cigarette. Had not, that is, until last Tuesday afternoon when, the tension that rode him demanding some form of release, he'd walked into a cigar store near his building and purchased a carton of the filter-tip 100s and the inexpensive plastic lighter. His first cigarette had induced lightheadedness. His second had instilled a quasi-calming effect. By the time he'd finished his third, Brett was hooked again. He had purchased his second carton that morning before entering the building.

Slicing a glance at the clock, Brett punched out the butt in the ashtray his secretary had unearthed for him, then immediately lighted another. His smile containing equal measures of self-disgust and self-amusement, Brett reached for his telephone. This morning Jo did not answer as usual.

"Yes, sir?" Her voice came crisply to him over the wire.

I'm *sir* again. Brett's twisted lips smoothed into a genuine smile. How long would it be, he wondered, before he was again Brett to her? Inside his head he could hear the exciting sound of her passion-thickened voice whispering his name.

"Mr. Renninger?" Jo's crispness had fled before confusion at his silence.

"You have to be told?" Brett drawled slowly.

"You want me in your office?"

In my office. In my apartment. In my bed. Anywhere and everywhere, Brett tormented himself with the tantalizing thought an instant before replying to her leading question.

"If you can find the time, Ms. Lawrence."

"Now?"

"If you will." Brett sighed loudly, exaggeratedly, then gently replaced the receiver.

The moment Jo walked into his office Brett felt the presence of the invisible wall she'd erected between them. The presence was as cold and forbidding as her expression. If he was any judge of women, and Brett had cultivated a discernment since Sondra, he was in for a very chilly period. His nerves tightening with tension, Brett waved her to a chair, then wondered what in hell he'd say to her. Perhaps, he mused, clearing the air would melt the ice. But first he needed a weed. Lighting a fresh cigarette from the end of his last one, Brett watched Jo's eyes flicker from him to the half-empty pack and then back to him again, a frown drawing a faint line on her brow.

"I—I didn't know that you smoked!" she blurted starkly.

"I don't . . . or, at least, I didn't." Now Brett frowned. "I used to," he explained. "I quit some time ago."

"But obviously . . . " she began.

"I started again," he said sharply.

"Why?" Jo retorted just as sharply, displaying little evidence of employee constraint.

Why? Why? The word echoed mockingly inside his head. Why, because I've got the hots for my brother's woman, Brett wanted to snarl, and it's driving me insane, that's why. The weeds are a substitute satisfaction, you beautiful bit— Brett clamped the lid on his thoughts. Longing to fondle something much softer, Brett fondled the plastic lighter.

"Maybe the pressure of business is finally getting to me," he answered dryly. "How are you feeling?" His sudden change in topic startled her and, for some perverse reason, that pleased him. Watch it, Renninger, he warned himself. If you derive

137

pleasure from drawing the mildest reaction from her, you're in bigger trouble than you imagined.

"*I'm* feeling fine." She eyed him uncertainly, then shrugged, as if thinking *why not?* Are you all right?" she asked warily.

Brett started to laugh, choked on the smoke he'd just drawn into his lungs, then coughed violently. "You're priceless," he gasped, gulping air into his tortured lungs. "The look on your face!" As the coughing fit subsided, he shook his head. "Were you wondering if you should call for help?"

"Will I need it?" Jo arched a dark brown questioningly.

There's a distinct possibility you will. Brett shrugged off the urge to voice the observation. Now was not the time. There was something he had to say first.

"Jo, about last week . . . "

"I don't want to talk about it!" she interrupted sharply. "Do you have work for me to do?"

"We're going to talk about it whether you want to or—"

"No!" Jumping out of the chair, she stood trembling and poised for flight. "If you have nothing for me to do—"

"SIT DOWN!" Brett barked the command. "I'll tell you when you may leave this office."

Her eyes shooting sparks at him, her delicate nostrils flaring with rebellious agitation, Jo defied his authority. "You can't make me . . . "

"Who the hell's going to stop me?" Partly amused, partly angry, Brett flung the question at her arrogantly. Jo did the one and only thing that could stop him cold. Calmly lifting the telephone receiver, she stared at him coolly as she punched the button for his secretary.

"Mrs. Jenkins, get me Wolf Renninger in Florida, please," she instructed the woman quietly. "I'll wait till you've made the connection."

"Damn you, Jo! Hang that phone up." Brett was so furious he had to push the order through his gritted teeth. You should have known better, you fool, he lashed himself scathingly. You really should have known better. Why did you assume, even for one wild moment, that she'd let you order her around? She's got the ear of the big prowler, his ear and every other vital part of him. You, big mouth, are only his baby brother! Berating himself, Brett watched as she spoke into the receiver.

"Cancel that Florida call, Mrs. Jenkins. We've resolved the problem." Cradling the receiver gently, Jo looked at him impassively. "We have resolved the problem. Haven't we?"

Leaning back in his chair, Brett studied her through narrowed lids. "You really would have called him, wouldn't you?"

"Yes," Jo replied simply. "I really would have called him."

"Because I raised my voice to you, you'd have taken the risk of disturbing him," Brett persisted coldly. "Regardless of his condition, or what a whining call from you might do to him, you would have called him?"

Even though Jo's features tightened, she answered coldly, "That's right, I would have." She pause to draw a deep breath, then coldly reinforced her position. "Let's have one thing clear here and now, *Mr.* Renninger, sir. I am your *brother's* assistant, not yours. At least, fortunately, not on a permanent basis. I am not a lackey. I am not a go-for. I am not the resident whipping boy. And I will not be spoken to like any of the above. If you are in a foul mood, find someone else to snap at." A derisive smile curled her lips. "You can always call Richard Colby," she suggested sweetly. "And chew him out." Her smile hardened. "May I leave now?"

Taut with anger, Brett curled his fingers around the chair arms to keep himself from springing from the seat and sprinting around the desk to her. He wanted to slap her smirking face. He wanted to shake the living hell out of her. But, more than anything else, he wanted to kiss her insolent mouth. You are in big trouble, boy, Brett advised himself, running a calculating glance over her. This one's got you tied in knots that would make a sailor blanch. Play it cool, chum, play it cool.

"Sit down, please," he said in a carefully controlled monotone.

"Why?" Jo didn't move.

Somehow Brett contained the curse that danced on the tip of his tongue. Forcing himself to relax, he sat up straight and folded his hands on his desk. One could hardly throttle a woman if one's hands were folded! "This is a business office, and . . . "

"Oh! You noticed, finally," Jo taunted coolly.

Of course, one could always *unfold* one's hands. Brett didn't. Instead, he drew a deep, cautioning breath. "You're right," he admitted, swallowing the taste of gall. "I stepped out of line . . . " He paused, then added firmly, "Here." He paused again, but her only reaction was a tightening of her lips. "It won't happen again." Once more he paused briefly. "Here."

"Why do I feel less than reassured?" Jo murmured tersely.

Brett could feel his facial muscles tightening with the insult. "I said I'll keep all our discussions on an impersonal basis here in the office. If I give you my word on it, will you sit down?"

Jo stared directly into Brett's eyes for several seconds, then slowly, stiffly sank to the very edge of the chair. Brett knew the elation he felt at her compliance was out of proportion to the situation, yet he savored the acknowledgment of her acceptance of his word. Staring into the hazel depths of her eyes, he nodded his head slightly. "Thank you." His husky tone caused a ripple in her mask of withdrawal, and that sent his elation up a notch. God! he mused, visually crawling into a hazel ensnarement. With very little effort, this gal could slip a ring through my nose and keep me grinning throughout the entire process! Time to pull your head together, Renninger, before you find yourself down for the count. Think of something, anything, but get your concentration back on the business of buildings.

"The Vermont project is underway." The suddenness of his stark statement shattered the tension Brett could feel sneaking along his nerve ends. It shattered a great deal of Jo's assumed composure as well. Two hazel traps blinked in momentary confusion, releasing their captive. "It would have been less awkward for me up there if you had seen fit to inform me of Wolf's decision to contract Sean Delheny for the job."

"But I didn't know he had!" Jo protested. "How many times do we have to go over this argument?" she added impatiently. "Brett, I will tell you once more that I had thought Wolf had scrapped the whole idea."

"Well, at least I'm Brett again." Brett was barely aware of murmuring the thought aloud. Jo hastened to assure him the status quo could revert at an instant's notice.

"For as long as you behave by maintaining a professional attitude."

The "behave" got to him. "I'm not a little boy, Jo," he purred with deliberate silkiness. "Be very careful of how you speak to me. You cannot remain in the building forever." He smiled gently, very gently. "Are you receiving my message?"

The expression that flashed across Jo's face activated a curl of excitement in Brett's lower region. She had obviously received his message loud and clear, and, although she now had her expression in rigid control, for a fleeting instant he had read blatant eagerness on her face. Oh, yes, my sweet, the time for A S A draws closer and closer for both of us, he promised silently.

"Brett, I did not know about Wolf contracting Sean Delheny." Jo's quiet but forceful disclaimer snapped the erotic thread Brett was weaving. Consigning his designing plans for their future of sensuality to the edge of his mind, he brought his concentration back to the cold world of business.

"Okay, but I felt like a fool. First of all, I didn't even know Casey was a woman! Then I find out Sean had his nose out of joint because he hadn't been included in our first meeting." Brett shook his head in memory. "As I said, I felt pretty foolish when Casey introduced me to Sean."

"I'm sorry. I could have saved you that embarrassment. I just never thought to tell you the architect was a woman. Of course, I knew that Casey and Sean were married, and that Sean was a building contractor, but . . . " She let her voice trail off as she shrugged lightly.

Brett's shrug reflected hers. "It's over and done with. Sean is now officially under contract. I suggested a few minor changes in design, which Casey is working on now, but, for all intents and purposes, the project is underway." Without consciously thinking about it, Brett lighted another cigarette, drawing in deeply before continuing. "Before I left Vermont I tossed the ball into your court. I instructed both the Delhenys to send their reports to you." Pushing his chair back abruptly, he stood up and strolled to the wide window behind his desk to stare up at the overcast sky. When Jo didn't respond for several seconds, Brett turned back to her. "Can you handle it?"

"Yes."

A tiny smile quirked the corners of Brett's lips as he silently applauded the simplicity of her affirmation. In effect, what Jo was telling him with her quiet assertion was "I'm good at my job, and I know it." In that respect Brett could empathize with her; he felt exactly the same way about himself. Brett went momentarily still with the realization of sharing yet another character trait with Jo. In his mind, he slowly ticked off the things they had in common. They were both good at their chosen work and knew it. They both had a somewhat offbeat sense of humor. They both enjoyed good food, especially of the breakfast variety. During the hours Brett had spent in Jo's apartment while she'd been sleeping, he had made a tour of the rooms. On completion of his inspection he'd decided her taste was excellent—very likely because it reflected his own. And, last but definitely not least, they shared a mutual physical hunger. The parallels were enlightening . . . and a little scary. Brett was positive he did not want to feel this affinity with *any* woman, let alone another man's woman!

"You don't believe me?" Jo's strained tone fragmented Brett's conjecturing.

"What?" Brett shook his head to clear his mind. "Oh, yes, of

142

course I believe you. I . . . ah . . . was thinking of something else." Something I wish I'd never considered, he added mutely. "Understand, if there are any snags, or major problems, we'll work them out together but, well, I'd like the freedom to get on with an idea of my own."

Jo's immediate interest was evidenced by her alert expression and the eagerness of her blurted, "What idea?"

"I'm considering a complex, a very large complex, in the Pocono Mountains in Pennsylvania." His gaze steady on her taut form, Brett waited to see if she'd react at all. He didn't have long to wait. Jo was still for a moment, then, an appreciative smile baring her white teeth, she nodded her head once.

"Can you get the property?" She shot the question at him hopefully.

"There's a realtor negotiating the deal now, but I want to be there." He lifted his shoulders. "The man is completely qualified yet"—he smiled deprecatingly—"I want to be there."

"Of course you do." Jo's return smile said tomes more than her simple words.

A gentle quiet settled between them. An understanding quiet Brett had never before experienced with a woman. It was good. They both felt it and reacted to it. Neither one of them moved, nor did they break that fragile quiet with speech. But they spoke to each other with mirroring smiles and glances that touched and locked. Jo, a wondering look widening her eyes, finally snapped the both of them back to the here and now.

"When are you leaving?"

There was an odd, almost frightened edge to her carefully controlled voice that Brett was in complete communion with. He felt it himself, the accord, or *simpatico*, or whatever it was that shimmered between them—it kind of frightened him too. He also was careful of betraying no nuances in his tone.

"I can clear my desk by Wednesday," Brett said hopefully.

"Then go," she chided softly. "I'll mind the store."

Brett grinned, unknowingly revealing his relief at her willingness to assume command in his absence. When he'd gone to Vermont three weeks previously he'd had everything under control. Now things were beginning to hum a bit—the way things usually did when the youngest of the Renningers got into gear—and it was a definite relief to know he had a second in command in New York who was the equal to Richard Colby in Atlanta. Still grinning, he walked back to his desk. Propping a hip on the edge of the cluttered surface, Brett picked up a thick manila envelope and handed it to Jo.

"The Vermont project thus far. Skim over it. If you have any questions, jot them down. We'll confer tomorrow afternoon." Brett arched a pale eyebrow at her. "Okay?"

"Yes."

Again that simple matter-of-factness. Damned if she isn't something else, Brett mused, watching her rise and move to the door. As Jo reached for the knob, another consideration struck him.

"By the way—" He halted her action. "I've fully briefed Marsha on the project. As the New England manager, she will be at your disposal."

Five minutes later, Brett still stared at the door Jo had closed so very carefully behind her. What the hell had happened to all that understanding that had been flowing back and forth between them? Suddenly Jo had turned into the queen of ice! Surely it could not have been because he'd suggested she utilize the talents of another employee? But then, what the hell had chased all the warmth from her eyes and voice? All he'd done was mention the New England area manager and Jo had turned on the frost. Women! Shaking his head, Brett circled his desk and sat down. Just when a man thought he was beginning to understand a female, she spins and throws one at him from left field!

As arranged, Brett met with Jo on Tuesday afternoon. The minute she entered his office Brett sighed with the realization that she had apparently applied her makeup with Jack Frost's paintbrush; he was still getting the ice treatment. Their meeting was terse, brief, and to the point. She claimed to have no questions whatever. Brett took her word for it. The minute she left his office, Brett called Marsha front and center.

"Has Jo been in touch with you about the Vermont deal?" Brett shot the question at Marsha before she'd even seated herself.

"No." Marsha made no attempt to conceal her surprise, or her curiosity.

"Why?"

"No special reason," Brett hedged. "I was merely wondering."

"She's the one, isn't she?" Marsha murmured sympathetically.

"What one?" Brett's tone leveled a definite warning.

"Oh, Brett." Marsha chose to ignore the danger. "You know 'what one'. The one whose memory kept you from performing at"—she paused at the sudden stiffness about him, but went on fearlessly—"full capacity, shall we say?"

Brett's reaction was immediate and startling. "Damn it, Marsha!" he snarled, jumping to his feet to stalk to the window, then back again. "Do I taunt you by reminding you of your failure that night?"

"I'm not taunting you, Brett."

"Then what the hell—"

"Brett," she cut in gently. "You're laying a smoke screen, and you know it. Jo is the one, isn't she?"

"Yes," he grated harshly. "Christ! Am I that transparent?"

"Of course not." Marsha smiled. "And you know it. But I was with you when you came back last week, remember. I could actually feel the tension between the two of you. And I saw your face when it became obvious that she was ill. Poor Brett, you've got it pretty bad, haven't you?"

"Sometimes bad." Brett smiled whimsically. "And sometimes good. But at all times frustrating."

"As to that, I have a million questions." She held up her hand

145

at the frown that drew his brows together. "None of which I'd dare ask. But isn't there any way you can resolve the situation?"

"Oh, my dear Marsha, I fully intend to resolve the situation," Brett assured her softly. "In my own time, and in my own way."

"There are times"—Marsha grinned—"my dear Brett, when you actually give me the shivers."

"Oh, sure," Brett said dismissively. Moving restlessly, he strolled to the window. "By the way, are you all settled in?" he asked idly.

"To what? The job or the apartment?"

"Both," he grinned. "But primarily the job."

"Fairly well." She grinned back. "Why do I have this sensation you have a particular reason for asking?"

"Maybe because I have a particular reason for asking," he retorted dryly. "I'm going to hit the road again on Wednesday," he explained seriously. "I was wondering if you had any questions before I leave."

"Where are you off to this time?" Not for a minute did Marsha think the query impertinent, which said much for the closeness that had developed between them in the brief time they'd known each other.

"The Pocono Mountains in Pennsylvania. I'm considering a condo complex there," Brett explained sketchily.

"For the skiers?"

Brett smiled. Marsha was sharp, but she was not quite as sharp as Jo. Jo had immediately picked up on his motivation. Oddly, knowing Jo was half a step ahead of most pleased him immensely.

"Partly." He nodded. "But I suspect that, before too long, that area will be booming the way the Jersey coast is now."

"Legalized gambling?" Marsha's eyes widened.

"The possibility is there." Brett shrugged. "What the hell, Columbus took a chance."

"And he's dead," Marsha drawled, straightfaced.

"Yes, well, nobody gets out of this life alive," Brett out-drawled her. "Well, do you have any questions?"

"None that I can think of offhand," she assured him.

"In that case, I have an assignment for you." Choosing his words carefully, Brett continued, "While I'm away I'd like you to use your connection with Casey Delheny to keep abreast of what's going on up there." Restless again, he measured the carpet in strides. "Jo has been put in complete charge but—"

"You don't trust her?" Marsha asked softly.

"I trust her implicitly!" His tone suddenly harsh, Brett stopped pacing to glare at her. "*But*, should she require assistance, I want you armed with the necessary data."

"Oh, boy," Marsha breathed softly. "You do have it bad." Before he could bite her head off, which he appeared ready to do, she asked, just as softly, "Are we friends, Brett?"

"You know we are," Brett snapped. "But that does not give you the right to—"

"Brett." Marsha silenced him with a wave of her hand. "Let me give you a bit of"—she shook her head at his scowling look—"not advice, but information. You know, the grapevine in this building is very alive and very active. I've picked up a few interesting bits and pieces since I've been here."

Positive she was going to say Wolf's name, and equally positive he did not want to hear it, Brett tried to shut her up. "I'm not interested in company gossip, Marsha."

"Then you should be," Marsha insisted, determined to have her say. "I'm told she's frigid."

"What!" With the memory of Jo's eager mouth, the way she melted against him, and her eyes, smokey with desire, teasing his mind, Brett was hard put not to laugh.

"Or afraid of men, or something. At any rate, she appears to have little or nothing to do with them. And they have tried, boy, have they tried! Apparently every eligible, and not so eligible, man in this building has approached her at one time or another.

147

The rebuff is made gently, and very politely, but it is definitely a rebuff." Marsha shrugged. "I just thought you should know."

"And now I do," Brett replied roughly. "And now the subject is closed." No sane person argued when Brett used that roughly threatening tone of voice. Marsha knew better than to set a precedent.

Brett was away from the office for ten days. Ten days during which he was very busy, and strangely lonely, and tormented by thoughts of Jo. Only once did he give thought to his last conversation with Marsha, and then only fleetingly. Incredible as it seemed, apparently no one at the office had an inkling of the affair between Wolf and his assistant. That fact confirmed Brett's opinion of the two of them: Wolf and Jo were intelligent individuals.

One consideration did occur at regular intervals during those ten days, and that was his stated trust in Jo. Did he trust her? Brett asked himself repeatedly. Always, he answered his question with a question: How could he trust a woman who was involved with a married man? Yet, after days of self-questioning, Brett finally answered his conscience with the truth: He would trust her with his life.

It didn't make much sense, at least not Brett's kind of sense, but there it was, like it or not. He trusted her. He loved her.

On the flight back to New York, Brett told himself he was as dead as Columbus!

It was raining when Brett landed at Newark. It was raining when he dashed from the taxi to the doors of the Renninger Building. The cabbie had told Brett the radio newscaster had said there was a possibility of the rain turning to snow. The front desk receptionist informed him the TV newscaster had said there was a chance of snow. Not one of them told him what he wanted to know. After ten days of longing for her, missing her, the only subject of interest to Brett was Jo Lawrence.

On entering his office, Brett's first act was to ask his secretary

148

to call Jo and request she join him. "And phrase it to her exactly that way," he instructed the shocked, middle-aged secretarial wizard.

To pass the time while waiting for Jo's arrival, Brett lighted a cigarette, then drummed on his desk with the tips of his fingers. Beginning to feel a trifle foolish staring fixedly at the wood-grained door, he swung his gaze to the window, then wished he hadn't. The direction of the wind was driving the rain against the pane and, intermingling with the drops striking the glass, Brett could discern the occasional splat of a snowflake.

"Whoever heard of snow a week and a half before Thanksgiving?" he muttered in disgust.

"I beg your pardon?"

"There's snow mixed with that rain!" Brett growled, swinging around to confront the tormenter of his nights. Then Jo smiled at his disgruntlement, making him feel more a fool than before. God! She's all I think about for over a week and, when I finally get back, I complain about snow! You had better nail this woman down pretty soon, old son, Brett advised himself. For if you don't, they're going to come and cart you away!

"Well, don't blame me." Jo actually laughed at him. "I didn't order it."

Lost in his own thoughts, Brett stared at her in confusion a moment. Then the dawn broke in his mind. The snow! "Oh, well, I'm not used to the stuff. The South doesn't get a great deal of it."

"Do tell!" Jo gave a fair imitation of a Southern drawl.

Brett was immediately suspicious. Why was she so downright chipper this afternoon? One word sprang into his mind. A name. A name he didn't even want to think, let alone say aloud. Nonetheless, there it was. Wolf! Had she been in contact with her lover? Damn it, if she had he'd beat her!

"You appear to be in fine spirits today," he probed carefully.

"And why not?" Jo grinned. "I received the report you sent me three days ago." Her grin widened into a full, breathtaking

149

smile. "You closed the deal on the property you wanted. I think that's plenty of reason for high spirits. Don't you?"

Brett nodded, grinned, and just sat staring at her. She is so damn beautiful, he thought achingly. Her smile alone brightens the dismal day. In concession to the weather, Jo was dressed in a full, dove-gray wool skirt and a pullover sweater in hot pink that clung to her figure to the point of making Brett's hands itch. Her long, slim legs were encased to the knee in black stack-heeled boots of soft, pliant leather. Considering the overall picture she presented, Brett decided she looked terrific. He also decided he'd love to undress her, very, very slowly. The beginnings of a frown marring her face drew him, reluctantly, out of the promise of a delightfully erotic daydream.

"Now the work begins on it," he said abruptly.

"Have you decided on an architect?"

"I was considering Casey Delheny," Brett said thoughtfully. "I was really impressed with her designs for Vermont. What do you think?" Brett's question was not rhetorical. He really wanted her opinion, and he let it show in his tone.

"I think Casey's an excellent choice. Wolf thought so too. He'd inspected several of the buildings she'd designed and was very impressed. He also approved of the work of her interior designers."

Although Brett was not pleased with her use of Wolf as a reference, he let it slide. "Yes, I've seen some of her buildings myself, and I like the work of her interior designers as well. Okay, we'll go with Casey and let her use her own people."

"Do you always make decisions this quickly?" Jo laughed in a tone slightly tinged with awe.

"Usually." Brett shrugged nonchalantly.

"But don't you have to consult with headquarters?"

"Are you kidding?" Brett grinned. "I consulted with headquarters until I was afraid the phone lines would melt between Pennsylvania and Florida." His grin widened. "And do you want to know what the final word from the head honcho was?"

Of course Jo nodded. "Mama told me, and these are her exact words, 'You picked up the ball, now run with it.' " Brett laughed out loud.

"Incredible!"

"I suppose." Brett shrugged. "But then, Renninger's is not run like most companies. In the first place it is entirely family owned and managed. Madam President *gives* orders, she does not take them." A gentle smile curved his lips. "In the second place, Mother gave each one of her sons the opportunity to do one complete job on his own. It was my turn. The Pocono project will be my baby."

"But what if you fail?" Jo blurted.

"No problem," Brett drawled. "She'll kill me."

Jo stared at him aghast for an instant, then joined him in laughter. "I think I'd like your mother," she said, when she could finally speak.

"I know Mother would like you," he assured her. "In fact, she wants to meet you."

"Me?" Jo blinked in astonishment. "Why would she want to meet me?" She eyed him warily. "And how would you know?"

"She told me." Brett met her wary glance with a smile. "While we were burning up Bell Tel's East Coast lines, she asked me how I was muddling along without the redoubtable Richard Colby. I told her I was indeed not muddling, but skimming, as I had Richard's double in drag in the New York office." Jo's gasp produced a slashing grin from Brett. "Again I quote my revered mother: 'I have got to meet the woman *you* admit is as competent as Richard!' she said quite seriously."

"Yes, well, the next time your mother is in New York, perhaps she'll peek into my office." Everything about Jo's attitude told Brett she didn't believe a word he said. "Now, back to the business at hand. Are you going to have the preliminary specs for the building drawn up by our people, or are you going with a general contractor?"

"What I said to my mother was incorrect." Brett groaned.

"You are not like Richard. You are much, much more of a slave driver." Jo frowned. Brett got back to the business at hand. "I've decided to use Sean Delheny as general contractor. As with Casey, I've seen some of his work. I've also discussed it with the people he's worked for. The decision was unanimous: Sean is one damned good ramrod. He's done some fast-tracking."

Jo was well aware that the term fast-tracking applied to bonuses earned for a construction job completed ahead of schedule. Jo was also well aware of Sean's track record. He was very careful. He was very good. He got a job done right, usually ahead of time. Brett knew she made it her business to be aware of such things.

"Does Sean know he's been appointed for yet another Renninger project?" Jo asked dryly.

"Of course." Brett acted shocked, as if she should have known better than to even ask. "He's in the mountains now, checking out the local talent for subcontracting. I plan to confer with him again after Thanksgiving."

"Which reminds me," Jo sat up straighter in her chair. "I'm going to be out of the office most of Thanksgiving week. I'm going home for the holiday. I still have some vacation time due me."

"No problem." Brett shrugged. "Clear it with personnel."

Long after Jo had gone back to her own office, Brett sat, again contemplating the grain in the wood door. All his hopes of the previous ten days metaphorically laughing at him as they floated out the window. There were four days left to this week, four days in which he had one hell of a lot of work to catch up on. Next week she'd be gone. Come to that, so would he, as he had to fly to Atlanta to brief and be briefed by Richard. Then he was off again to Florida for Thanksgiving. A schedule, Brett decided glumly, that allowed little time for seduction.

Pushing his chair back, Brett shoved his suddenly tired body erect and stalked to the window to glare out at the rain that was rapidly changing to snow. At first he had envisioned taking Jo

152

to his own bed. Then, growing desperate, he'd decided *her* bed would do just as well. Now, in a state of constant frustration, he'd happily make use of any damned bed or reasonably flat surface!

I think I was happier, he thought irritably, when all I wanted to do was strangle her.

During the remainder of that week, Brett saw more of Marsha than he did of Jo. A minor crisis had cropped up at a Renninger motel nearing completion in Massachusetts, and Marsha had come to Brett, mad as hell, because the ramrod of the project flatly refused to deal with a woman. When reason and diplomacy failed to budge the jerk, Brett had resolved the problem by telling the man to "Eat what you're served, or get the hell away from the table." If the injection of instant education didn't exactly cure the man's ailment, it did treat the existing symptoms; the ape decided he could work with Marsha.

In Atlanta, to Brett's immense relief, he found that Richard had everything under control, as usual.

"Are you attempting to ingratiate yourself into my office?" Their conference concluded, Brett and Richard were relaxing over a drink in one of Brett's favorite bars.

"Of course." Richard nodded. "The way I figure it, at the pace you've been working at since you and Sondra separated, you'll begin to burn out any day now." His grin was pure Machiavellian. "I intend to be prepared when Madam Pres finds herself in need of a new head man in Atlanta."

Free of tension for the first time in over a month, Brett leaned back in his chair and raised his glass in salute. "Good luck," he drawled, a grin lightening the new lines of strain on his handsome face.

Brett could afford the salute and the encouragement, very simply because he knew his assistant had no designs on his position. Richard Colby, small, dapper, urbane to his fingertips, was quite satisfied in his position as first assistant, and Brett knew it. Of course, Richard knew Brett knew it. Richard's mild threat was as close as he'd come to asking Brett to slow down. Brett, though appreciating Richard's concern, had no intention of paying heed to it.

Brett was in Florida barely long enough to sit down at the overloaded dinner table with the Renninger clan. Within the eighteen hours he was at the farm Brett learned that: Wolf was mending, if slowly; Micki was well, and pleased with the way Wolf was mending; their offspring were full of sun and the devil; Eric and his family were happily increasing, as Eric's wife was pregnant with their third child; his sister Di was smugly displaying her son's ability to perform back flips, and his mother was, as always, the indestructible head of Renninger Corporation—and all the assorted younger Renningers.

Then Brett was off again, this time to Pennsylvania and his prearranged meeting with Sean Delheny. Not once during Brett's quick visit to the farm had JoAnne Lawrence's name been mentioned. Not once had the image of JoAnne Lawrence been far from Brett's mind. In fact, by the time Brett returned to the New York office in early December, his thoughts of Jo had become so obsessive he was afraid that if he didn't see her soon he'd begin snarling at everyone around him like a dog with distemper.

Brett began snarling upon arrival at his office the following morning. He had wakened early feeling good with anticipation and had even caught himself whistling while standing under the shower. Walking to the office briskly in the cold December air, he had counted the blocks and then the pavement squares to his building. Entering the outer office, Brett had politely asked Ms. Jenkins to buzz Jo and request her to join him. Ms. Jenkins reply stopped him cold two paces from his office door.

"Ms. Lawrence isn't in, sir. She flew to Vermont yesterday."

Later, through Marsha and his second assistant, a young eager beaver named Bob Kempten, Brett learned that Casey Delheny had called about some technical problem and Jo had decided to investigate personally. By the time Jo returned, two days later, most of Brett's staff were circling him from a distance, as if he were a rabid dog. Determined he'd see her the minute she was back in her office, Brett left a terse note for her on her desk. The message consisted of three words: Get in here.

"You wanted to see me?" Jo asked as she gently closed the door to Brett's office.

Brett was standing at the window, trying to stare holes through the low-hanging, dirty-gray clouds. At the sound of his door being opened every muscle and nerve in his body tensed, but when he turned to face her he presented a picture of total relaxation. At the sight of her, her cheeks pink from the cold, her dark hair tousled from the brisk wind, and her lips slick with freshly applied gloss, Brett had to clamp his back teeth together to control the urge to go to her and pull her into his arms.

"What was Casey's problem?" Brett tossed the question at Jo as he strolled to his desk. As if, at this moment, I care, he thought, reaching for the pack of cigarettes on his desk to give his hands something to do instead of reaching for her.

"Nothing really earth shattering, and nothing I couldn't handle."

Every one of Brett's senses screamed an alert. There was something wrong here, something in Jo's tone. Eyelids narrowing, Brett studied her more closely, his sharpened glance probing past the glow imbued by being out of doors. Her eyes were opaque, refusing an observer access to her thoughts. Her features were carefully controlled, devoid of expression. Her attitude was of polite, cool detachment. All the questions he'd planned to ask her about Vermont fled before the confusion that fogged Brett's mind.

Before he'd left New York for Atlanta they had been on friendly, almost warm terms. Now Jo looked at him as if he were a stranger, and a not too appealing one at that. What could have possibly happened to change her? Brett wondered. And in such a short amount of time?

155

"Are you . . . all right?" Brett inquired gently, carefully feeling his way.

"Actually, no." Jo's lips tightened.

Brett's chest tightened too. "Is it something to do with that trouble in Vermont?" Even as Brett asked the question Jo was shaking her head in the negative. "What then?" he demanded, if softly.

Jo drew a deep breath, which nearly drew a groan past his compressed lips; Jo did fill a sweater to advantage.

"I'm not feeling right." She hesitated, then rushed on, too quickly. "I don't feel exactly ill, but I don't feel exactly well either. I'm . . . I'm tired all the time. Perhaps it's a holdover from the virus I contracted a few weeks ago."

Garbage. Brett knew Jo was lying, he *knew* it . . . yet, why? "Have you consulted a doctor about your symptoms?" Brett knew the answer to that too. He was right.

"No." Not a muscle in her face moved, only her lips. "I-I think all I need is some rest." Now she hesitated again, as if girding herself for battle. "I've used up all my vacation but, with your permission"—she grimaced, as if the last word was distasteful to her—"I'd like to take a leave of absence the last two weeks of this month."

"Jo—" Brett began, only to be cut off at once.

"That's not all . . . sir."

Sir again! Brett very nearly winced. Controlling the need to go to her and shake some life, some emotion, into her and evoke some *response* from her, Brett muttered, "Go on. What else do you want?"

"Permission to stay at the motel in Ocean City." Jo stared at him coolly.

"You want to go to the beach in December!" Brett exclaimed in an amazed shout.

"I want to rest!" Jo shouted back, revealing tension for the first time since entering his office. "It will be quiet there. And I love

156

the sea. May I stay in one of the rooms there?" she insisted, her tone again without inflection.

"Aren't you going home for Christmas?"

"No!" The denial shot out of her.

Brett now had part of the answer, but only part of it. He was sure something had happened while she'd been home at Thanksgiving, and apparently that something had been unpleasant. Brett was equally sure that was not the complete answer. Her attitude toward *him* had changed drastically, so it was also something to do with him that had caused this cold front she was presenting. But what had he done? Brett raked his mind and came up blank. If she'd only talk to him, or scream at him . . . but, from her attitude, it was obvious she was not going to budge from behind her icy mask. Damn it, he raged inwardly, what can I do but let her have what she wants? Nothing.

"If you're going to stay there the entire two weeks, one room won't do," he said flatly. "You'll get cabin fever before the first week is out. Stay in the apartment."

"But . . . "

"Don't argue!" Brett was skating very close to the edge of his patience, and it showed. Jo subsided at once. "I'll call Wolf's housekeeper, Mrs. Jorgeson, and ask her to have the utilities turned on and to clean the place for you." Standing abruptly, he slid his hand into his pocket and withdrew a gold keyring. After working two of the keys off the ring, he leaned across the desk and handed them to her. "I'll also let security know you're coming." A sardonic smile twitched at his lips. "I don't think you'd enjoy spending Christmas in the slammer for breaking and entering."

Jo's expression didn't change, in as much as she still showed no expression at all. "Thank you." Her voice had a cool, withdrawn quality that sent a shiver through Brett.

Brett mentally gnawed at the problem of Jo's attitude long after she'd left his office. In fact, he was still racking his brain for an answer after her leave of absence had officially begun. He

157

saw little of her during the two-week interval, and what he did see of her alarmed him. She was pale, she looked liked she was not getting enough sleep, and she was much too subdued. The Jo Lawrence he had come to love had been anything but subdued.

As Christmas grew nearer, and the office employees grew merrier, Brett's worry and frustration jelled into determination. Four days before Christmas he reached the end of his patience. Whether Jo liked it or not, she was going to get company. Damn it! He owned the place, didn't he?

Late that afternoon Brett signed the release for the employees' Christmas bonuses, locked his desk, and pushed his chair back. As he was shrugging into his coat the phone rang. Snatching up the receiver impatiently, Brett growled, "Ms. Jenkins, I told you I was leaving. I'm taking no calls."

"I'm sorry, Mr. Renninger, but I was sure you'd want to speak to this party."

Brett immediately thought of Jo. "Who is it?"

"The boss."

Brett smiled at the wizard's dry tone. Hell, he didn't know she was capable of dry humor! "You're right, Ms. Jenkins. I'll take the call." The moment Brett heard the switch click in, he drawled with his usual insolence, "Yes, sir?"

"I should have beaten you as a child," his mother said decisively, then added maternally, "You are coming to the farm for Christmas, aren't you?"

"Yes, of course," Brett assured her. "I should get there late in the afternoon on Christmas Eve."

"Good, we'll see you then," Violet said briskly. "By the way, if your Ms. Lawrence has no other plans, bring her with you," she tacked on as an afterthought.

Brett mulled over his mother's invitation all the way to Ocean City. Even though she had expressed a desire to meet Jo, it seemed odd to Brett that his mother had chosen this particular time to do it. Christmas was always a family time at the Renninger manse, wherever that happened to be when the holiday rolled around. There was, of course, one unavoidable consideration, and that was that Wolf had made a special request of Violet to include Jo. Merely speculating on that possibility torched a blaze of anger inside Brett.

By the time he drove onto the motel parking lot, Brett had mulled himself into a fury. Deep inside his conscience, Brett knew he had no right to demand anything from Jo. At the same time, consciously Brett knew he was about to demand everything from her.

The small car, parked near the entrance doors, looked slightly forlorn on the large lot. As he pulled the Porsche up beside it, the term run-about slithered into Brett's mind. Had Wolf signed his name to a check for the toy? Brett tormented himself with the query as he strode to the wide glass doors. After making sure the doors were securely locked again behind him, Brett took the stairs two at a time, then loped along the hallway to the apartment. Key at the ready, he hesitated a moment, then unlocked the door and stepped inside.

Jo was standing with her back to the oversized window, having obviously spun around at the sound of his entrance. She did not look frightened, or even surprised. In fact, Brett had the strange sensation that she'd been expecting him. His anger changing to an even more basic emotion, Brett stood still for a moment, eating her with his eyes. Even though it was still early evening, Jo was dressed for bed in a lilac-and-orchid striped silk robe over a paler orchid nightgown. Her face was free of makeup and her hair was slightly mussed. Brett decided to muss it even more.

Without as much as a word, watching her eyes, Brett walked to her, shedding his suede jacket and dropping it to the floor as he went. With cool deliberation he walked right into her, a primitive thrill leaping in his loins at the shock of their colliding bodies. Then the aching emptiness of his arms was filled with the softness of her and his restlessly moving hands delighted in the

159

silk material covering her back. Still staring into her eyes, Brett read surrender in the soft hazel depths.

The clean scent of her filling his senses, the feel of her soft breasts crushed to his chest, and his own now-raging desire snapped the thread of communication between Brett and his conscience. Damn Wolf! Damn the whole damned world! He must have this woman.

Giving Jo time to protest, or turn her head aside if she wanted to, Brett lowered his head slowly. The fact that Jo did neither, but parted her lips instead, set Brett's heart racing. Gently, gently, he cautioned himself as he touched his lips to hers. But then, at Jo's instant response, all thoughts of caution dissolved in the blood that went rushing through his veins. Suddenly filled with the need to conquer, Brett pressed his mouth against hers, unmindful of the low growl that swelled his vocal chords. Jo reacted by clasping his head to pull him deeper into her mouth.

Sliding his hands down her back, Brett grasped her rounded bottom and lifted her up to meet the urgent thrust of his body. At the same time he inserted his tongue into the sweet moistness of her mouth. Jo rewarded Brett's efforts with a low groan. Sweeping her into his arms, Brett strode to the bedroom, his lips locked on hers. Coming to a stop beside the bed, he allowed himself the pleasure of sliding her body down his as he settled her on her feet.

Every one of Brett's senses urged him to rip the robe and nightgown from Jo's body then tear his own clothes off. Clamping hard on his back teeth, Brett brought every ounce of control he possessed into play. He had waited too long for her to rush the moment. No, there'd be no ripping or tearing here. No hurried, frantic coupling. Brett fully intended to enjoy every minute of the love play. He fully intended Jo to enjoy it as well.

Slowly, tenderly, Brett removed the robe and nightgown, then stepped back to feast his eyes on her. Beautiful, God, she's beautiful, he thought, inching his gaze over Jo's nakedness. Her breasts were not large, but firm and high. Her waist curved in

160

neatly before flaring out again to rounded hips. Her legs were long, shapely as a dancer's, tapering to slim ankles and feet. And her thighs! Brett's gaze lingered on Jo's smooth thighs a moment, then slowly rose to meet her eyes.

"Brett . . . " It was the first word spoken, and her only word. The plea drew his eyes to her face.

"It will be good, Jo. I promise," Brett said in a hoarse voice he hardly recognized as his own. "Do you believe me?"

Jo swallowed, then wet her lips, making Brett long for the feel of her pink tongue in his mouth. "I—I want to believe you, but you don't understand. . . . "

"I don't need to understand," Brett cut her off urgently, positive she was going to attempt to tell him about Wolf. "It *will* be good. I swear to you."

Tugging the spread, blanket, and top sheet free, Brett tossed them to the bottom of the bed, then, lifting Jo again, he lay her in the middle of the mattress. Straightening, Brett swiftly shed his clothes, his gaze locked on hers. When, finally, he stood before her as God had made him, he searched her face for signs of approval—or disapproval. Brett was not unaware of his attractiveness to women. Many of the women he'd dated, and slept with, had been articulate in their praise of his masculine good looks. Now, stripped of all the expensive trappings, Brett trembled as he watched Jo's eyes examine him. His trembling increased with excitement when he saw her eyes widen on sight of his arousal. Brett's excitement building, he watched her gaze shy away from, then return to his manhood before climbing up his body to his face.

"I—I'm not sure I can . . . "

That's as far as Jo got before, sliding on to the bed beside her, Brett closed her mouth with his own. Yet Jo's attempt at protest had shaken him. The prospect of rejection goading him, Brett set out to seduce her.

His lips teased hers. His teeth nibbled on the tender flesh inside. His tongue made gentle forays into the recess of her

161

mouth, then thrust deeply over and over until she moaned and clung to him, silently-begging for more. At the tiny sound Brett deserted Jo's lips to plant stinging kisses down her neck to the hollow at the base of her throat. The flutter of Jo's pulse against the tip of Brett's tongue set fire to his blood. Enjoying the sensation of liquid flames racing through his body, Brett ventured farther south. His lips adored the satiny smoothness of her breasts, his tongue worshipped the hardening nipples. Driven now by a passion running rampant, Brett closed his lips over one rigid nipple and drew gently, shivering with the resultant tightening in his loins.

His hands stroking Jo's softness, learning all the places that caused a movement or murmur of response from her, Brett imprinted his lips onto the skin of her body. His own ardor rising, he dipped his tongue into her navel, then slid his moistened tongue the length of her abdomen and around the perimeter of her dark triangle. Loving his work, Brett tongue-kissed Jo's legs to her insteps, then backtracked up the inside of her thigh. When his lips reached their desired destination, Jo stiffened.

"Brett, no! I . . . "

It was too late. Determined not to be denied, Brett tasted the honied sweetness of her. His hands clasped to her hips, he kissed and caressed her silky warmth. Jo remained stiff for a moment, then a smile touched Brett's lips as he felt her begin to move slowly, then with increasing frenzy, her breath rasping through her moaning throat.

"Brett, Brett, please . . . oh, please . . . "

In all of his fantasies about Jo, never had he hoped to hear her plead for him to love her. Sliding his body up between her thighs, Brett placed his lips lightly to hers.

"Did I promise you it would be good?" he whispered into her mouth.

"Yes!" she gasped, sending a shudder through his body.

"And have I pleased you so far?" he murmured, nipping at her lower lip.

"Yes," she moaned, sending a shaft of near pain into the lower part of his body.

"Shall I continue?" he teased, sliding his tongue along her teeth.

"Oh, yes," she sobbed, sending his control into retreat.

Brett talked to himself to keep from rushing and ruining it all: Take your time. There's no hurry now. You've waited and waited what seems like forever for this. Wrest every ounce of sweetness from it.

All the while he was advising himself, Brett was moving over Jo. Gently he settled himself between her enticingly soft thighs, pausing a moment to stroke her heated core with one hand while caressing a breast with the other. The movement of Jo's hips encouraged entrance and, sliding his hands beneath her, Brett lifted her to meet him. Then, slowly, savoring every incremental movement, Brett penetrated into the satiny sheath that felt like it was fashioned for him alone. Deep within her warmth, Brett felt himself savoring every sensation as he and Jo moved in slow rhythm as one.

The slow savoring could not last. For the first time in his adult life Brett's control shattered completely. Never had he experienced the fullness of the love act—a joining of mind and soul as well as flesh—and only now with this most magnificent of women. Increasing the tempo, Brett moved faster, and still faster, thrusting his body against and into hers, thrilling to the feel of her legs embracing him tightly, exulting to the strength with which she thrust her body against his.

Brett's body was bathed in sweat and his hands felt the slippery wetness of Jo's, and still he prolonged the final moment, waiting for her. When that moment happened for her, he stilled, holding her close, absorbing the shudders into his own body. When her shock waves had subsided, Brett began moving again, stroking deeper, and yet deeper, desperate to possess, equally

163

desperate to be possessed. The explosion came within seconds of her own, and now Jo clutched him to her to cushion the reverberations.

When total sanity returned, Brett carefully moved from Jo's body to the bed. Without a word he drew her into his arms, close to his side. Then, his lips at her forehead, he murmured, "Thank you, water baby. Now, go to sleep."

Long after Jo's even breathing indicated to Brett that she was sleeping deeply, he lay awake, holding her soft body tightly to his own. Staring into the darkness, Brett attempted to sort out the tangle of conflicting emotions vying for supremacy in his mind. First and foremost was the indisputable fact that what he'd just been through had been *the* most shattering sexual experience he'd ever had. Even thinking it seemed strange, yet Jo had somehow enveloped him totally, not merely physically but spiritually as well! Stranger still was the stark realization that, not only did he not mind the . . . ensnarement, for want of a better word . . . he was actually rejoicing in it. He loved it! Hell, now, to himself, holding Jo close in a pitch-dark room, Brett felt free to revel in the truth that he loved her!

Pushing all other considerations aside, Brett whispered the words aloud.

"I love you, JoAnne Lawrence, completely, unconditionally, and, very likely, forever."

The vow at last spoken, even to one who could not hear, Brett sighed contentedly and went to sleep.

CHAPTER EIGHT

The sound of the wind, moaning like a soul in torment, woke Jo. Lying still, she listened to the shiver-inducing noise as gusts beat against the wide bedroom window in ineffectual fury. It was no longer dark beyond the pane, yet still not fully light, the time of morning when the lowest temperature reading is usually registered. In her mind, Jo pictured the ocean and breakers whipped to whitecapped frenzy by the gale. All that potentially destructive elemental force, she mused sleepily. So very near.

A smile of contentment curved her kiss-swollen lips. She was warm and safe. The warmth came, Jo acknowledged, not so much from the covers tucked around her shoulders but from the heat radiating from the body beside hers. The feeling of safety came not from being inside a roof and four walls but from being enclosed within two strong, masculine arms. Dismissing the weather as not worth consideration, Jo snuggled closer to Brett's body, luxuriating in the delicious sensation of his nakedness against her own.

God, he was wonderful! A grin tugged at Jo's lips. *She* was wonderful too! She was a woman! Not merely a female, but a living, breathing, sexually responsive woman! Brett had proved

165

it to her. Proved it in the most primitive way possible. He had made her his, figuratively as well as literally. Brett did not know it, and Jo prayed he never would, but with his possession of her he had earned himself a slave. Jo had been in love with him last night. This morning, what she felt for him came so close to adoration, it scared the wits out of her. Still, perhaps enslavement was worth the price for enlightenment. All her fears and insecurities concerning her ability to respond physically to a man had been swept from her mind by the pulsating rush of sexual fulfillment.

Go to hell, Gary Devlin!

Jo gulped back a gurgle of laughter and snuggled still closer to Brett. She felt terrific! She felt fantastic! She felt . . . Jo compressed her lips to contain a fresh surge of laughter. She *felt* Brett's hand stroking slowly up the inside of her thigh!

"Are you trying to tell me something with all your wiggling around?" Brett's breath whispered over Jo's temple an instant before his tongue outlined the edge of her ear.

"I—I was just thinking how cold the wind sounds, and how warm it is in here," Jo explained, her breath catching as his hand found the apex of her thighs. The entrapped breath vibrated in her throat producing a tiny gasp when his long fingers began combing through the dark thicket.

"I have a feeling it's going to go from warm to red hot very quickly if you continue wiggling your fanny like that." Brett punctuated his assertion by stabbing the tip of his tongue into her ear.

Jo's tiny gasp matured into a deep-throated moan as Brett's fingers slid lower to explore the moist heat of her core. And it was heated! The realization was both a shock and a delight to her. She, JoAnne Lawrence, the woman who had believed herself incapable of responding physically to any man, had become meltingly hot by the simple process of snuggling closer to Brett's warm, naked body. She was ready for him! She was actually ready for him! To a sexually experienced woman that sudden

166

arousal would not have come as a surprise. To Jo it seemed a miracle.

Go with the flow. The buzz phrase drifted through Jo's mind and, reacting to it, she moved her hips sensuously. Brett reacted to her movement by exploring the region in depth. Soft, inarticulate sounds she was barely aware of making tickling the back of her throat, Jo arched her body, instinctively inviting deeper penetration.

"You like that, do you?" Brett murmured into her ear.

"Yes!" Jo admitted between shallow gasps. "Oh, yes!"

"Then you might return the favor," he chided softly.

Return the favor? For an instant Jo's passion-clouded mind grappled with his request. What . . . Oh! Did Brett mean for her to . . . ? But, of course, what else could he mean? she thought fuzzily. Were men also turned on by having their bodies stroked and caressed? Brett answered the question for her in a low groan.

"Touch me, Jo! Please. You can't imagine how long I've ached for you to touch me."

Shyly, hesitantly, Jo lifted her hand and placed her palm against his chest. Then, slowly, she stroked, a growing sense of wonder widening her eyes at the smoothness of his skin. When her fingers brushed lightly over the flat male nipples she paused, a question rising to tantalize her mind. All too vividly Jo remembered the piercing pleasure she had experienced from the touch of Brett's lips to her breasts. Would Brett experience a similar reaction? Intrigued by the idea, Jo shifted her body around until she was positioned almost on top of him. With a soft sign, Brett obligingly made a half turn onto his back. Lowering her head, Jo dropped a string of delicate kisses across his chest. When her lips reached the tight nipple she hesitated and a shiver rippled through Brett's body.

"Jo, please, don't stop now!"

His hoarse, excitement-tinged groan encouraging her on, Jo closed her lips around the taut bud and laved it gently with her tongue. Amazingly, Brett gasped and actually writhed beneath her. His response had the strangest effect on Jo. She was suddenly filled with a heady sense of power. *She* could make him writhe in pleasure! How marvelous! At the same time, Jo recognized that her own sexual tension was increasing. She'd had no idea of how exciting making love to a man could be!

All timidity forgotten, Jo continued to explore Brett's body with her lips. By the time she dipped her tongue into his navel, Brett's breathing had a raspy, uneven sound and his hands moved restlessly over her upper arms and shoulders. All the while her lips dropped tiny kisses, her palms were absorbing the feel of his skin. At his navel she again hesitated briefly, then bravely skimmed her lips down the concave of his abdomen to a hair-rough thigh. Now Brett's hands were in her hair, stroking, tugging gently in a silent plea for her to bestow the ultimate caress.

Understanding immediately, Jo stilled for an instant. During that instant a minibattle raged. Could she? Did she want to? No! Yes! Damn it! Was she not a woman after all? Brett's hips thrust provocatively. The feeling of power washed over her again. Swiftly, before she could change her mind, Jo bent her head, sank her fingertips into his hard buttocks, and granted his mute request. Brett's low groan of intense pleasure urging her on, Jo caressed him gently, finding to her amazement that the more pleasure she gave him, the more she received herself.

Brett withstood Jo's ministrations for several moments, then he grasped her shoulders and growled softly, "Come up here and kiss my mouth, water baby, I want to feel your body covering mine."

Slowly, tormentingly, pausing at strategic spots to kiss teasingly, Jo sinuously slid up his body, unashamedly reveling in Brett's raspingly uttered words of praise.

"You're fantastic, do you know that? You've made me want you so badly I'm trembling all over." Then, when her mouth lightly touched his: "God! The scent of you! The feel of you! The taste of you!"

Digging his fingers into her hair, he pulled her head to his, his mouth taking hers hungrily, his tongue a hot spear branding her mouth as his own. Brett's lips locked onto hers, he grasped her by the hips and lifted her up, then settled her onto his body, branding her again with another spear.

Gasping aloud at the depth of his penetration, Jo let her head drop back and began to move her body in a slow, undulating motion.

"Yes, Yes," Brett crooned unevenly. "Perfect. God! You're perfect."

The lazy tempo was maintained for several minutes during which Jo felt the tension twisting into a wildness inside. She moaned as Brett's hands stroked lovingly over her tautly arched neck to her shoulders and then to her aching breasts before settling firmly on her hips. Slowly, directing her with his hands, Brett increased the tempo, his own body arching to meet hers. His action fed the wildness growing in her, and, grasping his wrists with her hands, Jo accelerated the tempo to a frenzied crescendo. Brett exploded under her. There was no holding back for him this time. Jo sensed his loss of control and gloried in the realization of having been the instrument of his loss. Reality· receding, Jo had the uncanny sensation of soaring through space, and then simultaneously they went crashing through the time barrier. For sweet, pulsating seconds time stood still while their entire beings experienced the highest of the highs. Then, slowly, gently, they drifted back to earth together.

Jo opened her eyes to the awareness of her head resting on Brett's shoulder, her face pressed to the curve of his neck. In gratitude and unspoken love she placed a kiss on his moist skin. Brett's arms tightened around her momentarily, then relaxed.

"Are you uncomfortable, darling?"

Wanting to lock the sound of it in her mind and heart, Jo closed her eyes at the endearment. Uncomfortable? How could she possibly tell him that, at this moment, she desired nothing more than to remain coupled to him forever? Dreamily, she

169

murmured something unintelligible and allowed him to disengage her body from his.

"Are you going to sleep again?" Brett teased, lightly caressing her thighs with one hand.

"I hope so," Jo murmured drowzily, lifting a lazy hand to cover a yawn.

"Self-indulgent wench," Brett chided. "I was hoping you'd come with me."

"With you?" Jo forced her heavy eyelids up. "Where are you going?"

"I thought I'd run on the beach." That quirky smile twitched his lips. "That is, after I've rested a bit. You do take the starch out of a man."

"Run on the beach!" Jo exclaimed, choosing to ignore the double meaning attached to his assertion. "Are you mad? It's cold out there! And windy! Don't you hear it screaming around the building?"

"I'd have to be stone deaf not to." He laughed. "I'm not afraid of the wind."

"I'm not either," Jo assured him around another yawn. "But that doesn't mean I want to run in it. Good night, Brett."

Brett's laughter grew stronger. "But it's morning, honey. See? It's broad daylight."

Casting a narrowed glance at the window, Jo obligingly observed the broad daylight, then she pulled the covers up to her chin and closed her eyes. "So it is," she agreed. "Good night, Brett." Inside her mind, Jo was savoring the taste of his "honey."

"It *is* cold out there." The statement was made through lips that moved against Jo's ear. "And you *are* so nice and warm." His hand wove an erotic pattern up her thigh to cup the tightly curled thicket. "Wonderfully warm." With his other hand Brett drew her head back into the curve of his neck. "Maybe I'll sleep awhile with you. *Then* I'll run on the beach."

The second time Jo woke that morning she noticed three things at once. The wind had died down; the sun was shining brightly; and she was alone in the bed. Apparently Brett had decided to run on the beach. In Jo's opinion, anybody who would even consider running on the beach, or anywhere else, on a cold December morning was slightly animal crackers, but, she thought shrugging, each to his own brand of self-torture. For Jo, the torture would come in the form of the first meal of the day. Jo was a lousy cook. She could knit like a dream, needles clicking away at a dizzying rate of speed while whipping up anything from a simple scarf to a full-length coat, but turn her loose in the kitchen and within minutes it was a disaster area.

After a warm, revitalizing shower, Jo tugged skin-tight jeans over her slender hips and pulled a thigh-length, baggy sweatshirt over her head, then winced as she stroked a brush through her mass of tangled hair. When the dark mop had been beaten into submission, Jo tossed the brush aside and padded barefoot out of the bedroom. She was standing at the kitchen sink, filling the electric percolator with cold water, when Brett swung into the apartment, out of breath, sweaty, and looking sexy as hell in a navy-and-white jogging suit.

"Hi!" he panted, flashing her an ice-melting grin. "If you give me ten minutes to jump in and out of the shower, I'll prepare brunch." Not waiting for a response, he loped across the living room and disappeared down the short hall to the bedroom.

Brunch yet! Jo smiled as she scooped coffee into the small basket. All the while she'd been showering, one worry had nagged at her mind: What would Brett's attitude toward her be now? The morning after! His spontaneous greeting and easy grin had laid that particular worry to rest. Oh, there were other worries and considerations Jo realized she'd eventually have to deal with, but they could wait until after she had fortified herself with food.

As if he'd timed it, Brett strode into the kitchen as the coffee-pot gurgled its last perk. Running a swift, encompassing glance over his lean frame, Jo decided he looked even sexier in tight, brushed denim jeans and a white velour pullover than he had in

171

the jogging outfit. Without hesitation, Brett drew her into his arms.

"Now I can wish you a proper good morning," he said, lowering his head to hers.

Brett's lips touched hers gently, almost tentatively, until he felt her part her lips in response, then his kiss deepened, although not in demand, but more like a learning process. Wanting to learn more herself, Jo put every ounce of herself into the meeting of mouths. When Brett drew back to gaze down at her, his eyes shimmering like silver, Jo promptly decided she'd adore being wished a proper good morning in that fashion every morning for the rest of her life. Smothering a sigh of regret for the impossibility of foolish dreams, she smiled tremulously back at him.

"How are you feeling?" The smile changed into a frown as Brett examined Jo's upturned face minutely. "When you left the office last week, you looked about ready to unravel. Are you feeling any better . . . now?"

Jo did not miss Brett's deliberate hesitation before the word now, and she knew he meant right now, since the night they'd spent together. Should she take a chance and tell him how deeply his lovemaking had affected her? Could she bare her soul to this man? Don't be a complete fool, the voice of cool logic warned scathingly. Remember what happened the last time you spoke of your feelings to a man. Staring up at Brett, Jo could actually hear the echo of Gary's taunting gibes. Gary's ridicule had been hard enough to take; somehow Jo knew she would not be able to bear it from Brett. No, Jo cautioned herself, play it cagy, play it down, but for God's sake, play it safe!

"I'm feeling much better." Jo avoided the word now. "I simply needed some rest . . . as I told you last week."

Brett's sigh revealed to Jo how disappointing her reply had been. Like all men, she thought in sudden irritation, he wanted his ego stroked! Well, damn it, women had egos too! And she sure hadn't heard any soul baring from him!

"If you're feeling so much better," Brett chided gently, "why

172

are you scowling at me in exactly the same way you were last week?"

"I'm hungry." Jo blurted the first excuse that came to mind. "I thought you said you were going to make brunch?"

From his expression, it was obvious that Brett didn't buy her disclaimer. But, fortunately, it immediately became obvious he was not going to push the issue. His grin back in place, if a trifle strained, he released her and stepped back.

"Okay, we'll leave it for now." A definite warning underlined his light tone. "Have you got anything interesting in the fridge?" Without waiting for a reply, he strode to the almond-toned appliance.

"I have the usual breakfast foods, eggs, bacon, juice," Jo enumerated, following him.

"Then I guess that will have to do." Brett sighed dramatically. "How about a bacon omelet? You wouldn't happen to have a green pepper and an onion, would you?"

Jo did, and the resultant meal was delicious. As she polished off the last bite of toast, Jo pondered on the hows and whys of Brett's culinary skill. He had whipped the meal together with the panache of a professional chef—making as many dishes dirty in the bargain. How had he learned to cook like that? And, more important, why? Brett had grown up in the proverbial lap of luxury. Why would anyone born to a family of wealth learn to cook? Especially a male? And this particular male didn't merely cook, he created!

All of a sudden Jo felt very uncomfortable. Musing on the circumstances of Brett's culinary expertise brought home the realization of how very little she knew about him. Brett was still virtually a stranger to her, and she had shared his bed! What must he think of her? Had she been merely a convenient, easy lay? A cold shudder rippled along Jo's spine. Unable to look at him, she lifted her cup and stared into her coffee. Oh, God! Jo thought bleakly. What had she let herself in for here? Loving

Brett as she now did, Jo felt sick at the idea of him using her simply to assuage a physical need.

"Were you planning to do anything today?" Brett's quiet voice shattered Jo's introspection.

"No." Jo forced herself to look at him. "There really isn't much to do in a resort town in December." Now she forced herself to smile. "I didn't come here to *do* anything. Remember? I came here to rest."

Jo's smile disintegrated at the memory of why she had needed to get away from everything. First there had been that disheartening visit home for Thanksgiving. Then, already feeling depressed, she had gone to Vermont, only to have Casey confirm what she had suspected about Brett and Marsha. And still, knowing they had been lovers before they came back to New York, she had not only not repulsed him, she had welcomed him into her bed, and herself! In the cold light of a winter morning, Jo told herself that loving Brett was no excuse for her self-indulgence. If she suffered later she had only herself to blame. But she could not think of it now, not with him sitting opposite her, frowning at her lengthy silence. Shaking herself out of her blue funk, Jo rose and began clearing the table, deciding she'd have to think it all through later.

"What's wrong?" Brett's fingers closed around Jo's wrist as she reached for his plate. "Why are you so quiet?"

"I'm always quiet." Jo made a feeble attempt at a smile. "Didn't you know? I have always been quiet. It comes from being an only child and being alone so much." She was babbling, she *knew* she was babbling, but Jo hoped that by expanding on his second question, she could avoid answering the first one.

"You're not alone now." Brett's tone implied a lot more than his flat statement. Jo sensed that he was telling her something that, in her emotionally confused mind, she simply wasn't hearing. Brett didn't give her time to ponder on his meaning. "You do realize I'm going to stay here with you, don't you? That is, at least through the twenty-third." The twenty-third was two days away. Two very short days, Jo thought, sighing and lowering her eyes to the long fingers lightly clasping her wrist. Two days in which to soak up the sight of him, the feel of him, and then he'd be gone until the next time he decided to add spice to his sexual life by changing bed partners. The thought hurt so badly Jo closed her eyes, blocking out the vision of implied imprisonment. An instant later Jo's eyes flew wide at Brett's soft pronouncement. "When I leave I'm taking you with me."

"Taking me with you?" Jo blurted, rather stupidly, she was sure. "Where?"

"To the farm." Brett's lips tightened, as if in anger. "In Florida."

"But I can't go . . . " Jo began in protest.

"Yes, you can. And you will." Brett's tone indicated there'd be no arguing over the matter. "I was instructed to, and this is an exact quote, 'Bring her with you.' "

"By whom?" Although she was positive the answer would be Wolf, Jo asked anyway. Wolf was the only person who knew her family situation. Thus Brett's answer came as a complete surprise.

"By Madam President, herself."

"Your mother!"

"The one and only," Brett concurred softly.

"But why?" Oh, God, had Wolf discussed her with his mother? And, in turn, had his mother taken pity on her? Jo felt sick. And more than a little angry. Damn it, she didn't want or need pity!

"Who knows what motivates the great minds?" Brett replied in a careless tone that was belied by the glitter of speculation in his eyes. It was patently obvious to Jo that something about his mother's invitation had angered Brett too. The realization reinforced her decision not to go, and, shaking her head sharply, she told him so.

"I won't go with you."

Jo was totally unprepared for the swiftness of Brett's reaction to her refusal to accompany him south. Rising abruptly to his feet, he gave a sharp tug on her wrist that impelled her against his hard chest. Releasing her wrist, he imprisoned her within his arms, crushing her soft breasts to the rock hardness of him.

"You will go with me," Brett contradicted with soft menace. "When I leave here on the twenty-third, and when I fly south on the twenty-fourth." Releasing her as abruptly as he'd caught her to him, he said briskly, "Now, let's get this mess cleaned up." His lips curved into a wickedly alluring smile. "I want to go back to bed."

"You can go straight to hell!" Really angry now, Jo planted her balled fists onto her slim hips. Who the hell did he think he was talking to . . . the upstairs maid? Was there an upstairs maid? Jo shrugged the irrelevant thought aside. Damn him! One night in the sack and he acted as if he owned her! Well, Madam President's fair-haired boy was about to learn that Jo Lawrence would not be owned . . . by anyone! She might love him but she'd be damned if she'd pander to him! She had learned the folly of pandering to a man the hard way. Never, never again, she vowed. "If you're feeling the need to work off the enormous breakfast you consumed," Jo said scathingly, "go beat your feet on the beach again." Her nastily voiced advice was followed by a loud gasp as she was immediately hauled into his arms.

"Oh, but I'd much prefer working off my 'enormous' meal by beating my body against yours," Brett purred with deliberate crudity. "Are you going to fight me?" One pale eyebrow arched elegantly. "Make me subdue you?" His lips twitched into a devilish smile. "How very intriguing."

"Let me go, Brett," Jo gritted warningly. "You'll get nothing from me by force." Jo groaned silently. If he didn't release her at once she'd be a goner! Already the melting process had begun, and she could feel the effects in the lower part of her body. Oh, God! Maybe the transition from female to woman had not been so wonderful after all. She was vulnerable to him now, much too vulnerable.

"Force!" Brett exclaimed on a soft burst of laughter. "Oh, honey, there'll be no need for me to use force." His liquid silver gaze seared her face. "Whether you realize it or not, your eyes are soft with desire. Your lips are parted, ready for mine. And"—his hands slid down her back to cup her derriere—"your hips are moving against mine very invitingly." Slowly, inexorably, he drew her against the hardness of his thighs and aroused manhood. "I accept your invitation," he murmured lowering his head. "Just as you are going to accept my mother's."

Jo wanted to scream a denial, and she would have if Brett's mouth had not taken hers so sweetly. Damn him, she sighed, mingling her breath with his. Damn him for being the only man able to ignite her physical fire! Fully cognizant of what she was doing, hating and loving it at one and the same time, Jo coiled her arms around Brett's strong neck and gave herself up to the moment.

The moment stretched into most of the afternoon! By the time Brett allowed Jo to drift into sleep, she was completely fulfilled and thoroughly exhausted. This man, she thought groggily, swiftly losing her hold on consciousness, has more than enough stamina to accommodate two women! Jo should have been upset by the observation, and she would have been if she had not drifted so far along the path to slumber.

The third time Jo woke it was to an oddly familiar stillness that was in no way connected to the fact that she was alone in the bed. Frowning as her mind groped for an explanation, Jo stared at the darkened bedroom window. A faint splat against the pane brought instant recognition. It was snowing!

Snow. Jo's pulses leaped with a ray of hope. If it were to snow long enough, and hard enough, maybe she and Brett would be stranded through Christmas! Savoring the possibility for more reasons than she cared to examine too closely, Jo snuggled deeper under the covers. She really should get up, she supposed vaguely. But then, she yawned, why should she? She was here to rest, wasn't she? And she certainly hadn't had a great amount of rest since Brett's arrival. The man was a sexual dynamo!

Groaning aloud, Jo rolled onto her side. Oh, damn! Jo was reminded of the last observation she'd made about him before falling asleep. Damn! Damn! Damn! Why had she gone to Vermont? Why had she gone home for Thanksgiving? Why had she ever been born? She didn't want to think about Vermont. She didn't want to think about Thanksgiving. She didn't want to think, period. The room was too quiet. Quiet was inductive to contemplation. Sighing in defeat, Jo flopped back onto her back and let memory have its way.

On arriving in Brookhaven, the small southeastern Pennsylvania town Jo had grown up in, she had been greeted warmly, if separately, by her parents. The evening before Thanksgiving had gone rather smoothly, Jo thought. But then, of course, there were church services to attend and a united false front to maintain for the benefit of her parents' fellow church members. Thanksgiving morning had not been too bad either, as her father had gone hunting, which put her mother into a good mood. That is, except for the note Jo's father had left on the kitchen table for her.

Her eyes beginning to sting, Jo lowered her lids and bit on her lip. If she lived forever she would never forget that note! How very like her father it had been, and all over an early phone call from Marybeth, a friend of Jo's from their high school days. He'd written:

My dear successful and independent daughter,
Marybeth will call you about nine thirty. She called earlier (would you believe seven thirty?) but I told her that, like most normal people on a holiday, you were still in bed. As you were still asleep, you could not answer the phone. Inasmuch as you could not answer the phone, Marybeth could

not talk to you, I told her to call again somewhere in the neighborhood of nine thirty, because I doubted you'd be up much before then. If you were to sleep till ten, and Marybeth calls at nine thirty, she still would not be able to speak to you. Anyway, if the phone rings at nine thirty, and you are awake to hear it, it will probably be Marybeth. Happy Thanksgiving, darling,

Daddy

At first Jo had laughed at the note, another in a long line of similar, whimsical missives. And then she had cried, because he was so dear and trying so hard to appear lighthearted in the face of his unhappiness. As fate would have it, her mother had entered the kitchen as Jo was wiping the tears from her cheeks. In response to her mother's concern over her tears, Jo had silently handed her the note. After skimming the lines, her mother had smiled bitterly.

"All men can be charming when it suits their purposes," Ellen Lawrence said dryly.

"Oh, Mother." Jo sighed, beginning to feel the familiar tightness in her stomach that usually appeared on her visits home. "Why do you always use that tone of voice when talking about Daddy?"

"Because he's a man," Ellen retorted. "I would have thought your experience with Gary Devlin would have taught you that they're all the same. They want one thing from a woman, then, once they get what they want, they no longer want her."

Jo remained perfectly still in hopes that her mother would expound on her subject. To date, this outburst was the closest Ellen had come to explaining the problem between herself and her husband, Mark.

"You'd do better to concentrate on your career," Ellen went on. "And forget the myth about finding happiness with a man. That kind of happiness exists only in fairy tales."

Jo knew from her mother's flat tone that the subject was now closed, and she had learned nothing of why she had always felt that she was hovering in the demarcation zone between opposing forces.

As usual, when Jo returned to New York the day after Thanksgiving, she felt depressed and vaguely responsible for the failure of her parents' marriage. Intellectually Jo knew she was in no way at fault, just as she knew, intellectually, she was not a cold, unresponsive woman like her mother. Lord, hadn't she lain awake night after night aching for the touch of one particular man? Somehow knowing something intellectually did not erase the scars carried over from childhood.

Jo sniffed in the silence of the bedroom. Then, as if her visit home hadn't been depressing enough, she had received that call from Casey Delheny! Why the hell hadn't she followed her first impulse and sent *her* assistant up to Vermont? Because she'd been hoping for a mental diversion, Jo derided herself. What she had found had had more the effect of a blow to the solar plexus. Oh, the technical problem regarding the application of one of Casey's designer's ideas to the existing plumbing plans had been relatively easy to unwrinkle. Relating to what Casey had confided to her over one too many drinks the night before Jo was due to return to New York was infinitely more difficult to handle.

"Are Brett and Marsha still together?" Casey had asked Jo morosely, swallowing almost half of her third martini.

"Together?" Jo had prompted softly, telling herself Casey, unhappy because of her lengthy separation from Sean, who was still in the Poconos, was talking through a gin-and-vermouth haze.

"Yes, you know, like in bed. That kind of together." Raising her glass, Casey gulped down the remainder of her drink. "The kind of together Sean and I have been doing damn little of lately." Waving her glass in the air, Casey indicated to their waiter that she wanted another drink. Tilting her head, she ran an assessing glance over Jo. "You know, I do believe Brett's even

180

more of a live wire than Wolf is." She laughed insinuatingly. "Businesswise *and* otherwise. I swear, he and Marsha spent every night together locked inside his room. Yet he was hard at work bright and early every morning."

Jo had returned to New York more depressed than before, even though she had suspected an affair between Brett and Marsha since he'd called her and as much as ordered her to find an apartment for Marsha. Walking into her office the morning she returned to find that insultingly terse note ordering her to "get in here" had been the absolute last straw for Jo. Suddenly bone weary, she had gone to Brett's office in a cold rage, prepared to resign if he refused her request for a leave of absence. She had to get away, to think and to rest.

Circles, circles, circles. Would this mental merry-go-round never end? Jo sighed. Lord, she was tired of her own thoughts! How many times must she plow over the same row before she found ground fertile enough to sprout some answers? Were there any answers? Jo moved restlessly between the tangled sheets, enjoying the sensuous feel of the fine percale against her naked skin. A smile of physical contentment softened the taut line of her mouth. Brett had given her the answer to one question, perhaps the most important one. Her initial response to him had been an outright revelation! Always before, with Gary, she had gone positively rigid the moment he began to enter. But then the moment of penetration had always come mere minutes after he had drawn her to him. Now, after experiencing Brett's lovemaking and the infinite care he took to arouse her body to the point of readiness that equaled his own, Jo realizied that Gary had only been interested in self-gratification, not mutual satisfaction. In the expertise stakes, one might say that Brett crossed the wire before Gary ever left the gate.

The rather silly analogy amused Jo. Pushing back the covers with one hand, Jo lifted her other hand to smother a giggle. Jumping off the bed, she shook her head in amazement; she never giggled! Giggling was strictly for teenage girls, usually in connec-

181

tion with teenage boys! Telling herself her gray matter was beginning to flake, Jo grabbed up her robe and strolled to the bathroom.

Standing under the stinging-hot shower spray, Jo came to terms with what she had already decided subconsciously. She would accept whatever Brett offered her of himself for as long as he offered it.

Turning around, she dropped her head to allow the hot spray to massage the tension out of the muscles in the back of her neck. Her decision was probably not a very intelligent one, Jo mused, sighing blissfully as the jet fingers reduced her muscles to rubber. I want him, she argued in her own defense, even if I have to share him. An image of Marsha Wenger rose to torment Jo's mind, and she gritted her teeth in determination. Bump Marsha Wenger! Brett's here now, with me, and I'll hang on to him for all I'm worth, even if it means going to Florida with him. And while I'm there, I just might strangle that blabbermouth Wolfgang Renninger!

Applying the same sharp intellect that had earned her the position of assistant to Wolf, Jo ruthlessly refused to use the old feminine cop-out of not being able to live without Brett. She could survive very well, if not too comfortably, without him and she knew it. Then again, why should she? At this moment in her life she was deeply in love, and she was Brett's, mind, body, and soul. When her time with him was over, she would accept the hand dealt to her without a wince. What the hell! Jo shrugged, oddly cold within the cascading hot water. She didn't want commitment either. Did she? Of course not, she assured herself bracingly. Jo was so consumed with her own rationalizing, she didn't hear the door being opened or feel a draft when the shower curtain was inched aside.

"Have you taken to sleeping in the shower now too, water baby?"

With a gasp that grew into a gurgle, due to water in the mouth,

Jo flung her head back to glare at Brett. "Are you trying to drown me?" she sputtered indignantly.

"I don't have to," Brett drawled dryly, unmindful of his shirt as he reached in to turn the water off. "You're doing a pretty good job of it yourself." Curling a now soaking wet arm around Jo's waist, he lifted her off her feet. "Out, water baby, before you wash yourself down the drain."

"Brett!" Jo protested his handling of her, although she didn't struggle. Only a complete idiot would take the chance of slipping out of one arm to land in a painful heap on the hard floor of a bathtub! "I was not falling asleep! I was letting the hot water work the ache out of my muscles!" Jo was so annoyed she was unaware of exactly what she was admitting to. As Brett set her carefully onto the fluffy bath mat, Jo shrugged off his arm. "And I wish you'd stop calling me that ridiculous name!"

"But I like that ridiculous name." Brett grinned. "I also like to look at you when you're all wet and slippery." The grin grew up to be a leer. "You are one sexy baby when you're wet." Bending to her, he licked a drop of water from the tip of her breast. "Hmmm . . . nectar," he murmured throatily, curling his tongue around the swiftly hardening bud before, very gently, closing his teeth on it. "And ambrosia." He passed judgment on the taste of her.

"You're positively mad!" Jo gasped, unconsciously arching her back to give him better access to his point of interest. "Oh, Brett . . . what are you doing?" Jo knew full well what he was doing; she could feel the results of his suckling lips through the nerve endings in her loins.

"You don't know?" Brett teased, skimming his tongue across her body from one breast tip to the other. "Maybe I'm not doing it right." Before her startled eyes, he dropped to his knees. "I guess I need a lot more practice. But first, I think I'll get rid of this sopping shirt." Straightening, he whipped the garment up his body and over his head, tossing it aside carelessly. It landed in the bathtub with a soft plop that neither he nor Jo heard.

Then, his hands clasping her lightly around her rib cage, his eyes watching hers, Brett enclosed one nipple inside his mouth.

It was the most incredibly erotic action Jo could imagine, Brett watching her, while she watched him make lover to her body! Lightheaded, feeling her knees begin to buckle, Jo grasped Brett's shoulders to keep from falling, a purring moan tickling the back of her throat.

"Ah . . . perhaps I am doing it right." He laughed softly. Slowly, tantalizingly, he lavished attention on her midsection, stringing moist kisses down to her navel. When he dipped the tip of his tongue into the indentation, Jo shuddered and gasped his name aloud. "You're trembling," he breathed against the damp skin stretched tautly over her abdomen. "From the cold outside, I wonder, or the heat inside?"

Quickly losing touch with reality, Jo sagged against him and, at the feel of his tongue dancing around the edge of her delta triangle, she lost all control of her legs and sank to the floor before him. It was a short, fast trip from her knees to her back. The soft fibers of the bath mat caressed Jo's spine while the prickly hair on Brett's chest caressed her breasts.

With her feet flat on the floor, and her knees bent and angled out, Jo should have been uncomfortable. She wasn't. Even the chafing sensation of Brett's jean-clan thighs against the inside of her own was more exciting than abrading. The realization of his arousal as he arched his body into hers was more exciting still. Brett's hands captured Jo's breasts as his mouth captured her lips. The assault on her senses was total. Spearing her tongue into his mouth, Jo dug her nails into his shoulders, glorying in the grunt of pleasure that exploded from his throat as he thrust his hips in reaction.

"I've got to get out of these damn jeans." He groaned, heaving himself up and away from her with obvious reluctance. "Stay warm for me, babe," he pleaded hoarsely, his hands fumbling with the belt buckle.

In fact, he didn't get completely out of the jeans. As Brett was about to lever himself to his feet, Jo called his name softly, beguilingly. The jeans, along with the silky very-brief briefs he wore underneath them, were forgotten the moment they pooled around his knees. Whispering her name in a voice made rough with urgency, Brett filled Jo's body with his own.

The tension building inside Jo coiled tightly, and still more tightly, until, Brett's name filling her mind in an endless scream and reverberating in the tiled room like an arching whimper, it snapped, springing her into near oblivion where she was conscious only of the ecstasy shuddering through her and the sound of her own hoarsely cried name beating against her eardrums.

Jo surfaced from the mind-blanketing fog of sensuality to the awareness of the crushing weight of Brett's collapsed body on hers and the soothing sensation of his hand stroking her hip. She was still wet, only now the moisture that sheened her body was the natural result of strenuous physical activity. Raising a lazily limp hand, she smoothed her palm down his equally slick back, her sensitized skin monitoring the responsive shiver that followed the path from shoulder to waist.

"God! You are one exciting woman," Brett rasped through uneven breaths, the tip of his tongue testing the saltiness of her skin. "I feel as though I've been pulled through the wringer and hung out to dry."

"Is that good?" Jo murmured, gliding her hand up his back to tangle her fingers in his sweat-dampened hair.

"Extremely good. In fact, it's what all the noise has been about all these many centuries." Brett laughed softly. "What do the French call it? The little death, or some such?"

"Some such." Jo sighed contentedly. "It must be true for I feel a little dead right now."

Brett's bark of delighted laughter pried her heavy eyelids up, and Jo stared, bemused, into his laughing face. Oh, happy saints, he was handsome when he laughed like that, but then, he was handsome when he didn't laugh like that too. At that moment,

185

Jo knew she could refuse him nothing. Apparently, possibly because of the dreamy expression on her face, Brett knew it too.

"You'll stay here with me through the twenty-third?" Brett was all seriousness now.

"Yes." Jo smiled as she felt his chest expand, then depress on a sigh of relief.

"And you'll go with me when I fly south on the twenty-fourth?" His chest expanded again, then became still as he held his breath.

"Yes." Jo's smile deepened as his sharply released breath feathered her cheek. Why ruin the effect by telling him she had decided to go with him before his exhausting inducement?

"Hmmm . . . have I told you you're beautiful?" Brett nibbled gently along Jo's jawline.

"Not nearly enough." Jo laughed as he nipped on her chin in tender punishment.

"And did I thank you for wringing me out so deliciously?" He teased her lips apart with his tongue.

"I think your wringing was more than enough thanks." Jo admitted to her own intense pleasure in his body.

"Do you suppose we could manage to drag our two wrung-out bodies into the shower?" Brett's eyes were silver bright in appreciation of her candid reply.

"I suppose we better had," Jo mimicked his heavily laid on drawl. "Because if I don't get up very soon, the fibers of this bath mat are going to be imbedded in my back, and your chest hair will be imbedded in my front."

Jo felt the expulsion of air into her mouth a millisecond before she heard his shout of laughter. Displaying what she considered a disgusting amount of energy, Brett eased his body carefully from hers, then sprang agilely to his feet. His shoulders still quaking with laughter, he kicked his legs free of jeans and briefs before bending to help her up. When Jo winced at the twinge of pain the sudden exertion caused in her thighs, Brett grinned wickedly.

"All that standing under a hot shower to ease overworked muscles for nothing," he commiserated falsely, making her aware now of what she had unconsciously admitted to him earlier. "But don't fret, darling. If the hot water doesn't work this time, just keep in mind what the physical fitness enthusiasts claim." Afraid to ask, Jo arched a delicately winged brow at him. "Why, that regular workouts will keep the muscles from tightening up." His grin telegraphed the punchline. "And I intend to work those muscles very regularly."

For two days Jo basked in the light of Brett's lovemaking and approval. And for two days she ate better than she had since leaving home at age nineteen. Brett did all the cooking. Jo did all the cleaning up. Personally, she thought she was getting the better of the bargain. In bed, Brett was demanding but gently so and, with his expert guidance, Jo emerged from behind her psychological wall of inhibitions. Never had she felt so free, so light, so at ease in the company of a man. Unselfconsciously, she teased him, sometimes dryly, other times wickedly. Brett, laughing often, responded in kind, leaving no doubt that he was enjoying himself every bit as much as she was.

Nervous apprehension began eating at Jo as the purring Porsche entered New York City. What would she find on arrival at the farm in Florida, besides a houseful of Renningers? Why had Brett's mother invited her there on a traditionally family-oriented holiday? Had Wolf related to his mother Jo's less-than-happy family situation? And if Wolf had turned blabbermouth, why? He's probably getting bored from inactivity, Jo answered her own question. Intermingled with the whys revolving in her mind was one recurring assertion. She did not want to go to Florida.

She was going to Florida. Jo examined the thought as the plane soared into the bright winter sunlight the following afternoon. She had coaxed and wheedled and pleaded to no avail the night before. Brett had remained adamant. Oh, he had loved

187

being coaxed, and wheedled, and pleaded with, and he laughingly admitted it, but he had remained adamant none the less.

Strangely, Brett had grown tense during the drive to the airport and had barely spoken to her since he'd buckled her into her seat belt. Now, sitting stiffly in her seat, Jo studied his rigid profile wondering what emotional tick had burrowed into his craw. He looked, she finally decided, like a man set in his determination to do a particularly unpleasant duty.

Trying to relax, Jo closed her eyes to the sight of Brett's harshly set features and her mind to futile speculation. But one thought persisted. Was Brett tired of her already? It was not a thought conducive to in-flight relaxation.

Relaxation in the form of sleep snuck up on Jo while she wasn't looking. She woke to the mild jolt of the wheels touching down and the realization that her seat belt had been fastened for her. Brett was busy stuffing papers into a large attache case and ignoring the fact that she sat beside him. The moment the plane came to a stop he stood up, only then deigning to notice her.

"I think you'll be warm enough if you drape this over your shoulders." Brett held up the golden-beige cashmere thigh-length coat Jo had worn onto the plane. "The pilot said the temperature is in the low fifties."

How wonderful, Jo thought wryly, turning her head to glance out the small window. He doesn't say one word from New York to Florida, then he gives me a weather report! As she could discern nothing in the darkness except the blue-tinged lights delineating the runway of the small, private landing field, Jo turned back to face him again. Brett's features still gave the impression of having been carved in granite. As she rose to her feet, hands smoothing the matching cashmere skirt she was wearing, Jo sighed tiredly. What the devil was bugging Brett, anyway? If he was bored with her company, why had he insisted she accompany him? For one mad second Jo was tempted to confront him with the question, then, mercifully, the madness subsided. In all honesty, Jo admitted to herself that she was afraid of what his answer would be. For all her self-assurances of a few days earlier that she would accept whatever Brett offered of himself for however long he offered it, she was beginning to live in fear of him walking away from her.

Standing mutely before Brett in the narrow aisle, Jo closed her eyes at the brief touch of his hands on her shoulders as he draped her coat over the emerald-green silk blouse she was wearing. How had it happened so quickly? How could it be that within a period of four days she knew that losing Brett would be as painful to her as losing a vital part of herself? Her throat closing in panic at the mere thought of his rejection of her, Jo preceded Brett to the door on legs suddenly unsteady.

The mild early-evening air felt balmy after the biting cold of New York, yet Jo wished herself back along the coast of Ocean City. The snow she had hoped would continue for days had lasted less than an hour but the wind had been blowing steadily, nipping at exposed cheeks and noses right up until they had boarded the small, sleek private jet.

On the ground, Jo could see little more than she'd viewed from the plane's window. Other than the lights positioned on the roof of the low building she assumed was a hangar, the surrounding area was as black as the inside of a leather glove. As Brett, his hand at her elbow, escorted her over the uneven ground, Jo began to discern the outline of a long vehicle as their destination. As they approached the car Jo saw a man standing beside it. When they were within three feet of him, he swung the back door open.

"Evenin', Mr. Brett," the man greeted laconically.

"Hello, Josh," Brett replied in the most civil tone Jo had heard from him in hours. "The mild weather feels good after the cold up north." Brett grinned, handing Jo inside the roomy backseat of what she could now see was a black Cadillac limousine.

"Gunna rain," Josh replied with the implied wisdom of a native.

"Perhaps you're right." Brett shrugged. "But it feels good just the same," he tacked on, settling his long frame beside Jo on the plush seat as their bags were loaded into the trunk.

"Wouldn't know, never been up north," Josh grunted before closing the door smartly.

As the car rolled smoothly onto a blacktop secondary road, Brett sliced a glance at Jo. A glance Jo felt all the way down to her toes.

"Are you comfortable?"

What would he say if I said no? Jo wondered. Brett's behavior in combination with her nervousness was making her irritable.

"Yes." How could one not be comfortable enscounced in the back of a luxurious car? she thought waspishly. "Is it very far to the farm?"

"No. Not far," Brett replied slowly, then, in an oddly intense tone: "Are you getting anxious?"

"Anxious?" Jo frowned. Why did he sound so uptight? *He* didn't have to walk into a houseful of strangers. Thank heavens Wolf would be there! "A little," she admitted. "It will be wonderful to see Wolf again."

"Thanks."

Astounded at the bitter note in Brett's tone, Jo stared at his averted head for several minutes. What in the world? Why had he said "thanks"? And in that tone? Surely he hadn't taken her eagerness to see Wolf again as an insult to him in his capacity as replacement employer? Brett had simply never struck her as the type of man who'd need employee adoration—loyalty, yes, adoration, no. Brett was too confident of himself to feel petty jealousy over his brother's popularity. So then, why the bitter thanks? Shaking her head in utter confusion, Jo turned away to glance out the window. All she saw was total blackness created by a combination of night and smokey-gray windowpanes. Actually feeling Brett withdraw into himself, Jo stared at the blackness, biting her lip to keep from demanding he tell the driver to turn around and take her back to the airfield.

By the time the car glided to a stop in front of the house, Jo's nervousness had drowned in the flood of her rising anger. How dare Brett insist she come south with him only to ignore her? Damn him! She'd enjoy this unexpected, unwanted holiday if it killed her!

Stepping out of the car, Jo stifled a groan. The horse farm, Brett had called it. So, naturally, she'd been expecting a farmhouse! Or perhaps a ranch house, maybe. What Jo was looking at was an elegant structure that would have looked right at home dead center on any antebellum plantation! The house was illuminated by spotlights on the outside and a blaze of indoor lights from every window on the ground floor.

As they mounted the three wide steps to the front door, it was flung open by a small, wiry woman who looked to be in her late sixties. Hands on her hips, the woman waited until Jo and Brett had stepped over the threshold, then she lambasted Brett in the tone of a field marshal.

"Well, young man, it's about time you got here." Dark, still-young eyes snapped a quick encompassing glance over Brett. "Much later and you would have missed Christmas Eve altogether." Now the dark eyes did their snapping dance over Jo. "And you must be Ms. Lawrence?"

"Yes, this is Ms. Lawrence," Brett answered for Jo, who was busy staring at his smiling face in consternation. How could he leap the distance between bitterness and lightheartedness so effortlessly? Jo wondered. The sound of her name shattered her bemusement. "Jo, this is Elania Calaveri, housekeeper to my mother and friend to us all."

"How do you do?" Jo murmured, offering her hand.

"So so," Elania replied surprisingly. "My arthritis is acting up. It's going to rain."

Jo had to hold her breath to keep from laughing. Brett made no attempt at self-containment. Laughing aloud, he wrapped the small woman in his arms and hugged her tight. "Josh said the same thing, so I guess it must be true."

"Of course it's true," Elania scolded. "Josh is no fool." Disentangling herself from Brett's embrace, she held out her hand. "I'll take care of your coats and bags. The gang's in the living room." She frowned at Brett. "Your mother expected you before dark. Now get in there. Supper will be in an hour."

Throughout Elania's tirade, Jo had been glancing around the enormous hall, admiring the wide, curving staircase, aware of the murmur of voices issuing from behind two oversized doors to her left. Feeling somewhat as if she'd stepped back into history, Jo was barely aware of Brett slipping the coat from her shoulders to hand it to Elania.

"Do you like the house?" he asked softly, his gaze following hers as it touched a beautifully made parson's bench along one wall.

"Like it?" Jo breathed in awe. "It's absolutely beautiful." Dragging her enthralled gaze from the rich patina of the parquet floor, she looked at him in amazement. "You grew up in this house?"

"Off and on," Brett drawled. "When I wasn't in the house in Miami, or the original family homestead in Lancaster, Pennsylvania."

"Your family's from Pennsylvania?" Jo exclaimed.

"Yes," Brett frowned. "I assumed you knew that."

"But . . . how would I have . . . "

"Brett Renninger!" Elania interrupted impatiently. "Your mother is waiting. You can show Ms. Lawrence over the house after dinner."

"Yes, of course." As if he suddenly remembered he wasn't speaking to her, Brett's face closed up again. "Come along, Jo. Mother's waiting." An odd grimace fleetingly twisted his lips. "They are all waiting."

Shepherding Jo across the wide hall, Brett slid the two intricately carved doors apart and motioned for Jo to precede him into the living room. As she stepped through the portal Jo did not actually see the generously proportioned room, or the many exquisite pieces of furniture that adorned it, or even the people

192

who reposed on the delicately crafted, probably priceless, chairs and settees, although she was aware of all of them. From the moment of entrance, Jo's gaze homed in on the man sitting in a wheelchair, his left leg encased in a hip-to-toe cast that stuck out straight as a board in front of him, his left arm nestled close to his chest inside a sling, and his right arm outstretched, palm up, to her. As Jo had noted months ago, there was very little facial resemblance between the man beckoning to her and the man standing behind her. As if drawn by a magnet, Jo unhesitatingly crossed the room to Wolf Renninger.

"Ah . . . " Wolf's masculinely attractive voice revealed satisfaction. "There's my girl." When Jo placed her hand in his, Wolf's fingers tightened in reassurance. "How are you, Jo?"

"I'm . . . I'm fine, Wolf," Jo finally managed to whisper around the thickness in her throat. Blinking her eyes against a surge of hot moisture, she smiled tremulously at the man she loved almost as much as her father and easily as much as she would have an older brother. Wolf's year-round golden tan had faded somewhat from confinement to the house, and he had lost weight but, in essence, he was the same ruggedly attractive man upon whose broad shoulder Jo had cried—not once but several times. This tough-tender man was the only living person Jo had ever confided in about her mixed-up emotional state. And now, the realization flashed through Jo's mind, that state had progressed from unsettled to near chaos. Pushing all thoughts of herself aside, Jo studied him intently. "How are *you*?"

"As you see"—Wolf laughed, indicating his immobilized left side— "out of commission." A grin lit his face, revealing even white teeth. "But only temporarily. We'll talk later, Jo, but now—" His right hand covered a slim one resting on the arm of the chair. "You remember my wife, Micki?"

"Yes, of course." Jo's glance shifted to the woman sitting on Wolf's right. Jo had met Micki on several occasions and each time her original opinion that Micki was the perfect mate for Wolf had been reinforced. After two months in the Florida sunshine, Micki was tan, and healthy looking, and more lovely than ever. Jo's smile was soft and genuine. "You're looking very well, Mrs. Renninger," Jo complimented quietly. "The climate? Or your husband's improvement?"

"A little of both, I'm sure." Micki smiled serenely. "But more the latter than the former," she hastened to add when Wolf's dark brows drew together in a mock frown. "You're looking as beautiful as ever yourself," Micki returned Jo's compliment. Before Jo could respond, Wolf made a motion with his hand for Jo to turn around.

"And now, my dear." Wolf grinned. "Gird yourself to meet . . . " He paused for dramatic effect. "The Boss." Wolf's eyes telegraphed the message that he was fully aware of her nervousness. His smiled confided that he was also fully aware that Jo would never betray her nervousness. Her composure intact, Jo turned to face the president of Renninger Corporation, actually amused with the realization of how very well Wolf knew her. "Mother," Wolf said gently as Jo crossed the room to the fair, still-beautiful woman, "my assistant, JoAnne Lawrence."

"How do you do, Mrs. Renninger?" Jo murmured in a tone of complete self-containment. "Thank you for inviting me."

"The pleasure is ours, JoAnne," Violet Renninger assured Jo, then on a delightfully light laugh, she exclaimed, "We must use first names here! Do you realize there are three Mrs. Renningers in this room?" Waving her left hand, she said, "We'll take the introductions as we sit." Turning to her left, she said, "This is my second son, Eric."

Jo pivoted to face the man patiently standing next to his mother and felt the breath catch in her throat. Eric Renninger was the most incredibly handsome man Jo had ever seen. Dark-haired like Wolf, Eric had sapphire-blue eyes that sparkled with good humor and a singularly endearing smile.

"I feel I know you, JoAnne," he said warmly. "I've heard so much about you." Before Jo could ask the stock question, Eric answered it. "All of it good. So good, in fact, that, if ever either one of my brothers gives you as much as an uncomfortable moment, you call me. I'll have an office ready for you within twenty-four hours."

Feeling the tension being drawn out of her by these warm welcoming people, Jo laughed easily. "Thank you, Eric. I'll definitely keep your offer in mind."

Releasing the hand Jo had offered to him, Eric made a half turn to his left. "And this very pregant lady is my wife, Doris. Darling, the much raved-about JoAnne Lawrence."

Doris Renninger was Jo's second shock within minutes. Compared to Eric's heart-stopping good looks, Doris was actually plain—except for the most arrestingly lustrous eyes Jo had ever gazed into. Dark brown with gold highlights, Doris's eyes glowed with an inner beauty.

"How do you do, JoAnne?" Doris smiled. "I'm sure this must be an ordeal for you, so I'll simply keep the ball rolling. The woman sitting next to me is the baby of this clan. Diane, called Di by all."

Di, as fair as her mother and brother Brett, had the same attractive smile that Jo was beginning to think of as pure Renninger. "Hello, JoAnne," Di chirped. "Besides yourself, I am the only woman in this room who is not a Renninger. And all because of this good-looking dude standing by me. JoAnne, I'd like you to meet my husband, Hank Carlton."

"The pleasure is mine, JoAnne," Hank assured in a rich baritone, taking Jo's hand in a warm, solid grip.

"And mine. Thank you, Hank," Jo replied, beginning to feel a trifle groggy. At that moment, Violet revealed how astute she was.

"You must be parched by now," she said crisply. "Will you have a cocktail? Or a glass of wine?"

"White wine would be lovely." Jo turned to smile at her hostess. "Thank you." Relieved as she was, Jo knew there was more to come. "But where are the children?"

"Having their supper in the kitchen, fortunately." Violet's

softened eyes belied her last word. "They'll be descending on us soon enough. Hank, would you get JoAnne a glass of wine? And you, child, take that chair beside Wolf. Maybe *you* can keep him in line."

"Fat chance." Wolf chuckled, echoing Jo's exact thoughts.

"Now," Violet went on in an aggrieved mother tone, "where *is* Brett?"

"Right here, sir." Brett's tone was deliberately insolent and drew every eye in the room to where he lounged lazily yet elegantly against the closed double doors. "I didn't want to intrude on Jo's . . . ah . . . moment of excitement." As he spoke, he pushed his slender frame away from the doors and strolled into the room, a cynical smile playing on his chiseled lips.

Watching him, Jo felt a thrill, both of apprehension and appreciation. Why the sarcasm and cynicism? she wondered in confusion. While, at the same time, she accepted the fact that, although Brett wasn't quite as rugged looking as Wolf or as handsome as Eric, he was the only male she really cared to gaze upon. Sighing for her own seemingly hopeless love, Jo observed Brett's greetings to his family from beneath lowered lashes. As Brett made his way, hugging the women, shaking hands with the men, around the room, Jo registered the increased rate of her heartbeats. When Brett came to a stop in front of Micki, Jo felt a stab of pain in her chest at the softness of his eyes and the tenderness in his smile.

"And how are you, darling?" he murmured, bending to kiss Micki's tan cheek.

"I'm fine . . . now, Brett," Micki murmured back. "Welcome home."

"Thank you, love." He held her hand a moment longer, then he cocked his head at Wolf, his eyes sharply assessing. "Well, big prowler, you look like you might just make it," he drawled in the same insolent tone he'd used earlier.

"You can bet your Porsche I'll make it, baby brother," Wolf

196

retorted, every bit as insolently. "If only for the pleasure it will give me to boot your ass out of my office."

Everyone in the room, including Brett, laughed, except for Jo, as Violet gently chided her eldest. "Behave yourself, Wolfgang!"

Jo's initial foray into the Renninger stronghold presaged the entire visit. The children were children. Delightful in their excitement of the day to come. Christmas day dawned, not cold and bright as Jo was accustomed to but mild and rainy, as Elania and Josh had predicted. The day, as all happy days are wont to do, seemed to flash by in a continuous din of laughter and family camaraderie. Though Jo had been fearful of receiving gifts proffered by people she had just met, the Renningers displayed both breeding and tact by offering none.

By the time the small jet with Jo and Brett enscounced inside soared again into the blue sky, its nose pointed north, Jo's mind was a seething mass of emotions and impressions, some good, some bad. The good impressions derived from eight days spent in the company of a truly "together" family whom, in the security of their affections for one another, had unhesitatingly included Jo within their circle of bantering communion. Savoring the memories of each day, most of which were rainy or gray outside, all of which were sun-bright inside, Jo tucked them away in a safe corner of her mind, to be taken out and enjoyed whenever she felt down.

Every one of Jo's bad impressions had been instilled by Brett. Though he had appeared to be relaxed and every bit as holiday-spirited as the rest of his family, Jo had seen through his light-hearted facade, possibly because she had come to know him so intimately. Throughout their entire visit, Brett had treated Jo with unfailing politeness. In fact, so very polite had he been, Jo had been repeatedly tempted to smack his face!

Now, sitting beside him as stiffly as she had on the flight south, Jo tried, as she had continuously over the past eight days, to equate this silent, hostile man with the ardent, laughing lover she'd come to know in the apartment in Ocean City.

Failing miserably in her attempt to understand Brett, Jo spent every quiet mile of the flight preparing herself for his leave-taking. A mask of cool composure blanking her face, Jo writhed with pain inside, knowing the pain was only a tiny measure of the agony that would strike her with Brett's final good-bye.

CHAPTER NINE

His facial muscles beginning to ache from being kept under rigid control, Brett curled his long fingers inward and grasped the arms of the seat to keep himself from reaching out to pull Jo into a hard embrace. Smothering a sigh, Brett faced the ills tormenting him. His arms ached to hold Jo's softness close. His lips burned with the need to crush her mouth. His body screamed to lose itself in the velvety warmth of hers.

Damn. And damn. And double damn! Brett had been mentally swearing, sometimes mildly, other times violently, for the better part of nine days. There was a knot in his stomach that felt like a rock. His neck was stiff from tension. And, after eight days of celibacy, he felt mean with frustration. Exerting every ounce of control he possessed, Brett sat statue still, staring straight ahead, positive that if he moved he'd explode, his bitterness and incrimination destroying the woman he both loved and hated.

You need help, buster!

Right.

A muscle twitched at the corner of Brett's jaw. God helps those . . . Great! Terrific! Now I'm not only talking to myself,

I'm answering myself! They're going to find a quiet room for you, Brett cautioned himself scathingly, if you don't do something, and soon, about this crazy situation. But what the hell *can* a man do when he finds himself involved with a woman who belongs to another man? Another man who just happens to be his own brother. Resting his head against the seat back, Brett closed his eyes.

There has to be some way, some answer.

Sure, there's an answer to everything. All you have to do is find it! The problem teased and tormented Brett as the jet streaked through the winter sky. One by one he rejected each solution that his mind presented for inspection.

The most obvious solution was, of course, to simply walk away from her. To do what? Brett wondered. Merely asking himself the question was enlightening. Always before, through any kind of personal upheaval, including the last months he'd been with Sondra, Brett had invariably found surcease in his work. The business of speculating on real estate had excited him from the first time he'd ventured into his mother's office at the advanced age of ten. Now the very thought of the work waiting for him in his office merely added to the weariness Brett was experiencing.

Weariness, and frustration, and anger. Three very debilitating emotions. Brett's nervous system had become ragged from those emotions, and others, during the last nine days. You had better get your head together, chum, Brett advised himself wryly. If you're not careful, your blood pressure is going to go up and your natural resistance is going to go down. God! What an unholy mess!

Wolf.

Brett exhaled a long, drawn-out sigh, no longer caring if the woman sitting beside him heard or not. Never, never would he forget the joyful expression that had momentarily set Jo's face aglow at her first sight of Wolf. Brett was positive none of the others in the room had seen that fleeting, betraying look of love

200

on Jo's face—with the possible exception of Wolf himself. But then, Wolf's rugged features had worn a like expression.

Moving restlessly in his seat, Brett could see again Wolf's outstretched arm, could hear the emotion in his brother's voice as Wolf growled, "There's my girl." Brett's teeth clamped together in much the same way they had on Christmas Eve, but then it had been to keep himself from snarling "Wrong, Wolf, Jo is *my* girl now." And that had only been the beginning of a week full of instances when Brett had not only wanted to snarl but to lash out both verbally and physically.

They had all fallen in love with her, every one of them. His mother; Eric, Doris, Di, Hank, all the kids, Elania, and even, before Jo had been there two full days, Micki. Brett sighed again. If nothing else, he could congratulate himself on a job well done in convincing Micki of Wolf's fidelity!

Jo was depressed now. Brett felt he could actually feel the vibrations of sadness that enveloped her. Yet, up until the moment he had handed her into the car to leave for the airfield, she had been lighthearted and carefree, seemingly content simply to be within the radius of Wolf, Micki or no Micki.

How many times during their visit had he conquered the urge to grab hold of her to shake some sense into her? Brett smiled in derision. About as many times as he'd conquered the need to go to her room during the night to restake her and his claim.

What the hell had they talked about? The question stabbed at Brett's mind at regular intervals. On the three separate occasions Wolf and Jo had been closeted together in Wolf's bedroom, of all places, what had they discussed? It sure as hell had not been one Brett Renninger, for Jo had emerged from those meetings flushed and laughing! She wasn't laughing now. In fact, Brett had the distinct impression Jo was within a hairsbreadth of breaking into sobs.

Brett realized with a jolt that he had never seen Jo cry. Not even when she'd become so suddenly and violently sick in the office had she given way to tears. She had been appalled at soiling his shoes and the carpet and the car, but she had not wept. And another time, her eyes had welled up—but she hadn't given in. If she cries now, he thought savagely, I'll beat her; then she'll really have something to cry about!

Brett shifted position, as if unable to find comfort in the confining seat. The discomfort was in his head, not his butt, and Brett knew it. He also knew that were she to lose a single tear, he would haul her into his arms, promising anything, anything in an effort to stem the flow.

Lord! What a mess!

You have a problem, my son?

Yes, Lord. You see, I love my brother but I love his woman too.

That is not very bright of you, my son.

But, Lord! How many women does one man need? Besides, I thought the wolf mated for life.

You're definitely losing it, Renninger, Brett chided himself in wry self-amusement. You keep playing these funny little games in your mind and you are going to find yourself weaving baskets instead of building condos for the rich and near rich. You have *got* to resolve this situation one way or another, and soon!

All wry self-amusement fled before a rising flood of despair. What could he do? Exactly what in hell could he do? Perhaps if they talked about it. But what would he say? Could I stand to hear Jo say she loves Wolf and could never give him up, even if it meant ending her relationship with me? Brett asked himself. No, I could not stand it, he replied honestly. Could not. As far as Brett could see he had two choices. He could accept the status quo, or he could take a walk.

Jo was too close. How could he think clearly with her sitting less than two feet away? It had been over a week since he'd held her in his arms. And, damn it, it had been the same length of time since she'd held him.

Brett was a proud man and he knew it. Now, although the taste was vile, he swallowed that pride. He *wanted* the feel of Jo's arms holding him close to her softness. He *yearned* for the touch of her fingers stroking through his hair. He *longed* for the sound of her voice whispering love words against his lips. Walking away would not erase the wanting, the yearning, the longing, and Brett knew it. He would just have to learn to live with the status quo.

"Brett."

Brett came slowly, reluctantly out of a half sleep in which he was reliving the days spent along the shore with Jo. Turning his head, he opened his eyes to stare into hazel depths darkened by disillusionment. God! He'd give his soul to be able to set those amber flecks glimmering like gold in happiness.

"It's time to fasten your seat belt for landing."

Brett nodded in answer and, straightening his cramped body, turned away. Even her voice has a dead, toneless sound, Brett thought tiredly, automatically engaging his belt. Taking Jo to the farm had been a mistake, just as he'd known it would be. What arrogance had led him to hope that three days and four nights with him would be enough to wipe the memory of Wolf out of her mind? For, in truth, that was what he had hoped for. But they had been such wonderfully contented days, and such satisfyingly ecstatic nights. Brett had convinced himself Jo had become as lost in him as he was in her. At any rate, he qualified mentally, he had tried to convince himself. Yet, even before they'd boarded the plane the tightness had begun in his insides, and it had continued unabated until now he had the sensation of carrying a rock around in his gut.

"Will there be a car waiting?"

"Yes, of course." Brett was immediately sorry for the impatience edging his tone. For God's sake, man, he berated himself, she asked a simple, quiet question! Was it really necessary to snap at her? It's either snap or beg, and I sure as hell cannot and will not do that!

Jo asked no further questions, nor did she make any remark whatever from the time they left the plane till the limousine drew up in front of her apartment. Brett broke the silence once, to inquire if Jo's car had been returned to New York from Ocean City.

"Yes, sir," Doug replied promptly. "I drove it in myself. It's parked in the garage at Ms. Lawrence's apartment."

Telling Doug to wait for him, Brett followed Jo out of the car and into the building. Traversing the hall beside her, Brett felt his lips twist in a grimace when Jo dug the large oddly shaped key from her purse. At the door to her apartment, he frowned at her trembling fingers as she stabbed at the slot in the lock.

"You're tired." Brett was careful to keep his tone free of inflection as he set her case inside the door. "We'll talk later. After you've had some rest." Jo's reaction startled him in its swiftness.

"No!" Jo spun to face him. "We will *not* talk later." Her eyes were no longer sad. They actually seemed to shoot sparks at him. Her voice was no longer quiet. Her tone was razor sharp with anger. "I don't know what sort of game you think you are playing, Brett, but you can deal me out of it. I thought I could . . ." Jo paused, as if to steady herself. "But I can't . . ." Her breath caught, then she repeated, on a sigh, "I just can't." Very slowly, very quietly, Jo closed the door in his face.

His body rigid, Brett stood frozen for one full minute, then, swinging around, he strode back to the elevator. What prompted him to do it, Brett had no idea yet, as he approached the security guard's desk he paused, then stopped.

"Do you remember who I am?" Brett ask the guard arrogantly.

"Yes, sir, Mr. Renninger." The man snapped to attention smartly. "Ms. Lawrence gave you clearance to enter at will two days before Christmas."

"That's correct." Brett's lips smiled at the man. "I wanted that point quite clear. I may be back some time later this evening, and I did not want any hassle over admittance. I will not have

Ms. Lawrence unnecessarily disturbed. Are we in accord?" Brett deliberately arched one brow imperiously.

"Yes, sir."

What a bastard you are, Brett accused himself wryly as he pushed through the entrance doors. But then, if you never take a step, you never get anywhere, in *any* direction, he exonerated his rather overbearing behavior.

In the car, Brett gnawed on the wisdom of returning to see Jo later that evening. He *knew* his attitude had been less than charming throughout their stay at the farm. On reflection, he admitted he'd acted out the part of the name he'd moments ago called himself to the letter. Why couldn't he just go to Jo and confess that he was so miserable, because he was so miserable?

On entering Wolf's apartment, Brett set his suitcase aside, tossed his jacket onto a chair, poured himself a double shot of Scotch then, telling himself he had to be hungry since he'd eaten nothing since early that morning, ambled into the kitchen. Opting for eggs, as he was certainly not in the mood to wax creative, he popped two slices of bread into the toaster while melting butter in a small frying pan. Breaking two eggs neatly in one hand, he dropped them, yolks intact, into the sizzling butter. A moment later he turned away from the stove to butter the toast, then, turning back, he grasped the handle of the pan to shift it gently back and forth a few times before, with a slight snap of his wrist, the eggs slid up and over, perfectly flipped. Brett waited another moment, then lifted the pan from the burner to slide the over light eggs onto a plate. He had taken three steps to the table when, spinning around, he walked to the sink to dump the combined eggs and toast into the disposal. Brett tossed back the last of his whisky as the mechanism ate his supper.

My mother would have a fit!

Smiling not unlike a devilish young boy, Brett returned to the living room for a second helping of his liquid meal. His second double shot tempered with ice and water, Brett climbed the stairs to his bedroom. Between long sips at his drink he undressed slowly. Glass in hand, he strolled into the bathroom where, again between sips, he brushed his teeth, shaved his face, and showered his body—this action minus the glass. By the time Brett had pulled on suede slacks, a soft sweater, and ankle boots, his glass was empty. Retracing his steps, he went back to the bar. After carefully measuring three-fourths whisky, one-fourth water, and adding two ice cubes, he lifted the glass.

"No!"

The glass landed on the smooth surface of the bar with a crash, its spilled contents unnoticed by the man who was scooping his jacket from the chair on his way toward the door.

His bootheels hitting the sidewalk with a muffled thud, Brett strode purposefully in the direction of Jo's apartment. Damned if he'd lie awake one more night, aching with the memory of how good their lovemaking had been! Damned if he'd give up on a relationship he *knew* would be satisfying to the both of them—if she'd give it a chance to get off the ground! And damned if he'd let her get away with closing the door in his face!

Plunging a hand into his coat pocket, Brett withdrew a cigarette and brought it to his chilled lips. Raising the plastic lighter, he cupped his hand over the end to shield the flame from the cold wind. The lighter clicked on, then off again. His movements uneven from the anger coursing through his body, Brett grasped the unlit cigarette from his lips and flung it to the street.

"No!" He growled softly, harshly. "No more substitutes to pacify frustration!"

At his destination, Brett nodded curtly to the doorman, and a moment later he dipped his head again to the security guard. Neither man attempted to impede his progress.

At Jo's door, Brett stabbed the button to her doorbell with quick impatient motions of his forefinger. Nothing. Grumbling an expletive that would very likely have shocked the neighbors, had they heard it, Brett slipped his hand into his slacks pocket and withdrew his gold keyring. Detaching the large key from the others, he unlocked the door and stepped inside.

"Jo?"

Nothing.

"Jo?" Brett crossed the living room to the bedroom. "Where are you?" Brett's question was answered not by a voice but by the sound of the shower in the bathroom. As he entered the room, the sound came to an abrupt stop. Standing in the middle of the room, facing the bathroom door, Brett waited. Two minutes. Five minutes. Nuts! He was pulling the sweater up over his shoulders when Jo came out of the bathroom tying the sash on the striped robe she'd worn in the apartment in Ocean City.

"Brett!" His name exploded from her lips with a gasp. "How did you get in here?"

"I'm a second-story man in my off hours," Brett muttered through the soft wool.

"And what do you think you're doing?" Jo demanded, charging across the room to stand before him, hands on hips.

"I'm getting undressed for bed." Staring her in the eyes, Brett tossed the sweater aside and began working on his belt buckle.

"Like hell you are!" Jo choked in fury.

"Like hell I'm not," Brett corrected softly. "It seems bed is the one place you and I can communicate. And, the way I feel right now, I just might communicate through most of the night." As he lowered the zipper on the slacks, Brett watched Jo stiffen with outrage. Well, he shrugged mentally, at least when she's furious she talks to me.

"You know," she finally managed through gritted teeth, "for an educated man, you certainly have a flair for crudity."

"Nothing crude about it," Brett contradicted smoothly. "And you know it." Slowly, deliberately, he let his eyes caress her body, feeling a quickness in his loins at the realization that she was wearing nothing but satiny skin underneath the classy, sexy robe. "I said we'll talk later," he went on softly, unselfconsciously stepping out of both slacks and briefs. "And we will talk . . . later." By now Jo's eyes were wide, her gorgeous lashes fluttering, her breath coming in short, angry puffs. God! Brett marveled. She is one beautiful woman.

Reaching out, Brett caught the tie belt of her robe and began loosening the knot.

"Brett!" Her throat worked spasmodically as she swallowed. "Brett, you can't do this! I won't let you."

Brett slid the loop free.

"Brett! Stop this!" Jo demanded in an unconvincing whisper.

The knot untied, Brett gently slid the silky material off Jo's trembling shoulders. Dropping his arms, he stood still, drinking in the longed-for sight of her. It had been nine nights since he'd held the slim loveliness of her close to his own hardness. It seemed more like nineteen years. Stifling a groan, Brett reached out again, this time to lightly grasp her shoulders. The feel of her under his hands set off a chain reaction Brett could not have controlled had his life depended on it. Sliding his hands urgently down her back, Brett drew the warmth and softness of Jo against him, a sigh of real pain escaping his tightly constricted throat.

"Jo . . . my Jo."

Brett, unaware he was saying it all, felt he needed to say so much, much more, yet all that came out was her name. The tips of her breasts touched his chest with the effect of electric probes, creating shock waves that spiraled wildly through his body. Brett's arms tightened convulsively, crushing her to him. His hands, hungry to touch her everywhere at once, moved with restless abandon from her shoulders to the base of her spine and back again.

"Oh, Brett! Oh, Brett."

There was a universe of mixed-up meanings contained in the husky, defeated sound that whispered into Brett's mind as well as his ears. His mind, totally absorbed with the overriding need to make her finally, irrevocably his, caught only the nuance of passion in her tone. Elation singing through him, Brett took her mouth with commanding force. Jo's capitulation was immediate and frenzied. Her hands skimmed the length of his body to grasp his buttocks, fingers clenching, urging the ultimate intimacy.

Brett literally went wild. Shuddering with the desire rocketing through his body, he began moving, backing her to the bed. Then he was on the bed, on Jo, in Jo, taking, taking, wanting more, and yet more, greedily demanding she give everything of herself, his body quivering in exultation of the primitive possession, his mind chanting: mine, mine, mine.

It was over very quickly. His head thrown back, Brett could feel the tug of strain on the taut tendons in his neck. Striving, driving, propelling himself to the very limit of endurance, Brett gasped harshly at the intensity of near pain at his moment of culmination, reveling in the echoing gasp that was torn from Jo's throat.

In a state of complete collapse, Brett lay with his head against Jo's breast, dragging great gulps of air. Brett lay still while his body went through the process of regeneration. His mind, emerging from the fog of sensuality, began clicking away like a well-made timepiece.

Never, never, not even that first time with Jo in Ocean City had Brett so completely lost contact with reality during the act of lovemaking. And never had he wished to remain so completely lost. Even in his exhausted condition a burst of adrenaline shot through his system at the memory of what he'd just experienced. Brett had always doubted the existence of the absolute sexual pinnacle. He doubted no longer.

Monitoring Jo's still-rapid heartbeat, a thrill snaked through Brett's insides. Jo had not surrendered! The thrill changed direction to skitter up his spine. Jo had *not* surrendered! If he had been impatient, rough, demanding, and he had, Jo had been equally so. He had witnessed the same tautness cording her slim white neck that had tightened his with tension. He had felt the sting of her oval nails in his buttocks as her fingers flexed and gripped in a frantic effort to draw him deeper and yet deeper into her body as if in craving to absorb him totally within her being. His lips now tasted the salty flavor of her sweat-sheened skin. Joyous delight followed the path of the thrill. In no way had she surrendered!

I love her! I love her. With my mind, with my body, with my soul! God! Why can't she love me too?

Brett felt an unfamiliar hot sting in his eyes and his brain went numb for an instant. He could not! He could not! He hadn't wept since his father's death during that stupid yacht race! Holy Mother of God! What *was* he going to do? The mere possibility of losing Jo now froze his heartbeats. I can't let her go, Brett's mind roared back to life. I cannot let her go.

The slight stirring of Jo's body beneath him alerted Brett to the realization that he was very likely crushing her slim frame with his weight. Easing himself from her, he stretched out beside her on the now-rumpled spread. Brett knew he should move, if only to get under the spread. Jo was so quiet. Was she sleeping? Shifting onto his side, Brett gazed down on her, a tender smile curving his lips at the sight of the dark swath of hair partially covering her face. Raising his hand to her face, he gently smoothed the swath away from her temple before trailing his fingers to her cheek. Several obstinate silky strands clung to Jo's eyelashes. Being careful not to startle her, Brett brushed her lashes with his fingertips, then became absolutely still.

Jo's lashes were wet! Her face was *wet!* Why was she crying? Had he hurt her! But she had not cried out, had not withdrawn in any way! Quite the opposite, she had attacked, consumed, devoured! As if, as if . . . A chill pervaded Brett's body. Jo had responded to him with all the fervor of a woman with the man she . . . No! Brett closed his eyes in an attempt to block out a face. He could not close his mind to the taunting whisper of a name.

Wolf.

Brett shook his head sharply once.

No. No. Please, no. He didn't want to hear it. Still, he had to know.

210

"Why are you crying?" His voice was soft, but tight with strain. "Did I hurt you?"

"No!" Jo's lids flew up and her head moved briefly on the pillow.

"Then why are you crying?" he insisted.

"It . . . it's nothing, really." The nothing started a fresh flow trickling down her cheeks. "I'm . . . being silly."

"Is it him?" To keep from shouting, Brett whispered. "Were you thinking of him?" Suddenly incensed, he leaned over her, his face close to hers. Teeth clenched, he rasped, "Was *he* in your mind . . . while *I* was in your body?"

"Brett!" Wide-eyed, Jo stared at him. "I don't . . . "

"Was he?" Brett's shout cut across her voice.

"NO!" Jo shouted back at him. "It's over, Brett. I swear it's over. It's been . . . "

"All right!" Brett again cut her off harshly. "I don't want a blow by blow of the ending." He leaned even closer to her. "As long as it is completely over. I want your word on that, Jo. I won't allow you to use my body to appease a hunger for another man."

"Use *you*?" Jo exclaimed on a shriek. "How—"

"Your word, Jo," Brett inserted quietly, ominously.

"You have it!" Jo actually snarled at him. "And don't you ever, ever again accuse *me* of using *you*. Do you understand?"

"Perfectly." Brett's teeth snapped together. Now what? Brett wondered, returning her glare fiercely. Well, when in doubt . . . kiss the bitch! Closing the inches that separated them, Brett covered her mouth with his own.

At first Jo's lips remained stiff and tightly closed. Then they softened. Then they parted. Then they grew warm. The warmth quickly turned to heat. Heat burst into flames. Instant replay; another conflagration. Tongues pierced, hands searched, bodies melded, one into the other. Who owned whom?

Normal breathing restored, Brett drew Jo's sleep-heavy body close to his own. Already half asleep himself, the thought wafted

211

through his mind again. Who owned whom? Beginning to drift, Brett lifted a hand to smother a yawn.

Who owned whom? Who cares?

The automatic alarm that jangled inside Brett's head every working morning at seven fifteen pried his eyes open the next morning. His eyes wide open, he frowned. When, he asked himself, had he and Jo made the move from on top of the spread to beneath the covers? Memory stirred and Brett vaguely recalled waking in the night feeling chilled. Rousing Jo, he had coaxed her up enough to allow him to pull the spread and covers down. She was back to sleep before he'd finished tucking the blankets around the two of them.

Throwing his arms over his head, Brett stretched his body awake. Lord, he was hungry. He needed some food. He needed a shower. But, first, he needed a kiss. Turning onto his side, he propped his head up on one hand. His expression soft, Brett studied the woman he loved. In sleep, Jo was even more beautiful, but in a different way. She looked younger than her twenty-eight years, defenseless, more vulnerable. Staring at Jo's sleep-flushed cheeks, her tender mouth, and her wildly disordered hair, Brett felt his throat constrict with emotion.

How could it be possible, Brett mused, to want to protect to the death and inflict pain on a woman at one and the same time? For Brett did suddenly feel fiercely, savagely protective of her. Yet there had been times, and probably would be again, when he wanted to hurt her. Strange. Frowning in concentration, Brett raked his mind for a single memory, a single instance when he'd ever felt so very strongly about another woman. His mind came up blank. Oh, he'd experienced the usual instinctive protectiveness for Sondra. Sondra had been his wife and as his wife she deserved his protection. Brett smiled. What he'd felt for Sondra paled to transparent in comparison to what he was feeling now for Jo. Brett's smile broadened in self-derision. Of course, he had faced the fact long ago that what he'd felt for Sondra had more to do with self-indulgence and infatuation than love. The woman he gazed upon now Brett loved with every fiber of his being. Brett's smile vanished.

On consideration, the whole concept was pretty damned scary!

Brett lowered his head, then caught himself up short less than an inch from her lips. Don't wake her, let her sleep, his conscience advised. She gave you infinite pleasure during the night, not once but several times. Let her sleep, she has earned it. His smile back in place, Brett eased his body away from Jo's and off the bed.

Twenty-odd minutes later Brett was tugging his crumpled sweater over his head when a slight movement on the bed caught his attention. Pulling the garment into place, he glanced up to find Jo watching him guardedly.

"Good morning." Brett offered the greeting in a neutral tone.

Jo continued to watch him unblinkingly, her expression wary. "Good morning," she responded in a sleep-husky murmur. "Have you eaten?"

"Not yet." Brett stood still, his hands at his sides, regarding her closely. What was she thinking? The alert, somewhat fearful expression in her eyes puzzled him. It was almost as if she was waiting for an inevitable blow to fall. Why? Unable to come up with an answer, Brett shrugged. "I thought I'd stop for something to eat on my way back to the apartment."

"I see," Jo replied tonelessly.

What does she see? Brett felt a stirring of anger. What the hell was going on in that beautiful head of hers? Jo ended his fruitless search for answers.

"You were going to leave without waking me?"

The mild reproach in her voice put a spur to his anger. "Of course not!" Brett was barely aware of his fingers curling into his palms. Cool it, chum, he cautioned himself. Make haste slowly here. What had he expected from her this morning? The query was rhetorical, and Brett knew it. He'd expected Jo to be as she'd been on the mornings they'd wakened together in Ocean City . . . warm, responsive, smiling. The disappointment that lanced through Brett robbed him of a portion of the energy he'd felt on awakening. Choosing his words carefully, Brett went on, "I had every intention of waking you. I put the coffee on to brew. It should be ready in a few minutes." A small smile Brett didn't particularly like shadowed Jo's lips.

"The holidays are over," she said flatly.

"Jo, what . . . ?"

"You'd better go," she interrupted impatiently. "You'll be late. And so will I."

Now what in hell . . . ? Brett frowned. Was she throwing him out? After last night? Oh, no! No way! Brett's balled hands tightened into hard fists. "I was going to suggest you take an extra day off."

"Why?" Jo shot the word at him.

Why? Brett was hard put not to laugh. God! He'd have thought it was obvious. He had loved her to a standstill; she'd been exhausted when he'd finally allowed her to rest. Come to that, so had he . . . and he felt, or at least he *had* felt, like he could fight his weight in wildcats. An unknowing, sardonic smile played on his lips. Hell! He was having trouble fighting his weight in JoAnne Lawrences! Exasperation serrated the edge of Brett's tone.

"Why not?"

"I don't want to stay home!"

"Then don't!" Brett snapped. Immediately regretting his loss of patience, Brett drew a deep calming breath. Jo was still lying flat on the bed, the covers up to her chin. Very probably, Brett decided, because she was naked. He didn't like the connotations to that consideration. During their time together by the ocean, Jo had been completely unselfconscious with him. An uncomfortable sensation of defeat crawled along the floor of his stomach. Hanging on to his temper, Brett explained calmly, "You had requested a leave to rest. What with one thing and another" —he shrugged—"you've had very little of it. I thought you could take the day to just . . . catch up."

"I'm fine," she assured him quietly.

"Okay, then I'll see you in the office?" Brett lifted one eyebrow slightly.

"Yes."

Brett didn't move. Staring into her eyes, he waited to see if Jo would say anything else. She didn't. She stared back at him, her expression also one of waiting. Say it. Now. The command flashed from Brett's brain to his lips.

"I'll transfer my things tonight." Barely breathing, Brett watched Jo's eyes flicker and widen, observed the sudden rigidity of her body.

"W-what . . . " Jo stopped to clear her throat before continuing in a husky whisper, "What are you saying?"

"I'm moving in with you." Brett heard the steel underlining his soft statement. From her expression of shock, it was obvious Jo heard it too.

"Brett, is . . ." Jo paused to moisten her lips with the tip of her tongue. "Is that wise?" Grasping the covers in one hand, she sat up to stare at him in consternation. "I mean, word of it will zing through the office grapevine within a week!"

Brett had to put a clamp on the elation that was dancing wildly through his system. He had won! Hot damn! He had won! Jo had not denied him the right to share her world or her body! She was simply concerned about propriety! He swallowed a whoop of laughter.

"Need I tell you what the office gossips can do to, and with, themselves?" he drawled. The amusement swelled at Jo's expression of censure. How in hell, after being Wolf's mistress, had she retained her naivete? The query killed Brett's amusement. Why had he had to think of Wolf, and the role he'd played in Jo's life, now? A fresh spurt of anger threatened to swamp his elation. *Had* played, Brett repeated in an effort to contain his emotions. The operative word here is *had*. While calming himself, Brett let his eyes feast on Jo's invitingly disheveled appearance. Taking one step toward her, Brett caught himself up short. You've got

215

to go to work, Renninger, he cautioned in an attempt to quell the sudden need to hold Jo in his arms. Get started on the day, he advised himself. The night will come more swiftly if you keep busy in the interim.

"Why are you staring at me like that?" The wariness was back in Jo's expression and her voice cracked with uncertainty.

"I'm thinking about having you for breakfast," Brett answered softly, his elation soaring again as her wariness and uncertainty were washed away by a look of surprised delight.

"I think you'd probably work a lot better on bacon and eggs," Jo replied, straightfaced.

This time Brett made no effort to contain his laughter. "I'd say you are probably right," he agreed, grinning. "Even though it won't be near as much fun." Brett held his breath. Was the tension gone for good? Was the easiness between them back to stay?

"Perhaps not," Jo murmured. Then, to Brett's delight, she fluttered her long lashes at him coyly. "You could always plan on having me for dessert. Anticipation sharpens the appetite, you know."

Brett took another step toward her. "If my appetite gets any sharper," he growled, "I'll slash myself on it and bleed to death." Brett had no qualms whatever about admitting to Jo how very much he desired her. Hadn't he admitted as much silently, with his body, throughout the long night?

"Poor darling," Jo cooed. The "darling" electrified Brett; still, he could appreciate her teasing. "So neglected. So deprived. How long has it been, dear, since a woman took pity on you?"

Sheer enjoyment of her tempered Brett's arousal. Laughing softly, he strode to the bed. "I don't want 'a woman.' I want *one* woman." Bending to her, he brushed her mouth with his lips, afraid to allow himself a deeper taste of her. He *had* to get to work! "And that one woman had better rustle her rump because, if she's late to work, I'll dock her pay."

216

Leaning back, Jo surveyed him with a superior expression. "In case you've forgotten, I am a sal-ar-ied employee." She smirked.

"Yes, I know." Brett smiled sweetly. "But then I could always demote you *and* put you on an hourly wage. I'm sure Bob Kempten would jump at the chance to have your job." Brett regretted the teasing barb the minute he uttered it. Jo was Wolf's assistant. How many times had she reminded him of that fact? Too many. Well, if she had plans of beating him to death using Wolf's name as a stick, he had certainly given her the perfect opportunity to get off the first whack.

"Oh, I'm quite sure you're right." Jo's purring voice sent a chill down Brett's spine. Here it comes, he thought tiredly. "But would he also jump at the chance to sit on your lap?"

The breath Brett was fully aware of holding sighed silently through his grinning lips. "Are you going to sit on my lap?" he asked with exaggerated eagerness.

Jo's expression turned woeful. "I'm a loyal employee." She sighed loudly. "If I must, I must."

Brett's laughter bounced off the walls. You had better get your can out of here, ol' buddy, he urged himself. Or there is no way you'll see the inside of your office this day. Still laughing softly, Brett spun away from the bed to stride across the room. Scooping his jacket off the chair he'd tossed it onto the night before, he slanted a devilish glance at Jo.

"Move it, water baby," he ordered gently. "I want to see you in my office at nine thirty." Still grinning, he sauntered out of the bedroom.

That evening, as promised, Brett transferred his clothing and few personal belongings to Jo's place, ignoring the taunting thought that he was moving out of Wolf's apartment into Wolf's apartment. As he stowed his shaving gear onto the medicine cabinet shelf Jo had cleared for him, Brett decided to contact a real estate agent about finding another place for them.

Surprisingly, they made the adjustment of living together very quickly and, within two weeks Brett wondered how he'd ever thought he was content living alone. They learned and accepted each others faults—in Jo's case, her habit of kicking her shoes off the moment she entered the apartment and forgetting to pick them up again; Brett did it for her. In Brett's case, his failure to replace the cap on the toothpaste tube; Jo did that for him. They worked together well. They played together joyously. They laughed together often.

Near the end of January Brett asked Jo if she'd like to go skiing. Jo's response was less than enthusiastic.

"I don't know how to ski, Brett. And, to be honest, I'm not all that eager to learn how."

"You could give it a try, honey," Brett coaxed, itching to get on the slopes again. "If you don't like it, you could always relax by the fire with a hot toddy while I attempt to break a leg."

Jo hesitated but Brett gave her such a woebegone expression she laughingly relented and agreed to go with him, exactly as he'd hoped she would.

"Terrific!" Brett exclaimed as eagerly as a kid might have. Jumping out of his chair, he walked restlessly around the living room, unaware of the gentle smile curving Jo's lips as she watched him. "Let's see now." He began making plans aloud. "Accommodations are no problem. I've retained the room at that motel up in Vermont for office space in case I needed it." Brett was equally unaware of the slight tightening of Jo's lips. "I have that meeting in Atlanta next week." Jo had absolutely refused to go to Atlanta with him. Brett was still not completely reconciled to her stand on Atlanta but, with this new victory, he decided to stop badgering her about it. "Suppose we say the week after next?" One brow lifted quizzically, he swung to face her. "Okay?"

"You love skiing that much?" Jo laughed.

"Yes," Brett answered simply. "And I haven't stepped into boots once this winter."

This time Brett was fully aware of Jo's gentle smile. "Okay," she agreed softly. "The week after next."

Brett thanked Jo, twice, after they'd turned out the light in the bedroom that night.

Atlanta was a drag for Brett, even though the meeting he'd set up with a local realtor proved satisfying to both of them. Brett missed Jo as much as he would have the loss of his right arm. His impatience to get all existing details cleared up did not go unnoticed by Richard Colby.

"Is she beautiful?" Richard asked out of the blue while they were discussing swamp drainage, of all things, the day before Brett's departure.

"Very," Brett responded immediately. Then, his tone dangerous, Brett retorted, "Why?"

"No reason." Richard, unperturbed by Brett's tone, smiled easily. "It's obvious you can't wait to get back to her. Why wait till tomorrow? We can clean this drainage thing up by dinnertime. I can handle all the nitpicking details myself. There's no reason you could not fly back to New York tonight." His smile broadened. "Unless, that is, you're enthralled with my company."

Brett's smile was as broad as Richard's. "Thanks, buddy. Remind me to give you a raise."

"Why do you think I made the suggestion?" Richard drawled dryly.

It was late by the time Brett let himself into the dark, silent apartment. Moving cautiously but unerringly, he made his way through the living room to the bedroom. Inside the bedroom he placed his case carefully out of the way, then stood still to allow his eyes to adjust to the unrelenting darkness. When he had his bearings, Brett walked softly to the side of the room's one large window to tug gently on the cord that worked the draperies. The heavy, lined drapes slid silently apart giving access to a pale shaft of moonlight. A low moaning sound froze Brett in his tracks as he turned from the window. Every sense alerted, he focused his gaze on the moonlight-washed figure lying on the bed.

Jo moaned again and, frowning with concern, Brett crossed to

219

the bed in three long strides. The sight that met his eyes stole Brett's breath.

Jo was lying on her back in the center of the bed, her arms flung wide, her fingers grasping at the sheet, nails scratching the smooth surface. Her naked body was only partially covered, and even as Brett stared her legs thrashed about, dislodging the blankets completely. Gazing transfixed at her white skin gleaming in the moonlight, Brett felt a kick of desire in his loins. A sighing sound drew his eyes to her face. Her head moved restlessly as another sigh whispered through her slightly parted lips.

She's dreaming, Brett concluded in bemusement. Watching her legs, Brett's heartbeat accelerated. She's dreaming she's making love! Brett closed his eyes as another low moan sent a shiver of excitement careening through his body. Barely conscious of what he was doing, Brett opened his eyes, then, fastening his gaze on her writhing body, he began to undress. When the last piece of his constricting clothing had been discarded, Brett stepped up to the bed. Sliding onto the cool sheet beside Jo, he ran one palm lightly from her ankle to her hip. Immediately Jo's leg moved to press against his hand and a low groan of need murmured from deep in her throat. Brett was sliding his hand over her rib cage when a chilling thought stopped him cold.

Who is she dreaming she's making love with?

Watching her, wanting to know, not wanting to know, Brett closed his mind to the visage and name of one man. She's mine, he raged silently. Awake or asleep, Jo is mine! Blocking out the idea that what he was doing could very well be wrong, Brett deliberately took possession of her silky-skinned breast.

"Brett."

Not even a whisper, hardly more than a sigh, yet his name swelled to a joyous crescendo in Brett's mind. Jo was dreaming *he* was making love to her! Unhesitatingly, Brett carefully slid his body between her soft thighs, determined to make her dream a reality. Covering her gently, yet not joining their bodies, Brett touched Jo's parted lips with his own. Before entering her, Brett wanted her fully conscious of who was doing what to whom. The touch of his lips and hands feather light, Brett adored her body.

"Brett?" Jo's voice was fuzzy. She was not yet fully awake.

"Yes, love?" Brett murmured, kissing the corner of her mouth.

"Oh, Brett. Is it really you?" Jo was coming out of sleep, but falling into passion. Her hands forsaking the sheet, she grasped Brett instead.

"Yes, love," Brett assured softly. "It's really me." He gave her the feel of his tongue along her bottom lip for proof.

"I missed you so." Jo's arms tightened; her thighs relaxed. "Don't make me wait. Please." She arched her body to his with the plea and sighed when Brett granted it.

Moving slowly at first, savoring the velvety softness of her, Brett twined his fingers in Jo's hair and kissed her tenderly on her cheeks, her eyes, her chin. When his lips brushed hers she groaned.

"Kiss me. Love me. Oh, Brett, I need you." The moan deepened into a sob. "I need you." That's when the brainstorm hit him. Teasing her with his body's slow strokes, Brett brushed Jo's quivering lips again.

"Marry me, Jo." Brett's voice was low but firm with conviction.

"What!" Jo's heavy lashes fluttered, then lifted. She stared at him with passion-clouded eyes. "What did you say?"

"Marry me." Brett increased his stroke, restraining a smile at the immediate response she made with her body.

"But . . ."

"We're good together, love," He brushed her lips harder. "You know we're good together. Not just like this." Brett thrust against her, then slowed again. "We're good together in everything."

"Brett, we can't!" Jo's breathing was shallow now and getting more shallow with each passing instant. "We don't . . . "

Brett closed her mouth with his own, certain he didn't want

221

to hear whatever she was going to say. He let his tongue match the motion of his body. When Jo was clinging to him, whimpering in need, Brett denied her his mouth.

"Will you marry me, Jo?" Brett stopped moving entirely.

Jo seemed unable to open her eyes. "Brett . . . please," she wailed.

"Will you marry me, Jo?" Brett kissed her very hard, and very fast.

"Yes."

The whisper trembled through Jo's lips. Relief trembled through Brett's body. Strength, power, followed on the heels of relief and, positive he could fly at that moment if he so wished, Brett gave in to the fire raging in his body.

Sated physically, satisfied emotionally, content in his mind, Brett lay cradling Jo's relaxed body close to his own. "Are you asleep?" Moving his head slowly, he brushed a few damp tendrils away from her temple with his lips.

"Yes." Jo's warm breath tingled the skin on his chest.

Lifting one hand to her chin, Brett turned her face up to his. "You won't back out. Will you, Jo?" he asked quietly, staring directly into her love-softened eyes.

"No, Brett, I won't back out."

Brett fought the urge to close his eyes in relief. Although he wasn't overjoyed at the underlying note of calm acceptance in Jo's tone, he consoled himself with the realization that her tone had also contained firm conviction. For now, Brett decided he could live with the knowledge that Jo would not attempt to repudiate her agreement to legalize their union on the grounds of duress. They could make it work, he *would* make it work, Brett vowed. He had to because he really had no other choice; Brett knew he could not let Jo go now. Brett knew also that he belonged to Jo every bit as much as he felt she belonged to him. It was somewhat scary but, Brett shrugged mentally, there it was. Bending to her, he kissed her tenderly.

"We can be married in Vermont next week." The suggestion

made, Brett held his breath, waiting for her reaction. He didn't have to hold his breath long.

Jo's eyes, suddenly clear, alert, widened in shock. "Next week?" Her voice cracked and she cleared her throat. "Vermont? Brett, I can't be ready to get married in less than a week!"

Positive he detected a note of panic creeping into her tone, Brett tightened his grasp on Jo's chin. "You can be ready." To punctuate his assertion he kissed her deeply. "You *will* be ready." His mouth crushed hers again. "We will be married"—another brief kiss—"next week . . . in Vermont. I'm sure Casey and Sean will be delighted to stand witness." Brett's punishing kisses were beginning to backlash. Feeling his body harden with renewed passion, Brett conveyed his need to Jo with his mouth, and his tongue, and his groaning words.

"Say yes again, Jo, please."

"To which question?" Jo gasped as he trailed his fingers from her chin to her breast. "The one you're asking with your words? Or the one you're asking with your body?"

Laughing softly, Brett sucked gently on her lower lip. "Say yes to both."

"Yes to both," Jo parroted at once, then qualified, "On one condition."

As by now the fire racing through Brett had consumed his brain, he would have consented to almost anything. "Name it," he murmured into her mouth.

"This time"—Jo hesitated, then rushed on—"I want to make love to you."

This was a condition? Laughter shook Brett's body. Flinging his arms wide, Brett threw himself back away from her to lay stretched out on the bed. "Take me," he cried, grinning wickedly. "I'm yours."

Brett was to remember his words several times over the days that followed. And, everytime he did, he felt again the thrill he'd experienced in being taken by Jo. Lord! When that exceptional woman decided she was going to make love to a man, she put her heart and soul into the effort. Days later Brett's body still tingled from the effective way she'd tormented him with her soft, caressing hands and her sweet, hungry mouth. Marriage to Jo, Brett decided, still lost in bemusement, should prove to be one interesting experiment.

Surprisingly, as the days until their departure for Vermont shortened, Brett found himself growing more and more nervous. Why the tension? Why the jumpiness? Why the crawly sensation in his stomach? Brett quizzed himself repeatedly. It was not as if he were being coerced into matrimony. Quite the contrary. If a charge of coercion were to be leveled, *he'd* be the guilty party. Strange, he thought, he had no recollection of any nervousness at all before he and Sondra were married. There were moments, many in number, when Brett wished he hadn't quit smoking . . . again. Brett's thinking process danced around the edges of the answer to his uptight feeling right up till he and Jo arrived in Vermont.

As Brett had predicted, Casey and Sean were both delighted and flattered to be asked to witness the nuptials. Casey, bubbling over with the news that she was pregnant, threw herself into the wedding spirit and, by the time the legalities were taken care of, had made all the arrangements for the ceremony.

Brett and Jo were married in a picturesque New England church on a Thursday morning in early February. Immediately following the brief service, Casey and Sean whisked them off to an equally picturesque but decidedly elegant restaurant for a champagne wedding breakfast that lasted through four bottles of the expensive wine and most of the afternoon. From the restaurant, the Delhenys poured Brett and Jo into a cab with the advice to do everything they might do.

"Which should take you until sometime tomorrow afternoon," Casey confided laughingly.

It was then that Brett, not drunk by a long shot, but feeling little pain, faced the reason for his nervousness during the previous week. In a word, Brett identified his malady. That word was fear. The cause and symptoms had vanished when Jo signed her name to the marriage certificate.

The first thing Brett did after he'd locked the motel room door was kiss his new bride, satisfyingly and thoroughly. The second thing he did was lift the telephone receiver and dial his mother's private office number in Florida. When his mother answered in her endearingly brisk tone, Brett, wasting no time on formalities, went directly to the reason for his call.

"Jo and I were married this morning, Mother." Not being able to resist, Brett added insolently, "We'll accept a large check for a wedding present." From behind him, Brett heard Jo's shocked gasp and grinned. His grin widened at his mother's retort.

"You'll accept what I choose to give you, smart ass." There was a telling pause, then Violet said solemnly, "Congratulations, Brett. JoAnne is a lovely young woman." Violet's tone changed to reveal confusion and a tinge of hurt feelings. "But why didn't you let us know? You could have been married at the farm."

"I've done that. Remember?" Brett's grin was gone, replaced by a grimace. Brett had coolly and deliberately chosen not to inform his family about his plans simply because he knew his mother would suggest the farm as a perfect site for the wedding. Brett's reason for not wanting to be married at the farm had absolutely nothing to do with memories of Sondra and everything to do with Wolf being in residence there. At his mother's sharply indrawn breath and murmured "Oh, Brett, how foolish of me. I'm sorry," Brett made an effort to soften his rough tone. "It's all right, sir, forget it. Besides, I wanted to go skiing on my honeymoon."

Following his mother's request, Brett handed the phone to Jo, then stood patiently while she responded to her new mother-in-law's well wishes. When the connection to Florida had been broken, Brett again handed the receiver to Jo.

"Your turn to face the firing squad," he teased. "But make it quick, love, your bridegroom is getting itchy."

Wondering at the odd expression on Jo's face, Brett studied

her as she placed the call. There was something wrong with Jo's family situation, Brett knew. Something that had hurt her. And, although Brett knew Jo had informed her parents that she was getting married, it was obvious she was not happy about making this call. Brett listened intently to Jo's short, terse conversation, anger stirring when she winced at something that was said to her. The moment she'd replaced the receiver, Brett enfolded Jo in his arms.

"It's all right, water baby," Brett soothed as she began to weep. "Don't cry, love."

"You don't understand," Jo sniffed, burrowing into his chest. "Talking to my mother always makes me cry. You see, my mother and father hate each other. And it's so sad . . . They're both so very unhappy."

What could he say to comfort her? Coming from a happy family, Brett hadn't the vaguest idea. So, instead of words, he comforted her with caresses. Jo didn't cry very long.

CHAPTER TEN

Jo woke to the delicious sensation of her husband's lips exploring her face.

Her husband! A shiver of pleasure rippled through Jo's mind and body. Brett's arm, bent at the elbow, made a V on her chest; his fingers combed through the tangled mass of her hair. Circling his wrist with her hand, Jo lifted it to peer at the face of the slim gold watch he'd forgotten to remove in the heat of the moment the night before. The digits pulsed to eleven fifteen. She had been Mrs. Brett Renninger for over twenty-four hours!

Eleven fifteen! Good heavens! Jo stared at the watch in disbelief. She never slept past nine in the morning, not even on her days off or on holidays! Of course, that was before one very handsome man breezed into her life, and her bed, keeping her awake until the darkness of night gave sway to the pearl gray of predawn. A memory thrill tiptoed down Jo's spine. Had any bride ever had a more ardent bridegroom? Had any bride ever experienced such consummate ecstasy? Jo very seriously doubted it. But, even so, it was time to get up! Even if she infinitely preferred to lay luxuriating in her marriage bed.

"Brett?"

"Hmmm?" Brett's warm breath caressed her ear.

"Do you know what time it is?" Gulping back a gasp, Jo managed a steady tone.

"Time to make love to you again?" Brett responded immediately, hopefully, gently nipping at her earlobe.

Jo tried, and failed, to suppress the laughter that bubbled into her throat. "What are you?" she demanded in a falsely stern voice. "Some kind of sex maniac?"

"No," Brett denied calmly, poking the tip of his tongue into her ear. "I'm every kind of sex maniac." Raising his head, Brett gazed at her with eyes so soft with tenderness, Jo's throat closed with emotion. "But," he qualified seriously, "I only suffer this libido madness when in the company of one particular woman. The rest of the female population is absolutely safe from me."

Even Marsha Wenger? Jo, cautioning herself against being stupid, ordered the question to remain silent. As far as she knew, Brett had not seen Marsha outside the office since he'd followed her to Ocean City. Marsha's loss is my gain, Jo decided with a feeling of ruthlessness she had never before experienced. Brett is *mine!*

"Have you been eating raw oysters and swallowing vitamin E capsules while I wasn't looking?" she teased, banishing all consideration of Marsha.

"Not necessary," Brett murmured, the quirk at the corners of his mouth telegraphing the coming grin. "Merely touching you here—" His wrist slipped out of her hand and his fingers blazed a fiery trail from her throat to the tip of one breast. "And here—" His fingers drew a straight, tantalizing line down her body. "And especially *here*—" His fingers slid into the moist warmth of her. "Is all the aphrodisiac I need." Brett moved his fingers enticingly and Jo, her breathing already erratic, arched her hips into his hand. All traces of Brett's grin disappeared as his eyes swept down over her body.

Jo felt the heat rising in her in reaction to his close scrutiny of her responsiveness. Watching her intently, Brett stroked a particularly sensitive spot, his eyes flaring silver with passion when her body writhed in pleasurable agony. Embarrassed by having him witness her abandoned response, Jo tensed her muscles in an attempt to withdraw from his maddening fingers.

"Brett . . . what are . . . you doing?" Jo pushed the protest out between short, rasping breaths.

"There are many ways of giving and receiving pleasure, love," Brett said softly, continuing his mind-divorcing slow stroke. "Together you and I are going to explore most of them. Relax, darling," he husked, luring the tension out of Jo's muscles. "Enjoy. I am."

Jo was beyond protest. Closing her eyes, she surrendered to the moment and the clamoring demand of her body for release. Jo knew Brett was watching her every frantic move, hearing her every labored breath but, suddenly, inexplicably, she no longer cared. Instinct or unformed intelligent reason routed all shame. Brett was her husband, the man she loved more than her own life. How could she feel shame in loving his lovemaking? She couldn't. Sighing in relief, Jo reveled in the enjoyment Brett offered her, thinking, vaguely, his turn would come.

Jo's vague thoughts proved correct some fifteen or twenty minutes later. When the last of his shudders had subsided, and his weight was a sweet heaviness on her seemingly boneless body, Brett lifted his head to kiss her softly. "I love—" He paused—because he was still out of breath? Jo wondered, afraid to think or even hope—then, disappointingly, he went on, "being with you, being around you, being in you." As if, no matter how much he had, he couldn't get enough of her, Brett kissed her again. "You love it too, don't you?"

"Yes," Jo admitted, swallowing the tightness in her throat that presaged tears in her eyes. "I love it too." The sense of defeat, of disappointment, was crushing. She had known Brett was not in love with her, still Jo had dared to hope. Hope gone, Jo consoled herself with the thought that, although Brett was not in love with her, he was not in love with any other woman either.

The very idea of Brett loving another woman made Jo tremble in fear of losing him.

"Are you cold, love?" Brett asked at once, then answered for her. "Of course you are." Carefully lifting his weight from her, Brett rolled to the edge of the bed and sat up. "Come along, darling. A hot shower will warm you up." Tilting his perfectly sculpted head, Brett slanted a teasing look at her. "Then, after you're all nice and warm, I'll take you skiing, and you can get cold all over again."

Pushing all thoughts of being unloved, and all consideration of other women from her mind, Jo arched one brow and taunted dryly, "Why are you so good to me?" The instant the gibe was out of her mouth Jo realized she'd let herself wide open for a zinger. Brett's slow grin told her she was right.

"Because you're such a hot number in the sack," he shot back every bit as dryly. "And because I had the proper up-dragging," he added, deadpan.

Jo refused to acknowledge the twinge of pain Brett's taunt had inflicted. He was obviously teasing, besides, with him, she *was* a hot number in the sack. Instead of feeling hurt, Jo chided herself, you should feel complimented. Not two years ago another man had damned near convinced you you were a walking, talking iceberg! You should be thankful for what you do have, not cry for what you don't have. And, right now, you have a husband who dearly loves to tease. Get with it, girl!

"Dragging is the perfect term," Jo rejoined, getting with it for all she was worth. "Insofar as your mind being dragged through the dirt, that is."

Leaning to her, Brett scowled threateningly. "Are you implying I have a dirty mind?"

"Oh, no." Jo smiled sweetly. "I'm *declaring* you have a dirty mind." Jo was up and running to the bathroom before she'd finished speaking, flicking the lock on the door a hairsbreadth before Brett reached it.

"Let me in, love," he coaxed, rattling the knob. "I promise I won't beat you . . . much."

Standing inside the door, Jo rested her forehead against the wood panel. She hated being separated from him, even by a hollow door. Dear God! Jo thought wonderingly, How is it possible to love so deeply? If he ever leaves me I'll . . . I'll . . .

"Jo." Brett's forlorn tone brought a smile to Jo's lips. "Please let me in."

"Will you buy me diamonds?"

"Yes."

"Will you buy me furs?"

"Yes, yes."

By now, tears running unheeded down her cheeks, Jo was shaking with laughter.

"How about a Maserati?"

"Are you crazy?" he bellowed. "Do you have any idea what they cost?"

Brushing impatiently at her wet cheeks, Jo unlocked the door.

Although Brett extended their stay in Vermont, the days disappeared like spring snow in warm sunshine. They spent most of their afternoons skiing, Brett on the high runs, Jo with the beginners. Their nights and mornings they spent alone, usually in bed. They were sitting in bed on their last morning, sipping coffee, when Brett asked casually . . . far too casually:

"What if you're pregnant?"

"I'm not," Jo answered calmly, ignoring the sudden wish that she was.

"How do you know?" Brett persisted. "We've certainly tried hard enough."

"I'm on the pill, Brett." Drawing a deep breath, Jo looked him straight in the eyes. What was he probing for? Jo speculated, searching his eyes for an answer. Was he hoping she was pregnant? Was he praying she wasn't? His eyes darkened with confusion and something else Jo could not identify.

"Since when?" Brett's quiet voice made Jo uneasy.

"Since the day you moved into my apartment," Jo replied in her self-enforced calm. "I already had the prescription. All I had to do was have it refilled." Jo grew chilled at Brett's sudden shuttered, withdrawn expression.

"Of course." He smiled wryly, increasing Jo's chill. "How stupid of me." Moving with a swiftness that startled Jo, he slid off the bed and stood up. "I guess we'd better pack. We have a long drive ahead of us."

Brett remained terse and withdrawn throughout the entire drive back to New York. Both confused and hurt by his quick change in attitude, Jo gave up her frustrating, fruitless attempts to draw him into conversation forty-five minutes into the trip.

Watching his expensively gloved hands control the powerful sports car with effortless ease, Jo sighed silently. This was not the first time Brett had coldly shut himself away from her without explanation. Was he opposed to her taking birth control pills? If so, why hadn't he simply told her he was? She'd like nothing better than to flush the things down the toilet. God! Jo shivered in the warmth of the car's heater. A good screaming match would be preferable to this freeze-out.

Sliding down into the supple leather of the bucket seat, Jo rested her head on the high seat back and closed her eyes. Would she ever understand this complex man she'd married? She knew his body intimately and his mind not at all. What motivates him? she mused. He works like a Trojan, yet doesn't need the money he accumulates. He laughs and teases like a carefree boy, then broods like an overburdened man. He amuses me. He confuses me. He scares me to death. Unaware of the sharp-eyed glances the object of her thoughts slanted at her periodically, Jo sighed in longing for the carefree boy who amuses.

Jo opened her eyes briefly when she heard a clicking sound, then closed them again as Brett finished sliding a tape into the machine attached to the underside of the dashboard. The music that filled the small interior of the car surprised her. If she'd been

232

asked to guess what kind of music Brett enjoyed, her last guess would have been Paul Williams, yet that's who she was now listening to! Losing herself in the singer's odd yet enchanting voice, Jo let her thoughts drift.

There was a danger in allowing one's thoughts to drift, Jo found to her chagrin. Unfettered, thoughts tended to drift in the wrong direction. Unwelcomed by Jo, the memory of her two phone calls to her mother sidled into her mind. Sighing again, she gave the memories free rein, hoping she'd then be able to put them out of her mind. Jo had made the first call to her mother the day after Brett's wildly unorthodox proposal of marriage. Quite like Brett had done when he'd phoned his mother after the fact, Jo had not beat around the bush.

"I'm getting married next week," Jo had said starkly, wincing at her mother's gasp of dismay.

"You're out of your mind!" Ellen had exclaimed angrily. Not "do you love him?" Or even "to whom?" Just "You're out of your mind."

Jo had dug her nails into her palm in reaction to the scorn in her mother's voice. Controlling her tone with sheer will, Jo had replied, "Perhaps so but, nevertheless, I'm getting married." Then, though unasked, she offered the name of the groom. "I'm going to marry Brett Renninger."

"Your boss?" Ellen asked with sudden interest.

"Yes." Jo had been totally unprepared for her mother's next words.

"Well, when the bubble bursts, at least you'll have money to fall back on."

"I'd never accept money from Brett like that, Mother," Jo had said with quiet determination.

"Now I'm convinced you're crazy," Ellen had retorted disgustedly. "Well, I won't waste my time wishing you happiness. The rich ones are even worse than the men without money. They can always buy their way out, and they know it. What I do wish

233

s that you'll change your mind before it's too late. Live with him, if you must. But think twice before you commit yourself."

Jo stirred restlessly, wondering when Brett had changed the tape. Now the sexy voice of Neil Diamond swirled around her head from the car's four speakers.

"Are you hungry?" Brett's voice was soft but the unexpected sound of it startled Jo into opening her eyes.

"No." Thinking the denial too uncompromising, Jo added quietly, "Are you?"

"No."

Anger flared inside Jo's mind. Arrogant beast! Apparently being uncompromising doesn't bother him! I should have listened to my mother! Jo regretted the thought immediately. No! She was not sorry she'd married Brett. Even if she did long to punch his lights out at this moment! Closing her eyes, Jo deliberately dredged up the memory of her second phone call to her mother. Knowing Brett was listening to her side of the conversation, Jo had chosen her words very carefully.

"It's Jo, Mother," she'd said with all the lightness she could muster. "I'm calling from Vermont to tell you Brett and I were married this morning."

"You have my deepest sympathy." Ellen sighed before adding, "Is he there with you now?"

"Yes, Mother." Jo had fought to keep her tone even.

"Tell him I said he's to take good care of you, even though I know he probably won't." There'd been a pause, then her mother had gone on in a muffled tone, "I love you, honey. I wish . . . I wish . . . well, it doesn't matter what I wish. I *do* hope you'll be happy, but . . . " Her voice trailed away.

Feeling the hot sting of tears behind her lashes, Jo opened her eyes and sat up abruptly, shaking her head sharply to dislodge the sound of her mother's sad voice.

"What the hell?" Brett sliced a frown at her. "What's the matter?"

"Nothing. It's nothing. I got a cramp in my neck from my

234

awkward position," Jo improvised, lifting her hand to rub the side of her neck. "It's fine now."

Brett returned his attention to the highway but his frown remained in place. "Even so, I think it's time we stopped to stretch and, while we're doing it, we might as well eat something."

The restaurant Brett found was unpretentious but clean and the food was superior. Jo ate less than half her dinner. Brett drank his. When he motioned the waiter to indicate he'd like a third Rob Roy, Jo reached out impulsively to grasp his hand.

"Brett! You've got quite a distance to drive. If you expect me to get into the car with you, don't have another drink."

Brett Renninger was not at all used to being told what to do, and Jo knew it. She also knew there was no way she'd ride in a car with a driver who was not only in a foul mood, but three sheets to the wind as well. Her resolve rock hard, Jo stared defiantly into Brett's icy, narrow-lidded eyes. Amazingly, Brett relented first, albeit angrily.

"A wife of little more than a week," he sneered, waving the waiter away. "And already you're issuing ultimatums." Brett extracted several bills from his wallet and tossed them on top of the check the waiter slid discreetly onto the table. Glancing back at Jo, he pinned her to her seat with eyes the color of cold steel. "This is the second time I've backed down to an ultimatum from you." Brett's voice was as steely as his eyes. Jo, her spine tingling with apprehension, had a memory flash of their confrontation in his office the day she'd lifted the phone to call Wolf in Florida. Raising her chin, Jo managed, just, to meet his stare unflinchingly. "Three strikes and you're out, sweetie," Brett said grittily. "Don't push your luck . . . or me too damn far."

Jo's gasp burst into the tension hovering in the air between them. Was Brett threatening her? Well, of course he was! Jo swallowed the taste of panic. What, exactly, was he threatening her with? The promise of physical retaliation? Jo rejected the idea at once. Without knowing how she knew, Jo was positive

235

Brett would never raise his hand to her in violence. Then what form would his retaliation take? The answer that stole into Jo's mind was accompanied by a choking nausea in her throat. He'd said "three strikes and you're out." Out as in: out of a job? Out of his life? Out of his sight? Out of a husband? Jo was very much afraid Brett meant every one of the outs that marched through her rattled brain.

The nausea lasted only a moment, then fled before the onslaught of fury. If Brett Renninger thought he could frighten her into quivering submission, he was in for a very rude awakening! Gritting her teeth, Jo leaned across the table to enable him to hear the rage in her soft voice.

"Don't you ever threaten me again. *You* are the one who followed me to Ocean City. *You* are the one who moved into *my* apartment. *You* are the one who insisted on marriage." Jo paused to gulp air into her constricted lungs, then, forcing her teeth apart, made a threat of her own . . . or at least attempted to.

"If you ever threaten me again, I'll . . . I'll. . ."

"You'll what?" Brett inserted in a quiet tone that in no way concealed his own fury. "Call the big prowler?"

"I don't need Wolf to protect me from you," Jo retorted. "Now, if you are tired of me, or bored with this situation you forced the both of us into, take a hike!" Pushing her chair back, Jo jumped to her feet, grabbed her coat, and, still glaring at Brett, underlined her position. "I don't need you, Brett," she lied convincingly. "I don't need any of the Renningers." Sliding the coat around her shoulders, Jo strode out of the restaurant.

For the remainder of the drive to New York the sports car took on the qualities of an abandoned tomb. There were moments when Jo was certain the silence would shatter her eardrums.

It was early evening when they arrived at the apartment. Jo's fury had long since burned itself out. By the time she walked into her bedroom, Jo was combating an overwhelming feeling of loss. Disregarding Brett's warning, she had issued one final ultimatum. She had figuratively pointed out the direction of the door. Now Jo was terrified Brett would literally walk out of it. Throwing her coat at the chair she had spent weeks shopping for, Jo stood in the middle of the room, stiff as a board and scared witless.

"Jo?" As soft as it was, Brett's voice jerked Jo around to face him.

"What?" Jo was amazed at the steadiness she'd managed to convey. In actuality, she was afraid to hear whatever he was about to say.

"I'm not at all tired of you." Brett walked to her slowly as he made the tension-relieving statement. As he drew near, Jo could see that all his anger was gone too.

"You're not?" Jo had to fight the urge to fling herself into his arms.

"No." Brett shook his head, a conciliatory smile tugging at his lips. "I'm also not bored with our situation."

"Then . . . why . . . ?" Jo gazed at him in confusion, her eyes begging for an explanation.

"It was the mention of a preexisting prescription for birth control pills." Brett shrugged, as if trying to rid himself of an unbearable weight. "No man likes to be reminded of his predecessor." Raising his hand, he touched her hair very gently. "I'm . . . sorry." Brett's hesitation was telling; he did not make apologies often. The relief that washed through Jo was shocking in its intensity.

"I'm sorry too," she whispered, blinking against a sudden rush of tears.

Jo gulped back a sob as she was hauled into Brett's arms. God! It was heaven, like being ushered into a warm room after standing naked in the freezing night. Burying her face in his chest, she slid her arms beneath his jacket and around his waist.

"Honey, are you crying?" The concern in Brett's voice was nearly Jo's undoing.

"No." Sniffing, Jo rubbed her face against his rough wool sweater.

Brett's long fingers caught her chin to lift her face to his scrutiny. "You are crying. And I'm a bastard for making you cry. Honey, don't." He brought his other hand up to brush at the tears. Bending low, close to her ear, Brett whispered in a teasing drawl, "If you stop crying, I'll buy you the Maserati."

A bubble of happiness burst inside Jo, creating shock waves of laughter that could not be contained. "And the diamonds?" She sniffed through a peel of laughter.

"And the diamonds." Brett sighed exaggeratedly.

"And the furs?" Jo fluttered her lashes at him.

"I'm afraid the furs will cost you," Brett said seriously.

Jo's laughter died in her throat, killed by the abrupt change in his voice. "Cost me?" she repeated blankly. "What will it cost me?"

"You'll probably consider the price too steep, but . . . " Brett paused, his tone solemn, then, he went on quietly, "I'd prefer it if you didn't take the pill anymore."

"Not take it!" Caught off guard, Jo stared at him in consternation. If things were different between them, if he loved her instead of loving to be with her, around her—Jo shivered in memory—in her, she'd glory in conceiving, carrying, and bearing his child. But Brett did *not* love her. He did not yearn to have proof of that love expressed in the form of a child. Brett's sole reason for asking her to discontinue the pill had more to do with pride than any other emotion. In his own words, Brett did not like being reminded of his predecessor—Gary Devlin. Still, after basking in the warmth of his arms and recent concern, Jo shuddered with the fear of having him revert back to the cold stranger he'd been all day. Could she refuse his request? Dare she refuse him?

"Tough decision, huh?" Brett's soft voice held a betraying thread of tension, tension that Jo now knew could quickly change to icy withdrawal.

Jo's sigh was the harbinger of her approaching capitulation. She didn't like it. In fact, she resented his use of coercion, especially this type of coercion, yet she knew she would yield in the end. She really hadn't much of a choice. It was either give way or face the cold stranger. Damn! Her mother was right, Jo thought distractedly. Being in love hurt in more ways than Jo had ever thought there *were* ways! If Jo had once believed Gary was a manipulator, she now knew he was a piker in comparison to Brett Renninger; Brett was a master of the art!

"Jo?" Brett was losing patience. He was attempting concealment with his low tone and the tender way he brushed her forehead with his lips, but Jo could hear the warning knell of impatience loud and clear.

Jo's face sought comfort in his sweater again. "All right, Brett." Tightening her arms around his waist, Jo clung to his lean frame in silent, possessive desperation, facing the unpalatable truth that she would very likely do anything to keep him satisfied—and with her. "I'll stop taking them . . . if that's what you want."

"Yes. That *is* what I want."

Holding him tightly, Jo could feel the tension easing out of his body. Could feel that tension being replaced by an unmistakable quickening. Brett's long thigh muscles tightened to press against hers in an urgent, demanding way. Moving his body suggestively, Brett made Jo excitingly aware of his arousal.

"You won't be sorry, love." Brett's caressing words were every bit as enticing as his body language. "I promise, you won't be sorry."

Jo's capitulation was complete; she was his, mind, body, and soul. Of course she knew it and, if his triumphant laughter as he urged her toward the bed could be used as an indicator, Brett knew it too.

The month of February seemed even shorter than usual for Jo. Except for a few minor irritants, and one glaringly jarring incident, Jo sailed through the cold, snowy month wrapped in a warm cocoon of marital bliss.

As the one glaring incident occurred when Brett tenderly draped a breathtakingly beautiful, full-length sable coat over her shoulders the day after he'd witnessed her disposal of the controversial pill, Jo was also wrapped in the cocooning warmth of shockingly expensive fur, even though she had resisted the gift on general principle. There was too much the feeling of payment about the coat. When Jo tried to explain her feelings to Brett, *he* took offense.

"Payment?" he barked, pulling her face close to his by tugging on the wide collar. "What do you mean? Not, I hope, like in 'for services rendered'?"

As that was exactly what she had meant, Jo winced and bit her lip, thereby giving herself away. Jo did not want a sable coat. She had never wanted any kind of fur coat. Warily studying Brett's frowning face, Jo ran her palms over the luxurious fur while advising herself to be prudent. From the look of him, she would have to be completely mad to refuse his gift on any grounds.

"It . . . it is a beautiful coat," she offered lamely, sighing when his frown deepened.

"I know *that!*" Now Brett narrowed his eyes. "*I* chose it. I did not call the shop and order it. I went to the store and picked it out for you." All the time he was speaking his voice grew softer, causing Jo's skin to tingle in warning. "But whether or not the damn thing is beautiful is beside the point. You didn't answer my question."

"Brett . . . "

"No!" Brett cut her off roughly. "I think I don't want to hear your answer. Please just say thank you, Jo."

Jo said thank you. As a matter of fact, Jo said thank you in more than words. Less than an hour after he'd sprung the coat on her, he was smiling again. Jo fully realized that to keep him smiling at her she'd wear the coat, and, to keep him so deliciously ardent, she'd even wear it to bed if he asked her to! Marriage was a compromise—wasn't it? Besides, she felt singularly honored by Brett's assurance that he had personally selected the garment. She knew the schedule Brett maintained better than any other person, including his secretary. Brett's days began early and ended late, and every hour between was packed with meetings, conferences, reports to go over, phone calls to receive or make, and various other details he insisted on seeing to himself. That Brett had thought enough of her to take the time to shop, when she knew full well his loathing for shopping, was a compliment to her. Jo accepted his compliment gratefully and told her sense of moral insult to cool it. Her principles had not been compromised! Since when did a husband have to pay for favors?

The irritants that marred Jo's otherwise euphoric month of wedded bliss were simply that, irritants, all concerned with the office. The major irritant was the mere sight of Marsha Wenger. Fortunately Jo saw the New England area manager seldom, but every time she did see Marsha, Jo smiled coolly and cursed silently. That what she was experiencing was rampant jealousy, Jo readily admitted—to herself. It was a new emotion, one Jo was positive she could very well have done without. She hated it and the mean way it made her feel, but there it was, all blatant and green eyed. Strangely, Jo had never felt the slightest twinge of jealousy over Gary, and the females had fluttered all over him wherever they had gone. Reluctantly, Jo faced the fact that what she had felt for Gary had been infatuation . . . and a rather shallow infatuation at that. She hadn't been in love with Gary at all, merely in love with the idea of being in love! It was a home truth Jo accepted, then put from her mind. Perhaps everyone had to experience the trauma of near love to appreciate the real thing when it finally did come along.

Early in March, Brett was away for the longest five days Jo had ever lived through. Both Brett and Sean were in the Poconos, ironing out some labor union wrinkles, and while he was away Jo began to understand Casey's attitude of the previous December. At the time, Casey had been frustrated and bitchy, and all because Sean had been away. During the five days, and what seemed like twice as many nights, that Brett was away, Jo was tormented by a like frustration and bitchiness. Thinking about Casey had given Jo some purpose though. In an effort to fill the lonely evening hours, Jo's knitting needles clicked away at a furious pace. A tiny, delicately fashioned pair of booties in a soft shade of yellow appeared the first night she was alone. Jo's industry of the second night produced a small matching cap. By the time Jo put her work aside on the third night, her eyes stinging from strain, her yarn was over half gone and an infant's sweater was easily discernable as it grew beneath her needles. The fourth night of Brett's absence the knitting lay forgotten as Jo worked on a report she'd brought home from the office. But, on the fifth and, Jo fervently hoped, the last night, she was busy knit, purl, knit, purling, when she heard the sound of a key turning the lock on the front door. The furious clicking stopped as, joy leaping through her entire body, Jo glanced up to see Brett stride into the room.

Brett looked tired, and windblown, and cold, and absolutely beautiful. He was outfitted in dark corduroy jeans, low boots, and a thigh-length, pile-lined suede jacket, and he looked like he'd just left the project site. Jo, both surprised and delighted by his early return, opened her mouth, but before the words of welcome and question could be formed, Brett explained in three terse words.

"I missed you."

Jo stopped breathing at the expression in Brett's eyes as he crossed the room to where she was sitting. His eyes, shot with silver, raked her face avidly before slowly drifting down over her body. When his glance touched the knitting, still clutched in her hands, his glance held, a frown drawing his brows together.

"Why do I get this uncanny image of a nineteen forties Holly-

242

wood scenario?" Brett's eyes remained fastened on the knitting as he muttered the question.

Bemused by the query, probably because she was still tingling all over in reaction to his admittance of having missed her, Jo shook her head in confusion. Nineteen forties? Hollywood? It was Jo's turn to frown. What the devil was Brett talking about?

"I'm afraid I don't understand, Brett. What scenario?"

Jo's baffled tone drew his intent gaze to her face. "Oh, you know." Brett's reply was oddly terse. "You must have seen it on the late-late movie at least once. It's the scene in which the young wife uses this type"—a quick movement of his hand indicated the knitting Jo was still clutching—"of contrivance to tell the young husband the 'big' news."

Jo's frown deepened. Feeling extremely dense, she glanced down at her work. Oh, gosh! Surely Brett didn't think . . . ? But of course he did. What else could he mean? Lifting her head, Jo studied Brett's face in an effort to discern his emotional reaction to his own hasty judgment. Her visual probe went unrewarded; Brett's expression was devoid of reaction. Whatever he was feeling, Brett was keeping it completely to himself.

"Brett, I think you might be jumping to the wrong conclusion here." Jo lay the knitting aside before continuing. "I'm knitting the sweater set for Casey's baby."

"Then you're not pregnant?" Brett's voice was flat, a trifle gritty, and maddeningly unrevealing.

Was he relieved? Was he disappointed? Jo didn't know, and not knowing was both frustrating and irritating. There had been moments during the last month when Jo had felt a closeness between them, a kind of coming together mentally that was every bit as exciting as their satisfying physical union. Jo longed for that closeness to mature. Having Brett lock his feelings away from her about something as important as the possibility of a child imbued in her the fear that their relationship had not progressed at all!

"No, Brett, I'm not pregnant." Jo sighed in sudden weariness.

"And damned glad of it." Brett's smile was cynical. "Right?"

Then and there Jo decided she hated his cynicism. Damn it, she *did* want his child! Jo also wanted to spend the rest of her life as his wife. But she was afraid. She was scared silly of this commitment they had rushed headlong into. Hell! Jo still wasn't even sure Brett liked her as a person, even though he no longer looked at her with open disdain. What were her chances of ever hearing him promise a lifetime commitment to her? As clearly as if Brett were speaking the words aloud at that minute, Jo heard his voice of months before: "While the fire rages, I intend to have you." It was the fear of the fire being consumed by its own intensity that made Jo answer:

"Yes, Brett, I am glad I'm not pregnant." Forcing herself to look into his eyes, Jo challenged him to declare himself on the issue. "Aren't you?"

Brett didn't quite pull off a shrug that was intended to be careless. "To tell you the truth, I really don't know. The possibility of you becoming pregnant has been on the fringes of my consciousness ever since I asked you to stop taking the pill." Removing his jacket, Brett walked slowly to the closet to hang it up. As he turned back to her he frowned. "I like kids. I've always enjoyed being around my nieces and nephew. I've never given much thought to having a child of my own." Brett's brief smile held traces of bitterness. "Sondra didn't want children either."

Jo shot to her feet. How dare he equate her with his former wife? If only half of what she'd heard about Sondra via the office grapevine was true, Sondra was nothing more than a playgirl, interested in no one except Sondra. Her feelings smarting from Brett's bitter dart, Jo planted her fists on her hips and glared at him.

"Back it up, Mr. Renninger!" Jo's voice trembled with hurt anger. "This seems to be your night for jumping to conclusions . . . all of them wrong! I did not say I don't want children. What I said was, I'm glad I'm not pregnant. I meant, at this time." Jo paused to draw breath and to try and get a grip on her turbulent emotions. Sondra indeed! She had no idea of the picture she presented to Brett in her silk robe with her hair a tumbled mass around her quivering shoulders and her hazel eyes flashing amber sparks at him. All Jo realized was she had to set Brett straight on this score once and for all.

"I also like kids! And, though you might find it extremely hard to believe, I have the required amount of maternal instincts!"

"Jo . . . "

"Let me finish!" Off and running, Jo trampled Brett's attempt to speak. "Good grief, man! We've only been married a month! We've hardly had a chance to become accustomed to each other, let alone a new individual! I just don't think now is . . . "

"JO!" Brett shouted her down. "Will you please shut up?"

Brett's bellow had the desired effect; Jo's mouth closed, her eyes opened wide in shock. Jo had seen Brett in a cold rage. She had seen him locked inside icy withdrawal. Once he had even raised his voice to her. But she had never actually heard him yell, at anyone. There was no way Jo could mask her surprise. She blinked once, then stared at him, the inside of her bottom lip caught between her teeth.

Brett, his nostrils flaring with his rate of inhalation, took the two steps necessary to bring him to within inches of Jo. Lifting his hand, Brett raked long fingers through his hair, ruffling the thick ash-blond waves. "I get the message, Jo." Brett sighed, then smiled apologetically. "And, of course, you're right. We haven't become accustomed to each other yet." His hand moved from his hair to hers, not raking now but stroking, smoothing. "We're going to have to work on the mutual learning process." Brett's tone was soft now, gentling. "Okay?"

Staring into his eyes, as soft as the feathers on a gray dove, Jo felt all the tension and irritation drain out of her. It was always the same. All Brett had to do was lower his voice and look at her tenderly, and she was completely his. It's not fair! A small spark of defiance tried to make itself heard above the flutter of

Jo's pulse. It is simply not fair for him to have this much control over me, when I have no effect whatever on him. Well, that wasn't quite true and Jo admitted it. She did have some effect. Jo could see the effect on Brett's body and in the tiny flame beginning to leap in his eyes. Jo knew she had the power to arouse Brett's body. There had been moments when she'd connected with his mind. Why couldn't she touch his heart?

"Okay, Brett." Jo acceded to his request in a whisper that betrayed the unhappiness her thoughts had churned up. Not even hearing the sound of her own voice, and unaware of the cloudy sadness dulling her eyes, Jo could only guess at the strange expression that moved spasmodically over Brett's face. Had it been anyone else, Jo would have concluded the expression was one of quickly suppressed pain. But not Brett; Brett had no reason to feel pain and every reason to feel triumphant. Brett had won . . . again. "How do you suggest we go about this learning process?" Jo recognized the stupidity of her question even as she voiced it. Damn this man for owning the ability to rattle her so effortlessly!

Brett's lips twitched in the quirky smile that had become so very endearing to Jo. "I know how I'd like to go about it," he said teasingly. "I've slept alone for four nights." The quirk progressed at its usual rate into a grin. "Let me rephrase that statement. I tried to sleep alone for four nights. I did not succeed very well. I missed you like hell, Jo." By the time Brett had finished speaking the grin was gone.

Jo was long past deciphering Brett's intricately simplistic admission. Merely knowing he had missed her was enough, for now. "I—I missed you too, Brett, that's why I picked up the knitting in the first place. I didn't know what to do without you here." The murmured confession escaped through Jo's unguarded mental barriers while she was otherwise occupied by becoming lost inside the gray prison of Brett's eyes. Vaguely, Jo wondered why the flame in those gray depths suddenly leaped wildly. As it was where Jo had wanted to be since he'd walked

246

into the room, she never entertained the thought of resistance when Brett drew her into his arms. Home. Jo sighed with relief. The scent of him, his aftershave, the hint of whisky on his breath, even the faint, woolly odor of his sweater, all were now the scents of home to Jo.

"I was going to suggest we go the usual route in our learning process." Brett's lips skimmed her forehead. "You know, open a bottle of wine, get comfortable on the sofa, and talk until we run out of words." As if drawn by a lure too enticing to resist, his lips made a direct path down her small nose to her mouth. "But, on consideration, four days without you is three and a half days too long. We'll still have a bottle of wine, but I think we'll drink it in bed." Brett's lips teased Jo's for mind-bending seconds. "After we've communicated in a more basic language," he whispered into her mouth.

Brett proceeded to converse very fluently without speaking a syllable. He began the dialogue with his lips, and his tongue, and his hands. Then, with his body, Brett presented a brilliant dissertation on communication. Distracted by sensations seemingly tripping over each other as they raced crazily through her body, Jo was ignorant of the fact that her own silent thesis was being presented with equal eloquence.

Brett eventually did get around to opening a bottle of wine, but only after they had both had a short, reviving nap and a long, revitalizing shower. Brett went to the kitchen while Jo remade the thoroughly disordered bed. Clad in the striped silk robe, she was reclining against the headboard when Brett strolled into the bedroom, a bottle of white wine and two glasses in one hand and a tray of sandwiches in the other.

"It's a good thing this is Friday night," he observed dryly. "As I'm planning to lay siege to your mind, and your body, through most of it."

"Actually, I was thinking of going into the office tomorrow," Jo lied unconvincingly. In truth, she had glumly looked forward to pacing the apartment till he came home. "There's a report I should finish to have ready for mailing on Monday."

Placing the tray of sandwiches on her legs, Brett slid onto the bed beside Jo and poured wine for the both of them before bothering to reply. "I could give you my opinion on your report," he drawled, arching one brow as he lifted his glass to her in a silent salute. "But I seem to recall shocking you the last time I gave a similar opinion concerning one of my suits." His devilish eyes made a liar of his innocent expression. "I believe you were in the bathtub at the time."

"Conjured up a rather strange picture too," Jo speculated thoughtfully. "Sounds exceedingly dull to me. I mean, really, a suit and a report?" She yawned delicately.

Brett fell apart and, in the process, splashed wine on his chest and the mid-thigh-length navy blue toweling robe he was wearing. When his roar of laughter subsided to a low chuckle, he shook his head in bemused amazement. "You are the only woman I have ever known who could do this to me," Brett confessed around a grin. "Come to think of it, I don't know anyone else who can make me laugh like you can." Sobering, he leaned to her to kiss her gently. "It feels good to laugh with you." When Brett lifted his head he was smiling. "Come to that, practically everything we do together makes me feel good. How about you?" he probed blatantly.

Jo's smile was a reflection of Brett's. "Makes me feel good too," she offered softly. "For the most part, I've enjoyed our being together."

"For the most part," Brett repeated quietly. "Well, that's a start." Picking up a piece of sandwich, he examined the ham-and-cheese filling as if he'd never seen it before. "Time for the learning process to begin, I think." Taking a tentative bite, he chewed it thoroughly and washed it down with a healthy swallow of wine. "I already know you are terrific at your job, knit like a wizard, and can't cook worth a damn," Brett finally con-

248

tinued. "What other talents, or lack thereof, are contained within the beautiful package you call yourself?"

"I'm great in bed." It was not a declaration but a question, if a teasing one. Although Brett obviously understood, he chose to treat Jo's query as a statement of fact.

"Granted." Brett's concurrence was made in all seriousness. "What else? And please feel free to elaborate."

Jo hesitated briefly, then, thinking—what have I got to lose?—opened her mind, if not her heart, to him. "I am, by nature, quiet. But I think I told you that before?" Jo arched a brow at him in question; Brett nodded. "I like almost all kinds of music, from classical to country western. I love movies, especially science fiction. I have a passion for clothes that by far exceed my budget."

"No longer," Brett inserted at this point of her litany. "I'll take care of your clothing bills."

Jo stiffened noticably. It was the sable-fur dilemma all over again. The last thing Jo wanted to do was stir Brett's anger. On the other hand, she didn't want him paying her bills either. Why having Brett assume financial responsibility for her should make her feel like a kept woman, Jo didn't know, unless it had something to do with Brett not loving her. Jo had conscious knowledge of being his wife; the emotional impact was missing. She would much prefer to pay her own bills. Now, for Jo, the problem was how to convey her feelings to him. Brett was way ahead of her.

"Don't say it, Jo," he warned softly. "We've got the beginnings of a good picnic going here." Jo was well aware Brett was not referring to the impromptu supper he'd put together. "Don't rain on it."

"Brett . . . I—" Jo faltered. Was her independence really worth the price of this tenuous reaching out they had embarked on? She *was* Brett's wife, all legal and binding—or at least as binding as any marriage could be in this enlightened age. Leave it, her common sense advised. Meet him halfway, see what develops.

You have nothing to lose and the world to gain. "I play a fair hand of poker."

Brett stared at her blankly for an instant, then a grin of mixed delight and relief instilled animation; he grinned like a summer-time-happy boy. As if he were suddenly starving, Brett wolfed down another sandwich. Waving his hand at the depleted plate, he ordered her to follow suit. "Dig in, honey." Brett's grin removed the sting from the barb that trailed his invitation. "*I* do know how to put a sandwich together."

They ate and drank in silence until the plate and bottle were empty, then Brett made himself comfortable by stretching his long length out full and throwing his arms over his head.

"I'm going to toss another responsibility at you next week," he told her lazily.

Busy brushing bits of breadcrumbs off the sheet, Jo didn't even look up. "Really?" she replied idly. "What sort of responsibility?"

"I'm going to put you to interviewing applicants." He yawned. "The job bores the hell out of me."

"Applicants?" Jo glanced up to frown at him. The only applicants Brett ever personally interviewed were for managerial positions, and, to Jo's knowledge, there were no positions of that type open. "Applicants for what?"

"New England area manager." Brett exhaled in exasperation. "We've got less than a month to replace Marsha, Jo."

Marsha! Jo froze. Marsha was leaving the firm? At first the news thrilled Jo. Then the thrill was chased by apprehension. Why was Marsha leaving? And why hadn't Jo known about it? Had Brett deliberately kept the information from her for reasons of his own? Jo could think of only one reason Brett would have for keeping silent, and that reason did not bear thinking about. Pushing a sudden, explicit image of Brett and Marsha together in much the same way Jo and he were now, Jo made a production out of finding the last, tiniest crumb.

"Why is Marsha quitting?" Jo directed her question at the smooth sheet.

Brett hesitated for seconds that were pure agony for Jo. "Well," he began slowly, "I know all she'd say was her reason was personal but—" Again he hesitated, drawing Jo's nerves to quivering tautness. "What the hell, you are not only my assistant but my wife. Marsha's going to follow her husband."

Jo could not have been more stunned if Brett had told her Marsha was going to have a sex-change operation! Added to Jo's bafflement at Brett's seeming assumption that she'd known of Marsha's intention to leave the company, Brett's revelation of a heretofore unheard of husband left Jo totally speechless. Had she been beating her emotions to death since December for nothing? Had there ever been anything personal between Brett and Marsha? And does being in love make jackasses of everybody? This last consideration jolted Jo out of contemplation and into speech.

"Brett, let's clarify a few details here." Jo's voice contained a harsh undertone. She was fed up. She never had liked playing games, and this love game was starting to get to her. As Jo had never particularly liked mysteries either, she wasn't about to tolerate Marsha's. "Detail one," she said flatly. "I knew nothing about Marsha's resignation. Detail two: I knew nothing about a husband."

"Former husband," Brett inserted.

"Former or otherwise," Jo bit angrily. "Which brings about detail three: I was under the impression that you and she had indulged in a flaming affair last October in Vermont." Sitting up straight, Jo stared Brett directly in the eyes, defying him to deny an alliance with Marsha. When Brett didn't respond immediately, Jo added, "And what the hell do you mean, former husband? If they are no longer married, why is she chucking an excellent job to follow him?"

"Are you finished?" Brett asked softly. "Or are there more details on your list?"

"I'm finished." And very likely in more ways than one, she

added silently. But, good grief, how long could she go on living with this silliness? Jo demanded of herself. Sex, in itself, was not a panacea, the be-all and end-all of any relationship . . . let alone marriage! There had to be more or, if there was not, then her mother was right!

"Detail one." Brett's quietly controlled voice intruded on Jo's introspection and riveted her attention. "I honestly believed you did know of Marsha's resignation. She tendered it this past Monday." He regarded her steadily. "I thought I'd mentioned it before I left for the mountains. I'm sorry, but I was rushed. Okay?"

Jo let a nod suffice for reply. If he was on a roll, she certainly wasn't going to call a halt now.

"Detail number two is a little more involved. Marsha has been unhappily divorced for over a year. The marriage fell apart because Marsha, admittedly, neglected it in favor of her career." Brett shrugged. "Apparently, like most men, Marsha's husband labored under the illusion that he should come first. When he discovered he didn't, he sought comfort elsewhere."

"How delightful!" Jo exclaimed. "He sounds like a real charmer. And Marsha is going to repress her ambition to chase *him*?" Incensed at the very idea of what Marsha was doing, Jo momentarily forgot how relieved she'd felt on hearing of the woman's intentions mere moments ago.

Brett's expression hardened at her outburst. "Why the hell must it always come to this?" he demanded angrily. "Why do all career women feel they must carry this equality banner to the outer limits?"

"Because that's where it belongs!" Jo retorted.

"But, damn it, Jo!" Brett shot back. "Is there no workable solution? Men are only going to back up so far! When they have reached the wall, then what happens? Something has got to give."

"You mean some*one* has got to give!" Jo protested. "And, of course, that someone had better be female!"

252

"Not necessarily," Brett denied Jo's allegation.

"Oh, but it is in the case of Marsha, isn't it?" Jo sneered. She was angry, really angry, and yet she was trembling with excitement. She was actually loving every minute of this argument! Geared for mental battle, Jo missed the significance of her enjoyment, and that was that the lines of communication were wide open!

"Jo!" Brett shouted in exasperation. "Marsha loves the man. She has been miserable for over a year! But she has decided to meet him halfway . . . no more. Can you honestly sit there and insist she's wrong?"

"Brett, how can you insist she is only meeting him halfway?" Jo argued heatedly. "She's giving up her job. She's going to him. What, exactly, is *he* doing? No! Don't tell me, I know. *He* is waiting for her to come to her senses! Right?"

"I don't believe this! I positively do not believe this." Brett glanced around the room as if seeking guidance. "We are actually fighting over another couple's marital problems!"

"Yes," Jo responded impulsively. "Isn't it fun?"

Brett grinned, then sobered almost at once. "It would be, if we didn't have a few problems of our own." Brett met Jo's glance and held it. "There was no affair in October." He hesitated, then went on determinedly, "But not for lack of trying on my part."

Jo sat perfectly still, staring at him, while her conscience went to work on her. She longed to dissect his last statement, but did she have the right? No, she did not, her conscience advised. In actual fact, she'd had no right to ask him about October in the first place. Obviously Brett had assumed she'd pounce on his admission.

"No questions?" he probed, a strange note of disappointment edging his voice. "Aren't you curious . . . at all?"

Jo sighed. "Yes, I'm curious. But it really is none of my business. Is it?" After the effervescence of their argument, Jo felt flat. "What you did, and who you did it with, before we married, is, in fact, none of my business." Jo broke the hold his eyes attempted to maintain.

"And so, of course, I have no right to ask you about your previous affair." Brett's tone had a corresponding flatness, tinged with accusation.

So he did know about Gary! Jo raised her eyes to encounter a blank wall. Brett had withdrawn. The lines of communication had snapped. Following Brett's example, Jo mentally withdrew.

"Not in that manner." Jo was amazed at the distant sound of her own voice.

"It doesn't matter." Brett's shrug had the impact of a blow to Jo's heart.

He doesn't really want to know, because he really doesn't care! The thought froze Jo's mind. Moving carefully, as if afraid she'd shatter into a million shards of ice if she hurried, Jo slid off the bed and walked into the bathroom thinking. The learning process is now over.

CHAPTER ELEVEN

Brett sat behind his brother's desk, staring fixedly at an unopened pack of cigarettes lying within inches of his hand. He had placed the pack on the smooth surface as a reminder of his own avowal of no more pacifiers. But it had been a very long three weeks since he and Jo had reached dead end the night he'd returned from Pennsylvania.

Why hadn't they been able to break free of constraint since then? Brett was afraid he knew the answer and simply didn't want to face it. Damn it, if she loved me . . . The desk chair was shoved back roughly as Brett jerked to his feet.

Stalking to the window, Brett scowled down at the miniature people scurrying about their business twenty-six stories below. God! He wanted a cigarette! How many times had he fought down the desire to seek comfort in that unopened pack during the last three weeks? Brett smiled in self-derision. More times than he wanted to remember. The need for a cigarette was the least of the desires Brett fought against.

If she loved me.

Brett was relieved at the intrusive noise of the buzzer on the telephone. Swinging back to the desk, he scooped up the receiver.

Before he could speak the "Wizard" said, "Mrs. Renninger on line two, sir." Brett's distraction was evidenced by his subdued greeting to his mother. He forgot to call her sir.

"Yes, Mother?" he queried after pressing the proper button.

"Are you feeling all right?" Violet demanded in concern.

Brett frowned. "Yes, of course. Why?"

"If you have to ask, I must be working you too hard," Violet answered. Then, without warning, she sprang her news on him. "Wolf has been declared fit to go back to work. He has decided to remain at the farm until after Easter. That gives you a week and a half to clear up whatever you're on at the moment and regear your mind for Atlanta. You can bring him up to date when you and JoAnne come down for the holiday. You *were* planning to come down for Easter, weren't you?"

Brett was in no mood for pretense. "I really hadn't thought about it," he admitted starkly.

"And now you don't have to," she shot back at him. "It's family conclave time, Brett. I'm considering another branch on the Renninger's company tree. Wolf needs to be brought up to date. And you sound like you need a rest. When will you and JoAnne arrive?"

Brett couldn't deny the smile that curved his tight lips. "What rank did you carry in the marines?" As the question was moot, he went on through her laughter, "We'll fly down sometime during holy week. I cannot be more definitive at this point. Okay?"

"I guess it will have to be." Violet sighed. "Sometimes I think I trained my sons too well. Give my love to JoAnne, Brett."

Give my love to JoAnne. The phrase revolved in Brett's head long after he'd replaced the receiver.

I want to give my love to JoAnne.

Does JoAnne still love my brother?

Did JoAnne ever love my brother?

Does JoAnne know how to love?

Is Brett going completely mad?

Tune in tomorrow for the next thrilling installment of "Brett Renninger takes a header."

Brett came to his senses with the realization that he was in the process of opening the forbidden pacifier. Stupid ass, he berated himself, flinging the pack from him with such force it ricocheted off the wall to skim over the floor to where it came to rest under the desk. In disgust, Brett turned his back to glare out the window.

They had come so close that night, so very close to a breakthrough, to a meeting of the minds as well as of the flesh. Brett swallowed the bitter taste of defeat coated with self-destructive jealousy. Both emotions were unfamilar and unacceptable to him. Brett knew he would have to do something to rectify the situation, and soon. The question was what?

I hate this!

The silent cry came from the soul. There was nothing new or unique about the protest. Brett had been living with it now for what seemed like most of his life. Stalemate. To Brett, the marriage was in a position of stalemate. So what do you do? he taxed himself. Write it off? Brett refused to as much as consider calling it quits without a fight.

What had gone wrong? Brett's lips curved wryly. What had ever been right about it . . . other than the purely physical? Then again, there had been some moments, times when he and Jo had been in smooth accord. Those times had been a lure, a teaser, promising a rich relationship if they could bridge the gap.

That was what had been so exciting for a little while the night he'd come home from the Poconos. Brett could still feel the tremor of expectation that had shivered through him that night. For a brief, breathless moment, he had allowed himself to believe Jo was beginning to care for him. Jo had talked more openly than ever before, she had even revealed signs of resentment for Marsha. For an instant, Brett had actually convinced himself Jo's resentment was caused by jealousy. Euphoric, Brett had felt the time right to mention Jo's affair with Wolf. Jo's sudden, chilly silence had said more than any lengthy explanation. Jo had stopped talking and, during these interminable three weeks, had conversed on a surface level. It was only after they were in bed that Jo displayed animation.

Brett felt his body harden in reaction to a flashing image of Jo, her breathing shallow, her lips parted, writhing and moaning beneath him. Their physical union was as close as Brett had ever hoped to get to perfect. The strange thing was, his desire appeared to be feeding itself. The more Brett had of Jo, the more he wanted her! Satiation was transient. Hunger was self-renewing. Need. Need. Need.

Turning abruptly, Brett strode back to his desk. He didn't have time to indulge in wishful thinking. His movements purposeful, Brett drew a pile of reports to the center of the desk. After reading the first sheet of paper contained in the first report for the second time, he closed the folder and pushed the pile away again. Resting his head against the chair's high back, Brett stared sightless at the large photograph of the first Renninger-built condominium on the wall opposite his desk.

His concentration was a thing of the past. Perhaps his mother was right and he did need a rest. Brett's smile was both bitter and derisive. He certainly didn't expect to get much rest at the farm! Not if he had to play the role of watchdog around Jo and Wolf. At the thought, Brett went rigid in the well-padded chair.

Is this what being in love had brought him to? Brett shuddered at the idea of himself sniffing at the heels of his wife and brother.

God damn it! No! He'd see them both in hell first! She was not worth it. No woman alive was worth it! Damn Wolf! Damn Jo! And damn my own love for her! If, when Wolf is once again in residence behind this desk, they still want each other, I'll go back to Atlanta alone! I can live without her!

But, oh God, I love her!

A short distance down a wide, plushly carpeted hall, Jo sat in a similar, if smaller office, at a similar, if smaller desk, coming to a similar, if softer decision. Jo had not damned Wolf. Jo had not damned Brett. Jo had not even damned herself. Jo had reached the same conclusion as Brett. She would remain in New York when Brett went back to Atlanta.

The relationship they had so very suddenly dived into was crumbling with equal swiftness. How long could she go on living with a stranger? Jo had grown weary with the repetition of the question. How long could she bear coexistence with a man who was always polite, most times even pleasant, a searing flame in bed, but a stranger nonetheless?

Was it worth it? Jo lowered long lashes over eyes stinging with hot moisture. Another failure. Was she to go through life drifting in and out of affairs? Successful in her chosen career, ineffectual in any personal relationship? Or was her mother right after all? Was it all a hoax, a shimmering facade—this idea, or ideal, or a real, lasting love between a man and a woman?

Rebellion stirred deep inside Jo. If the whole concept of love was nothing more than a myth, then what was the purpose of life? Without the humanizing presence of love, romantic love, humans would be reduced to the lowest level, and life itself would become a barren waste. Every atom of intelligence Jo possessed rejected the cold precept. Her mother was wrong! She *had* to be wrong! Jo refused to view life as a grinding ordeal, or humans as automatons, untouched or unsoftened by the gentle kiss of love.

Why can't Brett love me?

Shivering, Jo opened her eyes to stare at the plain, narrow gold band on her left ring finger. Jo wanted to live to be a very old lady and still be wearing that gold band when she closed her eyes for the last time. But without Brett's love, the ring was valueless.

Reflective of her husband's actions, Jo pushed her chair away from the desk and walked to the window. If only Brett had not mentioned her affair with Gary in quite that accusing tone! Or was she too sensitive about that fiasco? Why couldn't they just sit down and talk like two intelligent, mature adults? Maybe she ought to look Brett straight in the eyes and say: I love you. Now what are you going to do about it? Jo sighed. She knew full well that it was the fear of Brett's answer that kept her from speaking to him about her feelings. Still, Jo knew that something would have to give, and soon. She simply could not continue to live in this void.

Jo stood at the window a long time, her thoughts revolving, always coming back to the same point. Something, or someone, would have to give. Jo had the very uncomfortable feeling that the someone would be JoAnne Lawrence Renninger.

Since their marriage, whenever Brett was in the office, he came for her when it was time to go home. It was after six before he strode into Jo's office that afternoon. As usual, the sight of him set Jo's pulses racing. Today Brett's grim expression increased the pulse rate to a gallop.

"Are you ready to leave?"

For all the work she'd accomplished, she might as well have stayed home in the first place! Jo refrained from offering the information. Come to that, there hadn't been all that much work to do! Had Brett been as idle as she these last weeks? Jo rejected the idea at once. From all reports, he had not allowed his first wife to interfere with his work, and he had been in love with her! Jo nodded in answer and began collecting her briefcase, hand-bag, gloves, and coat, suppressing the longing to have the power to interfere with his daily routine.

"Well, at least I'll soon be saying good-bye to this place." Brett made the thickly drawled observation as they entered the apartment.

Startled, and more than a little shocked, Jo's gaze trekked Brett's as he scanned the room. She would have sworn he liked the apartment! The full content of his statement hit her in a rush. Was Brett obliquely telling her he was leaving her? Jo's fear hid itself behind a calm tone.

"Are you going somewhere?" God! She sounded bored! And, from the sharp glance Brett sliced at her, he did not appreciate her enforced smoothness.

"*We* are going somewhere," Brett enunciated harshly. "I had a call from Mother today." Removing his coat, Brett held it in one hand and reached for Jo's with the other. "She is expecting us at the farm for Easter," he continued as he hung the garments in the closet. Jo felt pinned by his steely eyes when he turned to face her. "It's time to return to Atlanta." Brett walked to within a few inches of her before adding, "Wolf's ready to resume control of the New York office."

"But that's wonderful!" Jo momentarily forgot her own unhappiness on hearing about Wolf's recovery. Brett brought her back to earth with a crash.

"Are you going with me?" Brett's quiet tone conflicted with the muscle jumping in his jaw.

To where? Jo wondered in confusion. To Florida or Atlanta? And why was he suddenly so tense? And, damn it, why did he sound so relieved about leaving the apartment? Ask him, you fool! Jo opened her mouth, then closed it again, damning herself for the coward she'd become. Fortunately, Brett unwittingly gave her a reprieve.

"I told Mother we'd fly down the middle of next week," Brett went on when it became obvious she was not going to respond. "It seems there's a family conference awaiting us. Will Wednesday be convenient for you?"

"Yes, of course." Jo frowned. "What is the conference all about?"

"Who knows?" Brett shrugged. "But, knowing Mother, it will probably mean more work for all of us."

Brett breathed in deeply as the plane soared off the runway into the clear morning sky. After a week of figuratively holding his breath, it was a relief to breathe without constraint. At every minute of every hour of every day Brett had expected Jo to tell him she was not going with him. Now, with Jo strapped into the seat beside him, Brett allowed his taut body to relax. The ending would come soon enough. Until the final moment was upon him, Brett wanted her right where she was, by his side.

My beautiful, fragile-looking, tough-as-a-marine wife. Brett smiled sadly inside his mind. Since meeting Jo the previous October, Brett had revised every one of his opinions about her but one. At that time, he had concluded that Jo was a confection spun of pure steel. Now Brett knew his conclusion had been correct. Then again, perhaps Marsha's theory held merit. Maybe Jo simply did not like men! Not once in the two months they had been together had Jo looked at another man with even a hint of interest. As to that, Jo hadn't revealed a hell of a lot of interest in him, either, except in the bedroom!

Brett had to clench his teeth against the bitter laughter that rose in his throat. Now, there's a switch! Weren't men forever getting rapped for being unable to communicate outside of the bedroom?

Crap!

Brett had never consciously thought about it before but, at that moment, he decided that most of what he'd heard and read about the differences between the sexes was simply that . . . so much crap. Once the obvious hurdle was cleared, the fact was there was very little difference between the male and the female.

The fact denoted equality.

The thought sprang into Brett's mind and refused to be dislodged. In all honesty, he had to admit, at least to himself, that Jo was indeed his equal. How often had he heard the expression "she thinks like a man"? As far as Brett was concerned that expression was more of the same crap. He had witnessed Jo in action. Jo did not think like a man. Jo thought like a highly intelligent human being. Brett personally knew several men who were not half as bright as she.

They should make a brilliant combination, Brett mused. The ideal team. So, why didn't they?

Because she does not love you.

Square one. From a distance that seemed like light-years, but was in fact not yet two full years, Brett acknowledged that the love he'd thought he'd felt for Sondra was as water compared to wine in what he felt for Jo. What he felt for Jo was a totally different kind of loving. Other than in the physical sense, he'd really not needed Sondra. Brett knew he needed Jo, in every sense known to man. If he required proof, all Brett had to do was remember the desperation he'd felt while making love to Jo ever since he'd received the phone call from his mother. For Brett, the act had gone far beyond the physical coupling of a man and a woman. In effect, what he had been attempting to do was draw the essence of Jo into himself; in a sense, to store up on her for a rainy day. And yet Brett still felt empty.

Emptiness has to be filled with something: Brett filled his personal void with anger. His fury was unreasonable and he knew it. Yet there it was, eating through him like a hot tongue of fire. Anger at Wolf, the brother he idolized. Anger at Jo, the woman he adored. Anger at himself, for getting involved in the first place. Brett's anger fostered determination. He could not . . . would not give Jo up without a fight!

The same black Cadillac with the same taciturn driver was waiting for them at the small airstrip in Florida, only this time the sun was shining brightly and the temperature hovered in the mid-seventies. There was not a hint of rain, either in the air or on the horizon.

Jo, grateful for Brett's suggestion that she wear light clothing, looked around with interest as they walked to the car. The airstrip and the small office-hangar had the appearance of having been plunked down in the middle of nowhere, so isolated were they.

Josh's greeting was every bit as terse and laconic as it had been in December. Brett's reply was as tight-lipped. Dismissing both men from her mind, Jo sat close to the smoked-glass window, her gaze skimming over the lush green pastureland they were driving through.

"Those trees are beautiful!" Jo exclaimed, indicating the huge pines that dotted the pastures and the large, tree-shaped cones that decorated the grass beneath the widely spread branches.

"Yes."

Brett's short reply robbed Jo of her delight in seeing Florida basking in the sunlight. Her first glimpse of sleek Thoroughbreds ambling serenely behind white rail fences restored her enthusiasm. Jo had never seen a Thoroughbred horse before, yet even she could recognize the fine lines and elegant appearance of the animals. It was not exactly love at first sight. Oh, the horses were very beautiful, but they were also very large. Jo decided she'd prefer to admire from a distance.

The drive seemed much shorter, and the house much larger, than before. As the car glided to a smooth stop in the curving driveway in front of the house, Jo was again struck by its likeness to pictures she'd seen of antebellum plantation homes. The word tranquility sprang to Jo's mind. As she stepped from the car, Jo fervently hoped she'd find a measure of that tranquility while she was within its walls. As Jo and Brett mounted the steps, the door was flung wide open.

Elania Calaveri was exactly as she had been in December. Jo smothered a bubble of laughter as the woman again took Brett to task.

"Well, what a surprise!" Elania exclaimed in mock amazement. "Only half of holy week gone and you're here already! Are you sick or something?" As they entered the imposing hall, the housekeeper directed her comments to Jo in a confiding manner. "Never could keep this hellion in one place for very long. He was always eager to be gone, even as a boy. He'd be up and out of the house so early, I had to teach the scamp to cook his own breakfast to make sure he'd get a decent meal inside him, as he seldom came home before dark."

Jo shot a gleaming glance at her scowling husband. One bursting sentence from Elania had cleared up the mystery of how and why Brett had learned to cook. Eager to be gone. The words reverberated in Jo's mind. Did that explain Brett's strained behavior of the past several weeks and his obvious relief about leaving the apartment soon? Was the adult Brett still the same as the boy—eager to be gone? Caught up in speculation, Jo missed Brett's greeting to Elania, snapping to attention when she heard her name.

"I'm sorry, I was . . . admiring the house and didn't hear what you said," she lied unevenly when Brett repeated her name impatiently.

"I said," Brett reiterated, "Elania has just told me that none of the others know we've arrived as they are in the dining room having lunch. Would you like to freshen up before we join them?"

Annoyed by Brett's too-quiet tone, Jo answered sharply, "Yes. If you don't mind?"

"If I had minded," Brett bit back, "I wouldn't have asked in the first place." Ignoring the tiny gasp that burst through Elania's suddenly tight lips, Brett ushered Jo up the stairs.

On her first visit to the house, Jo had been delighted with the bedroom Elania had escorted her to. Now she followed Brett as he swung in the opposite direction at the top of the wide staircase. Apparently, Jo mused, this side of the house contained the family bedrooms. A twinge of pain twisted in her chest as she wondered how much longer she'd be a member of the Renninger family.

The room Jo trailed Brett into was large and square and definitely masculine in decor. Jo loved it immediately. The absence of unnecessary clutter appealed to the Spartan in Jo. Standing just inside the door, Jo inventoried the rich dark-brown carpet and matching drapes, the bold broad stripes of alternating brown and white in the bedspread, and the stark white of unadorned walls. An overstuffed, comfortable-looking chair in a blazing red-orange gave the room focus and color. Jo did not have to be told that Brett had selected the decor himself. In some strange way the room was Brett.

"I love it." Jo might as well have said "I love you."

Brett's face relaxed at her stamp of approval. "Somehow I knew you would." He stared at her intently for a second, then indicated a door on the wall to her right with a wave of his hand. "The bathroom. You don't need to fuss, it's only family." A smile flickered over Brett's tautly drawn lips. "You always look perfect anyway."

Jo stared at him, unable to move for an instant. Would she ever get past the point of melting inside at the slightest suggestion of a smile from this man? It's not fair, Jo protested silently. It's simply not . . .

"If you don't move," Brett's sensuously warm voice drew her out of her thoughts, "I might be tempted to demonstrate the resiliency of the mattress on my bed." His lips curved invitingly. "Are you as hungry as I am?"

Incredibly Jo was suddenly starving, in exactly the manner Brett's slumberous eyes told her he was! How was it possible? Had they not skipped breakfast in favor of . . . Jo shivered in memory of the feast she and Brett had indulged in that morning. Fleetingly, Jo concluded that if they could remain in bed forever, they would have no marital problems. She wanted him, again, very badly, but, there was more to a marriage than that. There had to be. "Brett, I . . . " Jo's breath caught in her throat as he took a step toward her. "They are all down there," she finished lamely.

"And we are all up here." Brett took another slow step. "All two of us." His smile promised everything. "The perfect number for a luncheon party." One more step, and Jo felt like she was coming apart at the seams.

"But we haven't even seen Wolf yet!" Jo grabbed at the excuse in desperation. What if Elania had mentioned their arrival? What would they all think? The change in Brett was as confusing as it was sudden. His body stiffening with tension, Brett pivoted away from her.

"Yes, of course, Wolf." His back to her, Brett stood as still as if carved from rock, his voice as hard. "Will you go do whatever you have to do, so we can get out of this room?"

Jo wanted to scream. Jo wanted to throw things. She walked into the bathroom. How did one keep up with a man whose moods changed with mercurial swiftness? Jo stared at the pitifully wan face reflected in the mirror above the brown-and-white marbleized sink. With the eyes of a critic, she examined the makeup she'd applied so carefully that morning. Her pale cheeks were in need of a touch of the blusher brush. Her disordered hair needed taming. Jo pictured the needed articles inside the flight bag Brett had placed on the long double dresser as he'd entered the room. She could either go and get the bag, or ask Brett to hand it in to her. Jo's eyes avoided her face. Lifting her hands, she smoothed the mass of dark hair. She would not ask him for anything and, when she did walk out of the room, she would be ready to go downstairs. Brett was in a strange mood. He had been moody for weeks. The smell of showdown was in the air around them. Jo knew the slightest incident could trigger it. Raising her long lashes, Jo read the plea in her own dull hazel eyes; not now, not today, hold on to him as long as you can.

Jo's smoothing hands drifted down over the wheat-color suit jacket she wore over a crisp orange shirt, then down over hips covered in a pencil-slim skirt that partnered the jacket.

"Jo!"

Jo's hands stilled at Brett's impatient call. Dismissing the sad-eyed woman in the mirror, Jo opened the door and walked out of the room, her spine straight, her shoulders back, her head high, and her expectations gone. The sight of Brett had the usual, melting effect on Jo's senses. In casual slacks and sport coat, Brett didn't project quite the forbidding appearance as when he was decked out in battle array of conservative, three-piece business armor.

They descended the romantic staircase in an unromantic silence. As they neared the dining room the muted sound of genial conversation filtered through the closed double doors. Drawing a deep breath, Jo forced a smile to her stiff lips, prepared to follow Brett's lead in whatever image he created concerning their marriage.

Determined to play out the role of the happy bridegroom if it killed him, Brett pasted a parody of a smile on his face. His facial muscles ached in protest of the switch from down to up. Over the last weeks those muscles had grown used to the down position. As Brett followed Jo into the dining room, the ache was relieved by the scene that met his eyes. Brett frowned. Where were Eric and his family, and Di and her brood? The question spun out of his mind at the sound of his brother's voice.

"Will you look at the delicious creature!" Wolf's liquid-silver eyes swept Jo's willowy body. "What a delightful treat for dessert!"

Everyone laughed. Everyone but Brett. Cursing silently, Brett ordered a faint smile to his lips thinking, with shocking savagery, You touch her, big brother, and you're dead. Every muscle in Brett's body tightened. He hated it, yet there it was. Brett knew without doubt that should Wolf presume to lay one hand on Jo, he would find himself on the floor, on his back, and hurting like hell. Without conscious command his fingers curled into his palms, readying for action that didn't come.

"Wolf! Will you never learn to behave?" Violet chastised, bestowing a welcoming smile on Jo. "Come sit by me, JoAnne. It's long past time you were welcomed into the family." She shot an arched look at Brett.

"It's been a busy winter, Mother." Brett offered the lame excuse for not bringing Jo to visit sooner, then strode to where Wolf had risen in place at the end of the table. "You're looking good, big brother." The truth of his compliment brought an equal mixture of joy and pain to Brett. He had prayed for Wolf's recovery, while at the same time dreading it. Brett knew Wolf's return to vigor might well mean his own loss. The emotions in conflict inside him were tearing him apart.

Wolf's silver eyes darkened with concern. "I'm sorry I can't say the same about you. You look very tired, Brett." Wolf's glance sliced to Jo. "Are there problems?"

"No! I . . ."

"No more than usual," Brett cut across Jo's too-hurried denial. "I'll be glad to get back to running one region." Terminating the subject, Brett turned to kiss Micki's cheek in greeting, then frowningly directed his gaze back to his mother. "Eric and Di not here yet?"

"No. And they won't be coming." Violet waited till Brett seated himself opposite Jo before explaining. "Dirk is covered with chicken pox." She smiled in sympathy for Di's youngest child. "And, as Doris has been having mild cramps for several days, her doctor has forbidden her to travel."

"But it's not Doris's time yet. Is it?" Brett truthfully couldn't remember: he had had other, more important things on his mind since Christmas.

"Close enough," Violet drawled. "We might have another new member in the family by Easter."

His mother's comment elicited speculation from the others at the table about whether the new arrival would be a boy or a girl. Brett, making a show of eating the fish stew Elania set before him, let the conversation swirl around him as he studied his wife's animated face. A new baby. One month ago, for one flashing moment, Brett's heart had leaped with joy at the idea of a new baby. His baby. From Brett out of Jo. The spoon paused halfway between his mouth and the bowl. On the night he'd returned from Pennsylvania his hopes had soared with the suspicion that Jo was pregnant. But, had he hoped for a child, or to use the child to keep Jo with him? Brett slowly lowered the spoon to the bowl, his eyes hungry on Jo's face. Maybe not that night, but now, at this moment, Brett knew he wanted the child. Jo's child. Brett was painfully aware of the fact that he would probably never see that child.

"Brett!"

The exasperation that tinged his mother's tone was a clear

indication that it was not the first time she'd said his name. Shifting his gaze to Violet's face, Brett smiled ruefully. "Yes, Mother?"

"Are you feeling all right?" Violet's exasperation was overshadowed by concern. "You've barely touched your soup."

"I'm fine," Brett assured her quietly. "I was just wondering if the family conclave has been postponed . . . due to chicken pox and confinement."

"Not at all." Very motherlike, Violet searched Brett's face for telltale signs of illness.

"Brett's a big boy now, Mother. I'm sure he knows how to take care of himself," Wolf inserted dryly. "Even if handling both Atlanta and New York are too much for him."

Brett chose to ignore Wolf's taunt, which caused his mother's frown to darken. "How do you propose to have a family conclave with only half the family here?" In an effort to ease his mother's worry, Brett arched one pale brow exaggeratedly. Before his eyes, mother changed into Madam President.

"Have you ever heard of the conference line?"

Out of the corner of his eye, Brett caught the gleam of the appreciative grin that revealed Jo's even white teeth. Damn, she is beautiful! Dragging his concentration back to his mother, Brett nodded. "Yes, sir." His own grin wouldn't be denied when Brett heard Micki's soft laughter whisper down the length of the long, highly glossed table.

"That's more like it." Violet's expression of concern faded at Brett's apparent return to more normal behavior. "I've slated the conference for three o'clock. That will give you and JoAnne a chance to change clothes, or whatever."

Brett's inclination was to opt for the whatever but, for the moment, he focused his attention on getting through lunch without making a complete ass of himself. He'd already aroused his mother's concern and Wolf's taunting speculation. The last thing he needed was to create a scene at the lunch table. Elania would never forgive him!

Fortunately, Wolf chose to be briefed over the salad, and the remainder of the meal was consumed along with dry business details. By the time Brett and Jo went back upstairs to his bedroom less than forty-five minutes were left till conclave time.

Their cases were placed neatly side by side on the storage chest that ran the width of the bed at its base. Maintaining the cool silence that had enveloped them since leaving the dining room, Jo set to work immediately unpacking her case. Watching her from behind half-closed eyes Brett knew revealed both longing and desire, he shrugged out of his jacket, tossing it onto the foot of the bed as he strolled across the room. Dropping onto the padded chair, Brett sprawled with deceptive laziness, eyes now mere slits, watching her as she moved gracefully back and forth between suitcase and closet.

When her case was empty Jo closed the lid and snapped the locks. Would she, Brett mused, perform her wifely duty and unpack his case? She would. Brett felt a thrill shiver through his body at the sight of Jo's slim hands on his clothes.

You poor jerk! Brett sighed silently. You are positively besotted! When you can be turned on by observing a woman handling your faded Levis you have gone beyond the pale!

"Brett?" Jo's near whisper revealed the fact that she thought he was sleeping.

"Hmmm?" Brett raised his lids slightly, just enough to show her he was awake.

"Am I expected to attend this family conference?" Jo asked hesitantly.

"Are you a member of the family?" Brett laid the drawl on with a spade.

Jo responded indirectly. "I . . . I'm going to have a quick shower. I'll only be a moment."

"Take your time." Brett's smile mocked her. "We won't have to punch a time clock as we enter the boss's study." His smile disappeared as, with a toss of her head that betrayed her impatience with him, Jo strode into the bathroom.

271

Biting back a rather pungent, self-descriptive epithet, Brett jerked to his feet, crossing to the double dresser in four long strides to retrieve the shaving kit Jo had placed there. Tugging the zipper midway around the case, Brett inserted his fingers and withdrew a small velvet box. Flipping the lid, Brett stared down at the flawless, pear-shaped, three-carat diamond beautifully displayed in a delicate, intricately fashioned setting. Furs. Diamonds. The lid closed with a tiny snap. The Maserati was on order.

Sliding the top dresser drawer open, Brett dropped the box onto the neat pile of underwear inside, then slammed the drawer closed forcefully. Brett knew now that Jo could not be bought, either physically or emotionally. He had known it for some time. If Jo had been with Wolf, it had not been for the apartment, or the small car that was seldom moved out of the apartment parking area, or to advance herself in the company. If she had been with Wolf, it was because she had *wanted* to be with him.

Brett's body became absolutely still, while his mind pounced alertly on his last thought. Because she wanted to be with Wolf! Raising his head slowly, Brett stared into the wide, gray eyes reflected in the oversized mirror on the wall above the dresser. Because she *wanted* to be with Wolf!

She's with me now!

The gray eyes staring back at Brett suddenly glittered silver with hope. Could that mean . . . does Jo *want* to be with me? But Wolf's well now. A little thin, à little gaunt, but well! A shudder tore through Brett's slender frame.

Dear God! I have got to get her away from here!

There were twelve minutes left to go before the appointed hour of three when Jo rushed out of the bathroom. Clamping down on the urge to grab hold of her and run, Brett strode into the bathroom to replace her under a cold shower. When Brett walked back into the bedroom Jo was gone, as were the minutes till the hour of three. Pulling open the top dresser drawer, Brett smiled at the small velvet box before removing a pair of the silky navy very-brief briefs. Stepping into the faded Levis, Brett imagined he could feel the warmth of Jo's recent touch, smell her scent on the soft denim. A pale-blue chamois shirt, a double stamp into supple leather ankle boots, and Brett went striding out of the room, eight minutes late and primed to fight.

Four pairs of eyes swiveled to observe Brett's entrance into the study, and Eric's voice complained from the squawk box attached to the phone on Violet's desk.

"Hey! Where did everybody go?"

Sweeping a look over Brett that told him she was now "boss" not "Mother," Violet said crisply, "We are still here. And now your brother has condescended to join us." Brett met her drilling stare with calm detatchment.

"Congratulations, Brett." Eric's voice smiled. "You picked a winner this time."

Brett's eyes easily broke the hold of his mother's to stalk those of the "winner." "Thanks, Eric." Pride swelled inside Brett as Jo stared back at him serenely. It was as if she was saying, There's not a Renninger alive who can make me lose my composure. She is magnificent! The observation hardened Brett's determination to keep her. Refusing to release his visual hold on her, Brett added, "And how is your winner?"

"Doing fine," Eric assured. "You may be uncle again before the night is out."

"Then what the hell are you doing on this line?" Brett startled everyone, including himself, with his sudden harshness. "You should be with Doris, Eric." Brett felt the edge, of patience, of reason, of . . . whatever, looming closer. If he didn't do something soon to resolve this mess he'd created, Brett decided, he'd fall headfirst over that precarious edge.

A stunned silence held sway for an instant, then a soft voice issued from the squawk box. "Brett's right, you know." Di offered her opinion. "Eric should be with Doris, and I should be with Dirk. Mother, can we wind this meeting up fairly quickly?" Before Violet could respond, Di added, "Brett, Jo, I hope you'll be very happy. I'm holding my gift to you until you have a permanent address."

At that point Jo stole the initiative from Brett. Maintaining his oddly intense stare, and wondering what the devil was going on in his head, Jo infused warmth into her voice. "Thank you, Di. And you too, Eric. I'm keeping my fingers crossed for a boy."

Eric's laughter, and possible reply, were cut short by Violet's brisk voice. "Of course, Brett and Di are both right. We can have an in-depth meeting when everyone is well again. But there is one consideration I'd like you all to think about. Eric and I have discussed this and we are in complete accord. It's time for the company to expand again. I want to open another region—the northwest region, from Colorado west, including Oregon and Washington." She glanced at Brett. "I had considered giving Richard Colby the mid-Atlantic region and, as he was a bachelor, asking Brett to take over the new region." A soft smile curved her lips as she shifted her gaze to Jo. "But as Brett is now married . . ."

"We'll take it."

Jo blinked, for a second stunned by Brett's hard, decisive tone. Then swift anger rushed through her. How dare he presume to make decisions for her? Not that she would object to going to the Northwest or, for that matter, hell, as long as she was with him, but she would appreciate being consulted first! Breathing deeply, Jo managed to keep her tone neutral.

"Brett, I think we should discuss this in private." Jo's tone was belied by the flash of amber in her hazel eyes. "I don't know if I . . ."

"You'll do as your told." Brett's eyes glinted a warning for her to be silent; his tone was thick with ice. "Mother, we will take it."

"Brett!"

A chorus of voices, in varying degrees of shock, cried his name. Jo's was not one of them. Without even being aware of having moved, Jo was on her feet, her body shaking with humiliation and fury. Wolf was on his feet also, a protective alertness in his stance.

"Brett." The big prowler's voice commanded attention. "What in hell do you think you're doing? Apologize to Jo at once."

"Mind your own god-damned business, Wolf." Taut with anger, Brett ignored the collective gasp his snarling voice elicited. "Jo is *my* wife. I don't need you, or anyone else, to instruct me on how to handle her."

"Oh, sharp as a marble, you ass!" Eric's angry voice exploded from the squawk box.

There was more of the same, from Violet, from Di, from Micki, and from a now-incensed Wolf. Jo heard without hearing. Her eyes stinging with tears of shame, and hurt, and a jumbled mess of other emotions, she stared at the beauty of Brett's chiseled face until it blurred, then she ran, blocking out the angry voices that bounced off the paneled walls of Violet's study.

What had come over him? What had she done to turn Brett into a snarling dictator? Did he hate her so very much? The questions hammered in Jo's mind as she ran along the hall, through the spotless kitchen, and out the back door. Where could she go? Jo's tear-filled eyes swept the wide expanse of bricked courtyard behind the house, passing then slicing back to the two vehicles parked there. A jeep and a pickup truck, keys in the ignitions of each. If she could get to the airfield, or an airport . . .

No!

The protest was a rebellious scream inside Jo's mind. No, damn it! She would not run again! In effect, she had run from a bad situation—*not* of her making—when she'd left home at nineteen. If only in her mind, she had run from the pain and humiliation inflicted upon her by Gary. And, at least figuratively, she'd been running from a showdown with Brett since the first day she met him. How long could the mind employ evasive tactics? How many avenues of escape could her consciousness scurry along in avoidance of the truth? Besides, Jo had the uncomfortable feeling that if she ran now Brett would not follow her, and that would prove her mother's theory about love, and the relationships therein, correct. Sniffing, Jo shook her head in silent denial.

Ignoring the vehicles and the tears trickling down her face, Jo slid her fingers into the back pockets of her jeans and began pacing off the distance between the kitchen door and the four-car garage set to the right and rear of the house.

What the devil had come over Brett? Again. Jo came to an abrupt halt midway between house and garage, the single word repeating in her mind. Again? Yes, again. Even though there had been constraint between them since the night he'd returned from the Poconos, Brett had unfailingly treated her with polite consideration. What had caused his sudden harsh thoughtlessness? Jo raked her mind, examining every minute since their arrival at the house. A recent scene flashed into her memory, and, frowning, Jo relived it slowly.

"Are you as hungry as I am?"

The echo of Brett's sensuously warm voice tantalized her memory; he had certainly not been cold before lunch! But wait! Jo's frown deepened. Brett *had* turned cold before they'd gone down to join the family. What had she said to him? Something about the family waiting? No. That hadn't chilled his ardor. What then? Jo kicked at a tiny pebble in frustration; damn it, what else had she said? Memory clicked.

"But we haven't even seen Wolf yet!"

Wolf.

Wolf?

Jo went absolutely statue still. Brett had grown frigid at the mention of his brother's name . . . and not for the first time! It was almost as if Brett was jealous of Wolf, as if he believed . . . Oh my God! Could Brett really believe that she . . . and Wolf? Remembered images flashed through Jo's mind again, not entire scenes, but small, isolated fragments, beginning with Brett refusing to let her see Wolf after the accident.

Brett, warning her not to call Wolf while he was in Vermont. Brett, oddly backing down the time in his office when she'd lifted the phone to call Wolf. Brett, telling her they'd probably both regret it but that he had to have her. Brett, suddenly coldly remote when they'd come to the farm at Christmas time. Brett, withdrawing from her on learning about a preexisting prescription for birth control pills. Brett, mentioning her previous affair in that odd, intensely accusatory manner.

Could it be . . . could it possibly be . . . Jo spun around at the sound of the kitchen door closing, breath catching in her throat at the sight of Brett's face. His expression austere with grim determination, Brett walked to her with slow, measured strides. In the seconds required for him to reach her, Jo tried, and failed, to suppress the wild hope rioting through her. As he drew close, Brett's eyelids narrowed over eyes gleaming silvery with intent, increasing her hope tenfold. Could it be that the fire raging inside Brett was caused by love for her? Was Brett jealous over her? All this time? All this long wasted time?

Brett had reached the very edge; it was either fish or cut bait, and he sure as hell was not about to cut bait at this stage of the game! Stalking his wife, Brett conceded that he might have gone about it with more tact, but, tactless or not, Jo was going with him to Colorado! And, after the way his family had ganged up on him when Jo had run from his mother's study, Brett was perfectly primed for an argument.

She is mine, and I will not give her up.

The avowal revolved in his mind as Brett studied Jo's face through the slits of lids narrowed against the glare of late-afternoon sunlight. The evidence of tears on her cheeks gave him momentary pause. It was the second time he'd made her cry. Brett felt a twist of pain in his chest. Damn fool! You've hurt her again! I'll make it up to her, he soothed his stinging conscience, but I cannot give her up!

Two steps from her, Brett hesitated; he could not talk, or argue, with Jo in the courtyard, not with his mother, Wolf, Micki, *and* Elania for an audience! One step from her Brett reached out, grasped her wrist firmly with his hand, then, pivoting, strode back to the house, a gasping Jo stumbling behind him.

"Brett!" Jo gave an ineffectual tug of her arm. "Have you gone mad?"

"Be quiet." Brett snapped the order without turning his head. "You'll have plenty of time to talk when we're alone in our room."

When he got to the kitchen door, Brett thrust it open and strode through, tugging firmly on a now angrily sputtering Jo to keep her following him. If nothing else, his precipitous action had one good result, Brett thought with a grimace; Jo was no longer crying.

His gait unchecked, Brett loped along the hall. He had made it to the bottom of the stairs when the door to his mother's study was flung open and Wolf, Violet and Micki at his heels, rushed into the hallway, only to come to a dead stop at the sight of Brett literally dragging Jo through the house.

"For Christ's sake, Brett!" Wolf's voice held a note of sheer disbelief. "What in hell are you doing? Let her go!" Snaking out a long arm, Wolf caught Jo's other, flailing wrist.

At the command "let her go" all the accumulated months of frustration exploded inside Brett's mind. When Wolf put his hand on Jo, anger exploded out through Brett's mouth.

"Don't touch her!"

For long seconds shocked silence smothered response, then bedlam took over as everyone protested at once. Even Elania, coming from the living room to investigate the cause of all the noise, added her two cent's worth of condemnation. Brett's voice, coldly, frighteningly savage, cut through the babble.

"I want silence." Brett knew his objective was achieved through shock; he knew it and used it. "I assure you all that I have no intention of harming my wife." His eyes dropped to rest

278

deliberately on Wolf's fingers, curled around Jo's wrist. When he lifted his gaze, Brett's eyes had the look of opaque ice. "I told you not to touch her."

For whatever reason—curiosity, surprise, whatever—Wolf's hold on Jo's wrist relaxed, then fell away.

"Don't *ever* touch her again." Once again Brett spoke through an outburst of protest. "If you will all excuse us?" Tugging gently on Jo's arm, he started up the stairs. "Jo and I would like to have an argument in private."

Trailing Brett's anger-tightened body up the stairs and into their room, Jo felt excitement stir, then radiate through her system. Incredible, unbelievable as it seemed, Brett *was* jealous of Wolf. Why he was jealous of Wolf was the question Jo hoped soon to have the answer to. All these months! Why hadn't Brett simply asked her? Of all the lunkheads! Jo wasn't quite sure if she was referring to Brett or herself; they both fit the description! Hearing the door snap shut behind her, Jo spun to face her husband, trepidation closing her throat at the glittering glance he raked over her. Barely breathing, Jo watched his eyes until a flicker of movement caught her attention, drawing her gaze to his hands. The purposeful work of Brett's fingers as they unbuttoned his shirt opened Jo's throat enough to allow the passage of a startled squeak.

"What are you doing?"

His expression mocking her for asking the obvious, Brett yanked the shirt free of the jeans waistband and tossed it carelessly to the floor. His fingers found employment at his belt buckle as he began walking to her. Eyeing him warily, Jo edged toward the bathroom door.

"All right!" Jo felt rather proud of the steadiness of her tone; inside she was a jumbled bundle of excitement-tied nerve ends. "I know *what* you're doing. I thought we were going to talk."

His mocking smile deepening, Brett sauntered past her to drop onto the edge of the brightly colored chair. "I've changed my mind." His eyes laughed at her evasive edging toward the bathroom. Lifting one leg, he tugged at his boot; it landed on the floor with a soft thud. As he pulled at the other boot, Brett motioned at the bed with a brief nod of his head. "I've decided to give you a demonstration of the resiliency of the mattress after all."

"Brett . . ."

"You must admit," he went on, ignoring her attempt at protest, "the bed is the one place we communicate beautifully." The second boot plopped to the floor. "You had better get busy," he chided softly to the background sound of the descending zipper. "I'm way ahead of you."

Way ahead of you. Way ahead of you! A light clicked on in Jo's mind. Good grief! Had she left her reasoning power behind in the yard? Watching Brett's slim, muscularly corded length emerge from the jeans, Jo's adrenaline kicked all her senses into overtime. Brett may have been referring to her fully clothed state, but Jo interpreted his words in a different light. His cool detachment was nothing more than a facade! Introduce her to the bed's resiliency indeed! Brett was hell-bent on making a statement of ownership! He was not only jealous, he was running scared! Clamping her teeth together to contain a whoop of joy created by the wave of relief washing through her, Jo tore uncaringly at the buttons on her pure silk shirt. A raging fire? Jo's shirt landed unaimed on top of his. She'd show him an inferno!

Watching the play of emotions across her face, Brett knew the moment Jo reached a decision. When she began tearing at her clothes his already aroused manhood took on the quality of pure, painful iron. As her silky loveliness was exposed to his hungry stare an earlier thought reasserted itself.

She's with me now!

"Jo."

Brett wanted to say much more, so very much more, yet the only sound he could force through his constricted throat was the anguished whisper of her name. Consuming desire combined with a desperate need to claim erased all other consideration.

They both moved at the same instant.

There was no time for teasing kisses. There was no time for stroking caresses. There was no time for tiny erotic nuances. Mouths locked together in all-consuming need, they dropped to the bed, Brett thrusting into her on contact, Jo welcoming his invasion with a cry of exquisite pleasure. Never had their lovemaking been quite so fierce, or quite so savage, or quite so shatteringly satisfying.

The words that should have been said months before were purged from Brett's throat at the moment his life force erupted from his quivering body.

"I love you, Jo. Oh, God, how I love you!"

Sweet, sweet release. Release of tension. Release of fear. And, finally, unashamedly, release of long-pentup tears . . . both hers and his.

"Don't cry, darling!" Unmindful of her own wet cheeks, Jo brushed trembling fingertips over Brett's face. "It hurts me."

A tender smile softening his chiseled lips, Brett lowered his head to dry the salty moisture on her cheeks with his mouth. "You haven't said the words." Raising his head again, he gazed compellingly into her eyes. "Say it, Jo. Please. I need to hear it."

"I love you."

Jo felt the tremor that ripped through Brett's body in her palms still gripping his hips, in her body still pressed to his, and in her soul, now, at last, at one with his. Though complete, Jo was not so lost in euphoria she missed the significance of Brett's declaration without question. The significance thrilled her. Brett still labored under the illusion of a previous affair between her and his brother. What, Jo wondered mistily, had it cost Brett to make that declaration? Very likely a lot more than she'd ever know.

"You'll go to Colorado with me?" The uncertainty underlying Brett's tone drew Jo from speculation.

"I'd go to the moon with you." Jo's firm response brought a teasing gleam to his eyes.

"We've just been there."

Floating in contentment richer than whipped cream, Jo sighed as, levering his body a few inches from hers, Brett caressed her skin with his right hand. Long fingers drew a gasp of pleasure when they outlined the contour of one breast, the murmured confession that followed drew a gasp of dismay.

"I'd hate to have to admit the times I tormented myself with the thought of Wolf's hand stroking you like this."

"Brett—" Jo choked on the protest.

"Or," Brett continued raspily, "his mouth drinking from yours."

"Brett . . . please, listen."

"Or," Brett went on, unable to stop, "his body resting in the cradle of your thighs."

"Brett, stop this!" Releasing her hold on his hips, Jo brought her hands up to grasp his face, forcing him to look into her eyes. "There has never been anything personal between us. Never. *Ever.* Wolf has been my employer and my friend, nothing more." Jo sighed. "You should know better than I how very much Wolf adores Micki. I can't imagine where you ever got the idea that Wolf and I . . ."

Oh, God! Levering himself out of and off her completely, Brett lay beside Jo on his back, staring at the stark white ceiling. To believe the worse all these months, to live with the agony, day in, day out, only to find . . .

"He owns the apartment you live in." Started now, Brett had to have it all out.

"He does not own it!" Jo corrected, her tone revealing a hint of anger. "Wolf is holding the mortgage on it. Without his help I never could have managed it."

Brett turned his head to find Jo's eyes glaring at him. She was telling the truth and he knew it. Still he kept on, needing to hear it all. "He has a key to the place."

"Yes," Jo admitted readily on a sigh of exasperation. "He has a key. I gave it to him, but not, I assure you, for any unsavory purpose." Jo smiled wryly. "I have a bad habit, you see. I lock myself out on occasion."

Brett smiled, then laughed aloud as he gathered her close to his side. "Oh, hell, honey. I feel like such a jerk!"

"You should." Jo wasn't about to let him off the hook easily, not after the trauma of the last months. "Not for having the doubt in the first place, but for not asking me straight out if your suspicions were correct."

"Forgive me?" Brett hid his seriousness behind a grin. He'd take the rap, for there was no way he'd bring Micki's name into the discussion.

"Yes, of course." Jo snuggled closer to his warmth, shaking her head in wonder at her own obtuseness. "And here all the time I believed you were resenting Gary," she admitted in a murmur that turned to a yelp as Brett sat bolt upright.

"Who in the hell is Gary? And why in the hell didn't I know about him before now?" Brett asked angrily.

"Brett, you had to have realized there was someone before you," Jo said carefully.

"Yeah, sure, but I thought it was—"

"And now you know it wasn't," Jo interrupted gently. "Gary was the first, the only one before you." Praying that he wouldn't spoil what they had just found together, Jo explained her one disastrous affair in minute detail.

His expression contemplative, Brett stared down at Jo for long seconds when her recital was finished. He didn't like the idea of Gary Devlin, and not only for the hell he'd put Jo through. "Were you in love with him?" The question was a mild form of self-torture. Contrarily, he wanted her to say yes and no at the same time. Yes, because he couldn't abide the idea that Jo would live with a man she didn't love. And no, because he hated the mere thought that she'd loved a man before him. It was irrational. Brett knew it was irrational. Hadn't he thought himself in love with Sondra?

"I thought I was," Jo finally replied, unknowingly voicing

Brett's last consideration. "Of course I know now that I was merely infatuated with him. But it's too late to change things now, isn't it?"

"Yes." Bending to her, Brett brushed his lips over hers. "And it no longer matters." Surprisingly, it didn't, Brett realized in relief. Hell! Screw Devlin! "I don't mind not being first." His movement swift, Brett nipped gently at her lower lip. "As long as you make damned sure I'm the last."

"And what about you?" Jo arched a forbidding brow at him. "No more Marshas?"

"Jo, I told you . . ."

"What you told me, exactly, was 'Not for lack of trying on my part.' " Jo repeated his exact words. "I would like an explanation of that remark." The demand made, Jo held her breath. She knew she really had no right to an answer, but then, neither had he, and she'd been honest with him. Deep down, where she lived, Jo knew she was testing not only his love for her but his trust in her as well. When Brett smiled her personal world settled into place.

"The explanation is simple." Brett's hesitation was hardly noticable. Damn it, man, he scorned himself, she trusted you, it's your turn. "I meant exactly what I said. We were alone in Marsha's apartment in Vermont. We were undressed. We were in bed together." Brett paused as Jo's eyelids closed to conceal her pain. "Look at me, love." When her lashes lifted he stared into her eyes. "I was thinking about you, and I couldn't make it. Do you understand what I'm saying? I could not make it with another woman. I *wanted* you."

Jo blinked against a fresh swell of hot moisture and trembled with a fresh surge of hot response. Lord! Jo felt sure that if Brett touched her now he'd burn his hands! Lifting her hands, she grasped him around the waist to guide his body onto hers. "And now that you have me," she whispered, "what are you going to do with me?"

"I've been thinking about that," Brett answered solemnly, his eyes betraying his growing heat.

"And?" Jo prompted, moving against him sensuously to speed up his thinking process.

"I've decided to keep you." In retaliation, Brett angled his hips into hers, smiling at her gasp of pleasure. "And let the fire rage forever."

THE GAME
IS PLAYED

CHAPTER ONE

'YOU can get dressed now, Mrs Ortega, and I'll see you in my office in a few minutes.' Helen smiled gently at the timid young woman with the dark expressive eyes, then turned and left the examining room.

Ten minutes later, after seeing the beaming girl out of her consulting office, Helen lit a cigarette and leaned back into her desk chair with a contented sigh. Maria Ortega's delight in having her maternal expectations confirmed had given her an all-over good feeling. Even after five years of private practice Helen still felt the same satisfaction on diagnosing a wanted pregnancy as she had the first time.

A buzz and blinking light on her desk phone brought Helen upright in her chair, hand reaching for the receiver.

'Yes, Alice?'

The no-nonsense voice of her R.N. Alice Kelly answered crisply. 'Jolene Johnson is on the phone, Doctor. I think you'll want to speak to her yourself. I'll have her chart on your desk in a minute.'

'Thank you, Alice.' A long, slender forefinger touched the blinking button and in a tone professionally confident she asked, 'What's the problem, Jolene?' Automatically glancing at the clock, Helen noted the time: one fifteen. Fifteen minutes into her half day.

Every Wednesday Alice scheduled patients no later than twelve thirty or twelve forty-five, depending on the medical requirements, in order to have the office clear of patients by one o'clock, thereby giving Helen one free afternoon a week. Helen hoped to one day achieve that free afternoon.

Now as she glanced at the clock she gave a small sigh. She had so wanted to get to that lecture at Temple this afternoon.

'I don't know if it is a problem, Dr Cassidy.' Jolene Johnson's young voice wavered unsurely. 'But Tim insisted I call you.'

Thoughts of free afternoons and lectures banished, Helen replied soothingly, 'Suppose you tell me why your husband insisted you call me and we'll take it from there.'

'Well, I have this odd little trickle. It's the strangest sensation. It started after lunch when I stood up to clear the table and it happened twice while I did the dishes. It's not like the book says happens when the water sac breaks, and I have no pain or anything, but it does feel funny.'

As the girl was speaking Alice quietly entered the room and placed the open folder on Helen's desk. Helen nodded her thanks, lifted her oversize, dark-framed reading glasses from the desk, and slid them into place, her eyes scanning the neatly typed sheets for pertinent facts while a picture of Jolene Johnson rose in her mind. A pretty girl of average height and weight, she was twenty-three years old, married two years, and was one week into her ninth month of pregnancy.

'Your husband was right, Jolene.' Helen's voice was calm, unhurried. 'I want you to get yourself ready and go to the hospital.'

'But, Doctor, I don't even have any pain!'

'I know, Jolene, but although you've had no gush of water, you are leaking and I want you in the hospital. I'll call so they'll be expecting you.'

'Eh—I—' The beginning of fear in the young woman's voice was unmistakable. 'Okay, if you say so.' Then more softly. 'Doctor, do you think something's wrong?'

'I doubt it, Jolene.'

Helen's eyes had completed their perusal of the girl's chart and her voice was confident with the medical data she'd read. Jolene's pregnancy had been normal so far, with no indication of any irregularities. She'd have to examine the girl, of course, but she felt sure the girl and the baby were in no danger.

'Don't be alarmed. The hospital staff will take good care of you and I'll be in to see you later this afternoon.'

Helen's quiet tone had the hoped-for calming effect, for the lessening of tension was evident in Jolene's voice.

'All right, Doctor, I'll do whatever you say, and thank you.'

Helen sighed as she replaced the receiver and handed the chart to the silently waiting Alice.

'Trouble?' Alice asked quietly. The tall, rawboned woman had been a nurse for over twenty-five years. She had seen much, said little, and was impressed with very few. Helen Cassidy was one of those few.

'I hope not.' Helen sighed again. Well, so much for free half days. 'The girl's leaking but has no pain. Nothing very unusual so far, but we'll see.'

Alice nodded briefly, then turned and left the room. Helen sat staring at the clock. If she left now, she'd be able to hear some of the lecture, but hearing part of a lecture wouldn't do her much good, so—she shrugged her slim shoulders resignedly—maybe next time.

In sudden decision Helen pushed her chair back, went to the closet, and removed her fur-trimmed storm coat. January was being very unkind to the east coast this year, and the coat, along with the knee-high suede boots she wore, were not only fashionable, but necessary.

She slipped into the coat, dug in her capacious bag for her car keys, slung the bag's strap over her shoulder, and left the room, slowing her steps but not stopping as she passed Alice's desk.

'I'm going for lunch.' She named a restaurant. 'And then to the hospital, if you need me.'

'Why don't you do yourself a favour and have a good meal for a change?' Alice chided dryly. 'You're beginning to resemble your own shadow.'

Helen heard the words as she closed the outer door. She was still smiling wryly as she unlocked the door to her Monte Carlo and slid behind the wheel. Alice had been on a fatten-up-the-boss campaign for several weeks now, and although her remarks were often pointedly barbed, they had failed to penetrate Helen's composure.

She was slender. She always had been slender. She probably always would be slender. End of story. Helen frowned. True she had been skipping some meals lately in order to keep up with her increasingly heavy schedule. Also true she had lost a few pounds, but at her age that was better than gaining weight.

An hour and a half later Helen walked into Jolene Johnson's hospital room and paused, a smile tugging at her lips. The head nurse stood by the bed, one hand outspread on the expectant mother's distended abdomen, her voice a dry, reassuring drawl.

'It's still in the attic. Relax, honey, it's going to be a long day.'

As Helen moved quietly into the room the nurse turned and stepped back from the bed, a warm smile transforming her otherwise plain face.

'Hello, Doctor.' Her tone matched her smile in warmth. 'Jolene's doing just fine. All prepped and ready to go. At Mother Nature's convenience of course.'

The tug at Helen's lips turned into a full smile. This brash young woman was the most flip, while at the same time, the most efficient nurse she had ever worked with.

'Thank you, Kathy.'

The nurse nodded at Helen, sent a bracing grin at Jolene, and swung out of the room, whistling softly through her teeth.

Laughing, Helen placed her fingers on Jolene's wrist to take her pulse, eyes shifting to her watch. Jolene began speaking the moment Helen removed her fingers.

'Doctor, tell me the truth. Am I going to lose my baby?'

Helen paused in the process of adjusting her stethoscope, glancing at the girl sharply. 'No, of course not. Whatever gave you that idea?'

'Well.' Jolene's lips trembled. 'I'm not due for almost a month and I have this horrible feeling that something's wrong.'

'Just a moment,' Helen murmured, then proceeded to give the young woman a quick, but thorough, examination. When she finished, she straightened and looked Jolene squarely in the eyes. 'There is no indication that anything is "wrong". Now what I want you to do is relax. You may use the bathroom but I don't want you out of bed for any other purpose. I want you to rest.'

'All right, Doctor,' Jolene said softly. Then hesitantly, 'May Tim come in?'

'Yes, for a little while,' Helen replied, then added firmly, 'but I want you to rest. The nurse will be taking your temperature and blood pressure hourly. Don't be alarmed, it's a precautionary measure. You are open to infection now and I want a periodic check just in case.' She squeezed the girl's hand before adding. 'Now relax and don't worry. I'll be back later to check your progress.'

Helen walked out of the room, paused a few minutes to speak to Kathy, informing her she'd be in the cafeteria if needed, then left the section.

As she walked along the halls towards the lunchroom, Helen smiled, nodded, and spoke to several of the doctors and nurses she passed, totally unaware of the admiring glances cast at her retreating back.

Looking tall and slender, her honey-gold hair drawn smoothly back from her classically beautiful face into a neat coil at the back of her head, Helen presented a picture of cool, calm professionalism. She lived up to that picture completely. It seemed she had always known she would become a doctor and had worked steadily towards that goal. During premed she had decided to specialise in gynaecology and obstetrics and, except for a few minor and one major emotional entanglements, had concentrated all her energy in that direction.

Now, after five years of private practice and a flawless record, Helen had the reputation of being brilliant in her profession and coldly emotionless. She knew it, and she didn't care. In fact she encouraged the attitude. Even in the seventies achieving recognition in the professions was not easy for a woman. It took that little bit extra in dedication and hard work. Within her own sphere Helen had made it. If the cost was occasional weariness, due to a gruelling workload, and periodic loneliness, due to her withdrawn attitude, Helen paid the bill and considered the price as minimal.

She had what she wanted. She led a well-ordered existence doing the work she loved. If, at rare intervals, the warm female inside yearned for male companionship, she squashed the yearning ruthlessly.

Helen was of the opinion that in any emotional encounter the odds were heavily stacked in the male's favour. She had been burned, badly, while still in her early twenties and had promised herself that never again would a man get the chance to hurt her. It had taken months for the emotional wounds to heal, and the scars still remained, a searing reminder of the arrogance of the male animal called man.

As she left the lunchroom, after having a soothing cup of tea, Helen heard her name paged. She went to the main desk in the lobby, lifted the phone, and gave her name. After a short pause Alice's voice came calm over the wire.

'Better put on your roller skates, Doctor, I think you are going to be a mite rushed. Mr Darren just called. He's bringing his wife to the hospital now. Her contractions are four minutes apart. Good luck.'

There was a small click as Alice hung up. Replacing her own receiver, Helen turned away from the desk with a silent groan. Why do they do it? she asked herself as she stepped into the elevator. Why do some of these young women wait at home until the last moment? Are they afraid and trying to put off the inevitable as long as possible? Or are they trying to prove how unafraid they are? Helen truly didn't know. What she did know was she could live without these last-minute rush jobs. And she had thought Kristeen Darren had more sense.

By the time Helen walked into the delivery room, properly capped, gowned, and shod, Kristeen was only minutes away from motherhood.

'Good afternoon, Kristeen.' Helen's voice filtered coolly through the mask, which covered the lower half of her face. Above the mask her hazel eyes smiled warmly at the pale young woman. 'Longing to have it over with and hold your baby in your arms?'

'Yes, Doctor,' Kristeen began a smile that turned to a gasp as a hard contraction gripped her.

Helen's eyes shot a question at the anaesthetist, who nodded and murmured, 'Ready to go.'

Less than twenty minutes later Helen walked out of the delivery room, leaving behind a very tired but ecstatically happy mother of a perfectly formed baby daughter.

After cleaning up, Helen went into Jolene Johnson's

room, evicted young Tim Johnson with the assurance
that he would be called when the time came, and spent
the following twenty-five minutes examining Jolene and
talking down her renewed anxieties.

'I want you to rest,' she reiterated as she was leaving
the room. 'Sleep if possible. Conserve your strength for
when your labour does begin. And don't worry, I'll be
back later.'

She was standing at the nurses' station, making nota-
tions on Jolene's chart and talking with Kathy when a
nurse and a young student nurse rushed up to the desk all
flustered and excited.

'You should have seen what we just bumped into,
Kathy,' the nurse, a dark-haired, attractive young
woman in her midtwenties, said breathlessly.

Kathy eyed the two in amusement. 'Good to look at,
was he?' she asked dryly.

'Good!' The petite student gushed. 'He was totally
bad. Tall, red-haired, blue-eyed, and shoulders like a
Pittsburgh Steelers linebacker. What a hunk,' she
finished in an awed tone.

Kathy, obviously unimpressed, shot a long suffering
glance at Helen, who, lips twitching, opened her eyes
innocently wide and fluttered naturally long, silky lashes
at her, then turned and walked away without a word.
Behind her she heard Kathy laugh softly, and the
student nurse proclaim, 'No kidding, Kath, he really was
a hunk.'

A smile still tugging the corners of her mouth, Helen
pushed through the heavy swing doors that separated
the labour and delivery rooms from the maternity section, thinking that, as Kristeen Darren was probably
settled into a room by now, she may as well look in on
her before leaving the floor.

The smile left her face on hearing her name mentioned as she approached the nurses' station.

'If Dr Cassidy walked in now, we'd all catch hell.' The irate nurse, standing with her back to Helen, was so agitated, she missed the warning shake of the head from the grey-haired nurse she was speaking to. 'But I can't budge them.'

Before the older woman, who was facing both Helen and the angry nurse, could respond, Helen asked quietly, 'What's the problem Nancee?'

'Oh!' Nancee spun around, her face flushed with exasperation. 'Doctor, it's the people in Mrs Darren's room. There are five people in there, besides her husband. I've told them that, so soon after delivery, there should be no one in there *except* her husband, but they just ignored me. I understand that they're prominent people, and I didn't want to cause any trouble by calling security, but Mrs Darren looks exhausted.'

'There are six people around that bed?' The tone of Helen's voice sent a chill of apprehension down the spines of both nurses.

'I've tried to—' Nancee began.

'I'll go help her clear the room.' The older nurse cut in.

'No, I'll do it,' Helen stated grimly. 'You two have more important things to do than trying to coax a group of unthinking people into behaving rationally.'

Ignoring the anxious look the two women exchanged, Helen squared her shoulders and walked the short distance to the room in question. Pausing in the open doorway, Helen's eyes circled the room slowly, missing nothing.

Kristeen Darren did indeed look exhausted, even though her eyes were bright with excitement and pride. Her small pale hand was clasped tightly in a larger one, which obviously belonged to her husband, who, Helen noted with a frown, was sitting on the bed beside her. On either side of the bed were two older couples who Helen correctly identified as the respective grandparents. And at the foot of the bed was a young man, somewhere around thirty, Helen judged, who could be no one other than the 'totally bad hunk,' the giddy young student nurse had been starry-eyed over.

Helen's eyes lingered long seconds on the man. Up to a point the student's assessments had been correct. But only up to a point. He *was* tall and his shoulders did look like they belonged on a Pittsburgh Steelers linebacker. But this was no mere 'hunk'. This was more like bad news for all females. And his hair could not really be described as red. It was more of a deep chestnut-brown, the red highlights gleaming in the glare from the overhead light. And the face was shatteringly masculine. At least the profile, which was what Helen viewed, was.

'Is this party strictly family or may anyone join in?'

The caustic question, spoken in Helen's most professional, icy tone, jerked five startled faces towards her. Before anyone could protest or even open their mouths, Helen added, 'As it seems to have slipped everyone's mind, might I remind you that this woman has just given birth, and although she did not have a very hard delivery, it is never easy. She is tired. She needs rest, and as I want to examine her, I will give you thirty seconds to vacate this room.'

The startled expressions changed to embarrassment on all the faces but one. The 'hunk' turned, giving Helen the full impact of rugged good looks, an ice-blue stare, and a voice loaded with cool, male confidence.

'You must forgive us, Doctor.' The smooth, deep voice held not a hint of apology. 'This is the first child born in both families for some twenty-odd years and I'm afraid we've all been slightly carried away with her advent.' His eyes shifted briefly to Kristeen, clearly his sister, then swung back to Helen. 'But I see you are right. Kristeen does look very tired.' His eyes took on the glint of devilment. 'If you would step out of the doorway, we will all file quietly out and leave you to do your job.'

A shaft of hot anger stiffened Helen's already straight spine. This silken-mouthed young man was most assuredly overdue for his comeuppance. 'Thank you,' she snapped acidly, then turned away as if he were of no importance at all and addressed his brother-in-law in a pleasant tone.

'I'm sorry, Mr Darren, but you really must leave now. If you have any questions about your wife's condition, please wait in the hall. I'll only be a few minutes.'

As she was speaking she heard the muffled movements as the others left the room. When she finished, she favoured the new father with her most disarming smile.

That young man grinned sheepishly as he grasped his wife's hand.

'No, Doctor, I'm sorry. We were all thoughtless and inconsiderate.' He gazed down at his wife, his eyes warm with love. 'I'm so proud of her, we all are, and yet we remained, tiring her even more. Our only excuse, as Marsh said, is that we got carried away. I have no questions, as you filled me in perfectly after the baby was born.' He bent, kissed his wife lingeringly on the mouth, murmured a few love words to her, then straightened, released his hand, and stretched it out to Helen. 'I'll get out of here now. Thank you, Doctor, for everything.'

Clasping his hand, Helen laughed softly. 'I didn't do anything. Kristeen did all the hard work.'

The moment he was out of the room, Kristeen said quietly, 'I must apologise for my brother, Dr Cassidy. I know he made you angry, but you see, Marsh is used to issuing orders, not taking them.'

'No matter,' Helen brushed aside the subject of that young man. 'Let's see how you've progressed.' She did a routine check, asked a few questions, then, as she removed her stethoscope, pronounced, 'Very good. Now, if you behave yourself, get some rest, and eat a good dinner, you may have visitors this evening.' She started to move away from the bed, then paused and glanced archly over her shoulder. 'Two at a time, please.'

'Yes, Doctor.' Kristeen promised meekly.

The hall was clear of Kristeen's visitor except for the 'hunk' who leaned lazily against the wall next to the doorway, speculatively eyeing the passing nurses. As though he were invisible, Helen stepped by him briskly and headed down the hall. Silently, effortlessly, he fell into step beside her.

'I'd like a word with you, Doctor,' the deep voice requested blandly.

Helen felt her hackles rise, followed by shocked surprise. What was it about this man that put her back up? For in all truth she had felt it the moment she'd clapped eyes on him.

'What about?' She bristled.

'Temper, temper,' he murmured, then, at the flash of her eyes, 'my sister, among other things.'

Helen's steps didn't falter as she turned her head and raised her eyebrows at him in question.

'I've been told I was rude and owe you an apology by'—he raised his left hand and ticked off the fingers one by one with his right forefinger—'my mother, my father, my brother-in-law, and his most respected parents. By way of an apology let me buy you dinner.'

Coming to a full stop in front of the doors into the labour and delivery section, Helen turned to face him, shaking her head. 'No, thank you, Mr—'

'Kirk, Marshall Kirk. Most people call me Marsh.'

'I am not most people,' Helen elucidated clearly. 'Now if you will excuse me, I have a patient waiting.' On the last word she pushed the door open, stepped through, and let it swing back in his face.

Jolene's condition was stable and unchanged. She had not had a twinge of pain, and as she was getting bored and restless with her confinement, Helen sat talking to her for some time. After briefly outlining the procedures she would take if Jolene did not go into labour within a reasonable length of time, Helen left the girl and stopped at the desk to speak to Kathy.

'Slow day,' Kathy drawled, glancing at the clock. 'And unless things start happening mighty quickly, I'll be off duty long before Jolene is wheeled into delivery.'

Nodding in agreement, Helen's eyes followed Kathy's to the large wall clock, then flickered in surprise. It was almost six thirty! She had been in the section almost an hour and a half. No wonder she was beginning to feel slightly wilted and vaguely empty. Informing Kathy that she was off in search of sustenance, Helen left the section. The sight that met her eyes as she walked through the swing doors brought her to a shocked standstill. Propped against the wall, head back, eyes closed, stood Marshall Kirk, looking, strangely, neither uncomfortable nor out of place. On hearing the door swish closed, his eyes opened and appraised her with cool deliberation.

'Surely you haven't been here all this time, Mr Kirk?' The frank admiration in that level blue stare put an edge on Helen's tongue.

'I assure you I have, Dr Cassidy.' The sardonic emphasis he placed on her name rattled Helen, giving an even sharper edge to her tone.

'But why?'

Sighing wearly, exaggeratedly, he closed his eyes. When he lifted the lids, he fixed her with an ice-blue gaze so intense that Helen felt a shiver curl up the back of her neck.

'I told you I wanted to talk to you about my sister. I also invited you to have dinner with me, by way of an apology.'

Fighting the urge to rub the back of her neck, wondering at the odd catch in her throat, she rushed her words just a little. 'That's not necessary, we can talk in the lounge right here or in the—'

'I know it's not necessary,' he interrupted smoothly. 'But it is now'—he glanced at the slim gold watch on his wrist—'close to seven. I assume you're hungry. I know I am. Why not have our discussion in a congenial atmosphere and feed the inner person as well?'

Helen stared at him wordlessly for a long second. What was it about this young man? She felt unnerved, a very rare sensation for her, and she didn't know why. Which, of course, unnerved her even more. His attitude, of polite interest, could not be faulted. Nor could his tone, for he sounded pleasantly reasonable. So what was it? Unable to find an answer, or a reason for refusing his invitation, Helen hedged.

'Mr Kirk, I—'

'Yes, Dr Cassidy?' He prodded gently.

'Very well,' Helen sighed in defeat, then added firmly, 'but I cannot go far or be gone too long. I have a patient in there'—she nodded at the large swing doors—'that I want to keep an eye on.'

'Is she in labour?' he asked interestedly.

'Not yet.' She shook her head. 'But that's why I want to keep an eye on her.'

'Whatever you say, Doctor.' He paused, obviously thinking, then offered, 'There's a small place, fairly close by, an old, renovated inn, would that do?'

'Yes, anywhere, as long as it's close by.' Unsure she'd been wise in accepting him, Helen's tone was almost curt. 'I'll need a few minutes. I must call my answering service, get my coat and bag and—'

'Take your time,' he cut in. 'I'll go get my car and wait for you at the main entrance.'

Without waiting for a reply, he strode off down the corridor.

Her teeth nibbling at her lower lip, Helen watched him walk away, an uncomfortable feeling of foreboding stealing over her. She opened her mouth to call him back, tell him she'd changed her mind, then closed it again with a snap. *Don't be ridiculous*, she chided herself scathingly, there is nothing the least bit threatening about this man. He is exactly as he seems. A well-bred, urbane young man interested in the welfare of his sister. That his eyes seemed to have the power to demoralize her she put down to the fact that it had been a long day and that hunger was making her fanciful. Giving herself a mental shake, she walked away quickly.

He was waiting for her, standing beside a pale blue Lincoln Continental, hands thrust into the pockets of a perfectly cut tan cashmere topcoat. As her eyes ran over the luxurious garment Helen realized, with a start, that it was the first time she'd noticed his attire. If asked, she doubted if she could describe what he had on under the coat. Strange, she mused, hurrying towards the car, she usually took note of the total person, so to speak. Indeed, she could describe what Kristeen's parents, her husband, and his parents had been wearing, down to the snakeskin shoes the older Mrs Darren wore on her small feet. Strange.

Preoccupied with her thoughts, Helen was only vaguely aware he'd helped her into the car and slid behind the wheel beside her, when his quiet voice brought her musings to an end.

'Problems?'

'What?' She blinked in confusion, then laughed softly. 'No. No problems. I was just thinking.'

One dark eyebrow went up questioningly and she was

again subjected to that strangely intent blue gaze, then, with a small shrug and a murmured 'Good,' he turned away and set the car in motion.

A nervous, panicky feeling invaded her stomach and Helen turned her head to glance out of the side window, her teeth again punishing her lower lip. *What in the world*, she thought frantically, *is the matter with me?* She caught herself edging closer to the door and sat perfectly still with shock, her thoughts running wild. *Surely I'm not afraid of him?* Her hands went clammy as her stomach gave a small lurch. But that's preposterous, she told herself sternly. Over the last few years she had met, and had been unaffected by, a number of prominent and powerful men, some of whom had been extremely good-looking. What was it about this man? That she would react at all to him would have been curious. But this! This moist-palmed, all-over crawly sensation was mind bending. And to top it all off, he had to be at least five or six years her junior.

'You really are in a brown study.' Once more that deep, quiet voice cut into her thoughts. 'Wondering what your husband will say when he finds out you've had dinner with another man?'

It was a deliberate probe and she knew it. For some reason it irritated her.

'I'm not married, Mr Kirk.' Helen paused, then added bitingly, 'As I suspect you already know, since I wear no rings.'

To her surprise he laughed easily, slanting her a quick, glittering glance.

'No, Doctor, I didn't know, as a lack of rings today is no indication of a woman's marital status.' All amusement was gone, replaced by mild disgust 'Quite a few of the young marrieds I know refuse to adorn their fingers with anything as possessive as a man's ring.'

The knife-edged sarcasm to his tone shocked her

and she stared at him in amazement. What in the world was he attacking her for? Did he think she was lying. The thought that he might brought her chin up in anger.

'I assure you, sir'—she bit heavily on the last word—'I have no so mistreated male hidden away.'

'Temper, temper.' He repeated his chiding admonition of a few hours earlier, then, 'Ah, saved by our arrival at our destination.'

The inn was old, but beautifully renovated. The decor was rustic, the lighting soft, and the fire that blazed in the huge stone fireplace infused the room with a warmth and welcome that went a long way in draining the anger from Helen.

Sipping at a predinner glass of white wine, Helen studied him over the rim of the glass, taking deliberate note of his clothes. His brown herringbone sport coat and opened-necked cream-coloured silk shirt looked casually elegant, as did the way he leaned back lazily in his chair, sipping his own wine. His eyes scanned the room disinterestedly, yet Helen had the feeling that not the smallest detail escaped their perusal. And for some unknown reason he scared the hell out of her.

'Will I pass muster, Doctor?'

Helen felt her cheeks grow warm at the amused taunt. She would have vowed he had not observed her study. Deciding attack was the best form of defence, she gave him a level stare.

'Does it matter, Mr Kirk?' she asked dryly. 'You are a very attractive young man, as I'm sure you know. I'm sorry if I was staring, but I can't believe you give a damn if you pass muster or not.'

The sound of his soft laughter was more potent than the wine. The words that followed the laughter hit her like a blast of sobering cold air.

'Oh, but that's where you're wrong, Doctor. Your

opinion of me is very important. For you see, my lady doctor, I fully intend to rectify the nudity of your left ring finger by encircling it with my wedding ring.'

CHAPTER TWO

STUNNED, speechless, thought and feeling momentarily turned off, Helen sat staring at him while the colour slowly drained from her face.

Marsh stared back at her calmly, his cool blue eyes studying her reaction almost clinically.

She opened her mouth, then closed it again. How did one respond to a statement like that? If he'd issued it flippantly or teasingly, she'd have known exactly what to say, but he had been serious, deadly serious.

Feeling returned with anger that surged through her body and up under the delicate skin that covered her cheeks. Helen gritted her teeth against the hot, uncomfortable feeling.

'Mr Kirk—' she began.

'Yes, ma'am?' Now he was teasing, the light of devilry casting a shimmery gleam on his eyes. Leaning across the table, he caught her hand in his, and when she tried to pull away, his grip tightened, almost painfully.

'If you call me "Mr Kirk" again, in that tone of voice, I swear I'll—The name's Marsh. Got that?'

Too angry to speak Helen nodded, glancing pointedly at the large hand covering her own. When she glanced up, her eyes were as cold as her voice.

'Yes, I've got that, Marsh.' Her voice lowered, but lost none of its brittleness. 'Now if you don't remove your hand, I swear I'll stab you with my salad fork.'

His soft laughter rippled across the table, surrounding her in a sudden, surprising warmth. His fingers tightened, somehow adding to the warmth, then he released her.

'Beautiful,' he murmured. 'My instincts were right. No wonder I fell in love the minute you started snapping at me in Kris's room.'

Staring at him in astonishment, Helen froze in her chair, her eyes wide with disbelief at what she'd heard, disbelief and a touch of fear. Was this man some kind of nut? What had she let herself in for coming out with him? Glancing around the room like a cornered animal, Helen's eyes stopped on the waiter approaching the table with their dinner. Thoughts tumbled chaotically through her mind as she watched the waiter weave around the tables in the crowded room. Should she say she was feeling ill? Ask the waiter to call her a cab, while insisting Marsh stay and have his dinner?

'Relax, love.' Marsh's soft tone cut gently into her thoughts. 'And get that hunted look off your face. I'm not planning to abduct you or harm you in any way.'

Helen's eyes swung from the waiter back to his and caught, held captive by the tenderness she found there. When the waiter stopped at the table, he sat back, his eyes refusing to release hers. The moment the waiter had finished serving and left the table, Marsh leaned towards her again.

'I promise I'll take you directly back to the hospital when we've finished.' That blue gaze remained compellingly steady. 'I also promise my pursuit will be ruthless.' He smiled at the small gasp that Helen couldn't smother, then commanded gently, 'Eat your dinner, you're beginning to look hollow eyed. There is all the time in the world to discuss this later. By the way—' he paused, frowned. 'What the hell is your first name?'

The very abruptness of his tone brought an automatic response from her.

'Helen.'

'Helen,' he repeated softly, his eyes moving slowly

over her·face. She could feel the touch of those eyes, and a tiny shiver trickled down her spine.

'Yes,' he finally murmured. 'I like it. It suits you.' He picked up his fork, held it suspended in midair. 'By the way, Helen, I must warn you. My intentions are strictly honourable.'

Helen was trembling. This conversation, this whole situation, was unreal. She had never seen him before this afternoon, yet there he sat, coolly telling her he intended to marry her. And those eyes! What was it about his eyes that set her pulses racing, caused this tight, breathless feeling in her chest? The room around her seemed to recede into a shrouded fog, the diners' voices grew dim and blurred. For a brief second out of time she was alone with him in that room. She did not know him, and yet it was as if she had known him forever. The mystical thought brought with it a dart of fear, followed by a shaft of excitement.

'Eat your meal before it gets cold, Helen.' His tone was that of a concerned parent, coaxing a peckish child. It was exactly what was needed to break the spell of unreality surrounding her.

The room refocused, the voices took on human quality, and Helen began eating. Slowly, methodically, she made inroads into her food, tasting nothing. He watched her silently until she was almost finished.

'I didn't mean to frighten you, Helen. I only meant to make my position clear.'

The very gentleness of his tone struck a nerve. Who the hell did he think he was? And did he think he was speaking to a toddling child? Or a doddering ancient? The food in her stomach infused steel into her backbone and her head came up with a snap.

'You haven't frightened me in the least,' she lied. 'I've been around a few years, Marsh.' She hesitated, then underlined. 'A few more than you I think, and it will take a little more than a weird proposal of marriage to frighten me.'

'Weird or not, I meant every word.'

She had had enough. She was tired. It had been one very long day.

'If you don't mind, I'd like to go back to the hospital now.'

'Of course.' His sharp eyes contradicted his bland tone, and his following words gave her the eerie feeling he could read her mind. 'You're tired and your day isn't in yet. Let's go.'

As they made their way out of the room he placed a hand lightly at the small of her back. It was an impersonal touch, and yet Helen felt a tingle at the base of her spine that moved slowly, shiveringly up to her hairline. Annoyed, confused by her reaction to his slightest touch, she shrugged his hand away, quickening her step.

They were almost back to the hospital when she remembered the reason she'd gone with him in the first place.

'You said you wanted to talk about your sister.' She glanced at his profile, sharply etched in the glare of the headlights from the oncoming traffic. A good profile; strong, determined, attractive. Trying to ignore her sudden lack of breath, she continued with a false calmness. 'What is it about your sister's condition that bothers you?'

'Not a thing.' The calm reply was directed at the street.

'But you said—'

'I lied.' He shot a mocking glance at her. 'I figured it was the only thing I could say that might get you to go with me, and I had to talk to you alone, tell you.'

Helen felt that strange, disoriented feeling surrounding her again, and she shook her head violently to dispel it. 'You don't even know me,' she whispered hoarsely.

He stopped the car at the hospital's main entrance, then turned to face her.

'I will before too long.' He lifted his hand from the steering wheel to cup her face, draw her to him. His thumb moved caressingly, disturbingly, back and forth across her cheekbone, then slowly to the corner of her mouth. 'Don't look so shattered, love.' His head moved closer, closer, and Helen couldn't tear her eyes away from his mouth. His lips a mere whisper away from hers, he murmured, 'I don't understand it myself, darling. If I believed in reincarnation, I'd believe we have been lovers for a long, long time. I don't know. Hell, I don't even care. But I do know this. While I stood waiting for you in that hall, I knew I loved you and that you were mine.'

Stunned, Helen's eyes widened as he spoke those incredible words, one thought screaming through her mind: *I've got to get out of this car*. His eyes held hers, motionless, breathless. His breath was warm against her face, the smell of the wine he'd had with dinner, mingled with the musky scent of his cologne, was intoxicating. When he finished speaking, she moistened parched lips, gave a strangled 'No.'

Too late. His mouth touched hers in a kiss so sweet, so tender, it was almost reverent in its gentleness. It destroyed her resistance and with a sigh she went limp inside the arms that were suddenly around her, hard and possessive. His lips left hers, moved searingly over her cheek, ruffled the hair at her temple.

'You're trembling,' he said softly into her ear. 'I know how you feel. I feel it too. Oh, God, Helen, I don't know what's happening. I've never felt like this before in my life.'

Unsure, frightened, not at all the cool, self-contained

woman she knew herself to be, Helen stirred, tried to move away from him.

'I—I must go. I have a patient.'

'No.' His arms tightened. 'Not yet.'

His mouth sought hers again, but she twisted her head, began to struggle. The word 'patient' had pierced the curtain of mistiness that had covered her mind, tore the veil of enchantment that had encircled her.

'Let me go, Marsh.' Her voice was steady, controlled, the moment of madness had passed. 'I want to go in . . . now.'

Marsh sighed deeply but loosened his arms, then reached across her to open the door. 'Okay, love, go to work.' Dipping his head quickly, he gave her a fast, hard kiss. 'I'll call you tomorrow.'

'No. Marsh, I don't—'

A long finger came up to touch her lips, silencing her. 'I'll call you tomorrow. Now go.'

She went. Out of the car, up the steps, through the door, and across the lobby, practically at a run.

Waiting for the elevator, Helen glanced at her watch, then looked closer. Nine forty-five? That couldn't be the correct time! She swung around and her eyes flew to the large wall clock in the lobby. Nine forty-six. How could that be? The elevator doors slid back silently, and a frown marring her smooth brow, Helen stepped inside. She had been gone less than three hours, and yet it seemed such a long time since she'd left the hospital. Hours. Days. Half a lifetime.

A cold shudder shook her body as inside her head his voice whispered over and over again, 'I don't know how. Hell, I don't even care. I knew I loved you and that you were mine.'

The words jarred in her mind, tore at her nerves, like the needle caught on a badly scarred record. Nails digging into her palms, Helen stared, sightlessly, as the doors slid open at her floor. The doors whooshed softly as they came together and the car gave a mild lurch before it began to move up again. The lurch, mild as it had been, startled Helen back to awareness. Looking up at the floor indicator, she grimaced in self-disgust and stretched her hand out to touch the button of her floor number again. *What a fool you are*, she told herself bleakly. *You must need a vacation very badly*. The doors slid open once more and this time she stepped out quickly, walked down the hall with a determined pace.

Kathy was leaving Jolene's room as Helen crossed the floor towards it.

'Hang in there, Jo, you're doing fine.' The nurse spoke over her shoulder, then turning, she flashed a smile at Helen. 'That little lady means business, Doctor. She went into labour not long after you left and she's gone from one stage to the other like that.' Raising her hand, she snapped her fingers three times in succession. 'I just might have this baby before I go off duty, after all.' She grinned.

Helen grinned back, a sense of normalcy returning with the easy flippancy of Kathy's tone. Marshall Kirk and the bizarre events of the last few hours were pushed to the back of her mind as Helen went into Jolene's room.

Several hours later Helen stood in another elevator, her fingers idly playing with the keys in her hand. Jolene's son, born less than an hour before, had weighed in at seven pounds two ounces, a lusty male, squalling his resentment of the whole procedure. Jolene was doing fine, sleepily content now that her fears were unrealised. A tender smile curved Helen's lips as she remembered the bubbling joy young Tim Johnson had displayed on hearing her news.

The car stopped at the sixth floor and Helen stepped out and walked slowly along the hall to her apartment at

the front of the building, a sudden thought wiping the
smile from her lips. Tim Johnson had seemed so very
young to her, and yet he could not be more than a few
years younger than Marshall Kirk!

Hand none too steady, Helen unlocked her door,
stepped inside, then leaned back against the smooth
panels in sudden weariness. Memories of the few hours
she'd spent with him flooded her mind, while a small
shiver raced down her spine. What had possessed him to
say what he had to her? Closing her eyes, she could
almost hear his softly murmured words, feel his warm
breath against her skin. Remembering the way she'd
melted against him, her breath caught painfully in her
throat. What had possessed her?

Opening her eyes, Helen pushed herself away from
the door, hung her coat in the closet just inside the door;
then walked unerringly through the dark living room to
the small hallway that led to her bedroom. A flick of a
switch cast a soft glow on the muted green and blue
decor in the room, lent a sheen to the expensive dark
wood furniture. Moving slowly, Helen sat down on the
vanity bench, unzipped, then tugged the boots from her
feet. Uncharacteristically she tossed the boots in the
direction of her closet, then lifted her hands to remove
the pins that held her hair in a neat coil. Freed, her
honey-gold mane flowed rich and full to her shoulders,
and Helen's fingers pushed through it to massage the
scalp at the back of her head, gasping softly as the same
tingling she'd experienced earlier that evening spread up
her neck and under her fingers.

Stop it, she told herself harshly. *Stop thinking about
him. He's a young man probably looking for a diversion,
and an older woman is a challenge.* Her eyes shifted to
the mirror, momentarily studying her reflection. The
makeup she had carefully applied that morning, and
touched up before going to dinner, had worn off, leaving

exposed her clear skin, now pale and somewhat taut, with tiny lines of strain at the corners of her eyes and mouth.

It was a beautiful face and Helen knew it. She would be a fool not to know it and she had never been that. The honey fairness, the classic bone structure, the full soft mouth were gifts from her mother. Her height, her clear hazel eyes, and her determination were gifts from her father. Helen recognised and accepted those gifts with gratitude.

Now staring into those hazel eyes, Helen silently told her reflection, *he'll find no challenge here*. She had no intentions of getting involved with any men, let alone a younger one.

The mirrored eyes seemed to mock her knowingly. There was an attraction between them, she'd be a fool to deny that. The antagonism she'd felt on first sight should have warned her. Yet, she had never experienced anything like that before. How could she have known?

There was very little Helen didn't know about sex, except the actual participation in it. And that, she thought, biting her lip, was the most important part. What she had garnered from textbooks and lectures hardly qualified her as an expert. She knew what happened and the correct terms to define it, but without any real experience she was, in essence, abysmally ignorant.

Without conscious thought Helen brushed her hair and prepared for bed, her mind refusing to let go of the subject. She had come close, very close, to that real experience but she had backed away, almost at the last moment. And because of that long-ago fiasco she was still, unbelievable as it seemed, even to her sometimes, a virgin at thirty-five.

Slipping into bed, Helen lay still, eyes closed, wishing she'd not allowed her thoughts to stray in the direction they had. If she was still innocent, there had to be a reason, and her wandering thoughts had led to that reason. With a soft sigh of protest Helen saw a picture of a handsome, curly haired, laughing young man. Carl Engle, the man she had been engaged to while still in college.

Moving restlessly, she turned onto her side, trying to escape the memories crowding in on her.

She had been in love as only the very young can be, misty-eyed, seeing only perfection in the chosen one. They had seemed perfectly matched. They had shared the same interests in books, plays, music, movies, sports, and, most importantly, medicine. They had had wonderful times together; even studying had been fun, as long as they studied together. She had been seeing him exclusively for some months when he asked her to marry him and she had accepted him with only one condition: they would not marry until she received her M.D. Carl, who was planning on specialising in paediatrics, had agreed with a laughing 'Of course. We'll make a great team. You'll deliver them and I'll take over from there.'

Helen groaned and rolled onto her other side, her eyes tightly shut, as if trying to shut out the past. She was so tired, why did she have to think of Carl tonight? Marshall Kirk's face replaced Carl's in her mind and with another groan she gave up. Pushing the covers back, she left the bed, slipped into her robe, lit a cigarette, and walked to the large square window in the wall that ran parallel to her bed. Drawing deeply on her cigarette, she stared at the dark streets six floors below, lit, at this late hour, only occasionally by the headlights of a passing car. Glancing up, her eyes scanned the sky, following the blinking lights of a passing Jet Liner. The night was cold and clear, the stars very bright, seemingly very close. A shudder rippled through Helen's body and she drew jerkily on the cigarette. The stars had seemed very bright and close on that other night too.

She and Carl had been engaged six months and she was very happy, if vaguely discontent. Knowing what the discontent stemmed from was little consolation. Helen had been carefully brought up by loving, protective parents whose views on sex were rigid to the point of puritanical. She had been gently, but firmly, taught that a girl 'saves herself' for her wedding night. The nights came, more often as the months went by, that Carl's love-making became heated and his soft voice cajoled her coaxingly to give in. She had been tempted, filled with the longing to belong to him completely, to be part of him. But her parents had done their job well, and she had stopped him before reaching the no-turning point. In consequence she was left with mingled feelings of guilt and frustration. Guilt for having the perfectly normal urges that seared through her body, frustration at having to deny those urges.

That was the emotional situation on, what Helen had always thought of since, *that night*. They had driven over into Jersey to join friends at a beer and pizza bar to celebrate the end of first term. It had been a fun evening, with lots of laughter, as they solved the world's problems, decided who would win the up-coming Oscars, and discussed the merits of the latest rock groups. By the time the party broke up, Carl was mellow with beer and feeling very friendly. Instead of heading straight for the Ben Franklin Bridge to Philly he found a country road and parked the car off the side of the road under the trees.

Another shudder, stronger this time, shook Helen's slim frame and her arms came up to hug herself, her nails digging into the soft flesh of her upper arms. To this day every word, every act that had occurred in that car that night, was as clear in her mind as it had been then.

'Why are we stopping?' she had asked, glancing out the window apprehensively. The area was very dark and desolate, and the idea of being stranded there scared her. 'Is there something wrong with the car?'

Laughing softly, Carl had turned to her, pulled her into his arms. 'No, honey, there's nothing wrong with the car. I just couldn't wait to kiss you.' His arms loosened, hands moving between them to undo the buttons on her coat. When the buttons were free he pushed the coat open, down, and off her shoulders, tugging it off.

'Carl!' she'd cried. 'I'm cold.'

The coat was tossed behind him as he slid from under the steering wheel, pushing her along the seat towards the door. 'You won't be for long. I'm gonna keep you warm.' His jacket followed hers, then his arms were around her again, jerking her against him with such force, it knocked the breath from her body.

'Carl, what—'

She got no further for his mouth crashed onto hers, jolting her head back with the impact. His lips were moist and urgent, his tongue an assault, and his hand, moving roughly over her back, slid between them to grasp painfully at her breast.

Shocked and angry at his rough handling, Helen had tried to twist away, her hand pushing at his shoulders. Her resistance seemed to inflame him and his arm slid around her again, crushed her against him. His lips slipped wetly from hers, slid slowly down the side of her neck.

'Come into the backseat with me.'

His slurred words caused the first twinge of fear. It was not an invitation. It was an order.

'Carl, you know how I feel about that. I want—'

She gasped in shock and pain as his teeth ground together on the soft skin at the curve of her neck.

'Carl! Stop you're hurti—Oh!'

She hadn't seen his hand move, only felt the pain as his palm hit her cheek. His mouth caught hers again, grinding her lips against her teeth. Near panic, blinded by tears, Helen struggled, pushing against him frantically. Suddenly she was free as, pulling away from her, he slid back across the seat, cursing as he flung her coat and his jacket onto the floor, out of his way. He pushed his door open, then slammed it so hard behind him that the car rocked.

Sitting huddled and trembling on the seat, tears running down her face, Helen had thought he'd gone to cool off and she jumped when she heard him yank open the backseat door behind her. The door next to her was flung open, and with a grated 'Get out,' he reached in, grabbed her arm, and dragged her out of the car and around the backseat door. 'Get in,' he grated.

Nearly hysterical, Helen hit out at him, screaming, 'No, I won't get in. I want you to take me home, now. I—'

'Damn you, get in.'

This time it was his fist that hit her face, and barely conscious, Helen didn't even feel her shins scrape against the side of the car or her head strike the opposite armrest when he shoved her in and onto the seat. The next instant his body was on hers, pressing her back against the upholstery, one hand moving up under her sweater to clutch her breast, the other sliding up her leg under her skirt.

Her face, her whole head, throbbed with pain and she couldn't seem to focus her eyes. She felt groggy and sick to her stomach and still she fought him wildly, silently.

'It's your own fault, Helen. You and your damned wait-till-the-wedding-night bit. Well, I can't wait anymore, and I won't.'

His mouth crushed hers and his larger body, pressing

down on hers, subdued her struggles, cut off her air. Consciousness slipping away from her, Helen hadn't heard the car stop behind them, but she did hear the sharp rap against the window, did hear the not-unpleasant voice of the patrolman when he called, 'Break it up, kids. You're not allowed to park here.' Not waiting for a response, he strolled back to the patrol car.

Jerking away from her, Carl stared out the back window, cursing softly at the retreating, straight back. Then, turning, he looped his legs over the back of the front seat and pushed himself up and over. Glancing in the rearview mirror at the patrol car, obviously waiting for him to move, he cursed again, then snarled, 'Well, are you coming up or not?'

Curled on the backseat, swallowing hard against the sobs that tore at her throat, Helen didn't bother to answer him. He waited a moment, cursed again, shrugged into his jacket, threw hers over the seat to her, then reached out to slam the door closed with a snapped 'Will you shut the damned door?'

Moving slowly, Helen straightened and closed the back door. Then, pulling her coat around her shoulders, she rested her pounding head back against the seat and closed her eyes, gulping down the nausea rising from her churning stomach. They were almost back to her dormitory before Carl broke the strained silence.

'I'm sorry I hit you, Helen,' he began softly, then his tone hardened. 'But a man can take just so much. We're going to be married anyway, so what the hell difference does it make if we go to bed together now? No normal man could be expected to wait years to make love to his girl.'

Again Helen didn't respond and she was ready when he stopped the car in front of her dorm. Without speaking, she pushed open the door, jumped out, threw his ring onto the front seat, and ran up the walk to the safety of the dorm, ignoring his call to wait.

Now, over ten years later, Helen stood staring out her bedroom window at a night very much like that other night, her face cold and uncompromising. Sighing deeply, she turned from the window, walked to the nightstand by the bed, shook another cigarette from the pack, and lit it, her eyes pensive.

Over the years she had gone out with many men, had proposals from several and a few propositions, but something inside seemed frozen and she could not respond to any of them. Intellectually she knew that all men did not become brutal when frustrated, but emotionally she could not handle a close relationship, and when a light goodnight kiss began to deepen into something more or a male hand began to wander, she withdrew coldly, her manner shutting the man out as effectively as if she'd closed a door between them.

She had never been able to control her withdrawal, nor had she tried very hard to control it. In her opinion any woman who'd put herself in the position of receiving that kind of punishment twice was a fool.

Moving around the room restlessly, Helen tried to figure out what had happened to her built-in warning alarm that evening. Not only had she relaxed in Marshall Kirk's arms, she had, if only for a moment, returned his kiss. And the fluttering breathlessness that gripped her when he turned that steady blue gaze on her confounded her completely. *What the hell*, she derided herself, *got into you?* Strangely her mind shied away from delving too deeply for answers, and shaking her head sharply, she told herself to forget him. Which, of course, brought a picture of him to her mind.

Grimacing in self-derision, Helen dragged harshly on her cigarette, then crushed it out in the ashtray. Glancing at the clock, she groaned aloud. It was almost four and her alarm would ring at seven, she had to get some sleep.

As she slid between the sheets and drew the blanket around her shoulders, Marsh's murmured words taunted her mind. 'I knew I loved you and that you were mine.'

'Not on your young life, Kirk,' she whispered aloud, then closed her eyes and drifted into sleep.

CHAPTER THREE

'I DON'T know what it is, Doctor.' Alice's voice was heavy with exasperation. 'But I think everybody has a bad case of the Januaries.'

Including me, Helen thought, a small smile tugging at her lips at the nurse's caustic tone.

'What now?' she sighed, cradling the phone against her shoulder as she lit a cigarette. It was her first one since lunchtime, and that had been over four hours ago. As usual for a Thursday the office had been full all day and that, plus her lack of sleep the night before, was beginning to tell on her. By the tone of her voice Helen suspected Alice was also beginning to feel a little hassled.

'There is a patient in the other examining room, there are four more still in the waiting room, and I have a Mr Kirk on the line who insists on speaking to you. I've told him you are very busy, but—'

'It's all right,' she cut in wearily. 'I'll talk to him.'

There was a short, somewhat shocked, paused and then a click.

'What can I do for you Mr Kirk?' she asked coolly.

Soft laughter skimmed through the wire to tickle her ear.

'Do you want the proper answer or the truth?'

'I'm keeping a patient waiting.' Helen's tone plunged five degrees.

'Where have I heard that before?' he wondered aloud, then, 'okay, I'll be brief. What time should I pick you up for dinner, and where?'

Caught off guard by his casual assumption that she'd

go with him, Helen searched for words. 'Mr Kirk,' she began after several long seconds.

'Yes, darling?' It was a smooth warning Helen couldn't ignore.

'Marsh.' She bit the name out through clenched teeth.

'That's better,' he crooned.

'Marsh,' she repeated coldly. 'I do not have time to play telephone games. I had very little sleep last night and a very busy day today *and* I won't be through here for another hour and a half. I am tired and I don't feel like going out to dinner.'

'Okay,' he replied easily. 'Come right to my place when you leave the office and we'll eat in.'

This man had a positive talent for striking her speechless.

'I certainly will not come to your place,' she finally snapped.

'I'm inviting you for dinner, Helen.' The amusement in his voice made her feel very young and naive. 'Not for a long, illicit weekend.'

'I don't—'

'Good Lord, Helen,' he cut in briskly, all amusement gone. 'You're not afraid of me, are you?'

'No, of course not, but—'

'No, of course not,' Marsh mimicked. 'I'll expect you in about two hours.' He rattled off an address, then his tone went low with warning. 'And if you're more than fifteen minutes late, I'll come looking for you.'

The line went dead before she could answer him, and Helen stared at the receiver, anger, mixed with a flutter in her stomach she refused to acknowledge, bringing a twinge of pink to her pale cheeks. Of all the arrogant gall, she fumed. Just who in the hell did he think he was anyway? Well, he could go whistle up his hallway. She had no intention of going to his place for dinner, or anything else.

The following hour and fifteen minutes seemed to fly by and Helen caught herself glancing at her watch more and more frequently. By the time she ushered her last patient out of her office, Helen was having a hard time hiding her nervousness. Would he really carry out his threat to come looking for her? Of course he wouldn't, she told herself bracingly. Of course he would, her self chided positively.

Undecided, Helen fidgeted, moving things around on her desk aimlessly. Alice came to the door to say good-night, a puzzled expression on her face at Helen's unusual behaviour. Her mind playing a tug of war with 'to go or not to go,' Helen didn't notice Alice's concerned look.

The second hand on her desk clock seemed to be sweeping the minutes away in less than thirty seconds each. Finally, with barely enough time left to reach his apartment within the time limit he'd set, Helen dashed into the changing room that connected her two examining rooms. Fingers trembling, she smoothed her hair, tucked a few loose tendrils into the neat coil, then did a quick repair job on her makeup.

Tension kept Helen's fingers curled tightly around the steering wheel as she inched her way through the early evening traffic, her eyes darting to her watch at every stop sign and red light. The address Marsh had given her was a large, fairly new condominium just outside the city limits, with a spacious parking area off to one side.

A security guard sat at a counterlike desk just inside the wide glass entrance doors, and the first thing Helen noticed was the clock that sat on the desktop next to a registration book. She was two minutes inside his time limit. She gave her name and the security guard said politely, 'Oh, yes, Dr Cassidy, Mr Kirk called down that he was expecting you. You may go right up. Apartment eight-oh-two to the left of the elevator.'

He indicated the elevator across the foyer behind him, then bent to write something in the register. *Probably my name and the time of arrival*, Helen mused as she crossed the dark red-carpeted floor.

A few seconds later, standing before the door marked 802, Helen drew a deep breath, held it, and touched her finger to the lighted doorbell button. The door was opened almost immediately, convincing her that the guard had announced her arrival, and once again she was held motionless in a hypnotic blue gaze.

'Perfect timing,' Marsh murmured, pulling the door wide as he stepped back. 'I had just decided to give you a few more minutes before going on the hunt.' His mouth curving into a smile, he taunted, 'Are you coming in or are you going to bolt for the exit?'

Giving a good imitation of a careless shrug, Helen exhaled slowly, broke the hold of his eyes, and stepped inside. Every nerve in her body seemed to jump when the door clicked shut behind her and hum like live electrical wires when she felt his hands on her shoulders.

'I'll take your coat.'

His soft voice, close to her ear, turned a mundane statement into a caress, and Helen bit down hard on her lip to try and still the shakiness of her fingers fumbling at her coat buttons.

When he turned away to hang up her coat, Helen's eyes swept the oversize living room, glimpsed the dining room behind an intricately worked wrought-iron room divider. The colours in the room merged and blurred before her eyes as she was spun around and into his arms.

'I thought you'd never get here.'

Marsh's eyes had a dark, smouldering look and his voice was a rasp from deep in his throat.

Helen's arms came up between them, her hands pushing ineffectively against his shoulders.

'Marsh—'

His head swooped low and his mouth caught her parted lips, silencing her protests. His lips were hard with the demand for her submission, his kiss possessive, consuming.

Feeling reason beginning to slip away, Helen's mind sent an order to her hands to pull his head away. Her hands lifted, her fingers slid into his hair, but somewhere along the line the order became garbled and instead of tugging at his hair, her hands grasped his head, drawing him closer. At once his arms tightened, moulded her against the long, taut length of his body. His mouth searched hers hungrily, making her senses swim crazily and igniting a spark that quickly leaped into a searing flame that danced wildly from her lips to her toes. Teetering on the edge of surrender, Helen murmured a soft protest when his mouth left hers. Leaving a trail of fire, his lips moved slowly over her cheek. His teeth, nibbling at her lobe, sent a shaft of alarm through her, and reason scuttled back where it belonged. Her hands dropped onto his shoulders and pushed, using all the strength she possessed.

'Marsh, stop, I've got to call my service.'

'Later,' he growled against the side of her neck. 'Helen, I've waited all last night and all day today to hold you like this. You can call your service later.'

His lips found, caressed, the hollow at the base of her throat, and Helen, her breathing growing shallow and uneven, knew that if she didn't put some distance between them her will would turn to water. She pleaded, 'Marsh, please. I must let them know where I can be reached. Let me go, please.'

For a long moment she thought he was going to disregard her plea, then, with a low moan, his arms dropped and he stepped back, a rueful smile curving his mouth.

'Be my guest.'

He waved his hand negligently at the living room, and turning, Helen's eyes sought, then found, the phone resting on an octagonal-shaped cabinet table at the end of a long sofa, which was covered in a gold furry material.

On legs she was none too sure would support her, Helen made her way to the phone, stumbling a little when she caught her boot heel in the deep plush of the chocolate-brown carpet.

'Careful, love.'

The softly spoken caution threatened to sap the remaining strength from her legs, and Helen sank onto the corner of the sofa with a soft sigh of relief. As she punched out the services number on the push buttons, she heard Marsh walk across the room and glanced up to see him disappear into the dining room.

'Come into the dining room.'

His call, obviously from the kitchen, came as she replaced the receiver, and drawing a steadying breath, Helen rose and walked into the room just as he emerged from an opposite door.

'I hope you like Chinese food.' He grinned easily. 'I stopped and picked it up on my way home.'

He held a long-stemmed glass, three quarters full of white wine, in each hand and he moved with such casual ease, Helen felt a hot flash of anger. What had happened to all the tension that had tautened his entire body only a few minutes ago? She felt on the point of collapse, while he looked relaxed and unaffected. Could he flick his emotions on and off like a light switch?

'Are you going to take the wine?' His chiding tone made her aware of the glass he was holding out to her. 'Or are you going to scowl at it all night?'

Embarrassed now, not only by her present vagueness but by her response and subsequent reaction to his advance, she lifted her eyes and stared into his with a steadiness she was far from feeling.

'Is white the correct wine for Chinese food?' Her attempt at lightness didn't fall too short of the mark.

'Who cares?' His shoulders lifted eloquently. 'I drink what I like with whatever I choose to eat.' His eyes glittered as he placed the glass into her hand. 'I please myself and never worry about what others deem correct.'

Positive his last remark held a double meaning, also positive she would not be able to eat a thing, Helen allowed Marsh to seat her at the table. When he went back into the kitchen for the food, she sipped tentatively at her wine, identified it as an excellent Chenin Blanc, then drank some more in an effort to relax the tightness in her throat.

Marsh hadn't forgotten a thing. He began talking the minute they'd started on their wonton soup and kept up a steady flow of light conversation right through the chicken chow mein, fried rice, and shrimp egg rolls. By the time she bit into her almond cookie, Helen had not only relaxed, she found herself laughing delightedly as he recounted the Christmas Day antics of a friend's youngster.

'Give me a minute to clear the table and stack the dishwasher, then we can have our coffee in the living room,' Marsh said when the last cookie crumb had disappeared. 'Or would you prefer more wine?'

'No, thank you.' Helen shook her head emphatically. 'I've had more than enough. But I would love some coffee and I'll help you with the cleaning up.'

They made fast work of the table and dishes, then Helen preceded him into the living room, sat on the sofa, and watched as he placed a tray with the coffee things on the low coffee table in front of him, then turned and walked to the stereo unit along the wall next to the dining room entrance. He selected a long-playing record from a large, solidly packed record cabinet, put it on the machine, then came back to her and, to her amazement, instead of seating himself in the opposite chair or on the sofa beside her, he dropped onto the floor, stretched his long legs out, and rested his back against the cushion, next to her legs.

The opening strains of Tchaikovsky's *Romeo and Juliet* filled the room as she poured the coffee, handed him his, then sat back, her eyes following the direction of his to the flickering coils of a conal-shaped electric fireplace set in the wall between two large drapery-covered windows.

They sat in listening silence, both of them held in quiet captivity to the composer's genius. Even when Marsh held up his cup for a refill, she filled the cup and added more to her own without either uttering a murmur. When he finished his coffee, he placed the cup on the tray, shifted his shoulders, and rested his head against her thigh.

Replete with food, heavy lidded from lack of sleep the night before, Helen let her head drop back against the sofa and closed her eyes, the hauntingly beautiful music moving through her body like a living thing. Unaware of her actions, her hand dropped idly to his head, slim fingers slid slowly through the silken strands of his hair.

Trembling, her emotions almost painfully in tune with the music's throbbing finale, it seemed the most natural thing in the world when his fingers circled her wrist, drew her hand across his face to his mouth. His lips, moving sensuously on her palm, sent a spreading warmth up her arm, increasing the trembling, robbing her of breath.

'Marsh.'

Her soft involuntary gasp set him in motion. Grasping her wrist, he levered himself up and onto the sofa beside her, drawing her arm around his neck as his head moved towards hers. His free hand caught her chin, tilted her head back, ready for his mouth. His kiss was the exact opposite of the night before. His lips, hard and demanding, forced hers apart, took arrogant possession of her mouth with driving urgency. His hands moved between them to expertly dispatch the buttons of her shirt. A sensation strangely like déjà vu flashed through her. It was gone in a moment, replaced by the new, exciting sensations his hands, sliding around her waist, sent shivering through her body.

Holding her firmly, he turned her, lowered her slowly to the soft cushions, and without knowing quite how he'd managed it, she felt his long length stretched out partly beside, partly on top of her.

His mouth released hers, went to the hollow at the base of her throat, his lips, the tip of his tongue, teasing a soft moan from her constricted throat.

'Marsh, you must stop. I'm so sleepy. I have to go home, get to bed.. Oh, Marsh—'

His lips had moved down, in a fiery straight line, to explore the shadowed hollow between her breasts.

'You don't have to go anywhere.' His warm breath tingled tantalizingly over her skin as his mouth moved back to hover over hers. 'Your service knows where to reach you. If you're that sleepy, you can sleep here, with me.'

'No, I—' His lips touched hers lightly, fleetingly. 'I can't stay here.' Her lower lip was caught between his. 'It's—it's out of the question.' His teeth nibbled gently at the sensitive inner ridge of her lip. Her voice sank to a low cry. 'Oh, Marsh, kiss me.'

His mouth crushed hers, causing a shudder to ripple along the length of her body. The flick of his tongue against her teeth drove her hands to his chest, trembling fingers fighting his shirt buttons. When her palms slid over his hair-roughened skin, he lifted his head, groaned, 'Stay with me, Helen. Sleep with me. Let me show you what you do to me.'

'I can't—I—what are you doing?'

He was on his feet, lifting her in his arms. Turning, he carried her across the room, through a doorway. 'You said you wanted to go to bed.' He kicked the door closed, walked to the bed, then stood her on her feet in front of him.

'Not here!' Her hands were drawn back to his chest as if magnetized. 'Marsh, I can't stay here. Stop that!'

Disregarding her order, his fingers continued to tug the pins from her hair. When her hair was free of its confining coil, his hands dropped to her shoulders. With a minimum of effort her shirt was removed, dropped carelessly onto the floor. 'Marsh, don't,' she pleaded softly. 'I want to go home.'

Again that odd flash of déjà vu struck her. In confusion she wondered what had caused it, then her thoughts became blurred as Marsh's lips found a sensitive spot behind her ear.

'You're so beautiful, Helen.' Her legs went weak at his low tone, the enticing movement of his lips on her skin. 'Stay with me.' His hands slid smoothly over her back. His fingers flipped open her bra with easy expertise. The lacy wisp of material landed on top of her shirt. 'I want you so desperately.' His hands slid around her rib cage.

'Marsh, no!'

His mouth silenced her weak protest at the same moment as his hands moved up and over the full mounds of her aching breasts. Reason fled and with a soft sigh she wound her arms around his neck, clinging as he slowly lowered her onto the bed. His mouth devoured hers, his tongue teased hers. Her skirt was twisted around her hips, and one hand deserted a hard-tipped mound to caress her nylon-clad thigh.

Moaning softly, barely aware of what she was doing, her hands came up to clasp his head, fingers digging into his hair ruthlessly to pull him closer, wanting more and more of his mouth.

She heard him groan before he moved over her, his solid weight pushing her into the firm mattress. Suddenly she froze. The feeling of déjà vu gripped her and she was being pressed against a cold car seat. Carl's face rose before her, filling her mind with fear. Tearing at his hair, she forced his mouth from hers with a hoarse cry.

'Damn you, stop it.'

Marsh jerked away from her as if he'd been shot.

'Helen, what is it? Did I hurt you?'

Shaking with remembered panic, she didn't hear the words. All that registered was that the voice was male, and it terrified her. Cringing away from him, she brought her forearm up across her face, fingers spread to ward off a blow. The voice that whispered through her lips belonged to a younger woman.

'Don't hit me again, please.'

Marsh froze, staring at her in disbelief.

'Hit you? Helen, what the hell—'

'Carl, please don't.' She was sobbing now. 'Please.'

At the sound of the other man's name. Marsh's face went rigid, lids narrowing over eyes ice-blue with fury.

'He hit you?' He gritted. 'This . . . Carl . . . he dared to hit you?' His tone went low with menace. 'If I ever find him, I'll kill him.'

His cold tone, the words that were not a boast or even a threat, but a statement in the absolute, broke the hold of memory gripping Helen's mind. The back of her hand slid down to cover her mouth.

'Oh, God, Marsh.' Her eyes went wide to stare into his. 'It was so real, so horribly real. It was all happening again.'

Sitting up fully, he grasped her shoulders, pulled her

up, over his legs. Cradling her in his arms like a child, he asked, 'When did it happen?'

Closing her eyes, she sighed wearily, 'Long ago. So very long ago, and yet it seemed so real just now, as if it were all happening again.' A shudder tore through her body, and his arms tightened protectively. She buried her face in the wiry mat of curls on his chest, her wet tears making a few strands glisten.

'He raped you?'

The words came softly from his lips, but Helen heard the tone that spoke of tightly controlled rage.

'No. No.' She shook her head, her forehead rubbing against his chest.

'A—a patrol car stopped. The patrolman told him he'd have to move along.'

Helen felt the shiver that slithered through his tough body, heard the sigh that escaped his lips. His arms tightened still more.

'You called to the cop for help?'

'No.' Silent tears slid down her cheeks. 'You don't understand, Marsh, I was engaged to him.' She shivered. 'I thought I wanted to spend the rest of my life with him.'

'Don't cry, love.' His fingers brushed at her wet cheeks, smoothed the hair back from her temples. 'You've been afraid ever since?'

'I guess so.' She gave a small shrug.

'This has happened before, when you've been with other men?' He paused, then added stiffly, 'Or is it me that repels you?'

'It has never happened before because I've never been with any other men. I don't know—'

'What?'

He went completely still. After several seconds Helen lifted her head to see his face. The face he turned to her was one of total astonishment.

'You have never been—?' He broke off, his voice mirroring his expression. 'Helen, are you still a—'

'Yes.' Helen rushed before he could say the word. 'Yes, yes. There has never been anyone.'

'Well, I will be damned.' He murmured softly. 'I've changed my mind.' He bent his head, kissed her lightly, a small smile tugging at his lips. 'I'm not going to kill him. I'm going to thank him for saving you for me.'

'He didn't save me for you or anyone else,' Helen snapped. 'I lost my head tonight but it won't happen again.'

His hand caught her face, drew it close to his.

'Not for a little while, maybe. I'm going to give you time to get to know me. I'm going to get to know you. But it will happen again. Nothing can stop it. I told you you are mine. Nothing you do can change it. A little while ago, before the memories caught you, you were mine. We're going to be fantastic together.'

He released her abruptly and stood up. 'But not tonight. Right now I'm going to get the hell out of here so you can get dressed. Then I'm going to take you home.' Bending swiftly, he kissed the tip of each full breast, then brought his lips to her mouth. 'You have a beautiful body,' he whispered between short, hard kisses. 'I love it and I love you. You may not be ready to face it yet, but you love me too.'

Laughing softly at her outraged gasp, he strode across the room, bathing the room in light by the flick of a switch as he went through the doorway.

The moment the door closed, Helen jumped off the bed. She was wide awake, all her earlier sleepiness banished by the events of the last hour. Moving slowly, she tried to explain away the strange experience, make some logic of it in her own mind. What she'd told Marsh was true; nothing like it had ever happened to her before. She'd had frightening nightmares for some months after the incident, but they had eventually faded. During the last few years she'd rarely thought about it, and when she did, the memory was triggered by odd, unrelated incidents. Even meeting Carl, which she did occasionally, had not disturbed her. Except, her reasoning qualified, that very first time, and she had come away from that meeting with her head high, her poise and cool composure intact.

Helen used the bathroom that was off his bedroom, absently admiring the masculine-looking marbled black and white tile, the large snow-white bathsheets. The long glass shelf under the medicine cabinet held just three items: his shaving cream, his aftershave, and the cologne that, on his skin, had the power to make her senses swim.

Fully aware of her surroundings now, Helen went back into the bedroom, her eyes making a cool survey. The bed, which she'd only seen in semidarkness before, was king-size and, right now, very rumpled. Like the bathroom, Marsh's bedroom reflected the man. Totally masculine, with an understated core of warmth.

Agitated at herself for her softened attitude towards him, Helen tossed back her hair impatiently. Within minutes she slipped into her bra and shirt, then on hands and knees she retrieved most of the hairpins he'd dropped carelessly to the floor.

Rising to her feet, she raked her fingers through her tangled hair. Wincing at the twinge of pain on her scalp, she walked to the door, pulled it open and called irritably, 'Marsh, will you hand me my handbag, please? I need my hairbrush.'

Tapping her foot impatiently, Helen watched him scoop her bag off the floor beside the sofa, then saunter to her, a smile curving his lips at her disgruntled expression. His eyes slid over her slowly, thoroughly, before coming back to study her face, her hair.

'I don't know why you want your brush,' he teased, his eyes glinting with devilry. 'You look ravishing with your hair all wild around your face.' He paused, head tilted to the side, considering before adding softly, 'Or is the correct word "ravished"?'

Giving him a sour look, Helen snatched the bag from his hand, rummaged in it for the brush, then, tossing the bag onto the bed, she turned her back to him and walked to stand in front of the large mirror above the double dresser.

His reflection told her that his eyes followed her every move and, made nervous by his perusal, she pulled the brush through her knotted mane with unnecessary force. Tears sprang to her eyes from the self-inflicted pain. Pausing in midstroke, she blinked her lids rapidly to clear her vision and thus missed the reflection beside her own growing larger. The sound of his voice close behind her made her jump.

'What are you punishing yourself for, love?' His fingers plucked the brush from her hand. 'Nothing happened here tonight that shouldn't have happened long ago.' Very slowly, very gently, he drew the brush through her hair. 'Don't misunderstand. I am, egotistically, very happy that it did not. You are mine and the thought that you have belonged, however briefly, to another—or several other—men has been tearing my guts apart since I left you at the hospital last night.'

The brush was tossed onto the dresser, and with a shiver she felt his hand draw aside her now-smooth and shining mane, felt his lips caress the sensitive skin on the back of her neck. The shiver increasing in intensity, she heard him draw deeply the scent of her into his lungs, felt the delicious tingle of his breath as he exhaled slowly.

'I'm nearly out of my mind with love for you, Helen. And I want you so badly, I can taste it. But I can wait until my lovemaking doesn't activate the ugly memories.

Until I hear, from your own lips, that you want me every bit as badly as I want you. But, dear God, love, I hope the waiting period is a short one.'

As he spoke he turned her around, into his arms, his intense blue gaze staring into her wide, wary eyes.

'Marsh,' she began firmly enough. 'I wish you wouldn't talk like this. I don't want to get invol—'

His mouth covered hers, effectively cutting off what she'd been about to say. Undaunted, Helen began speaking again the instant he lifted his head.

'Marsh, listen to me. I don't want any kind of emotional involvement. Besides which—' she hesitated, wet her dry lips, then said flatly. 'I'm older than you.'

A deep frown brought his dark, beautifully shaped eyebrows together. A tiny fire leaped in his eyes.

'Did you think I was unaware of that?' Just the sound of his quiet voice made her shiver. 'Exactly how old are you?'

Helen's eyelids lowered, then came up again defensively. Never before had she hestitated about stating her age. The fact that this man could make her feel defensive about, resentful of, her years was a shocking bit of self-knowledge she didn't want to face. In retaliation she forced a note of pride into her voice.

'Thirty-five.'

'And I'll be thirty-one in March.' His shrug was eloquent. 'I hardly think four years is just cause for argument.'

His blithe unconcern angered her. Jerking her shoulder away from his hand, she turned away.

'Four years can be very important.'

She was immediately swung back to face him. His hand grasped her chin, held it firmly.

'The only years that hold any importance for me any longer are the years we are going to spend together.'

At her wince the pressure on her chin was eased, although he did not let her go.

'I'm not going to argue about this anymore tonight, Helen.' He lowered his head and Helen's eyes became fascinated with his mouth. 'I knew from the moment I laid eyes on you that we belonged together. Nothing you say, nothing you do, is ever going to change that.'

His lips were almost touching hers and Helen tried to ignore and deny the warm curl of anticipation in her stomach.

'There isn't anywhere on this earth you could run to to get away from me, or yourself for that matter. Now close your eyes like a good girl, because I'm going to kiss you.'

And suiting action to words, he did, his arms sliding around her to draw her close against him. The kiss was long and deep and wildly arousing, and Helen could no more have stopped her arms from clinging to him, any more than she could stop the passage of time. She felt a tremor run through his body before he put her firmly from him. Eyes smouldering with smoky blue fire, he stepped back.

'I'm taking you home now. Because if I don't, I doubt you'll ever see the place again.'

He drove her car, brushing aside her protest with a careless 'I'll grab a cab back.'

Before they were halfway to her apartment, Helen was having trouble keeping her eyes open. Numb with fatigue, she finally gave up the battle and allowed her lids to drop, block out the hurtful glare from the headlights of the approaching cars.

'Where should I put the car? Do you have a designated space, or can you park anywhere?'

Marsh's quiet voice nudged her eyelids up. The car was motionless, the engine idling, at the entrance to the covered parking area adjacent to her apartment building.

'What? Oh, anywhere. It doesn't matter.'

Even fuzzy-minded Helen could not miss the indulgent expression on his face. A smile curving his lips, he set the car in motion and drove onto the parking lot.

Too tired to argue, Helen simply shrugged when he insisted on seeing her safely into her apartment.

While she hung her coat in the closet, Marsh used her phone to call for a cab to pick him up. Standing by the door, she watched him cradle the receiver, then walk to her, a tingle of apprehensive anticipation growing stronger with each step he took.

'I won't be able to see you tomorrow or Saturday.' He stopped in front of her, his tone regretful. 'I have previous commitments that I can't break without causing friction on the homefront.'

'Marsh, you don't have to explain your actions to me.' Helen was experiencing that trapped, panicky feeling again. 'You owe me nothing.'

He smiled, raised his hand to caress her face, then went on as if she hadn't said a word.

'I'll be bored out of my gourd, but I can't get out of it without hurting my mother's feelings. But I want to spend the whole day with you Sunday—if you're free.'

The feather-light touch of his fingers on her cheek set off a chain reaction along her nervous system. Her breathing growing shallow, she murmured, 'Yes, but—'

'Out.' Laughing softly, he shook his head at her. 'I'll take you out somewhere. I'll pick you up in the morning at . . . ?' He lifted a questioning eyebrow.

'Not too early,' she sighed, too tired to argue with him. 'Unless I have a call, I sleep late on Sunday.'

'Ten?'

Helen shivered with weariness, nodded.

'Okay.' Feeling her shiver against his fingers, his eyes grew sharp. 'Don't eat, we'll start the day with breakfast or brunch. How does a walk in the park sound?'

'In January?'

'Of course.' He laughed again. 'You'll see.'

His eyes moved over her face, clung for a moment on her mouth, then came back to her eyes.

'You're exhausted, love. Go to bed and go to sleep. Don't think. Don't speculate. Block everything out and sleep.'

His thumb stroked the dark smudges under her eyes as he lowered his head to hers and said softly, 'I love you, Helen.'

His lips, though firm, held no passion, no demand. Comforting warmth spread through her, easing the beginning ache at her temples. All too soon the warmth was removed, as moving away, he opened the door, murmured, 'Sleep well, love,' and was gone.

CHAPTER FOUR

SUNDAY dawned bright and cold. The end of January sunlight, glittering fiercely through Helen's bedroom windows, warned her not to go outdoors without her sunglasses.

Yawning hugely, stretching luxuriously, Helen glanced at the clock on her nightstand and gave a small yelp. Marsh would be arriving in less than an hour and here she lay, basking in the sun like a fat house cat. Scrambling out of bed, she grabbed her robe off the end of the bed and ran into the bathroom.

Helen felt good. Surprisingly she'd slept well the last few nights, including Thursday. She hadn't expected to, in fact, after Marsh had left her with his murmured, 'Sleep well, love,' she'd been convinced she wouldn't sleep at all. Contrarily she was asleep not three minutes after her head hit the pillow.

With two deliveries, plus the usual number of office patients, on Friday, and several hours in the operating room on Saturday, she'd tired herself enough to sleep on those two nights. The thought of Marsh, and what had happened in his bedroom, she'd managed to push to the back of her mind by concentrating fiercely on her work.

When, at the odd moments, the thought of him, the remembered feel of him, crept to the forefront of her mind, she'd gritted her teeth, fighting down the shakiness that assailed her. Afraid, and unwilling to examine exactly why, she'd silently battled against the memories, using sleep as an ally.

Her door chimes pealed at exactly ten o'clock. Fasten-

ing the belt to her slacks, Helen walked to the door and
pulled it open, her breath catching at the sight of him.
He was dressed for a day out of doors in brown corduroy
slacks, tan heavy knit sweater, and a fur-lined, high-
collared parka.

Before she could speak, he dipped his head and placed
his cold lips against hers.

'Good morning,' he murmured, his breath fresh and
tickly on her lips. 'May I come in?'

'Yes—yes, of course.' She stepped back to allow him
to walk by, then added hurriedly, 'I'm ready to leave.
All I have to do is put on my coat.'

A grin slashed his mouth, revealed perfect white
teeth. His eyes danced with gentle mockery.

'Although I'll admit to being tempted, I'm not going
to jump on you and drag you into the bedroom, Helen,
but'—his arm shot out, snaked around her waist, pulled
her to him—'I am going to kiss you properly.'

As he lowered his head his hands came up to cup her
face, cool fingers sliding over the smoothed back hair
above her ears.

'Marsh! Don't you dare touch those pins.'

Laughter rumbling in his throat, the tip of one finger
gently nudged the curved metal hair anchor back into
place under the neat coil.

'Spoilsport.'

The word was murmured against her lips, which,
unbidden, had parted to receive his. Several inches
separated him and Helen, yet he made no move to get
closer, as if deliberately denying his body the feel of
hers. His hands on her face, his mouth on hers, was their
only physical contact, yet Helen felt a warmth and
security flow through her that could not have been
stronger had he enfolded her in his arms, held her tightly
against his strong, hard body.

When he lifted his head, she had to bite back the soft

cry of protest that rose in her throat. Opening her eyes, she felt her breath cut off altogether at the intensity of his blue gaze. The fingers of his right hand trailed slowly down her cheek, over her lips, then with a sharp shake of his head he stepped back, a rueful smile twisting his mouth.

'I think we'd better get out of here,' he clipped tersely, going to the closet to get her coat.

Shaken, Helen stood mutely, automatically lifting her arms to the sleeves of her coat when he held it for her. When his hands dropped away from her shoulders, she found her voice.

'I must stop at the hospital.'

'Why?'

The sharp edge to his tone drove the fuzziness from her mind. The face she lifted to him was cool, composed.

'I must make my rounds. I have three post-op and four maternity patients to examine and release papers to sign for another—' Helen paused in midsentence, a look of concern shadowing her eyes. 'Marsh, the patient being released this morning is your sister.'

'I know that.' One dark brow went up in question. 'So?'

'Well—I—mm—I mean.' Helen faltered, then asked quickly, 'Were you planning to wait for me in the car?'

'Hell, no!' He snapped irritably. 'Do you know how cold it is out there? And I sure as hell didn't consider wasting gas to keep the car warm. If you don't want me trailing around behind you, leave Kris till last and I'll visit with her while you make your rounds.'

'But—' Helen hesitated, her fingers playing nervously with her coat buttons. 'Marsh, what will your sister think?'

'Who cares what she thinks?' He pulled the door open angrily. 'Now, can we go and get these rounds over with? I'm hungry.'

An uneasy silence rode with them all the way to the hospital. By the time Marsh stopped the car at the entrance, Helen's nerves were ragged.

'I'll park the car and see you later in Kris's room.'

Helen chose to ignore the anger that still laced his tone. She didn't want him to wait for her in his sister's room, simply because she didn't want Kristeen Darren to know that they were together.

'Why don't you wait for me in the lunchroom? Have some toast and a cup of—'

'Helen!' he exploded. 'Will you get on with it? At the rate we're moving it will be lunchtime before we get breakfast.'

Hot anger shot through her, and not bothering to reply, she slammed out of the car and into the building. *I must be out of my mind*, she fumed. *Why did I agree to spend the day with him? Did I, in fact, actually agree?*

Thoughts of the same nature seethed in her mind as Helen made her rounds, her cool outward appearance giving no hint of the anger that boiled in her veins. Not since Carl had she allowed a man to upset her like this. And the fact that he was younger than she was an added thorn. She was doing the work she loved and was completely satisfied with her life. She didn't need any man, let alone a smooth-talking rich kid who could issue orders like a marine sergeant.

By the time she walked into Kristeen Darren's room, Helen was in a cold fury and ready to tell Marshall Kirk to go to hell. The scene that met Helen's eyes as she walked through the doorway brought an abrupt halt to her angry stride.

Kristeen was sitting on the bed fully dressed, an impatient frown on her face. Her husband paced restlessly between the room's only window and the bed. Her mother sat, back rigid, in a chair beside the bed. And in the corner, sitting on a functional, straight-backed chair,

Marsh somehow managed to look lazily comfortable. Helen's eyes slid over him as if he were not there.

'I'm sorry I'm late, Kristeen.' She apologised briskly, drawing four pairs of eyes to her. 'I've signed your release, and they'll be bringing your baby to you in a minute. How are you feeling this morning?'

Her fingers on Kristeen's wrist, her eyes on her watch, Helen smiled and nodded understandably at the young woman's breathless tone.

'I'm fine, Doctor. Excited about taking my baby home.'

'Of course,' she murmured, adjusting her stethoscope. Satisfied with what she heard, Helen glanced at Kristeen as she removed the instrument. 'Okay, you may go. Do you have any questions about the instructions I gave you yesterday?'

'No, Doctor, everything's clear.'

'Fine. If you have any problem whatever, call my office.' Except for the cursory glance she'd given him on first entering the room, Helen had not looked at Marsh. She did not look at him now as, smiling warmly at the other three, she wished Kristeen good luck with her daughter, said she'd see her in six weeks, and turned to leave. Marsh's voice stopped her a foot from the door.

'Helen.'

The sound of her name in that smooth, too-soft tone sent a chill along her spine. Turning slowly, she met his eyes, her breath catching at the mocking slant of his lips, the flash of blue fire in his eyes.

Out of the corner of her eye Helen caught the confused glances that flew between Kristeen, her husband, and her mother. Using every ounce of willpower she possessed, Helen hung on to her cool.

'Yes?'

'You're finished now?'

Helen's teeth ground together at the warm note

Marsh had inflected into his voice. Just what did he think he was doing? she thought furiously, noting the sharp glance his mother turned at him. Her tone went from cool to cold.

'Yes.'

'Then, my love, can we now go and have breakfast? My stomach is beginning to feel divorced from the rest of my body.'

The soft gasps that came from the two women, the low whistle that Mike Darren emitted, grated against Helen's nerves. She could have happily hit him. Instead she nodded her head sharply and turned to the door. He was beside her before she had taken three steps, his arm sliding possessively around her waist.

'Take care, Kristeen,' he said lightly, shepherding Helen out of the room. 'I'll see you all later.'

Too angry to trust herself with words, Helen maintained a frigid silence as she retrieved her coat and followed him to his car. Spitting like an angry cat, she turned to him as soon as both car doors were closed.

'Damn you, Kirk,' she began heatedly, only to have him cut her off with a soft warning.

'Watch it, my sweet. I'll take just about anything from you, except your cursing me.'

'I'm not asking you to take anything at all from me,' she sputtered, growing more angry by the minute. 'And I want nothing from you. Not a meal, or a walk in the park, or your company. I'm going home.'

Helen turned to the door, hand groping for the release, and gave a sharp cry of pain when his hands grasped her shoulders, pulled her around to face him.

'You're not going anywhere,' he growled, giving her a not-too-gentle shake. 'At least not until you tell me what you're so mad about.'

'Oh, I'm not mad, Mr Kirk.' Helen returned his

growl. 'I'm way past mad. Try furious. Better yet, try incensed.'

'But why?' His confusion was unfeigned. As angry as she was, Helen had no doubt of that. For some reason it incited her even more.

'Why?' She choked. 'Why? What were you trying to do back there in Kristeen's room? Do you know?'

'Yes, I know,' he replied evenly. 'I was determined to make you acknowledge my existence. You would have walked out of that room without even looking at me, wouldn't you?'

'Yes,' she answered bluntly.

'Yes,' he repeated grimly. 'And that's why I stopped you.'

'And because I bruised your delicate ego, you mentioned our having breakfast together in a tone that suggested we spent the night together.'

'Oh,' he breathed out slowly. 'Now we get to the real reason for your anger. You didn't want anyone—not just my family, but anyone—to know we were together because you were afraid they'd wonder if we were sleeping together. That's why you wanted me to wait in the car or lunchroom.'

'Exactly.' Helen's face had taken on her cool, withdrawn, professional expression. Her tone held frigid hauteur. 'My reputation, both professionally and privately, is spotless. I fully intend to keep it that way. I will not have my name bandied about in speculative gossip.'

The laughter that met her stilted statement wiped the composure off Helen's face.

'Bandied about?' he gasped, between whoops of delight. 'Oh! I love it. Bandied about.' With an obvious effort he brought his roars under control. 'You straight-backed screwball. Where did you pull that chestnut from?'

Against her better judgment Helen felt her lips twitch

with humour. What a pompous ass she sounded. Where
had she pulled that chestnut from?

'Don't laugh at me, Marsh,' she scolded quietly. 'It's
not polite to ridicule your elders.'

Hot, swift anger wiped the amusement from his face,
cut off the laughter still rumbling in his chest. The abrupt
transition startled and frightened her.

'Damn you, Helen,' he snarled softly, fingers digging
painfully into her shoulders. 'What is this stupid hang-up
you have about our ages? You are not my *elder*.' Helen's
eyes widened as his face drew close to hers. 'You will not
speak to me as if I were a naughty boy.' His eyes glittered
with intent, robbing Helen of breath. 'A naughty man
maybe, but not a naughty boy.'

His lips, hard with anger, forced hers apart. The rigid
tip of his tongue flicked against her teeth, stirring an
unwanted curl of excitement in her midsection.

'You want a taste of the man, Helen?'

A seductive whisper, then his mouth crushed hers
hungrily, his tongue plunged to extract the sweetness as
a bee extracts honey from the blossom.

Helen's heart seemed to stop, then the beat increased
to thunder in her ears like the hoofbeats of a wildly
galloping horse. Good Lord! It was the last coherent
thought she had for several seconds. His hands turned
her, pushed her gently against the seat, and her breasts
were crushed by the weight of his chest.

An ache began, deep inside, that quickly grew to
enormous proportions. Giving in to the need to get
closer to him, Helen's arms encircled his waist, tightened convulsively.

His mouth left hers reluctantly, came back as if unwilling to have the moment end. Between slow,
languorous forays, he muttered, 'How long, Helen?
How long before you face reality and yourself? You
want me. I know you do.'

Helen brought her hand up, her fingers moving across his lips.

'Marsh, stop.' Her breathing was uneven, erratic. 'I don't want any emotional involvements. Oh, Marsh, please.' His lips were busy against her fingers, his teeth nipped playfully. 'There's no time in my life for a man.'

'Too late,' he murmured. His lips caught the tip of her ring finger, sucked gently. 'You've got a man in your life. At the moment a very hungry man.' He moved away from her, back behind the steering wheel, a rueful smile slanting his mouth. 'A hungry man in more ways than one. Are we going to go eat or are you going to sit there and watch me slowly starve to death?'

Helen welcomed his return to humour with a sigh of relief. Although his anger had been brief, it had been fierce and he had really frightened her. What would he be like, she wondered fleetingly, if he really let loose? She could only hope she never had to witness it, let alone be the cause of it. The mere thought made her feel cold all over. Shrugging to cover the shiver that shook her slim frame, Helen gave in.

'All right, Marsh, you win. We'll go eat.'

His smile grew into a rakish grin. 'At the risk of sounding conceited, I think I'd better warn you that I usually do. Win, that is.'

Later, sitting in a small restaurant, Helen toyed with her cheese omelette and watched, fascinated, while Marsh demolished a huge club sandwich and a double order of French fries. Their conversation had been minimal as he attacked the food like a man who was actually starving.

When he finished, he wiped his lips with his napkin, indicated to the waitress that he'd like his coffee cup refilled, sat back, and turned that unnerving blue gaze on her.

'Are you from Philly originally?'

Helen blinked with the suddenness of his question after the long silence. Nodding to the waitress who held the coffee pot paused over her cup, her eyebrows raised questioningly, Helen matched his casual tone. 'No, I was born up near Wilkes-Barre. My father was a G.P., had a surprisingly large practice considering the size of the community.'

'Was? Had?' He probed.

'He retired two years ago. He and my mother sold everything and moved to Phoenix, Arizona.' She lifted her gaze from her coffee cup, unaware of the touch of sadness he could see in her eyes, the wistfulness of her small smile. 'I miss them.'

'Of course.' His voice lost some of its casualness. 'You have other family here? Brothers, sisters?'

'No.' She shook her head. 'I have a younger brother, he's also in Phoenix. That's the main reason Mother and Dad decided to retire there. He, Rob, has two small children. My parents wanted to watch their grand-children grow up.' Helen's smile twisted wryly. 'They gave up the hope of seeing any grandchildren from me a long time ago.'

'Why?' Marsh's tone sharpened. 'You're not too old to have kids.'

Helen breathed deeply, lit a cigarette with sur-prisingly steady hands. 'I don't want children, Marsh.'

His eyes narrowed at the calm finality of her tone. Frowning, he reached across the table, slid a cigarette from her pack, lit it, then exhaled in a soft sigh. His shoulders lifted, came down again in an oddly resigned gesture.

'Okay.' His tone was flat, but steady. 'We won't have any.'

'Won't have any! Marsh—'

Helen stopped herself on hearing her own rising

voice. She glanced around quickly before continuing in a much lower, fiercer tone. 'Marsh, what are you talking about? You know my feelings on—'

'Not here.' Marsh rose, silencing her effectively. In the car she turned to him as soon as he'd slid behind the wheel. 'Not here, either,' he snapped with finality.

Helen was amazed at the number of people in Fairmont Park. It was very cold and the wind, though not strong, bit at her exposed skin with icy teeth. 'Incredible,' she murmured, after they'd been walking for some minutes. 'Is it like this every Sunday?'

'Yes.' He slanted a mocking glance at her. 'Helen, I find it hard to believe you didn't know. Don't you ever watch the local news on T.V.?'

'I rarely watch T.V. at all.' She replied, glancing around interestedly. 'I did know the park was a favourite spot for joggers but I had no idea there were this many people into jogging, let alone all these other people here.'

'You live a rather single-minded existence, don't you?' he chided.

'I never thought of it that way, but'—she shrugged—'I suppose I do. Which reminds me. Back at the restaurant you said—Marsh! What are you doing?'

He had taken her gloved left hand in his larger bare one. After tugging her glove off, he laced the fingers of his right hand through hers, then slipped their clasped hands into the deep fur-lined slash pocket of his jacket. When she tried to pull her hand free, his fingers tightened until she cried out in pain. 'Marsh, please.'

'Stop fighting me.' His fingers loosened, but not enough for her to slip free. 'And back at the restaurant I said that if you didn't want children we wouldn't have any.'

He was so unconcerned, so nonchalant, Helen was beginning to feel she'd get better results talking to one of the park's many trees. Fighting to hang on to her patience, she gritted slowly.

'That's right, *we* won't have any children. *We* won't have anything together for the simple reason we won't be together. What do I have to do to make you understand? I don't want a relationship. I don't want to be bothered by any man.' During this entire tirade Helen's tone had not risen above a harsh whisper. Now she drew a ragged breath and added in a more normal tone, 'Do I make myself clear?'

'Perfectly.'

It was what she'd wanted to hear, so why did his prompt, careless answer cause a sharp pain in her chest? No sooner had the thought skittered through her mind than he added blandly, 'There's only one problem, my love. You are already bothered by a man. This man. And this man plans to bother you one hell of a lot more before he's through.'

'Marsh,' Helen began angrily, but he cut in in that same bland tone.

'Let's shelve the subject for now and enjoy our walk. Are you cold?'

'Yes. No. A little.' Helen could have shouted at him, he had her so frustrated, she didn't know what she was saying. And his soft, delighted laughter didn't help much either. 'I mean I am a little cold but I'm enjoying the walk.'

'Good. Do you want to walk down to the river and see if there are any hardy souls crewing?'

Helen hesitated. If there were boats on the river, she'd like to see them. But then again, her nose was beginning to feel numb now and the wind off the water would be a lot colder, so she shivered and shook her head. 'I don't think so. Another day perhaps.'

'Chicken.' He taunted softly. 'Don't tell me you're a hothouse flower.'

'Coming from Wilkes Barre?' She laughed. 'You have got to be kidding. Why, when I was in the sixth grade I was the undisputed snowball champ.'

'Liar.'

Helen's laughter sang on the cold air, bringing a bemused expression to his eyes, a deepening timbre to his voice, 'What were you really like in sixth grade?'

'Quiet, studious, head-of-the-class type. You know.' She paused, looked away from him. 'I never wanted to be anything but a doctor. My mother despaired at my nose in a book, but my father was delighted. He had similar hopes for Rob too, but Rob had his own ideas.' She laughed again, a soft, reminiscent laugh. 'Rob's a charmer. Always has been. He could talk the face off an eight-day clock. A born salesman. And that's exactly what he is. Makes an excellent living at it too.'

'You miss him.' It was not a question. 'Were you very close?'

'Yes.' Helen closed her eyes against the sudden, sharp longing she felt for her distant family. 'While we were growing up we fought like a dog and cat. Nearly drove my mother mad. Our saving grace was that we also defended each other fiercely against outsiders.' She laughed again at a particular memory.

'Tell me,' Marsh prompted. 'Let me share the laughter.'

'It's silly.' Helen shook her head, still smiling. 'To this day Rob tells people that I was named Laura, after my mother, but I grew up a hell-en and it stuck.'

'You *do* miss him.' Inside the pocket his fingers squeezed hers, sending a shaft of exciting warmth up her arm. 'When did you see him last?'

'I flew out for a week last spring for his birthday.' She frowned, remembering. Her tone lost its sparkle, went flat. 'His thirty-first. I've always thought of Rob as my baby brother, Marsh, and he's a year older than you are.'

A tautness came into his body. She could feel it in the arm that rested against hers, in the tightening of his fingers. 'Do you think of me in the same vein?' Even his voice was taut.

'Marsh, I—'

'Do you?' Harsh now, rough, he stopped walking, turned to face her.

'No.' It was a shaken whisper, but she could not lie to him with that intent blue gaze on her. His deep sigh formed a misty cloud between them.

'It's a damned good thing,' he grated. 'Helen, unless you want to see some real fireworks, I think you'd better make a concentrated effort to forget the difference in our ages. Without too much prodding I could become positively paranoid about it.'

He leaned closer to her and his voice went very low. Not in self-consciousness of the people passing by, but in sheer intensity. 'I love you, Helen. I don't know *how* I know, but I *do* know that if there were ten or even fifteen years between us, I would still love you.'

'Marsh, I—I—' Shaken by his declaration, unsure, Helen searched for words.

'Leave it for now,' he said softly. The bone-crushing grip on her fingers was eased as the tension went out of his body. 'We came here to walk, let's walk.'

They had taken only a few steps when he jiggled her fingers, and requested, 'Tell me some more about your family.'

'No.' The eyes that met his sharp look were teasing. 'Tell me about yours. I'm curious to know what type people it takes to produce such a—a—'

'Bonehead?' he suggested dryly. 'Bulldog? Bast—'

'Marsh!'

His head was thrown back in laughter. Joyful, enchanting laughter that stole her breath, doubled the rate of her heartbeat. And before she realised what he was doing, he turned, bent his head, and caught her mouth with his, unconcerned with the giggles that came from a group of teenage girls passing by.

Helen felt as gauche as a teenager herself, feeling her cheeks grow hot when he lifted his head, grinned at her, and whispered, 'I do love kissing you.'

'You're a fool,' she whispered back, trying to sound stern, failing miserably.

'Yes, well, we'll go into that another time,' he warned. 'But now'—he resumed walking again, totally relaxed— 'my family. My mother's beautiful, as I'm sure you noticed.' He raised dark brows at her and she nodded. 'My father's rich, and I mean old guard, Society Hill, rich. Kris is a pet. She used to be a drag, trailing after me all the time, but even when she was a drag, she was a pet. I love them all, but I adore my grandfather.'

Helen looked up quickly, breath catching at the softness in his tone, his eyes. The strong lines of his face, the russet hair, those incredibly clear blue eyes, were becoming too familiar, too heart-wrenching important. In an effort to shake off her thoughts, Helen prompted, 'Your grandfather?'

'Yes,' He smiled. 'My grandfather. You'll like him,' he stated emphatically. 'And I know he's going to be crazy about you.' He laughed softly at some secret joke, then went on. 'My grandfather is definitely not old guard. A real scrapper still, and he's close to seventy-five. Chews me out regularly, enjoys every minute of it too. He started sixty years ago with a couple of hundred dollars, which was all that was left after his father died, and built it into a small empire. It keeps me running, trying to handle the damn thing.'

'Started what?'

'A small building and construction firm that is now a very large building and construction firm, plus assorted other interests he's picked up along the way.'

'So you do work for a living,' she chided. 'I did wonder. You're a construction worker?'

'Among other things.' That devastating grin flashed. 'My father wanted me to follow him into banking.' He grimaced. 'Can you see me as a banker?' Helen smiled, shook her head. 'Yeah, well, neither could I. Cullen couldn't either.'

'Cullen?'

'My grandfather. I've called him Cullen, on his insistence, for as long as I can remember. Drove my grandparents on my father's side up the wall.'

'Cullen is your mother's father.'

'Yes. Her mother died giving her life and although Cullen wanted a son, he never remarried. He told me there wasn't a woman alive who could replace his Megan. Anyway, after she died, he lived for his work and his daughter. I think he claimed me for himself about five minutes after I was born. My father didn't stand a chance against the old bear.'

'Your father gave in to him without a fight?' Helen asked incredulously, thinking of the battle anyone would have had trying to claim her brother away from her father.

'Hell, no.' Marsh chuckled. 'Dad's no slouch. The tug-of-war lasted through all the years I was growing up, with me in the middle, catching flak from both sides.'

They had retraced their steps back to the car and Helen was glad to slide onto the velour-upholstered seat, out of the cold air. She waited until he'd started the car and drove into the flow of traffic before observing, 'I'm surprised you weren't scarred by the war. Or were you?'

'It wasn't that kind of war.' He stopped at a stop sign and turned to give her an encompassing glance. 'You look frozen. Any warmth coming from the heater yet?'

'Yes, a little, but I'm fine.' Helen turned to study his features. 'What kind of war was it?'

'Friendly. Dad and Cullen get along fine, always did. I suppose you could say they fought their battle like a chess game, only I was the only chessman. One would move me this way, the other another way.'

'And your grandfather made the deciding move?' Helen couldn't decide if she was fascinated or appalled by the story.

'No.' Marsh grinned. 'I did.'

'But, Marsh, you said earlier that you ran the business, that must mean your grandfather's got what he wanted.'

'You think so?' he taunted softly. 'Ask him sometime.'

Helen had been so caught up in watching the play of emotions on his face, she hadn't once glanced out the window. When he drove the car into a small parking area, she looked around in confusion. The parking lot was adjacent to a small Italian restaurant in a part of the city she was unfamiliar with. Her eyes came back to him as he turned the key, cutting the engine.

'Why are we stopping here?'

'This is one of my favourite haunts. I'm addicted to their shrimp scampi.' Her widening eyes brought the grin back to his mouth. 'I walked off my lunch,' he defended himself carelessly. 'I'm hungry.' His eyes went over her face, dropped to her slim wrists. 'Some good, rich Italian food wouldn't hurt you either. Were you always so thin?'

'Oh, for heaven's sake,' Helen groaned, reaching for the door release. 'You sound like Alice.'

He was out of his door and around to hers in time to close it for her. 'Who's Alice?'

'My office nurse.'

'Oh, yes, the dragon I talked to on the phone

Thursday.' He held open the door into the restaurant for her to precede him inside, and as he helped her with her coat he asked wryly, 'Does Alice look as daunting as she sounds?'

'And as bossy.' Helen nodded. 'She has been nagging me for weeks about my weight.'

'I think I like Alice,' he murmured as a tall, swarthy man approached, a huge smile revealing glistening white teeth.

'Hiya, Marsh, haven't seen you for a while.' His bold, dark eyes slid over Helen appreciatively. When his eyes returned to Marsh they held a trace of envy. 'Where've you been hiding out, *compare?*'

Marsh put his hand out to clasp the other man's, a taunting grin curving his lips. 'Not hiding, Moe, working. Cullen's had me on the run for weeks.'

Moe looked at Helen, letting his glance linger deliberately a second before remarking, 'Not too much on the run. You've obviously had time for other things. Very beautiful other things.'

Marsh laughed aloud, and Helen couldn't help smiling back at the good-looking Moe. He was about the same age as Marsh, with black curly hair, dark brown eyes, and a sexy look about him that probably ensnared women in droves.

'Helen, this smart-mouthed Sicilian is Emilio Brenzini, Moe to you. He's the owner of this joint. He's also my best friend, I think.' Marsh turned a sardonic face to Moe. 'Moe, Helen Cassidy. Doctor Helen Cassidy, my future wife.'

Helen's shocked gasp was covered up by Moe's shouted, 'What? Hey, man, that's terrific. Come and sit down.' They were ushered to a small table covered with a blood-red cloth, matching napkins folded neatly beside carefully arranged flatware. When Moe moved behind Helen to hold her chair, she glared at Marsh, who smiled back sweetly. Choking back the angry words she wanted to spit at him, she forced a smile to her lips when Moe was again facing them.

'I just can't believe it,' Moe exclaimed in awe. 'Marshall Kirk, man about town, heartbreaker extraordinaire, brought down in his prime by a female sawbones.' His eyes glittered at Helen. 'What the hell did such a gorgeous creature as you see in this big number-counting lady killer?'

'Knock off the comedy routine, Moe,' Marsh drawled. 'And break out the wine. Helen and I were outside for hours and we need some warming up.'

'Okay, sweetheart.' Moe did a bad imitation of Bogart and walked away, chuckling to himself.

The moment he was out of sight Helen snapped, 'How dare you tell him that.'

'Why not?' Marsh answered blandly. 'You are going to be my wife.'

'No, I am not.' She gritted furiously. 'Do you understand? I am not. When Moe comes back, you tell him you were joking.'

'No.'

'Marsh, I'm warning you.' Seething, Helen had trouble enunciating her words. 'If you don't tell him, I will.'

Marsh eyed her dispassionately. 'Have fun,' he drawled. 'But personally I think you're going to sound pretty damned silly. Moe's going to wonder why you didn't deny it at once.'

Helen opened her mouth, closed it again, trying to collect some control. Then Moe was back, grinning happily as he poured the ruby-red wine.

'To both of you.' He lifted his glass, his face sobering as he turned to Helen. 'I should say I hope you'll be very happy but with this one'—he jerked his head at Marsh, a soft smile touching his lips—'I don't really think it's necessary. He is the best there is, Helen. Only a very foolish woman would not find happiness with him.' Then he turned to Marsh, glass going high in salute.

'Congratulations, *compare*. I begin to suspect that you are a very, very lucky man.'

CHAPTER FIVE

SLEEP eluding her, Helen lay on her back, staring at the pale white ceiling. It was late, several hours since Marsh had left, and yet her mind hung on to the day's happenings as tenaciously as a baby monkey hangs on to its mother.

She had said nothing to clarify the situation to Moe, of course. How could she after the sincerity of his toast to them?

Positive she'd choke if she tried to force food around the anger waiting to explode from her throat, Helen had surprised herself by not only eating but keeping pace with Marsh. The scampi was every bit as delicious as Marsh had claimed, but then, the antipasto, tossed salad, large slices of crispy crusted bread, and spumoni were the best Helen had ever eaten also. When they had drained the last drop of wine and were preparing to leave, Marsh reached for his wallet. Moe placed his hand on Marsh's arm and shook his head.

'This one's on me, buddy. Bring Helen over to meet Jeanette soon.' He laughed softly before adding, 'They've already got one thing in common.'

At Helen's questioning look Marsh explained, 'The medical profession, love. Jeanette is an anaesthetist.'

'Really? Where?' Those were her first unstrained words since Marsh had told Moe she was to be his wife. Moe named the hospital and Helen smiled, nodded. 'Yes, I'm familiar with it. They have excellent facilities and a first-rate staff. Does she enjoy her work?'

'Most of the time.' Moe's answer was laconic. 'Sometimes it all gets on top of her. You know, the job, taking

78

care of the kids, the house'—he grinned—'keeping me happy.'

Curious, Helen asked, 'How many children do you have?' His smug answer shocked her.

'Four. Five years of marriage and four *bambinos*. That's pretty good work, wouldn't you say, Doc?'

'Four babies and she keeps up the pace in O.R.?' Helen returned incredulously. 'Moe, you are married to a superwoman.

'Jeanette *is* a super person,' Marsh put in, edging her to the door. 'But don't think for a minute this buffoon doesn't take good care of her. She works by choice, and she has plenty of help in the house. The *gran signore* here gets his masculine ego kicks by giving people the impression he's got a master-slave marital arrangement. When in fact he'd drop onto his knees and kiss the hem of her uniform if she asked him to.'

'Without hesitation' was Moe's emphatic response.

Even now, hours later, Helen shook her head in wonder at Moe's wife. A date had been set, for the following Saturday, for Helen and Marsh to join Moe and Jeanette for dinner at the restaurant. Helen was looking forward to meeting her.

When, finally, they had left Emilio's, Helen had withdrawn into a cold silence. Marsh had not made an attempt to break that silence, although he had cast several searching glances at her.

Helen was mad, and she wanted him to know she was mad. She simmered with indignation all the way home, while he parked the car, rode up in the elevator with her, stood behind her as she turned the key in the lock. When she turned to give him a frosty goodnight, he reached around her, pushed the door open, spun her around, gave her a gentle shove, and followed her into the room. Eyes blazing, she'd whirled back to face him. He beat her to the draw.

'Okay, you're mad.' His voice was low, steady, unrepentent. 'So let's have it. Get it out of your system and then we'll talk calmly about it.'

'I don't want to talk about it,' Helen said coldly. 'You will have to make my apology next Saturday night. I am not going with you. I do not want to see you again. I do not want you to call me.' Breathing deeply, she stared into his impassive, expressionless face. 'Is that understood?'

'You're nuts, do you know that?'

The soft, taunting amusement in his tone drew a gasp from her. Before she could form words of retaliation, he stepped in front of her, grasped her shoulders, and gave her a light shake.

'For all your cool, self-contained act, it doesn't take much to set you off, does it?' His eyebrows arched and a knowing smile twitched his lips. 'Or is it me?' he chided softly. 'I have a hunch that if any other man had made that statement, you would have, very coolly, called him a liar.' His voice went softer still. 'I get to you, don't I? I rattle you and ruffle your feathers. I make you mad, but'—he lowered his head to within an inch of hers—'I can also make you laugh.' His mouth brushed hers, once, twice. 'But what really bothers you is that I excite you.' The tip of his tongue slid across her lips, parting them in a small, involuntary gasp. His mouth covered hers, his hands moved down her spine, moulding her against him.

At first she struggled against him, clenching her teeth and jaw tightly. But what he said was true. He did excite her, and that excitement curled around and through her, loosening her jaw, weakening her knees, driving her arms up and around his neck to cling helplessly while his mouth plundered hers.

Helen moved restlessly on the bed. Just thinking about him sparked off that excitement, sent it scampering wildly through her body. The words he'd whispered against her lips now brought a low moan from her throat.

'I want to sleep with you, Helen. Let me stay. Let me exorcise, once and for all, the fears that have kept your emotions frozen all these years.' He pulled her closer, his arms tightening. His breath danced across her ear. 'Trust me, love, I won't hurt you.'

'No, no.'

Her words had a desperate, panicky sound, even to her own ears, and he allowed her to move out of his arms, away from him. He watched her pull the ragged edges of her composure together, then he sighed softly and walked to the door.

'I'll call you tomorrow.'

'Marsh, I said—'

'Damn it, Helen,' he flared, 'don't fight me. Do you want me to come back over there? Prove to you that there's a woman inside that cool, professional veneer you've covered yourself with?'

She backed away warily, shaking her head in answer.

'All right then, play it cool for a while, see what develops. Now,' he sighed again, impatiently, 'what's the best time to call you tomorrow?'

'After six thirty. Here.'

Why had she given in to him? Helen silently asked her ceiling. Why did she let him brush aside her protests as if they meant nothing? Her mouth twisted in self-mockery. Maybe, because, if she was honest with herself, they meant exactly that: nothing.

Helen went rigid, fingers curling lightly around the bed-covers. The self-truth was a shocking jolt her stiffened body tried to reject. *Face it, Dr Cassidy*, she told herself derisively, *you're as human and vulnerable as the next woman. You* like *the breathlessness that intent, blue gaze causes. You* like *the feeling of weakness the touch of his hand on your body induces. You* like *the crazy riot of sensations his hungry mouth generates. For the first time in over ten years you have a physical need for a man. But why this particular man?*

Helen's mind darted in different directions in an effort to avoid answering her own question. It was quite true she'd felt no urges of a sexual nature since the night of Carl's assault. Filled with disgust, contempt, she had, for many months, withdrawn from any kind of personal contact with the opposite sex. As time passed and circumstances demanded she have some contact with men, the contempt lessened, and in a few cases was replaced by respect and admiration, but that was all. It was as if the part of her brain that controlled her emotional responses had closed shop—permanently. With the rest of her mind she could evaluate a man's potential and his accomplishments, and applaud them, but always as a contemporary, never, ever, as an interesting male.

Now, suddenly, this one man, this *younger* man, was arousing all kinds of needs and wants inside her.

'No, please.' It was a whispered cry into the room's darkness. The stiffness drained out of her body, replaced by a longing ache that made what she'd felt for Carl, before *that* night, seem mild and insipid by comparison.

Head moving from side to side on the pillow, Helen's eyes closed slowly. After all these years the emotional control centre in her brain was alert and functioning and sending out signals she could not deny. She wanted this man. She needed this man. *Damn it to hell*, she thought furiously, *I'm in love with him.*

No! I can't be, her reason rebelled. *I don't even know him and I never even found out what it is, exactly, he does. Then, irrelevantly, he's not even in the medical profession*. The irrationality of her thoughts struck her, and aloud she moaned, 'He is right, I am nuts.'

The bedcovers twisted around her squirming body as she fought against the insidious languor thoughts of him had produced. *I am not in love*, she told herself firmly. *Of course I'm not. This—this craziness is just that: physical craziness. Marsh is a good-looking—no, handsome—man. He has charm, and money, in abundance, and face it, he is downright sexy.* His eyes alone had the power to set off a chain reaction of sensations inside a woman. *And*, she rationalised, *I can surely handle my own physical attraction to him. I must. I cannot, I will not, expose myself to that kind of pain again. I'm a mature woman, not a silly young girl. And I certainly will not be an object of any man's pleasure. Most especially a young man.*

Helen winced. Why, when all the mature, sophisticated men she'd met had left her cold, did she react so strongly to him? His assertion that they were fated to come together she dismissed as nonsense. She was a physician. She was aware, if not fully understanding, of the age-old mystery of one person's chemistry striking sparks off of another. But it was totally incomprehensible to her why his was the only chemistry able to ignite hers, after all this time. She would not have it. She had worked too hard to allow a man, probably going through a phase in which he was attracted to older women, to disrupt her life.

For a long time Helen's thoughts ran on in the same vein, always coming back to the same conclusion. Since she could not order him to stay away—he paid no attention to her when she did—she'd go along with him, keeping him at arm's length, until the phase, or attraction, wore itself out.

Finally the plaguing ache left her body and she relaxed, grew drowsy. Her last coherent thought was he could not hurt her if she simply refused to allow herself to *be* hurt.

She held on to that thought all through office hours the next day, whenever Marsh invaded her mind. She was in the apartment not fifteen minutes when the phone rang. Going to the wall phone in the kitchen, Helen glanced at the clock, thinking it must be her service as Marsh was not due to call for a half hour.

'Dr Cassidy.' She spoke briskly into the receiver.

'I don't want to speak to Dr Cassidy,' the low voice taunted. 'I want to speak to Helen. Is she there?'

Steeling herself against the warmth the sound of his voice sent racing through her body, Helen asked cooly, 'Is there a difference?'

His soft laughter sent a shiver after the warmth. 'A very big difference,' he stated firmly. 'Dr Cassidy is a machine, Helen is a woman.'

Stung by his jibe, surprised at the swift shaft of pain it caused, Helen murmured, 'That wasn't very nice, Marsh.'

'When did I ever say I was nice?' he mocked. 'Oh, I have my moments, but not with you. I don't want to be nice to you. What I want to do is shake some sense into your rigid mind. But not tonight. I'll have to pass on that pleasure for the rest of the week.' He paused and his tone took on an edge Helen didn't understand. 'I'm going out of town for the rest of the week. I must make a circuit of several of my clients, clear up a few things.' Now he sounded annoyed, as if angry at the claim to his time. 'The damned incompetence of some bookkeepers today is not to be believed.' Again he paused, and his tone had a controlled, frustrated ring. 'I'll be back sometime Friday. I'll call you.'

'All right, Marsh.' Helen's calm reply gave away none of the confusion she was feeling. After wishing him a safe trip and hanging up the receiver, Helen moved around the kitchen, getting herself something to eat, her mind nagging at his tone.

Why had he been so annoyed? she wondered with a vague twinge of unease. After forcing down a cold sliced roast beef sandwich and a small salad, she brewed a pot of herb tea and carried it into the living room. As she sipped the hot, green liquid Helen speculated on the reason for his anger. Was it really caused by the need to visit clients or was it connected in some way with her?

Cup in hand, Helen moved restlessly around the taste-fully decorated room in a vain attempt to escape her thoughts. It didn't work. Her thoughts pursued her as she paced back and forth, into the kitchen to wash up her few dishes. He had been angry the night before. Angry and impatient and very likely frustrated with his failure at getting her into bed with him.

A shudder rippled through her body and she stood unmoving at the sink, the towel she'd been drying her hands on hanging forgotten in her fingers. Had he thought she'd be an easy conquest? Her behaviour the previous Thursday may have led him to believe so. Did he think, like many other people, that an unmarried woman in her mid-thirties was so desperate for male companionship that she'd hop into bed with almost any male?

Wincing, Helen tossed aside the towel and went back to pacing the living room. Unlike most women, reaching thirty, thirty-five, had not bothered her. Why should it? She was performing at the peak of her efficiency and she knew it. She lived well and had a comfortable sum of money in the bank. Her life was evolving as planned. What more could she possibly ask for? Up until now her answer to that would have been an emphatic nothing. But now the answer that shouted in her mind shook her with its intensity.

She wanted Marsh. She wanted the feel of his mouth

on hers, his arms tight around her, his body, hard and urgent, leaving her in no doubt that he wanted her as badly.

Becoming tired, yet unable to sit still, Helen continued to pace in a nervous, jerky manner that in itself was alien to her usual smooth movements. She did not feel like herself. She wasn't even sure what she did feel like. She didn't like it, but wasn't quite sure what to do about it.

Maybe, she decided clinically as she prepared for bed, she should have an affair with him, get him out of her system, let him get her out of his. She toyed with the idea a moment, then rejected it. No, she could not do that, for she felt positive that in an encounter or affair like that she would end up wounded if not crushed. While he, malelike, would blithely walk away, one Helen Cassidy forgotten, looking for new battlefields to conquer. No! She wasn't quite sure how she'd handle the situation, but she felt positive that if she played along with him, let him have it all his way, she'd be the one left torn and bleeding on this particular battlefield.

So ran her thoughts for the remainder of the week, and by the time her alarm rang on Friday morning she was thoroughly sick of them. Although it was an extremely busy week, with several deliveries and her office packed with patients, it had seemed like an endless one.

By the time her last patient left on Friday afternoon, Helen decided she'd been a fool to give the matter so much consideration. Without Marsh's proximity she had reached the point of observing the whole affair objectively and came to the conclusion that she was mountain climbing over molehills.

Her sense of balance restored, Helen went home with the conviction that she could handle one Marshall Kirk with one hand tied behind her back. Her right hand at that.

She would, she thought smugly, do exactly as Marsh had recommended: play it cool. She would go with him to have dinner with Moe and his wife and start the evening with a flat denial of Marsh's assertions of the previous Sunday.

Helen waited for his call until after midnight, her hard-fought balance slipping away as each hour died a slow death. And when, in the small hours, she did finally drift into an uneasy sleep, she felt actually bruised, as if she'd been beaten, and her pillow knew an unfamiliar dampness.

Her phone rang before her alarm, and as she had two patients due at any time, Helen snatched up the receiver on the second ring.

'Good morning, love, did I wake you?'

Marsh's soft voice sent an anticipatory shiver through Helen's body, and she had to clutch the receiver to keep from dropping it. How, she wondered, did he manage to sound so seductive at this hour of the morning.

'Yes.' And why did she have to sound so breathless and sleepy?

'I could tell,' he purred sexily. 'You sound warm and cuddly and'—he paused—'ready, and I wish like hell that I was there right now.'

Helen's mouth went dry, and she placed her hand over the receiver as if afraid he could actually see her wet her lips.

'No comeback?' Marsh taunted softly. 'No cutting reply? You must still be half asleep.' He laughed low in his throat. 'Or is it the other? Are you all warm . . . and so forth?'

The jarring noise of her alarm broke the spell his sensuous voice had caught her up in. So much for firm resolutions and objective reasoning, Helen thought wryly, her finger silencing the alarm's persistent ring.

'Actually.' How had she achieved that detached tone?

'I was confused for a moment as to who it was. It's been so long since I heard your voice.' A gentle, but effective, reminder that he'd said he'd call the night before.

His laughter appreciated the thrust. 'You lie so convincingly, darling. Is it one of your habits?' His laughter deepened at the half gasp her covering hand was not fast enough to blank out entirely. 'I know I said I'd call you last night but it was very late when I got in and I didn't want to disturb you—or did I manage to do that anyway?'

The soft insinuation brought a sparkle of anger, self-directed, to Helen's now-wide-awake hazel eyes. Biting back the few choice names she would have found much pleasure in calling him at this safe distance, she snapped waspishly, 'Marsh, I have to go to work. Did you call for a reason or just to annoy me?'

'Ah-ha, she's awake now, and the transformation has been made. There speaks the mechanical Dr Cassidy.'

'Marsh, have you been up all night?' Helen enunciated with exaggerated patience. 'You sound somewhat light-headed.'

'It's an affliction that attacks the minds of men when they're in love,' Marsh replied seriously. Then he added wickedly, 'And have the hots.'

'Not men,' she retaliated harshly. 'Callow youths.'

'Mind your tongue, Helen.' The bantering tone was gone, replaced by steel-edged anger.

'Marsh, it's after seven thirty.' Helen retreated quickly. 'I have to get ready for work. What, exactly, did you call for?'

'To find out what your early-morning voice sounds like,' he shot back smoothly. 'And to tell you I'll pick you up at seven.'

'All right, now I must go.'

'And, Helen? Give me a break and let your hair down. Bye, love.'

Fuming, Helen stood several seconds, listening to the dial tone before replacing the receiver, unsure if he had meant her to take his request literally or figuratively.

The morning went surprisingly well and before one thirty Helen found herself free for the day. About to leave the office, she turned back, picked up her phone, and called the hairdresser who occasionally cut and styled her hair. Yes, the young woman told her, if Helen could come right in, she could work her in.

When she let herself into her apartment several hours later, Helen's hair had been shampooed, shaped, and blown dry. It lay in soft curls and waves around her face and against her shoulders.

Later, as she was putting the finishing touches to her makeup, Helen paused to study the unfamiliar hairstyle. At first, the change being so radical from her usual smoothed-back neatness, Helen had not been sure if she liked it. But now, after living with it for some hours, she had to admit that the loose curls and waves framing her face softened the stubborn line of her chin, the curve of her cheek. Was she, perhaps, past the age for such a careless style? Her hazel eyes sharpened, searched thoroughly, but the thick mane, not quite brown, yet not quite blonde, revealed not a sign of grey. Well, maybe for the weekends, the rare evening out, she finally decided. But never, never for the office, the hospital. The one thing she didn't want while she was working was to appear, in any way, softened or vulnerable. At one minute to seven Helen stepped out of the elevator into the apartment building's small lobby and came face to face with Marsh. Without speaking, she watched his eyes widen, flicker with admiration and approval as they went over her hair, her face, then move down to the muted red of her wool coat. She could actually feel the touch of that blue gaze as it slowly travelled the length of her slim, sheer nylon-clad legs to her narrow feet, not at all covered by the few thin straps of her narrow-heeled sandals. When he raised his eyes to hers, Helen felt her heartbeat slow down then speed up into an alarmingly rapid thud. The expression in his eyes, on his strong, handsome face, was so blatantly sensual, all the moisture evaporated from her mouth and throat.

'You are one beautiful woman.' His voice was very low, yet each word was clear, distinct. 'Why in the hell do you ever pull your hair back off your face?'

Helen stared at her own reflection in his eyes, suddenly filled with an overwhelming desire to lose herself in their blue depths. Her lips parted, the tip of her tongue skimming over them wetly, but no words came. She heard him draw in his breath sharply, saw him lift his hands, take a step towards her before he brought himself up abruptly, a rueful smile twisting his lips.

'We had better get out of here, love,' he murmured hoarsely, 'before I do something that would very likely delight the people in this lobby but embarrass you.'

With that he stepped beside her, grasped her elbow, and hurried her towards the front entrance. It was only then that Helen became aware of the group of people in the lobby, laughing and talking about the evening ahead, calling a greeting to another couple as they came in the door and joined the group.

As they passed the group several pairs of eyes turned in their direction, and Helen could not help but see the sharp looks of interest and appreciation. Avid female glances took in Marsh's imposing figure; warm male eyes ran over her own.

With a jolt Helen realised that up until that point she and Marsh had been unobserved and that the eternity that had seemed to pass while she'd stared into his eyes had, in actuality, lasted only a few brief seconds.

Oddly shaken, Helen walked beside him in silence to the car, slid obediently onto the seat as he held the door.

Her mind numb, refusing to delve for any deep meaning in the incident, Helen stared through the windshield as Marsh slid behind the wheel, started the engine, and drove away from the parking lot.

When the stunned sensation left her, Helen stole a glance at Marsh's set profile. Her glance froze and held for long seconds before, with a smothered gasp, she forced her eyes back to the windshield. But the windshield couldn't hold her gaze, and slowly, almost against her will, her eyes crept back to fasten hungrily on his face. She had not realised how very much she'd missed him. In something very close to pain her eyes devoured the sight of him, soaked the image of him into her mind, her senses.

'Stop it, Helen.'

Helen blinked at the raw harshness of his voice, stammered, 'W—what?'

'You know damn well what,' he rasped. 'I can *feel* your eyes on me. We have a date with Moe and Jeanette, but if you don't look away, I'm going to say the hell with it, turn the car around, and take you to my place.'

'Marsh—I—' Helen began tremulously.

'I mean it, Helen.' He cut across her words roughly. 'The way I feel right this minute, I could park this car at the first empty spot I find and make love to you and not give a damn if we drew an audience.'

A shiver of excited anticipation slid down Helen's spine, then shocked at her reaction to his threat, she practically jumped away from him and glued her eyes to the side window.

'That's better.' His tone had smoothed out and it now held amusement. Helen gritted her teeth and a few moments later greeted with a sigh of relief the bright red neon sign that spelled out the name EMILIO'S.

There was an awkward stiffness between them as they left the car and walked to the restaurant, but the awkwardness soon dissolved when exposed to the sincere warmth of Moe's greeting. With unrestrained pride Moe drew his wife forward to introduce her to Helen.

At a quick, cursory glance Jeanette may have appeared simply pretty. But, as Helen's glance was neither quick nor cursory, she was struck by the beauty of Jeanette's mass of short, shiny black curls, her wide, dark brown eyes, which somehow managed to look both femininely soft and sharply intelligent at the same time.

With a flourish Moe ushered them to a table, telling them menus wouldn't be necessary as he and Jeanette had completely planned the meal from appetiser to dessert. When a small wiry waiter walked up to their table carrying a silver bucket containing a bottle with a foil-wrapped head, a happy grin spread across Moe's face.

'For my *compare* and his beautiful bride-to-be'—his hand grasped the neck of the bottle, lifted it to reveal the Dom Pérignon label—'nothing but the best.'

In frozen silence, a strained smile cracking her pale face, Helen heard the muffled pop of the cork as it was forced from the bottle by Moe's hand, hidden beneath a towel. Watching the golden liquid as it cascaded, bubbling, into the tulip-shaped glasses, Helen thought frantically: *Now is the time to speak, put an end to this pretence.*

In cloying panic she had the uncanny feeling that if she did not speak before the toast was given she'd be trapped into a situation from which she'd never get free. *That's ridiculous*, she told herself scathingly, casting about in her mind for light, joking words that would correct Marsh's statement of the week before without putting a damper on the party. She knew, already, that she was going to really like Moe and Jeanette and she didn't want to begin a friendship with a lie.

Unable to find the proper words, Helen's mind went

blank. The glasses were passed around, and Moe and Jeanette lifted theirs. Surprisingly it was Jeanette who offered the toast. Her smile, her entire face, revealing the affection she felt for him, she looked directly at Marsh.

'To our favourite man, who deserves the best.' She then looked at Helen, drawing her into the circle of affection. 'And to his woman, who obviously is.'

'*Bravissimo, cara,*' Moe applauded as he lifted his glass to his lips.

'*Grazie,*' Marsh replied simply before leaning across the table to kiss Jeanette's smiling mouth.

Self-schooled to show as little emotion as possible, Helen had listened to the toast, observed Marsh's reaction to it, and stared openly as the two men embraced each other, with a growing sense of wonder. Did these people always display their feelings this openly? Then all conjecture was sent flying as Moe's amazingly gentle lips touched hers. Startled, about to pull back and away, Marsh's chiding voice saved her from making a fool of herself.

'Enough already, you greedy Sicilian. It's my turn.'

The gentle lips were removed, replaced by an equally gentle pair. And yet there was a difference. A difference so electrifying, Helen felt the shock waves reverberate through her entire body. He must have felt it too for he lifted his head too swiftly, breathed, 'Later, love,' and turned a smiling face back to Moe and Jeanette.

The toast over, Helen relaxed and, before she was even aware of being drawn, found herself laughing and talking with Moe and Jeanette as if she'd known them for years. The minute they'd finished their after-dinner liqueur and coffee, Moe stood up, his grin directed at Marsh.

'Come with me, *paesano*, I got to show you my new ovens.'

Marsh rose but stood still when Jeanette placed a staying hand on his arm. Turning to her husband, she sighed exaggeratedly, 'Marsh doesn't want to see your ovens, Moe.'

Moe's eyes, as soulful as a scolded cocker spaniel, shifted from Marsh to Jeanette, then back to Marsh.

'Tell the heartless woman you want to see my new ovens, Marsh,' he pleaded petulantly.

His lips twitching, Marsh stared into Jeanette's laughing brown eyes and said seriously, 'I want to see Moe's new ovens, heartless woman.'

Jeanette's carefully controlled features dissolved into laughter. Waving one hand dismissively, she cried, 'Oh, for heaven's sake, go admire the new ovens, you two lunatics.'

Shaking her curly black head, Jeanette turned back to Helen with a grimace that quickly turned into a smile. 'I swear, sometimes I think that man loves his kitchens more than he loves me.'

'Kitchens?' Helen queried.

'Yes,' the black head nodded. 'He has three restaurants, even though this place, being the first, is his favourite.'

'Does he do any of the cooking?'

'Lord, yes!' Jeanette exclaimed. 'Here and at home. And what a cook!' She placed closed fingertips to her lips and kissed them. 'I have to starve myself during the working hours or there would be a lot more of me.'

'Well, if he cooked tonight's dinner,' Helen said laughingly, 'I can understand your problem.'

'You know, Helen.' Jeanette's tone went low, serious. 'When Moe came home raving about Marsh's beautiful woman, I thought, yeah, just another in a long line of beautiful women. But five minutes after we met, I knew you were not just a beautiful woman in any man's line. You're special, and that makes me happy, because

Marsh is also special and his happiness is very important to Moe and me.'

What could one possibly reply to a sentiment like that? Feeling anything she'd say would be vastly inadequate, Helen nevertheless began an attempt to tell Jeanette the truth.

'Jeanette, I don't know quite how to say this, but—'

'By your solemn expression, love.' Marsh inserted, 'I have a nasty suspicion my best friend's wife has been telling tales out of school.'

'Every chance I can,' Jeanette retorted. 'We girls have to stick together if we hope to keep you guys in line.'

The moment for taking Jeanette into her confidence was past, and Helen felt an odd relief at Marsh's interruption. Strangely she hated the idea of disappointing Moe and Jeanette.

CHAPTER SIX

IT was close to midnight before the party broke up. It seemed to Helen that they talked nonstop, one minute laughingly, the next seriously. There were even a few friendly arguments, which nobody won, ending happily with everyone agreeing to disagree. Helen amazed herself with her own participation. She couldn't remember the last time she'd entered into a free-for-all conversation so effortlessly, and she enjoyed every minute of it.

When the last of the other dinner patrons had left, Moe, Marsh, and a few of the waiters cleared a small area of floor space by moving several tables together, and Moe found some slow, late-night music on the stereo-FM radio behind the bar.

He then came to Helen and, with a courtly, old-world bow, requested the honour of the first dance. Moe was a good dancer; in fact he was the next thing to expert. Never very proficient herself, Helen found it hard to relax. When the music ended and was followed immediately by another, slower, number, Helen swirled out of one pair of arms into another.

Although he moved smoothly, evenly, Marsh was not nearly as expert as Moe and as his steps were less intricate, Helen followed his lead easier. As one song followed another and the tension of concentration seeped out of her body, Marsh's arms tightened. His steps grew slower until, locked together, they were simply swaying to the music, oblivious of the knowing smiles of Moe and Jeanette, the shadowy movements of the waiters as they unobtrusively cleared the tables.

On the way home, still in a mellow mood, Helen tipped her head back against the headrest and softly hummed one of the tunes they'd danced to.

'You like my friends?' Marsh's quiet tone blended with her mood, and she answered without hesitation.

'Very much.'

'I'm glad.' He was quiet a moment, then added softly, 'Maybe you'll introduce me to some of your friends sometime.'

The mood was shattered, and Helen sat up straight, alert and wary. Now she did hesitate, for although his voice was soft, his tone had taughtened.

'Maybe,' she said, hedging, 'sometime.'

His soft laughter mocked her but he didn't pursue the subject. Instead he taunted, 'Did you miss me this week?'

'Why?' Helen asked blandly, innocently. 'Were you away?'

This time his laughter filled the car, scurried down her spine.

'That'll cost you also,' he purred warningly. 'You are racking up quite a bill, woman. And I fully intend to make you pay in toto.'

'I don't have the vaguest idea what you're talking about.' Helen managed a light tone, despite the lick of excitement that shot through her veins.

'Oh, I think you do,' he mocked. 'Now answer my question. Did you miss me?'

'Well, maybe a little.' She returned his mocking tone. 'Like one might miss a persistent itch after it's gone.'

'Deeper and deeper,' he said, chuckling. 'You're going to need a ladder to get yourself out of the hole you're digging.'

He parked the car on the lot close to the building and grinned when she turned to say goodnight.

'Save your breath, I'm coming up with you.'

'But, Marsh, it's late and—'

'Save it.' He cut her off. 'I'm coming up with you, Helen. That almost kiss I got early this evening wore off long ago. Besides which, I thought you'd offer me a nightcap or at least a cup of coffee.'

'Coffee! At this hour?'

'You forget, I'm still young,' he teased roughly. 'Coffee never keeps me awake. Now stop stalling and let's go.'

They went, Helen at an irritated, impatient clip, Marsh at a long-legged saunter beside her. She only glanced at him once on the way up. One glance at his twitching lips, his blue eyes dancing with devilry, was enough to send her blood racing—with anger?—through her body.

Inside the apartment she flung her coat and bag onto a chair and stormed into the kitchen. His soft laughter, as he carefully hung up her coat, crawled up the back of her neck, made her scalp tingle.

She was pouring the water into the top of the automatic coffee maker when he entered the room, and after sliding the glass pot into place, Helen turned, eyes widening. He had not only removed his topcoat, but his jacket and tie as well, and had opened the top three buttons of his shirt. Turning away quickly, she pulled open the cabinet door, shaking fingers fumbling for cups. Damn him, she thought wildly, trying to concentrate on getting the cups safely out of the cabinet. *How can I hope to keep him at arm's length when he's already half undressed? And how in the world do I handle a man that simply laughs at me and refuses to be handled? More to the point, how do I handle myself when I know that what I want to do is finish the job he started on his shirt, feel his warm skin against my fingertips?*

Angry with him, with herself, with everything in general, she slid the cups from the shelf and banged them onto the countertop. Glaring at the coffee running into the pot, she snapped, 'Make yourself at home.'

'I intend to.'

She hadn't heard him move up behind her, and she jumped when his arms slid around her waist, drew her back against him. When his lips touched her cheek, she cried, 'Marsh, the coffee's ready.'

'So am I,' he murmured close to her ear, his hands moving slowly up her rib cage. 'God, I missed you,' he groaned. 'You may only have missed me like the absence of an itch, but this is one itch that is going to persist until you have to scratch. Helen.'

Helen's mouth went dry and her eyes closed against the sigh of urgency he put into her name. She gasped softly when his teeth nipped her lobe, then her eyes flew wide as his hands moved over her breasts.

'Marsh, stop.'

Her words whirled away as she was twirled inside his arms. His hungry mouth, covering hers, allowed no more words for several moments. Feeling her resolve, her determination, melt under the heat of his obvious desire, Helen pushed at his chest, head moving back and forth in agitation.

'Marsh, the coffee.'

'The hell with the coffee,' he growled harshly. 'Helen, I've barely thought of anything but this all week. Now will you be quiet and let me kiss you?'

'No.' She pushed harder against his chest. 'Marsh, you—you wanted the damn coffee and you're going to drink it or you're going to go home.'

He sighed, but his hands dropped to his sides. 'All right, I'll drink the coffee.' He gave in, then qualified. 'If you'll join me.'

The room crackled with tension as she filled the cups, placed them, along with cream and sugar, on the table. Sitting opposite him, sipping nervously at the brew she didn't want, Helen could feel the tension like a tangible presence. When he spoke, the calm normalcy of his tone struck her like a dash of cold water.

'Were you very busy this week?'

'Yes.'

Try as she did, she could not come up with any other words. The silence yawned in front of her again, and her head jerked up when he blandly asked, 'What's that you say? Did I have a busy week? As a matter of fact I did.' His eyes bored into hers. 'Even though I seemed to spend as much time in the air as on the ground. Altoona, Harrisburg, Pittsburgh.'

He stopped abruptly, his eyes refusing to release hers. But he had achieved his purpose, he had reignited her curiosity about his work.

'Your grandfather's building and construction firm extends throughout the state?'

The blue gaze softened and he smiled.

'No, but he does have business interests not only throughout the state but along the entire East Coast.'

'I see.'

Helen sipped her coffee, then stared into the creamy brew. She really didn't know any more than she had before. When she looked up, she was caught by the waiting stillness about Marsh, the hint of amusement in his eyes. *He's not going to volunteer a thing*, she thought frustratedly. *He's going to sit there, silently laughing at me, and make me ask. The hell with it*, she fumed, *and him. I don't even care what he does*.

With elaborate casualness she got up, walked to the counter, and refilled her cup with coffee she wanted even less than the first cup. When he held out his cup to her, his lips twitching, she refilled it and handed it back to him, fighting down the urge to upend it over his head. She was going to ask. She knew she was going to ask and she resented him for it. Why was so it important to her anyway? The less she knew about him the better. Right?

'Do you handle all your grandfather's interests?' Well, at least she'd managed an unconcerned tone, she congratulated herself.

'Mostly,' he replied laconically. 'But I wasn't on Cullen's business this trip. I was on my own.'

Helen glanced up hopefully, but he was calmly drinking his coffee, his eyes mocking her over the cup's rim. *Damn him,* she thought furiously. *Why is he doing this?* 'because he knows,' reason told her. *He knows how much I hate this need to know everything about him. God, can he read my mind?* It was not the first time she'd wondered about that, and the idea, as ridiculous as it was, made her uneasy. Placing her cup carefully in the saucer, Helen sighed in defeat.

'What is your business, Marsh?'

'Now, that hardly hurt at all, did it?' Marsh mocked softly. Then all traces of mocking were gone, but the amusement deepened, danced in his eyes. 'I'm an accountant.'

'An accountant!'

At her tone of astonished disbelief his laughter escaped, danced across the table and along her nerve ends. 'An accountant,' he repeated dryly. 'Don't I look like an accountant?'

'Hardly.' Helen had control of herself now, her dryness matched his. 'Does King Kong look like a monkey?'

'Do I look like King Kong?' His laughter deepened and Helen felt a strange, melting sensation inside. Her own eyes sparkling with amusement, she answered sweetly, 'Only when you're angry.'

He was up and around the table before Helen even finished speaking, and still laughing, he pulled her out of her chair and into his arms.

'You want to play Fay Wray?' He grinned suggestively.

'To an accountant?' Helen taunted.

'Ah, but you see, love,' he said in the same suggestive tone, 'accountants know all about figures.' His hands moved slowly down her back, over her hips. 'And you've got one of the best I've ever handled.'

'And you've handled so many?' Helen shot back, annoyed at the twinge of pain the memory of Jeanette's words about Marsh's women sent tearing through her chest.

'Enough,' he admitted lazily. His arms tightened, drawing her close to his muscle-tautened frame. 'Helen,' he murmured urgently. 'You're driving me crazy.' His mouth was a driving force that pushed her head back, crushed the resistance out of her.

Feeling her body soften traitorously against him, Helen sighed fatalistically. She *had* missed him. She had missed *this*. Her hands, imprisoned between them, inched to the centre of his chest. She heard his sharply indrawn breath when her fingers began undoing the buttons still fastened on his shirt, and when she paused, heard him groan, 'Good God, love, don't stop.'

His lips left a fiery, hungry trail down her arched throat; his hands moved restlessly over her shoulders, her back, her hips. His lips back tracked to the sensitive skin behind her ear. His voice was a hoarse, exciting seducement. 'I love you. I love you. It's been such a long week. Helen, don't send me home, let me stay with you.'

'Marsh, oh, Marsh.' Helen could hardly speak. Her breath came in short, quick gasps through her parted lips. The shirt was open and she felt him shudder when her fingers tentatively stroked his heated skin.

'More, more.' His mouth hovered tantalisingly over hers. Her hands pushed away the silky material of his shirt as they slid up his chest, over his shoulders. With a low moan his mouth crushed hers in a demand she no longer could, or wanted to, deny.

The ring of the wall phone, not three feet from Helen's head, was a shrill intrusion of reality. It was a call she couldn't ignore, and on the second ring she struggled against him. Cursing softly, Marsh released her reluctantly.

With shaking hands Helen grasped the receiver, drew a deep breath, and huskily said, 'Dr Cassidy.'

'Sorry to waken you, Doctor,' the voice of the never-seen person who worked for her service said apologetically. 'I just had a call from a Mr Rayburn. He said his wife's labour pains are ten minutes apart and she's spotting, and he is taking her to the hospital.'

'Thank you.' Helen's husky, sleepy-sounding tone had brisked to wide-awake alertness. Without even looking at Marsh, she swung through the doorway to the living room, calling to him over her shoulder, 'Marsh, you may as well go home. I have to go to the hospital and I have no idea how long I'll be.'

He caught up with her halfway across the living room, grasping her arm to spin her around to face him.

'I'll drive you and wait for you.'

Impatient to be gone, Helen shrugged his hand from her arm. 'Don't be silly! I told you I have no idea how long it will take. It's one thirty in the morning. Go home, get some sleep.'

'But I don't mind—'

'Marsh, please,' Helen interrupted sharply. Cold reality, and the knowledge of how close she'd come to sharing her bed with him, put an edge on her tongue. 'I have to go and I want to change my clothes. Will you just go home?'

'Would you object if I wait while you change and walk down to your car with you?' Marsh asked sarcastically. 'As you said, it is one thirty in the morning.'

'Oh, all right,' Helen replied ungraciously, turning to run into the bedroom.

When she came hurrying back a few minutes later, he was standing at the door, holding her coat and hand-bag.

'Marsh, I—I'm sorry I was so sharp with you,' Helen apologised haltingly, sliding her arms into the sleeves of her coat. 'It's just that I . . . well—'

'Don't worry about it.' His hands tightened a second on her shoulders before he removed them and turned to open the door. 'Had you scared for a minute there in the kitchen, didn't I?' he teased as she walked by him into the hall. His good humour was entirely restored and the devil gleam was back in his eyes.

'I don't understand.' Flustered, Helen stepped into the elevator, then turned deliberately widened, questioning eyes to him.

'You understand perfectly,' he said softly, tormenting her. 'I'm going to get you and you know it. It's just a matter of time.' He paused, grinning ruefully. 'And an uninterrupted opportunity.'

As they stepped out of the apartment entrance, for the second time that night, they were met by a swirl of snowflakes.

'I hope this doesn't amount to anything.' Marsh frowned, looking up at the dirty grey sky.

'Why, don't you like snow, Marsh?' Helen had always liked snow.

'As a rule it doesn't bother me one way or the other,' he answered, taking her keys from her fingers as they reached her car. He unlocked the door, handed her keys back, then opened the door for her and added, 'But tonight, at who knows what time, my girl's going to be driving home in it, so I hope it doesn't amount to any-thing.'

Before she could say anything he kissed her hard on

the mouth and strode across the lot in the direction of his car, parked some distance away.

His girl! His *girl!* Helen wasn't sure if she was amused or angry. His girl indeed. As she drove off the lot Marsh's car was two bright headlights reflected in her rearview mirror. And the reflection was there, every time she glanced in the mirror, all the way to the hospital. Now she was sure she was angry.

After parking her car in the section marked DOCTORS ONLY, Helen flung out of the car and across the lot to where the big Lincoln sat idling quietly. He slid out of the car when she reached the front fender. Walking with jerky, angry steps around the door, she snapped, 'What do you think you're doing? I asked you to go home.'

Without a word he pulled her into his arms, kissed her roughly.

'And I'm going home,' he grated when he lifted his head. 'I wanted to make sure you got here safely, and to tell you to call me when you get home.'

'But I don't know what time it will be.' She started walking towards a side entrance, Marsh close beside her.

'That doesn't matter,' he stated flatly.

'Marsh, I do this all the time,' Helen reasoned.

'And people get stopped and attacked in their cars more and more all the time.' His tone was adamant, final. 'Helen, I mean it. Promise you'll call or I'll wait right here.'

'All right, I promise.' Helen yanked open the door. 'Now will you go and let me get to the delivery room before that baby does?'

'Okay, I'll go. Don't forget.'

Helen was gone, practically running down the long hall to the elevators.

It was a hard delivery and Helen felt exhausted when she finally let herself into her living room close to three thirty. At least she hadn't had to face treacherous driving conditions, as the snow squall had moved off and the streets were dry.

The baby was a large one and had taken quite a bit out of his mother, not to mention Helen. Like a sleep-walker she went into the bedroom and undressed, thinking light-headedly that even at birth most males gave a woman an undue amount of trouble. After washing her face and hands, Helen sat on the side of her bed, lit a cigarette, and picked up the phone.

'Helen?' Marsh's voice questioned after the first ring.

'Yes, Marsh.' Helen spoke softly, tiredly. 'I'm home.'

'You sound beat, love. Was it bad?' Deep concern laced his tone.

'For a while there,' she sighed. 'But Mrs Rayburn is fine and so is her son and I'm half asleep sitting here.'

'I can hear that,' he murmured. 'I wish I was there to hold you, reward you. Go to bed, love. I'll call you tomorrow afternoon. By the way, my parents would like you to come for dinner tomorrow, or should I say tonight, but I'll tell you more about that when I call. Goodnight, love.'

Helen murmured goodnight, replaced the receiver, then sat up with a start. His parents' for dinner! Whatever for? Good grief! Was she to be brought home to Mother and Dad for approval? Was Marsh out of his mind to think she'd stand for that? And what did he mean by reward me?

Too many questions in a mind too tired to search for answers. Helen crushed out her cigarette, switched off the light, crawled into bed, and was instantly asleep.

The phone remained considerately silent all Sunday morning, and Helen slept until after noon. She was glancing over the paper, sipping at her second cup of coffee, when the instrument issued its insistent cry. It was Marsh, and she was ready for him.

'What was all that business about dinner at your

parents' home?' Helen began the moment he'd finished saying, 'Good morning, love, did you sleep well?'

There was a long pause, then he asked smoothly, 'Are you always this prickly when you first wake up?'

'Only when I've been sent to sleep with the threat of being paraded for approval, like a horse at an auction,' she replied acidly.

'Only with the very best Thoroughbred fillies, darling.' He laughed softly. 'What gave you the idea you were going to be paraded?'

'It smacks too much of "bring the girl home for inspection before you do anything stupid, son,"' Helen retorted. 'Really, Marsh, why else would they invite me?'

'Because they want to meet you? Get to know you?' His amusement curled along the line to her.

'Why now? All of a sudden?' she asked bluntly.

'All right, Helen.' His voice sobered, grew serious. 'I admit that Mother asked a few discreet questions after we left Kris's room together. I'm also sure she had already talked to my father about it, as he was there during the'—he paused—'questioning.'

'And?' Helen prompted.

'I told them I'd asked you to marry me.'

The calm statement almost had the power to curl Helen's hair.

'Marsh, you didn't!' Helen fairly screamed into the mouthpiece.

'Don't fall apart, love.' He was laughing again. 'I was honest. I told them you'd turned me down—for now.'

'Marshall Kirk,' Helen gritted, 'if you're trying to get yourself strangled, you are going about it in the right way. I can't go.'

'You'd better,' he warned. 'I've told them we'll be there at seven. It won't be all that bad, love. Kris and Mike will be there, and as an extra added attraction they've invited Cullen. You can sit back and watch my father and the old bear take verbal potshots at each other.'

Good Lord, the whole family! Helen groaned. *Am I going prematurely senile? I must be or I wouldn't put up with this silliness. Why should I volunteer to endure this meet-the-family routine? I haven't the slightest intention of getting involved with him in any way, let alone marry him.* The scene in that very kitchen the night before returned to mock her, and she groaned again.

'Helen? What's the matter?' His sharp query made her aware of how long she'd been quiet. His next question assured her he'd heard her soft groan. 'Are you crying?'

'I never cry,' she answered bitingly. 'I don't have the time.'

'But you *do* have time for dinner tonight.' He bit back. 'And I *will* come for you at six thirty.' The bite turned into a threat. 'And you'd *better* be ready.'

Helen simmered, just below boiling point, all afternoon. Marsh's parting thrust, 'You'd *better* be ready,' stabbing at her mind like the tip of a red-hot poker.

You fool! she berated herself unmercifully. *You stupid fool! You have no sense at all?* Silently, as if to another person, she dressed herself down as harshly as a tough top sergeant might a raw recruit. *You, a professional—whose very pride is in that cool professionalism—are you going to meekly submit to the dictates of a man? What can you be thinking of? You are not a twittering teenager. You are not a fresh-faced young woman, just starting out. You have earned your pride, your confidence, your independence. And you did it by yourself, without the support, the consideration of any male.*

Although the day waned, Helen's self-directed fury did not. As she went about washing the few dishes in the sink, making her bed, straightening the apartment, her mental tirade continued.

Now, now when you've reached the point in life where you hold that pride, that independence, tightly in your hands, are you going to fling it all away for the brief assuagement of your resurrected physical needs? And don't, for one minute, try to convince yourself it will be anything but brief.

At five forty-five, her soft lips twisted in self-derision, Helen stepped under the shower. Still scolding silently, she told her invisible target, *The very idea of a woman like you is a challenge to the Marshall Kirks of this world. He says he loves you. In all probability he would say or do anything to get what he wants.*

Helen stepped out of the shower, scooped up a towel, and began patting herself dry. *And what does he want, you ask?* Helen went still, a wry smile tugging at her lips as she gazed into the hazel eyes of the recipient of her condemnation, reflected in the full-length mirror on the back of the bathroom door. *Okay, you asked for it. I'll tell you exactly what he wants. He wants the power to make you come to heel, like a well-trained puppy, at his mildest command. He wants the exquisite satisfaction of knowing he has brought the very cool, so very professional, Dr Cassidy to her knees. And when he is sated with that satisfaction, he will take a walk—and forget to come back. Are you willing,* Helen asked those watchful, reflected eyes, *to deny everything you've worked so hard for, for a few moments of mindless bliss that can only be found in this one man's arms?*

Helen blinked, and her head snapped up. The answer was there, in the clear hazel eyes staring back at her. Silently, yet loud and clear, those eyes proclaimed, 'No way.'

Her self-denouncement completed, Helen dressed slowly, carefully, a secret smile softening the contours of her face. She had tried, and failed, to convince Marsh of her disinterest in any kind of male-female relationship. He had, figuratively, backed her into a corner. She refused to cower in that corner. Her intelligent father and gentle mother had not raised a female fool. She would play Marsh's game, and beat him at it.

The doorbell rang at exactly six thirty. Composing her features, squaring her shoulders, Helen went to open the door, a smile of welcome curving her lips. The smile wavered at the sheer, overpowering look of him, then strengthened at the memory of her resolve.

He was dressed in a dark suit and silk shirt, which matched exactly the colour of his eyes, and a patterned tie, which contrasted, yet complemented, his attire. The overall effect was one of elegantly covered, raw masculinity. His gleaming, not-quite red hair had been - slightly tousled by the wind. His grey topcoat had been tossed carelessly over one broad shoulder, and his casually arrogant stance gave him the look of a well-dressed hell-raiser.

'Good eve—' He broke off midword, a stunned expression on his face, as his eyes made a slow tour of her body, while her own expression returned the compliment.

Without speaking, Helen moved back to allow him to enter, then closed the door quietly and turned to face him.

After long deliberation she had dressed in a long, narrow black velvet skirt with a snugly fitting matching vest over a smoky-coloured, long-sleeved chiffon blouse. A single strand of milky-white pearls (a gift from her brother when she had graduated from medical school) glowed around her slender throat. The warm admiration in his eyes told her she'd chosen well.

'Black on black,' he murmured when her eyes met his. 'Very effective with your hair, your fair skin, and the pearls.' His voice deepened huskily. 'You're beautiful, Helen.'

A thrill of excitement shot through Helen, followed by a shaft of elation. He had called the game and dealt out the cards on the day they met. Now, she decided, was the time for her to pick up her hand and play her first card.

Helen's eyes lifted to his. 'Thank you. You—you're beautiful too.' She laughed softly. 'I suppose a woman shouldn't tell a man he's beautiful, but you are, you know. A beautiful male animal.'

A flame ignited in his eyes and he drew his breath in very slowly. As he exhaled, equally slowly, he moved to stand close to her.

'I don't know if a woman is supposed to tell a man that,' he murmured. 'But I know this man likes hearing it.' His hands came up to cup her face. 'Tell me more. Tell me why you think I'm beautiful.'

'I don't know if I can explain, exactly.' Helen searched for words. 'Certainly you are very attractive, but you know that. You dress well. Instead of simply covering your body, your clothes enhance it, proclaim your masculinity.'

His thumb moved caressingly over her cheek, and Helen paused to run her tongue over suddenly dry lips.

'An invitation if I ever saw one,' he whispered, bending his head to touch his mouth to hers. 'Is there more?' he whispered against her lips.

'You make me laugh, even when I'm angry,' Helen whispered back. 'And you make me breathless, most of the time.'

'Are you breathless now?'

'Yes.'

'And me.' His mouth crushed hers, sending the room spinning around her head.

When he lifted his head and the room settled back into

place, Helen drew deep breaths to calm her racing senses. 'Marsh, we must go, your parents are expecting us.'

'I know,' he groaned. 'Helen, will you let me stay?'

It was time to play the second card. Lifting her hand to his face, she trailed her slim fingers across his cheek, over his firm lips. 'Marsh, please, be patient with me. Let me get to know you, feel . . . easier . . . with you. It's been a long time since I've felt safe with a man.' She shuddered and felt his lips kiss her finger. 'I don't want what happened that night in your apartment to happen again.' She slid her hand from his mouth, across his face, and around his neck to draw his head close to hers. Her lips against his, she pleaded, 'Please, Marsh.'

Helen felt a ripple run through his body and heard his soft sigh before he answered tersely, 'All right, love, I won't pressure you. But I think it's only fair to warn you that I want you very badly and I'm going to do every damned thing I can think of to warm that core of ice that's deep inside you.'

He stepped back, his eyes eating her, then he shook his head and muttered, 'We'd better leave.'

CHAPTER SEVEN

HELEN shivered, but not from the outside cold. The warmth from the car's heater protected them from the biting winds and subzero temperature. The soft music from the tape deck added to that warmth. The chill was inside Helen, deep inside. The shiver stemmed from two different sources. One of them was excitement, the other, fear. The elements of both those emotions had Helen at near-fever pitch.

The feeling of power that had surged through her at Marsh's reaction to her small advance had generated an excitement Helen had never experienced before. It was heady, exhilarating, while at the same time, she realised, a little dangerous. And then there was the tiny fear that had begun with Marsh's words. Taken at face value they were innocuous enough. But could she take them at face value? There was the seed of her growing fear. '*I'm going to do every damned thing I can think of to warm that core of ice.*' A simple straightforward promise? Or something more? Perhaps she was reading words between the lines that simply were not there, but his tone, everything about him, had been so intense that a small alarm had sounded inside her mind.

'You're very quiet,' Marsh said softly into her thoughts. 'You're not nervous about meeting the family, are you?'

All traces of his earlier intensity were gone, and telling herself she was being overimaginative, Helen turned to him with a smile.

'A little,' she admitted. 'Mostly of your grandfather. He sounds a very formidable character.'

113

'Oh, he is that.' Marsh laughed. 'But he's a pushover for a beautiful woman. And an absolute lapdog for one with intelligence as well as beauty. You, love, will have him eating out of your hand fifteen minutes after you're there.'

'Your confidence in my feminine prowess is overwhelming,' Helen murmured dryly, secretly elated. He thought she was beautiful. He thought she was intelligent. She was a challenge to his manhood, and he wanted to overcome that challenge by possessing her physically. *Nothing very complicated or scary about that*, she assured herself. *You, Doctor, have been chasing shadows that just are not there. Relax and enjoy the game until the final card is played.*

Marsh's parents' home loomed large and imposing, the many brightly lit windows a beacon in the winter-night darkness. From the moment she stepped inside the door Helen could feel the wealth and good taste of its owners surround her. The family, the very correct butler informed Marsh, were in the small rear sitting room. Following his ramrod-straight back across the wide hall, Helen chanced a glance at Marsh and received a slow, exaggerated wink in return.

The small rear sitting room was not really at the rear and not small at all, and very, very elegant. Helen judged that the furniture, paintings, and exquisite decorations in the room had probably cost more than she could earn if she worked flat out until she was ninety. A room definitely not for small children, she thought, wondering if Marsh and his sister had been barred from it while they were growing up.

Marsh's mother, a tall, attractive woman in her mid-fifties, came across the room to greet them, her head high, rich auburn hair gleaming in the room's soft light.

'Good evening, Dr Cassidy.' Kathleen Kirk's voice was deep and cultured, and held a note of real welcoming warmth that was reassuring. 'I'm so pleased you were free to join us this evening.'

'Thank you for inviting me,' Helen replied softly, studying the older woman as she placed her hand in the one outstretched to her. Although she was tall, she was delicately formed and the fine skin covering her face still held a faint, youthful glow despite the fine lines around her dark blue eyes.

During the brief exchange two men had come to stand behind Mrs Kirk, and as she released Helen's hand she stepped to the side, said pleasantly, 'My husband, George,' nodding to a sandy-haired, distinguished-looking man not much taller than herself.

Helen took his hand, searching in vain for a re-semblance to Marsh, as she murmured, 'Mr Kirk'. Then she turned her head and caught her breath at Mrs Kirk's, 'And my father, Cullen Hannlon.'

The resemblance here was uncanny. Helen knew that Marsh's grandfather had to be in his mid-seventies, yet nothing about him betrayed that fact. As tall as Marsh, his shoulders almost as broad, Cullen Hannlon stood straight, his large frame unbowed by time. He fitted Marsh's name for him perfectly, for he was truly a bear of a man. The light blue eyes that held hers were the exact shade of his grandson's and they glowed with the same intent sharpness, and Helen would have bet her eyeteeth that his luxuriant shock of white hair had, in years past, been the same not-quite red as Marsh's.

Her hand was grasped, not taken, by his large, hard-fingered, brown one, which reminded Helen of tough old leather. His entire appearance contrasted oddly with his deep, gentle voice.

'Well, Helen.' No title from this quarter, Helen thought with amusement. 'We finally meet. Of course,' he teased, squeezing her hand. 'Now that I see you I can understand why Marsh wanted to keep you to himself.

You, my dear, are an extraordinarily beautiful woman.'

Before Helen could find words to reply to this un-believable old man, she heard Marsh laugh softly behind her and say sardonically, 'You're wasting your time and breath, Cullen. Helen is immune to flattery.'

Cullen favoured Helen with a secret smile before turning suddenly fierce blue eyes on his grandson. 'If you really believe that, son, you are a fool. And I know you are anything but that. No woman is immune to flattery, as indeed no man is; *if* it's the right kind of flattery.'

Sauntering beside her as his mother ushered them into the room, Marsh's laughter deepened and he whispered close to her ear, 'Imagine what he must have been like when he was young.'

I don't have to imagine anything, Helen thought wryly. *All I have to do is turn my head and look at you.* The thought that Marsh would very likely be exactly the same as Cullen when he grew old was a strangely exciting one, and Helen quickly squashed it by thinking, *I won't be there to see it.* Forcing her mind away from the oddly bereft sensation her thoughts created, Helen turned her attention to what Mrs Kirk was saying.

'You know my daughter, Kristeen, and her husband, Mike, of course.'

Helen smiled at the young couple, seating herself on the delicately upholstered chair beside the matching settee they shared. 'Hello, Kristeen, how are you? Mr Darren. And how is your daughter?'

'She's perfect, Doctor, thank you.' Kristeen smiled shyly. 'And I feel wonderful. I wouldn't dare feel any other way after the amount of fussing this family of mine has done over me.'

'Fussing, hell!' Cullen snorted impatiently. 'This family has lost one woman through childbirth. I don't want to live through that again, so behave yourself, young woman, and let us care for you.'

Although a smile played at her soft mouth, Kristeen answered demurely, 'Yes, Grandfather.'

'Father, please,' Kathleen murmured softly, silencingly.

On his first statement Helen's eyes, full of questions, had swung to Cullen's, and now, although he grasped his daughter's shoulder gently, he answered the question. 'I lost my wife three weeks after Kathleen was born.' His voice was steady, yet Helen could sense the wealth of sorrow he still felt from his loss. 'Megan had had a hard delivery and she was very weak. I was just getting started in the construction business and couldn't afford a full-time nurse.'

His eyes darkened with pain, and Helen said urgently, 'Mr Hannlon, please don't. This isn't necessary.' Her eyes flew to Marsh with a silent plea for help, but he didn't see her. His eyes were fastened on his grandfather, and incredibly Cullen's pain was reflected in them.

'She was so delighted with our daughter, she found pleasure in caring for her, even though it drained the little strength she had.' He went on in that same quiet tone. 'She was eighteen, I was twenty-one. Twenty-one,' he repeated softly, then his eyes sharpened on Helen's. 'Do you have any idea, I wonder, what losing his soul-mate can do to a man?'

Helen felt trapped, pinned by those intense blue eyes, and she had the unreal, weird sensation that he was trying to tell her something important. Mentally shrugging off the feeling as compassion for his still obviously deep grief, Helen searched for suitable words.

'I—I don't know, sir. I've never lost a patient or had to bring that kind of news to a husband. I can't even imagine—'

Marsh's soft voice saved Helen from floundering

further, but in so doing he confused her even more, for there was a definite warning in his tone.

'Enough said, Cullen.'

The old man's eyes shot a challenge at his grandson, one Marsh's very stance conveyed he was ready to meet. For several seconds the room seemed electrically charged and Helen could see her own confusion mirrored on the faces of the others as matching pairs of blue eyes silently duelled. Mr Kirk relieved the tension with a dry gibe, addressed to Helen, but aimed at his son.

'May I get you an aperitif, Helen? You may need some alcoholic fortitude, as your escort seems to be spoiling for an argument.'

'I'll get it.' Marsh shot a grin at his father and a broad wink at his grandfather. 'But let me assure you, she does not need it. I've tried arguing with Helen. I invariably lose.'

'Good for Helen.' Kathleen Kirk's smile stole the sting from her barb. 'You are much too sure of yourself.'

Later Helen was to wonder why she had hesitated over Marsh's parents' invitation. She had a delightful time. Kristeen and Mike were a lively couple, full of interesting and funny stories of times spent with their wide assortment of friends. Marsh periodically dropped dry, witty comments into their narrative as they shared some of their friends. Helen was surprised to find that Mr and Mrs Kirk were very well acquainted with several of her friends and colleagues, and that paved the way for further easy conversation.

But for Helen the most enjoyable part of the evening came from watching, in fascinated amusement, the thrust and parry between Cullen Hannlon and George Kirk. The play swung back and forth, George Kirk's wry, caustic lunges effortlessly deflected by Cullen's dry, acerbic ripostes. Helen had never witnessed anything quite like it before in her life.

Glancing at Marsh, Helen saw her own amusement mirrored in his eyes. That he got a kick out of watching the two men was obvious. Equally obvious was the deep love and respect he had for them. Knowing this warmed her, but for the life of her she couldn't figure out why. Why should it matter to her one way or the other, she asked herself, if he was capable of feeling abiding love, loyalty, respect?

When he took her home, Marsh kept to his promise not to pressure her. With a murmured, 'I'll call you,' he kissed her gently and left her staring after him in uncertain amazement.

It was towards the end of the following week that Helen first felt an uncomfortable twinge about Marsh's behaviour. The fact that she couldn't exactly pinpoint what it was about his attitude made her uneasy. He was considerate and attentive, without actually dancing attendance on her, and yet there was something. It nagged her, but she couldn't quite put her finger on why.

January slipped into February and their relationship seemed at an impasse. Helen was seeing Marsh on an average of four nights a week, and surprisingly he did not call her on the nights she didn't see him. More surprising still was that he was adhering completely to his no-pressure promise. Was he losing interest? It was a question Helen asked herself more and more frequently as the days went by.

On the surface Marsh seemed as determined as before, at times more so. On the evening of Valentine's Day Kristeen and Mike were having a small get-together of friends, the first since their baby's birth, and they had asked Helen and Marsh to join them.

'I don't think so,' Helen hedged when Marsh relayed Kris's invitation.

'Why not?' he asked, surprised. 'I thought you liked Kris and Mike.'

'I do,' Helen replied promptly, then hesitated. She couldn't very well tell him she thought it unadvisable to get too involved with his family and friends, so she offered, lamely, 'But it will be young married couples, won't it? I just don't think I'd fit in.'

'Not fit in?' he exclaimed. 'Helen, that's ridiculous. Of course you'd fit in. It will do you good to be around young women who are not your patients. Besides which'—he grinned—'I already told them we'd come.'

He takes too much on himself, Helen fumed in frustration. *I really ought to put him back in his place.* She didn't at once, and then the moment was gone as he went on blandly to tell her who would be there. Not a large group, he informed her. Just a few close friends he shared with Kris and Mike.

On the fourteenth Marsh arrived at the apartment with a large elaborately decorated heart-shaped box of chocolates and a card, almost as large, that was covered with cupids and flowers and gushy sentiment. Reading the card, Helen frowned, unable to believe he really went in for that sort of mush, then, glancing up, she smiled ruefully at the devil gleam in his eye.

'There are times I'm convinced you are really quite mad, Marsh,' she said, her tone deliberately crushing. It didn't work. He laughed at her, taunted, 'I am quite mad. For you. I couldn't resist the urge to watch your face as you read it.' He paused, then chided, nodding at the candy, 'Aren't you going to offer me a piece?'

'You're impossible,' Helen murmured, tugging at the end of the large bow on the ribbon that surrounded the box. Glancing up to smile at him, she felt her heartbeats quicken, her mouth go dry. The gleam had disappeared and there was a waiting stillness about him that warned her. Lifting the heart-shaped lid carefully, she bit her lip, then sat down slowly. At the *V* of the heart several pieces of the candy had been removed and in their place was nestled a small jeweller's box.

For a moment, thinking that the box contained a ring, pure panic gripped her. Then reason reasserted itself as she realised the box was larger, flatter than a ring box. With trembling fingers she removed the box, lifted the lid, a small gasp whispering through her lips. In the glow from the lamp beside her chair the gold inside the box seemed to glitter and wink at her. Very carefully she extracted the intricately worked and, at the price of gold, obviously expensive chains, one for the neck and a smaller one for the wrist.

Handling the delicate pieces gently, Helen looked up at the silently waiting man in front of her, her eyes unknowingly telegraphing her words.

'Marsh, they're beautiful, but I—'

'Don't say it, Helen,' Marsh warned softly. He lifted the candy box from her lap and slid it onto the end table. 'Stand up and I'll fasten them on for you.'

Standing on legs that felt none too steady, Helen watched as he clasped the small chain on her wrist. The chain was loose and slid partway down the back of her hand.

'I didn't realise your wrist was so slender,' he said softly. 'Should I have it made smaller for you?'

A sudden, unreasonable feeling of possessiveness gripped her, and not even knowing why, she didn't want to remove the chain. 'No!' Too hasty, she chided herself, tempering it with a small laugh. 'I think I like it loose like that.'

'Yes.' Marsh murmured, studying the effect of the gold against her skin. 'Something sexy about it.' His eyes lifted to hers and what they told her sent her pulses racing.

Without waiting to see if she'd reply, he moved

around her to fasten the neck chain. He brushed her hair to one side, and Helen felt a chill at the touch of his fingers on the sensitive skin at the back of her neck. The chain was fastened, then his hands encircled her throat.

'They look like fine slave chains,' he breathed softly. 'Do they make you my slave, Helen?'

The chill turned into a strong shiver that zigzagged the length of her spine, down the back of her legs.

'Marsh . . . oh, Marsh, stop.'

It was a strangled protest against his mouth, moving along the side of her neck; his hands, moving down the silky material of her blouse, over the firm mounds of her breasts.

'How long are you going to hold out, Helen?' his breath whispered against her skin. Then she was turned around into his arms, his hands holding her tightly to the hard length of his body. 'How long should the slave be allowed to torture her master?' His hands fastened on her hips, drawing her still closer, making her all too aware of his meaning.

Helen gasped at the word 'master,' but her retort was lost inside his mouth. His kiss was a hungry, urgent demand, and Helen's hands, which had grasped his wrists to pull his hands away from her hips, slid up his arms to his shoulders and clung. He hadn't kissed her like this in weeks, and until that moment Helen hadn't fully realised how much she'd wanted him to. The realisation was a sobering one. Giving a firm push against his shoulders, she stepped back away from him.

'Marsh, stop it,' she cried shakily. 'If you think my accepting these gives you the right to—' She paused, fingers fumbling at the clasp on the wrist chain. 'You can take it back.'

'Leave it,' Marsh snapped, his large hand covering her fingers, stilling their trembling. 'There are no strings on it, or anything else I may give you. Not even on myself.'

He drew a harsh breath, then added more softly, 'You know what I want, Helen. I made my feelings clear at the beginning. But you can set the rules, you make the conditions. Only, for God's sake, do it soon. Don't let me hang indefinitely.'

Helen felt shaken and confused. Oh, yes, she thought wildly, she knew what he wanted. He wanted a bed partner, the triumph of subduing the cool, *older* lady doctor. Were there rules and conditions to that kind of relationship? If there were, Helen was positive that, for all his assurances to the contrary, he fully intended to set them.

He waited several minutes, and when she didn't speak or respond in anyway, he spun away, walked to the closet, yanked her coat from the hanger, and snapped, 'Let's get out of here. Kris and Mike are probably wondering where we are.'

Still without speaking, Helen slipped into the coat, buttoned up with a calmness she was far from feeling inside. He was angry. Really angry. His eyes held a chilling coldness he'd never turned on her before. His control seemed to crack when she returned his stare with a forced coolness of her own.

'You're enjoying every minute of this, aren't you?' he ground through clenched teeth.

'I don't know what you mean.'

'Of course not,' he taunted silkily. 'Have your fun while you can, love, because your line's about played out.'

Marsh maintained a cool, withdrawn silence during the entire twenty-five-minute drive to his sister's home. Helen's nerves, already frayed when they left the apartment, stretched and grew more taut as each silent second followed another. She was twisting the narrow chain around her wrist, on the verge of telling him to turn the car around and take her home, when he pulled up and parked along the curb in front of a row of fairly new, modern town houses. There were other cars parked along the curb and two, bumper to bumper, in the narrow driveway that led to a garage adjacent to the house.

When Marsh walked through the doorway of his sister's house, he left outside the cold, angry man he'd been for over a half hour. A slight widening of her eyes was her only outward reaction to his sudden change, but he saw it and shook his head once sharply at her before turning a smiling face to the people gathered inside the long living room.

Besides Kris and Mike there were four other couples in the room. Names were tossed at her casually, with an aside from Marsh not to worry, he'd sort them out for her later, but although the surnames were lost, she caught and held on to the first names. There were Bob and Donna, and Charles and Irene, all the same age as Kris and Mike. Then there were Ray and Betty, and Grant and Mary Ellen, a few years older than the others, more Marsh's age.

There were no awkward moments. The introductions dispensed with, Helen was drawn into the conversation so effortlessly, it had her wondering if the whole thing had been rehearsed. She would reject the idea a short time later.

Before many minutes had passed, Helen reached the conclusion that the affection these people obviously held for each other was a holdover from childhood. They accepted her without question because she was with Marsh, it was as simple as that.

Marsh slipped into a chair and the conversation with an easy camaraderie. Letting the conversation swirl around her, Helen observed him, as she had the evening she'd been at his parents' home. All traces of his earlier tension and anger were gone. He laughed often, a delightful sound that drew a reciprocal response from the others. It soon became evident to Helen as she watched him that, although he genuinely liked all the guests, there was a special bond between him and Grant.

Their banter back and forth, as they argued over a recent Philadelphia 76ers game, was much the same as Marsh indulged in with Moe. Listening more to the tone of their voices rather than their words, Helen glanced up in surprise when Grant asked, 'Don't you agree, Helen?'

'I'm sorry.' Helen smiled apologetically. 'I'm afraid I wasn't listening.'

'Grant said that it looks like the 76ers may have a winning year.' Marsh's tone held a faint trace of annoyance. 'He asked if you agree with him.'

'I have no idea.' Helen met Marsh's cool glance with equal coolness before turning to Grant with a warm smile. 'I don't follow basketball at all.' A teasing note covered her serious tone. 'Does that make me a traitor to my city?'

'If it does, you have plenty of company,' Mary Ellen answered for her husband.

'I thought you liked basketball.' Grant's pleasant, ordinary face held an injured look that matched his tone.

'I do.' Mary Ellen Laughed. 'I also like watching the Eagles play football, the Flyers play hockey, and the Phillies play baseball, but not necessarily as a steady diet.'

Grant turned to Marsh with eyebrows raised exaggerately high. 'Do you get the feeling our conversation has been boring the ladies?'

'The thought has occurred,' Marsh replied dryly. 'Perhaps we should hit the ball into their court and let them choose a topic.'

It was all the encouragement Mary Ellen needed. Eyes bright with amusement, she launched into a hilarious account of a comedy-of-errors skiing trip she and Grant had taken the previous year.

During the course of the evening Helen learned, from Mary Ellen, that her assumption about the closeness between Marsh and Grant was correct. They had been friends from grade school, were in fact closer than most brothers. Marsh had been best man at their wedding and was their son's godfather. A sudden stifled, closed-in sensation feathered over Helen when Mary Ellen finished, 'Both Grant and I unashamedly adore Marsh and would love to see him content and happy with a family of his own.' Her eyes sought the man in question, a gentle smile curved her lips as she studied him. 'Marsh will be thirty-one next month,' she said softly. 'And though he claims to be having a ball in his bachelor existence, everyone who loves him knows it's a lie. He's a steady, roots-deep-in-the-ground sort of man; he's ready to settle down.' Her eyes swung to Helen's face, her smile deepened. 'The problem *has* been finding the right woman.'

Unease joined the stifled sensations rippling along Helen's nerves, and changing the subject quickly, she figuratively backed away from Mary Ellen's none too subtle revelations.

Midway through the evening Kris announced that a light supper had been set out on the dining room table. After serving herself sparingly from the wide assortment of food, Helen followed Marsh back to the living room and allowed him to draw her down onto a large pouf beside his chair.

'What do you think of Grant?' His bland tone didn't deceive her for a second. She could actually feel the intentness with which he awaited her answer.

'I like him.' She answered with frank honesty. 'And I think the easygoing manner he shows to the world is a facade that disguises a very determined man.' She glanced up at him, smiled slightly. 'I think he could give a woman a very bad time, if he was so inclined.'

'Couldn't we all?' Marsh slanted her a wicked glance and laughed softy. 'But I'm inclined to think that Mary Ellen could probably give him a damned good run for his money, if *she* was so inclined.' His grin was every bit as wicked as his glance. 'You want to try *me* on?'

Ignoring the lightning shaft of excitement that zigzagged through her, Helen returned his stare thoughtfully then replied coolly, 'You'd lose, you know.'

His soft laughter was a gentle assault on her senses. 'Not on your stethoscope, sweetheart.'

Even though his tone had been teasing, Helen felt a chill of warning replace the excitement deep inside. She had no time to analyse the feeling however as he went on quietly. 'I've invited Grant and Mary Ellen to join us for dinner at my apartment Saturday night.' He arched an inquiring eyebrow at her. 'All right?'

'Yes, of course,' Helen replied. 'But right now I think I'd better go home. I have a full schedule tomorrow.'

After the usual time-consuming flurry of leave-taking and when they were finally in the car, Helen asked curiously, 'Were you planning to cook dinner yourself?'

'And poison some of my best friends?' Marsh asked seriously. 'No, love, I'll let Moe do the honours this time. Unless'—he shot her a teasing glance—'you'd like to do it.'

For one insane moment Helen was actually tempted, then common sense reasserted itself. 'I'll pass, thank you.' As he stopped at a stop sign at that moment, she turned to look at him directly, her eyes cool. 'I'm not in the least domestic.' Another card, unplanned, was placed onto the invisible table between them.

Marsh played a trump. 'It doesn't matter, I can always *hire* domestic help.'

They both knew they were no longer talking about the

upcoming dinner, and thinking it judicious to play her cards more carefully in future, Helen remained silent. Could he, she wondered, be aware that she'd dealt herself a hand in this game he was playing? The thought nagged at her for some minutes, then she dismissed it as ridiculous. He was far too sure of himself to ever consider the possibility.

Helen was late arriving for dinner. Marsh had said they'd eat at seven thirty but, as Grant and Mary Ellen were coming at seven for predinner drinks, he'd pick her up at six thirty.

Just before five Helen received an emergency call from the hospital. A self-induced abortion case had been brought in, she was informed. A young girl, still in her teens. As the girl's mother, frantic with worry, was a patient of Helen's, she had insisted, hysterically, that Helen be called.

Helen recognised the woman's name immediately and said she'd be there as soon as possible. She left the apartment without a thought to Marsh's dinner, her mind on the possible physical damage to the girl, and the mental damage to the mother.

The woman had come to Helen with a minor problem the same week she'd opened her office and returned for twice-yearly checkups ever since. Honest, hardworking and unassuming, she had made a career of taking care of her husband, raising her family. Helen knew what the young girl's action could do to the woman. So much for the joys and rewards of family life, Helen thought cynically as she drove to the hospital.

It was not until she had parked her car, illegally, in the emergency entrance and was striding towards the wide glass doors, that she remembered Marsh.

Stopping at the nurses station, Helen asked where the girl was, if someone could take care of her car, and would the nurse make a phone call for her. In that order. The nurse, a middle-aged veteran, echoed Helen's brisk tone. The girl was being prepped for O.R.; she could rest easy about her car; and, certainly, the phone call would be made.

Helen asked for a piece of paper, on which she scribbled Marsh's name and phone number, then she told the nurse tersely, 'Just tell him there's been an emergency and I'll get there as soon as I can. And thank you.'

The nurse's quiet 'You're welcome, Doctor' floated on the empty air where Helen had stood. Moving at a fast clip towards the elevators, Helen glanced at the large wall clock. It was twenty-three minutes since she'd received the call.

It was messy and touch and go, and the hands on the O.R. wall clock moved inexorably from number to number, but Helen saved the young girl's life.

Exhausted, filled with rage and bitter frustration at the idea that in an age of almost instant legal abortion on demand, a young girl, terrified at the results of her own foolishness, would inflict such damage on herself rather than go to her parents, Helen cleaned up and went to the lounge where those parents waited.

On entering the room, Helen's eyes went first to the girl's father. Of medium height, stockily built, the man held his face in such rigid control, it looked as if it were carved in stone. Shifting her gaze, Helen's eyes met the anxious, tear-drenched eyes of his wife. Lips quivering, the woman whispered, 'Doctor?'

'She'll live,' Helen stated bluntly, steeling herself against the fresh tears that ran down the woman's pale cheeks.

'Thank God.' The low, choked-out prayer came from the husband. 'May we see her?'

Helen's eyes swung back to his, now suspiciously

bright with moisture. 'She'll be in recovery for a while.' Compassion tugged at her heart, softened her tone. 'You both look on the verge of collapse. Why don't you take your wife down to the lunchroom, have some coffee and something to eat.' She underlined the last three words heavily.

'Was there much damage, Doctor?' The woman had gained control of herself. Her eyes were clear, steady.

'Some,' Helen sighed. 'But she is alive and will recover. We'll discuss the damage, both physical and mental, later. Right now I prescribe a strong shot of caffeine for both of you.' She was rewarded with a weak smile. 'The nurse at the floor station will tell you when you can see her. If you can arrange to be in the hospital tomorrow morning when I make my rounds, we'll talk after I've examined your daughter.'

'We'll be here.' The man beat his wife into speech.

After again advising them to have something to eat, Helen left the room and went to collect her coat and bag, not even bothering to repair her makeup.

Marsh opened the door seconds after Helen touched the bell and, after a quick glance at her face, murmured, 'Was it bad?'

'Yes,' she answered simply as she entered the apartment's tiny foyer.

Standing behind her, holding her coat as she slipped out of it, he asked. 'A hard delivery?'

'No.' Helen turned to face him, waited until he'd hung up her coat and turned around again before adding, 'A young girl tried to commit suicide the hard way.'

'Abortion?' Incredulity laced his tone.

'Yes.'

His eyes, tinged with concern, searched her face. 'Is she all right?'

'She's alive,' Helen sighed wearily. 'Oh, Marsh, it was grim.' Without hesitation, without even thinking, she walked right into him, rested her forehead against his chest.

For a split second he was still, then his arms came around her, tightened protectively. 'It's all right, love,' he murmured against her hair. 'You're home.'

Too tired, for the moment, to think, she barely heard his words, let alone the meaning behind them. His hand moved and tugged at her hair to turn her face up to his. In fascination Helen watched his firm mouth lowering slowly to hers, lost to the presence of the two people sitting in the living room unashamedly watching the tableau with interest.

Marsh's mouth was tender, gentle with hers. As the kiss lengthened, deepened, Helen felt the tensions and frustrations of the last hours drain out of her. Sighing deeply, she returned his kiss fervently. Her hands were moving up his chest to his neck when he suddenly stepped back, a rueful smile curving his lips.

'We have guests, love,' he said softly. 'Come have a drink and relax a little before dinner.'

Marsh turned her towards the living room, his arm, angled from shoulder to waist across her back, holding her close to his side. Helen felt the warmth of embarrassment mount her cheeks on encountering the expressions of concern for her, written clearly on the faces of Grant and Mary Ellen.

'Come sit by me, Helen, while Marsh gets your drink,' Mary Ellen invited warmly. 'You look completely shattered.'

With a tired smile Helen sank onto the sofa beside Mary Ellen, accepted the glass of wine Marsh handed her, took a small sip, smiled her appreciation and thanks to him, then turned her attention to what Mary Ellen was saying.

'We couldn't help but overhear what you said when you came in. What a horrible thing to do.'

'Yes,' Helen agreed. 'It was pretty horrible for her parents too. I am of the opinion that raising children can be heartbreaking at times.'

'But rewarding as well,' Mary Ellen assured firmly. 'Grant and I have had a few bad moments with our two boys, but I wouldn't give them up for the world.' She turned her serious gaze onto her husband. 'Would you, Grant?'

'No,' Grant answered simply. 'I think that by the time they are fully grown the good times will have, by far, outweighed the bad.'

'I think on that profound note, we'll go have dinner,' Marsh said, quietly reaching for Helen's hand.

Conversation was easy and relaxed while they ate Moe's expertly prepared veal scallopini.

'Do you ski, Helen?' Mary Ellen asked suddenly, pausing in the act of spooning up the rich dessert Moe had concocted.

'Yes,' Helen admitted, adding, 'not expertly, but well enough to handle the smaller slopes.'

'And I know Marsh is very good.' Mary Ellen's eyes lit with an idea. 'Grant and I, along with several other couples, are going up to the Poconos next Thursday for a long weekend of skiing. Why don't you two join us?'

'I don't think—' That was as far as Helen got with her refusal, for Marsh quietly interrupted her.

'Sounds good to me.' He lifted an eyebrow at her. 'What do you say, Helen? Do you think you could get someone to fill in for you? You could stand a break, especially after today.'

'Well, I suppose I could, but—'

'The hospital won't fall apart in four days, Helen,' Marsh urged.

'Well—' Helen hesitated, then gave in. 'Let me see if I can arrange something.'

Leaving the table, Helen went to the phone in the

living room, dialed, then spoke quietly a few moments. When she turned back to the others, she was smiling.

'All set.' Helen's eyes sought, then found the blue ones. 'Dr Munziack will be on call for me. He owes me one.' Her smile deepened. 'As a matter of fact he owes me several. I can be ready to leave as soon as I've made my rounds Thursday morning.'

The remainder of the evening was spent in making plans and generally getting to know each other. Marsh went to the stereo and placed a record on the machine, then waited for the music to begin to adjust the volume. Helen glaced up in surprise on hearing the opening strains of Tchaikovsky's *Fifth Symphony*. Marsh grinned at her, shrugged.

'What can I tell you?' His grin widened. 'I'm a Tchaikovsky nut.'

Helen managed to keep a straight face, but her amusement came through in her tone. 'And all this time I thought it was a ploy you used when—ah—entertaining.'

Laughing softly, he strolled across the room to her, placed a hand on her shoulder, and gave her a punishing squeeze, blandly ignoring the confused glances Grant and Mary Ellen exchanged.

It was not until later that night when Helen lay on her bed, tired yet sleepless, that the closed-in feeling returned. Only now it was so much stronger, so cloying, Helen sat up quickly, breathing deeply. Marsh was drawing her slowly, but inexorably, into his life. His words of earlier that night crept into her mind. 'It's all right, love. You're home.'

She slid down onto the pillows again, her mind worrying at his words. Calmer now, her thinking process coolly detached, Helen reached the conclusion that Marsh had decided to pull out all stops. He had every intention of winning this particular game. *And you*, she told herself dismally, *are playing right into his hands.* Her last coherent thought as she drifted into sleep was that the last thing she should be considering now was a long weekend in the mountains with him.

CHAPTER EIGHT

THAT same thought nagged at her all day Monday and Tuesday, kept her unusually quiet during dinner Tuesday night. When, over coffee, Marsh finally commented on her preoccupation, she pleaded fatigue, lack of sleep. It was a perfectly legitimate excuse, as she'd had a late delivery Monday night and it had been after three when she'd dropped onto her bed to fall asleep immediately.

'You really do need a rest,' Marsh said softly. 'I'm glad we decided to go. You can take it easy for four whole days.'

'On the slopes?' The 'we' got to her, put a slight sting in her voice.

'There's no law that says you have to ski, Helen,' Marsh admonished softly. 'You can laze around the fireplace all day if you want to.' His eyes narrowed on her face. 'You look like you've about had it. I'm going to take you home so you can have an early night.' His tone lowered, caressed. 'We have the long weekend to be together.'

Maybe if his tone hadn't been quite so caressing, hadn't held that hint of what he expected from their weekend away together, Helen would not have bolted. Oh, most definitely she had to get away. But from him, not with him.

It seemed that whenever Helen got a break between patients on Wednesday she had a phone call to make. The first one to Dr Stanley Munziack who assured her it would be no hardship for him if she extended her four-day weekend into a full week. At her lunchtime break

135

she called the airport and was informed there was a seat available on the late-night flight to Phoenix. In mid-afternoon she called her mother and was told, 'Of course your father will meet the plane.' And finally, after her last patient had left, she called her answering service.

After a light supper that she barely touched Helen packed her suitcase, her eyes going to her small bedside clock every few minutes. Although they had agreed not to see each other that night, Marsh had said he would call. When the phone rang, Helen's hand clutched, crushed, the blouse she was holding and with a muttered 'Damn', she let it drop into a silky heap on the bed before, taking a deep breath, she reached for the receiver.

'Dr Cassidy.' Helen's voice was overcool with trying to cover her guilty nervousness.

'What's wrong, Helen?' Marsh's tone was sharp with concern. 'Are you all right?'

'Yes, of course I'm all right,' she answered a little less coolly. 'I'm just tired and a little harried with the packing.'

'You? Harried?' His tone held real astonishment. 'You really are tired. Did I catch you right in the middle of it?'

'Yes, and I would really like to get it finished, Marsh.' Helen caught her lower lip between her teeth, fighting down the urge to tell him the truth.

'Okay.' He laughed softly. 'I can take a hint. I'll call you in the morning, early, to make sure you haven't overslept.'

Helen stood with her hand on the receiver long moments after she'd replaced it. Without halfway trying, she could imagine Marsh's reaction in the morning when her service informed him that Dr Cassidy was out of town and no, they didn't know where she'd gone.

The flight, late that night, was quiet and uneventful, and although she didn't think she'd be able to, Helen slept through most of it. Her father, tall, slim, was waiting for her, a smile of eager expectancy on his sun-weathered face.

With a feeling of coming home, being safe, Helen walked into his outstretched arms, closed her eyes against the sudden hot sting of tears.

'What's this?' Robert Cassidy felt the shiver that rippled through his daughter's slim frame, and grasping her shoulders, he held her away from him, studied her face carefully. Noting the brightness of her eyes, his brows rose slowly.

'A man, Helen?'

Helen didn't even consider pretence. He was the one person she could never fool with her cool exterior. In fact there were times while Helen was growing up that he seemed to know what she was going to do before she did. And now, her feelings raw and she more vulnerable than she'd ever been before in her life, she didn't even try.

'Yes.'

That one softly murmured word spoke volumes to him, and his eyes sharpened while his tone softened.

'Want to talk about it?'

'No.' Helen gave a quick shake of her head, then smiled ruefully. 'At least not tonight.' She paused before adding, 'I have to think it through for myself first, Dad. Right now I'm uncertain as to how to handle this and I don't like the feeling, it's not me.'

'That's for sure.' One arm draped over her shoulders, Robert paced his long stride to hers as they went to pick up her suitcase. In tune mentally, as they had always been, they dropped the subject, Robert knowing that when she was ready Helen would tell him, if not everything, enough to put him in the picture.

Her mother was waiting at the door of the small ranch-style home her parents had bought on the outskirts of Phoenix, her still-lovely face mirroring her happiness at seeing her firstborn. For the second time in less than an hour Helen was enfolded within loving arms and again felt the quick rush of tears.

No less shrewd than her husband Laura Cassidy was quick to notice the change in her daughter.

'Darling, what's wrong?' she asked anxiously. 'Are you ill?'

The words, so similar to the ones Marsh had said to her just a few hours ago, brought a fresh surge of moisture. What was wrong with her anyway? Helen thought irritably. She hadn't been this quick to tears during adolescence. With a determined effort she controlled her features, steadied her voice.

'No, Mother, I'm not ill,' she answered firmly. 'The last couple of weeks have been hectic, I'm very tired. Nothing more serious than that.'

'Well, that's a relief,' Laura sighed deeply, her sentiments reflected on her face. 'Come sit down. I have a pot of herb tea ready for you, and as soon as you've had a cup it's bed for you.'

Helen's laughter was a warm, natural reaction to her mother's dictate. Not since her fifteenth year had she heard that note of firmness in her mother's voice.

'Oh, Mother.' Helen bestowed a brief hug on her parent. 'It's so good to see you.'

Surrounded by parental love, cocooned within the silence of her father's tacit patience, Helen slept deeply and refreshingly, undisturbed by uneasy thoughts of a handsome young man bent on possession.

Rob's welcome was no less enthusiastic than their parents' had been, as was his pretty, somewhat flighty wife and their two fresh-faced boys. But as their mother and father had done the previous evening, he saw at once that all was not well with her.

'What's the problem, big sister?' Rob asked bluntly the first time they were alone for a minute.

'Mind your own business, Sonny,' Helen quipped gently, returning the grin he threw her at her deliberate use of his childhood nickname.

'The subject not open for discussion, Helen?'

'Not just yet, Rob,' she answered softly. They were standing together at the barbecue grill at the end of the large patio outside the kitchen of Rob's much larger ranch-style home a few miles from her parents'. In between brushing globs of sauce on the chicken sizzling on the grill, Rob slanted her a sharp-eyed glance.

'Will you answer one question?' He turned to face her fully, his gaze level.

'Depends on the question,' Helen hedged.

'Daddy.' The voice of Rob's eldest filtered through the kitchen screen door.

'In a minute, Chuck,' Rob tossed over his shoulder, his eyes locked on hers. Then, his tone lower, he asked, 'Is there a man involved?'

'Yes, but that's all I'm saying.'

'Daddy, Mommy said you should come in for the salad things.' Chuck's young voice was a shade louder.

'Paint your chicken, Sonny,' Helen gibed, grinning as she turned towards the house. 'I'll help Chuck with the salad.'

Rob's hand caught her arm, held her still a moment. 'If you need me, want someone to tell your troubles to, I'm here, big sister.'

Something lodged, painfully, in Helen's throat at his gentle tone. Her slim hand covered his, tightened briefly in thanks. Turning quickly, she hurried towards the house, a tiny break in her voice as she called, 'Daddy's busy, Chuck. I'll help you.'

In the general confusion of fixing a salad with Chuck,

fussing over her youngest nephew, Mike, when he woke from his nap, and receiving a rundown from her sister-in-law of both boys' activities since she'd last seen them, Helen was able to bring her shaky emotions under control.

The week passed pleasantly and much too fast. As her tension eased and her usual confidence reasserted itself, Helen lost the urge to confide in her family.

In the afternoon of the day before Helen's scheduled return to Philly, she had a few minutes alone with her father in the tiny room everyone teasingly referred to as 'Dad's study.' Feeling she owed her father some sort of an explanation, yet not sure how to begin, Helen sighed with relief when her father ended the short uncomfortable silence.

'Feeling better, Helen?'

'Yes, Dad, I—' Helen hesitated, searching for words. His astuteness made it unnecessary.

'You look better too.' Robert studied her carefully, warmly. 'If you don't want to talk about it, Helen, then don't. But just remember, I'm here for you if you need me.'

Not for the first time, Helen gave a silent thanks for the family she'd been blessed with. Her mother had fussed over her all week, coaxing her to eat, to rest, but though her eyes mirrored her concern, she had not questioned her once. And now her father's words had echoed Rob's. 'If you need me, I'm here.' They would not pry or in any way presume to infringe on her privacy, but quietly, lovingly, they let her know they were there for her. It helped.

'Thanks, Dad.' Helen smiled her gratitude. 'I'd really rather not talk about it. Right now I'm feeling a little unsure of myself with this man, who, if you don't mind, will remain nameless.' Robert nodded his head briefly. 'Please don't worry and don't let Mother and Rob worry either.' Her voice firmed with determination. 'I'll resolve it.'

'Of course you will.' Robert's tone was equally firm. 'We all need breathing space at times, Helen, when things seem to crowd in, threaten to overwhelm us. You have a good head on your shoulders. I doubt there's little you can't handle.'

But then, Helen thought wryly, *you don't know Marshall Kirk.*

Her flight home was every bit as uneventful as the one west had been. She boarded the plane feeling more relaxed than she had in weeks, but tension began building as the big jet drew ever nearer to the East Coast.

There was Marsh's justifiable anger to be faced. What had been his reaction to her disappearance? Perhaps, after his initial irritation cooled, he had put her from his mind and gone about the business of finding a more accommodating companion. The mere thought of him with another woman brought a mixture of pain and self-derision. *Do you know,* she asked herself bitingly, *what exactly you do want?* Flipping open the magazine her father had bought for her, she flipped through the pages, not yet ready to face a truthful answer to her own question.

It was early evening when Helen entered her apartment. After depositing her suitcase in the bedroom, she went into the kitchen, made herself a cup of tea, then called her service for messages left while she was gone. The crisp voice at the other end of the line rattled on for several minutes and ended with, 'And a Mr Kirk has called twice a day, morning and evening, every day. He was very put-out the first morning, insisted I tell him where you were. I had some difficulty convincing him I had no idea where you'd gone.'

'Yes . . . well, I'll take care of it,' Helen said softly. 'Thank you.'

Her finger pressed the disconnect button, then moved to press Marsh's number. While his phone rang, she draw a deep breath, steeling herself for his anger.

'Hello.' The voice was so harsh, so ragged sounding, Helen was not sure it was he.

'Marsh?' ·

There was silence for a full ten seconds before Helen heard his breath being expelled very slowly.

'Where were you?' His very softness threw her off balance, robbed her of speech. 'Helen, I've been damned near out of my mind. Where were you?' The tone was rough now, demanding an answer.

'With my family.' Helen found her voice, even managed to keep it steady. 'In Arizona. I was tired, Marsh, and I just couldn't face that skiing trip. I'm sorry but—'

'Who cares about the stupid skiing trip?' he cut in roughly. 'Are you all right?'

'Yes, of course, but—'

'No buts,' Marsh again cut in. 'If you had to get away for a while, then you did. I told you no strings, Helen, I meant it.' His voice went low, held a hint of amusement. 'I've got you running scared, haven't I?'

'Scared?' she scoffed, a little shakily. 'Of you? You flatter yourself.'

His soft laughter hummed along the wire to tickle her ear, tinge her cheeks pink. 'Do I? I don't think so,' he drawled. 'Why don't you give up? You're going to lose, Helen.'

'I don't know what you mean,' she snapped. 'I must hang up now, I have some more calls to make.'

'Okay, coward.' Helen shivered as he laughed again. 'One more thing and I'll let you go.' His tone softened. 'Do you feel rested now?'

Suspicious of his tone but not sure why, Helen hesitated a second before admitting, 'Yes.'

'Good, then you'll be up to having dinner with Cullen tomorrow night.' Before she could object, refuse, he whispered, 'Goodnight, love,' and hung up.

Cullen was the perfect host, charming and amusing. Helen knew, for she had seen at unguarded moments that everyone was speculating about the seriousness of her and Marsh's relationship. Everyone, that was, except Cullen. In the relatively short amount of time they were with him, she was left in little doubt that the 'old bear' was no longer speculating. He had reached the conclusion that the young 'cub' had found a mate. He made no attempt to hide the fact that his conclusion pleased him.

Helen did not like deceiving anyone. But most especially she did not like deceiving Cullen. If he was an 'old bear,' he was an extremely gentle one, at least with her. After that evening the game became not only nerve-racking but distasteful, and Helen told herself repeatedly to end it.

Curiosity kept her from following the dictates of her own common sense. How long, she wondered, would Marsh drag out the farce? As the weeks slipped by, Helen became certain that the game was losing its appeal for him, for he made no overt moves towards her. Since the night he gave her the gold chains and his promise of no pressure, he had not been in her apartment. When he brought her home, it was to the door, where, with a light, passionless kiss and a casual goodnight, he left her.

But still he made no indication that he was ready to either abandon or end the game, even though the challenge she had represented had apparently lost its allure. Helen, barely able to face her own accusing eyes in the mirror, doggedly followed his lead.

What did she think she was doing? The question repeated itself with monotonous regularity. He was becoming a habit, a habit, moveover, that was growing stronger with each passing day. Being with him was torment, being away from him was agony. She wanted him desperately and the intensity of that growing desperation confused and frightened her. At times she lost sight of what the game was all about and longed for the feel of his arms around her, his hard body pressed to hers. She had no basis of comparison for her feelings except the time she had spent with Carl, and even in that, the comparison was minute. At no time, either while they were dating or after they had become engaged, had her feelings for Carl ever made her lose sight of her goal. And so she worried. Worried about her own increasing need to be with him. Worried about the thoughts that tormented her late in the night, driving her out of her bed to pace the floor restlessly. Worried about the end that had to come soon if she was to retain a shred of her self-respect.

Marsh seemed in no way concerned with similar worries. And seemingly without being aware he was doing it, he was wearing down her resistance. He took it for granted that she would spend most of her free time with him and had taken to calling her at the office to inform her of the plans he'd made, the invitations he'd accepted for both of them.

Sundays they were together exclusively. Hour by hour, hand in hand, they walked. They explored Germantown, strolled on the cobblestone street by the brick houses in Elfreth's Alley, a one-block-long street near the river-front that is one of the oldest streets in America. They spent hours in Independence Hall and the National Historical Park and seriously discussed the possibility of the first United States flag being made in the Betsy Ross House. Then they went back into Fairmont Park; this time Marsh succeeded in drawing her down to the river to watch the sculling crews working out. Sunday nights were the only nights Helen had no difficulty sleeping. With all the exercise and fresh air she was usually out cold within minutes after sliding between the sheets.

By mid-March Helen had a problem. On Saturday afternoon, after ushering her last patient out of her office, she sat staring at the square, white, gold-embossed invitation she held gingerly in one hand. A frown creasing her forehead, she read, then reread, the gold script. The invitation was for a retirement party of the following Saturday to honour the much-respected and very well-liked head of OB-GYN. at the hospital. True, it gave very short notice of the affair, but as she knew the man's decision to retire had been on the spur of the moment because of health reasons, this was not why Helen frowned.

Her problem was Marsh. As the invitation had been issued to Helen and guest, she was, of course, at liberty to ask him to escort her. But that was the fly in her particular ointment. Thus far she had deliberately avoided introducing him to any of her small circle of friends. At regular intervals he had chided her about it, but she had dodged his sardonic barbs with the excuse that her friends, most with full family lives, were in an after-the-holidays entertaining slump. As it was now over two months since the holiday season, Helen knew there were large holes in the excuse and she had been searching her mind for a replacement.

Now, tucked in with the usual mundane Saturday mail, was an invitation she could not very well ignore. Helen's friends, knowing her as well as possible, had thought little of her absence—except that she might be overworking. They knew that she was a very private person, that she preferred a quiet evening of conversation or a really good concert, to overcrowded parties, whether in private homes or the organised ones in large hotels or country clubs. But they also knew of the true affection she had for her imminent chief and would be surprised if she bypassed his party.

Tapping the card with a neatly trimmed, unpainted fingernail, Helen wondered what to do. She knew Marsh. She also knew that if she told him that she could not see him next Saturday night he would torment her subtly until she told him why. She could lie, of course, but somehow the thought of lying outright to him was repulsive to her. When her phone buzzed, Helen tossed the card onto her desk with relief. Lifting the receiver, she pressed the blinking button and said briskly, 'Dr Cassidy.'

Without preliminaries Marsh inquired, 'Are you almost through there, Helen?'

'Yes, why?'

'No little mother about to increase the population? No meetings? No hairdresser appointment or shopping to do?'

'No,' Helen answered patiently. 'Why, Marsh?'

'I'm stranded at a construction site and hoped I could coax you into picking me up.' Marsh hesitated, then bribed. 'I'll buy you lunch.'

'What do you mean you're stranded? Where is your car?'

'I put it in the garage this morning for inspection,' he explained. 'It won't be ready until later this afternoon. As a matter of fact you could drop me at the garage after we've had lunch, okay?'

'Yes, of course I'll pick you up,' Helen agreed at once. 'But what construction site are you stranded at, and why?' Helen's puzzlement was obvious. 'I mean—why are you at *any* construction site?'

'It's one of Cullen's babies.' Marsh laughed 'There

was a snarl up here, and as always, he called and told me to come straighten it out.'

'And did you?' Helen asked dryly.

'Just about.' He spoke with equal dryness. He gave her directions to the site, which was located some distance outside the city, then said, 'When you get here, park the car and come into the trailer office.' A hint of laughter touched his tone. 'Just in case the unsnarler gets snarled.'

As Helen prepared to leave the office her glance was caught by the white card on her desk. After a moment's hesitation she picked it up, slipped it back into its envelope, and stuffed it into the depths of her handbag. Giving a mental shrug, she thought, *I'll decide about that later.*

She found the site without difficulty, and after parking the car, she made her way carefully over the uneven and still frozen ground, pausing to read the large white sign posted on the wooden fence that completely surrounded the site. The sign informed her that the construction under way would result in a high-rise apartment complex, that it had been designed by the architectural firm of Wanner, Freebold, and Wanner, and was being erected by the Hannlon Building and Construction Firm, Cullen Hannlon, President.

A small smile curved Helen's lips as she read the last, then her eyes perplexed, her gaze returned to the name Wanner.

'Learning anything?'

Helen jumped at the sound of the teasing voice close to her ear. Not bothering to answer his question, she murmured, 'That name Wanner seems vaguely familiar.'

'I'm not surprised.' Marsh laughed softly. 'You were introduced to it a few weeks ago.' At her confused stare he nudged. 'Grant? Mary Ellen?'

'Oh!' Helen's eyes cleared and she smiled, remembering. 'Last names barely registered that night. I was relieved I could hold on to the first.'

'Grant's the second Wanner,' he offered. 'The firm was started by his father and uncle. Grant joined it as a very junior member when he got out of school. He's really very good,' he added. 'As a matter of fact he designed this building.'

While he was talking, Marsh led her to a small trailer some yards away and guided her up the steps and into what appeared to be a shambles. Watching her expression as her eyes circled the mess, Marsh laughed aloud.

'Don't be deceived, love. I assure you the construction boss knows exactly where everything is and can lay his hand on whatever he wants at a moment's notice.' Strolling into the trailer's tiny kitchen area, he asked. 'Would you like some coffee?'

Helen opened her mouth to say 'Yes, please,' but nothing came out. Lips forming a large *O* her eyes went wide at the loud sound of gears grinding, tyres screeching, and then the scream of a man. Before she could close her mouth, blink her eyes, Marsh was by her and lunging out the door, the last part of his growled 'Son of a—' lost to her. In half an instant she was spinning around, running after him, stumbling over the torn-up, slippery earth.

Dodging ice-skimmed puddles of water, Helen tried to make sense of the blurred scene that met her eyes. Men were running from all directions towards a large piece of machinery lying drunkenly on its side. As she reached the fringes of the crowded men Helen could hear Marsh's voice, sharp, clear, issuing orders tersely. One man detached himself from the group, ran towards another large machine.

From inside the circle of men Helen heard the

agonised speech of a man, heard him groan, and her hand pushed against a rock-hard male arm.

'Let me through,' she ordered as sharply as Marsh had. 'I'm a doctor.'

Moving aside respectfully, the man tapped the shoulder of the man in front of him, relaying Helen's order. Moving through the men, Helen took in the situation. When the machine had toppled over, it had trapped the driver and crushed his leg against the ground, and now half in, half out, of the thing, the man lay in a crumpled heap in the driver's seat. His lips were twisted in pain, his eyes were glazed, and his face was grey with shock.

Without a thought to the sheer nylon that gave no protection whatever to her knees, Helen dropped to the ground beside him, her fingers going to his wrist. Not liking what she felt, she ordered softly, 'Marsh, you have got to move this monster off of him.' Not for a minute doubting his ability to do so.

'We will,' Marsh said just as softly. 'An ambulance has been called. I've sent for blankets and—' A man walked up beside him, handed him a white box with a red cross on it. 'And here's the first-aid box. There's a syringe of morphine inside.'

Without questioning or even looking up, Helen held out her hand. A saturated piece of cotton was placed in her fingers, and after swabbing the man's arm, Helen administered the injection. Working quickly, carefully, her hands firm, yet gentle, she covered as much of the man's body as she could with the blankets Marsh handed her. While she worked, Helen was aware of the machine being backed into position beside the disabled one, of chains being fixed into place. When Marsh grasped her elbow, she stood up and stepped back.

In a strained hush everyone watched as, motor growling, chains rattling over winches, the shuddering machine was set aright. Whispering, 'Oh, God,' Helen watched the injured man's leg dangle crookedly over the side of the machine. Then with a barked, 'Don't touch him,' she stopped the men's move towards him. Marsh beside her, she walked up to that leg.

'Is there a scissors in that box?'

'Yes.'

Seconds later Helen was snipping away, quickly, but cautiously, at the blood-soaked material. Her eyes closed briefly when the leg was exposed. The leg was mangled, literally crushed, and with the weight of inadequacy pushing on her mind, she didn't know where to begin. She drew a deep breath, then gave a silent, thankful prayer of relief on hearing the scream of the ambulance siren.

The construction crew guiding the driver, the ambulance was backed as closely as possible to the injured man and two paramedics jumped out and went into action. Working with them, Helen helped cushion and immobilise the leg with an inflatable plastic casing, then the man was moved carefully onto the litter. Strangely Helen knew one of the paramedics, as she had delivered his first and only child, and after sliding the litter into the long vehicle, he slapped the door shut, smiled, winked, and murmured, 'Good work, Doc.'

Feeling the praise unearned, Helen nevertheless returned his smile with a soft 'Thank you.'

As the paramedics climbed back into the ambulance, a hard arm slid around her back.

'I'd like to follow along to the hospital, if you don't mind. There'll be questions to answer, forms to fill out. And I'll have to call Cullen, give him a report on the man's condition.'

'Yes, of course. But you do realise it may be some time before any definite word is given out.' Breathlessly she moved beside him as, striding along, he half dragged, half carried, her over the rough ground towards her car.

'I know.' He gave her a small smile. 'But it's got to be done and I've got to do it. The man has no family here.'

The drive was a short one, as they took the man to a local hospital. For the following forty-five minutes Helen stood with Marsh as he filled out form after form, answered questions. Helen was asked questions also, but at last it was all finished and the desk nurse said, 'If you'd like to wait in the lounge, Doctor, Mr Kirk, the doctor will have some information for you as soon as possible.'

About to walk away, Marsh turned back to the nurse.

'If we're wanted, we'll be in the coffee shop.' He paused, then asked, 'There is a coffee shop?'

The nurse smiled, nodded, and gave them directions.

'Not exactly what I had in mind when I promised you lunch.' Marsh smiled ruefully twenty-five minutes later when the waitress walked away after serving them their food.

'But I love chicken noodle soup.' Helen smiled, indicating the steaming bowl in front of her. And with a wave of her hand, over her sandwich, added, 'And I've been a cheeseburger freak since I was a kid.' She sipped at the cup cradled in her hands. 'The coffee is hot and really very good. It's an excellent lunch, Marsh.' Her eyes teased him. 'And you can't beat the prices.'

'You're a cheap date.' Marsh's warmly glowing eyes teased back. 'Remind me to invite you out to lunch again sometime.'

It was after four thirty when they returned to the waiting lounge, and after only a few tense moments Helen suddenly remembered something. Standing up, she held out her hand to Marsh, palm up.

'Give me your car keys.'

Without question Marsh stood up, plunged his hand

into his pocket, then, glancing up, curiously asked. 'What for?'

'I'm going to go for your car,' she answered simply. 'I'll ask the desk nurse to call a cab for me and go get your car.'

'Helen, that's not necessary,' Marsh said softly.

'I know.' Her eyes were teasing again. 'But I hate hanging around hospital waiting rooms. Now give me the keys and the address of the garage and I'll be back before you can even miss me.'

'I seriously doubt that,' he drawled, dropping the keys into her hand.

It was after six when they finally left the hospital, relief on hearing the man would not lose his leg rendering a spring to their step. Marsh walked Helen to her car, unlocked and opened the door for her before asking, 'Can you be ready by eight?'

'Ready for what?'

'For dinner.' Marsh grinned. 'Maybe a bowl of soup and a cheeseburger would hold you for hours but I have a suspicion that in another hour or so I'm going to be looking forward to a steak. So can you be ready?'

'I'm really very tired, Marsh, and—'

'Nothing fancy,' Marsh promised. 'And I plan to take you home as soon as we've finished dinner.'

Helen was vaguely unsettled by his words, but with a sigh she agreed.

There was nothing fancy about the restaurant Marsh took her to. But it was clean and quiet and the food was delicious and the wine was good.

Later, standing in the hallway in front of her open apartment door, Marsh cupped her face in his hands, kissed her softly.

'You were pretty wonderful today, Helen,' he murmured. 'Some day, very soon, you and I are going to have a long, serious discussion. But right now you look too tired to think properly, let alone talk.' He kissed her again, then dropped his hands. 'Go inside, go to bed. I'll call you late in the morning.'

Lying in bed, Helen closed her eyes, as if by doing so, she could close out the certainty painfully searing her mind. He was ready to make his move, play his high card, and she knew it. And the knowing hurt, more than she had ever dreamed it would.

CHAPTER NINE

By midmorning Sunday Helen had come to terms with her emotions. Although, when embarking on this charade, she had not fully considered the possibly painful ramifications to herself, she could not throw in her hand now. No, pride demanded she play the hand to the last card, then pick up what emotional chips were left and go home.

When Marsh called, Helen was able to talk to him calmly, but she wasn't yet ready to see him. In an easy tone she could hardly believe she'd achieved, she told him she didn't want to go out that afternoon, as she had a hundred personal things she had to catch up on.

'A full hundred?' he mocked. 'Are you trying to put off the inevitable, love?'

Helen felt a sinking sensation in the pit of her stomach. Marsh hadn't called her 'love' in that tone for weeks. She was right. He was ready for the big play.

Her eyes closed against the renewed pain. She should have felt relieved, thankful that it would be over soon. She didn't. She felt sick, and suddenly very tired.

'Helen?'

She'd been quiet very long. Too long.

'Yes, Marsh.'

'Are you all right?' The concern in his voice, which he made no effort to hide, deepened her pain. 'I mean, are you feeling all right?'

'Yes, of course.' Helen forced a light laugh. 'I'm sorry, Marsh, I'm afraid I'm still a little sleep-vacant.'

Helen winced at the lie. 'I haven't been up very long and I don't have the mental process together yet.'

'I can't wait to hear what you'll have to say when you get it together.' He laughed, then chided, 'Do you think you will have your hundred personal chores finished by dinnertime? I'll make reservations somewhere.'

Again she hesitated, but only briefly this time.

'All right, Marsh, but I want to have an early night. I'm scheduled for O.R. early tomorrow morning.' At least that was the truth.

'Something serious?'

'Yes.' She would say no more.

'Okay, love, you're the boss. I'll pick you up at six thirty and you can be back home and tucked in for the night by ten.'

Alone, Helen added silently.

The restaurant was a new one for Helen. Spanish in decor, with a lot of black wrought iron complemented by dark red tablecloths and carpet. The menu was a disappointment, being entirely American. The closest Helen got to Spain was the bottle of imported sangría, compliments of the house, that was included with every—expensive—meal.

After dinner Helen played with the stem of her tiny cordial glass, staring at the Tia Maria inside.

'Are you going to admire it or drink it?' Marsh teased.

Startled out of her reverie, Helen glanced up, saw his own Drambuie was gone. A red-jacketed waiter stopped at their table, refilled the coffee cups. When he walked away again, Marsh pinned her with curious eyes.

'Something bothering you, Helen?'

'No.' Her fingertip circled the rim of the small glass. *You are certainly not playing this very intelligently,* she told herself bleakly. *Perhaps it's time to throw a card that will put him off balance, just a little.* 'I was just wondering if you'd care to escort me to a party Saturday night.'

'Of course,' he replied promptly. 'Did you doubt that I would?'

'I wasn't sure.' Helen shrugged. 'I'm afraid it won't be a very lively affair, but I don't want to miss it.'

'What sort of party is it?'

'Retirement.' Helen sipped her drink, smiled gently. 'My chief in OB. He's a nice man and a brilliant surgeon. I'm going to miss him and I would like to go.'

'So we'll go,' Marsh said easily, then his eyes narrowed slightly. 'But now something bothers me.'

'What?' Helen answered warily.

'Why you even hesitated about mentioning it. Did you really think I wouldn't want to go with you?' He paused and his tone grew an edge. 'Or were you hating the idea that you'd finally have to introduce me to some of your friends?'

'Marsh!' Helen's shocked tone hid the curl of unease she felt.

'Don't play the innocent with me, love.' He rapped softly. 'You didn't really think I'd bought those lame excuses, did you? I knew all along why you were dodging that particular issue. Part of it, the biggest part, was this damned hang-up you have about our age difference.' He leaned back lazily in his chair; his eyes refuted that laziness. Very softly he warned, 'I'm not exactly stupid, you know.'

A chill of apprehension trickled down Helen's spine. She was sure he was giving her a definite warning about something—but what? For a brief, panicky second Helen felt sure he knew she was playing him at his own game. Then common sense took over. She had made her position clear from the beginning, had told him bluntly she wanted no involvement of any kind. There was no reason whatever for him to be suspicious. Once again his pride had been touched and he didn't like it. And so the warning; it was as simple as that.

When Marsh didn't pursue the subject, Helen convinced herself her diagnosis was correct.

During the week Helen changed her mind about what to wear for the party at least four times. At one point she even convinced herself she needed something new. Never had she been so nervous about going out somewhere. After long mental arguments she finally scrapped the idea of a new gown. She *had* a new gown. She'd bought it for the holidays and never worn it. And though the calendar said it was just about spring, the temperature said it was still very much winter.

On Saturday night, standing fully dressed in front of her mirror, Helen still wasn't sure of her dress. There was very little of it, at least the top part of it, and Helen wondered for the tenth time if it was right for her. Its cut was deceptively simple, with a rather deep *V* neckline and straight, clingy skirt slit up the right side to the knee. The sleeves were of free-flowing chiffon, almost the same as no covering at all. About the only thing that did please Helen was the shimmery midnight-blue colour. Marsh's gift chains were the only jewellery she wore. She had coiled her hair back, telling herself the severe style offset the gown's more daring effect.

'Very elegant.'

They were Marsh's first words when she opened the door to him and they echoed her thought about his appearance. In black tux and white ruffled shirt, the only word to describe him was devastating.

The party was being held in the ballroom of one of the city's largest hotels. Helen had not been in the room five minutes before she saw her own opinion of Marsh's looks reflected in the eyes of a dozen women. The sudden mixture of feelings those devouring female eyes sent searing through her made her want to run for the nearest exit. Pride, jealousy, and, Lord help her, possessiveness raged through her like a raging bull gone mad. It made her feel a little sick. It made her feel a little angry. But, worst of all, it made her feel foolish, and that she could not bear.

With a smile on her lips that was pure honey, and tasted in her mouth like straight acid, Helen introduced Marsh to friends as they moved around the room. Helen was aware of more than one pair of eyebrows raised over eyes full of shocked disbelief, and she could imagine what everyone was thinking. She was rarely ever seen with a man, and when she was, it was usually with a close friend who was the husband of a closer friend. People who were her friends knew she simply did not indulge. Now here she was, not only with a man they had never met before, but a younger one as well. Helen had a feeling of certainty that the postparty conversations between husbands and wives would be loaded with speculation.

Marsh seemed sublimely unaware of it all. The glittery, assessing glances from women of varying ages, the raised brows, even the sharp inspection from her chief, apparently went over his head. But Helen saw it, and she didn't like it, not any of it.

Along the one end of the long room a table had been placed for the retiree and his family. In front of that, placed informally, were the other tables. Beyond them a large space had been left clear for dancing, and at the other end a small combo awaited their cue to begin playing. Along the far wall a long buffet table had been set up, and next to that was an almost equally long bar.

Marsh found a table, tucked against a pillar, barely big enough for two and that's where they sat, turning down, with a smile, the numerous offers from friends to join them. Helen knew it was real friendship that prompted the offers, friendship and a big dash of curiosity.

After the short speeches were made and the toasts

given, the party's planner invited everyone to help himself to the food and the dance floor.

To the background music of a popular new ballad, Marsh asked, 'Do you want something to eat or drink?'

'Not yet.' Helen shook her head.

'Good, let's dance.'

All the way to the dance floor Helen was called to, waved at, but Marsh would not let her stop. A smile on his lips, his hand firmly grasping hers, he kept moving, until, reaching the dancing area, he turned her into his arms with an exaggerated sigh.

'I had no idea you had so many friends,' he groaned. 'Didn't you mention that only some of your friends would be here tonight?'

'They aren't all close friends, Marsh.' Helen laughed softly. 'There are quite a few people here I only see at the hospital.' Her smile remained, but her tone went dry. 'I think you're the one causing all this sudden interest in me.'

'I can't imagine why,' he drawled. 'I'm really very ordinary.'

Oh, sure, Helen thought, *about as much as Pavarotti is ordinary compared to other singers.*

An attractive young nurse, a Linda something-or-other, not at all shy or reticent, tapped Helen on the shoulder. Glancing around, Helen's eyes went wide with surprise at the young woman's words.

'Can I cut in, Doctor?' She smiled beautifully. 'I was just saying to the girls I'm with that your escort is the best-looking man on the dance floor and—well—they dared me to cut in on you.'

Astounded, Helen didn't know what to say until, flicking a glance at Marsh, she saw the amusement tugging at his lips.

'But of course,' she purred sweetly. 'I was dying for something to drink anyway.' Moving out of Marsh's arms, away from his mocking eyes, she wiggled her fingers at him. 'Have fun.'

Helen accepted the glass of champagne from the bartender and took a large swallow, her eyes gleaming with fury. *And he says the difference in our ages doesn't matter*, she fumed. She swallowed some more of the wine, then looked at the glass as if seeing it for the first time. *No wonder I feel like a fool*, she thought bitterly, *I am one. And if I'm not careful, in another minute I'll be a smashed fool.*

'Good evening, Helen. It's been a long time.'

The deep-timbred voice jerked her mind away from her own shortcomings and her head around to stare into the handsome face of Carl Engle.

'Oh! Hello, Carl.' Helen smiled coolly. 'You startled me.'

'I'm sorry, I didn't mean to.' He smiled warmly. 'May I get you more wine?'

Helen frowned at the empty glass in her hand. She didn't even remember finishing it.

'Yes, please.' Even though she didn't want it, Helen decided she'd look like even more of a fool standing around with an empty glass in her hand.

While Carl spoke to the waiter, then waited for a fresh glass of wine, Helen studied him unobtrusively. She had seen him at various functions over the last few years, but this was the first time she looked, really looked, at him.

There was not a hint of grey in the fair hair that contrasted beautifully with the deep tan on his handsome face. And he had matured into a handsome man, Helen admitted. Tall, still slim, his brown eyes bright and alert, he'd catch the eye of more than his share of females. Helen felt a strange sensation at the thought. If he had exercised some judgment, acquired a little maturity while still in college, he would probably be her

husband today. For some unknown reason Helen was
very glad he hadn't and wasn't.

'Are you here alone?' He turned back to her, the smile
deepening, revealing even white teeth.

'No, I came with—'

'Me.' Marsh finished the sentence for her, his eyes
sombre as they went slowly over Carl.

'Carl Engle, Marshall Kirk.' Helen introduced
quietly. Marsh's eyes narrowed a fleeting second, but it
was the only indication he gave that he'd ever heard the
name before. So much, Helen thought wryly, for his
saying he'd thank Carl if he ever met him.

Two arms were extended, hands were clasped and
almost immediately released.

'Kirk.' Carl mused. 'Any connection to the account-
ing firm of Kirk and Terrell?'

'The same Kirk,' Marsh answered quietly.

'I've heard some very good things about your firm,'
Carl murmured. 'You're connected with Hannlon
Construction also, aren't you?'

'My grandfather,' Marsh admitted.

'I know your sister, Kristeen,' Carl said, then smiled
at Marsh's raised brows. 'I'm your niece's paediatrician.'
Before Marsh could reply, Carl smiled at Helen.
'Another patient to thank you for, Dr Cassidy.'

'The choice is theirs.' Helen shrugged. 'If they ask for
a recommendation, I supply three names.'

'Well, thank you for including me in the three.' Carl
laughed. 'Now, as the saying goes, may I have the next
dance?'

'Excuse me,' Marsh inserted before Helen could think
of a polite way of saying no. 'I promised Helen I'd take
her to the buffet as soon as that dance was finished.'

'Of course,' Carl replied. 'Maybe later.'

Marsh smiled thinly in answer, grasped Helen's arm,
and led her towards the end of the long table.

'I distinctly remember telling you I was not hungry,' Helen chided coolly.

'I distinctly remember you telling me you were not thirsty,' Marsh retorted, one eyebrow arched at her half-empty glass.

They ate in silence, Helen picking disinterestedly at the small amount of food on her plate. When Marsh had cleaned off his plate, he tossed his napkin on top of it and pinned her with very cool blue eyes.

'Did you want to dance with him?' His tone was cold and, Helen thought, somehow condemning. Her hackles rose.

'Would it have mattered if I did?' She didn't wait for him to answer, adding sweetly, 'Did you enjoy your dance?'

Watching his eyes narrow, Helen felt sick. Even to herself she sounded like a jealous, possessive woman.

'Not particularly,' he finally answered. 'I'm not turned on by gushy, clingy females.'

'Too bad,' she purred, looking beyond him. 'There's another, probably the gushiest, heading this way. I imagine they'll all ask you now.'

Helen recognised the girl coming towards them, for it was the student who had referred to Marsh as 'totally bad' on the day Helen met him.

When she stopped at their table, Marsh stood up, a charming polite smile on his lips.

'Oh, Mr Kirk.' The girl actually did gush. 'Doctor, I hope you don't mind, but Linda will be unbearable for the rest of the night if the rest of us don't get a dance.'

'How many are the rest of you?' Marsh asked warily.

'Four,' the girl answered brightly. 'Including me.'

Helen saw Marsh's lips tighten, but before he could say a word, she laughed softly. 'Four's not many. Go along, Marsh.' She dismissed him airily. 'I'm perfectly happy here . . . by myself.'

Marsh made a motion with his hand for the girl to precede him, then before following her, he turned a thunderous look on Helen. 'You'll pay for this, woman,' he whispered harshly.

Helen watched his retreating back, deriving a malicious pleasure in the stiffness of it. He certainly didn't like being manipulated.

'Time for that dance now, Helen?' Carl stood beside her, an expectant smile on his face.

'Yes, thank you.' Helen smiled, thinking, *Well, why not? Anything's better than sitting here like the proverbial wallflower.*

Carl had always been a good dancer, smooth, easy to follow, and after a few minutes Helen felt some of the angry tautness leave her.

'You've matured into a beautiful woman, Helen.' Carl's voice was low, oddly urgent.

A tiny smile touching her lips at his unknowing echo of her earlier thoughts about him, she glanced up.'

'Thank you.'

'Have you ever forgiven me, Helen?' he asked abruptly.

Helen's glance wavered, then grew steady again. 'There's nothing to forgive, for nothing really happened.' *No actual rape that is*, she amended mentally, *only two blows, the second with your fist*. 'I never think of it.' She lied. *Then what*, she chided herself, *were you sobbing about in Marsh's arms that night?*

'We could have made it together.'

'What?' His incredible words shocked her out of her thoughts.

'You and I,' he explained softly. 'We could have made it very good.' He drew her a little closer, and amazed at his cool presumption, Helen didn't resist. In fact she was hardly aware of him, for she had just caught a glimpse of

Marsh with yet another girl in his arms, a little older, much prettier than the others.

'We still could, Helen.' The urgent voice tried to draw her attention.

'How?' Helen wasn't even sure of what he was saying. All she was sure of was the hot jealousy running through her veins and the sick shame that jealousy spawned.

'Don't be naive, darling.' Carl's lips touched her hair as he brought her closer still. 'My wife would never know, and even if she did, I doubt if she'd care.'

His lips, as well as his words, brushing her ear, brought her alert. She knew his wife and had heard of the number of mistresses he'd had.

'I find that a little hard to believe,' she said carefully.

'You needn't, I assure you.' Again his arms tightened, and Helen felt anger replace her jealousy. 'My wife's a little girl playing house. Only in her case the dolls are our children and the playhouse furniture is life-sized. As long as her little domain is not threatened, she couldn't care less what I do.' He paused then added fatuously, 'You do understand, I have no intention of threatening that domain.'

Of course not, Helen thought furiously, *you're not stupid. Why lose the goodwill of a very prominent and influential father-in-law, if you can have your cake and eat it.* Helen placed her hands on his chest, about to push him away while she told him exactly what she thought of him. She didn't get a chance to do either.

'May I cut in?' Marsh's voice was low, deceptively quiet. 'I believe you promised me this dance, Helen.' His arm slid around her waist, his fingers gripped painfully.

'Yes, of course.' Helen was suddenly breathless with apprehension. Good Lord, she couldn't allow him to make a scene *here*. 'And then, if you don't mind, I'd like to go home.'

Marsh nodded, started to turn her away, but Carl, seeming to think her words were a good sign for him, said softly, 'I'll call you, Helen.'

'No, you won't.'

Flat, final, the words hung between the two men like a sword. Marsh's eyes cold, detached, bored into Carl's. Carl's dropped first as, with a shrug, he smiled faintly and walked away.

'Marsh, really, you—'

'Be quiet, Helen.' Marsh's tone matched his eyes for coldness. 'Do you want to dance or do you want to go home?'

'I—' Helen drew a deep breath. 'I think we'd better go.'

Without a word he turned on his heel, grasped her arm, and headed for the door. After hasty farewells to their host Helen found herself rushed to the cloakroom. Marsh asked for his car to be brought around, and as they stepped out of the door Helen gasped. There was at least three inches of snow on the ground and it was still coming down hard.

Driving was bad, requiring all Marsh's concentration, and the distance to her apartment was covered in silence. Helen could feel his anger beating against her like storm-tossed waves. Knowing there would be a confrontation when they got to her place, Helen almost dreaded arriving home. To her surprise he did not drive onto the parking lot, but pulled up, motor running, under the marquee that protected the entrance. She hesitated a second but when he didn't speak or even look at her, she slid across the seat, got out, closed the door carefully, and ran into the building.

Inside her apartment Helen went straight to her bedroom. She was wearing thin-strap evening sandals and her feet had gotten soaked in her short dash through the snow to the car. Now she felt chilled to the bone, not only from her foot soaking. She stripped, then took a hot shower, slipped into her nightgown and quilted, belted robe, and started for the kitchen to make a cup of tea.

The doorbell's ring stopped her in the kitchen doorway. Now who in the world? Helen glanced at the clock. At this hour? The ring came again, short, angry sounding. Helen walked slowly to the door, checked to see if the chain was in place, then opened the door two inches.

Marsh stood in the hall looking every bit as angry as he had when he'd dropped her off less than forty-five minutes ago. He also looked the tough construction worker he'd once been, dressed in a suede, fur-lined jacket, brushed-denim jeans, and what looked like logging boots laced almost to the knee.

'What do you want?' Slipping the chain, Helen stepped back. He walked in far enough to close the door. One eyebrow arched mockingly.

'There are a few questions I want answers to.' He slipped out of his jacket.

'But why didn't you ask them when you brought me home?' She moved away from him edgily.

'I wanted to get the car home.' He bent over, began unlacing his boots.

'But—'

'I have one of the company's four-wheel-drive pickups,' he answered before she could ask. After tugging the boots off, he padded across the room to her. His eyes were cool, direct.

'Do you still feel something for him?'

Helen gasped. She didn't know what she'd been expecting, but it certainly hadn't been that.

'Carl?'

The confusion in her tone seemed to anger him even more. Grasping her shoulders painfully, he pulled her close to him.

'Yes, Carl,' he gritted through clenched teeth. 'While you were in his arms.' His lips twisted, his tone grew sarcastic. 'While you were held so very closely in his arms, dancing, did you find you still feel something for him?'

'No.' It was stated simply, positively, but it didn't satisfy him.

'Then why did you allow him to practically crawl all over you?' he snapped. 'What was he saying to you?'

Helen could have cried aloud. She didn't want to answer him. He was mad enough already. She hesitated a moment. It was a moment too long.

'Answer me, Helen.' He gave her a little shake. 'What did he say?'

'He suggested an . . . arrangement.' She sighed. 'He also assured me his wife would not interfere. You men are wonderful creatures, aren't you?' she ended bitterly.

A flame flared in Marsh's eyes. 'It takes two to play that kind of game. A man *and* a woman.' His fingers dug into her arms. 'What did you tell him?'

'I wanted to tell him to go to hell.' Helen's eyes flashed back at him. 'But you showed up before I could.'

Helen could actually see the anger seep out of him. His face became less rigid; his fingers relaxed their punishing hold.

'If he calls you,' he spat out, 'or tries to see you—'

'I'm sure he won't,' Helen said quickly, feeling his fingers tighten again. 'I think you made it very clear that he shouldn't.'

'He'd better not.' He drew her closer, his fingers loosening again, massaging her tender skin. Then her eyes widened as he breathed softly, 'You're mine, Helen. And the game is over.'

'No, I'm—'

His mouth caught her parted lips, silencing her. If the

kiss had been rough or hard, she could have fought him. It was neither. Gently, tenderly, his mouth put his stamp of ownership on her. Melting, trembling, she felt his hand slide down her back, his arm gather her tightly to him. His mouth left hers, moved slowly across her cheek to her ear.

'Helen, Helen.' The voice that whispered her name was raw. 'Oh, God, I love you. Hold me, love. Please hold me.'

Helen's arms slid up and around his neck, and she closed her eyes against the quick hot sting inside. Turning her face into the side of this neck, she breathed in deeply. His cologne, plus the male scent of him, confused her thinking.

'Marsh,' she whispered, trying to hang on to her evaporating reason. 'You—we shouldn't.'

'Yes, we should.' His warm breath feathered her ear, tickled its way down the length of her body. 'We should have long ago.'

His mouth left a fiery trace over her face, back to her lips. And now she was ready for the driving force that crushed her mouth, made dust of her resistance. Tiny little sparks burst into flames inside her. Flames that leaped higher and higher as his mouth grew more demanding.

Her own hunger aroused, Helen returned his kiss, barely aware of what he was doing, when she felt his hands loosen her belt, pull her arms down, slide her robe off. But she was aware of his hands moving over the silky material of her nightgown, was aware of the sudden need to feel those hands against her skin. The awareness brought momentary sanity. Tearing her mouth from his, she gasped for air, finally found her voice.

'Marsh, no.' Helen couldn't breath properly and she paused to draw a short, shallow breath. She shuddered as his lips nibbled along the strained cord in her neck.

'Oh, Marsh, no.' It was a feeble protest against his hands sliding the gown's narrow straps from her shoulders. The gown slid to the floor silently, and then Helen's body became electrically charged at the touch of his hands. His lips found the beginning swell of her breasts and she moaned softly. Moving lazily, the tip of his tongue driving the flame yet higher, his mouth retraced the trail to her lips. Reason was gone, common sense was gone; all that was left was the ache to be with him. Sliding her arms around his neck, she dug her fingers into his hair. Lifting his head, he stared down at her, his breathing ragged.

'Sweet Lord, I can't wait anymore,' he whispered hoarsely. 'I won't wait anymore.'

Bending swiftly, he swung her up into his arms and carried her into the bedroom. He laid her gently onto the bed, then straightened, his eyes caressing her as he pulled his silky knit sweater over his head and tossed it into a corner. When his hand went to the snap at the waistband of his jeans, Helen closed her eyes. He was beside her in seconds, his skin warm and firm against hers. 'Marsh, I—'

'I love you,' he whispered fiercely, his mouth closing off any further protests from her. His hands brought every inch of her skin tinglingly alive, his mouth drove her to the edge of madness. Aching, moaning deep in her throat, she opened her eyes wide when he ordered, 'Tell me you love me.'

'I love you,' she repeated weakly.

'Again.'

'I love you.' A little stronger this time.

'Again.'

'I love you. I love you. Damn you, I love you.'

'Good.' Blatant satisfaction coated his tone.

Her nails punished him, but he laughed softly. 'You have a hunger almost as great as mine, love.' He kissed her, his tongue probing until she arched uncontrollably against him.

'What do you want, love?' he teased.

'Don't,' she pleaded.

'Tell me what you want,' he demanded relentlessly.

'You,' she sobbed. 'I want you. Don't torture me, Marsh, please.'

'Torture? You don't know the meaning of the word.' His lips teased hers, the tip of his tongue ran along the outline of her upper lip. 'I wanted to hear you say it, Helen. I had to hear it.' His body shifted, blanketing hers, and with a whispered, but definite 'Now,' his lips ceased their teasing, became hard, urgent.

It was everything a younger Helen had once hoped it would be. And much, much more than her imagination had ever dared hope for. Slowly, gently, Marsh guided her through the first fleeting moments of discomfort, then, his passion unleashed, he introduced her to a world she'd never dreamed existed. A world of pure sensation, of tension almost unbearable, of pleasure so exquisite that it held a thread of pain. Finer, yet more defined, the sweet bud of agony slowly blossomed. When it burst into full bloom there was soaring joy, shuddering victory, and one brief moment of unconsciousness that filled Helen with wonder. And the most incredible thing was that the near perfection could be repeated, as Marsh proved at regular intervals, over and over again. It was after four in the morning before Marsh, with a softly taunted 'Quitter,' let her drift into sleep.

The eerie silence that smothers the world with a heavy snowfall woke Helen late in the morning. Without moving, she opened her eyelids slowly. The space on the bed beside her was empty. Turning her head, her eyes come to his tall form, standing in front of the window. Barely breathing, she studied that form, a sharp pain stabbing at her heart. He had pulled on his jeans, but nothing else, and with his fingers tucked into his back pockets, his muscles bunched tautly in his arms across his shoulders. Head up, sombre-faced, he stared out through the window, a quality of waiting about him.

Waiting for what? To laugh? To crow over his triumph? To be prepared to smile indulgently as she meekly accepted his terms? Helen squirmed inwardly at her own thoughts, hating herself for her own weakness—almost hating him for taking advantage of that weakness.

Her eyes closed again, covering the pain and despair he could have easily read had he turned his head. She knew what she looked like in the morning. She faced that reality every day. Face pale, tiny lines of strain and years around her eyes and mouth. And this morning she would look even worse with her hair a tangled mess framing her pale face.

Helen would have been more shocked had someone thrust a mirror in front of her, forced her to open her eyes. The afterglow of love still tinged her cheeks; the tiny lines of strain had smoothed out, been partially erased by the release of tension; and the disarray of her hair gave her an untamed, sensual look. In essence the image she would have seen reflected in a mirror, and that Marsh did see when he turned his head, was of a breath-takingly beautiful woman. But no one did place a mirror in front of her, and Helen was convinced, on opening her eyes and finding Marsh's brooding ones on her, that what those hooded eyes observed displeased him.

Unable to bear those unreadable eyes on her, the taut, waiting stillness that held him, her hands curled into tight, determined fists under the covers. He had played his ace to her king, but if he thought he had won the game he was in for a shock. She still held one card and she would let *him* squirm awhile before she played it. The veneer of cool professionalism was pulled into place. In a voice withdrawn, detached from all the happenings of the past night, Helen clipped, 'Are you happy now? Are you satisfied?'

CHAPTER TEN

MARSH didn't move. A flame leaped brightly in his blue eyes, then was instantly, deliberately, quenched.

'Am I satisfied?' His voice, devoid of emotion, had a frighteningly dead sound. 'For the moment yes. Am I happy? Now? No.'

Well, Helen thought dismally, you certainly couldn't argue with a statement as definite as that. It wasn't quite what she had expected, but then, when had he ever done anything quite like she'd expected?

'Helen, about last night—'

No! a voice screamed inside her head. No, she would not listen to terms or possible plans or—maybe—rejection, not while she still lay on the battlefield of her own defeat.

'Marsh,' she interrupted quickly. 'I want to have a shower, get dressed.' Dragging the sheet with her, she sat up.

'Helen,' Marsh gritted impatiently, 'we have got to talk about—'

'Marsh, please.' She again cut him off. 'Will you leave this room so I can get up?'

His body stiffened, and she could see the battle that raged inside him. Then, with a curt nod, he turned and strode across the room, scooping his sweater off the floor in passing, and left the room, closing the door with an angry snap.

Fighting the urge to run after him, to agree to everything and anything he wanted, Helen slid off the bed and ran into the bathroom.

Twenty minutes later she walked into the kitchen to face him, her resolve strengthened, her course clearly mapped out in her mind.

He had made a pot of coffee and stood leaning against the counter, a cup of steaming brew cradled in his hands. Her small kitchen radio played softly in the background. When she entered the room, he set down his cup, filled a matching one for her, handed it to her, then tilted his head at the only window in the room.

'I've just heard a weather report,' he said quietly. 'We had over a foot of snow during the night and it's still snowing heavily. The weather bureau is calling for another three to five inches.'

A very safe subject, Helen thought cynically, the weather. Falling in with his lead, she murmured, 'Driving is going to be a nightmare. It's a good thing you took your car home.'

He nodded and polished off half his coffee in several swallows. The subject of the weather exhausted, a strained, uneasy silence vibrated between them. They both jumped at the sudden, discordant ring from the phone. Helen snatched up the receiver on the second ring, beating her service to it.

'Dr Cassidy.'

'Doctor, this is David Stewart. My wife fell a little while ago and is in labour.' The man rushed all in one breath. Gasping quickly, he hurried on. 'What the hell am I going to do? I can't even get my car out of the garage.'

Conjuring up a mental picture of Cheryl Stewart, Helen asked calmly, 'How far apart are the contractions?'

'I don't know,' he answered distractedly, then, 'just a minute, my mother-in-law is timing it now.' There was a short pause, then, 'Five minutes, Doctor.'

'Mr Stewart, give me your address, then go hold your

wife's hand.' Helen's calm voice soothed. 'I'll send an ambulance out and meet you at the hospital.'

'But can an ambulance get out here in this mess?' His voice was now frantic. Hearing an outcry of pain in the background, Helen knew why. This was the Stewarts' first baby.

'I'm sure it can, Mr Stewart, if you get off the line and let me call for one.'

The line went dead. A small smile pulling at her lips, Helen put through the call for an ambulance. The dispatcher's harried 'As soon as possible, Doctor' erased the smile, triggered a curl of unease. Her face thoughtful, Helen replaced the receiver. Glancing around at Marsh, she tossed the address to him.

'Can you get me out there?'

'Yes.' He caught on at once. 'You don't feel right about this?'

'I'm probably running you on a wild-goose chase.' Helen smiled apologetically. 'But no, I don't feel right about it.'

'So jump into your boots, grab your coat, and let's go.' He was already moving towards the living room.

Helen did exactly as he suggested. Less than ten minutes later, ready to go out the door, Helen paused, turned back to Marsh.

'In the closet, at the far end of the shelf, there's a black bag. Will you get it for me, please?'

Walking to the elevator, bag in his hand, Marsh lifted a questioning eyebrow at Helen.

'I don't even know what made me think of it. I've never used it,' she explained softly. 'My father gave it to me when I entered premed.' She hesitated, a gentle smile curling her lips. 'He had hoped I'd follow him into general practice.'

As Helen had predicted earlier, driving was a nightmare. Even with the four-wheel drive, negotiating the truck through the heavy wet snow required all Marsh's concentration, and as Helen was busy with her own thoughts, the drive was completed in near silence. When Marsh turned onto the street where the Stewarts lived, Helen sighed with a mixture of relief and disappointment. She had hoped to see an ambulance, if only the retreating lights of one, but the street was empty, the snow virgin, smooth.

As he parked the truck Marsh grunted, 'At least a path's been shovelled to the kerb.' Stepping out, he advised, 'Slide under the wheel and get out this side.'

David Stewart had the door open before they were halfway up the walk.

'Where the hell is that ambulance, Doctor?' His voice was heavy with strain, his face pale. 'Her pains are getting closer.'

'They'll get here as soon as they can.' Helen's tone was soothing as she walked into the small foyer. She removed her coat, then went still at the outcry of a woman in pain. 'Where is she? I'll—'

'I don't think this baby is going to wait for an ambulance. Come with me, Doctor.

Helen moved automatically towards the older woman who stood in an archway that led off the living room. Without another word the woman turned and led the way along a short hallway and into a bedroom. Cheryl Stewart lay on the bed, her face drawn with pain, her brow wet with sweat.

'Oh, Doctor,' she gasped. 'I'm so glad to see you. The pains are very bad.'

'She's been very good up until now, Doctor,' Cheryl's mother offered. 'I managed to get a plastic sheet and towels under her before her water broke.'

Drawing the covering sheet away, Helen nodded her approval. It required the briefest examination to ascertain the truth of the older woman's statement. This baby was not going to wait for anything. Cheryl gasped with the onslaught of another contraction, and Helen urged, 'Don't fight it, Cheryl, go with it.'

About to call to Marsh to bring her bag, Helen smiled in gratitude when he placed it beside her, asking, 'What can I do to help?'

'I think there's a packaged pair of gloves in there. Will you get them for me?'

After that she simply had to ask for what she wanted and it was handed to her. Sheets were draped, tentlike, over the girl's legs, and speaking quietly, encouragingly, Helen delivered the baby.

'Stop pushing now,' Helen instructed Cheryl when she held the baby's head and one shoulder in her hands. Then to Marsh, 'The syringe ready?'

'Right here,' came the calm reply.

Guiding the small form with her hands, Helen drew the baby into the world, then taking the syringe Marsh handed her, she cleaned the tiny mouth and nostrils of birth mucus. The infant sputtered, then began to cry, and Helen placed the red-faced child on Cheryl's stomach.

'You have a beautiful son, Cheryl,' she told the exhausted girl.

When she was satisfied that the baby was breathing spontaneously, Helen cut the lifeline cord, unaware that the ambulance had arrived or that the two attendants waited in the hall to take over.

They entered the room as she swabbed the blood from the baby's face.

'Okay, let's go,' Helen ordered briskly, wrapping the baby up warmly while the attendants carefully covered Cheryl. 'I'll suture in the hospital. Marsh, if you'll follow behind with Mr Stewart, I'll ride in the ambulance.'

Marsh nodded, holding her coat for her, and as she

slipped into it he whispered, 'That was beautiful, Helen. You're fantastic.'

It had stopped snowing and the streets were in somewhat better condition by the time they returned to the Stewart house several hours later. After dropping off a much happier-looking David, Marsh suggested they go to his apartment for something to eat.

'No, Marsh.' Helen shook her head firmly. 'There's plenty of food in my fridge. Besides which, I need a shower. I'm tired. I want to go home and get comfortable.' She didn't bother to add that her tiredness stemmed more from her lack of sleep the night before than the events of the day. She wasn't quite ready to tackle that subject yet.

After a relaxing shower Helen prepared a quick meal of canned soup and bacon, lettuce, and tomato sandwiches. Although they kept the conversation light and general while they ate, Helen could feel the tension of the morning tautening between them again. When the supper things were cleared away, they carried their coffee into the living room. Coffee cup in hand, Marsh paced back and forth for several minutes, then came to an abrupt halt in front of Helen.

'Can we talk now?'

'There is nothing to talk about.' Glancing up, Helen saw his lips tighten.

'Last night was nothing?' he asked sharply.

'I didn't say that.' Helen stood up, walked to the window. Her back to him, she said, 'What I meant was, it doesn't change anything.'

'Really?' Marsh mocked dryly. 'I'd have thought it changed everything.' A small smile replaced the mockery on his lips. 'Helen, I told you at the beginning that my intentions were honourable. I'm asking you to marry me.'

'No,' Helen answered at once, afraid to give herself

time to think, to weaken. 'It wouldn't work. My life suits me just as it is. I want no commitments, no strings.'

'All right, we'll play it your way.' His smile deepened as he slowly crossed the room to her. 'We'll live together without ceremony. You can move into my place or'—at her frown—'I'll move in here.' He shrugged, coming to a stop before her. 'It doesn't matter where, as long as I know that when you leave the office or the hospital or wherever, you'll be coming home to me. There'll be no commitments, no strings, no pressures, I promise.'

'No, Marsh.' Feeling sick, Helen watched the smile leave his face, his eyes narrow.

'I believe you said you love me last night,' he said quietly.

'That admission was forced out of me,' Helen snapped.

'And that changes it?' he snapped back. 'I also believe I told you I love you—at least fifty times.'

'And *I'm* positive you believe it—now.' Helen backed away from the sudden flare in his eyes. 'And I'm positive you believe you could be content with the arrangement you've suggested.' Holding up her hand to prevent him from interrupting, she hurried on. 'But I'm also very positive that the day would come when that arrangement would not be enough, when you'd ask for more, and I'm not prepared to play the three traditional roles. Not even for you.'

'What are you talking about?' Marsh was obviously confused. 'What three roles?'

Her heart feeling like a lead weight in her chest, Helen looked him squarely in the eyes and coldly, flatly, threw down her ace of trump.

'The cook in your kitchen, the madonna in your nursery, the mistress in your bed. For whether you believe it now or not, Marsh, I'm positive that the day will come when you'll come home hungry at dinnertime and I won't be here, either to make a meal or go out with you for one, and you'll resent it. And I don't need that.'

'Helen.'

'And the nights will come,' Helen went on, as if he hadn't spoken, 'when, after I've been called out, you'll lay alone on the bed and the dissatisfaction will grow. And I don't need that.'

'Helen.'

There was a low, angry warning in his tone now, and yet Helen went on.

'And the day will surely come when the desire for an extension of yourself, in the form of a child, will bring that resentment and dissatisfaction to an angry confrontation. *And I don't need that.*'

Finished now, Helen stood before him, waiting for his reaction. Finally, when she was beginning to think he would not reply at all, he said softly, 'In other words you don't need me. Is that what you're saying?'

Helen's throat closed painfully, but telling herself she had to say it, she lifted her head, pushed the word out.

'Yes.'

His face went pale and for one flashing instant seemed to contort with pain. In that instant Helen thought she saw raw agony in his eyes, then his head snapped up arrogantly, his jaw hardened, and his eyes went dead.

'Well, that's clear enough.' His tone was devoid of expression. 'I won't bother you again, Helen.'

Fingers curled into her hand, nails digging into her palm, Helen stared into the empty space where he'd stood. Eyes hot with a sudden sting, she heard him stamp into his boots, open the door. Teeth biting down hard on her lip, she kept herself from crying out to him to stop.

Let him go, she silently wept. *Now the game is played.*

For the following two weeks Helen worked at a gruelling pace. When she wasn't at the hospital or in the office, she attended every lecture offered—on her own subject of OB–GYN as well as others. She spent as little time as possible in her apartment and saw nothing at all of her friends. Telling herself that the empty, dead feeling inside would pass more quickly if she kept herself busy, she kept busy for all she was worth.

She had just returned home from the hospital on Monday night, two weeks after she had sent Marsh away, when she answered her doorbell and found Kris in the hall.

'I'm sorry to bother you so late, Helen,' she apologised after Helen had asked her to come in, 'but I've been here several times in the last couple of days and you've always been out.'

'I've been rather busy,' Helen said warily. 'What did you want to see me about?' Helen knew, of course. She hoped she was wrong, but she wasn't.

'Marsh,' Kris answered bluntly.

'Kris, I don't—' Helen began.

'Helen, I don't know what happened between you two and I have no intention of asking. But I love him and I'm worried about him and there's something I think you should know.'

Helen had continued to stand after asking Kris to sit down, but now, fear whispering through her mind, her legs suddenly weak, she sank onto a chair.

'Worried about him? Why? What's wrong with him?'

'I don't know if anything is,' Kris answered distractedly. 'Oh, let me explain. Two weeks ago today I took the baby over to Mother's and went shopping. When I returned, I heard voices from the library, and as the door was partially open, I thought Mother was probably in there with Dad, so I walked towards it. Just before I reached the door, the voices became louder and I stopped.' Kris wet her lips. 'I did not mean to eavesdrop, but I was so shocked by what I heard, I couldn't seem to move.'

'Kris,' Helen inserted quickly, 'if you overheard a private family conversation, I don't think you should be repeating it.'

'I have to, Helen,' Kris pleaded, 'so you'll understand why I'm here.' Helen started to shake her head, but Kris rushed on. 'I heard my father say to Marsh, "What do you intend? Good Lord, Son, this woman has an excellent reputation. Are you going to marry her?" I would have moved on then, Helen, really I would. But the odd sound of Marsh's voice kept me motionless. "She doesn't want me" was all he answered then, but he sounded so strange.'

'Kris, please.' Helen stood up again, moved around restlessly.

'Then Dad asked him what he was going to do, or something like that.' Kris went on relentlessly. 'And Marsh almost shouted at him.' Kris bit her lip. 'Helen, I've never heard Marsh raise his voice to my father before. Still in that odd tone he said, "I don't know. Right now I'm bleeding to death inside and I simply don't care." He walked out of the room then and right by me, as if I weren't there. When he got to the door, I called to him, asked him where he was going. He turned and looked through me. Then he smiled very gently and said, "Very probably to hell." '

Helen felt as if something had given way inside, and she sat down again very quickly.

'That was the last any of us saw of him. We haven't heard a word from him and have no idea where he is. I know Mother is very upset, and although he doesn't say anything, Dad's beginning to worry too. But there is one person who may know where he is.'

Cullen. The name flashed into Helen's mind at the same moment Kris said, 'My grandfather. I've been to see him, but all he'll tell me is Marsh can take care of himself and I'm not to worry.'

'Then don't,' Helen advised, now more than a little concerned herself.

'Oh, Helen,' Kris sighed. 'How does one not worry about the welfare of someone they love? I can't help but worry. This is just not like Marsh.' She hesitated, then suggested tentatively, 'If you went to Grandfather, I think he might tell you.'

'I can't do that, Kris.' Helen was out of her chair again. 'I—I have no right to question your grandfather about Marsh.'

'Just think about it, please.' Kris stood up and walked to the door. 'I must go. Mike is waiting in the car.' Before she walked out of the door, she urged, 'At least think about it, Helen.'

'I can't, Kris,' was all Helen could find to say.

Three days later Helen stood in front of the large door of the imposing edifice Cullen Hannlon called home. Kris had called her at the office that afternoon to inform her that there had still been no word from Marsh. Unable to bear her own fears and uncertainties any longer, Helen had come to the house directly from the office.

The door was opened by a pleasant-faced woman close to Cullen's own age. Helen asked to see Mr Hannlon, then gave her name and was ushered inside and along a wide beautifully panelled hall so swiftly that she almost felt she had been expected. The woman stopped at a door midway down the hall, tapped lightly, then pushed the door open and motioned Helen inside.

Cullen Hannlon stood beside a long narrow window, a smile on his still-handsome face.

'Ah, Helen, come in, come in,' he urged. 'I've been standing here enjoying the sunshine. This more spring-like weather feels so good after that snow a few weeks ago. But come, sit down. Can I get you some coffee or a drink?'

'No, nothing, thank you,' Helen murmured, wondering where to begin. 'Mr Hannlon, I—I—'

'Kris has been talking to you, hasn't she?' He smiled knowingly. 'I was afraid she would.'

'Do you know where he is?' Helen asked bluntly.

'Yes.' He was equally blunt. 'But I can't tell you. I gave him my word.'

'But—'

'No, Helen, I'm sorry.' He really did sound sorry; he also sounded adamant. 'I don't know what the problem is, but I do know my grandson's hurting. He went away on my suggestion and with my word that I'd tell no one where he is. I don't think you would ask me to break my word to him.'

'No,' Helen whispered. 'Of course not.'

'But I can tell you this,' he said gently. 'He will be back within two weeks. Should I tell him you were here?' This last was added hopefully.

Helen rose quickly. 'No, please don't. I need some time myself.' She paused, then admitted, to herself as well as him, 'To reorganise my thinking.'

I love him. Nothing has changed that; nothing ever will.

Helen lost count of the times she faced that fact during the next two weeks. With a suddenness that was shattering, she realised that without him her work, her independence, everything she had counted as precious, had very little meaning to her. She longed to see him, feel his strong arms draw her close against his hard body. It was spring and she wanted to walk in the park with him. She didn't hear a word from, or about, him.

Towards the end of that week Helen had a rough delivery. Rough in two ways. The breech birth in itself was difficult. The fact that her patient was her oldest and closest friend made it doubly so.

She had first met Estelle while in her first year of premed. Being the daughter of Helen's favourite professor, Estelle had been at home the first time Helen had been invited to his house. They had very few similar interests, and yet they became fast friends. The friendship had endured the years.

Estelle, scatterbrained and happy-go-lucky, surprised everyone, except possibly Helen, by marrying a serious-minded English professor ten years her senior. Everyone said the union could not possibly work. Everyone was wrong. Estelle and John balanced each other perfectly. There was only one unhappy note in their marriage: Estelle's inability to carry a child full term. After her third miscarriage, at the age of thirty-one, Estelle was strongly advised by Helen not to get pregnant again.

Estelle, being Estelle, disregarded Helen's advice and came to her two years later to confirm her pregnancy. And Helen, being Helen, was determined to see this child born. And now, after a pregnancy spent almost entirely in bed, a very long, hard labour and an extremely difficult delivery, Helen smiled with joy at both mother and son.

The new father was gently adoring when he was allowed a few minutes with his exhausted wife, proud as a prancing stallion when he viewed his offspring, and full of praise when he rejoined Helen in the waiting lounge.

'I want to buy you dinner.' He grinned as he crossed the room to her. 'I want to buy you champagne.' Pulling her to him, he gave her a bear hug. 'God, Helen, I want to buy you the moon.'

'I'll settle for dinner,' Helen told him solemnly, her eyes teasing.

He picked the most expensive restaurant in one of the

largest hotels. As they had no reservations, they were informed they could be served if they didn't mind a short wait. His high spirits undaunted, John told the maître d' they'd be in the bar and led Helen to it. Some forty-five minutes later they were called to their table. Told they should take their drinks with them, they left the bar drinks in hand. Crossing the threshold into the dining room, Helen came to a jarring stop.

Coming towards her, a lovely, young brunette on his arm, was the man Helen had spent almost four weeks being sick over. In the few seconds it took for Marsh and the girl to come up to her, Helen noted detail. Marsh looked well, relaxed, and, as he was smiling, happy. The girl, chattering away, looked equally happy. And why not? Helen asked herself bitterly. The girl's left hand rested on his forearm and on the ring finger rested a diamond solitaire big enough to choke a small horse.

The advantage was Helen's, as she had time to compose her features. Smiling down at the girl, Marsh didn't see her until he was practically on top of her.

'Good evening, Helen.'

Nothing registered on his face. No emotion, nothing. Helen went him one better—she smiled. 'Marsh.'

Marsh's cool blue eyes swept their glasses, then Helen's and John's smiling faces.

'A celebration?' His tone was mildly curious.

'Of the best kind,' John answered for her. 'This beautiful woman has just made me the happiest man in the state.'

Helen didn't bother to correct the wrong impression John had given.

'Congratulations,' Marsh said dryly, his eyes mocking Helen and the words she'd spoken against marriage just a few weeks before.

'Thank you.' John grinned, accepting Marsh's good wishes at face value.

'Excuse me.' The brunette's voice was soft but insistent. 'Marsh, we have to go. I don't want to be late for my own engagement party.'

'Of course,' Marsh said at once, then with a brief nod at Helen and John, he led the girl from the room.

Three hours later, pacing back and forth on her living room carpet, Helen was still amazed at the way she'd handled herself. Not only had she eaten her dinner, she had laughed and held up her end of the conversation. Now she wasn't at all sure her dinner would stay down and she was a great deal closer to tears than laughter. In an effort to keep the tears from escaping, she whipped herself into a rage.

You are not only a fool, she silently stormed, *you're an absolute nitwit. For weeks you've been dragging yourself from day to day, aching for the sight of him. Like an innocent child you talked yourself into believing every word he said. Convinced yourself your life was pointless without him. While he's out getting engaged to a young girl.*

Hands clenched into fists, she paced. Never had she known such anger. Anger at Marsh? Anger at herself? Her mind tried to shy away from the questions, not quite ready to face the final, self-commitment. With no place left to hide, exposed to herself, her mind screamed, *Dammit, he is mine.*

When the doorbell pealed, Helen swung blazing eyes to the door. It was Marsh. She knew it and she was tempted to ignore it. When it rang again, she strode across the room, flipped the lock, and yanked the door open. Without a word Marsh stormed by her, tossed his suit coat at a chair, then, eyes blazing as hotly as hers, turned to confront her.

'Who the hell is he?' he rasped harshly.

'None of your damned business,' Helen snapped.

Biting off a curse, Marsh closed the space between

them. Grasping her shoulders, he pulled her against his body with such force the air exploded from her lungs.

'It is my damned business,' he snarled. 'You are mine, Helen.' He jerked his head in the direction of the bedroom. 'I made you mine in there. Now get on that phone and call what's-his-name and tell him to run along. He can't have you.'

Sheer fury ripped through Helen. Of all the arrogant swine. Talk about wanting to have your cake and eat it all at the same time. He actually came from his own engagement party to tell her she belonged to him and couldn't have another man.

Twisting out of his arms, she spun away from him, then spun back, her voice icy.

'You—you . . . boy.' She flung at him. 'Get out of here before I hit you.' Incensed, raging, no longer thinking, she cried, 'To think I went to that old man.'

'You went to Cullen? Why?'

She was long past noticing how still he'd grown, how tight was his tone.

'To find out where you were.' Helen was near to shouting. She didn't care. Her laughter was not pretty. 'I was ready to crawl on my knees to you. I must have been out of my—'

She was pulled against him, her words drowning inside his mouth. It was heaven. It was hell. And though Helen didn't want it to ever stop, she pushed him away.

'I told you to get out of here.' Her voice was cold, flat, all signs of her fiery anger gone. 'Go back to your party, your friends, your fiancée.'

'My fiancée! I don't—' Marsh went silent, his eyes incredulous. 'You're jealous?' The incredulity changed to wonder. 'Helen, you're jealous.'

Helen stepped back warily, unsure of his awed tone, the light that leaped into his eyes.

'Helen, love,' Marsh murmured, 'that girl is Grant's sister. She's been another Kris to me. That engagement party tonight was for her and a young guy named Robert, who decided he couldn't live another day without her. Just exactly as I decided the same about you in January.' He walked to her slowly, drew her gently into his arms. 'Nothing's changed that,' he whispered. 'Nothing ever will.'

Tiny fingers crawled up Helen's scalp, and she experienced that eerie sensation he'd caused before.

'Oh, Marsh.'

'What's-his-name has got to go,' he groaned. 'Helen, love, haven't you realised yet that we belong to each other, together? I won't let you send me away again. I can't and continue to function normally.'

'What's-his-name is the husband of my best friend,' Helen explained softly, her hand going to his face with the need to touch him. 'She and I together successfully brought their first child into the world late this afternoon. He insisted on buying me dinner. That's what we were celebrating.'

'Oh, God.' His mouth moved over her face as if imprinting her likeness on his lips. 'I don't ever want to live through a period like the last couple of hours again. Helen, I was so mad, I thought I'd blow apart. The thought of you with another man— He shuddered and brought his mouth back to hers to kiss her violently.

'I know,' she whispered when she could breathe again. 'I was going through the same thing.' Her voice went rough. 'Marsh, where have you been these past weeks? I was sick with worry.' Before he could answer, she slid her fingers over his lips, shook her head. 'No, it doesn't matter. I love you. I want to spend the rest of my life with you. With commitments or without. With strings or without. That doesn't matter either.' Then, very softly, she repeated his words of weeks ago. 'The only thing that does matter is when you finally do come, from the office, or wherever, you'll be coming to me.'

The sunshine, streaming through the bedroom windows, had a golden autumnal glow. Marsh, whistling softly, came through the bedroom door.

'Coffee's ready and the juice is poured, love. Are you going to laze away half the holiday in bed or are you going to get up and have breakfast with me?'

At the mention of food Helen groaned and rolled onto her side away from him.

A smile curving his lips, Marsh sauntered to Helen's side of the bed, dropped onto his haunches, leaned forward, and tickled her ear with his tongue.

'If you're not up in thirty seconds, I'm going to crawl back in there with you, and I don't care if we never make it to Mother's for Thanksgiving dinner.'

With a murmured 'Good morning,' Helen slid one arm around his neck and sought the lips now teasing her cheek. When his wake-up kiss started to deepen, she pushed gently against his shoulders. 'Go back to the kitchen,' Helen whispered breathlessly, evading his still-hungry mouth. 'I'll be with you in a minute.'

Marsh grinned, stole another quick kiss, then rose and strolled out of the room, again whistling softly.

After rinsing her face and brushing her teeth, Helen followed him to the kitchen, impatient with the weariness of her body. As she entered the kitchen the room swirled before her eyes, and groaning a soft protest against the light-headedness, she grasped the back of a kitchen chair.

'Helen?' Marsh's sharp tone barely penetrated the mistiness, but she felt his strength when he scooped her up into his arms. 'What's the matter? Are you coming down with something?' The questions were rapped anxiously at her as he strode through the living room into the bedroom.

'No, Marsh, I'm not sick.' Off her feet she felt the fuzziness pass and she smiled weakly at him. 'I'm pregnant.'

Marsh froze. Even his face looked frozen. 'How?' At her arched glance he sighed, 'I mean, I thought you were taking precautions.'

'I stopped.'

'Why, Helen? I told you it didn't matter.'

'It suddenly mattered very much to me.' She hid her face against his chest as he set her on her feet. 'I wanted to have our baby, Marsh.'

The sound of his sharply indrawn breath came clearly to her as he turned her around in his arms, then spread his hands wide over her still flat belly. 'Is it safe for you, love?'

'Yes, Marsh. I'm seeing an excellent obstetrician.'

'Are you sure?' he murmured against her hair. 'Are you very, very sure?'

'Very, very sure.' Helen's hands covered his, the narrow gold band on her left ring finger brushing against its counterpart on his. 'It will be all right, I promise you. We are going to have a beautiful baby, Marsh.'

SUMMER STORM
Catherine Hart

"Hart offers a gripping, sympathetic portrait of the Cheyenne as a proud people caught in turmoil by an encroaching world."

—*Publishers Weekly*

SUMMER STORM. Soft and warm as a sweet summer rain, Summer Storm could be tamed only by Windrider, a brave leader of the Cheyenne. Though she had given her heart to another, he vowed their tumultuous joining would be climaxed in a whirlwind of ecstasy.

_____2465-9 $3.95 US/$4.95 CAN

De:

_____

Para:

_____

Fecha:

_____

Jesús siempre

Sarah Young

GRUPO NELSON
Una división de Thomas Nelson Publishers
Desde 1798

NASHVILLE   MÉXICO DF.   RÍO DE JANEIRO

© 2017 por Grupo Nelson®
Publicado en Nashville, Tennessee, Estados Unidos de América.
Grupo Nelson es una subsidiaria que pertenece completamente a
Thomas Nelson.
Grupo Nelson es una marca registrada de Thomas Nelson.
www.gruponelson.com

Título en inglés: *Jesus Always*
© 2016 por Sarah Young
Publicado por Thomas Nelson

Editora en Jefe: *Graciela Lelli*
Traducción: *Eugenio Orellana*
Adaptación del diseño al español: *Grupo Nivel Uno, Inc.*

ISBN: 978-0-71809-311-2

Impreso en Estados Unidos de América
16 17 18 19 20 DCI 6 5 4 3 2 1

Dedico este libro a Jesús: mi Señor y
mi Dios, mi Salvador y Amigo.

Llegaré entonces al altar de Dios,
del Dios de mi alegría y mi deleite.
—SALMOS 43.4

Me has dado a conocer la senda de la vida;
me llenarás de alegría en tu presencia,
y de dicha eterna a tu derecha.
—SALMOS 16.11

Ustedes lo aman a pesar de no haberlo visto;
y aunque no lo ven ahora,
creen en él y se alegran con un
gozo indescriptible y glorioso.
—1 PEDRO 1.8

Reconocimientos

Es una bendición para mí trabajar con un equipo tan talentoso: Jennifer Gott, mi directora del proyecto editorial, ha trabajado con denuedo en la producción de este libro, desempeñando una variedad de funciones de manera muy eficiente. Estoy agradecida con Kris Bearss, mi editor, que conoce mi trabajo maravillosamente bien y edita mis escritos con el toque exacto. Finalmente, siento gratitud hacia mi editora, Laura Minchew, quien tiene una gran abundancia de ideas creativas y además «pastorea» mis publicaciones.

Introducción

Escribir *Jesús siempre* ha sido una verdadera maratón para mí. Lo empecé en septiembre de 2012 mientras todavía vivía en Perth, Australia. En el año 2013, mi esposo y yo volvimos a los Estados Unidos, un cambio realmente complicado al ir de un punto en el planeta a otro. A lo largo de medio año viví abriendo y cerrando maletas. Nos quedamos en siete hogares diferentes, yendo y viniendo entre uno y otro múltiples veces. No hace falta decirlo, pero durante estos seis meses no avancé mucho en el libro.

Cuando finalmente nos instalamos en nuestra casa permanente en Tennessee, me sentí feliz de poder retomar la escritura. Trabajar en *Jesús siempre* se convirtió en mi prioridad número uno: para terminar de escribir este libro decidí posponer una serie de actividades importantes. Fue un placer y un privilegio poder separar tiempo a fin de concentrarme en Jesús y su Palabra.

Jesús siempre ha sido concebido para acrecentar su gozo y fortalecer su relación con Jesús. Si usted le pertenece a él, su historia tiene un final indescriptiblemente feliz, sea cual fuere la situación que esté viviendo en este momento. Y el solo hecho de saber que su historia finaliza tan maravillosamente bien puede llenar de gozo su presente. Si no conoce aun a Cristo como su Salvador, le aseguro que estoy orando por usted cada día para que le pida que perdone sus pecados y le conceda el glorioso regalo de la vida eterna. Entonces podrá también experimentar el asombroso gozo de ser el amigo amado de Jesús.

Durante muchos años, desde agosto de 2001, he tenido que luchar con la enfermedad. En mi búsqueda de salud he visitado a numerosos doctores y recurrido a una variedad de tratamientos médicos. Sigo teniendo serias limitaciones en mi vida, pero he encontrado el gozo para seguir viviendo.

Mi incapacidad de estarme moviendo de un lado al otro me ha dado más tiempo para enfocarme en Jesús y disfrutar de su Presencia. También me ha provisto de oportunidades para pasar tiempo con amigos queridos y conocidos. Ya no manejo debido al vértigo crónico que padezco desde 2008. Como resultado, amigos de buen corazón me han llevado a varios lugares, quedándose a menudo conmigo durante largas horas de espera en las consultas médicas. Pasar tiempo con esta gente extraordinaria ha sido una fuente de mucha alegría para mí.

Llevar una vida de quietud me ha ayudado a buscar y encontrar pequeños tesoros que le dan brillo a mi día: un cardenal o una urraca azul en vuelo, una «coincidencia» que me recuerda que Dios está obrando aun en los detalles de mi vida. Trato de dedicar un tiempo cada día para escribir en mi cuaderno algo de las recientes bendiciones que he recibido. Lo llamo mi «Libro de gratitud». Observar las cosas buenas y agradecerle a Dios por ellas me anima y cambia mi perspectiva, ayudándome a ver mi vida a través de un prisma de gratitud.

Me encanta la historia de aquel minero anciano y débil cuyo cuerpo se había desgastado por sus muchos años de duro trabajo en las minas. En su humilde hogar había una mesa con un pequeño pocillo lleno de avena. En su mano tiznada de carbón sostenía un pedazo de pan y se aprestaba a servirse su pobre desayuno. Sin embargo, primero se arrodilló junto a la mesa y alegremente exclamó una y otra vez: «¡Todo esto, y también Jesús! ¡Todo esto, y también Jesús!».

Esta historia me inspira y ayuda a entender la hermosa verdad de que tener a Jesús en mi vida significa que estoy siendo bendecida más allá de mi fe. Estoy convencida de que la gratitud es uno de los ingredientes más importantes de un corazón gozoso.

Me gusta cantar por las mañanas esta canción breve y sencilla: «Este es el día que el Señor ha hecho. Regocijémonos y alegrémonos en él». Eso me ayuda a ver el día como un regalo precioso de Dios y a recordar que hasta cada aliento que respiro proviene de él.

El subtítulo de *Jesús siempre* es *Abrace el gozo en su presencia*. Abrazamos el Gozo al abrazar a Jesús: al amarlo, confiar en él, estar en comunicación con él. Podemos optar por vivir de esta manera aun en los tiempos más difíciles. En realidad, mientras más duras resulten nuestras circunstancias, más brillante será nuestro Gozo, en vívido contraste con el oscuro telón de fondo de la adversidad. De esta manera hacemos la Luz de la Presencia de Jesús visible a las personas que nos rodean.

Considero a la Biblia un tesoro apreciable; es la única Palabra de Dios inspirada, inerrante e incambiable. Me gozo leyéndola, meditando en la *profundidad de las riquezas de la sabiduría y el conocimiento de Dios*. Durante los últimos cinco años, memorizar las Escrituras se ha convertido en algo cada vez más precioso para mí. ¡Es muy consolador tener la Palabra de Dios en mi corazón todo el tiempo, guiándome y alentándome día y noche!

Como todos mis libros devocionales, *Jesús siempre* ha sido escrito desde la perspectiva de Jesús hablándole a usted, el lector. Debido a que reverencio la Biblia, siempre me esfuerzo para lograr que mis escritos se correspondan con la verdad bíblica. Incluyo principios de las Escrituras en los devocionales (indicados en cursivas), y cada sección es seguida por tres o cuatro referencias bíblicas. Lo animo a que busque y lea estos versículos cuidadosamente. ¡Son palabras de Vida! Unos cuantos de los devocionales que aparecen en este libro reflejan ideas que se encuentran en *Jesús vive*. Las he incluido en *Jesús siempre* para aumentar el «cociente de gozo» en el libro.

Desde la publicación de *Jesús te llama*, he orado diariamente por las personas que están leyendo mis libros. Con el paso de los años, estas oraciones se han hecho más extensas cubriendo una variedad de temas. Aun cuando he estado hospitalizada, no he dejado pasar un día sin orar por mis lectores. Lo considero una responsabilidad que me ha dado Dios y un privilegio gratificante. Me siento feliz de agregar a los lectores de *Jesús siempre* a esta preciosa comunidad. Una de mis oraciones diarias más fervientes es que el Señor traiga a muchos lectores a su Reino de *Gozo inexpresable y glorioso*.

Querido lector, mientras usted recorre las páginas de este libro, mi deseo es que abrace el Gozo de una relación íntima con Jesús. Él está con usted en todo tiempo y en su Presencia hay *plenitud de Gozo*.

¡ABUNDANTES BENDICIONES!

Sarah Young

Enero

*Tu palabra es una lámpara
que guía mis pie,
y una luz para mi camino.*

SALMOS 119.105, NTV

NO TE QUEDES EN EL PASADO. ¡Mira, yo estoy haciendo algo nuevo! Al comenzar otro año, alégrate de que no dejo de hacer cosas nuevas en tu vida. No permitas que las desilusiones y los fracasos recientes te definan o disminuyan tus expectativas. ¡Este es el momento de disfrutar de un nuevo comienzo! Yo soy un Dios con una creatividad sin límites; espera a ver las cosas sorprendentes que haré este año y tendrán que ver contigo.

El día de hoy es un regalo precioso. El momento presente es donde me encuentro contigo, mi amado. Así que búscame a lo largo de *este día que he hecho.* Lo he preparado cuidadosamente para ti, con tierna atención por cada detalle. Quiero que te *regocijes y te alegres en él.*

Identifica las señales de mi Presencia amorosa mientras vas por *la senda de la vida.* Busca los pequeños placeres que he sembrado a lo largo de tu ruta, a veces en lugares sorprendentes, y agradéceme por cada uno de ellos. Tu agradecimiento te mantendrá cerca de mí y te ayudará a encontrar el Gozo en tu viaje.

ISAÍAS 43.18, 19; SALMOS 118.24;
SALMOS 16.11

Enero 2

¡Yo soy tu Gozo! Estas cuatro palabras pueden iluminar tu vida. Ya que estoy siempre contigo, *el Gozo de mi Presencia* siempre se encuentra accesible para ti. Puedes llegar a mi Presencia a través de tu confianza en mí, de tu amor por mí. Intenta decir: «Jesús, tú eres mi Gozo». Mi Luz brillará sobre ti y dentro de ti al *alegrarte en mí*, tu Salvador. Medita en todo lo que he hecho por ti y en todo lo que soy para ti. Esto te llevará más allá de tus circunstancias.

Cuando te convertiste en mi seguidor, te di poder para elevarte por sobre las condiciones de tu vida. Te llené con mi Espíritu, y este Santo Ayudador tiene Poder ilimitado. Prometí que *volvería y te llevaría conmigo* al cielo, *para que estés donde yo estoy* para siempre. Cuando tu mundo parezca oscuro, ilumina tu perspectiva enfocándote en mí. Descansa en mi Presencia y escúchame decir: «¡Mi amado, yo soy tu Gozo!».

SALMOS 21.6; FILIPENSES 4.4;
JUAN 14.3

QUÉDENSE QUIETOS, RECONOZCAN *que yo soy Dios*. Muchos cristianos están familiarizados con este mandamiento, pero no tanto como para tomarlo en serio. Sin embargo, para quienes lo *hacen*, las bendiciones fluyen como *corrientes de agua viva*. En la medida en que estos creyentes permanecen en quietud —concentrados en mí y mi Palabra— su percepción de mí se expandirá y la importancia de sus problemas disminuirá.

Quiero que participes de estas bendiciones, mi amado. Aparta tiempo. Aparta tiempo para estar conmigo. Mientras descansas en mi Presencia, esclarezco tus pensamientos y te ayudo a ver las cosas más bíblicamente. Recuerda: *mi Palabra es una lámpara que guía tus pasos y alumbra tu camino*. Los pensamientos bíblicos van alumbrando delante de ti, de modo que no tengas posibilidad de extraviarte.

Es absolutamente importante saber no solo que *yo soy* Dios, sino que *yo te hice y eres mío*. Tú eres una *oveja de mi prado*. Las ovejas tienen una comprensión bastante limitada en cuanto a lo que su pastor está haciendo por ella, pero de todos modos lo siguen. De igual manera, como mi «oveja», tu deber es confiar en mí e ir a donde yo te guíe.

SALMOS 46.10; JUAN 7.38;
SALMOS 119.105; SALMOS 100.3

Enero 4

HALLA TU GOZO EN MÍ, porque yo soy tu Fuerza. Resulta vital que mantengas vivo tu Gozo, especialmente cuando te encuentras en medio de las angustias de la adversidad. Cada vez que estés luchando con las dificultades, necesitas tener cuidado de tus pensamientos y lo que dices. Si le prestas demasiada atención a todas las cosas que están mal, te vas a sentir más y más desalentado, y tu fuerza tenderá a agotarse. Tan pronto como te des cuenta de que eso está sucediendo, detén de inmediato este proceso que te hiere. Vuélvete a mí y pídeme que te ayude con todas tus luchas.

Dedica un tiempo a alabarme. Pronuncia o canta palabras de adoración. Lee pasajes bíblicos que te ayuden a regocijarte en mí.

Recuerda que tus problemas son temporales, pero que yo soy eterno e igual de eterna es tu relación conmigo. Al hallar tu Gozo en mí y deleitarte en *mi amor inagotable* hacia ti, tus fuerzas se acrecentarán. ¡Este es *el Gozo del Señor*, que es tuyo todo el tiempo y hasta la eternidad!

NEHEMÍAS 8.10; SALMOS 66.1-3;
SALMOS 143.8

Deja que *mi consuelo*, mi consolación, *lleven Gozo a tu alma.* Cuando la ansiedad se acumule sobre ti, acércate a mí y *vuelca tu corazón.* Luego quédate quieto en mi Presencia mientras yo te consuelo y te ayudo a ver las cosas desde mi perspectiva. ¡Yo te hago recordar que tienes un destino celestial, porque indudablemente te encuentras camino de la Gloria! Infundo mi Gozo y mi Paz en tu corazón, mente y alma.

Cuando estás contento, este Gozo cambia la forma en que ves el mundo a tu alrededor. Y aunque notes mucha oscuridad, también podrás *ver* la Luz de mi Presencia alumbrando de forma continua. Además, el Gozo en tu alma te dará optimismo y firmeza para superar los muchos problemas que pudieras tener en tu vida. Una vez que hayas alcanzado esta perspectiva, descubrirás que puedes consolar a otros que estén pasando por tribulaciones. Y estos otros encontrarán en ti la consolación que tú has hallado en mí. Así, tu Gozo se hará contagioso, «infectando» las almas de *todos* los que te rodean.

Salmos 94.19; Salmos 62.8;
2 Corintios 1.3, 4

Enero 6

Es POSIBLE que mis seguidores experimenten alegría y miedo al mismo tiempo. Cuando un ángel les dijo a las mujeres que fueron a mi tumba que yo había resucitado de la muerte, ellas se sintieron «asustadas pero muy alegres». No dejes que el miedo te prive de experimentar el Gozo de mi Presencia. Esto no es un lujo reservado para los tiempos en que tus problemas —y las crisis en el mundo— parezcan bajo control. Mi amorosa Presencia es tuya para que la disfrutes hoy, mañana y siempre.

No des lugar a una vida sin alegría al permitir que las preocupaciones por el presente o el futuro te agobien. En cambio, recuerda que *ni lo presente ni lo por venir, ni los poderes, ni cosa alguna en toda la creación, podrá apartarte de mi Amor.*

Cuéntame tus miedos, exprésame libremente tus pensamientos y sentimientos. Relájate en mi Presencia y entrégame todas tus preocupaciones. Luego pídeme que te bendiga con mi Gozo, el cual *nadie te quitará.*

MATEO 28.8; ROMANOS 8.38, 39;
JUAN 16.22

7

MIENTRAS MÁS VUELVAS tus pensamientos a mí, más disfrutarás de mi *perfecta Paz*. Este es un reto desafiante, pero también es un don glorioso. *Yo, el Pastor de tu alma*, estoy siempre cerca de ti.

Entrena tu mente para apartarla de otras cosas y que se concentre en mí. Cuando experimentes algo hermoso, agradécemelo. Cuando un ser querido te produzca gozo, recuerda que yo soy la fuente de esa alegría. Coloca recordatorios de mi Presencia en tu casa, automóvil y oficina. También es sabio memorizar versículos bíblicos, porque todos confluyen en mí.

Volver tus pensamientos hacia mí es prueba de que te inspiro confianza. Incluso ciertas cosas desagradables como el dolor y los problemas pueden recordarte comunicarte conmigo. Enfocarte en mi Presencia te protege de quedarte atascado en los problemas, de estar pensando una y otra vez en ellos sin hacer ningún tipo de progreso.

Sé creativo para buscar nuevas formas de volver tus pensamientos a mí. Así podrás disfrutar del maravilloso don de mi Paz.

ISAÍAS 26.3; 1 PEDRO 2.25;
FILIPENSES 4.6, 7

¡EN MÍ, TÚ PUEDES DESCUBRIR UN *Gozo inexpresable y plenitud de Gloria*! Esta clase de placer no la podrás encontrar en ninguna otra parte; está disponible solo en tu relación conmigo. Por eso, confía en mí, mi amado, y avanza con seguridad por el camino de la vida. Mientras vamos juntos, encontrarás muchos obstáculos, algunos muy dolorosos. Espera estas dificultades cada día y no dejes que te desvíen de tu curso ni que la adversidad te prive de alegrarte en mí. En mi Presencia las profundas penas pueden coexistir con un Gozo aun más profundo.

Tu vida conmigo es una aventura, y en un viaje aventurado siempre hay peligros. Pídeme que te dé valor para que puedas enfrentar las pruebas con fortaleza. Mantén tu esperanza fuertemente sujeta a mí y a la recompensa celestial que te espera. Tu Gozo se expandirá astronómicamente, más allá de todo lo que te puedas imaginar, cuando llegues a tu hogar eterno. ¡Allí me verás *cara a Cara*, y tu Gozo no conocerá fronteras!

1 PEDRO 1.8; 2 CORINTIOS 6.10;
1 CORINTIOS 13.12

¡Yo soy tu Tesoro! A veces te sientes cansado, llevado de un lado a otro por las personas y las circunstancias. Tu anhelo de significado y conexión profunda te lleva a más y más actividad. Aun cuando tu cuerpo puede estar quieto, tu mente tiende a correr, anticipándose a los problemas futuros y buscando soluciones. Necesitas recordar que *todos los tesoros de la sabiduría y el conocimiento se encuentran escondidos en mí.* Trae con frecuencia a tu memoria esta gloriosa verdad y declara en un susurro: «Jesús, tú eres mi Tesoro. En ti estoy completo».

Cuando me aprecias sobre todo lo demás y me haces tu *Primer Amor,* te estás protegiendo de tener sentimientos divididos. Siempre que sientas que tus pensamientos se extravían, entrena tu mente para que regrese al Único que te llena completamente. Esto le da un enfoque a tu vida y te ayuda a permanecer cerca de mí. Vivir cerca de mí y disfrutar de mi Presencia implica *obedecer mis mandamientos.* Te estoy diciendo esto *para que tengas mi Gozo y así tu Gozo sea completo.*

COLOSENSES 2.2, 3; APOCALIPSIS 2.4;
JUAN 15.10, 11

TEN CUIDADO DE PENSAR EN EXCESO EN LAS COSAS, obsesionándote con ciertos asuntos sin importancia. Cuando tu mente está ociosa, tiendes a planificar: a tratar de entender las cosas, a hacer decisiones antes de que en realidad necesites hacerlas. Esta es una manera improductiva de tratar de controlarlo todo, además de ser una pérdida de tiempo precioso. A menudo, terminas pensando en otras cosas o simplemente olvidándote de la decisión que habías hecho. Hay un tiempo para planificar, pero definitivamente no debemos hacerlo *todo* el tiempo… o incluso la mayor parte del tiempo.

Trata de vivir en el momento presente, donde mi Presencia te espera continuamente. Refréscate en mi cercanía, dejando que mi Amor trabaje en tu ser interior. Relájate conmigo, poniendo a un lado tus problemas para que puedas estar atento a mí y recibir más de mi Amor. *Tu alma tiene sed de mí*, pero a menudo no te das cuenta de lo que realmente estás anhelando: ser consciente de mi Presencia. Déjame *llevarte junto a aguas tranquilas y restaurar tu alma*. Del mismo modo que los enamorados no necesitan decir mucho para tener una comunicación profunda, así debe ser tu relación conmigo, el Amor de tu alma.

EFESIOS 3.17-19; SALMOS 63.1;
SALMOS 23.2, 3

Hay un tiempo para todo, *y todo lo que se hace debajo del cielo tiene su hora.* Cuando buscas mi rostro y mi voluntad —buscando orientación— puedo mostrarte el siguiente paso en tu caminar sin revelarte el momento en que darás ese paso. En lugar de ir a toda velocidad tan pronto sabes cuál es el próximo paso, debes esperar hasta que te muestre *cuándo* quiero que avances.

Hay un tiempo para todo. Esto significa que incluso en los momentos más gratificantes de la vida hay que dar paso a algo nuevo. Mientras que algunos de mis seguidores se muestran impacientes por avanzar a un nuevo territorio, otros se detienen cuando estoy claramente dirigiéndolos para que sigan adelante. Pasar de un tiempo tranquilo y confortable en la vida a una nueva situación puede causar miedo, sobre todo a aquellos a los que no les gustan los cambios. Sin embargo, quiero que confíes en mí lo suficiente como para que te aferres a mí y vayas a donde yo te guíe *cuando* yo lo quiera. *Tu vida entera está en mis manos.*

Eclesiastés 3.1; Isaías 43.19;
2 Corintios 5.17; Salmos 31.15

SÉ VALIENTE Y NO TE DESANIMES, porque yo estoy contigo adondequiera que vayas. Es fácil para mis seguidores sentirse asustados y pesimistas cuando las voces dominantes de este mundo hablan con tanta fuerza contra ellos. Ver la vida a través de lentes sesgadas e incrédulas sin duda que desmoraliza a cualquiera. El valor cristiano es el antídoto contra esta influencia venenosa, y se nutre por medio de la convicción de que estoy siempre contigo.

Es importante recordar que lo que puedes ver de la realidad es solo una parte muy pequeña del todo. Cuando Elías estaba profundamente desalentado, dijo que él era *el único* que había permanecido fiel. Sin embargo, había millares en Israel que no se habían inclinado ante Baal. Elías estaba cegado por su aislamiento y su desánimo. Del mismo modo, el criado de Eliseo se encontraba aterrorizado, ya que no podía percibir lo que veía Eliseo: *caballos y carros de fuego alrededor* de ellos para protegerlos de las fuerzas enemigas. Amado, yo no solo estoy contigo, sino que tengo recursos ilimitados para ayudarte. ¡Así que mira más allá de la apariencia de las cosas, y *no tengas miedo!*

JOSUÉ 1.9; 1 REYES 19.14;
2 REYES 6.17; MATEO 14.27

¡CONMIGO TODAS LAS COSAS SON POSIBLES! Deja que estas poderosas palabras iluminen tu mente y alienten tu corazón. Rehúsate a ser intimidado por la forma en que las cosas se ven en el momento. Yo te estoy preparando para que *vivas por fe, no por vista.*

El sentido de la vista es un regalo espectacular que proviene de mí, a fin de que sea utilizado de forma alegre y agradecida. Sin embargo, es fácil quedar hipnotizado por todos los estímulos visuales que te rodean y olvidarte de mí. La fe es un tipo de visión que te conecta conmigo. En lugar de concentrarte en el mundo visible, atrévete a confiar en mí y en mis promesas.

Vive cerca de mí, tu Salvador y Amigo, pero recuerda: también soy Dios infinito. Cuando viví en tu planeta, mis *milagrosas señales revelaron mi Gloria, y mis discípulos pusieron su fe en mí.* Yo continúo haciendo milagros en tu mundo, de acuerdo con mi voluntad y propósitos. Trata de alinear tu voluntad con la mía y ver las cosas desde mi perspectiva. Ejerce tu fe para pedir cosas grandes, y obsérvame trabajar con esperanza.

MARCOS 10.27; 2 CORINTIOS 5.7;
JUAN 2.11; MIQUEAS 7.7

Enero 14

Yo TE CONOZCO MUY BIEN. Sé absolutamente todo acerca de ti, y te amo con un *Amor perfecto e inagotable*. Muchas personas andan en busca de una mayor comprensión y aceptación de sí mismas. Implícito en su búsqueda está un deseo de encontrar a alguien que realmente las entienda y acepte como son. Yo soy ese Alguien que puede satisfacer plenamente este anhelo tan profundamente arraigado en ti. Es en tu relación conmigo que descubres lo que realmente eres.

Te animo a que seas auténtico conmigo, entregándome todas tus pretensiones y abriéndote totalmente a mí. Al acercarte, pronuncia estas palabras inspiradas: «*Examíname, oh Dios, y sondea mi corazón; ponme a prueba y sondea mis pensamientos*». En la Luz de mi santa mirada, verás cosas que necesitas cambiar. Sin embargo, no te desesperes; yo te ayudaré. Continúa descansando en mi Presencia, recibiendo mi Amor que fluye libremente hacia ti en la medida en que te abres a mí. Dale tiempo a este poderoso Amor para que penetre profundamente en tu vida, llenando espacios vacíos y desbordándose en gozosa adoración. ¡Regocíjate porque eres perfectamente conocido y para siempre amado!

1 CORINTIOS 13.12; SALMOS 147.11;
SALMOS 139.23, 24

LA VIDA CRISTIANA tiene que ver por completo con confiar en mí. En los buenos tiempos *y* también en los malos. Yo soy el Señor de todas tus circunstancias, por eso quiero estar involucrado en cada aspecto de tu vida. En menos de un segundo puedes conectarte conmigo, confirmando tu confianza en mí, aquí y ahora. Cuando tu mundo te parezca oscuro y tú de todas maneras confíes en mí, mi Luz brillará poderosa a través de ti. Tu demostración de fe trascendente anulará las fuerzas espirituales del mal y mi Luz sobrenatural que se expresa a través de ti bendecirá y fortalecerá a las personas que te rodean.

Aferrarte a mí en la oscuridad requiere que persistas en ejercer tu fuerza de voluntad. No obstante, mientras te estás asiendo firmemente a mí, recuerda: el agarre de mi mano sobre la tuya es eterno. ¡Nunca te soltaré! Además, mi Espíritu te ayudará a mantenerte conectado conmigo. Cuando te sientas a punto de desfallecer, pídele que te ayude: «¡Ayúdame, Espíritu Santo!». Esta breve oración te permitirá beneficiarte de sus recursos ilimitados, incluso cuando tus circunstancias se vean oscuras y amenazantes. ¡Mi Luz *sigue brillando* con un resplandor insuperable!

1 JUAN 1.7; SALMOS 62.8; SALMOS 139.10;
JUAN 1.5

Enero 16

CUANDO LAS COSAS NO TE ESTÉN saliendo como tú quieres, no te acongojes. Deja lo que estés haciendo y respira. Profundamente. *Busca mi Rostro,* pasa unos momentos disfrutando de mi Presencia. Cuéntame sobre los asuntos que te están preocupando. Yo te ayudaré a ver las cosas desde mi perspectiva y a separar lo que es importante de lo que no lo es. Además, voy a abrir el camino ante ti para que avances en confiada dependencia, manteniendo la comunicación conmigo.

Tu deseo de estar en control de todo es a menudo el culpable detrás de tu frustración. Planeas tu día y esperas que los demás se comporten de manera que hagan que tus planes se cumplan. Cuando tal cosa no ocurre, te ves enfrentado a una crisis. Tendrás que decidir si resentirte o confiar en mí. Recuerda que el que está en control de todo soy yo y que *mis caminos son más altos que los tuyos, como los cielos son más altos que la tierra.* En lugar de perturbarte por los contratiempos que experimenta tu agenda, usa esos contratiempos como recordatorios: Yo soy tu Dios Salvador y tú eres mi amado seguidor. Tranquilízate confiando en mi control soberano y *en mi amor inagotable.*

SALMOS 27.8; ISAÍAS 55.9; SALMOS 43.5;
SALMOS 13.5

TE TRAJE A UN LUGAR ESPACIOSO. Te rescaté porque me agradé de ti. Estás en un espacioso lugar de salvación, salvado de ser un *esclavo del pecado.* Tu salvación es lo más grande, el regalo más espléndido que podrías recibir jamás. Nunca dejes de darme las gracias por este regalo infinitamente precioso. Por las mañanas cuando te despiertes, regocíjate porque te he adoptado para que seas parte de mi familia real. Por las noches, antes de irte a dormir, alábame por mi gracia gloriosa. Vive de tal manera que ayudes a otros a verme como el manantial de Vida abundante e inacabable.

Yo me deleité en ti no porque haya algún mérito en tu persona, sino porque te escogí para gozarme en ti y en mi espléndido amor por ti. Ya que tus mejores esfuerzos nunca podrían ser suficientes para salvarte, te vestí con mi propia justicia perfecta. Usa este *vestido de salvación* con gratitud, con gozo desbordante. Recuerda que eres realeza en mi reino, donde mi Gloria y Luz brillan eternamente. *Vive como un hijo de la Luz,* arropado seguramente en mi justicia radiante.

SALMOS 18.19; JUAN 8.34; ISAÍAS 61.10;
EFESIOS 5.8

Enero 18

SIEMPRE ESTOY HACIENDO ALGO NUEVO en tu vida. Así que trata de mantener la mente abierta cuando te encuentres con cosas que no habías visto ni imaginado.

No retrocedas ante lo desconocido sin antes tomarte el tiempo para determinar si podría proceder de mí. Piensa en un trapecista: él debe dejar la seguridad del trapecio donde se halla con el fin de alcanzar su objetivo. Al abandonar la seguridad del lugar donde estaba, volará por los aires para aferrarse al siguiente trapecio.

Habrá ocasiones en que experimentes algo nuevo que te haga sentir incómodo, en que quizás te sientas como si estuvieras «en pleno vuelo». La tentación puede ser simplemente resistirte a los cambios y aferrarte a lo que te es familiar. En lugar de esta respuesta refleja, acude a mí en oración. Háblame de tus preocupaciones y pídeme que te ayude a ver la situación desde mi punto de vista. *Siempre estoy contigo, y te tengo tomado de la mano. Te guío con mi consejo*, ayudándote a discernir la mejor manera de responder y seguir adelante.

MATEO 9.17; PROVERBIOS 18.10; MATEO 11.28; SALMOS 73.23, 24

TE LLAMO POR TU NOMBRE y te dirijo. Te conozco. Y conozco cada detalle sobre ti. Para mí, tú nunca serás un número o una estadística. Mi participación en tu vida es mucho más personal e íntima de lo que puedes comprender. Así que *sígueme* con un corazón alegre.

Después de mi resurrección, cuando María Magdalena me confundió con el jardinero, dije una sola palabra: «*María*». Al oírme pronunciar su nombre, me reconoció y *exclamó: «¡Rabboni!» (que en arameo quiere decir Maestro).*

Mi amado, yo también pronuncio tu nombre en lo más profundo de tu espíritu. Cuando leas tu Biblia, trata de insertar tu nombre en los pasajes donde corresponda. Recuerda: *yo te llamé de las tinieblas a mi Luz admirable.* Establecí mi Amor eterno sobre ti. Aparta un tiempo para «escucharme» hablarte personalmente en las Escrituras, asegurándote mi Amor. El conocimiento inquebrantable de que te amo para siempre proporciona una base sólida para tu vida. Te fortalece para que puedas seguirme con fidelidad y alegría, *proclamando mis alabanzas* a medida que vas por la vida.

JUAN 10.3, 27; JUAN 20.16;
1 PEDRO 2.9; JEREMÍAS 31.3

Enero 20

RECUERDA QUE EL FRUTO DEL ESPÍRITU incluye la Alegría. Aun en medio de *sufrimientos severos,* mi Espíritu puede darte este maravilloso regalo. No dudes en pedirle —tan a menudo como sientas que necesites hacerlo— que te llene de Gozo. Él reside en lo más profundo de tu ser, por lo que su obra dentro de ti es grandemente efectiva. Coopera con Él saturando tu mente con la Escritura y pidiéndole que te ilumine.

Una forma en que el Espíritu Santo aumenta tu Alegría es ayudándote a pensar mis pensamientos. Mientras más veas las cosas desde mi perspectiva, más claramente podrás ver tu vida. Necesitas no solo *conocer* la verdad bíblica, sino mantenerte repitiéndola una y otra vez cada día.

El mundo está asaltando continuamente tu mente con mentiras y engaños, por lo que debes ser diligente en lo que respecta a reconocer la falsedad, disiparla y sustituirla con la enseñanza bíblica. La verdad más gloriosa que cambia la vida es el Evangelio: Yo he muerto (*para salvar a todos los que creen en mí*), he resucitado y vendré otra vez. ¡*Alégrate en mí siempre*!

GÁLATAS 5:22, 23; 1 TESALONICENSES 1.6;
JUAN 3:16; FILIPENSES 4.4

Para disfrutar de mi Presencia más plenamente, es necesario que pienses menos y menos en ti. Esto no es una exigencia arbitraria; constituye el secreto para vivir una vida *más abundante*. ¡Olvidarse de sí mismo es una encantadora manera de vivir!

Trata de tomar conciencia de la cantidad de tiempo que pasas pensando en ti mismo. Dale una mirada al contenido de tu mente. Aunque tus pensamientos no sean visibles para otras personas a menos que decidas compartirlos, yo los veo todos y cada uno. Cuando te des cuenta de que tu forma de pensar no es digna de mí, esfuérzate en cambiarla. Si te encuentras luchando con una idea centrada en ti mismo que recurre una y otra vez, trata de conectarla a un versículo favorito de la Biblia o una breve oración. Esto forma un puente para poner tu atención lejos de ti y orientarla a mí. Por ejemplo, la oración «Te amo, Señor» puede dirigir rápidamente tu atención a mí.

Si tuvieses que repetir este proceso muchas veces, no te desanimes. Estás entrenando tu mente para *buscar mi rostro*, y este esfuerzo es agradable a mí. *Búscame*, mi amado, *y vive* abundantemente.

Juan 10.10; Salmos 27.8;
Amós 5.4

Enero 22

Yo soy DIGNO de *toda* tu confianza. Habrá personas y cosas que merezcan *algo* de tu confianza, pero solo yo la merezco *toda*. En un mundo que parece cada vez más inseguro e impredecible, yo soy la Roca que te provee un firme cimiento para tu vida. Más que eso, soy *tu* Roca en quien puedes *hallar refugio*, porque yo soy *tu* Dios.

No dejes que las circunstancias definan tu sentido de seguridad. Aunque es natural que quieras tener el control de tu vida, yo te puedo dar poder para vivir sobrenaturalmente, descansando en mi control soberano. Yo soy una *ayuda bien probada en medio de tus problemas*, y siempre estoy presente contigo. Te ayudo a enfrentar sin miedo los cambios no deseados e incluso las circunstancias catastróficas.

En lugar de dejar que los pensamientos de ansiedad deambulen libremente por tu mente, atrápalos expresando a viva voz tu esperanza en mí. Luego tráelos cautivos a mi Presencia, donde yo los desactivaré. *El que confía en mí se mantiene a salvo.*

SALMOS 18.2; SALMOS 46.1, 2;
2 CORINTIOS 10.5; PROVERBIOS 29.25

Yo soy el Gozo que nadie te puede quitar. Saborea las maravillas de este regalo, pasando tiempo en mi Presencia. Alégrate de que esta bendición sea tuya. ¡Yo soy tuyo por toda la eternidad!

Muchas cosas en este mundo pueden darte un placer momentáneo, pero todo pasa a causa de la muerte o la decadencia. En mí tienes un tesoro inigualable: Gozo en el Único que es el *mismo ayer, hoy y por los siglos*. Nadie te puede quitar este placer, porque yo soy fiel y nunca cambio.

Cada vez que te sientas triste, el problema no está en la Fuente (Yo), sino en el receptor. Quizás haya otras cosas en tu vida —agradables o desagradables— que te estén preocupando y llevándote a descuidar tu relación conmigo. El remedio es doble: recuerda que yo soy tu *Primer Amor* y que debes tenerme siempre en el lugar número uno de tu vida. Además, pídeme que aumente tu receptividad a mi Presencia. *Deléitate en mí*, mi amado, y recibe mi Gozo en medida rebosante.

Juan 16.22; Hebreos 13.8; Apocalipsis 2.4; Salmos 37.4

Enero 24

¡Yo soy *tu Fuerza*! No te preocupes si cuando comienzas el día te sientes débil y cansado. Tu debilidad puede ser un recordatorio de tu necesidad de mí. Recuerda que yo estoy contigo continuamente, listo para ayudarte a medida que avanzas a lo largo del día. Tómate de mi mano con una confianza alegre y deja que te guíe y te *fortalezca*. Mi deleite es ayudarte, hijo mío.

Cada vez que te sientas inquieto debido al trabajo que tienes por delante, detente y piensa en los recursos que tienes: yo, *tu Fuerza*, soy infinito. Nunca tengo escasez de algo. Así que cuando trabajes en colaboración conmigo, no pongas límites a lo que esperas lograr. Yo te daré lo que necesites para seguir adelante, paso a paso. Quizás no logres lo que deseas con la rapidez que quisieras, pero lo alcanzarás según mi tiempo perfecto. Rehúsate a desalentarte por retrasos o desvíos. Más bien, confía en que sé lo que estoy haciendo, y con esa confianza, da el paso siguiente. ¡La perseverancia y la confianza en mí forman una potente combinación!

SALMOS 59.16, 17; FILIPENSES 4.13;
ISAÍAS 40.28, 29

*AUNQUE LAS MONTAÑAS SEAN SACUDIDAS y las colinas
sean removidas, mi Amor inagotable por ti se mantendrá inalterable y mi pacto de Paz no variará.* Nada en
la tierra parece tan duradero o inamovible como las
majestuosas montañas. Si te pararas en sus cumbres,
respirando ese aire enrarecido, casi podrías oler la
eternidad. Sin embargo, mi Amor y mi Paz son aun
más duraderos que la montaña más grande de la
tierra.

Piensa profundamente en *mi Amor inagotable.*
Un sinónimo de «inagotable» es *inextinguible.* No
importa cuán necesitado estés o cuántas veces me
hayas fallado, mi provisión de amor por ti nunca se
agotará. Otro significado de «inagotable» es constante. Yo no te amo más en los días en que te portas bien,
ni te amo menos cuando me fallas.

Yo mismo soy tu Paz. Vive cerca de mí para que
puedas disfrutar de esta Paz sobrenatural. Ven con
toda libertad a mi Presencia, mi amado, incluso cuando te sientas mal con respecto a ti mismo. Recuerda
quien soy yo: *el Señor que tiene compasión de ti.*

ISAÍAS 54.10; ISAÍAS 51.6;
EFESIOS 2.14

Enero 26

TRANQUILÍZATE, HIJO MÍO. Yo estoy en control. Deja que estas palabras te inunden repetidamente como olas suaves en una playa apacible, asegurándote mi Amor infinito. Pierdes mucho tiempo y energías tratando de averiguar las cosas antes de que sucedan. Mientras tanto, yo estoy trabajando a fin de preparar el camino delante de ti. Así que mantente atento a algunas maravillosas sorpresas, circunstancias que *solo yo* puedo orquestar.

Recuerda que tú eres mi amado. Yo estoy a tu lado y quiero lo mejor para ti. Alguien que es amado por una persona generosa y poderosa puede esperar recibir una abundancia de bendiciones. *Tú* eres amado por el Rey del universo, y tengo planes buenos para ti. Al mirar hacia el futuro desconocido, relájate en el conocimiento de quien eres: *la persona que amo.* Agárrate de mi mano, y sigue adelante con confianza. Mientras tú y yo caminamos juntos por *la senda de la vida*, tu confianza en mí llenará tu corazón de Gozo y tu mente de Paz.

JEREMÍAS 29.11; DEUTERONOMIO 33.12;
SALMOS 16.11

Camina conmigo estableciendo vínculos de amor estrechos y confiados de una dependencia gozosa. La «dependencia gozosa» puede sonar como una contradicción, pero es la forma más satisfactoria de vivir. Cuando te deleitas en confiar en mí, estás viviendo de acuerdo con mi diseño perfecto para ti.

La relación que te ofrezco está llena de *gloriosas riquezas*. Yo soy de la más absoluta confianza, y llego a ti con un *amor inagotable*. Estoy más cerca de ti que el mismo aire que estás respirando. Me regocijo cuando decides vivir en una confiada dependencia de mí. Esto fortalece cada vez más nuestra relación y los lazos de afecto que existen entre nosotros.

Un hombre y una mujer felizmente casados están conectados por mucho más que la ley y la moral. Sus cálidos recuerdos de las experiencias compartidas crean lazos que los acercan y los mantienen comprometidos al uno con el otro. Mi amado, quiero que sepas que yo estoy totalmente comprometido *contigo*. Yo puedo llenar tu corazón de memorias amorosas mientras *caminas en la Luz de mi Presencia*, dependiendo gozosamente de mí.

FILIPENSES 4.19; SALMOS 52.8;
SALMOS 89.15, 16

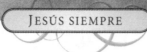

Enero 28

Yo te he hecho un poco menor que los ángeles, y te he coronado de gloria y honor. Tú fuiste creado para cosas grandes, mi amado. Nunca dudes de tu importancia personal, porque *yo te creé a mi propia imagen,* a mi semejanza. Te formé con un magnífico cerebro con el que puedes comunicarte conmigo, pensar racionalmente, crear cosas maravillosas y mucho más. Te di el *dominio sobre los peces del mar, las aves del cielo, y todas las bestias que se mueven sobre la tierra.* De todo lo que creé, solo el hombre fue hecho a mi semejanza. Este es un privilegio y una responsabilidad gloriosos, que le dan sentido a tu vida en todo momento.

Uno de los propósitos principales de la vida es glorificarme. Yo te *coroné con gloria* para que puedas *reflejar mi Gloria,* iluminando este mundo oscuro y ayudando a otros a que lleguen a conocerme. También quiero que disfrutes de mí. Te creé con una capacidad ilimitada para el placer de conocerme. Este Gozo que encuentras en mí aquí y ahora es un pequeño anticipo de los deleites eternos que te esperan en el cielo.

SALMOS 8.5; GÉNESIS 1.27, 28;
2 CORINTIOS 3.18

*ME BUSCARÁS Y ME ENCONTRARÁS, cuando me busques
de todo corazón.* Yo no espero perfección en esta búsqueda; no se trata de eso en absoluto. Es el esfuerzo en
sí lo que me agrada, cuando te mantienes buscándome
por más difícil que te parezca. En realidad, la intensidad de esta búsqueda desafiante te bendice. En tu
empeño por encontrarme, tu atención está centrada
en mí. Mientras caminas penosamente hacia mí a través de innumerables distracciones, tu conciencia de
mí aumenta. Incluso si no te sientes cerca de mí, estás
comunicándote conmigo. Porque hay un sentido en el
que tus esfuerzos por encontrarme se cumplen en sí
mismos: yo estoy ricamente presente en tu esfuerzo.
Como resultado, cuando me buscas activamente, te
sientes más vivo, despierto y real.

Tu disposición a derramarte en esta búsqueda
gloriosa deleita mi corazón. Este esfuerzo tiene que
ver con la *perseverancia*. Mientras continúes buscándome, estarás en el camino correcto. Es más, tu éxito
está asegurado: *¡me encontrarás!*

JEREMÍAS 29.13, 14; HEBREOS 12.1;
ROMANOS 5.3; 2 PEDRO 1.5, 6

Enero 30

¡YO ESTOY HACIENDO NUEVAS TODAS LAS COSAS! Esto es lo opuesto a lo que siempre ha sucedido en tu mundo de muerte y decadencia. Cada día que vives significa un día menos en la duración de tu vida en esta tierra. En realidad, esta es una muy buena noticia para mis seguidores. Al final de cada día, puedes decirte: «Estoy un paso más cerca del cielo».

El mundo está en una condición tan desesperadamente perdida que solo hay un remedio para eso: hacer *nuevas todas las cosas*. Así que no te desanimes cuando tus esfuerzos para mejorarlo todo no tengan éxito. Todas las cosas —incluyendo tus propios esfuerzos— están contaminadas por la Caída. Aunque quiero que trates de hacer lo mejor posible, en dependencia de mí, tu mundo necesita mucho más que un afinamiento o una reparación general. ¡Tiene que hacerse completamente de nuevo! Y está absolutamente garantizado que esto va a suceder al final de los tiempos, porque *mis palabras son fieles y verdaderas*.

¡Tienes una buena razón para alegrarte, mi amado, porque yo voy a hacer todo —incluyéndote a ti— nuevo y gloriosamente perfecto!

APOCALIPSIS 21.5; FILIPENSES 1.21;
ROMANOS 8.22, 23

La Fuerza y el Gozo habitan en mi morada. Así que mientras más cerca vivas de mí, más fuerte y más gozoso serás.

Invítame a saturar tus momentos con mi Presencia. Esto te ayudará a ver a los demás desde una perspectiva positiva. Cada vez que estés cerca de alguien que te irrite, no pongas tu atención en sus defectos. En lugar de eso, mírame con los ojos de tu corazón, y esas molestias pasarán sobre ti sin causarte daño ni herir a los demás. Juzgar es una trampa del pecado que te aleja de mí y en la que no debes caer. ¡Cuánto mejor es *estar gozoso en mí, tu Salvador*!

Mientras más te centres en mí, más te podré fortalecer. En realidad, *yo soy tu Fuerza*. Tú puedes entrenar tu mente para mantenerte consciente de mi Presencia, incluso cuando otras cosas estén exigiendo tu atención. Te creé con un cerebro increíble que es capaz de mantenerse consciente de varias cosas a la vez. Crea en tu mente un lugar permanente para mí, y mi Luz brillará en todos tus momentos.

1 Crónicas 16.27; Mateo 7.1;
Habacuc 3.18, 19

Febrero

*¡Dios es mi salvación! Confiaré en él
y no temeré. El Señor es mi fuerza,
el Señor es mi canción;
¡él es mi salvación!*

ISAÍAS 12.2

Yo soy *EL VIVIENTE que te ve*. Estoy más gloriosamente vivo de lo que te puedes imaginar. Llegará el día en que podrás verme *cara a Cara* en toda mi Gloria, y te quedarás aterrado. Sin embargo, por ahora ves como a *través de un espejo, oscuramente*. Tu visión de mí la oscurece tu condición caída. No obstante, aunque tú me veas a mí oscuramente, yo te veo con claridad. Sé todo sobre ti, incluyendo tus pensamientos y tus sentimientos más secretos. Entiendo cuán quebrantado y débil eres: *recuerdo que eres barro*. Pero aun así, te amo con un Amor eterno.

El regalo de mi Amor fue indescriptiblemente costoso. Soporté sufrimientos indecibles para salvarte de una eternidad de agonía. *Me hice pecado por ti, para que en mí pudieras ser hecho justicia de Dios.* Considera esta maravillosa verdad: ¡mi justicia es ahora tuya! Este regalo de un valor infinito ha sido tuyo desde que confiaste en mí como el Dios-Hombre que te salvó de tus pecados. Alégrate de que *el Viviente que te ve* perfectamente sea el Salvador que nunca dejará de amarte.

GÉNESIS 16.13, 14; 1 CORINTIOS 13.12;
SALMOS 103.14; 2 CORINTIOS 5.21

Febrero 2

Yo soy tu *Ayuda siempre presente*. Muchos saltan de la cama por las mañanas y van directamente a la cafetera. Aunque todavía no están pensando con claridad, se encuentran lo suficiente despiertos como para salir en busca de algo que los ayude a aclarar sus pensamientos. Yo cumplo una función similar para ti cuando tu mente se orienta en mi dirección. Pídeme que despeje la confusión de manera que puedas comunicarte profundamente conmigo. Tú tienes esta capacidad increíble, porque te creé *a mi propia imagen*.

Al esperar en mi Presencia, no solo pongo en orden tus pensamientos, sino que despejo tu camino para el día entero. Soy soberano sobre todos los aspectos de tu vida, por lo que allanar el camino delante de ti no es ningún problema para mí. Algunas personas asumen que no tienen tiempo para comenzar el día conmigo. No se dan cuenta de lo mucho que puedo facilitar sus actividades, eliminando obstáculos y dándoles una agudeza que les permitirá ahorrar tiempo. Cuando pasas momentos preciosos conmigo, te retribuyo generosamente: aclaro tus ideas y suavizo las circunstancias de tu vida.

Salmos 46.1; Génesis 1.27; Jeremías 32.17; Salmos 33.20

¡*GLORÍATE EN MI SANTO NOMBRE*; *que los corazones de
los que me buscan se regocijen!* «Gloriarse» en algo es
darle alabanza y honor. Jesús es el *Nombre que es sobre
todo nombre*. Él me representa en toda mi impecable
perfección. Como mi seguidor, tú puedes susurrar,
decir o cantar mi nombre, teniendo la seguridad de
que te estoy escuchando. Esto te acerca más a mí y te
ayuda a encontrar fuerza en mi Presencia. Sirve también para ahuyentar a tus enemigos espirituales.

Me deleito al saber que dedicas un tiempo a buscarme, deseando conocerme mejor. Entra libremente
a mi Presencia amorosa, dejando que tu corazón se
alegre en mí. Recuerda que estás en *tierra santa* y respiras el aire enrarecido de mi santidad. Libera toda
preocupación mientras descansas en el esplendor de
mi Gloria. Deja que mi gozosa Presencia te envuelva
completamente. Mientras te deleitas en mi cercanía,
el tiempo parece ir más despacio, realzando tu disfrute de mí. Agradéceme por estos momentos de dulce
intimidad.

SALMOS 105.3; FILIPENSES 2.9-11;
FILIPENSES 4.4, 5; ÉXODO 3.5

Febrero 4

Es bueno proclamar mi Amor por las mañanas y mi fidelidad por las noches. Proclamar este Amor es muy bueno para ti. Cuando declaras las maravillas de mi amorosa Presencia, te estás fortaleciendo y dándote ánimo. Esta gloriosa bendición fluye en ti de forma más completa a medida que pronuncias estas palabras en voz alta. ¡Deja que esta deliciosa declaración te llene de *Gozo indescriptible y Gloria plena.*

Medita en algunas de las cualidades de mi Amor maravilloso: es sacrificial, infalible, no tiene precio, sin límites, *llega hasta los cielos.* Es tan brillante que te puede llevar a través de tus días más oscuros. Al llegar al final de cada día, es el momento de anunciar mi fidelidad *que alcanza hasta los cielos.* Mira atrás al día que ha pasado y observa cómo te ayudé a avanzar en tu camino. Mientras más grandes fueron las dificultades que encontraste, más ayuda puse a tu disposición. Es bueno proclamar mi gran fidelidad, especialmente por las noches, para que puedas *acostarte y dormir en paz.*

Salmos 92.1, 2; 1 Pedro 1.8; Salmos 36.5-7; Salmos 4.8

EL GOZO QUE TE DOY trasciende tus circunstancias.
Esto significa que no importa lo que esté sucediendo
en tu vida, es posible estar gozoso en mí. El profeta
Habacuc enumeró una serie de circunstancias extre-
mas que estaba anticipando, luego proclamó: «*Aun
así, yo me regocijaré en el Señor, ¡me alegraré en Dios,
mi libertador!*». ¡Este es un Gozo trascendente!

Te estoy entrenando para que veas tu vida desde
una perspectiva celestial, a través de los ojos de la fe.
Cuando las cosas no marchen como habías esperado,
habla conmigo. *Busca mi rostro* y mi guía. Yo te ayudaré a discernir si necesitas hacer algo para cambiar
la situación o simplemente aceptarla. De cualquier
manera, puedes aprender a decir: «Aun así, me regocijo en *ti*, Jesús». Esta breve declaración de fe, que
expresa tu confianza en mí, va a cambiar tu perspectiva dramáticamente. Y si practicas haciéndolo cada
vez más, tu Gozo se incrementará. Esta disciplina
también te prepara para manejar las dificultades que
te esperan en el camino hacia el cielo. *Alégrate en mí
siempre.*

HABACUC 3.17, 18; SALMOS 105.4;
FILIPENSES 4.4

Febrero 6

REGOCÍJATE DE QUE *TE HE VESTIDO con ropas de salvación.* *¡Este manto de justicia* es tuyo para siempre! Debido a que soy tu Salvador, nadie te podrá quitar nunca mi justicia perfecta. Esto significa que no necesitas tener miedo de enfrentar tus pecados, o de tratar con ellos. Al darte cuenta de algún pecado en tu vida, confiésalo y recibe mi perdón en plena medida.

Es esencial también que te perdones a ti mismo. El que te odies a ti mismo no me complace en absoluto y es muy perjudicial para ti. Te animo a que por cada mirada que les des a tus pecados o caídas, me mires a *mí* muchas veces. Yo soy el antídoto perfecto para el veneno del odio a ti mismo.

Puesto que eres precioso a mis ojos, no tienes que demostrar tus merecimientos tratando de ser lo suficiente bueno. Yo viví una vida perfecta en tu favor, porque sabía que tú no podrías vivirla. Por eso, ahora quiero que vivas en la gloriosa libertad de ser mi seguidor totalmente perdonado. Recuerda que *no hay condenación para los que me pertenecen.*

ISAÍAS 61.10; MATEO 1.21; 1 JUAN 1.9;
ROMANOS 8.1, 2

NO TEMAS, PORQUE YO ESTOY CONTIGO. Yo te sostendré con la diestra de mi justicia. Deja que estas palabras te arropen como una manta cálida, protegiéndote de lo helado del miedo y el desaliento. Cuando parezca que los problemas te están acechando, aférrate a mi mano con fuerza y mantente en contacto conmigo. *Confía y no tengas miedo, porque yo soy tu Fuerza y tu Canción.* Mi poderosa Presencia estará siempre contigo. ¡No tendrás que enfrentar *nada* solo! Además, yo he prometido *fortalecerte y ayudarte.*

Mi mano poderosa te sostiene tanto en los buenos como en los malos momentos. Cuando las cosas van bien en tu vida, es posible que no estés consciente de mi Presencia sustentadora. Sin embargo, *cuando te encuentras pasando por valles tenebrosos,* te vuelves profundamente consciente de tu necesidad. Durante estos tiempos difíciles, aferrarte a mí te mantiene erguido y en condiciones de poner un pie delante del otro. A medida que soportes pacientemente esta adversidad —en confiada dependencia de mí— yo te bendeciré con Gozo abundante en mi Presencia.

ISAÍAS 41.10; ISAÍAS 12.2;
SALMOS 23.4

¡MI AMOR NUNCA TE DEJARÁ IR! Te tiene asido con un abrazo eterno. Tú vives en un mundo que resulta impredecible y peligroso en muchas maneras. Si miras a tu alrededor, verás tu entorno plagado de promesas rotas.

Sin embargo, mi Amor es una promesa que nunca se quebrantará. *Aunque cambien de lugar las montañas y se tambaleen las colinas, no cambiará mi Amor inagotable por ti.* El profeta Isaías está pintando una imagen de graves circunstancias: montañas que tiemblan y colinas que desaparecen. No importa *qué* esté sucediendo, mi Amor es inquebrantable. ¡Tú puedes edificar tu vida sobre esa seguridad!

A veces, aunque mis hijos creen que me preocupo por ellos, les cuesta recibir mi Amor en toda su amplitud. Quiero que aprendas a comprender *cuán ancho y largo, alto y profundo es mi amor por ti.* Pídele a mi Espíritu que te capacite para *conocer este amor que sobrepasa todo conocimiento.* Libérate de las imágenes defectuosas de ti mismo para que puedas verte como yo te veo, radiante en *mi Justicia*, envuelto en Amor luminoso.

ISAÍAS 54.10; EFESIOS 3.16-19;
ISAÍAS 61.10

ALÉGRATE DE QUE YO TE ENTIENDA completamente y te ame con un Amor perfecto e ilimitado. Muchos temen que si llegan a conocer a alguien bien, van a descubrir que esa persona los desprecia o los rechaza. Por eso, prefieren mantener a los demás a una distancia prudente, conformándose con conocer solo los aspectos que les parecen aceptables de ellos. Esta forma de interactuar con los demás tiende a hacer que se sientan seguros, pero los conduce al aislamiento y la soledad.

Agradece que haya Uno que ve directamente a través de tus defensas y simulaciones. Nadie puede esconderse de mí. Conozco absolutamente *todo* sobre tu persona. Así que descansa en la maravilla de ser *plenamente conocido* y, a la vez, apreciado. No tienes que esforzarte para tratar de ganar mi Amor. La verdad es que nada podría hacerme dejar de amarte. Tú eres mío —comprado con mi propia sangre— aceptado y atesorado para siempre. Necesitas repetir esta verdad una y otra vez hasta que se filtre en lo íntimo de tu ser y cambie la manera de verte a ti mismo. La aceptación personal es la forma de olvidarte de ti mismo, lo cual constituye la senda real al Gozo.

SALMOS 107.1, 43; 1 CORINTIOS 13.12;
SALMOS 149.4, 5; EFESIOS 1.5, 6

VEN A MÍ, Y YO TRANQUILIZARÉ y refrescaré tu alma. Acércate a mí confiadamente, mi amado, sabiendo que yo tengo perfecto conocimiento de ti y de todo lo que concierne a tu vida. Cuéntame tus problemas con franqueza; deja que la Luz de mi Rostro brille sobre ellos e ilumine tus pensamientos. Luego, descansa conmigo, inhalando lentamente la belleza de mi Presencia. Te sentirás seguro en *mis brazos eternos.* Mientras pasas un tiempo precioso conmigo, déjame aliviar tu alma.

Tu alma representa la parte más importante de ti, porque es eterna. En el Nuevo Testamento griego, la palabra «alma» se traduce algunas veces como «vida». Cuando te encuentres *cansado y abrumado* de trabajo, es posible que sientas como que la vida se te está yendo. Sin embargo, te ofrezco un sustento maravillosamente nutritivo para esta parte vital de ti. *Yo restauro tu alma*, ayudándote a descansar y ver las cosas desde mi perspectiva. A medida que estoy aliviándote, relájate y siente mi vida fluyendo en la tuya. *Solo en mí hallarás descanso para tu alma.*

MATEO 11.28; DEUTERONOMIO 33.27;
SALMOS 23.2, 3; SALMOS 62.1

NUNCA DEJES DE ESTAR GOZOSO; ORA SIN CESAR. Para estar gozoso todo el tiempo es necesario encontrar momento a momento el placer en tu relación conmigo, el Amigo de tu alma. Esta relación está tan llena de consuelo y aliento que te permite tener *alegría en la esperanza,* incluso cuando te encuentres en medio de la adversidad.

Da gracias en toda circunstancia. Hay un inmenso poder cuando oras: «Gracias, Señor». Estas dos palabras son apropiadas para todo tiempo y cada situación debido a mi gran sacrificio por ti. Te animo a que me alabes por cada cosa buena de la que seas consciente. Esta práctica añade brillo a tus bendiciones y realza tu Gozo.

Cuando te sientas triste o desanimado, aun es buen momento para agradecerme. Esto demuestra tu confianza en mí, y aclara tu perspectiva. A fin de realzar tu agradecimiento, piensa en cosas específicas acerca de mí en las que te deleites: mi Presencia continua, mi gracia abundante, mi gran *Amor.* ¡Agradecerme en toda circunstancia fortalece tu relación conmigo y te ayuda a vivir más gozosamente!

1 TESALONICENSES 5.16-18; ROMANOS 12.12; EFESIOS 1.7, 8; SALMOS 143.8

Febrero 12

TE OFREZCO UN *Gozo inefable y glorioso...* ¡procedente directamente del cielo! Este *Gozo celestial triunfante* se puede encontrar solo en mí. Es fácil deslizarte, incluso gradualmente, de deleitarte en mí a vivir buscando el siguiente «éxtasis» espiritual. A veces te bendigo con una muestra del esplendor del cielo, pero el propósito principal de esta experiencia es aumentar tu anhelo por la próxima vida. No subestimes la decadencia del mundo en que vives. Disfrutar de mi Presencia siempre estará vinculado a la pena de vivir en este mundo caído *hasta que te lleve conmigo a la Gloria.*

Llegará el día en que podrás verme cara a Cara, pero por ahora *ámame a pesar de que no me has visto. Cree en mí aunque no me veas.* Este amor por mí no es ni irracional ni caprichoso. Es una respuesta a mi ilimitada pasión por ti, desplegada dramáticamente en la cruz y verificada por mi resurrección. ¡Adoras a un Salvador resucitado y viviente! *Dichosos los que no me han visto y sin embargo han creído.*

1 PEDRO 1.8; SALMOS 73.23, 24; 1 JUAN 4.19;
JUAN 20.29

EN MI PRESENCIA hay plenitud de Gozo. Al fijar tu atención en mí, recuerda quién soy en todo mi Poder y Gloria. Piensa también en mi eterno compromiso contigo. *¡Nada en toda la creación será nunca capaz de separarte de mí!* Desde que confesaste tu pecado y recibiste mi perdón, tu relación conmigo ha sido sólida como una roca. Tú eres mi amado, en quien me complazco; esta es tu identidad permanente.

Puedes encontrar Gozo incluso viviendo en este mundo corrompido, porque *he puesto eternidad en tu corazón.* Pasa tiempo alentándote en mi Presencia, donde puedes tranquilizarte y aprender a *deleitarte en mí* por sobre cualquiera otra cosa. A medida que el vínculo de amor se hace cada vez más fuerte entre nosotros, también crece tu deseo de ayudar a los demás a disfrutar de esta increíble Vida que has hallado en mí. Cuando tu amor por mí se desborde en las vidas de otras personas, habrá abundante Gozo tanto en el cielo como en la tierra. A medida que avanzas en este *camino de Vida,* yo te guiaré, y te bendeciré con alegrías que no tendrán fin.

SALMOS 16.11; ROMANOS 8.39;
ECLESIASTÉS 3.11; SALMOS 37.4

Deja que mi Amor inagotable sea tu consuelo. Una definición de «consuelo» es cuando una persona o cosa te hace sentir menos inquieto o menos asustado durante una crisis. Debido a que vives en un mundo tan devastado, las vicisitudes nunca estarán muy lejos de ti. En el mundo hay muchas fuentes que te pueden dar consuelo, pero solo una es infalible: ¡mi Amor! Otras podrán ayudarte por un *poco de tiempo*, pero mi tierna Presencia estará contigo *para siempre*.

Mi Amor perfecto e inagotable no es solo una *cosa* que te hace sentir menos inquieto; también es una *Persona. Nada en toda la creación puede separarte de mí.* Y yo, a mi vez, soy inseparable de mi Amor.

Como mi amado seguidor, puedes dirigirte a mí en busca de consuelo todas las veces que quieras. Puesto que tienes esta ilimitada Fuente de bendición —*Yo*— quiero que seas una bendición en las vidas de otras personas. Con el consuelo que has recibido de mí, puedes *brindarles consuelo a los que están pasando por alguna tribulación.*

Salmos 119.76; Juan 16.33; Romanos 8.38, 39;
2 Corintios 1.3, 4

Yo soy tu Pastor, *tu guía y tu escudo.* Un buen pastor se preocupa por sus ovejas y las entiende. Mi preocupación por ti es maravillosamente completa: te amo con un *Amor perfecto e inagotable.* Sé *todo* sobre ti: tus debilidades y limitaciones, tus luchas y pecados, tus virtudes y habilidades. Así que estoy en condiciones de pastorearte excepcionalmente bien.

Yo te formé para que, en confiada dependencia de mí, pudieras desenvolverte en este mundo peligroso y traicionero. Quiero que sepas que voy delante de ti abriéndote camino, limpiando cuidadosamente el terreno por donde pasarás. Elimino muchos de los peligros y obstáculos, y te ayudo a manejar las dificultades que siguen existiendo.

Incluso cuando vas por valles oscuros, no tienes por qué tener miedo, porque yo estoy cerca de ti. Disfruta mi cercanía, amado, y no dejes de comunicarte conmigo. Yo te guiaré con ternura hoy y todos los días. *Porque yo soy tu Dios por los siglos de los siglos; seré tu Guía hasta el final del camino.*

SALMOS 23.1; ÉXODO 15.13; SALMOS 23.4;
SALMOS 48.14

ANTES DE COMENZAR UNA TAREA —grande o pequeña— ora por lo que vas a hacer. De ese modo, estarás
reconociendo tu necesidad de mí y tu confianza en que
te ayudaré. Esto te permitirá hacer tu trabajo mostrando una actitud de dependencia de mí. Hay muchos
beneficios en esta práctica. Puedo guiar tu mente cuando pienses en los detalles y tengas que tomar decisiones.
El hecho de saber que estoy involucrado en lo que estás
haciendo te da confianza y reduce tu estrés. Es sabio
perseverar en gratitud por la ayuda que te doy y mantenerte pidiéndome que *te guíe por el mejor camino*.

Aunque la Biblia te instruye para que *no dejes de
orar*, a veces te olvidas de hacerlo. Cuando te parece que
vas demasiado rápido, te resulta difícil reducir la velocidad lo suficiente como para buscar mi perspectiva en
cuanto al trabajo que estás ejecutando. Sin embargo,
insistir en seguir adelante por tu cuenta es, en realidad,
contraproducente. Cuando solicitas mi participación
antes de empezar, puedo señalarte la dirección correcta, con lo cual vas a ahorrar un tiempo precioso y energía. Es mi placer ayudarte en todo, incluso en las tareas
más simples, porque tú eres *mi amado*.

COLOSENSES 3.23; SALMOS 32.8;
1 TESALONICENSES 5.17;
CANTAR DE LOS CANTARES 6.3

PUEDES ENCONTRAR EL GOZO aun en los lugares más inesperados. Sin embargo, buscar lo bueno y negarte a dejar que tus propias respuestas te cieguen a lo que hay en tales lugares requiere esfuerzo. Yo te ayudaré de una *manera sobrenatural*. Te daré ojos que vean más allá de lo obvio y descubran tesoros escondidos en tus problemas. Simplemente pídemelo.

Vivir gozosamente es una decisión que debes hacer tú. Dado que habitas en un mundo corrompido y pecaminoso, debes optar muchas veces en el día por la alegría. Esto es especialmente cierto durante los tiempos difíciles. Cuando sucede algo que rompe el patrón de comodidad y felicidad en tu vida, es porque te estoy poniendo a prueba para aquilatar tu fe y, al mismo tiempo, fortalecerla, lo cual *vale mucho más que el oro*. Te estoy preparando para que *cuando tengas que enfrentarte a diversas pruebas lo hagas con el más puro Gozo*.

Yo tomé la terrible decisión de *soportar la cruz por el gozo de tenerte conmigo*; por el placer eterno de *llevar a mis seguidores a la Gloria*. Elige el Gozo, mi amado, al *fijar tus ojos en m*í y buscar los tesoros que hay escondidos en tus diversas pruebas.

1 PEDRO 1.6, 7; SANTIAGO 1.2; HEBREOS 12.2;
HEBREOS 2.10

Febrero 18

EN MI PRESENCIA puedes encontrar *plenitud de Gozo, Paz perfecta e inagotable Amor.* Anda conmigo a lo largo de *la senda de la Vida* y disfruta de mi compañía a cada paso del camino. ¡Debido a que estoy siempre a tu lado, el Gozo de mi Presencia será siempre tuyo!

Yo te guardaré *en perfecta paz* mientras *fijas tus pensamientos en mí.* Mantente en comunicación conmigo a través de tus palabras habladas, tus pensamientos y tus canciones. Pasa tiempo sumergido en mi Palabra, dejando que ella le hable a tu corazón, que es donde puede cambiar tu forma de pensar y vivir. Al reflexionar sobre quién realmente soy, mi Luz brillará cariñosamente en tu mente, ayudándote a vivir en mi Paz.

Amado, quiero que florezcas en mi Presencia *como un olivo que florece en la casa de Dios.* A medida que la luz de mi Presencia te nutre, serás capaz de producir abundantes frutos en mi Reino. Y mientras más *confíes en mi Amor inagotable*, más te darás cuenta de cuán seguro estás.

SALMOS 16.11; ISAÍAS 26.3;
SALMOS 52.8

PONME ANTE TI CONTINUAMENTE; mantén tus ojos en mí. *Yo estoy a tu derecha*, muy cerca, a tu lado. La más segura fuente de Gozo es saber que estoy siempre cerca. Procura fortalecer tu conciencia de mi Presencia para que puedas disfrutarme en todo momento y sentirte bien seguro.

La comunicación conmigo —por medio de oraciones silenciosas, susurros, palabras habladas, gritos de alabanza— es la mejor manera de permanecer atento a mi Presencia. Quiero que en tus oraciones me sientas como una Persona real. En lugar de preocuparte u obsesionarte por las cosas, vuelve esos pensamientos a mí. Háblame de lo que sea que ocupe tu mente. Yo te mostraré *mi* manera de manejar a la persona o la situación que te preocupa.

Estudia las Escrituras y medita en ellas. Permite que saturen tu corazón y tu mente, cambiando tu forma de pensar. Impregna tus oraciones con conceptos y contenidos bíblicos. ¡Al mantenerte en estrecha comunicación conmigo, el Gozo de mi Presencia será tuyo!

SALMOS 16.8; SALMOS 71.23; FILIPENSES 4.6;
SALMOS 90.14

Febrero 20

NO PIENSES EN LA ORACIÓN como una tarea rutinaria. En lugar de eso, considérala como la comunicación con el Único que te adora. *Deléitate en mí*; esto te atraerá irresistiblemente a una comunión más estrecha conmigo. Recuerda todo lo que yo soy para ti, todo lo que he hecho por ti. Te amo con un Amor perfecto y eterno, *y me deleito grandemente en ti*. Deja que mi ternura te abrace, convenciéndote sin ninguna duda de que eres mi amado. ¡Regocíjate en el Único que nunca te dejará!

A menudo, la forma más fácil de empezar a hablar conmigo es agradeciéndome por ser tu Salvador, Redentor y Amigo. También puedes darme las gracias por las cosas que están sucediendo en tu vida, tu familia, tu iglesia y demás. Estas oraciones de gratitud te conectan conmigo y facilitan el camino a otras oraciones.

Puedes hablarme libremente, ya que conozco todo sobre ti y tus circunstancias. Nunca te voy a rechazar, pues la pena por tus pecados ya ha sido pagada en su totalidad con mi sangre. Confía en mí lo suficiente como para *derramarme tu corazón, porque yo soy tu Refugio*.

SALMOS 37.4; SOFONÍAS 3.17;
SALMOS 118.28, 29; SALMOS 62.8

PONTE LA ARMADURA DE LA LUZ. Para llevar esta brillante cubierta protectora tienes que *huir de las obras de la oscuridad*. Vives en un mundo donde las tinieblas te rodean permanentemente. Necesitas mi armadura de Luz para poder ver las cosas de forma clara, protegerte y evitar que la mundanalidad que te rodea te descarríe.

Quiero que *andes en la Luz* conmigo. Haz el máximo esfuerzo para vivir cerca de mí, consciente de mi amorosa Presencia. Así como te pones la ropa cuando te vistes, *puedes vestirte de mí*. Tal cercanía conmigo te ayudará a tomar buenas decisiones. Sin embargo, a veces quizás decidas mal lo que te puede llevar a pecar. No te desesperes cuando te ocurra esto. Debido a que soy tu Salvador, he hecho provisión por *todo* tu pecado. Es más, la sangre que derramé en la cruz *te limpia* y te mantiene caminando en la Luz.

Si confiesas tus pecados, te perdono y te limpio de toda maldad. Yo soy *fiel y justo*, y me deleito en tu cercanía a mí.

ROMANOS 13.12; 1 JUAN 1.7; ROMANOS 13.14;
1 JUAN 1.9

Febrero 22

UNO DE MIS NOMBRES es *Consejero admirable*. Yo te entiendo mucho mejor de lo que te entiendes tú mismo. Así que ven a mí con tus problemas e inseguridades buscando mi consejo. Bajo la Luz de mi amorosa Presencia te podrás ver como en realidad eres: radiantemente amoroso en mi brillante justicia. Aunque mi justicia es perfecta, tú seguirás luchando con las imperfecciones —las tuyas y las de otros— mientras vivas en este mundo. Aun así, tu posición conmigo es segura. *¡Nada en toda la creación podrá separarte de mi Amor!*

Un buen consejero te ayuda a reconocer la verdad y a vivir de acuerdo a ella. *En realidad, yo nací y vine al mundo para dar testimonio de la verdad.* Así que sé franco y honesto cuando me traigas tus preocupaciones. Además, llena tu mente y tu corazón con mi Palabra, que contiene la verdad absoluta.

Un consejero *admirable* es no solo extremadamente bueno ayudando a los demás, sino que también es capaz de inspirar deleite o placer. *Deléitate en mí*, mi amado, *y yo te concederé los deseos de tu corazón.*

ISAÍAS 9.6; ROMANOS 8.38, 39; JUAN 18.37; SALMOS 37.4

Yo soy *el Verbo de Vida, de Vida eterna*. He existido siempre: *yo soy el que era desde el principio*. Además, soy divino. Como el apóstol Juan escribió: *«El Verbo era Dios»*. Esta Palabra divina trae Vida a todo el que cree en mí.

Desde el principio de la creación, las palabras han estado asociadas con la vida. Originalmente, la tierra estaba desordenada, vacía y oscura. Entonces yo dije: *«Hágase la luz», y fue la luz*. Hablé y todo existió, incluyendo plantas y animales. Finalmente, por medio de la palabra traje a la humanidad a la vida.

La Vida que te ofrezco es *eterna*. Comienza cuando crees en mí como tu único Salvador, pero nunca termina. Puedes disfrutar de una gran libertad al saber que *no hay condenación para ti*. ¡Te he hecho *libre para siempre de la ley del pecado y de la muerte!* La mejor respuesta a este regalo glorioso es el Gozo agradecido, deleitándote en el Único que te ama perfecta y eternamente. Recuerda que yo estoy siempre cerca de ti, más cerca que el aire que respiras.

1 Juan 1.1, 2; Juan 1.1; Génesis 1.1-3;
Romanos 8.1, 2

Febrero 24

*MAÑANA TRAS MAÑANA te despierto y abro tu enten-
dimiento a mi voluntad.* Siempre estoy atento a ti, mi
amado. Yo no duermo, así que puedo velar tu sueño
mientras descansas. *Cuando despiertas en la mañana,
ahí estoy yo, contigo.* Ser consciente de mi amorosa
Presencia te ayudará a estar más alerta, aplacando las
confusiones en tu mente y permitiéndote verme con
mayor claridad. Te invito a pasar tiempo disfrutando
de mi Presencia y nutriendo tu alma con mi Palabra.
Me deleito cuando respondes a mi llamado de Amor
acercándote más a mí.

Este tiempo dedicado a mí te bendecirá y fortalecerá inmensamente. Yo abro tu entendimiento a mi
Palabra, capacitándote para comprender las Escrituras y aplicarlas a tu vida. Al hacer planes para el día
de hoy, te ayudaré a discernir mi voluntad. Esta colaboración conmigo te capacitará para manejar *cualquier cosa* que se te presente durante el día. Te estoy
preparando para *confiar en mí en todo momento y* en
cualquier circunstancia.

ISAÍAS 50.4; SALMOS 139.17, 18; SANTIAGO 4.8;
SALMOS 62.8

LA LUZ DE MI GLORIA brilla sobre ti, mi amado. Búscame con un espíritu de adoración. Deja que el resplandor de mi Amor caiga sobre ti y alcance hasta
las mayores profundidades de tu ser. Saborea esos
momentos a solas conmigo. Los estoy usando para
hacer que seas más como yo. Mientras más mantengas
tu mirada en mí —en los momentos de tranquilidad *y*
en el ajetreo del día— mejor podrás *reflejar mi Gloria*
a otras personas.

Mantenerte consciente de mí cuando estás ocupado puede ser todo un reto. Sin embargo, te he creado
con una mente tan asombrosa que puede permitirte
funcionar en más de un asunto al mismo tiempo. La
práctica de mi Presencia implica dedicarle un tiempo a tu relación conmigo. Esta práctica tiene muchos
beneficios. Cuando estás consciente de que estoy contigo, es menos probable que hagas o digas algo que me
desagrade. Cuando estás luchando con circunstancias
difíciles o sentimientos dolorosos, estar consciente de
mi Presencia te da valor y consuelo. Yo puedo usar
todas las cosas en tu vida para bien, *transformándote a
mi semejanza con una Gloria siempre en aumento.*

HEBREOS 12.2; 2 CORINTIOS 3.18;
ROMANOS 8.28

Febrero 26

EL HOMBRE MIRA LA APARIENCIA exterior, pero yo miro el corazón. La capacidad de ver es un gran don. Al observar y admirar la belleza de la naturaleza te ofrezco destellos de mi Gloria. Las grandes pinturas, las esculturas y la cinematografía pueden ayudarte a abrir los ojos de tu alma. Alégrate con estos gloriosos regalos, pero no te conviertas en un esclavo de las apariencias. Yo estoy principalmente interesado en el estado de tu corazón, y obro para crear belleza en él.

Es muy importante que separes tiempo para nutrir tu corazón. *Sobre toda cosa guardada, guarda tu corazón, porque de él mana la vida.* Tu corazón es una fuente de abundante provisión. ¡Puesto que me perteneces, mi propia vida fluye a través de ti! Sin embargo, para mantener esta Vida fluyendo de forma abundante, debes proteger tu corazón de las malas influencias y alimentarlo con el estudio de la Biblia y la oración.

Ajustar tus prioridades según mis enseñanzas puede ser muy liberador. Cuando no te guste el aspecto de las cosas en tu mundo, cierra los ojos y fíjate en quién soy. Recuerda que *yo soy Emanuel: Dios contigo.*

1 SAMUEL 16.7; PROVERBIOS 4.23;
MATEO 1.23

Yo vine al mundo como una Luz, para que todo el que cree en mí no permanezca en tinieblas. Sin embargo, no solo traje luz al mundo, sino que yo mismo soy *la Luz que se mantiene brillando en la oscuridad.* ¡Y puesto que soy infinito y todopoderoso, nada puede extinguir esta luminosidad.

Cuando creíste en mí, llegaste a ser un *hijo de Luz* y la brillantez inundó tu ser interior. Esto te ayuda a ver las cosas desde mi perspectiva, tanto las del mundo como las de tu corazón. La iluminación del contenido de tu corazón puede ser muy incómoda; no obstante, te conduce al arrepentimiento y a caminar en mis pisadas, que es el camino hacia la libertad.

Regocíjate en tu clara perspectiva. *El dios de este siglo ha enceguecido el entendimiento de los incrédulos, para que no puedan ver la Luz del evangelio de mi Gloria.* Sin embargo, debido a que tú eres un ser muy querido para mí, tienes la *Luz del conocimiento de mi Gloria* brillando en tu corazón. ¡Regocíjate grandemente!

JUAN 12.46; JUAN 1.5; 1 TESALONICENSES 5.5;
2 CORINTIOS 4.4, 6

Febrero 28

TÚ NO ERES EXTRAÑO para mí, mi amado. *Antes que te formara en el vientre ya te conocía.* Mi conocimiento de ti ha continuado sin interrupción: a través de tu entrada en este mundo y a lo largo de tu vida. Así como el experto alfarero se deleita en la obra que sale de sus manos, yo me gozo en transformarte cada vez más para que llegues a ser aquel que tenía la intención que fueras cuando te creé.

Una implicación de mi Presencia ininterrumpida en tu vida es que nunca estarás solo. Aunque entiendo que eres humano y que tu capacidad de atención es limitada, te estoy preparando para que seas cada vez más consciente de mí. Habrá ocasiones en que en medio del sufrimiento pienses que estás solo o abandonado. Sin embargo, yo sufrí solo en la cruz para que tú nunca estuvieras solo en tus luchas. *Siempre estarás conmigo; yo te sostengo de tu mano derecha.*

El último enemigo al que tendrás que enfrentarte es la muerte, pero mi crucifixión y resurrección han diezmado a ese enemigo. Así que confía en mí para te guíe a través de tu vida y *después te acoja en la Gloria.*

JEREMÍAS 1.5; SALMOS 139.16;
SALMOS 73.23, 24

61

Yo TE LLAMÉ DE LAS TINIEBLAS a mi Luz admirable. Te *saqué no solo de la oscuridad,* sino que te hice parte de mi familia real. Te vestí con mi propio *manto de justicia,* lo que te habilita perfectamente para que pertenezcas a mi reino. Tú eres uno *de mi pueblo especial:* me perteneces, y yo me deleito en ti.

He optado por utilizar seres imperfectos como tú para *proclamar mis obras maravillosas.* Sé que no podrás hacerlo tan bien como querrías. En realidad, sin mi ayuda es imposible que lo logres. Esta brecha entre mi llamado en tu vida y tu capacidad de responder es parte de mi plan. Te ayuda a reconocer tu insuficiencia más absoluta. Debido a que eres mío, te permito conectar tu incapacidad a mi ilimitada suficiencia. En lugar de preocuparte de tu insuficiencia, preocúpate de permanecer cerca de mí. En todo lo que hagas, confía conscientemente en mi ayuda, viviendo en la jubilosa maravilla del olvido de ti mismo. Al acudir a mí para todo lo que necesitas, tu rostro reflejará la Luz de mi incomparable Gloria.

1 Pedro 2.9; Isaías 61.10; Juan 15.5;
2 Corintios 3.18

Marzo

*De su plenitud todos hemos
recibido gracia sobre gracia.*

Juan 1.16

Yo TE DOY Gozo en tu paso por el mundo. Este regalo centelleante no es un lujo; ¡es una necesidad! En el camino encontrarás obstáculos, así como curvas cerradas, subidas y bajadas. Sin el Gozo en tu corazón, *te cansarás y te desalentarás.*

El Gozo que te doy no depende de las circunstancias. ¡Las trasciende! Esta es la razón por la que las personas pobres son a menudo más felices que las que tienen riquezas. Enfermos, e incluso muriendo, las personas pueden sentir gozo cuando confían en mí como su Salvador, Señor y Amigo.

Trata de difundir el Gozo en el mundo que te rodea. Deja que mi Luz se refleje en tu forma de ser mediante tus sonrisas, tu risa, tus palabras. El Espíritu Santo te capacitará para hacerlo en la medida que le des espacio en tu vida. Pídele que te llene de un deleite contagioso. Concéntrate en estar cerca de mí, y yo te guiaré a lo largo del *camino de la Vida. En mi Presencia hay plenitud de Gozo.*

HEBREOS 12.3; HABACUC 3.17, 18;
SALMOS 16.11

Marzo 2

¡MIS CAMINOS ESTÁN MÁS ALLÁ DE TU COMPRENSIÓN! Ven a mí con un corazón humilde, inclinándote ante mi inteligencia infinita. Renuncia a tu deseo de entenderme; acepta el hecho de que muchas cosas superan tus posibilidades de comprensión. Debido a que yo soy infinito y tú eres finito, las limitaciones de tu mente hacen que sea imposible que entiendas muchos de los hechos que ocurren en tu vida y en el mundo. Por eso es vital que dejes espacio para el *misterio* en la forma en que ves el desarrollo de los hechos.

Eres privilegiado al saber muchas cosas que antiguamente eran misterios, cosas *que se habían mantenido ocultas por siglos y generaciones*. El Nuevo Testamento está lleno de revelaciones que se hicieron conocidas a través de mi encarnación, vida, muerte y resurrección. ¡Tú eres inconmensurablemente bendecido por tener hoy este conocimiento inapreciable!

Con todo, las formas en que obro en tu mundo son a menudo misteriosas para ti. Están más allá de tu comprensión. Por eso tienes que hacer una decisión: resistirte o inclinarte ante mí con asombro y adoración. ¡Maravíllate ante la *profundidad de las riquezas de mi sabiduría y conocimiento*!

ROMANOS 11.33; PROVERBIOS 3.5;
COLOSENSES 1.26

MI AMOR TE BUSCA CADA DÍA DE TU VIDA. Así que identifica las señales de mi tierna Presencia mientras avanzas a través de tu jornada diaria. Yo me revelo a ti en una gran variedad de formas y maneras: palabras surgidas de las Escrituras justo cuando más las necesitas, palabras dichas a través de otras personas, «coincidencias» orquestada por mi Espíritu, la belleza de la creación, y por medio de otras muchas cosas. Mi Amor por ti no es pasivo; te busca activamente y cuando te encuentra, se hace evidente en tu vida. Invítame para que abra los ojos de tu corazón de manera que puedas «verme» bendiciéndote en miles de formas pequeñas o grandes.

Quiero que no solo recibas mis abundantes bendiciones, sino que las anotes con cuidado. *Atesóralas y medita en ellas en tu corazón.* Dame las gracias por las formas en que las hago realidad en tu vida; escribe algunas de ellas de manera que puedas disfrutarlas una y otra vez. Estas señales de mi Presencia te fortalecen y te preparan para cuando se presenten las dificultades. Recuerda que *nada en toda la creación puede separarte de mi Amor.*

SALMOS 23.6; SALMOS 119.11; LUCAS 2.19;
ROMANOS 8.39

Marzo 4

¡DICHOSOS SON TODOS LOS QUE ESPERAN EN MÍ! Esperar pacientemente no es fácil, no obstante, resulta muy bueno para ti. Elaboras planes con mucha anticipación, tomas decisiones definitivas y haces que las cosas *ocurran*. Hay un tiempo para eso, pero este no es el momento. Ahora es tiempo de que te sientes ante mi Presencia, confiando en mí con todo tu ser. Esta disciplina te traerá una abundancia de bendiciones.

Algunas de las cosas buenas que te ofrezco se encuentran en el futuro. Mientras esperas obedientemente en mí, estás aumentando el valor de aquellas cosas que aún no se han convertido en bendiciones. Debido a que ellas están veladas en el misterio del futuro, no las puedes ver con claridad. Para el tiempo presente hay otras bendiciones. El mismo proceso de esperar en mí es beneficioso. Mantén tu alma a la expectativa mientras me buscas con esperanza. Sé consciente de que yo estoy en control y puedes descansar en mi bondad. Aunque no entiendas por qué tienes que esperar tanto, yo te bendigo al decidirte a *confiar en mí con todo su corazón*.

ISAÍAS 30.18; SALMOS 143.8;
PROVERBIOS 3.5

Yo ME PREOCUPO POR TI. Cuando te sientas solo y vulnerable, expuesto a los «elementos» de un mundo caído, detente y recuérdate a ti mismo: «Jesús cuida de mí». Este recuerdo te traerá consuelo y te ayudará a sentirte descansado. Te impedirá obsesionarte por el futuro, intentando averiguar y anticipar lo que sucederá.

Cuando las circunstancias sean confusas y no sepas qué camino tomar, recuerda que yo no aparto mis ojos de ti. Sé todo sobre tu vida y tu situación. También conozco el futuro. Un niño de una buena familia con los recursos adecuados no necesita saber la forma en que sus padres le proveerán mañana, la próxima semana, o el próximo año. Tú perteneces a la mejor familia que te puedas imaginar, y mis recursos son absolutamente ilimitados. Por lo tanto, tráeme todas tus necesidades y preocupaciones. Confíamelas y vive tranquilo, como un hijo del *Rey de reyes*. Relájate y regocíjate, porque yo tengo buen cuidado de ti.

1 PEDRO 5.7; ISAÍAS 58.11;
APOCALIPSIS 19.16

Marzo 6

No SIENTAS MIEDO *cuando vayas por valles tenebrosos.* Mi Presencia radiante brilla en *ese lugar profundo y oscuro,* fortaleciéndote, alentándote y consolándote. Ya que *nunca duermo,* estoy en condiciones de mantener sobre ti una vigilancia constante. Por lo demás, ningún valle es tan profundo, ningún foso es tan oscuro, que yo no pueda verlo todo hasta el fondo mismo.

Incluso si de vez en cuando te alejas de mí y caes en un *pozo de desesperación,* puedes contar con que yo te rescataré. Cuando clamas a mí, *te levanto del lodo y del pantano y pongo tus pies sobre una roca,* dándote *un lugar firme donde puedas estar.* Encuentra consuelo en mi compromiso de ayudarte, incluso cuando tropieces y caigas.

Cada vez que comiences a sentir miedo, recuerda que *estoy contigo.* He prometido que *nunca te dejaré. Yo mismo, en persona, te precedo* en el camino de la vida. Cuando sientas que vas atravesando el valle de la adversidad, deja que estas palabras de consuelo fluyan en tu mente: «*No temeré mal alguno, porque tú estarás conmigo*».

SALMOS 23.4; SALMOS 121.2, 3;
SALMOS 40.1, 2; DEUTERONOMIO 31.8

BIENAVENTURADOS LOS QUE SE GOZAN en mi Nombre todo el día y se regocijan en mi justicia. Este Nombre me representa en todos mis gloriosos atributos. Usado correctamente, te acerca a mi amorosa Presencia. Muchas personas abusan de mi Nombre utilizándolo como una palabrota. Oír este abuso verbal me es extremadamente ofensivo. Sin embargo, mis seguidores pueden pronunciar amorosamente la palabra «Jesús» durante todo el día para regocijarse en mí y pedir mi ayuda. *Yo soy Dios tu Salvador, y te ayudaré para la Gloria de mi Nombre.*

Te invito a que te regocijes en mi justicia. «Regocijarte» es estar encantado, eufórico, alegre y jubiloso, especialmente por el triunfo o el éxito. Justo antes de morir en la cruz dije: «*¡Todo se ha cumplido!*». Estaba anunciando la realización del mayor triunfo imaginable: la victoria sobre el pecado y la muerte para todo el que cree en mí. A través de este logro supremo, mi justicia ha sido acreditada a ti para siempre, mi amado. *Te he cubierto con el manto de justicia.* ¡Usa mis gloriosas *ropas de salvación* con deleite, euforia, júbilo y alegría!

SALMOS 89.16; SALMOS 79.9;
JUAN 19.30; ISAÍAS 61.10

Marzo 8

Yo TE CAPACITO *para que permanezcas en las alturas.*
Este término «las alturas» puede referirse a un sinnúmero de cosas. Tomado de forma literal, significa que
algo está físicamente muy arriba. Esta es una forma
apropiada de describir las altas cumbres de una montaña o los pisos más altos de un rascacielos. Tomado en
sentido figurado, el término puede referirse al placer
eufórico *o* a algo muy diferente: experiencias importantes llenas de responsabilidad. Si aspiras a alcanzar
las alturas, sobre todo los lugares más altos de logros y
reconocimientos, debes prepararte para asumir las responsabilidades que acompañan el éxito. Sin embargo,
no te olvides de disfrutar de la satisfacción de experimentar cosas buenas conmigo, a través de mí y para mí.

Debido a que eres mío, puedes *mantenerte firme,
con el cinturón de la verdad bien abrochado alrededor
de tu cintura y la coraza de justicia en su lugar.* Todas
mis enseñanzas son verdades absolutas, *porque yo soy
la Verdad.* Esto te da una base firme, una roca sólida
sobre la cual pararte. Mi perfecta justicia se ha acreditado a tu cuenta para siempre. ¡No importa la cantidad de problemas con que te encuentres en la vida,
esta justicia podrá mantenerte en pie!

2 SAMUEL 22.34; EFESIOS 6.14; JUAN 14.6;
ROMANOS 3.22

MIS CAMINOS SON MISTERIOSOS e impredecibles, pero son buenos. Cuando observamos los acontecimientos mundiales —con tanta maldad rampante— es fácil sentir miedo y desanimarse. Seguramente tú no puedes comprender por qué permito tanta crueldad y sufrimiento. La dificultad radica en el hecho de que yo soy infinito y tú no lo eres. Muchas cosas están simplemente más allá de tu comprensión. Sin embargo, no te desesperes. Cuando llegues al límite de tu capacidad de entender, confiar en mí te llevará adelante. Afirma tu *confianza en mí* mediante oraciones silenciosas y habladas. ¡Mantén la comunicación conmigo!

No te quedes atrapado en la postura de demandar saber por qué. Esa es una pregunta equivocada. Las preguntas correctas son: «¿Cómo quieres que vea esta situación?» y «¿Qué quieres que haga ahora?». No se puede cambiar el pasado, por lo que comienza con el momento presente y trata de encontrar mi camino en lo adelante. Confía en mí un día, un momento, una vez. *No temas, porque yo estoy contigo. Te fortaleceré y te ayudaré.*

PROVERBIOS 3.5; ECLESIASTÉS 8.17;
SALMOS 37.12, 13; ISAÍAS 41.10

Marzo 10

DE LA PLENITUD DE MI GRACIA, tú has recibido una bendición tras otra. Detente un momento, mi amado, y piensa en el asombroso don de la salvación *por gracia mediante la fe* en mí. Debido a que es totalmente un regalo, *no resultado de las obras*, esta salvación está segura. Tu parte es recibir lo que he logrado para ti en la cruz, creyendo con la fe que te fue dada. Este Amor y este favor inmerecidos son tuyos para siempre. ¡Mi gracia tiene un valor infinito!

Múltiples bendiciones fluyen de la gracia debido a su extraordinaria plenitud. Los sentimientos de culpa se derriten bajo la cálida Luz de mi perdón. Tu identidad como un *hijo de Dios* le da a tu vida sentido y propósito. Tu relación con otras personas mejora a medida que te relacionas con ellas demostrando amor y perdón.

La mejor respuesta a mi gracia abundante es un corazón lleno de gratitud. Dedica un tiempo cada día a pensar en mí y agradecerme por las bendiciones de tu vida. Esto protege tu corazón de la mala hierba de la ingratitud que brota tan fácilmente. ¡*Sé agradecido*!

JUAN 1.16; EFESIOS 2.8, 9; JUAN 1.12;
COLOSENSES 3.15

PROCURA VIVIR EN EL PRESENTE... *¡conmigo!* Tu vida es un regalo que te he hecho y que consiste de millones y millones de momentos. Estos incontables y pequeños dones que te he dado pueden pasar fácilmente inadvertidos sin que hagas uso de ellos. El mejor remedio para tal error es llenar tus momentos con mi Presencia. Puedes comenzar tu día conectándote conmigo y orando: «Gracias, Jesús, por este precioso día de vida. Ayúdame a ser consciente de tu Presencia conmigo».

El agradecimiento te mantiene unido a mí y anclado en el presente. La preocupación, por otra parte, te empuja hacia el futuro, donde terminarás deambulando en lugares estériles de incertidumbre. Sin embargo, siempre podrás volver a mí si me dices en un susurro: «Señor, ayúdame».

Para vivir constantemente en el presente, trata de ser más agradecido. Mira a tu alrededor e intenta ubicar los muchos regalos que derramo sobre ti. Cuando vayas a darme las gracias por estas bendiciones, hazlo con entusiasmo y alegría. Esto aumentará tu agradecimiento e intensificará tu habilidad de entender cuán bendecido realmente eres.

SALMOS 118.24; COLOSENSES 2.6, 7;
SALMOS 13.5; 2 CORINTIOS 9.15

Marzo 12

EL GOZO QUE TIENES EN MÍ es independiente de tus circunstancias. *En mi Presencia hay plenitud de Gozo,* y tú nunca estás separado de mí. *Búscame* mientras caminas por el sendero del día de hoy. Yo me deleito en revelarme a ti. A veces me comunico contigo a través de grandes e inconfundibles formas, «coincidencias» que son claramente la obra de mis manos. En otras ocasiones revelo mi Presencia invisible de maneras muy sutiles. A menudo son tan personales que otros no las notan. Sin embargo, estas manifestaciones tan sutiles pueden ser una fuente de Gozo profundo e íntimo.

Mientras más atención pongas, más claramente podrás encontrarme en los detalles de tu vida. Así que trata de mantenerte alerta. ¡No dejes de buscarme!

Llena tu mente y tu corazón con las Escrituras, en las que me revelo con mayor claridad. Deja que mis promesas penetren en tu pensamiento y mantente cerca de mí. *Escucha mi voz. Yo te conozco, y tú me sigues. Yo te doy vida eterna y nadie te podrá arrebatar de mi mano.* ¡Regocíjate!

SALMOS 16.11; JEREMÍAS 29.13;
JUAN 10.27, 28

NO TE QUEDES VIVIENDO EN EL PASADO, mi amado. Es cierto que del pasado se puede aprender, pero no dejes que se convierta en tu enfoque primario. Por mucho que quieras hacerlo, no es posible deshacer las cosas que ya han ocurrido. En lugar de desear lo imposible, ven a mí y *ábreme tu corazón*. Recuerda que yo soy *tu Refugio*; *confía en mí en todo momento*.

Refuerza tu confianza en mí diciendo lo más frecuentemente que puedas: «Confío en ti, Jesús». Pronunciar estas cuatro palabras puede iluminar tu día de inmediato, despejando las negras nubes de preocupación por medio de una simple confianza en mí, como la de un niño.

¡Yo estoy haciendo algo nuevo! No dejes de descubrir todo lo que estoy logrando en tu vida. Pídeme que abra los ojos de tu mente y tu corazón para que puedas ver las muchas oportunidades que he puesto a lo largo de tu camino. No caigas en la rutina de reparar solo en las mismas cosas viejas, porque puedes perderte la bendición de las nuevas. Recuerda que yo puedo abrir un camino donde pareciera que nadie podría hacerlo. *¡Conmigo todo es posible!*

ISAÍAS 43.18, 19; SALMOS 62.8;
MATEO 19.26

Marzo 14

Yo *ME DELEITO EN TI CON CÁNTICOS*. Abre tu corazón, mente y espíritu para recibir mis más ricas bendiciones. Debido a que eres mi hijo comprado con mi sangre, mi Amor por ti fluye continuamente desde *el trono de la gracia*. Mírame y recibe todo lo que tengo para ti. Escucha y me oirás cantar canciones de Gozo por mi *gran complacencia en ti*. Puedes acercarte a mí valientemente, con la confianza que te da el saber que eres a *quien yo amo*.

El mundo te enseña que el amor es condicional; que depende del desempeño, la apariencia y el estatus. A pesar de que no crees esta mentira, la constante embestida de este mensaje en los medios de comunicación puede penetrar tu pensamiento. Es por eso que resulta tan importante dedicar un tiempo a enfocarte en mí, saturándote de mi Presencia, absorbiendo mi Palabra.

Separar tiempo para estar a solas conmigo es contracultural, por lo que esta práctica requiere disciplina y determinación. Sin embargo, bien vale el esfuerzo. Vivir cerca de mí ilumina tu vida inmensamente. *En mí está la fuente de Vida; en mi Luz tú ves la Luz.*

SOFONÍAS 3.17; HEBREOS 4.16;
DEUTERONOMIO 33.12; SALMOS 36.9

Yo sostengo a todos los que caen y levanto a todos los agobiados. Hay ocasiones en que solo tú y yo sabemos que has caído. La tentación a veces es no darle importancia a lo que has hecho (o dejado de hacer). Es posible que no te acongojen los sentimientos de vergüenza, pero en lo íntimo de tu ser te sientes inquieto e intranquilo, ligeramente culpable. Aun en momentos como esos, yo no dejo de amarte de forma perfecta. A veces te muestro mi Amor por ti de maneras inesperadas, como por ejemplo humillándote y deleitándote al mismo tiempo. Esto agudiza tu conciencia de haber pecado e intensifica tu deseo de confesarlo y acercarte a mí. Mientras retornas al lugar que te corresponde, mi redimido, tu inquietud da lugar a la calma. Así es como te levanto cuando has tropezado.

Recuerda que puedo hacer que *todas las cosas* —incluyendo tus fracasos— *ayuden a bien, porque tú me amas y has sido llamado conforme a mi propósito.* Darte cuenta de lo mucho que te aprecio incluso cuando no estás viviendo bien profundiza tu relación conmigo. También ayuda a que te relajes y te regocijes en *mi inagotable amor.*

Salmos 145.14; Romanos 8.28;
Lamentaciones 3.22, 23

Yo soy el antídoto para la soledad. *Porque yo soy el Señor, tu Dios, quien te sostiene de tu mano derecha y te dice: «No temas, yo te ayudaré».* Cierra tu diestra, como si estuvieras agarrado a la mía. Este gesto simbólico te ayudará a sentirte conectado a mí, a mi Presencia viva. Cada vez que te empieces a sentir solo o temeroso, reconéctate.

Háblame de lo que estás sintiendo y las luchas que enfrentas. Yo las conozco, pero te hace bien decírmelas. Pasa tiempo disfrutando en la Luz de mi Presencia, dándote cuenta de lo seguro que estás en mí. *Yo estoy contigo* cada nanosegundo de tu vida. ¡Nunca te encuentras solo!

Busca mi rostro y mi perspectiva para tu vida. A veces es bueno que escribas tus preocupaciones. Aclara tus pensamientos y lleva un registro de tus plegarias. Esto también te ayuda a entregarme tus problemas. *Yo estoy contigo* continuamente.

Isaías 41.13; Mateo 28.20; Salmos 27.4;
Génesis 28.15

NADA EN TODA LA CREACIÓN puede separarte de mi Amor. Detente a pensar y reflexionar en el increíble contenido de esta promesa. Tú vives en un mundo donde las separaciones abundan: las esposas de sus maridos, los hijos de sus padres, los amigos de sus amigos, los sueños de la infancia de las realidades de la edad adulta. Sin embargo, hay una terrible separación que tú nunca tendrás que enfrentar: el aislamiento de mi amorosa Presencia.

Quiero que te conectes a mí con una confianza tenaz. Eso te dará fuerzas para hacerle frente a la incertidumbre de vivir en un mundo inestable y corrompido. Si olvidas que mi amor nunca te fallará, los pensamientos de ansiedad te pueden asaltar y llenarte de miedo. Cuando te sientas invadido por el temor, agárrate de mi mano con la confianza de un niño que se refugia en la mano de su papá. Descansa en la protección de mi Presencia, y recuerda que *el perfecto Amor echa fuera el temor.*

La mayor riqueza en la tierra es ínfima en comparación con las riquezas de mi amor sin límites. Este es mi regalo para todos los que me siguen. *¡Cuán precioso es mi gran Amor!*

ROMANOS 8.38, 39; ISAÍAS 30.15; 1 JUAN 4.18;
SALMOS 36.7

Marzo 18

Esfuérzate por vivir más plenamente en el presente, rehusándote a *preocuparte por el mañana*. Esforzarse implica dedicar seriamente energía a algo; y por lo general, eso incluye lucha. Deberás ejercer un esfuerzo continuo si quieres vivir el tiempo presente en mi Presencia. Te invito a que me conviertas en la más importante búsqueda de tu vida cotidiana.

Es esencial resistir la tentación a sentirte preocupado. Es cierto que vives en un mundo caído, lleno de pecado y batallas, donde nunca faltarán cosas que te quieran provocar ansiedad, pero no te olvides de que *cada día tiene sus propios problemas*. Yo calibro con cuidado la cantidad de dificultades que encontrarás en un día determinado. Y sé exactamente cuántas de esas dificultades podrás manejar con mi ayuda. Yo estoy siempre cerca, listo para fortalecerte, animarte y consolarte.

Mantenerte cerca de mí es la mejor manera de vivir en el presente. Cuando tus pensamientos quieran divagar, tráelos sin demora a mí. Regresa a mí con alegría, mi amado. *Me deleitaré en ti con gozo, me alegraré por ti con cánticos.*

Mateo 6.34; Isaías 41.10; Sofonías 3.17

TÚ ESTARÁS PREPARADO PARA TODO al vivir en una relación conmigo. Descansa en mi Presencia mientras te *infundo fuerza interior*. Como eres un hijo del Rey de reyes, eres capaz de mucho más de lo que crees. Sin embargo, para beneficiarte totalmente de tu posición privilegiada, necesitas pasar mucho tiempo conmigo. Al relajarte en mi Presencia —deleitándote en mí y abriéndome tu corazón— te lleno de fuerza interior. Ese tiempo que pasamos juntos no solo es placentero, sino que resulta fortalecedor.

Cuando las muchas ocupaciones te presionan, la tentación es posponer tu tiempo conmigo y sumergirte en las actividades del día. No obstante, al igual que un desayuno saludable te ayuda a funcionar mucho mejor, así ocurrirá cuando alimentes tu alma con la dieta adecuada que te ofrezco. Disfruta mi Palabra, pidiéndole a mi Espíritu que la haga parte de tu propia vida. Saborea estas palabras de Vida. Tu relación viviente conmigo te ayudará a enfrentar cada nuevo día con confianza, preparado para cualquier cosa que se te presente.

FILIPENSES 4.13; SALMOS 37.4;
SALMOS 5.3

Marzo 20

¡DETÉN ESA INCESANTE PREOCUPACIÓN por planificar! Trae tu mente desde el futuro al momento presente, donde te espera mi amorosa Presencia. *Búscame* con una sonrisa en el corazón, sabiendo que yo me deleito en ti. Háblame acerca de todo lo que te preocupa y las tareas pendientes que tienes sobre tus hombros. Pídeme que te ayude a establecer tus prioridades de acuerdo con mi voluntad. Luego, vuelve a concentrarte en mí y en el trabajo que te ocupa. Invitarme a tus actividades aumenta tu Gozo y te ayuda a ser más efectivo.

Cuando necesites hacer un alto, recuerda que yo soy tu lugar de descanso. Mis *brazos eternos* estarán siempre disponibles para sostenerte y abrazarte. Si te relajas en mi compañía —esperando conmigo por unos momentos— eso demuestra la confianza genuina que me tienes. Mientras te preparas para volver a tus tareas, haz el esfuerzo de incluirme en tus planes. Eso te protegerá de preocupaciones y también te ayudará a mantenerte cerca de mí, disfrutando de mi Presencia.

LUCAS 12.25, 26; SALMOS 62.5, 6;
DEUTERONOMIO 33.27

TE ESTOY ENTRENANDO no solo para soportar tus dificultades, sino para transformarlas en Gloria. Esta no es una proeza humana, y requiere la ayuda sobrenatural de mi Espíritu. Cuando los problemas te están pesando demasiado, tu tendencia natural es acelerar tu ritmo de vida, buscando frenéticamente las respuestas. Sin embargo, lo que necesitas en tales momentos es *reducir el paso* y buscar mi Rostro. Invita a mi Espíritu para que te ayude mientras analizas tus dificultades conmigo. Luego, *pon tus peticiones delante de mí y espera la respuesta.*

Aun cuando esperes con expectación, quizás yo no responda a tus oraciones todo lo rápido que desearías. Ten en cuenta que siempre estoy haciendo algo importante en tu vida, más que simplemente solucionando tus problemas. Tus luchas son parte de una batalla mucho más grande, y la forma en que las manejes puede contribuir a los resultados con significado eterno. Cuando respondes a tus tribulaciones confiando en mí y *orando con acción de gracias*, me estás glorificando. Además, con el tiempo, tu práctica de orar persistentemente hará una gran diferencia en ti. Mi amado *coronado de Gloria.*

SALMOS 5.3; FILIPENSES 4.6;
SALMOS 8.5

Marzo 22

ALÉGRATE, MI AMADO, porque mi sacrificio en la cruz absorbió toda tu culpa: pasada, presente y futura. *No hay condenación para los que están en mí.* Tu estatus como mi seguidor libre de culpa es una buena razón para que estés gozoso cada día de tu vida. Desde la Caída en el Jardín del Edén, el peor problema de la humanidad ha sido el pecado. Mi muerte sacrificial proveyó la solución a este terrible problema. El evangelio trae la mejor noticia imaginable: tomé tu pecado —*me hice pecado por ti*— y te di mi justicia perfecta. ¡Esta es una transacción eterna increíble!

Quiero que aprendas a disfrutar más plenamente de tu condición de estar libre de culpa en mi reino. *¡A través de mí, la ley del Espíritu de vida te hizo libre!* Esta no es una invitación a que te sumerjas en un estilo de vida pecaminoso. En cambio, te estoy invitando a vivir jubilosamente, deleitándote en el privilegio glorioso de pertenecerme para siempre. Esta es tu verdadera identidad, y le da momento a momento sentido a tu vida. Alégrate de saber quién eres en realidad: un amado *hijo de Dios.*

ROMANOS 8.1, 2; GÉNESIS 3.6, 7;
2 CORINTIOS 5.21; JUAN 1.11, 12

Yo soy el Resucitado; *tu Dios vivo.* ¡Celebra el Gozo de servir a un Salvador que está exuberantemente vivo! Regocíjate también en mi promesa de estar contigo siempre a lo largo del tiempo y la eternidad. Estas verdades te pueden sostener a través de las más grandes pruebas o decepciones que pudieres encontrar en el camino. Así que anda confiadamente a lo largo del camino de la Vida conmigo, el Único que nunca te soltará de su mano.

Piensa en lo que te ofrezco: yo mismo, perdón de *todos* tus pecados, disfrutes para siempre en el cielo. Todo esto es tan extraordinario y espléndido que no podrías comprenderlo en su totalidad. Por eso es que adorarme resulta tan importante: es una manera tan poderosa de conectarte conmigo que trasciende tu capacidad de comprensión. También proclama mi Presencia. Existen numerosas formas de adorarme: entonando himnos y canciones de alabanza, estudiando y memorizando mi Palabra, orando individualmente y con otros, disfrutando de las maravillas de mi creación. Servir y amar a los demás con mi Amor también puede ser una forma de adoración. *Lo que sea que hagas, hazlo todo para la Gloria de Dios… ¡mi Gloria!*

Mateo 28.5, 6; Salmos 42.2;
Colosenses 2.2, 3; 1 Corintios 10.31

Marzo 24

No importa cuán insuficiente te sientas, siempre puedes venir a mí en busca de ayuda. No necesitas ir a un lugar especial o asumir determinada postura para *buscar mi Rostro*. Tampoco necesitas utilizar un lenguaje elegante ni trabajar para ganar mi favor. Siempre te miro con buenos ojos, porque te veo vestido con el manto de mi justicia. Yo estoy vivo en ti, y entiendo perfectamente tus pensamientos. Por eso, una simple mirada —una mirada de fe— es suficiente para contar con mi ayuda.

Tiendes a malgastar energía tratando de determinar si tus recursos son adecuados para el día. Te mantienes controlando tu «indicador de potencia» en lugar de buscarme a mí para que te provea lo que necesitas. ¡Cuánto mejor es simplemente reconocer tu insuficiencia cuando despiertas! Eso te libera para que confíes en mí. Si te mantienes en contacto conmigo, voy a poner el suficiente Poder a tu disposición para satisfacer tus necesidades cuando se presenten. Mantente esperando en mí, tu *ayudador siempre presente*. Y tu fuerza será igual a las exigencias de tu día.

Salmos 105.4; Isaías 61.10; Salmos 46.1;
Deuteronomio 33.25

Yo soy la Resurrección y la Vida. El que cree en mí vivirá, aunque muera. Yo le dije esta verdad a Marta cuando su hermano Lázaro había muerto, y ella me creyó. Poco después, mandé a Lázaro a salir de su tumba, y lo hizo. Aunque finalmente murió de nuevo —como todos— él sabía que iba a volver a resucitar a la Vida, como cada creyente lo hará.

Poco antes de mi crucifixión, les enseñé a mis discípulos: *«Yo soy el Camino, la Verdad y la Vida».* Yo soy todo lo que tú pudieras necesitar, para esta vida y la siguiente. Soy el Tesoro que abarca todos los tesoros. ¡Esta verdad puede simplificar tu vida inmensamente! Yo soy la respuesta a todas tus luchas, el Gozo que abarca todo tiempo y circunstancia. Puedo hacer soportables los tiempos más duros y los buenos momentos absolutamente maravillosos. Así que *ven a mí* tal como estás, mi amado; hazme partícipe cada vez más de tu vida. Regocíjate mientras vas andando conmigo; el Camino que te guía siempre y la Resurrección que te da la Vida eterna.

JUAN 11.25, 43, 44; JUAN 14.6;
COLOSENSES 2.2, 3; MATEO 11.28

Marzo 26

PÍDEME QUE AUMENTE tu sentido de gratitud. Esto le dará luminosidad a tu día y dispondrá tu corazón para mí. Trata de «verme» en medio de tus circunstancias. Busca atisbos de mi Presencia invisible mientras vas por *la senda de la Vida*. El sentido de gratitud no solo abre tu corazón, sino también tus ojos. Al conocerme íntimamente, me podrás encontrar en multitud de pequeños detalles, así como en el panorama completo de tu vida. Aparta un tiempo para darte cuenta de todas mis bendiciones —pequeñas y grandes— y agradéceme por ellas. Esta práctica te ayudará a disfrutar de mis muchos dones.

Pídeme también que te entrene en lo que respecta a confiar en mí de un modo más constante. Una confianza bien desarrollada te permitirá atravesar los terrenos peligrosos sin tropezar. Mientras más desafiante sea tu caminar, más frecuentemente necesitarás expresarme tu confianza. Puedes orar: «Señor, *yo confío en tu gran Amor*». Esta breve oración te recordará que me encuentro contigo, que estoy cuidando de ti, y que mi Amor por ti es eterno. Regocíjate, mi amado, porque yo soy verdaderamente digno de tu gratitud y tu confianza.

COLOSENSES 2.6, 7; SALMOS 16.11;
SALMOS 52.8

MEDIANTE MI RESURRECCIÓN de entre los muertos, tú tienes un renacer a una esperanza viva. Toda mi obra en ti tiene que ver con lo «nuevo». Debido a que me perteneces, eres *una nueva creación*; *¡lo viejo ha pasado, lo nuevo ha llegado!* Tu adopción en mi familia real se produjo instantáneamente en el momento en que confiaste en mí como tu Salvador. En ese instante, tu estatus espiritual cambió de muerte a vida. A Vida eterna. *En el cielo, tienes reservada una herencia indestructible, incontaminada e inmarchitable.*

Sin ninguna duda eres una nueva creación con el Espíritu Santo viviendo en ti. Sin embargo, tu conversión a la fe cristiana fue solo el *comienzo* de la obra que estoy haciendo en ti. Necesitas *que te haga nuevo en la actitud de tu mente y ponga en ti el nuevo yo* para que cada vez seas más piadoso, justo y santo. Este es un esfuerzo de por vida que te estará preparando para la Gloria celestial. Así que recibe esta asignación con valor y gratitud. Mantente alerta e identifica todas las cosas maravillosas que estoy haciendo en tu vida.

1 PEDRO 1.3, 4; 2 CORINTIOS 5.17;
EFESIOS 4.22-24; ROMANOS 6.4

Marzo 28

AL LLEGAR A CONOCERME más íntimamente, vas siendo más consciente de tus pecados. Esto te enfrenta a la imperiosa necesidad de hacer una elección: enfocarte en tus defectos y fallas o regocijarte en mi glorioso don de la salvación. Si mantienes tu atención en mi sacrificio por tus pecados, vivirás con la conciencia gozosa de que eres maravillosamente amado. *No hay mayor Amor que el mío*, ¡y es tuyo para siempre! La mejor respuesta a tan insondable don es *amarme con todo tu corazón*.

Trágicamente, muchas personas piensan que yo tengo poco, o incluso nada, que perdonarles. Han sido engañadas por la mentira dominante de que no existe una verdad absoluta. Creen que el bien y el mal son términos relativos, por lo que no ven la necesidad de un Salvador. Estas personas que viven engañadas no buscan mi perdón, y sus pecados permanecen sin ser perdonados. Uno de los engaños que el maligno lleva a cabo es oscurecer sus mentes. Sin embargo, *yo soy la Luz del mundo*, y mi Luz puede brillar en sus vidas a través de ti. Debido a que tú eres mi seguidor, *nunca andarás en las tinieblas, sino que tendrás la Luz de la Vida.*

SALMOS 13.5, 6; JUAN 15.13; MATEO 22.37, 38; JUAN 8.12

Si andas en la Luz —viviendo cerca de mí— *mi sangre te limpiará continuamente de todo pecado.* Cuando seas consciente de tus pecados, quiero que los confieses y busques mi ayuda para hacer los cambios necesarios. No obstante, tu estatus conmigo no se basa en confesar tus pecados lo suficientemente rápido o en detalle. Lo único que te mantiene en una buena relación conmigo es *mi* perfecta justicia, que te di libre y permanentemente cuando te uniste a mi familia eterna. Dado que eres mío, vestido gloriosamente *con un manto de justicia,* te invito a venir con confianza a mi Presencia luminosa.

Andar a la Luz de mi Presencia te bendecirá de múltiples maneras. Las cosas buenas serán mejores y las cosas malas serán más soportables cuando las compartas conmigo. Al deleitarte en mi Amor-Luz, podrás amar a otros creyentes más plenamente y *tener compañerismo* con ellos. Habrá menos probabilidades de que tropieces y caigas, porque los pecados serán notoriamente obvios bajo mi santa Luz. *Regocíjate en mi Nombre a lo largo del día*, disfrutando de mi Presencia y *mi justicia*.

1 Juan 1.7; Isaías 61.10; Salmos 89.15, 16

Yo soy LA LUZ de lo alto que desciende sobre ti para dar luz a los que habitan en tinieblas. A veces tus circunstancias son tan difíciles y confusas que te sientes como si estuvieras rodeado de tinieblas. Tu mente ofrece varias soluciones a tus problemas, pero ya las has intentado todas sin éxito. Por eso, impotente y frustrado, te preocupas y te preguntas qué hacer. En momentos como esos, necesitas alzar la mirada y posarla en mi Luz que brilla sobre ti. Mírame con la confianza de un niño, descansando en mi Presencia. Deja por un tiempo de buscarles solución a tus problemas. *Quédate quieto, y reconoce que yo soy Dios.*

Mientras descansas en mi Presencia, recuerda que yo soy el *Príncipe de Paz*. Mientras más lleno estés de mí, más paciente serás. Aspira de mí en cada aliento. Después de descansar conmigo, háblame de tus problemas, confiando en que yo te puedo ayudar a resolverlos. Permanece cerca de mí, hijo mío y yo *guiaré tus pasos por la senda de la Paz.*

Lucas 1.78, 79; Salmos 46.10; Isaías 9.6

ALÉGRATE DE QUE TU NOMBRE está *escrito en el cielo*, en el libro de la Vida. Debido a que eres mío, tienes un Gozo que es independiente de las circunstancias. Haz recibido una Vida eterna que *nunca* nadie te quitará. *Los que son justificados* (mediante la fe en mí como su Salvador resucitado) *son también glorificados*. Hay un sentido muy real de encontrarte ya *sentado conmigo en las regiones celestiales*.

El Gozo es el derecho de nacimiento de todos los que me pertenecen. Este derecho puede coexistir con las circunstancias más difíciles y desgarradoras. Así que ven a mí cada mañana con las manos dispuestas y el corazón receptivo, diciendo: «Señor Jesús, recibo tu Gozo». Luego, espera conmigo mientras la Luz de mi Presencia brilla sobre ti, alcanzando hasta las más grandes profundidades de lo íntimo de tu ser. De esta manera te estoy fortaleciendo, preparándote para el día que tienes por delante.

Mientras avanzas en tu jornada, vuelve a mí por Gozo fresco todas las veces que lo creas necesario. Yo soy un Dios de abundancia ilimitada, por lo que siempre tengo más que suficiente para ti.

LUCAS 10.20; ROMANOS 8.30;
EFESIOS 2.6

Abril

«El Señor te bendiga y te guarde;
el Señor te mire con agrado y
te extienda su amor».

NÚMEROS 6.24, 25

Yo ME DELEITO en iluminar tu perspectiva. Es por eso que me aventuré en tu mundo, sabiendo claramente cuál sería el terrible precio que tendría que pagar. Vine *a abrir los ojos a los ciegos, a libertar a los presos de las cárceles y a liberar de las mazmorras a los que habitan en tinieblas.* Cuando te encuentres prisionero de la ingratitud, pídeme que abra tus ojos y te libere de ese lugar oscuro. Y lo haré.

Te ha correspondido vivir en una sociedad de derecho, por lo que necesitas contrarrestar los mensajes que te dicen que mereces más. Una forma es anotando algunas cosas por las que estás agradecido cada día. Esto cambiará tu enfoque de lo que te gustaría tener a las bendiciones que ya tienes.

Saturar tu mente con las Escrituras te puede ayudar a ver las cosas desde mi perspectiva infinitamente sabia. Mi Palabra *es más cortante que toda espada de doble filo.* La uso para llevar a cabo una cirugía espiritual en *los pensamientos y las intenciones de tu corazón.* En la medida que las Escrituras iluminen tu punto de vista, yo te sacaré de la mazmorra de la ingratitud, liberándote para que disfrutes de los placeres de un corazón agradecido.

ISAÍAS 42.7; SALMOS 119.105; HEBREOS 4.12

Abril 2

CREER EN MÍ TIENE muchos efectos beneficiosos... ¡incluyendo *el Gozo que es indescriptible y lleno de Gloria*! Si algo es inexpresable se debe a que resulta demasiado grande y maravilloso como para explicarlo. No obstante, aunque no se puede explicar, sí se puede experimentar. Ven a mi Presencia expectante; abre por completo tu corazón ante mí. El Gozo que puedes tener conmigo es triunfante y está lleno de la Gloria celestial. ¡Yo triunfé sobre el pecado y la muerte de una vez y para siempre! Esto abre el camino al cielo para todos los que creen en mí.

No importa cuántas dificultades tengas que enfrentar, *la victoria de tu fe —la salvación de tu alma—* está asegurada. Esto es así para todos los que realmente confían en mí como su Dios y Salvador. Al gozarte ante la perspectiva de tu futuro glorioso en el cielo, *deja que tu luz alumbre a otras personas*. Mi Espíritu, el Espíritu de verdad, te ayudará a hablar la verdad en la vida de otros. Alíate conmigo, porque *yo vine al mundo a dar testimonio de la verdad*. Únete a mí en esta búsqueda para que las *personas que viven en la oscuridad* me puedan encontrar y empezar a vivir en mi *gran Luz*.

1 PEDRO 1.8, 9; MATEO 5.16; JUAN 18.37;
ISAÍAS 9.2

MÍRAME, AMADO MÍO, porque *mi Rostro está brillando sobre ti.* Asómbrate ante la Gloria de mi santidad y deja que la Luz de mi Amor inunde lo íntimo de tu ser. Recuerda que *yo habito en tu corazón a través de la fe.* Soy, simultáneamente, el Señor del universo —que yo creé y controlo— y el Salvador que vive dentro de ti. Mi majestuosa grandeza y mi apacible humildad se combinan para darte todo lo que necesitas. ¡Tú eres rico más allá de tu más exagerada imaginación.

Debido a que vives en un mundo terriblemente quebrantado, puede resultarte difícil recordar que perteneces a la realeza; que has sido adoptado en la familia del *Rey de reyes.* Tu peregrinar por este mundo te puede llevar por caminos de dolor y problemas, por desiertos de privación y angustia. Sin embargo, no permitas que te sorprendan estas duras pruebas; más bien, tómalas con calma, confiando en el Único que nunca te abandonará. A su debido tiempo te llevaré al reino de mi Gloria-Luz donde *no habrá más noche.*

NÚMEROS 6.24, 25; EFESIOS 3.16, 17;
APOCALIPSIS 19.16; APOCALIPSIS 21.25

Abril 4

Tus tiempos están en mis manos. Mis santas manos son absolutamente capaces de cuidar de ti y satisfacer tus necesidades. Quiero que te relajes en mi cuidado soberano, confiando en que siempre haré lo mejor por ti. Debido a que soy totalmente confiable, puedes sentirte seguro de dejar a mi cuidado tanto los «qués» como los «cuándos» de tu vida.

Mientras permanezcas a este lado del cielo, tendrás que someterte a la realidad del tiempo. Piensa en los siguientes ejemplos: una novia para cuya boda se ha fijado la fecha puede anhelar que el tiempo pase rápido a fin de llegar cuanto antes a aquel feliz día. Sin embargo, su anhelo no cambia el ritmo de las horas, de modo que tendrá que esperar. Una persona que está sufriendo dolores puede anhelar el alivio y desear que sea inmediato, pero también debe esperar. No obstante, yo vivo por sobre la tiranía del tiempo; soy su Amo. Si estás luchando con la realidad de tener que esperar por algo, vuélvete a mí en confiada aceptación de los hechos. No luches contra lo que no puedes cambiar. En lugar de eso, regocíjate en el conocimiento de que el Amo del Tiempo entiende tus luchas y te ama *con un Amor eterno.*

SALMOS 31.14, 15; SALMOS 62.8;
JEREMÍAS 31.3

¡Quiero que saques agua *del pozo de la salvación con Gozo!* Saber que te he salvado para siempre de tus pecados puede ser una fuente de Gozo en tu vida diaria. Debido a que me conoces como tu Salvador, tienes dentro de ti *un manantial de agua que brota para vida eterna.* ¡Piensa en la enormidad de este regalo asombroso y alégrate! Trata de comenzar y terminar cada día agradeciéndome por todo lo que te he provisto.

Mi don de la salvación ha sido diseñado para bendecirte no solo a ti, sino a todos los que te rodean. Al confiar en mí, *corrientes de agua viva fluirán del interior de tu ser.* Pídele a mi Espíritu, que habita en tu interior, que bendiga a otros a través de ti, fluyendo hacia sus vidas. Una forma de hacer esta petición es orando: «Espíritu Santo, *piensa* a través de mí; vive a través de mí; ama a través de mí». Mientras sus corrientes de agua viva están pasando por medio de ti a los corazones de otras personas, ¡yo los llenaré a ellos *y* a ti con Gozo!

Isaías 12.3; Juan 4.13, 14;
Juan 7.38

Abril 6

AUN CUANDO EN OCASIONES pudieras tener la sensación de que caminas sin rumbo fijo, *tus pasos están siendo dirigidos por mí*. Cuando el camino que tienes por delante se vea oscurecido por la incertidumbre, lo mejor que puedes hacer es aferrarte a mí. Imagínate a un niño de corta edad caminando por una calle llena de gente en compañía de un adulto. El niño tal vez se sienta abrumado al pensar que podría perderse en medio de esa multitud. No obstante, si se mantiene agarrado de la mano del adulto, no se perderá, sino que llegará sano y salvo a su destino. Del mismo modo, si te aferras a mi mano asegurándote de mi ayuda y dirección, estarás a salvo.

Aunque quizás no conozcas el camino por donde tienes que ir, conoces al Único que es *el Camino*. Debido a que soy soberano sobre tu vida, *dirijo tus pasos y los hago seguros*, aunque te parezca que vas caminando al azar. Háblame sobre tus incertidumbres y tu temor por tomar alguna decisión equivocada. La elección más importante que debes hacer momento a momento es mantener la comunicación conmigo. De esa manera te mantendrás aferrado a mí. *Así* es como podrás confiar en mi Presencia guiadora para mantenerte a salvo.

PROVERBIOS 20.24; JUAN 14.6;
PROVERBIOS 16.9; 2 CORINTIOS 5.7

Yo te doy vida eterna, y no perecerás jamás, ni nadie te arrebatará de mi mano. Esta es una asombrosa buena noticia para todos los que me conocen como su Salvador. ¡La herencia que te he prometido es mucho más gloriosa que cualquier cosa que te pudieras imaginar! El don de la Vida eterna provee una Luz que brilla incluso en tus días más oscuros. Así que deja que este brillo te invite a seguir adelante, protegiéndote para que no te desanimes. No permitas que las circunstancias difíciles o la maldad de este mundo te depriman. En lugar de eso, mira hacia adelante a la Gloria que te espera. A la distancia, más allá del horizonte, la verás centelleando.

Es posible que en tu peregrinar por la vida tengas que pasar por aguas profundas. Cuando tal cosa ocurra, recuerda: *yo estaré contigo cuando pases a través de las aguas. Ellas no te arrasarán.* Mantente agarrado de mi mano en confiada dependencia, seguro de que te amo y que *nada podrá separarte de mí.* En lugar de tenerle miedo a los desafíos que pudieran esperarte más adelante, trata de disfrutar de la aventura de caminar conmigo a través de tu vida.

Juan 10.27, 28; 1 Pedro 1.3, 4; Isaías 43.2; Romanos 8.38, 39

Abril 8

DEBES ESTAR SIEMPRE PREPARADO para dar respuesta a todos los que te pregunten por la razón de tu esperanza. Es más fácil obedecer esta orden cuando te sientes bien descansado y tu vida está fluyendo sin problemas que cuando te encuentras agotado y decaído. Sin embargo, *este* puede ser el momento en que tu respuesta esperanzadora tenga el mayor impacto. Así que convierte en tu meta el estar *siempre* preparado. También necesitas estar listo para responder a *todo* el que te pregunte por la razón de tu optimismo. Es tentador juzgar a algunas personas como pobres candidatos para aprender sobre mí y lo que yo significo para ti. Sin embargo, solo *yo* conozco sus corazones y los planes que tengo para ellos.

Una preparación esencial para que des una buena respuesta es vivir con la seguridad de mi Presencia y confiando plenamente en mí como tu Esperanza. Esto te mantendrá firme cuando tengas que enfrentar los continuos altibajos de tu vida. Cada vez que te encuentres luchando, date ánimo meditando en las verdades del evangelio y mirándome a mí, tu gloriosa Esperanza.

1 PEDRO 3.15; ROMANOS 5.5; SALMOS 27.4

MANTENTE SIEMPRE DISPUESTO A SEGUIRME, mi amado. Entrégate más plenamente a mí y a mi propósito para ti. No te concentres solo en lo que quieres, pues te puedes perder las cosas que he preparado para ti. Relájate conmigo mientras *te transformo por la renovación de tu mente,* estableciendo lo nuevo de mí en lo íntimo de tu ser. Créeme lo suficiente como para dejar a un lado tus expectativas y demandas. *Quédate quieto, y reconoce que yo soy Dios.*

A veces obstruyes las cosas que deseas al intentar demasiado vehementemente hacer que todo vaya de acuerdo a tu voluntad y tiempo. Yo conozco los deseos de tu corazón, y también conozco la mejor manera de alcanzar esas metas. En lugar de esforzarte por tener el control para conseguir lo que quieres, *busca mi Rostro.* Háblame francamente y descansa en mi Presencia. Cuando te sientas más tranquilo, invítame a que te muestre el camino que tienes por adelante. *Yo te guiaré por el mejor camino para tu vida. Te ayudaré y velaré por ti.*

ROMANOS 12.2; SALMOS 46.10; 1 CRÓNICAS
16.11; SALMOS 32.8

Abril 10

*MI AMOR ES TAN GRANDE que alcanza hasta los cielos;
mi fidelidad se extiende por el firmamento.* Puedes sentir una maravillosa seguridad en este Amor que no
tiene fronteras ni límites. Mi fidelidad tampoco los
tiene.

Responde a estos regalos maravillosos adorándome. Mientras más me exaltes, más podrás *reflejar mi
Gloria* a otras personas. Esta es la obra del Espíritu,
que te está *transformando a mi semejanza con cada vez
mayor Gloria.* A medida que te acerques a mí a través de la adoración, te iré cambiando profundamente,
equipándote para que me des a conocer a los demás.

Mi Amor no solo alcanza hasta los cielos, sino
que desciende sobre ti desde las regiones celestiales.
No dejes de mantener tu mirada en mí, mi amado. Me
verás sonriéndote en radiante aprobación. Mi Amor
ilimitado cae continuamente sobre ti como copos de
nieve celestiales que se funden en tu rostro vuelto
hacia lo alto. No importa lo dolorosas que sean tus
circunstancias, este Amor es suficiente para sustentarte. Algún día vas a ascender al cielo en él. Yo espero
ansiosamente el momento cuando *te acoja en la Gloria...* ¡para que estés conmigo siempre!

SALMOS 57.9, 10; 2 CORINTIOS 3.18;
NÚMEROS 6.25, 26; SALMOS 73.23, 24

PROCURA PENSAR MIS PENSAMIENTOS más y más. Busca la ayuda de mi Espíritu en este esfuerzo, *porque la mente controlada por el Espíritu es Vida y Paz.*

Cuando las preocupaciones de este mundo te estén presionando, dedica un tiempo a reflexionar en mi Presencia. Descansa en mí, mi amado. Deja que mis *brazos eternos* te estrechen en Paz. Tómate un descanso de tus preocupaciones y *fija tus pensamientos* en mí. Combina la tranquilidad con la lectura de las Escrituras, hablarme y cantarme alabanzas. También puedes utilizar versículos de la Biblia en tus oraciones. Cuando tus pensamientos y oraciones se impregnen de las Escrituras, podrás tener más confianza en ellos.

Quiero que *seas transformado mediante la renovación de tu mente.* El mundo ejerce sobre ti cantidades masivas de presión a través de sus omnipresentes comunicaciones electrónicas. En lugar de dejar que el mundo y sus artilugios formen tu pensamiento, invítame para que yo transforme tu manera de pensar. Al renovar tu mente, tus ideales y actitudes me reflejarán cada vez más.

ROMANOS 8.6; DEUTERONOMIO 33.27;
HEBREOS 3.1; ROMANOS 12.2

Abril 12

TU RELACIÓN CONMIGO TRASCIENDE todas tus circunstancias. Es por eso que puedes alabarme y disfrutar de mi Presencia en medio de las dificultades más oscuras. Para encontrarte conmigo en tales momentos, tienes que ejercitar tu fe, pero yo estoy siempre cerca.

Como cristiano, vives en dos planos simultáneamente: el mundo natural, donde abundan las situaciones adversas; y el mundo sobrenatural, en el que reino de forma suprema. Los músculos de tu confianza te capacitan para experimentar mi Presencia aun en tus momentos más difíciles. En verdad, las pruebas pueden tanto fortalecer tu fe como ayudarte a discernir cuánto realmente confías en mí.

Quiero que trabajes en el fortalecimiento de tus músculos de la confianza. Una forma es llenando tu mente y corazón con las Escrituras. Otra es *buscando mi Rostro continuamente*. En lugar de quedarte atascado en la introspección, vuelve tus pensamientos hacia mí. Convierte esto en una práctica frecuente para afirmar tu fe en mí ya sea que te sientas seguro o inadecuado. Recuerda que tu adecuación descansa en tu relación conmigo. ¡Yo te *preparo para todo infundiéndote fuerza interior*!

SANTIAGO 1.2, 3; SALMOS 105.4;
FILIPENSES 4.13

TRATA DE INCLUIRME en más de tus momentos viviendo en una gozosa dependencia de mí. *Yo estoy contigo en constante vigilia.* Nada de lo que hagas escapa de mi vista. Ni un trabajo ni una oportunidad son demasiado pequeños para que no me pidas ayuda. En realidad, tu propia existencia, incluyendo cada aliento que exhalas, depende de mi Poder sustentador.

Cuando tienes por delante un trabajo difícil, usualmente recuerdas que debes orar al respecto, tanto antes de empezar como cuando ya estás en medio de ese reto desafiante. Interrumpes tu trabajo con breves oraciones, tales como: «Ayúdame, Señor» o «Gracias, Jesús». Estas comunicaciones aumentan tanto tu confianza en mí como tu gratitud por mi Presencia continua. Sin embargo, cuando te involucras en tareas menos desafiantes, a menudo te olvidas de mí y te lanzas adelante por tu propia cuenta. Es posible que experimentes algún grado de éxito, pero te pierdes de obtener una bendición mucho mayor que estaba a tu disposición si hubieses pedido mi ayuda. O puedes fracasar lamentablemente, mientras que si hubieses dependido de mí, te habría llevado al éxito. Es mejor que confíes en mí en *todo* lo que hagas. Tengo bendiciones esperándote.

GÉNESIS 28.15; HEBREOS 1.3; PROVERBIOS 3.6

Abril 14

YA NO ERES TU PROPIO DUEÑO, porque fuiste comprado por un precio. Y ese precio fue exorbitante: ¡mi propia Vida! Al sacrificarme por tus pecados, pasé por dolores y humillaciones insoportables. Este fue un regalo de un valor infinito, un acto de Amor indescriptible. Sin embargo, solo aquellos que reconocen su pecaminosidad y su necesidad de un Salvador pueden recibir este asombroso regalo de Amor. Escucha la invitación que hago: *«Vengan a mí todos los que están cansados y agobiados, y yo les daré descanso».* El pecado es una terrible carga que aplasta y agobia, pero yo he pagado el precio *completo* para quitarlo de ti para siempre.

Cuando te despiertes cada mañana, dite: «Yo no soy mío. Pertenezco a Jesús». Luego, mientras el día transcurre y especialmente cuando hagas planes o tomes decisiones, no olvides de quién eres. Saber que me perteneces te ayudará a mantenerte en *la senda de la Paz.* Este conocimiento satisface necesidades profundamente arraigadas. Puedes encontrar seguridad espiritual y emocional, recordando que *eres mío,* mi amado.

1 CORINTIOS 6.19, 20; MATEO 11.28;
LUCAS 1.76-79

Puedes confiar en el Único que murió por ti. En este mundo de impostores y estafadores resulta difícil creer en alguien. La gente habla de requerirles a otros que se «ganen» su confianza y se prueben a sí mismos. Yo soy la Persona por excelencia que se ha ganado el derecho a ser confiable. Por tu bien, dejé la gloriosa perfección del cielo y comencé a vivir en tu mundo como un niño desvalido que nació en un establo. Durante treinta y tres años resistí todas las tentaciones para que mi sacrificio por los pecadores fuera suficiente. Viví una vida perfecta y voluntariamente di mi cuerpo para que fuera torturado y ejecutado a fin de pagar el castigo completo por el pecado. Como resultado de mi muerte y resurrección, *¡todo el que cree en mí, tiene vida eterna.*

Quiero que te apoyes con confianza en mí, no solo como tu Salvador, sino también como el Dios-Amigo que no te deja solo. Ya te he demostrado cuán confiable soy. Ahora te invito a que te relajes en mi Presencia amorosa y a que confíes en mí. Háblame de tus esperanzas y temores. *Deposita toda tu ansiedad sobre mí, porque yo cuido de ti.*

2 Corintios 8.9; Juan 3.36;
1 Pedro 5.7

Abril 16

ESTE ES EL DÍA QUE YO HE HECHO. Te invito a regocijarte en este día compartiéndolo conmigo. Mientras más de mí tengas en tu vida, más feliz serás.

Invítame a participar de tus momentos contándome lo que sea que te esté preocupando, cualquiera cosa que ocupe tu mente. Tus conversaciones conmigo cambiarán radicalmente tu forma de pensar. Si has venido preocupándote por algo trivial, incluirme en tus pensamientos te ayudará a reconocer lo absurdo que es hacer tal cosa. Si estás atrapado en el pasado, deseando cambiar lo que ya sucedió, mi amorosa Presencia te traerá de nuevo al presente. Yo te puedo ayudar a manejar lo que sea que estés enfrentando.

Trata de encontrar el Gozo en este día que he hecho para ti. He escondido pequeños placeres a lo largo de tu jornada. Búscalos y dame las gracias por cada uno que encuentres. Muchas de las pequeñas cosas que hacen las delicias de tu corazón son exclusivas para ti. Te conozco tan íntimamente que puedo proporcionarte justo lo que necesitas para ser feliz. ¡*Regocíjate*, mi amado!

SALMOS 118.24; 1 TESALONICENSES 5.16-18;
SALMOS 139.1-3

Fija la mirada en mí con alegría. Fuiste *hecho* para el Gozo, y yo soy en tu vida la Fuente desbordante e ilimitada de deleite.

Nunca carezco de nada, porque soy infinito. Si extraes demasiado de otros placeres, terminarán decepcionándote. La naturaleza de la adicción implica que el adicto necesita más y más de una sustancia para obtener el mismo efecto que antes. Esta es una trampa autodestructiva. Sin embargo, mientras más te enfocas en *mí*, menos tendrás que depender de otras cosas. Puedes disfrutar de lo bueno que te proveo, pero no necesitas aferrarte a ello tratando de obtener cada posible sorbo de placer.

Aprende a fijar la mirada en mí incluso cuando el mundo desfile ante ti. Susurra mi nombre para recordarte que estoy cerca, y háblame de lo que te preocupa. Agradéceme por las cosas que disfrutas, mi amado: un techo seguro, comida, la luz y el calor del sol, el brillo de las estrellas, y *especialmente mi gloriosa Presencia*. Busca mi rostro y mi voluntad; *mírame a mí y a mi fuerza*.

Hebreos 12.2; Juan 15.11; 1 Timoteo 1.17; Salmos 105.4

Abril 18

AGRADÉCEME POR EL DON GLORIOSO del perdón. Yo soy tu Dios-Salvador, y el Único que podía darte esta bendición. Incurrí en un costo exorbitante para procurar este regalo para ti. *Al recibirme y creer en mi Nombre*, recibiste el perdón y llegaste a ser mi hijo. Este Nombre, Jesús, significa *el Señor salva*. Para recibir este don de la salvación necesitabas creer en mí como tu única Esperanza, Aquel que te podía liberar de todos tus pecados.

No hay condenación para los que están en mí. Quiero que disfrutes la maravilla de caminar a través de la vida como mi seguidor… ¡totalmente perdonado! La mejor retribución a este don maravilloso es vivir en gratitud, procurando complacerme por encima de todo lo demás. No necesitas hacer cosas buenas para asegurarte mi Amor, porque ya es tuyo. Simplemente deja que tu deseo de agradarme fluya libremente desde tu corazón agradecido. Darme las gracias con frecuencia te ayudará a permanecer cerca de mí, listo para seguirme a donde te dirija. Regocíjate, mi amado, *porque a través de mí la ley del Espíritu de Vida te ha hecho libre.*

JUAN 1.12; HECHOS 4.12;
ROMANOS 8.1, 2

Tú me amas porque yo te amé primero. Mis ojos estaban puestos en ti desde mucho antes de que estuvieras interesado en mí. Me he dado cuenta de todo lo que te ha ocurrido y te he seguido a todas partes. Orquesté circunstancias y acontecimientos en tu vida para ayudarte a ver tu necesidad de mí. He puesto a personas y enseñanzas en tu camino que te digan la verdad sobre mí de formas que puedas entender. Mi Espíritu ha trabajado dentro de ti para darle vida a tu espíritu, capacitándote para que *me recibas y creas en mi Nombre.* Todo esto ha sido un resultado de mi más profundo y poderoso afecto por ti. *¡Te he amado con un Amor eterno!*

Mientras más te des cuenta de la inmensidad de mi pasión por ti, más intensamente podrá ser tu amor por *mí.* Esto te permitirá ir creciendo, poco a poco, hasta llegar a ser la persona que tenía la intención que fueras. Al pasar tiempo en mi tierna Presencia, se te hará más fácil deleitarte en mí y mostrarles bondad a otras personas. Cuando estés con ellas, pídeme que te ayude a mostrarles amor. *¡Mi* Amor!

1 Juan 4.19; Juan 1.12; Jeremías 31.3

Abril 20

ESTE DÍA DE VIDA ES UN REGALO precioso que yo te he
dado. Trátalo como el tesoro que es, dándole prioridad a la oración. Al observar cómo el día se extiende
ante ti, *busca mi Presencia* para que te ayude a discernir lo que es más importante. Establece prioridades
de acuerdo a mi voluntad, y úsalas para que te guíen
a medida que el día avanza. Esta práctica te ayudará
a tomar buenas decisiones sobre el uso de tu tiempo
y energía. Al llegar al final del día, te podrás sentir en
paz con las cosas que pudiste hacer, y también con lo
que no alcanzaste a lograr.

Te animo a que me invites a participar en todo
lo que hagas. La breve oración: «¡Ayúdame, Señor!»
es suficiente para involucrarme en tus actividades.
Me alegro cuando veo que me buscas continuamente porque me necesitas. Y quiero que te alegres en tu
necesidad, porque es un fuerte vínculo con mi Presencia radiante. Aunque vivir de un modo dependiente resulta contracultural, es una manera de vivir
bendecida, regocijándote en la Gloria de mi Presencia.

SALMOS 118.24; 1 CRÓNICAS 16.10, 11;
JUAN 15.5; JUDAS v. 24

EL FUTURO DE LOS JUSTOS ES EL GOZO. Esto significa que tus perspectivas son excelentes, mi amado. Yo viví una vida de perfecta justicia y morí en tu lugar, soportando todo el castigo por tus pecados. Tal cosa hizo posible que te cubriera con mi propio *manto de justicia*. Te invito a que uses las *vestiduras de salvación* con desbordante gratitud y Gozo.

Una actitud gozosa y agradecida te ayudará a vivir de acuerdo a mi voluntad. Comenzar tu día con esta actitud mental positiva te pondrá en el camino correcto. El agradecimiento aumenta el Gozo, el cual a su vez aumenta tu gratitud. Hay una encantadora sinergia entre estas dos actitudes. Cuando tu habilidad para sentirte contento parezca estar disminuyendo, energízala con una abundante dosis de acción de gracias. Leer salmos te puede ayudar con esto, al igual que cantar himnos o canciones de alabanza. Hacer una lista —mental o en un papel— de las bendiciones en tu vida es otra manera efectiva de dar gracias. Quiero que recuerdes las *grandes cosas que he hecho para ti*; esto *te llenará de alegría*.

PROVERBIOS 10.28; ISAÍAS 61.10;
SALMOS 13.6; SALMOS 126.3

Abril 22

¡NO TE PREOCUPES POR EL MAÑANA! Este es el más misericordioso de los mandatos. Entiendo la fragilidad humana; sé que *eres de barro*. Este mandato no está destinado a agobiarte o condenarte, sino a hacerte libre de las preocupaciones mundanales.

Justo antes de que les diera esta instrucción a mis seguidores hablé sobre cómo disfrutar de tal libertad. Recuerda que *tu Padre celestial conoce tus necesidades*. Al *buscar primero su reino y su justicia*, tu perspectiva cambia. La búsqueda de cosas temporales pasa a un segundo plano con respecto a las realidades invisibles y eternas: el avance de mi reino. Así que dedica más tiempo y energía al desarrollo de tu relación conmigo, buscando no solo mi Presencia, sino también mi voluntad. Prepárate para seguirme a donde sea que te guíe. Te llevaré por rutas colmadas de aventuras que llenarán tu vida de sentido.

Te creé para que disfrutes de mi Presencia en el presente, dejando tu futuro a mi cuidado. *Al deleitarte en mí, yo te concederé los deseos de tu corazón.*

MATEO 6.32-34; SALMOS 103.14;
SALMOS 37.4

Yo soy AQUEL QUE VINO DEL PADRE, *lleno de gracia
y de verdad.* Vine de Él y regresé a Él, porque yo soy
Dios, la segunda Persona de la Trinidad.

Entré en tu mundo para proveerte la forma de
tener una relación viva y eterna con tu Padre-Dios.
Las personas que no me conocen dicen a menudo que
para llegar a Dios hay muchos caminos. Sin embargo, esta afirmación es absolutamente falsa: *yo soy el
Camino, la Verdad y la Vida. Nadie llega al Padre, sino
por mí.*

Vengo a *ti,* mi amado, *lleno de gracia.* Debido a
que has confiado en mí para la salvación de tus pecados mediante mi muerte sacrificial en la cruz, no tienes nada que temer. No es necesario que le temas al
fracaso o tengas expectativas por debajo de lo esperado. Puesto que soy tu Salvador —y tú no podrías
haberte salvado a ti mismo— tu seguridad descansa en mi gracia. Alégrate de que sea fiel y suficiente.
Frente a todas las vicisitudes de este mundo, *en mí
tendrás Paz. ¡Yo he vencido al mundo!*

JUAN 1.14; JUAN 14.6; JUAN 16.33

Abril 24

Yo soy un escudo para todos los que se refugian en mí.
Hay días en que sientes la necesidad de mi Presencia
protectora. En otras ocasiones ni siquiera estás consciente de que necesitas protección, pero yo estoy continuamente cerca de ti, observándote. Me complazco
en ser tu Protector, por lo que siempre podrás encontrar un refugio en mí.

Una de las mejores maneras de convertirme en
tu Refugio es pasando tiempo conectado conmigo y
abriéndome tu corazón. Cuéntame sobre las cosas que
te han herido: las cosas injustas que te han hecho o
han dicho de ti. Confía en mi preocupación y en mi
deseo de sanar tus heridas. Además, conozco la verdad acerca de todo; mi punto de vista está absolutamente libre de insinuaciones y medias verdades.

Algo vital para tu sanidad física, emocional o
espiritual es saber que yo te entiendo. También es fundamental para que perdones a los que te han causado
algún daño. El perdón es por lo general un proceso,
de modo que mantente perdonando hasta que sientas
que has vencido en lo que respecta a esto. Regocíjate
en mí, mi amado, porque yo vine para *hacerte libre.*

SALMOS 18.30; SALMOS 62.8; JUAN 8.32

Yo soy la Verdad. ¡La Verdad inmutable y trascendente! Muchas personas creen que la verdad es relativa, dependiendo de la situación, la persona, o el día. Sin embargo, solo la verdad absoluta puede proporcionar un fundamento firme para tu vida. Todo lo demás es arena movediza.

Debido a que soy la Verdad infalible, *todos los tesoros de la sabiduría y el conocimiento* están ocultos en mí. Puedes encontrar todo lo que necesitas en tu relación conmigo. Yo te proveo el fundamento sobre el cual puedes construir tu vida. Yo mismo *soy* la Vida. ¡Así que mientras más cerca vivas de mí, más vivo te sentirás!

Muchas personas luchan con problemas de identidad, preguntándose quiénes realmente son y qué se supone que deberían hacer con sus vidas. No obstante, mientras más plenamente me conozcas —la *Verdad*— mejor podrás entenderte a ti mismo y comprender el significado de tu vida. Así es que haz todo lo posible para conocerme como en verdad soy. También quiero que estés siempre *preparado* para hablarles a otros acerca del Dios-Salvador que te redimió y *te hizo libre.*

JUAN 14.6; COLOSENSES 2.2, 3;
1 PEDRO 3.15; JUAN 8.32

Abril 26

EN EL CIELO *NO HABRÁ NOCHE, porque la Gloria de Dios lo iluminará.* No necesitarás horas nocturnas para dormir, porque tu cuerpo glorificado estará siempre pleno de energía. El cansancio es una de las principales cosas que las personas tienen que enfrentar en este mundo, en especial a medida que envejecen o se enferman. Sin embargo, en el cielo no habrá fatiga y, por lo tanto, no habrá necesidad de dormir.

La Luz-Gloria de los cielos será perfecta y brillante, sin un ápice de oscuridad en ella. Allí no habrá pecado, de modo que no habrá nada que esconder. Verás todo a través de ojos glorificados, como nunca antes has visto. Los colores serán más vivos; los rostros serán más vibrantes. Podrás ver por completo mi Rostro. Tu experiencia será mucho mayor que la de Moisés, quien tuvo que ocultarse en la hendidura de una roca, mientras mi Gloria pasaba. A él solo se le permitió ver mis espaldas, pero tú no tendrás tales limitaciones. ¡En el cielo, *me verás cara a Cara,* en toda mi Gloria!

APOCALIPSIS 21.23, 25; 1 JUAN 1.5;
ÉXODO 33.22, 23; 1 CORINTIOS 13.12

Estás preocupado por el miedo al fracaso, pero mi Amor por ti nunca va a fallar. Déjame describir lo que veo cuando te contemplo, mi amado. Luces regio, porque te he revestido con mi justicia y *coronado con gloria y honra*. Te ves *radiante*, especialmente cuando estás mirándome. Eres hermoso al reflejar mi Gloria. ¡En realidad, me alegras tanto que *me deleito en ti con gritos de Gozo!* Así es como te veo a través de mi visión llena de gracia.

Debido a que soy infinito, te puedo ver simultáneamente como eres ahora y como serás cuando estés en el cielo. Al verte en el presente, trabajo contigo en las cosas que necesitas cambiar. Al verte desde la perspectiva del cielo, te amo como si ya fueses perfecto.

Quiero que aprendas a mirarte a ti mismo —y a otros— a través del lente de mi Amor inagotable. Mientras perseveras en esto, te irás dando cuenta poco a poco de lo fácil que es amarse uno a uno mismo *y* a los demás.

HEBREOS 2.7; SALMOS 34.5;
2 CORINTIOS 3.18; SOFONÍAS 3.17

Abril 28

CONFÍA EN MÍ EN TODO MOMENTO. Ábreme tu corazón, porque yo soy tu Refugio. Mientras más confíes en mí, más eficazmente te podré ayudar. Confiar en mí resulta apropiado sin importar la situación en la que estés: alegre o triste, tranquilo o inquieto. En realidad, las cosas que te provocan estrés pueden servirte como recordatorios para *buscar mi Rostro*. Quiero que recuerdes que yo estoy contigo, cuidando de ti, incluso cuando la vida se pone difícil. Háblame de tus problemas y déjamelos a mí. Luego descansa en mi Presencia mientras obro a tu favor.

Reafírmate la verdad sobre mí. Usa palabras de las Escrituras para describirme: *«Tú eres mi refugio y mi fortaleza, el Dios en quien confío».* Sin duda que soy un refugio: un lugar seguro donde encontrar protección en medio de las tormentas de la vida. Proclamar o cantar estas verdades es una manera muy eficaz de mantenerte cerca de mí. Por tu mente de manera habitual están pasando innumerables pensamientos o fragmentos de pensamientos. En lugar de solo pensar en mí, háblame en voz alta; esto te permite concentrar tus pensamientos y tu confianza en mí.

SALMOS 62.8; 1 CRÓNICAS 16.11;
1 PEDRO 5.7; SALMOS 91.2

Yo soy digno de toda tu confianza. Así que no dejes que los acontecimientos del mundo te asusten. En lugar de eso, usa tu energía para confiar en mí y buscar evidencias de mi Presencia en el mundo. Susurra mi Nombre a fin de reconectar sin demora tu corazón y tu mente a mí. *Yo estoy cerca de todo el que me invoca.* Deja que te envuelva en mi Presencia permanente y te conforte con mi Paz.

Recuerda que soy a la vez amoroso y fiel. *¡Mi Amor llega hasta los cielos y mi fidelidad alcanza las nubes!* Esto significa que nunca podrás encontrar el final de mi Amor. Mi Amor es ilimitado y eterno. Por otra parte, puedes pararte en la Roca de mi fidelidad sin importar las circunstancias por las que estés atravesando.

De forma rutinaria, la gente suele poner su confianza en sus habilidades, su educación, las riquezas o las apariencias. No obstante, tú debes depositar tu confianza plenamente en mí… ¡el Salvador cuya muerte sacrificial y resurrección milagrosa te abrieron el camino *a la Gloria eterna!*

Salmos 145.18; Salmos 36.5;
2 Corintios 4.17

Abril 30

DÉJAME SATISFACERTE POR LAS MAÑANAS con mi Amor inagotable, para que puedas cantar con Gozo y vivir feliz a lo largo de tus días. La gente busca satisfacción de una gran variedad de maneras dañinas, muchas de las cuales son adictivas. Incluso las cosas buenas pueden no satisfacerte si las pones por encima de mí. Así que ven a mí cada mañana con tu sensación de vacuidad y tus anhelos. Permanece quieto en mi Presencia, comunicándote conmigo. Invítame a llenar tu vida de mi Amor ilimitado hasta que se derrame. Piensa *cuán ancho y largo, alto y profundo* es este vasto océano de bendición.

Sentirte satisfecho en mí por sobre toda otra cosa provee un sólido fundamento para tu vida. Construir sobre este cimiento sólido te capacita para estar contento mientras tu vida se va desarrollando. Sin embargo, todavía encontrarás dificultades, ya que vives en un mundo quebrantado, pero yo amorosamente te guiaré a lo largo de tu caminar mientras te aferras a mí confiadamente. De esta manera, tu vida tendrá sentido y te proporcionará satisfacciones mientras te diriges hacia tu meta final: ¡las puertas de la Gloria!

SALMOS 90.14; EFESIOS 3.17-19;
SALMOS 73.24

Mayo

«Yo he venido para que tengan vida,
y la tengan en abundancia
[al máximo; hasta que
sobreabunde]».

JUAN 10.10

EL MOMENTO PRESENTE ES EL PUNTO en el cual el tiempo se cruza con la eternidad. También es el lugar donde te puedes encontrar *conmigo*, tu Salvador eterno. Por eso, hasta donde te sea posible, mantén tus pensamientos centrados en el presente, disfrutando de mi Presencia aquí y ahora.

Invítame a participar en todas tus actividades. Pídeme que te ayude a *hacer tu trabajo de buena gana*. Trabajando juntos, tú y yo podremos hacer que tu carga se aligere y te permita ser más eficaz. Comparte conmigo no solo tu trabajo, sino también tu tiempo libre, agradeciéndome por ambos. Cuando algo te perturbe, no dejes que el miedo o los pensamientos obsesivos controlen tu mente. En su lugar, háblame sobre lo que te está robando la paz. Luego, *echa toda tu ansiedad sobre mí*, sabiendo que *yo cuido de ti*.

Si me lo pides, abriré tus ojos y despertaré tu corazón para que puedas ver con más detalles todo lo que contiene el presente. Me deleito en reunirme contigo cuando tu corazón se mantiene alerta. *Yo vine al mundo para que tengas vida en abundancia, tanto, que llegue a desbordarse.*

COLOSENSES 3.23; 1 PEDRO 5.7;
JUAN 10.10

Mayo 2

CONFIAR EN MÍ es la alternativa para no caer en la desesperación ni escapar de la irrealidad. Es posible que cuando te encuentres en medio de la adversidad te sea difícil pensar claramente. Sin embargo, es ahí cuando resulta de vital importancia tomar decisiones sabias. A veces parece como si las decisiones se arremolinaran a nuestro alrededor, esperando que agarremos la primera que encontremos a mano. No obstante, hay *una* opción que es siempre apropiada y eficaz: la decisión de *confiar en mí con todo el corazón y con toda la mente.*

Si estás a punto de caer en las profundidades de la desesperación, detente y expresa tu confianza en mí. ¡Susúrralo, dilo en voz alta, grítalo a los cuatro vientos! Dedica tiempo a reflexionar sobre todas las razones que tienes para *confiar en mí.* Recuerda y gózate en mi Amor *infinito e inagotable.*

Si has estado adormeciendo tu dolor por medio de negar la realidad, expresar tu confianza te puede poner en contacto con la Realidad superior: ¡yo! Confía en mí, mi amado, porque yo lo sé todo. Entiendo cada situación en lo que respecta a tus circunstancias, *y te ayudaré.*

PROVERBIOS 3.5; SALMOS 52.8;
ISAÍAS 41.13

Es SOLO CUANDO TRABAJO que todo funciona realmente bien. Cuando lo que estás haciendo me agrada, me uno a ti para ayudarte. A veces eres consciente de mi Presencia que te fortalece, y otras veces no. Sin embargo, mientras más veces vengas a mí buscando orientación y ayuda, más bendiciones derramaré sobre ti. Algunas de las bendiciones están orientadas al trabajo; otras son asuntos del corazón. Estar consciente de mi Presencia aumenta tu sensación de seguridad y te llena de Gozo.

Te estoy entrenando para que me busques dondequiera que te encuentres o en cualquier situación que te halles. Habrá ocasiones en las que tendrás que mirar *a través* de tus circunstancias para encontrar señales de mi Presencia radiante. Imagínate mirando a través de una ventana sucia hacia un magnífico jardín bañado por el sol. Si enfocas tu mirada en la suciedad de los vidrios, no podrás admirar la belleza exquisita del jardín. Así como puedes entrenar tus ojos para que vean el esplendor más allá de la ventana, puedes aprender a mirar a través de tus circunstancias y «ver» *mi Rostro brillando sobre* ti. Búscame y me encontrarás en todas partes.

COLOSENSES 1.29; HECHOS 2.28;
NÚMEROS 6.24, 25

Mayo 4

CONOZCO CADA UNA DE TUS TRIBULACIONES. *He recogido todas tus lágrimas y las he registrado en mi libro.* Así que no tengas miedo de llorar, o de las dificultades que provocan tus lágrimas. Tus problemas no son fortuitos o carecen de sentido. Te estoy convocando para que no solo confíes en mí, sino para que también tengas en cuenta mi soberanía. ¡Yo sé lo que estoy haciendo!

Debido a que mi perspectiva es infinita —ilimitada en cuanto a tiempo o espacio— las formas en que actúo en el mundo están a menudo más allá de tu comprensión. Si pudieras ver las cosas desde mi perspectiva como Dios, entenderías la perfección de mi voluntad revelada en mi Gloria. No obstante, por ahora solo *ves un pobre reflejo*, por lo que tienes que aprender a vivir con el misterio.

He recogido tus lágrimas en mi redoma porque eres extremadamente valioso para mí. Y llegará el día en que *enjugaré toda lágrima de tus ojos. No habrá más muerte, ni llanto, ni clamor, ni dolor.* ¡Regocíjate en este futuro celestial y glorioso que te espera!

SALMOS 56.8; 1 CORINTIOS 13.12;
APOCALIPSIS 21.4

QUIERO QUE MANTENGAS una actitud de agradecimiento. Este es el lugar más encantador, donde el Gozo de mi Presencia brilla calurosamente sobre ti.

A menudo oras fervientemente por algo hasta que recibes la respuesta que deseabas. Cuando te concedo tu petición, respondes con Gozo y gratitud. Sin embargo, tu tendencia es seguir adelante rápidamente al próximo asunto. Quiero que permanezcas por un tiempo mostrando una actitud de Gozo agradecido. En lugar de experimentar solo una breve explosión de gratitud, deja que este placer fluya libremente hacia tu futuro, adiestrándote para recordar lo que he hecho. Una forma de hacerlo es contándoselo a otros. Esto bendice tanto a los demás como a ti, a la vez que me pone muy contento a mí. Otra forma es escribiendo la oración-respuesta y colocándola en un lugar donde la puedas ver una y otra vez.

Mantente expresándome tu gratitud. Este agradecimiento te bendecirá doblemente: con recuerdos felices de las oraciones contestadas y con el placer de compartir tu Gozo conmigo.

SALMOS 95.2; 1 CORINTIOS 15.57;
1 CRÓNICAS 16.12

Mayo 6

ESTO ES LO QUE TE DIGO: *yo fui quien te hizo, te for-mó en el seno materno y te ayudará. No tengas mie-do.* Siempre he estado involucrado en tu vida, incluso antes de que nacieras. Debido a que eres mío, com-prado con mi propia sangre, puedes contar con mi promesa de ayudarte mientras vas viviendo en este mundo. Obtienes la victoria sobre el miedo confiando en mi *ayuda segura.*

El problema surge cuando miras demasiado tiem-po hacia el futuro, tratando de visualizar y controlar lo que todavía está por ocurrir. Persistir en mirar al futuro puede fácilmente convertirse en un problema de enfoque. Las malas hierbas de la preocupación y el miedo surgen rápidamente en este tipo de «suelo». Cuando te des cuenta de que esto está sucediendo, alé-jate de tus preocupaciones y vuélvete al Único que está amorosamente presente contigo. Alégrate de que *aún* estaré contigo cuando llegues a cada etapa del cami-no. Apóyate firme en mi Presencia, confiando en que puedo ayudarte hoy, *y todos los días de tu vida.*

ISAÍAS 44.2; SALMOS 46.1;
SALMOS 23.6

133

Tú ERES UN HIJO DE DIOS. El día llegará en que *me veas tal como soy.* Estarás cara a Cara conmigo en la Gloria. Hasta ese momento, te estoy preparando para *hacerte nuevo en la actitud de tu mente y ponerte el ropaje de tu nueva naturaleza.* Aunque tu nueva naturaleza está siendo conformada a mi imagen, este proceso no borra la esencia de quién eres. En lugar de eso, mientras más te *asemejes* a mí, más te desarrollarás como la persona exclusiva que diseñé que fueras.

Tú has sido un miembro de mi familia real desde el día en que confiaste en mí como tu Salvador. Por lo tanto, eres un *coheredero conmigo, compartiendo mi herencia.* Sin embargo, también *deberás compartir mi sufrimiento si vas a compartir mi Gloria.* Cuando enfrentes tiempos difíciles, búscame en medio de tus luchas. Pídeme que te ayude a soportar el sufrimiento en una manera digna de la familia del Rey. Todo lo que soportes te ayudará a ser más como yo. Recuerda el objetivo final: *¡Ver mi rostro en justicia, y sentirte satisfecho!*

1 JUAN 3.2; EFESIOS 4.23, 24;
ROMANOS 8.17; SALMOS 17.15

134

Yo TE HE RESCATADO DEL SEPULCRO; *te he coronado con Amor y compasión; te he colmado de bondad y estoy renovando tu juventud.*

Te he dado estos magníficos regalos porque *me gozo en ti.* Deja que mi deleite llegue hasta lo más profundo de tu ser, satisfaciendo tu alma. Aunque conozco tus pecados y defectos, mi Amor perfecto nunca flaquea. Ante todo, te veo como mi redimido, que lleva *una corona del paraíso y va envuelto en belleza eterna.*

Quiero que tu identidad como mi amado esté en el frente y el centro de tu mente, a pesar de que a menudo tus pensamientos se atascan en asuntos triviales, sobre todo cuando tu mente está desenfocada. Es por esto que te aconsejo que *permanezcas siempre alerta y perseveres en la oración.* Invítame a participar de tus circunstancias, incluyendo tus pensamientos, sentimientos y decisiones. Mantenerte comunicado conmigo te ayudará a centrarte menos en lo trivial y más en las realidades gloriosas. Mientras esperas en mi Presencia, *renovaré tus fuerzas.* ¡Independientemente de la edad que tienes, *siempre serás joven en mi Presencia!*

SALMOS 103.4, 5; SALMOS 149.4;
EFESIOS 6.18; ISAÍAS 40.31

Yo TE BUSCO EN EL LUGAR de tu necesidad más profunda. Así que ven a mí tal como estás, dejando atrás pretensiones y comportamientos. Eres totalmente transparente para mí. Sé todo sobre ti. Sin embargo, debido a que eres mío —redimido con mi sangre— siento por ti un Amor ilimitado e inacabable.

Pídele a mi Espíritu que te ayude a ser honesto y franco conmigo. No te avergüences de tus necesidades; más bien, úsalas para conectarte conmigo en humilde dependencia. Invítame a ser parte de tu vida. Recuerda que *yo soy el Alfarero y tú eres el barro*. La debilidad que me entregas es maleable en mis manos, y la uso para moldearte de acuerdo a mi voluntad.

Tu necesidad más profunda es *apoyarte en mí, creerme y confiar en mí*. Aceptar tu falta de fuerza te ayuda a apoyarte en mí, demostrando una dependencia no vergonzosa. Te estoy preparando para que confíes en mí —*con todo tu corazón y toda tu mente*— en un esfuerzo de toda la vida. Y la mejor manera de *no sentir miedo* es tener confianza en mí, *tu Fuerza*.

1 PEDRO 1.18, 19; ISAÍAS 64.8;
PROVERBIOS 3.5; ISAÍAS 12.2

Mayo 10

Tus DECISIONES SON IMPORTANTES, mi amado. Son una parte vital de mi obra transformadora en ti. Tú haces la mayor parte de tus decisiones solo, en la soledad de tu corazón y tu mente. Sin embargo, recuerda algo: ¡yo soy *Cristo en ti!* Conozco cada pensamiento antes de que lo pienses, cada decisión antes de que la lleves a cabo. Tu aceptación de que estoy al tanto de todo lo que ocurre dentro de ti puede protegerte de una vida descuidada y egoísta. Deja que tu deseo *me complazca*, al Único que te conoce tan íntimamente y cambia tu forma de pensar y vivir.

Es posible que hayas pensado que la mayor parte de tus decisiones resultan insignificantes, pero esto no es cierto. Una buena decisión que hagas hoy, por pequeña que sea, puede colocarte en una posición en la que lograrás algo muy importante. Una mala decisión, aparentemente sin importancia, puede conducirte a serios fracasos o pérdidas en el futuro. Aunque tus decisiones sin duda importan, recuerda que *no hay condenación para los que me pertenecen*. Yo soy capaz de ver todos tus defectos y fracasos, pero al mismo tiempo amarte con un *Amor glorioso e inagotable*.

COLOSENSES 1.27; 1 TESALONICENSES 4.1;
ROMANOS 8.1, 2; SALMOS 13.5

Soy tu Hermano y tu Amigo. Soy *el Primogénito entre muchos hermanos;* y tú estás *siendo conformado a mi imagen.* ¡Este es un privilegio sorprendente y una bendición! Algunos niños son bendecidos al tener un hermano mayor fuerte y cariñoso que los ayuda y protege. Tú tienes un Gran Hermano todopoderoso que está constantemente velando por tus intereses. Ni el más comprometido miembro de la familia o amigo puede estar contigo siempre, pero yo jamás me separo de tu lado. Yo soy el *Amigo más fiel que un hermano.*

Mi continua Presencia contigo nunca debería ser subestimada. Recuerda que tu fiel Amigo es también *Rey de reyes.* Si pudieras vislumbrarme en toda mi Gloria, entenderías por qué *Juan cayó a mis pies como muerto* cuando me vio. *¡Yo soy el Primero y el Último, el que estuvo muerto y vive por los siglos de los siglos!* Quiero que te relaciones conmigo con reverencia, pues yo soy tu Dios-Salvador. Recuerda que el glorioso don de la salvación es tuyo para siempre. Hónrame con gratitud.

Romanos 8.29; Proverbios 18.24;
Apocalipsis 17.14; Apocalipsis 1.17, 18

Mayo 12

ALÁBAME POR LA AYUDA de mi Presencia. En todo momento y toda circunstancia, es conveniente que ores: «Gracias, Jesús, por estar *conmigo* aquí y ahora». Es posible que no sientas mi Presencia, pero yo la he prometido… ¡y eso es suficiente!

Una parte importante de tu asignación como cristiano es confiar en que *yo estoy contigo siempre*. Con fe, háblame de tus pensamientos y sentimientos, de tus luchas y placeres. Cree que me preocupo por ti y escucho todas tus oraciones. Busca mi ayuda con confiada expectación. Mantente atento para ver todas las formas en que obro en ti y por medio de tu vida. Alégrate por el hecho de que tú y yo, juntos, podemos *hacer muchísimo más que todo lo que podrías pedir o imaginar. Mi Poder está trabajando dentro de ti*, sobre todo al conectarse con tu debilidad, ofrecida a mí para que se cumplan mis propósitos.

Recuerda que *nada es imposible para mí*. No te dejes intimidar por las circunstancias desalentadoras. ¡Alábame por la ayuda de mi Presencia!

SALMOS 42.5; MATEO 28.20;
EFESIOS 3.20; LUCAS 1.37

Deja de juzgar por las apariencias, y haz un juicio justo. Hice esta declaración en el templo de Jerusalén, enseñando que juzgar puede ser bueno pero también es posible que resulte malo. Estaba hablándoles a ciertas personas que me habían evaluado sobre la base de las apariencias: centrándose en la letra de la Ley más que en el espíritu de la Ley. Lo que hacían estaba mal, pero eso no significa que *todos* los juicios estén equivocados. Yo prohíbo las evaluaciones superficiales, autosuficientes e hipócritas. No obstante, sí quiero que mis seguidores hagan evaluaciones *justas* sobre la moral y los asuntos teológicos, basadas en la verdad bíblica.

En esta era de «tolerancia», existe una enorme presión sobre la gente para que se abstenga de hacer declaraciones que diferencien el bien del mal. El temor a ser catalogado como «intolerante» ha silenciado a muchas personas que saben hacer juicios justos. Quiero que tengas el valor de *decir la verdad con amor* mientras te guío a hacerlo. La mejor preparación es examinar las Escrituras y tu corazón. Luego, pídele a mi Espíritu que hable a través de ti y ame a los demás por medio de tu amor hacia ellos.

Juan 7.24; Mateo 7.1;
Efesios 4.15

Mayo 14

YO PUEDO EVITAR QUE TE CAIGAS. Sé lo débil que eres y cuán fácilmente pierdes el equilibrio si yo no estuviera allí para sostenerte. Estás *creciendo en la gracia,* pero la libertad completa del pecado no será posible mientras estés viviendo en este mundo caído. Por eso, necesitas mi ayuda continuamente.

Yo puedo *establecerte impecable* —irreprochable, perfecto, sin mancha— *ante la Presencia de mi Gloria,* porque *te he vestido con ropas de salvación y te he ataviado con el manto de justicia.* Quiero que lleves estas vestiduras reales con toda confianza. Tienes todo el derecho, ya que es mi justicia la que te salva, no la tuya.

El *Gozo inmenso* es para ti y para mí. Me deleito en ti ahora, pero este Gozo será inmensamente mayor cuando te unas a mí en la Gloria. El júbilo que experimentarás en el cielo no se puede describir; está mucho más allá que cualquier placer que hayas podido conocer en este mundo. ¡Nada puede robarte esta gloriosa *herencia indestructible, incontaminada e inmarchitable!*

JUDAS VV. 24, 25; 2 PEDRO 3.18;
ISAÍAS 61.10; 1 PEDRO 1.3, 4

MIENTRAS ME BUSCAS, te animo a que te *alegres y te regocijes en mí*. Tómate tu tiempo para alabarme con salmos y cánticos. Piensa en quién soy: yo habito en *esplendor, majestad y belleza*. Luego, recuerda cómo dejé la Gloria del cielo y vine al mundo para llevarte a mi reino de Vida eterna y Luz. Todo esto te ayudará a *gozarte en mí, tu Salvador*. Este Gozo te adentra más en mi santa Presencia, ayudándote a acercarte más a mí. ¡Y esta cercanía te da más motivos aún para alegrarte!

Ser una persona alegre te bendice no solo a ti, sino también a otros. Tu familia y tus amigos se beneficiarán de tu alegría, que puede contagiárseles a ellos. También podrás influir a muchos más allá de tu círculo íntimo. Cuando mis seguidores están alegres, hay más posibilidades de atraer a los incrédulos a mí. El Gozo brilla en marcado contraste con tu mundo cada vez más oscuro, y habrá quienes querrán saber más de ese Gozo. *Mantente siempre preparado para dar una respuesta a todos los que te pregunten por la razón de tu esperanza.*

SALMOS 70.4; SALMOS 96.6; HABACUC 3.18; 1 PEDRO 3.15

Mayo 16

CUANDO AL COMENZAR EL DÍA o iniciar un trabajo te sientas con poco ánimo, recuerda esto: *mi gracia es suficiente para ti.* El tiempo presente del verbo «ser» destaca la continua disponibilidad de mi gracia maravillosa. Así que no gastes energía lamentándote por lo débil que te sientes. En lugar de eso, abraza tu insuficiencia, alegrándote de que te ayude a darte cuenta de cuánto me necesitas. Ven a mí en busca de ayuda, y deléitate en mi infinita suficiencia. *Mi Poder se perfecciona en la debilidad.*

A medida que avanzas en alguna tarea mostrando una gozosa dependencia de mí, te sorprenderás al ver cuánto puedes realizar. Además, la calidad de tu trabajo será mejor en gran medida por medio de tu colaboración conmigo. Piensa en el asombroso privilegio de vivir y trabajar a mi lado, el *Rey de reyes y Señor de señores.* Trata de alinearte con mi voluntad, haciendo de ti mismo un *sacrificio vivo.* Esta es una forma de adoración que me complace. También hace que tu vida tenga sentido y sea alegre. ¡Es un pequeño anticipo del Gozo inmenso, glorioso e indescriptible que te espera en el cielo!

2 CORINTIOS 12.9; APOCALIPSIS 19.16;
ROMANOS 12.1; JUDAS V. 24

ENCOMIÉNDAME TUS PREOCUPACIONES, y yo te sosten-dré. Llevar tus propias cargas tú te produce desgaste. Tus hombros no fueron diseñados para soportar tanto peso; por eso quiero que aprendas a depositar tus cargas sobre mí. El primer paso es reconocer que algo te está agobiando. El segundo es examinar la dificultad para determinar si es tuya o de alguna otra persona. Si no es tuya, simplemente despreocúpate. Si es tuya, háblame sobre el problema, y yo te ayudaré a verlo desde mi perspectiva y te mostraré el camino que deberás seguir.

Mantente preparado para entrar en acción si es necesario, pero no dejes que los problemas te agobien al convertirse en tu enfoque central. ¡Leva a cabo un esfuerzo coordinado para depositar tus preocupaciones sobre mí, porque yo tengo hombros poderosos! Después, simplemente haz lo que sigue en gozosa dependencia de mí.

Anímate por mi promesa de sustentarte y pro-veerte lo que necesitas. *Yo supliré todas tus necesidades de acuerdo con mis riquezas en la Gloria.*

SALMOS 55.22; ISAÍAS 9.6;
FILIPENSES 4.19

Mayo 18

PARA AUMENTAR TU CONCIENCIA de mi Presencia, necesitas aprender el arte de olvidarte de ti mismo. No fuiste diseñado para la autocontemplación. Tristemente, la desobediencia de Adán y Eva en el Jardín del Edén hizo del egoísmo la tendencia natural de la raza humana. Esto es una trampa mortal, por lo cual te he provisto de los medios para que *vivas sobrenaturalmente*. Desde el momento en que me pediste que fuera tu Salvador, has tenido mi Espíritu viviendo en ti. Pídele a este Santo Ayudador que te libere de cualquiera forma de egocentrismo. Puedes orar tan a menudo como lo desees o necesites: «Ayúdame, Espíritu Santo».

Una cosa que nos atrapa en el ensimismamiento es preocuparnos demasiado acerca de cómo lucimos frente al espejo o ante los ojos de los demás. En lugar de convertirte en el objeto de tus pensamientos, mírame a mí y sé atento con las personas que te rodean. Pídele a mi Espíritu que te ayude a mirar más allá de ti mismo con ojos que realmente vean. Estás seguro en mis *brazos siempre* y completo en mi amorosa Presencia. Así que preocúpate de confiar en mí y demostrarme tu amor.

GÉNESIS 3.6, 7; ROMANOS 8.9; JUAN 15.26;
DEUTERONOMIO 33.27

BÚSCAME EN LOS LUGARES difíciles de tu vida. Me puedes encontrar en las oraciones contestadas, en la belleza y la sinceridad del Gozo. Sin embargo, también estoy tiernamente presente en las dificultades. En realidad, tus problemas son un suelo fértil para que crezca en ellos la gracia y encuentres mi amorosa Presencia con mayor profundidad y amplitud. Búscame en los tiempos oscuros, tanto pasados como presentes. Si te atormentan los recuerdos dolorosos y las experiencias hirientes, búscame en ellos. Yo los conozco todos y estoy listo para encontrarme allí contigo. Invítame a esos lugares quebrantados, y coopera conmigo para poner los pedazos una vez más juntos de maneras nuevas.

Si en el presente estás atravesando tiempos difíciles, recuerda que no debes soltarte de mi mano. Contra el oscuro telón de fondo de la adversidad, la *Luz de mi Presencia* brilla con luminosidad trascendente. Esta Luz te bendice abundantemente, proveyéndote tanto tranquilidad como orientación. Yo te mostraré paso a paso el camino que tienes por delante. Al caminar cerca de mí te atraeré a una intimidad más profunda y valiosa.

SALMOS 139.11, 12; JUAN 1.5;
SALMOS 73.23, 24

Mayo 20

Yo soy la Puerta; el que por mí entre, será salvo. Yo no soy una barrera bloqueada, sino una puerta abierta para ti y todos mis seguidores escogidos. Vine al mundo para que *tengas Vida y la tengas en abundancia.*

Una vida plena tiene significados diferentes para diferentes personas. Así que en tu búsqueda para vivir una vida abundante no compares tus circunstancias con las de otros. Tú no necesitas tener tanto dinero o muchos lujos como tu vecino a fin de vivir bien.

La piedad con contentamiento es gran ganancia. Quiero que te sientas satisfecho con mi provisión para ti. *Si tienes alimento y ropa* —las necesidades básicas de la vida— *siéntete contento con eso.* Si te doy más, responde con Gozo y agradecimiento. Sin embargo, no te aferres a lo que tienes o codicies lo que no posees. A lo único que puedes aferrarte sin dañar tu alma es a *mí.* No importa lo que poseas en este mundo, recuerda: ¡poco (o mucho) más Yo es igual a todo!

JUAN 10.9, 10; 1 TIMOTEO 6.6-8;
SALMOS 63.8; JUAN 3.16

ATESÓRAME POR ENCIMA de todo. Esto infundirá Gozo en tu corazón y tu mente. ¡También me glorificará! Atesorar algo es conservarlo, estimándolo como algo precioso. Yo te estoy preparando para que te aferres fuertemente a mí, tu Dios-Salvador y Compañero constante. Saber que nunca me separaré de tu lado puede aumentar tu Gozo y Paz inconmensurablemente. Además, estimarme como tu precioso Salvador fortalece tu deseo de mantenerme «en la mira» y vivir de acuerdo a mi voluntad.

Cuando me aprecias por sobre todo lo demás, las otras cosas pierden prioridad. Una forma de discernir lo que más aprecias es examinando tus pensamientos cuando tu mente está en reposo. Si no te gusta lo que encuentras, no te desesperes. Eso te puede enseñar a pensar en mí de una forma más constante. Es útil memorizar versículos de la Biblia, especialmente los que te acercan más a mí. Trata de colocar recordatorios de mi Presencia amorosa por toda tu casa y el lugar de trabajo. Y recuerda enrolar a mi Espíritu para que te ayude. Él se complace en hacerte regresar a mí.

MATEO 13.44; FILIPENSES 3.8, 9;
JUAN 14.26; JUAN 16.14

Mayo 22

QUIERO QUE CONOZCAS LA PROFUNDIDAD y la amplitud de *mi Amor que sobrepasa todo conocimiento*. Hay una enorme diferencia entre conocerme y saber acerca de mí. Del mismo modo, experimentar mi amorosa Presencia es muy diferente a conocer hechos sobre mi carácter. A fin de experimentar mi Presencia, necesitas la obra fortalecedora de mi Espíritu. Pídele que *te fortalezca con Poder en lo interior de tu ser*, de modo que puedas *conocer mi Amo*r en toda su extensión.

Desde el momento de tu salvación, he estado vivo en tu corazón. Mientras más espacio haces para mí allí, más te puedo llenar con mi Amor. Hay varias formas de ampliar este espacio en tu corazón. Es fundamental que pases tiempo conmigo, disfrutando de mi Presencia y estudiando mi Palabra. También resulta vital mantenerte comunicado conmigo. Como escribió el apóstol Pablo, *ora sin cesar*. Esta excelente práctica te mantendrá cerca de mí. Por último, deja que mi amor fluya hacia los demás a través de ti, tanto en palabras como en acciones. *Esto hará que mi amor en ti sea pleno.*

EFESIOS 3.16-19; HECHOS 4.12;
1 TESALONICENSES 5.17; 1 JUAN 4.11, 12

CUANDO EL CAMINO DELANTE de ti te parezca demasiado difícil, vuélvete a mí y dime: «Yo solo no puedo, pero *nosotros* (tú y yo juntos) *sí podremos*». Reconocer tu incapacidad para manejar las cosas por tu cuenta implica una dosis saludable de realidad. Sin embargo, esta es solo una parte de la ecuación, porque un sentido de ineptitud por sí mismo puede resultar paralizante. La parte más importante de la ecuación es reconocer mi Presencia permanente contigo y mi deseo de ayudarte.

Ábreme tu corazón. Pídeme que lleve tus cargas y te muestre el camino que tienes por delante. No malgastes tu energía preocupándote por cosas que están fuera de tu control. En lugar de eso, usa esa energía para conectarte conmigo. *Busca mi rostro continuamente.* Mantente listo para seguirme adondequiera que te lleve confiando en que yo te iré abriendo camino.

Atrévete a ver tu incapacidad como una puerta a mi Presencia. Considera tu caminar como una aventura en la que quieres que yo participe. Mantén la comunicación, disfrutando de mi compañía a medida que vamos caminando juntos.

FILIPENSES 4.13; SALMOS 62.8;
SALMOS 105.4

Mayo 24

HAY PAZ Y PLENITUD DE GOZO en mi amorosa Presencia. Búscame a medida que avanzas a través de este día. Yo estoy deseoso de que me encuentres. Nunca te pierdo de vista. Te cuido continuamente. Sin embargo, hay muchas formas en que tú puedes perderme de vista. La mayoría de ellas constituyen simplemente distracciones temporales, las cuales abundan en el mundo. El remedio es simple: ¡no te olvides de que yo estoy contigo!

Un problema mucho más serio es que abandones tu *Primer Amor*. Si te das cuenta de que esto ha sucedido, arrepiéntete y corre de nuevo a mí. Confiesa qué ídolos te han alejado de mí. Tómate tu tiempo para recibir mi perdón con acción de gracias. Colabora conmigo en el reordenamiento de tus prioridades, poniéndome primero en tu vida. Al pasar tiempo en mi Presencia, piensa en quién soy: el Rey del universo, la *Luz del mundo*. Disfruta en esta *Luz de la Vida*, para que puedas reflejarme a otros. Mientras permaneces deleitándote en mí, te llenaré de *Amor, Alegría y Paz*.

SALMOS 121.8; APOCALIPSIS 2.4; JUAN 8.12;
GÁLATAS 5.22, 23

AGRADÉCEME POR TODOS LOS desafíos en tu vida. Son regalos que te hago, oportunidades para crecer más fuerte y dependiente de mí. La mayoría de las personas piensa que mientras más fuertes se vuelven, menos dependientes serán. Sin embargo, en *mi* reino, la fuerza y la dependencia van de la mano. Esto se debe a que fuiste diseñado para caminar cerca de mí mientras vas por la vida. Las circunstancias difíciles hacen resaltar tu necesidad y te ayudan a confiar en mi suficiencia infinita.

Cuando las circunstancias se vuelven difíciles y las enfrentas confiando en mí, eres bendecido. Resulta vivificante atravesar aquellos retos que pensabas que eran demasiado grandes para ti. Cuando lo haces dependiendo de mí, nuestra relación se torna más fuerte.

Tu éxito en el manejo de las dificultades también aumenta tu sentido de seguridad. Ganas confianza de que tú y yo, *juntos*, podemos hacerle frente a cualquier tiempo difícil que el futuro pudiera traer. *Estás listo para lo que sea a través del Único que infunde fuerza interior en ti.* ¡Alégrate en mi suficiencia!

SANTIAGO 1.2; SALMOS 31.14-16;
FILIPENSES 4.13

Yo soy DIOS, TU ALEGRÍA Y TU DELEITE. Quiero que encuentres placer en mí y mi Palabra. Yo soy el Verbo siempre viviente: *en el principio* y para siempre. Por eso me puedes encontrar abundantemente en mi Palabra escrita, la Biblia. Mientras más y más interiorizas las Escrituras, experimentarás el deleite de mi Presencia de una forma cada vez más constante. Dedica un tiempo a meditar en los pasajes de la Biblia y memorizar algunos de ellos. Te ayudarán a superar las noches de insomnio y a salir victorioso de tus encuentros con la adversidad.

Saber que yo soy *tu alegría* puede evitar que te lamentes por tus circunstancias o que envidies a otros cuya situación pareciera mejor que la tuya. Debido a que no te dejo ni por un momento, tienes en tu vida una fuente de Gozo siempre presente. Encontrarás placer en mí a través de *regocijarte en mi Nombre todo el día*. Simplemente pronunciar «Jesús» como una oración puede levantarte el ánimo. Una excelente manera de *deleitarte en mí es regocijándote en mi justicia*, la cual te he otorgado amorosamente. ¡Este *manto de justicia* te cubrirá perfectamente y para siempre!

SALMOS 43.4; JUAN 1.1; SALMOS 89.16;
ISAÍAS 61.10

Mi reino no es de este mundo; es indestructible y eterno. Cuando observes a tu alrededor el mal impactante y los abusos de autoridad, no te desesperes. Poco antes que me detuvieran en Getsemaní, les dije a mis discípulos que *si hubiese querido, le habría pedido a mi Padre que mandara a doce legiones de ángeles* para que me rescataran. Sin embargo, ese no era el plan que habíamos elegido. Resultaba necesario que fuera crucificado para salvar *a todo el que invoque mi Nombre.*

Recuerda que tú eres parte de mi reino de eterna Vida y Luz. Mientras más oscuro llegue a ser tu planeta, más necesario será que te aferres a la esperanza que tienes en mí. A pesar de cómo se ven las cosas, yo estoy en control, y me mantengo cumpliendo mis propósitos de formas que no puedes entender. Aunque este mundo está terriblemente caído, es posible vivir en él con Gozo y Paz en el corazón. Como les dije a mis discípulos, así te digo a ti ahora: *¡Ten buen ánimo; yo he vencido al mundo!* Debido a que perteneces a mi reino, en *mí puedes tener Paz.*

Juan 18.36; Mateo 26.53; Hechos 2.21;
Juan 16.33

Mayo 28

Yo soy la Vid; tú eres una de las ramas. El que permanece en mí y yo en él, ese da fruto abundante. Separado de mí, sin la unión vital conmigo, no puedes hacer nada.

Piensa en esta gloriosa verdad: ¡yo estoy vivo en tu interior! Así como la savia fluye a través de las ramas de la vid, así mi Vida fluye a través de ti. Soy infinito y perfecto, pero he elegido vivir en ti. Esta intimidad que tienes conmigo resulta maravillosamente valiosa. Yo leo cada uno de tus pensamientos. Estoy consciente de todos tus sentimientos. Sé lo débil que eres, y estoy listo para fortalecerte con mi fuerza.

Si cooperas con mi Presencia que vive en ti y me pides que esté en control, puedes producir abundantes frutos; en cambio, si tratas de hacer las cosas con tus propias fuerzas, ignorando tu unión vital conmigo, es muy probable que te vayas de bruces. Cualquier cosa que *hagas* separado de mí no tendrá ningún valor en mi reino. Por lo tanto, nutre bien tu intimidad conmigo, mi amado. Deléitate en mi Presencia que da Vida.

JUAN 15.5; COLOSENSES 1.27; 2 CORINTIOS 12.9;
DEUTERONOMIO 33.12

AGRADÉCEME GOZOSAMENTE por perdonar *todos* tus
pecados: pasados, presentes y futuros; conocidos y
desconocidos. El perdón es tu mayor necesidad, y yo
he satisfecho esa necesidad perfectamente. ¡Y para
siempre! Yo soy *la Vida eterna que estaba con el Padre
y se ha manifestado a ti.* Debido a que crees en mí
como tu Salvador-Dios tienes Vida eterna. Deja que
esta maravillosa promesa te llene de Gozo y expulse
de tu vida el miedo al futuro. Tu futuro es glorioso y
seguro: *una herencia indestructible, incontaminada e
inmarchitable y que te está reservada en los cielos.* ¡La
mejor respuesta a este regalo infinito e inapreciable
es la gratitud!

Mientras más frecuentemente me expreses tu
agradecimiento, más gozosa será tu vida. Así que busca las cosas que alimenten tu gratitud. El mismo acto
de darme las gracias —de forma hablada o mediante
la palabra escrita, por medio de la oración silencio-
sa, susurros, gritos o cánticos de alabanza— aumenta
tu Gozo y te eleva por sobre tus circunstancias. Una
forma encantadora de expresar tu adoración es leer
salmos en voz alta. Regocíjate en mí, mi redimido,
porque nada puede separarte de mi Amor.

1 JUAN 1.2; JUAN 3.16; 1 PEDRO 1.3, 4;
ROMANOS 8.38, 39

YO SOY DIOS, Y TÚ NO LO ERES. Esto puede sonar duro, pero la verdad es que implica una bendita dosis de realidad. En el Jardín del Edén, Satanás tentó a Eva con el mismo deseo que había provocado que él mismo fuera expulsado del cielo: *ser como Dios*, intentando usurpar así mi posición divina. Eva sucumbió a esta tentación, al igual que Adán. Desde aquel tiempo, la naturaleza pecaminosa en los seres humanos los impulsa a actuar como si ellos fueran Dios, tratando de controlarlo todo y juzgándome cuando las circunstancias no van como les gustaría que fueran.

Recordar que tú *no* eres Dios te ayudará a vivir en libertad. No asumas responsabilidad alguna por asuntos que están fuera de tu control, lo cual incluye la *mayor* parte de los asuntos. Si te desentendieras de todo lo que no es tu responsabilidad, te librarías de llevar cargas innecesarias. Y podrías ser más eficaz en áreas donde sí tienes alguna forma de control. Además, podrías orar por todas tus preocupaciones, confiando en mi soberanía. Tráeme tus *oraciones con acciones de gracias y preséntame tus peticiones.* Vivir de esta manera te protegerá de la ansiedad y te bendecirá con la *Paz que sobrepasa todo entendimiento.*

LUCAS 10.18; GÉNESIS 3.5;
FILIPENSES 4.6, 7

SIGUE VIVIENDO ARRAIGADO y edificado en mí, y llenos de gratitud. La relación que tienes conmigo es diferente a cualquiera otra. Tú vives en mí, y yo vivo en ti. ¡Nunca vas a ningún lado sin mí! Este sorprendente grado de conexión proporciona un sólido fundamento para tu vida. Quiero que continúes construyendo sobre esta base, viviendo en la gozosa seguridad de mi Presencia.

El agradecimiento provee algunos de los más importantes pilares de tu vida. Mientras más de estos pilares uses, mejor será tu experiencia de vida. El agradecimiento amplía la capacidad de tu corazón para el Gozo abundante. También ayuda a soportar los sufrimientos sin caer en la desesperación o la autocompasión. Pase lo que pase, siempre puedes agradecerme por tu salvación eterna y *mi gran Amor*. Estas son bendiciones constantes e inmutables. Otras bendiciones —tales como tus relaciones, tus finanzas y tu salud— pueden cambiar con mucha frecuencia. ¡Yo te animo a que cuentes *ambos* tipos de bendiciones hasta que te desbordes de agradecimiento!

COLOSENSES 2.6, 7; COLOSENSES 1.27;
SALMOS 13.5, 6

Junio

Te cubrirá con sus plumas
y bajo sus alas hallarás refugio.
¡Su verdad será tu escudo
y tu baluarte!

SALMOS 91.4

Yo TE APRUEBO, mi hijo. Debido a que eres mío
—adoptado en mi familia real— te veo a través de los
ojos de la gracia. *Te escogí desde antes de la creación
del mundo para que fueras santo y sin mancha ante mis
ojos.* Yo sé que en tu vida diaria no logras llegar a la
altura de esta norma perfecta, pero te veo como santo
y sin mancha, porque esta es tu posición permanente
en mi reino. Por supuesto, yo no apruebo todo lo que
haces (o dejas de hacer). Aun así, *apruebo* tu verdadero yo, el que te creé para que fueses.

Sé cuánto deseas mi afirmación y lo difícil que es
para ti aceptarla. Quiero que aprendas a verte a ti mismo y a otros a través de la visión de la gracia. Si miras
con los ojos de la gracia, podrás concentrarte más en
lo que es bueno y correcto que en lo que es malo y
equivocado. Aprenderás a cooperar conmigo y a apreciar lo que estoy haciendo en tu vida: *transformándote
a mi semejanza con una Gloria cada vez mayor.* Yo no
solo te apruebo, sino que me *complazco* en ti.

EFESIOS 1.4; FILIPENSES 4.8;
2 CORINTIOS 3.18; SALMOS 149.4

Junio 2

FIJA TUS OJOS NO EN LO QUE SE VE, sino en lo que no se ve. Gastas demasiado tiempo y energía mental pensando en cosas triviales, en asuntos superficiales que no tienen ningún valor en mi reino. El sentido de la vista es un maravilloso regalo que te he dado, pero puede convertirse en una fuente de servidumbre si lo utilizas mal. Resulta fácil para ti contemplarte en el espejo y verte con una exactitud deslumbrante. Esto, combinado con las imágenes de los medios de comunicación de personas que parecen perfectas, hace que le dediques demasiada atención a tu apariencia. Lo mismo puede ocurrir con tu hogar o tu familia. Poner demasiado énfasis en las apariencias te distrae del placer de conocerme, el cual satisface el alma.

Cuando me buscas, disfrutas de la compañía de la única Persona perfecta que haya existido alguna vez, aunque mi perfección no estaba en mi apariencia, sino en mi carácter divino, sin pecado. Yo soy el Único que puede amarte con un *gran Amor* y darte una *Paz perfecta*. De modo que no pierdas tiempo pensando en trivialidades. En lugar de eso, *fija tus pensamientos en mí* y recibe mi Paz.

2 CORINTIOS 4.18; SALMOS 36.7;
ISAÍAS 26.3

Junio 3

TE INVITO A CONTEMPLAR *mi hermosura y buscarme* cada vez más. ¡Esta es una invitación muy deliciosa que te hago! Podrás vislumbrar algo de mi hermosura observando las maravillas de la naturaleza, a pesar de que tales atisbos son solamente un pequeño y débil reflejo de mi inmensa Gloria. En realidad, lo mejor aún está por venir, cuando me veas cara a Cara en el cielo. Por ahora, vislumbrar mi belleza requiere que te concentres en mi Presencia invisible a través de la oración y la meditación de mi Palabra.

Algo fundamental mientras me buscas es recordar que estoy continuamente contigo; que siempre estoy sintonizado con tu frecuencia y te estoy preparando para que seas cada vez más consciente de mí. Coloca recordatorios de mi Presencia en tu casa, automóvil y oficina. Susurrar mi nombre te recordará mi cercanía. Entona alabanzas. Lee o recita pasajes de las Escrituras en voz alta. Encuentra a otras personas que deseen conocerme más a fondo y comparte esta gloriosa misión con ellas. *Búscame como si fuera una necesidad vital; búscame con todo tu corazón.*

SALMOS 27.4; 1 CORINTIOS 13.12;
JEREMÍAS 29.13

Junio 4

¡Yo soy tu Gozo! Deja que estas palabras resuenen en tu mente y penetren en lo más íntimo de tu ser. Yo, tu Compañero que *nunca te dejará* solo, soy una ilimitada fuente de Gozo. Si realmente crees esto, puedes descansar en la verdad de que cada día de tu vida es un buen día. Niégate a utilizar el calificativo de «un día malo», incluso cuando pudieras estar luchando denodadamente con alguna contrariedad. Es posible que tus circunstancias sean muy duras, no obstante, yo estoy contigo, *sosteniéndote de tu mano derecha.* Hay algo bueno para encontrar en este día —y todos los días— gracias a mi Presencia constante y mi Amor inamovible.

¡Es posible que no seas rico según los criterios del mundo, pero *mi gran amor no tiene precio!* Este Amor te garantiza que podrás *encontrar refugio a la sombra de mis alas* sin importar lo que esté sucediendo. Además, te da acceso a *mi río de deleites.* Cuando tu mundo parezca cualquier cosa menos encantador, vuélvete a mí y bebe a tus anchas de este río encantador: mi amorosa Presencia. ¡Yo soy tu Gozo!

DEUTERONOMIO 31.8; SALMOS 73.23;
SALMOS 36.7, 8

Haz lo que puedas y déjame el resto a mí. Cuando estés enredado en una situación difícil, *ábreme tu corazón* sabiendo que yo te escucho y me preocupo. Descansa en mí, tu *Ayudador siempre presente si te encuentras en problemas.* Sin importar cuán ansioso estés por resolver una situación dada, no permitas que te robe la tranquilidad. Cuando hayas hecho todo lo posible, lo mejor es simplemente esperar y buscar reposo en mi Presencia. No te dejes atrapar por la mentira de que la vida no se puede disfrutar mientras no estén resueltos todos los problemas. *En el mundo tendrás aflicciones*, pero *en mí tendrás Paz...* ¡incluso en medio de la peor batalla.

Tu relación conmigo es de colaboración: tú y yo trabajando juntos. Acude a mí cuando busques ayuda y orientación. Haz todo lo posible y confía en que yo haré lo que no puedes hacer. En lugar de tratar de forzar las cosas procurando una conclusión prematura, relájate y pídeme que *te muestre el camino por donde debes segui*r, según mi tiempo. Sujétate de mi mano con la más profunda confianza, y disfruta tu jornada en mi Presencia.

SALMOS 62.8; SALMOS 46.1; JUAN 16.33;
SALMOS 143.8

Junio 6

¡Alimenta bien tu sentido de la gratitud, porque ese es el camino real que lleva al Gozo! De hecho, ningún placer está realmente completo sin que se exprese gratitud por él. Es bueno que les agradezcas a las personas a través de las cuales recibes bendiciones, pero recuerda que yo soy *Dios, de quien todas las bendiciones fluyen.* Por eso, alábame y *agradéceme* en todo momento y cada día. Esto nutre tu alma y completa tu Gozo. También realza tu relación conmigo, proporcionándote una manera fácil de acercarte a mí.

Como mi amado seguidor, has recibido el glorioso regalo de la gracia en la forma de un favor inmerecido. Nadie ni ningún conjunto de circunstancias podrán despojarte de este regalo espléndido. ¡Tú me perteneces para siempre! *Nada en toda la creación podrá separarte de mi Amor.*

Cuando te despiertes cada mañana, di: «Gracias, Jesús, por el regalo de este nuevo día». Y a medida que el día transcurra, busca las bendiciones y satisfacciones que están dispersas a lo largo de tu camino. ¡El mayor tesoro es mi Presencia contigo, porque yo soy el *Don inefable*!

Salmos 95.2; Efesios 2.8, 9;
Romanos 8.38, 39; 2 Corintios 9.15

SI ME TIENES A MÍ, tu Salvador, Señor y Amigo, tienes todo lo que realmente importa. Tal vez no poseas riquezas, fama o éxito, pero no te dejes desalentar por eso que no tienes. Como les dije a mis discípulos: *«¿Cuál será el beneficio si ganas el mundo entero pero pierdes tu alma?».* ¡Nada se puede comparar con el inestimable tesoro de la Vida eterna! Piensa en *aquel comerciante de joyas que andaba a la caza de las mejores perlas. Cuando encontró una que no tenía defecto, vendió todo y la compró.* Mi reino es así: ¡de un valor incalculable! Así que aprende a sentirte contento por tenerme a *mí,* mi amado, independientemente de lo que puede que no tengas en este mundo.

Compararse con los demás es la fuente de mucho descontento. Te animo a que hagas todo lo posible para evitar esta trampa mortal. Recuerda que tú eres mi creación única, redimido con mi sangre y exquisitamente precioso para mí. Mantente en gozosa comunicación conmigo, el Salvador que te ama inmensamente más de lo que puedes imaginar. Te iré transformando cada vez más hasta que llegues a ser la *obra maestra* que yo diseñé que fueras.

MATEO 16.26; MATEO 13.46; 1 TIMOTEO 6.6;
EFESIOS 2.10

Junio 8

¡MI AMOR TE HA CONQUISTADO Y *eres libre*! El Poder de mi Amor es tan grande que te ha esclavizado a mí. *Ya no eres tu propio dueño. Fuiste comprado por un precio*: mi sangre preciosa. Mientras más me ames, más vas a querer servirme con cada fibra de tu ser. Este servicio puede llenarte de Gozo celestial en la medida que te entregas a mí más plenamente.

Debido a que soy perfecto en todos mis caminos, te puedes rendir de todo corazón a mí sin miedo a que me pueda aprovechar de ti. Por el contrario, ser conquistado por mí es lo que te hace verdaderamente libre. Yo he invadido el lugar más íntimo de tu ser, y mi Espíritu viviendo en ti va tomando control de cada vez más territorio. *Donde está el Espíritu del Señor, allí hay libertad*. Quiero que *reflejes mi Gloria* a otros, porque te estoy *transformando a mi semejanza con una Gloria que crece de día en día*. ¡Regocíjate en la libertad que has encontrado en mí, y entrégate con agrado a mi Amor victorioso!

ROMANOS 6.18; 1 CORINTIOS 6.19, 20;
2 CORINTIOS 3.17, 18

SEPARADO DE MÍ NO PUEDES HACER NADA. Durante los días en que las tareas que te aguardan te parezcan abrumadoras, recuerda esto: yo estoy contigo listo para ayudarte. Tómate un momento para descansar en mi amorosa Presencia. Susurra: «*En realidad, el Señor está en este lugar*». Relájate, sabiendo que no estás destinado a ser autosuficiente. Yo te diseñé para que me necesitaras y dependieras de mí. Así es que *ven a mí* tal como eres, sin vergüenza ni pretensión. Háblame de los desafíos que estás enfrentando y lo incapaz que te sientes. Ora para que te muestre el camino que tengo para ti, pero en lugar de lanzarte locamente hacia adelante, da mejor pequeños pasos llenos de confianza, manteniendo la comunicación conmigo.

Yo soy la vid; tú eres una de mis ramas. Al permanecer conectado a mí, mi vida fluirá a través de ti, lo que te permitirá *dar mucho fruto.* No te preocupes por tener éxito a los ojos del mundo. Llevar fruto en mi reino significa *hacer las buenas obras que Dios dispuso de antemano.* Así es que vive cerca de mí, listo para hacer mi voluntad, y yo abriré el camino delante de ti.

JUAN 15.5; GÉNESIS 28.16;
MATEO 11.28, 29; EFESIOS 2.10

Junio 10

RECIBE MI GLORIA-FUERZA. Cuando los problemas en los que estás involucrado te exijan *perseverar por un tiempo largo*, procura no reaccionar apretando los dientes y mostrando un esquema mental sombrío. Esta actitud pasiva-negativa *no* es la forma en que quiero que afrontes las dificultades.

Yo soy soberano sobre las circunstancias de tu vida, por lo que siempre hay oportunidades de superarlas. No seas como el hombre aquel que *escondió el dinero de su señor en la tierra*, porque estaba descontento con sus circunstancias. Él se rindió y tomó el camino más fácil, culpando a su difícil situación en lugar de aprovechar al máximo su oportunidad. En realidad, mientras más difícil sea tu circunstancia, más podrás aprender de ella.

Gustoso te doy mi Gloria-fuerza. Esta fórmula es especialmente poderosa, porque el Espíritu mismo te da el poder *fortaleciéndote en lo íntimo de tu ser*. Además, mi ilimitada Gloria-fuerza te permite mantenerte fuerte, *soportando lo insoportable*. Dado que este poder es tan vasto, hay más que suficiente de él como para dejar que se *derrame sobre el Gozo*.

COLOSENSES 1.11; ISAÍAS 40.10;
MATEO 25.25; EFESIOS 3.16

MI PRESENCIA IRÁ CONTIGO, y *te daré descanso*. ¡Donde quiera que estés, donde quiera que vayas, yo estaré contigo! Esta es una declaración sorprendente, pero es verdad. Mi Presencia invisible es más *real* que la gente de carne y sangre que te rodea. Sin embargo, debes «verme» con los ojos del corazón y comunicarte conmigo a través de la oración, confiando en que de verdad te escucho y me preocupo por ti.

Te aseguro que tus oraciones son determinantes y yo las respondo, aunque no siempre de maneras que puedas ver ni en el tiempo en que desearías. Yo tengo en cuenta las oraciones de los creyentes en mi gobierno soberano de tu mundo de formas demasiado complejas para que las mentes finitas las puedan comprender. Recuerda: *como los cielos son más altos que la tierra, así son mis caminos y mis pensamientos más altos que los tuyos*.

Debido a que mis métodos de obrar en el mundo son a menudo tan misteriosos para ti, es importante que apartes un tiempo para *estar quieto y saber que yo soy Dios*. Siéntate tranquilo en mi Presencia, respirando en mi Paz, y yo te haré descansar.

ÉXODO 33.14; ISAÍAS 55.8, 9; SALMOS 46.10;
SALMOS 29.11

Junio 12

SI YO ESTOY CONTIGO, ¿quién podría estar contra ti? Mi amado, que no te quepa ninguna duda de que yo estoy contigo, pues tú eres mi seguidor. Por supuesto, esto no quiere decir que nunca nadie se te opondrá. Significa que tenerme a tu lado es el hecho más importante de tu existencia. ¡Independientemente de lo que pudiera suceder en tu vida, estás en el lado ganador! Yo ya obtuve la victoria a través de mi muerte y resurrección. Yo soy el eterno Vencedor, y tú compartes mi triunfo, sin importar la cantidad de adversidades con las que te encuentres en tu viaje al cielo. Por último, nada ni nadie puede derrotarte, ya que me perteneces para siempre.

Saber que tu futuro está completamente asegurado puede cambiar tu perspectiva de manera radical. En lugar de vivir a la defensiva —tratando con desesperación de protegerte del sufrimiento— aprende a seguirme valientemente a donde quiera que desee llevarte. Te estoy preparando no solo para que *busques mi Rostro* y me sigas, sino también para que disfrutes de la aventura de abandonarte a mí. Recuerda: yo soy tu *Ayuda segura en las pruebas y los problemas.*

ROMANOS 8.31; SALMOS 27.8;
SALMOS 46.1

Deja que mi Paz proteja tu mente y tu corazón. Recuerda que *yo estoy cerca*, así que *alégrate* en mi Presencia permanente. Pasa todo el tiempo que puedas conmigo, *presentándome tus peticiones con accion de gracia*. Esta es la forma de recibir mi *Paz que sobrepasa todo entendimiento*. De ese modo, *resguardo tu corazón y tu mente*. Este es un esfuerzo en colaboración. Tú y yo juntos. ¡Tú nunca tendrás que enfrentar algo solo!

Para los cristianos, la soledad es una ilusión… tan peligrosa, que puede conducir a la depresión o la autocompasión. El diablo y sus subordinados trabajan duro para obnubilar tu convicción de mi Presencia. Es crucial que te des cuenta de sus ataques y los resistas. Defiéndete con mi Palabra, que es *viva y poderosa*. Léela, medita en ella, memorízala, compártela.

Incluso, si te sientes solo, puedes hablar libremente conmigo, confiando en que *yo estoy contigo siempre*. Mientras más te comunicas conmigo, más convencido estarás de mi cercanía. *Resiste al diablo, y él huirá de ti. Acércate a mí, y yo me acercaré a ti.*

FILIPENSES 4.4-7; HEBREOS 4.12;
MATEO 28.20; SANTIAGO 4.7, 8

EL AMOR ES PACIENTE. Observa que el primer adjetivo que el apóstol Pablo usa para describir al amor es «paciente». Yo aprecio esta cualidad en mis seguidores, aunque no sea muy visible en la mayoría de las descripciones del amor del siglo veintiuno.

La gente paciente puede mantener la calma mientras soporta largas esperas o trata con personas o problemas difíciles. Te animo a que examines tu propia vida para ver cómo respondes a las esperas y las dificultades. Esto te dará una buena medida de cuán paciente —y amoroso— eres.

La «paciencia» aparece en cuarto lugar en la lista *del fruto del Espíritu*. Mi Espíritu te ayudará a crecer en este importante rasgo de tu carácter, especialmente si se lo pides. Algunos cristianos tienen miedo de orar pidiendo paciencia. Creen que les voy a responder sometiéndolos a severos sufrimientos y pruebas. Sin embargo, en mi reino el sufrimiento sirve a un importante propósito y las pruebas no son opcionales. *¡Vienen para que tu fe pueda ser probada como genuina y pueda resultar en alabanza, gloria y honra* a Dios!

1 CORINTIOS 13.4; GÁLATAS 5.22, 23;
1 PEDRO 1.6, 7

VEN A MÍ, MI AMADO. Continuamente te estoy invitando a que te acerques a mí. Guarda silencio en mi Presencia, y *fija tus pensamientos en mí*. Relájate y escucha cómo mi Amor te susurra en el corazón: *«Con Amor eterno te he amado»*. Medita en la gloriosa verdad de que *estoy contigo siempre*. Puedes edificar tu vida sobre esta realidad, sólida como una roca.

El mundo en que habitas está constantemente en proceso de cambio. Aquí no vas a encontrar un terreno sólido. Por eso te desafío a que te mantengas consciente de mi Presencia a medida que avanza el día. No lo vas a hacer perfectamente, pero yo te ayudaré cuando me lo pidas. Puedes orar así: «Señor Jesús, mantenme al tanto de tu Presencia». Permite que estas palabras tengan eco a través de tu corazón y tu mente. Aunque con cierta frecuencia tus pensamientos se van a otras partes, esta oración sencilla puede atraerte de nuevo a mí.

Mientras más forme parte de tu vida —al permanecer cerca de mí— más gozoso estarás y a más personas puedo bendecir a través de ti.

HEBREOS 3.1; JEREMÍAS 31.3;
MATEO 28.19, 20

Junio 16

Tengo buenas intenciones contigo. Pueden ser radicalmente diferentes de lo que esperabas, pero son buenas. *Yo soy la Luz, y en mí no hay oscuridad.* Busca mi Luz en todas tus circunstancias. Yo estoy abundantemente presente en tus momentos. Tu responsabilidad consiste en estar atento a mí y a los caminos que tengo para ti. A veces, esto requiere renunciar a cosas que habías planeado o soñado. Necesitas recordar y creer de todo corazón que *mi camino es perfecto*, pese a lo difícil que es.

Soy un escudo para todos los que buscan refugio en mí. Cuando te estés sintiendo afligido o con miedo, ven a mí y dime: «Señor, me refugio en *ti*». No te protejo de las cosas que puedes manejar, pues tienes una parte importante que jugar en este mundo. Sin embargo, te protejo de más peligros y dificultades de las que te puedes imaginar. Así que haz todos los esfuerzos necesarios para *vivir la vida que te he asignado*. Hazlo en gozosa dependencia de mí, y *tu alma será ricamente satisfecha*.

1 Juan 1.5; Salmos 18.30; 1 Corintios 7.17; Salmos 63.5

TRATA DE SER CADA VEZ MÁS RECEPTIVO y sensible a mí. Yo siempre me estoy involucrando activamente en tu vida. En lugar de intentar forzarme a que haga lo que deseas, *cuando* lo deseas, tranquilízate y fíjate en lo que ya estoy haciendo por ti. Vive de un modo receptivo, esperándome y confiando en mi manejo del tiempo. *Yo soy bueno con aquellos que confían en mí y me buscan.* Pídeme que abra tus ojos a fin de que puedas ver todo lo que tengo para ti. Tal conocimiento te ayudará a vivir responsablemente, listo para hacer mi voluntad.

A menudo, mis seguidores no logran ver las muchas bendiciones que derramo sobre ellos. Están tan ocupados en otras cosas que no perciben lo que está delante de sus ojos o están por recibir. Se olvidan de que yo soy Dios soberano y el manejo del tiempo es mi prerrogativa.

Quiero que confíes en mí lo suficiente como para dejar que te guíe. Cuando una pareja está bailando, uno de ellos conduce y el otro lo sigue; de lo contrario, habría confusión y torpeza. Danza *conmigo*, mi amado. Sígueme, mientras te guío con elegancia a través de la vida.

LAMENTACIONES 3.25; EFESIOS 5.17;
SALMOS 71.16; SALMOS 28.7

Junio 18

LA QUIETUD ES CADA VEZ MÁS DIFÍCIL de conseguir en este mundo inquieto y agitado. Tú debes esforzarte a fin de apartar un tiempo para mí. Cuando intentas reunirte tranquilamente conmigo, las distracciones te llegan de todos lados. Sin embargo, nuestra conexión íntima es digna de que se luche por ella, así es que no te rindas. Separa un tiempo sin interrupciones para estar conmigo. Concéntrate en un pasaje favorito de las Escrituras y respira hondo para relajarte. Recuerda que yo soy *Emanuel, Dios contigo*. Relájate en mi pacífica Presencia, dejando que tus preocupaciones se alejen. *Quédate quieto*, mi amado, *y reconoce que yo soy Dios*.

Mientras más tiempo mantengas la mirada en mí, más te regocijarás en mi majestuoso esplendor y más confianza tendrás en mi control soberano. *Aunque se desmorone la tierra y las montañas se hundan en el fondo del mar*, yo soy tu Refugio. En mi Presencia hay una estabilidad trascendente. Al reflexionar en la inmensidad de mi Poder y Gloria, tu perspectiva cambiará y tus problemas se verán más pequeños. *En este mundo tendrás aflicción, pero anímate. Yo he vencido al mundo.*

MATEO 1.23; SALMOS 46.10; SALMOS 46.1, 2; JUAN 16.33

Yo te guío por el camino de la sabiduría y te dirijo por sendas de rectitud. La sabiduría se puede definir como «la habilidad de hacer buenas decisiones basadas en el conocimiento y la experiencia». Por eso es tan importante que aprendas lo que es verdadero y apliques ese conocimiento a tu vida, sobre todo a tus decisiones. Puesto que *yo soy el Camino, la Verdad, y la Vida*, soy el mejor Guía que te puedas imaginar. También soy *el Verbo que estaba con Dios y es Dios*. El camino de la sabiduría que se encuentra en la Palabra escrita te guía de manera muy eficaz. Así que estudia mi Palabra y permanece cerca de mí mientras vas por el mundo.

Busca y sigue las *sendas de rectitud* que tengo para ti. No te prometo que vayan a ser siempre fáciles. No obstante, si caminas cerca de mí, tu andar será mucho menos tortuoso. Si miras hacia adelante, verás curvas y giros desconcertantes. Sin embargo, cuando miras hacia atrás al trecho que ya has cubierto, podrás ver que he estado contigo en cada instancia del camino, protegiéndote de los peligros, eliminando los obstáculos y enderezando tus veredas.

PROVERBIOS 4.11; JUAN 14.6;
JUAN 1.1

Junio 20

No te irrites por la gente malvada que prospera; no te inquietes por sus intrigas. En estos días de comunicación instantánea tienes acceso a tanta información y noticias que resulta fácil sentirte abrumado. No solo *oyes* hablar de gente mala y sus planes perversos, sino que también *ves* los detalles gráficos. Estas imágenes visuales tienen un poderoso impacto en tu química cerebral. Una dieta constante de tal catástrofe puede hacer de ti una persona ansiosa y temerosa.

Quiero que ores por los acontecimientos del mundo y busques la paz hasta donde seas capaz. Sin embargo, es crucial reconocer lo que puedes cambiar y lo que no. Preocuparte por cosas que están fuera de tu control drenará tu energía y te desalentará. En lugar de este enfoque doloroso, esfuérzate por *fijar tus pensamientos en mí.* Yo estoy contigo y para ti. *¡Deléitate en mí!*

Recuerda que yo soy un Dios de justicia y lo sé todo. Al final, voy a enderezar todo lo torcido. Así que *mantente quieto en mi Presencia, confiando en mí con un corazón firme mientras esperas que actúe.*

Salmos 37.7; Hebreos 3.1; Salmos 37.3, 4

¡Yo VIVO EN TI! Soy todo lo que pudieras necesitar en un Dios-Salvador, y estoy vivo en tu interior. Te lleno de Vida radiante y Amor. Quiero que mi Vida en ti se desborde e impacte a otras personas. Al interactuar con ellas, pídeme que viva y ame a través de ti. Cuando colabores conmigo de esta manera, mi luz se reflejará desde tu rostro y mi Amor le dará gracia a tus palabras.

En mí, tú estás completo. Todo lo que necesitas para tu salvación y tu crecimiento espiritual lo encuentras conmigo. Mediante *mi Poder divino* tienes todo lo necesario para perseverar en la Vida eterna que te he dado. También te doy un *conocimiento* íntimo de mí. Te invito a sincerarte y compartir conmigo en los niveles más profundos tanto tus luchas como tus deleites.

Encuentra descanso en mi obra terminada en la cruz y regocíjate de estar eternamente seguro conmigo. Disfruta de una rica satisfacción espiritual a través de conocer a tu amoroso Salvador y Amigo eterno.

GÁLATAS 2.20; 2 CORINTIOS 3.18;
COLOSENSES 2.9, 10; 2 PEDRO 1.3

CADA VEZ QUE TE SIENTAS TRISTE, quiero que pienses en la alegría jubilosa que te espera. Esto eliminará el dolor de la tristeza, porque te ayudará a recordar que tal estado de ánimo es solo temporal. Aunque con el tiempo esa tristeza tienda a hacerse más grande tratando de convencerte de que siempre serás un infeliz, eso no es más que una mentira. La verdad es que a *todos* mis seguidores les espera un Gozo infinito, garantizado por toda la eternidad. Esto es algo que *nadie te puede quitar.*

Tu paso por este mundo tiene muchos altibajos. Los tiempos de desaliento son difíciles, pero sirven a un propósito importante. Si confías en mí en medio de la adversidad, el dolor y las luchas, te ayudarán a mejorar y crecer más fuerte. Tus problemas son comparables a los dolores de parto. Los dolores de una mujer dando a luz son dolores muy reales. En medio del sufrimiento, ella puede preguntarse cuánto tiempo más podrá soportarlos. Sin embargo, tan ardua lucha produce un resultado maravilloso: un bebé precioso que viene al mundo. Mientras experimentas dolores a través de tus luchas terrenales, mantén tus ojos fijos en la recompensa prometida: ¡Gozo sin límites en el cielo! Incluso en medio de la tristeza, tu seguridad de mi Presencia, que implica una *plenitud de alegría*, aumentará.

JUAN 16.22; JUAN 16.21; SALMOS 16.11

Tu ciudadanía está en los cielos. Algún día *transformaré tu cuerpo terrenal para que sea como mi cuerpo glorioso*. Vas a tener una eternidad para disfrutar de tu cuerpo perfecto, glorificado. Así que no te preocupes demasiado por tu estado físico ahora. Muchos de mis seguidores se aferran desesperadamente a su vida terrenal cuando están a las puertas mismas del paraíso, pero una vez que se van y pasan a través de ese velo fino y entran en el cielo, experimentan un Gozo extático que supera cualquier cosa que alguna vez hayan imaginado.

Tu vida está en mis manos. Yo he planificado todos tus días, y sé exactamente cuántos te quedan. Debido a que *tu cuerpo es templo del Espíritu Santo*, espero que lo cuides, pero no quiero que te concentres demasiado en su condición. Esto te puede volver ansioso y distraerte de mi Presencia. Mejor, recibe cada día como un regalo precioso que te hago. Busca tanto los placeres como las responsabilidades que he puesto ante ti en tu camino. Toma mi mano con gozosa confianza; siempre estoy a tu lado.

FILIPENSES 3.20, 21; 1 CORINTIOS 2.9;
SALMOS 31.15; 1 CORINTIOS 6.19

Junio 24

TE ESTOY HACIENDO *NUEVO en tu actitud mental.* Vivir cerca de mí tiene que ver con la novedad y el cambio. Te estoy transformando *mediante la total renovación de tu mente.* Esta es una empresa de gran envergadura; vas a participar en el proceso de edificación hasta el día de tu muerte. Sin embargo, a diferencia de los materiales inanimados que los constructores usan para construir edificios, tú eres un «material» vivo y que respira. Te he dado la asombrosa habilidad de pensar y hacer decisiones importantes. Quiero que uses esta habilidad divina para cooperar conmigo mientras te transformo. Esto implica *deponer tu vieja naturaleza* —tu antigua manera de pensar y hacer las cosas— y *activar la nueva naturaleza.*

A fin de tomar decisiones buenas y piadosas, necesitas conocerme como en realidad soy. Búscame en mi Palabra; pídele a mi Espíritu que te ilumine, proyectando su Luz de modo que las Escrituras adquieran vida en ti. Mientras más decidido estás de vivir conforme a mi voluntad, más serás *como yo*, y más te deleitarás *caminando en la Luz de mi Presencia.*

EFESIOS 4.22-24; 2 CORINTIOS 5.17;
ROMANOS 12.2; SALMOS 89.15

REHÚSATE A PREOCUPARTE, MI AMADO. Saca de tu mente, con confianza y una actitud agradecida, esos pensamientos que te quitan el sueño. Afirma tu fe en mí mientras me alabas por todo lo que soy y todo lo que he hecho. Esta combinación de alabanza y confianza es potente. Ahuyenta la ansiedad y los poderes de la oscuridad. También fortalece tu relación conmigo. Es muy posible que todavía tengas preocupaciones legítimas contra las cuales estás luchando, pero yo te ayudaré con ellas. Mientras recuperas la calma, mira tus problemas a la Luz de mi Presencia y busca mi consejo. Deja que las Escrituras obren en tus pensamientos de modo que pueda comunicarme contigo con mayor claridad.

Tómate tu tiempo para agradecerme por las muchas cosas buenas que he hecho en tu vida. Quiero que expreses agradecimiento en tus oraciones, tus conversaciones con otros y tus pensamientos privados. Yo leo tus pensamientos continuamente, y me alegro cuando contienen gratitud. Agradéceme incluso por cosas que desearías que fueran diferentes. Este acto de fe te ayudará a liberarte de los pensamientos negativos. *Da gracias en todo; esta es mi voluntad para ti.*

SALMOS 31.14; SALMOS 32.8;
1 TESALONICENSES 5.18

Junio 26

Si yo estoy contigo, ¿quién podría estar en contra de ti? Es esencial que comprendas que en verdad *estoy* contigo. Esta es una promesa para todos mis seguidores. Cuando las cosas no marchan como tú quisieras y la gente en la que confiabas se pone en contra tuya, es fácil sentirte como si yo te hubiese abandonado. Es importante que en esos momentos te digas a ti mismo la verdad: yo no solo estoy *contigo* siempre, sino que también estoy *para* ti todo el tiempo. Esto es verdad en los días en que estás haciendo las cosas bien y en los días en que no es así; cuando los demás te tratan bien y cuando te maltratan.

Si en realidad entiendes y crees absolutamente que yo estoy *para ti*, entonces el miedo disminuirá y podrás enfrentar las adversidades con más calma. El hecho de saber que nunca te dejaré te debe dar confianza para no claudicar en los tiempos difíciles. ¡Yo te apruebo, mi amado, porque eres mío! Es *mi* opinión que tengo de ti la que prevalece y seguirá prevaleciendo por toda la eternidad. ¡Ninguna persona o cosa te *podrá separar de mi amorosa Presencia*!

ROMANOS 8.31; NÚMEROS 6.26;
ROMANOS 8.39

Yo ESTOY RICAMENTE presente en el mundo que te rodea, en la Palabra y en tu corazón a través de mi Espíritu. Pídeme que abra los ojos de tu corazón para que puedas «verme», porque yo estoy amorosamente presente en todos tus momentos. Es muy importante que separes tiempo para *buscar mi Presencia*. Esto requiere una disciplina mental persistente: dejar de pensar en los ídolos que te atraen y decidirte a dedicarme tus pensamientos. Yo soy la Palabra viviente, por lo que me encontrarás vibrantemente presente cuando me busques en las Escrituras.

Creé una belleza asombrosa en el mundo para que señalara al Único que lo hizo todo. *Sin mí, nada de lo que está hecho se habría hecho.* Cuando estés disfrutando de algo hermoso, dame las gracias. Esto me complace, y también aumenta la complacencia tuya. Cuando te encuentres en medio de dificultades o situaciones feas en este mundo quebrantado, confía también en mí. Mantén tus ojos puestos en mí en medio de tus momentos buenos *y* en los momentos difíciles. Encontrarás esperanza y consuelo a través del conocimiento de que *toda tu vida está en mis manos.*

1 CRÓNICAS 16.11; JUAN 1.3;
SALMOS 31.14, 15

Junio 28

TODO LO QUE TIENES ES UN REGALO que te he hecho, incluyendo cada aliento que respiras. Yo derramo tantas bendiciones sobre ti que es fácil que consideres algunos de mis preciosos dones como algo natural. Por ejemplo, la mayoría de la gente no reconoce la maravilla de estar inhalando mi Vida continuamente. Sin embargo, fue solo cuando soplé *mi hálito de Vida* en Adán que se *convirtió en un ser viviente.*

Mientras permaneces en silencio en mi Presencia, trata de agradecerme íntimamente cada vez que inhalas. Al exhalar, estarás afirmando tu confianza en mí. Mientras más frecuentemente practiques esto, más relajado te sentirás. Al pasar tiempo conmigo, te ayudaré a apreciar y agradecer las bendiciones que sueles pasar por alto: el cielo y los árboles, la luz y los colores, tus seres queridos y tus comodidades diarias. ¡La lista es interminable! Mientras más te fijes en las cosas buenas de tu vida, más clara será tu visión.

Por supuesto, tu mayor gratitud debería ser por la *Vida eterna*, que es tuya debido a que *creíste en mí.* ¡Este es el don eterno inapreciable que te llenará de un cada vez mayor *Gozo en mi Presencia!*

GÉNESIS 2.7; JUAN 3.16;
SALMOS 16.11

LOS QUE SIEMBRAN con lágrimas cosecharán con regocijo. Así que no subestimes tus lágrimas, mi hijo amado; para mí son preciosas. Algún día *enjugaré toda lágrima de tus ojos*, pero por ahora vives en un valle donde el llanto abunda. Así como el agua es necesaria para que las semillas se conviertan en plantas, tus lágrimas te ayudan a ser un cristiano más fuerte y gozoso. Tu disposición a participar del dolor de este mundo tan profundamente caído te proporciona un sentido más real de compasión. También aumenta tu capacidad para disfrutar del Gozo y tu habilidad para compartirlo conmigo en los tiempos buenos y los no tan buenos.

Los *cantos llenos de Gozo* han sido tu patrimonio desde que te convertiste en mi seguidor. No te olvides de este delicioso modo de adorarme y mejorar tu ánimo. A pesar de que es contrario a la intuición natural cantar alabanzas cuando te sientes triste, hacerlo es una forma poderosa de elevar tu corazón a mí. En la medida en que este Gozo en mí encuentra mi deleite en ti, puedes descansar en la Luz de mi Presencia. ¡Este es *el Gozo del Señor*!

SALMOS 126.5, 6; APOCALIPSIS 21.4;
ISAÍAS 62.4; NEHEMÍAS 8.10

Junio 30

CONFÍA EN MÍ Y NO TENGAS MIEDO. No te amedrentes por los acontecimientos del planeta o los informes noticiosos. Estos informes no son objetivos, ya que se presentan como si yo no existiera. Las noticias muestran pequeños trozos de acontecimientos mundiales en los que el elemento más importante ha sido cuidadosamente eliminado. *Mi Presencia en el mundo.* Mientras las empresas noticiosas filtran grandes cantidades de información, eliminan todo lo que tenga que ver conmigo y lo que estoy logrando en la tierra.

Cada vez que sientas que tu mundo es un lugar aterrorizante, vuélvete a mí y busca valor en mi Presencia. Sigue el ejemplo de David, que *se animó y puso su confianza en el Señor* cuando el pueblo estaba por apedrearlo. También podrás encontrar valor recordando quién soy yo. Piensa en mi impresionante Gloria y Poder; disfruta de mi Amor inagotable. Alégrate de que estás en un viaje venturoso conmigo cuyo destino final es el cielo. A medida que te mantengas centrado en mí y disfrutes de la rica relación que te ofrezco, el miedo va a ir desapareciendo y el Gozo se alzará de nuevo dentro de ti. Confía en mí con todo tu corazón, mi amado, porque *yo soy tu Fuerza y tu Canción.*

ISAÍAS 12.2; ÉXODO 33.14;
1 SAMUEL 30.6

Julio

«¡Yo no te olvidaré! Grabada te
llevo en las palmas de mis manos».

Isaías 49.15, 16

Yo TE HE GRABADO *en las palmas de mis manos,* y este es un compromiso eterno. Nada podría borrar ni destruir esta inscripción, porque tú eres mi posesión atesorada, comprada con sangre.

Grabar los metales preciosos es una práctica destinada a ser permanente. Sin embargo, el grabado puede deteriorarse con los años, y a veces los objetos en los que se ha hecho alguna inscripción se pierden, son robados o se funden. Por lo tanto, mi amado, pon primero lo primero. Los metales preciosos como el oro y la plata tienen *algún* valor en el mundo, *pero comparados con la grandeza insuperable de conocerme a mí son como basura.*

Ya que te encuentras escrito en las palmas de mis manos, puedes estar seguro de que siempre estarás visible para mí. A veces la gente anota algo en las palmas de sus manos para recordarlo más tarde. Yo te he grabado en mis palmas debido a que eres eternamente precioso para mí. Alégrate en la maravilla de saber que yo, el Rey del universo, te considero un tesoro inapreciable. Responde atesorándome tú a *mí* por encima de todo.

ISAÍAS 49.15, 16; FILIPENSES 3.8, 9;
SALMOS 43.4

Julio 2

Cuando ya no te queda aliento, yo te muestro el camino. Este es uno de los beneficios de la debilidad. Ella pone de manifiesto que no puedes avanzar sin mi ayuda. Si te estás sintiendo cansado o confundido, puedes optar por dejarte llevar por esos estados de ánimo o volverte incondicionalmente a mí. Derrama tu corazón libremente y luego descansa en la Presencia del Único que *conoce tu camino* a la perfección, hasta llegar al cielo mismo.

Continúa con la práctica de mantener tu mirada en mí incluso cuando te sientas fuerte y seguro. En realidad, es en tales ocasiones cuando estás más en riesgo de tomar la dirección equivocada. En lugar de asumir que conoces el siguiente paso de tu andar, prepárate para planificar en mi Presencia, pidiéndome que sea yo quien te guíe. Recuerda que *mis caminos y pensamientos son más altos que los tuyos, así como los cielos son más altos que la tierra.* Deja que estos recordatorios te inciten a adorarme, *al Excelso y Sublime, que vive para siempre* y descendió para ayudarte a ti.

SALMOS 142.3; ISAÍAS 55.9;
ISAÍAS 57.15

Yo soy el Señor tu Dios, que sostiene tu mano derecha, y te dice: No temas, yo te ayudaré. Es esencial que reconozcas y creas que yo no solo soy tu Salvador, sino también *tu Dios.* Muchas personas tratan de identificarme con un gran modelo humano, un mártir que lo sacrificó todo por los demás. No obstante, si yo fuera solo humano, tú todavía estarías *muerto en tus pecados.* ¡El Único que te sostiene de tu mano y calma tus temores es el Dios vivo! Alégrate al meditar en esta asombrosa verdad. Deléitate con la misteriosa maravilla de la Trinidad: Padre, Hijo y Espíritu. Un Dios.

Aparta un tiempo para esperar en mi Presencia. Háblame de tus problemas; *abre tu corazón delante de mí.* Escúchame cuando te digo: «No tengas miedo, mi amado. Yo estoy aquí, listo para ayudarte». No te condeno por tus miedos, pero quiero que los eches de ti con la esperanza y la confianza en mí. Y cuando confiadamente *esperes en mí, mi infalible Amor te acompañará.*

Isaías 41.13; Efesios 2.1; Salmos 62.8;
Salmos 33.22

Julio 4

A TODO AQUEL QUE VENCIERE, le daré a comer el fruto del Árbol de la Vida en el paraíso. Mi amado, en cierto sentido ya eres victorioso. *Porque a los que predestiné, yo también los llamé; y a los que llamé, también los justifiqué; y a los que justifiqué, también los glorifiqué.* Te traje de la oscuridad a mi reino de Luz; ¡esto significa que estás en camino a la Gloria! Ya tienes la victoria ganada, cumplida a través de mi obra terminada en la cruz.

En otro sentido debes luchar durante toda tu vida para ser victorioso. En este mundo te vas a encontrar con pruebas de fuego y tentaciones que pondrán de relieve tu pecaminosidad y tus debilidades. Esto puede llevarte al desaliento a medida que te das cuenta de tus múltiples fallas. Incluso te puede parecer que ya no me perteneces, pero no te dejes engañar por tales sentimientos. En lugar de eso, aférrate con todas tus fuerzas a mí, no te sueltes por nada de mi mano y confía en las indescriptibles maravillas del paraíso que son tu herencia prometida. La Luz en la ciudad celestial es deslumbradoramente brillante, porque *la Gloria de Dios la ilumina y el Cordero es su Lumbrera.*

APOCALIPSIS 2.7; ROMANOS 8.30;
APOCALIPSIS 21.23

CAMINA EN LA LUZ DE MI PRESENCIA. Esta encantadora manera de vivir implica *aclamarme, alegrarte en mi Nombre y regocijarte en mi justicia.* Aclamarme es alabarme de una manera decidida y entusiasta, a veces con gritos y aplausos. Cuando te regocijas en mi Nombre, encuentras Gozo en todo lo que soy: tu Salvador y Pastor, tu Señor y Dios, tu Rey Soberano, tu Amigo que te ama con un *gran Amor.* Puedes regocijarte en mi justicia, porque la he compartido contigo. Aunque continuarás pecando en esta vida, mi justicia perfecta ya ha sido acreditada en tu cuenta.

Cuando andas en mi Luz gloriosa, *mi sangre te limpia continuamente de todo pecado.* Al tratar de vivir cerca de mí, reconociendo que eres un pecador que necesita del perdón, mi santa luminosidad te purifica. Esta bendición es para todos los creyentes, por lo que hace posible que mis seguidores *tengan comunión unos con otros.* Así que, anda en la Luz conmigo, amigo mío. Pasa tiempo disfrutando de mi Presencia brillante y amorosa.

SALMOS 89.15, 16; SALMOS 31.16;
ROMANOS 3.22; 1 JUAN 1.7

Julio 6

Yo soy antes de todas las cosas, que por medio de mí forman un todo coherente. Siempre he sido y siempre seré. *Todas las cosas fueron creadas por mí: las cosas en el cielo y la tierra, visibles e invisibles.* ¡Yo soy Señor de la creación, de la iglesia, de todo! Adórame como tu vibrante Señor, *el Dios vivo.* Quiero que mis amados tengan sed de mí, así *como el ciervo jadea por las corrientes de las aguas.*

No te sientas satisfecho con solo pensar en mí o conocerme intelectualmente. Ten sed de un conocimiento experiencial de mí, basado en la sana verdad bíblica. Busca conocer *mi Amor que sobrepasa todo conocimiento.* Para lograrlo, vas a necesitar la ayuda de mi Espíritu.

Debes *ser fortalecido con gran Poder por medio del Espíritu Santo, que habita en lo íntimo de tu ser.* Invítalo a que te fortalezca y te guíe en esta amorosa aventura. Sin embargo, recuerda que *yo soy* el objetivo de tu búsqueda. Conviérteme en tu meta. ¡*Me buscarás y me hallarás, cuando me busques con todo tu corazón!*

Colosenses 1.16, 17; Salmos 42.1, 2;
Efesios 3.16-19; Jeremías 29.13

Yo soy la Puerta; el que por mí entra será salvo. Yo soy la única entrada a *la senda de la Vida*, de la Vida eterna. Si no entras a través de mí, nunca vas a encontrar la salvación de tus pecados.

Algunas personas comparan el viaje espiritual con escalar una montaña: hay muchos caminos que conducen a la cumbre, y todos los escaladores que tengan éxito terminarán en el mismo lugar, sin importar el camino que hayan tomado. A menudo se usa esta analogía para afirmar que todos los caminos a Dios son igualmente efectivos. ¡Nada podría estar más lejos de la verdad! Tú puedes entrar en la salvación solo por *mí*, la única Puerta verdadera.

Una vez que hayas atravesado esta Puerta, podrás disfrutar yendo por el camino de la Vida. No garantizo que sea un viaje fácil, pero sí te prometo estar contigo en todo momento. No importa qué dificultades puedan asaltarte en la jornada, *hay Gozo al encontrarse en mi Presencia*. Además, cada paso que das te acerca a la meta: tu hogar celestial.

JUAN 10.9; SALMOS 16.11; MATEO 1.21;
2 TIMOTEO 4.18

Julio 8

ME ACERCO A TI en el momento presente. Intenta disfrutar de mi Presencia ahora. La confianza y el agradecimiento son tus mejores aliados en esta búsqueda.

Cuando te regodeas en el pasado o te preocupas por el futuro, tu conciencia de mí se oscurece. Sin embargo, mientras más confías en mí, más completa será tu vida en el presente, donde mi Presencia te espera siempre. Dime con frecuencia: «Confío en ti, Señor Jesús». «¡*Cuánto te amo, Señor, fuerza mía!*». Estas breves oraciones te mantendrán cerca de mí, con la confianza de que yo estoy amorosamente velando por ti.

Es importante que crezcas no solo en lo que respecta a la confianza, sino también a la gratitud. Una actitud agradecida es esencial para vivir cerca de mí. La ingratitud me resulta ofensiva y te arrastra hacia abajo tanto en lo espiritual como emocionalmente. Recuerda que sin importar lo que esté sucediendo en tu vida o en el mundo, estamos *recibiendo un reino inconmovible*. Esto significa que tienes una razón constante e inquebrantable para *ser agradecido*. Permanece unido a mí y disfruta de mi Presencia, *dando gracias en toda situación*.

SALMOS 18.1; HEBREOS 12.28, 29;
1 TESALONICENSES 5.18

AL MIRARME CADA VEZ MÁS, harás que me convierta en el objeto de tu alegría. Cuando nos fijamos en el mundo de hoy, muchas cosas perturbadoras llaman nuestra atención. Si te concentras demasiado en esas cosas, vas a terminar profundamente desalentado. Mientras tanto, el Único que *está siempre contigo* te grita: «¡Estoy aquí! ¡Mírame, mi amado, y encuentra Gozo en mí!».

Mi Presencia te bendecirá siempre, incluso cuando esté solo en el fondo de tu mente. Puedes aprender a estar consciente de mí aunque te ocupes de otros asuntos. El magnífico cerebro que te di puede funcionar en varias tareas al mismo tiempo. Cuando estás haciendo algo que demanda una gran inversión de energía mental, tu conciencia de mi Presencia se vuelve sutil, aunque de todos modos resulta reconfortante y alentadora.

Haz de mí tu enfoque jubiloso. El enfoque *no* es escapismo. Por el contrario, tu concentración en mí te fortalecerá y te dará valor para enfrentar las dificultades en tu vida. Mientras más persistas en mirarme, más eficaz y gozoso serás.

SALMOS 105.4; SALMOS 73.23;
DEUTERONOMIO 31.6

Julio 10

Tú puedes ser un vencedor formidable por medio de mí, el Rey de Gloria que te ama. No importa lo que esté ocurriendo en este mundo quebrantado y caído o en tu propia vida, eres un triunfador. Yo obtuve la Victoria de una vez por todas a través de mi muerte sacrificial y mi milagrosa resurrección. *Mi gran Amor* ha logrado esta maravillosa conquista y ha hecho de ti mucho, mucho más que un vencedor. ¡Eres un heredero del reino de Vida eterna y Luz!

¡Nada te podrá apartar de mi Amor! Piensa en lo que significa tenerme a mí como Aquel que ama a tu alma en todo momento y para siempre. Tu alma es la parte eterna de ti, la parte que jamás podrá separarse de mí. No es lo que ves en el espejo o lo que otras personas ven en ti. Es la esencia de quien eres, el «verdadero tú» que está *siendo transformado con cada vez más Gloria*. Por lo tanto, no te desanimes por los defectos que veas en ti. En lugar de eso, recuerda que estás siendo continuamente *transformado a mi semejanza.* ¡Alégrate!

Romanos 8.37-39; Salmos 13.5, 6;
2 Corintios 3.18

Tu capacidad proviene de mí. Eso significa que no hay lugar para el orgullo por lo que logres en la vida. También significa que eres capaz de mucho más de lo que crees posible. La combinación de tus habilidades naturales y mi capacidad sobrenatural resulta muy efectiva. Te he llamado a que vivas en una alegre dependencia de mí, así es que no dudes en pedirme ayuda. Haz todos los esfuerzos necesarios para identificar mi voluntad para ti, escudriñando las Escrituras y *buscando mi Presencia*. También, procura recibir consejos sabios de otros cristianos. Yo te mostraré el camino por donde deberás ir de acuerdo con mi sabiduría y voluntad.

Pídele a mi Espíritu que te guíe al transitar por el camino que he elegido para ti. El Santo Ayudador te equipará y te capacitará para lograr mis propósitos en tu vida. Dame las gracias por todo: las habilidades que te he dado, las oportunidades que tienes ante ti y la capacitación de mi Espíritu para que logres cosas importantes en mi reino. Mantente en comunicación conmigo, disfrutando de mi compañía mientras vas avanzando por *la senda de la Vida*. ¡Te llenaré de alegría en mi Presencia!

2 Corintios 3.5; 1 Crónicas 16.10, 11;
1 Tesalonicenses 5.16-18; Salmos 16.11

Julio 12

QUIERO QUE CON ALEGRÍA SAQUES *agua de las fuentes de salvación*. Estas fuentes son insondablemente profundas y están llenas hasta los bordes de mis bendiciones. El valor de tu salvación es incalculable: mucho mayor que todas las fortunas terrenales del pasado, presente y futuro. Cuando tu vida en este mundo llegue a su fin, vivirás conmigo para *siempre* en un ambiente perfecto lleno de Gloria deslumbrante. Me adorarás con un número incalculable de mis seguidores, todos los cuales se relacionarán entre sí con un Amor maravilloso y responderán a mí con un Amor aun *más grande*. ¡Además, serás capaz de recibir Amor de mí en una medida inimaginable!

La seguridad de los placeres sempiternos que te esperan en el cielo te podrá ayudar a soportar tus luchas en este mundo. Entiendo las dificultades que estás enfrentando, pero recuerda: Yo soy *tu Fuerza y tu Canción*. Soy lo suficiente fuerte para llevarte adelante cuando sientas que no puedes seguir. Incluso te capacito para que cantes conmigo: en los días buenos *y* en los días difíciles. ¡Yo, *tu canción*, puedo llenarte de Gozo!

ISAÍAS 12.2, 3; 2 CORINTIOS 8.9;
SALMOS 16.11

A VECES NECESITAS AYUDA incluso para pedirme que te ayude. Cuando tratas de hacer varias cosas a la vez, te encuentras moviéndote cada vez más rápido, dejando una cosa sin terminar para empezar otra. Si el teléfono suena en esos momentos, tu nivel de estrés se eleva. La mejor manera de salirse de este torbellino es deteniendo todo, respirando hondo, susurrando mi Nombre y reconociendo tu necesidad de mi guía a través de los momentos de este día. Yo, amorosamente, te guiaré por *sendas de justicia por Amor de mi nombre*.

Mientras te estás preparando para hacer algo difícil, por lo general dedicas un tiempo a conseguir mi ayuda. Sin embargo, cuando estás enfrentando las tareas cotidianas, tiendes a llevarlas a cabo sin mí, como si fueras capaz de manejar estos asuntos solo. ¡Cuánto mejor es que intentes hacer *todo* en humilde dependencia de mí! Siempre que te dispongas a actuar de algún modo, pídeme que te ayude a detenerte y buscarme, dejándome que te muestre el camino por el cual avanzar en tu vida. *Yo te mostraré el camino que debes seguir.*

SALMOS 23.3; HECHOS 17.27;
SALMOS 32.8

Julio 14

Guarda silencio en mi Presencia y espera pacientemente en mí para actuar. La quietud es un bien escaso en este mundo. Muchas personas se juzgan a sí mismas y su día por lo mucho o poco que han logrado hacer. Descansar en mi Presencia no suele ser uno de esos logros. ¡Sin embargo, qué gran cantidad de bendiciones se pueden encontrar en este santo reposo!

La Paz y el Gozo abundan en mi Presencia, pero se necesita tiempo para que penetren hasta el interior de tu ser. También se necesita confianza. En lugar de quejarte y disgustarte cuando tus planes se vean frustrados, espera pacientemente a que yo actúe. Puedes *poner tu esperanza en mí*, porque yo soy el *Dios de tu salvación.* Ten la seguridad de que *te escucharé.* Es posible que no te conteste con la prontitud que desearías, pero siempre respondo a tus oraciones de la manera que más te conviene a ti.

No te irrites ante el éxito de la gente mala ni te inquietes por sus intrigas. Yo me río de los malvados, porque sé que les llegará su hora. Descansa en mí, mi amado. *Quédate quieto y reconoce que yo soy Dios.*

SALMOS 37.7; MIQUEAS 7.7;
SALMOS 37.13; SALMOS 46.10

¡MI AMOR ES MEJOR QUE LA VIDA MISMA! En calidad, cantidad o duración, mi Amor no tiene límites. Es infinitamente mejor que cualquiera cosa que este mundo pudiera ofrecerte, y nunca se agotará. *¡Cuán precioso es mi gran Amor!*

Piensa por un momento en la parábola *del comerciante que buscaba perlas finas y que cuando encontró una de gran valor, vendió todo lo que tenía y la compró.* Mi Amor es como esa perla: tan invaluable que vale la pena perder lo que sea a fin de asegurarlo para siempre.

Aunque para ganar mi Amor vale la pena incluso exponerse a perder la vida, lo que realmente ocurre es que, lejos de hacer que la pierdas, mi Amor enriquece tu vida. Este glorioso regalo provee un fundamento para construir sobre él, y mejora tus relaciones con otras personas. El hecho de saber que eres amado de una manera perfecta y eterna te ayuda a que llegues a ser la persona que yo diseñé que fueras. *Entender cuán ancho y largo, alto y profundo es mi Amor* por ti te conduce a la adoración. *¡Aquí* es donde tu intimidad conmigo crece a pasos agigantados, a medida que gozosamente celebras mi magnífica Presencia!

SALMOS 63.3; SALMOS 36.7; MATEO 13.45, 46;
EFESIOS 3.17, 18

Julio 16

ANUNCIA MI SALVACIÓN DÍA A DÍA. Necesitas recordar la verdad del evangelio a cada momento: *Porque por gracia has sido salvado mediante la fe, y esto no es tu propia obra; es un regalo, no un resultado de tu propio esfuerzo.* Esta verdad es muy contracultural. El mundo te dice que tienes que trabajar para ser lo suficiente bueno. Tu propia mente caída y tu corazón estarán de acuerdo con estos mensajes, a menos que estés vigilante. Es por eso que las Escrituras te advierten para que *te mantengas alerta.* El diablo es *el acusador* de mis seguidores. Sus acusaciones desalientan y derrotan a muchos cristianos, por lo que debes recordar con frecuencia la verdad del evangelio.

La mejor respuesta al glorioso regalo de la gracia es un corazón agradecido que se deleita en hacer mi voluntad. Es vital que anuncies el evangelio no solo a ti mismo, sino al mundo. *¡Proclama mi Gloria entre las naciones!* Trata de compartir esta buena noticia, tanto cerca (a familiares, amigos, compañeros de trabajo) como lejos (a las naciones). *Todos los pueblos* necesitan conocer la verdad sobre mí. Deja que tu gratitud te motive, te energice y te llene de Gozo.

SALMOS 96.2, 3; EFESIOS 2.8, 9; 1 PEDRO 5.8;
APOCALIPSIS 12.10

DICHOSOS AQUELLOS QUE HAN aprendido a aclamar-me. La palabra «aclamar» significa expresar aproba-ción de forma entusiasta. Esta no es una inclinación natural de la humanidad. Es algo que necesitas apren-der y practicar. Comienza con tus pensamientos. ¡En lugar de pensar en mí de maneras aburridas y repeti-tivas, medita en mi gloriosa grandeza! Yo hablé y el mundo existió. Formé a las personas a mi propia ima-gen y les di almas eternas. Creé belleza en el mundo y en todo el universo. Soy infinitamente más brillan-te que el más grande genio que te puedas imaginar. Mi sabiduría es *profunda*, y mi Amor es inagotable. Aprende a tener grandes pensamientos acerca de mí y exprésalos con entusiasmo. Los salmos proveen una excelente instrucción en esta búsqueda.

Alabarme también significa reconocer pública-mente mi excelencia. *Tú eres la luz del mundo*, porque me conoces como tu Dios-Salvador. Quiero que *dejes que tu luz brille delante de los hombres*; cuéntales de las maravillas de quien soy y todo lo que he hecho. *Proclama las obras maravillosas de Aquel que te llamó de las tinieblas a su Luz admirable.*

SALMOS 89.15; ROMANOS 11.33; MATEO 5.14-16;
1 PEDRO 2.9

Julio 18

¡ESTÉN SIEMPRE ALEGRES! Este es uno de los versículos más cortos de la Biblia, pero irradia Luz celestial.
Yo te hice a mi imagen, y te creé con la capacidad de
elegir el Gozo para cada momento de tu vida. Cuando
tu mente tiende a descender por caminos desagradables y sombríos, detenla con este mandato glorioso.
Comprueba cuántas veces al día puedes recordar que
debes alegrarte.

Es importante no solo regocijarse, sino también
debes pensar en los motivos específicos para estar
contento. Pueden ser tan sencillos como las provisio-
nes diarias: alimento, casa, ropa. Las relaciones con
los seres queridos también pueden ser una rica fuente de Gozo. Dado que tú eres mi amado, tu relación
conmigo es una fuente omnipresente de alegría. Estos
pensamientos gozosos iluminarán tanto tu mente
como tu corazón, capacitándote para encontrar más
placer en tu vida.

Elegir regocijarte te bendecirá a ti y a los que te
rodean. También fortalecerá tu relación conmigo.

1 TESALONICENSES 5.16; GÉNESIS 1.27;
FILIPENSES 4.4

Yo soy tu Socorro y tu Escudo. Préstale especial atención al pronombre posesivo, *tu*. Eso significa que no soy solo *una* Ayuda y *un* Escudo. Soy los *tuyos* para todos los tiempos y por toda la eternidad. Deja que este compromiso eterno te fortalezca y anime mientras caminas conmigo a lo largo de este día. *Nunca te dejaré ni te abandonaré.* ¡Puedes depender de mí!

Debido a que soy tu Ayuda, no es necesario que les temas a tus incapacidades. Cuando la tarea que tienes por delante parezca desalentadora, alégrate porque estoy listo para ayudarte. Reconoce francamente tu insuficiencia, y confía en mi suficiencia infinita. Tú y yo *juntos* podemos lograr cualquier cosa que esté dentro de mi voluntad.

Definitivamente, me necesitas como tu Escudo. Te protejo de muchos peligros: físicos, emocionales y espirituales. A veces eres consciente de mi obra protectora a tu favor, pero también te protejo de peligros que ni siquiera sospechas. Encuentra reposo en esta seguridad de mi Presencia velando por ti. *No temas peligro alguno,* mi amado, *porque yo estoy contigo.*

SALMOS 33.20; DEUTERONOMIO 31.8;
FILIPENSES 4.13; SALMOS 23.4

Julio 20

Aférrate a mí, mi amado, porque *mi mano derecha te sostiene.* Cuando te agarras de mí en infantil dependencia, estás demostrando tu compromiso conmigo. A veces utilizo los tiempos difíciles para refinar tu fe y probar que es genuina. Al aferrarte a mí en medio de la adversidad, tu fe se hace más fuerte y tú experimentas consuelo. Habiendo soportado diversas pruebas, ganas la confianza de que con mi ayuda puedes hacerles frente a las dificultades futuras. Eres cada vez más consciente de que yo siempre estaré disponible para ayudarte.

En medio de la noche o de tiempos difíciles, recuerda que mi diestra te sostiene. Esta mano que te sostiene es fuerte y justa; no hay límite para la cantidad de apoyo que te puede proporcionar. Por eso, cuando te sientas abrumado, no te rindas. En cambio, *recurre a mí y mi Fuerza.* Ten la seguridad de que mi mano poderosa es también justa, y que todo lo que te provee es bueno. *No temas, porque yo te fortaleceré y te ayudaré. Te sostendré con mi diestra victoriosa.*

Salmos 63.8; 1 Pedro 1.7; Salmos 105.4;
Isaías 41.10

LOS QUE ME MIRAN A MÍ, están radiantes. Yo soy el Sol que te alumbra de forma continua, incluso cuando tus circunstancias pudieran ser difíciles y el camino por delante luzca oscuro. Debido a que me conoces como Salvador, tienes una fuente de Luz que vence a la oscuridad. Yo te diseñé para que *reflejaras mi Gloria*, y lo haces mirándome, volviendo tu rostro hacia la Luz. Aparta un tiempo para permanecer quieto en mi Presencia, con tu rostro vuelto hacia arriba para absorber mi resplandor. Mientras más tiempo permanezcas en esta atmósfera de Luz radiante, más podré bendecirte y fortalecerte.

Cuando estés descansando conmigo, podrías susurrar las palabras de Jacob: «*En realidad, el Señor está en este lugar*». Yo estoy en todas partes en todo momento, por lo que esta declaración es siempre verdad, ya sea que sientas o no mi cercanía.

Dedicar un tiempo a disfrutar de mi Amor-Luz, solazándote en mi resplandor, puede elevar tu percepción de mi Presencia. Además, el tiempo pasado conmigo te ayuda a ser una luz en el mundo, irradiando mi Amor a todos los que tienes cerca.

SALMOS 34.5; 2 CORINTIOS 3.18;
GÉNESIS 28.16; MATEO 5.16

Julio 22

MEDIANTE MI RESURRECCIÓN de entre los muertos, *has recibido un nuevo nacimiento a una esperanza viva*. Yo morí en la cruz para pagar el castigo por los pecados de todos mis seguidores. Si hubiera permanecido muerto, *tu fe habría sido ilusoria* y hubieras estado espiritualmente muerto para siempre, siendo *todavía culpable por tus pecados*. ¡Por supuesto, era imposible que mi muerte fuera permanente, porque yo soy Dios! Como les dije claramente a los que se me oponían: *Mi Padre y yo somos Uno*.

Mi resurrección es un hecho histórico muy bien documentado. Este acontecimiento milagroso te abrió el camino para que pudieras experimentar el *nuevo nacimiento*. Al confesar tu pecado y confiar en mí como tu Salvador, te has convertido en uno de los míos, transitando por un camino que te lleva al cielo. ¡Debido a que soy tu Salvador viviente, vas por un camino de *esperanza viva*! La Luz de mi amorosa Presencia brilla sobre ti siempre, incluso en los momentos más oscuros y difíciles. Mírame a mí, mi amado. Deja que mi Amor-Luz brillante perfore la oscuridad y llene tu corazón de Gozo.

1 PEDRO 1.3; 1 CORINTIOS 15.17;
EFESIOS 2.1; JUAN 10.30

Yo soy Dios tu Libertador. No importa lo que esté sucediendo en el mundo, puedes *alegrarte en mí*. Tu planeta ha estado en una condición terriblemente caída desde la desobediencia de Adán y Eva. Ellos perdieron a sus dos primeros hijos de una manera desgarradora. Caín mató a su hermano menor, Abel, porque estaba celoso de él. Dios entonces lo castigó sentenciándolo a *ser un fugitivo errante* sobre la tierra.

Los efectos persistentes de la Caída siguen haciendo del mundo un lugar peligroso e incierto. Por eso, el reto que tienes ante ti cada día es estar siempre gozoso en medio del quebrantamiento en que yace el mundo. Recuérdate a menudo: «Jesús está conmigo y a mi favor. *Nada puede apartarme de su Amor*». Dedica tus energías a disfrutar de mi Presencia y de lo bueno que aún queda sobre la tierra. Usa tus dones para proyectar mi Luz en los lugares a los que te he dado acceso. *No tengas miedo de las malas noticias*, porque yo soy capaz de sacar algo bueno de lo malo. Entrena tu corazón para que se *mantenga firme, confiando en mí*, tu Salvador.

Habacuc 3.18; Génesis 4.12;
Romanos 8.39; Salmos 112.7

Julio 24

No TEMAS NI TE DESANIMES. Te estás preocupando anticipadamente por las incertidumbres que tienes por delante dejando que te amilanen. El miedo y el desánimo te están esperando en cualquier recodo del camino, listos para acompañarte si se lo permites. *Sin embargo, yo estoy siempre contigo, sosteniéndote de tu mano derecha*. Debido a que yo vivo más allá del tiempo, también estoy en el camino adelante, brillando intensamente, haciéndote señas para que fijes tu mirada en mí. Aférrate a mi mano y con paso resuelto pasa junto a aquellas oscuras presencias del miedo y la desesperación. Mantén la mirada en mi radiante Presencia que lanza rayos de *Amor* y *consuelo* inagotables.

Tu confianza proviene de saber que yo estoy continuamente contigo *y* ya estoy en tu futuro, preparando el camino delante de ti. Escúchame mientras te llamo... con palabras de advertencia y sabiduría, valor y esperanza: *No temas, porque yo estoy contigo. No te angusties, porque yo soy tu Dios. Te fortaleceré y te ayudaré; te sostendré con mi diestra victoriosa.*

DEUTERONOMIO 31.8; SALMOS 73.23;
SALMOS 119.76; ISAÍAS 41.10

Es en el momento presente que me encuentras más cerca de ti. Mi Presencia hoy es una fuente inagotable de Gozo… ¡siempre es día de fiesta! Estoy entrenándote para que *te alegres en mí siempre*. Esta es una elección de momento a momento. Es posible encontrar Gozo en mí, aun durante tus situaciones más difíciles. Siempre me encuentro cerca, por lo que estoy siempre disponible para ayudarte. Incluso te puedo llevar a través de tus experiencias más arduas.

Imagínate a una mujer que se ha comprometido con un hombre al que ama y admira profundamente. Su corazón se desborda de placer cada vez que piensa en su amado. Mientras él está en su mente, los problemas se pierden en el fondo de sus pensamientos, incapaces de atenuar su entusiasmo y emoción. Del mismo modo, cuando recuerdas que yo soy tu prometido y has hecho un compromiso conmigo para siempre, podrás encontrar placer en mí aun frente a las peores dificultades. La satisfacción del alma que encuentras en mí te ayuda a relacionarte bien con otras personas. Y al disfrutar de mi Presencia amorosa, con tu Gozo podrás ser de bendición para muchos.

Proverbios 15.15; Filipenses 4.4, 5;
Salmos 63.5; Deuteronomio 33.12

Julio 26

Yo DESPEJO EL CAMINO *debajo de tus pies para que tus tobillos no flaqueen.* Esto demuestra hasta qué punto llega mi participación en tu vida. Sé exactamente lo que hay delante de ti y cómo puedo alterar el camino por donde vas a transitar para que tu andar sea más fácil. A veces te permito ver lo que he hecho a tu favor. En otras ocasiones no te percatas de las dificultades de las que te he librado. De cualquier manera, el hecho de que ensanche el camino por donde pasarás demuestra cuán amorosamente estoy involucrado en tu vida.

Desde tu perspectiva, a menudo lo que hago te resulta misterioso. No te protejo, a ti ni a nadie, de *todas* las adversidades. Tampoco *yo* estuve protegido contra las adversidades durante los treinta y tres años que viví en tu mundo. ¡Al contrario, por tu bien sufrí de forma totalmente voluntaria dolores inimaginables, humillaciones y la agonía de la cruz! Cuando mi Padre se alejó de mí, experimenté un sufrimiento indecible. Sin embargo, debido a que estuve dispuesto a soportar tal aislamiento de Él, tú nunca tendrás que sufrir solo. ¡He prometido *estar contigo siempre*!

SALMOS 18.36; MATEO 27.46;
MATEO 28.20

EL QUE CREE EN MÍ, no cree solo en mí, sino en el que me envió. Cuando me ves a mí, estás viendo al que me envió. Vine al mundo no solo para ser tu Salvador, sino también para ayudarte a ver al Padre con mayor claridad. Él y yo siempre trabajamos en perfecta unidad. Como lo proclamé cuando enseñaba en el templo en Jerusalén: *«El Padre y yo somos uno».* Así que cuando busques vivir cerca de mí —*fijando tus ojos en mí*— de ninguna manera estarás ignorando a mi Padre.

La Trinidad, compuesta de Padre, Hijo y Espíritu Santo, es un gran regalo para ti; también es un misterio más allá de tu comprensión. Esta bendición de tres Personas en una enriquece en gran medida tu vida de oración. Puedes orar al Padre en mi Nombre; también me puedes hablar directamente a mí. Y el Espíritu Santo está continuamente disponible para ayudarte con tus oraciones. No dejes que los misterios de la Trinidad te perturben. ¡En lugar de eso, responde a estas maravillas con alabanza gozosa y adoración!

JUAN 12.44, 45; JUAN 10.30; HEBREOS 12.2;
SALMOS 150.6

Julio 28

Yo soy *EL VIVIENTE QUE TE VE* SIEMPRE. Yo veo lo más profundo de tu ser. Ni siquiera uno de tus pensamientos escapa a mi observación. Mi conocimiento íntimo de todo lo que tiene que ver contigo significa que nunca estás solo, tanto en los tiempos apacibles como en los tiempos turbulentos. También significa que quiero limpiar tus pensamientos de sus tendencias pecaminosas.

Cuando te encuentres pensando de una forma odiosa e hiriente, confiésamelo de inmediato. No me pidas solo que te perdone, sino que te cambie. No tienes que elaborar demasiado tu confesión, como si tuvieras que convencerme para que extienda mi gracia sobre ti. Yo pasé a través de una tortuosa ejecución y la separación absoluta de mi Padre, por eso puedo *echar tan lejos de ti tus transgresiones como lejos está el oriente del occidente.* ¡Me deleito en perdonarte!

Recuerda que incluso ahora te veo vestido con radiantes vestiduras: mi perfecta justicia. Y ya puedo ver en ti la gloriosa visión que tendrás cuando el cielo se convierta en tu hogar.

GÉNESIS 16.14; SALMOS 139.1, 2;
2 CORINTIOS 5.21; SALMOS 103.12

TE ESTOY ENTRENANDO *en la perseverancia.* Esta lección no es para los débiles de corazón. Sin embargo, es una rica bendición, una forma de compartir mi reino y mi sufrimiento.

Ya que mi reino es eterno, resulta de un valor infinito. He dejado en claro que para *participar en mi Gloria* es necesario *compartir mis sufrimientos.* Además, esta experiencia produce beneficios reales aquí y ahora: carácter.

La perseverancia solo puede desarrollarse a través de las pruebas. Así que haz todo lo que sea necesario para aceptar cualquier problema que te cause miedo. Tráelo a mi Presencia con acción de gracias, y reconoce tu disposición a soportarlo todo el tiempo que sea necesario. Pídeme que tome este problema feo y oscuro y lo transforme en algo encantador. A partir de la más desgarradora situación yo puedo tejer brillantes hilos dorados de Gloria. Quizás haya que esperar un tiempo para que el modelo precioso emerja, pero esta espera puede producir paciencia. ¡Alégrate, mi amado, porque estoy puliendo tu carácter hasta que brille con la Luz de mi Gloria!

APOCALIPSIS 1.9; ROMANOS 8.17;
FILIPENSES 2.14, 15

MI AMADO, *MIS BONDADES JAMÁS SE AGOTAN. Son nuevas cada mañana.* Así que puedes comenzar cada día con confianza, sabiendo que mi gran reserva de bendiciones está llena hasta el borde. Esta certidumbre te ayuda a *esperar en mí*, confiando a mi preocupación y cuidado tu larga espera por una respuesta a tus oraciones. Te aseguro que a ninguna de esas peticiones ha pasado inadvertida sin que me ocupe de ella. Quiero que bebas abundantemente de mi fuente de Amor ilimitado y compasión inagotable. Mientras esperas en mi Presencia, estos nutrientes divinos están libremente disponibles para ti.

Aunque quizás muchas de tus oraciones aun no tienen respuesta, puedes encontrar esperanza en *mi gran fidelidad.* Yo mantengo todas mis promesas según mi manera y tiempo perfectos. He prometido *darte la Paz* que puede desterrar los problemas y las angustias de tu corazón. Si te sientes cansado de esperar, recuerda que yo también espero; *que puedo tener piedad contigo y mostrarte compasión.* Me contengo hasta que estés listo para recibir las cosas que amorosamente te he preparado. *Dichosos son todos los que esperan en mí.*

LAMENTACIONES 3.22, 24; JUAN 14.27;
ISAÍAS 30.18

ANTES QUE ME LLAMES, YO TE RESPONDERÉ; todavía estarás hablando cuando ya te habré escuchado. Sé que a veces te sientes como si estuvieras solo, en la oscuridad. Te mantienes orando porque es lo que hay que hacer, pero te preguntas si tus oraciones producen algún cambio. Cuando te estés sintiendo de esta manera, es bueno que te detengas y recuerdes quién soy yo: *¡el Rey de la Gloria!* Yo trasciendo el tiempo. Pasado, presente y futuro son todos iguales para mí. Esta es la razón por la que puedo responderte antes de que me digas tu necesidad.

Ninguna oración tuya es desoída ni queda sin respuesta. Sin embargo, a veces tengo que decirte «No» o «Todavía no». En otras ocasiones tus oraciones reciben una respuesta que no puedes percibir. *Mi sabiduría es profunda,* está enormemente más allá de tu comprensión. Dedica un tiempo a pensar en las maravillas de mi inteligencia infinita y deléitate en mi Amor inagotable. Si persistes en esta adoración íntima, sabrás más allá de cualquiera duda que *nunca* estarás solo. ¡Eres mío!

ISAÍAS 65.24; SALMOS 24.10;
ROMANOS 11.33

Agosto

*Me has dado a conocer los
caminos de la vida; me llenarás
de alegría en tu presencia.*

HECHOS 2.28

VEN CON ANSIAS ANTE MI PRESENCIA, invitándome a que te *sacie con mi Amor*. El mejor tiempo para buscar mi Rostro es *por la mañana*, poco después de que te despiertes. Conectarte conmigo temprano marcará la pauta para el resto del día. Mi Amor inagotable satisface inmensamente: Te ayuda a saber que eres apreciado e importante. Te recuerda que *juntos*, tú y yo podemos manejar las circunstancias de tu día. Saber que eres amado por siempre te da energías y valor para atravesar victorioso las dificultades.

Tu encuentro con mi Presencia amorosa por la mañana temprano te equipa para *cantar de alegría*. Piensa en el asombroso privilegio de encontrarte, en la intimidad de tu casa, con quien es *Rey de reyes y Señor de señores*. Alégrate de que tu nombre está escrito con tinta indeleble en el *libro de la Vida del Cordero*. Aparta tiempo para disfrutar en mi Presencia. Habla o canta alabanzas; lee las Escrituras y ora. ¡Deléitate asimismo en la maravillosa verdad de que *nada en toda la creación te podrá apartarte de mi Amor!*

SALMOS 90.14; APOCALIPSIS 19.16;
APOCALIPSIS 21.27; ROMANOS 8.39

Yo soy tu Señor viviente, tu Roca, tu Dios-Salvador. Dedica un tiempo a pensar en mi grandeza y mi compromiso infinito contigo. Vives en una cultura en la que la gente se resiste a hacer compromisos. Incluso aquellos que dicen: «Sí, acepto», a menudo cambian de opinión a última hora. Sin embargo, yo soy tu Amigo para siempre y el Amor eterno de tu alma. ¡Puedes estar seguro de mi Amor!

En lugar de preocuparte por los problemas de tu vida y tu mundo, recuerda quién soy yo. No solo soy tu Señor viviente y tu Roca inmutable, sino que también soy *Dios tu Salvador*. ¡Debido a que soy el Dios eterno, mi muerte en la cruz por tus pecados *te salva por completo!* Así que no tienes que preocuparte de que vaya a dejar de amarte porque tu comportamiento pudiera no haber sido lo suficiente bueno. Es *mi* bondad y *mi* justicia las que te conservan seguro en mi Amor. Deja que mi compromiso interminable contigo sea un consuelo en tu caminar por este mundo lleno de problemas. Algún día vas a vivir conmigo en el paraíso.

SALMOS 18.46; HEBREOS 7.25;
2 CORINTIOS 5.21

ESPERA EN MI PRESENCIA. Hay muchos beneficios
—espirituales, emocionales y físicos— al pasar tiempo conmigo. Sin embargo, muchos de mis hijos creen
que esto es un lujo que no pueden permitirse. Aunque
saben que necesitan descansar y permanecer en quietud, persisten en su acelerado estilo de vida. Quiero
que *tú* organices tus prioridades de una manera tal
que puedas tener algunos momentos de descanso
conmigo. Voy a refrescar tu alma y fortalecerte para el
camino que queda por delante.

Ten valor. Vivir en este mundo quebrantado y
corrompido requiere valentía de tu parte. Puesto que
la valentía no es una característica en muchos de los
corazones de los seres humanos, vas a necesitar mi
ayuda para *ser fuerte y valiente*. A pesar de todos los
acontecimientos alarmantes en el mundo, no tienes
por qué sentirte aterrorizado o desanimado. Disci-
plínate para *tenerme en tus pensamientos* una y otra y
otra vez. Encuentra consuelo en mi promesa de *acompañarte dondequiera que vayas.*

Continúa en tus esfuerzos a fin de ser valiente, y
búscame para que te ayude. *Yo fortaleceré tu corazón.*

SALMOS 27.14; JOSUÉ 1.9;
HEBREOS 3.1

Agosto 4

¡NUNCA SUBESTIMES EL PODER DE LA ORACIÓN! Hay personas que cuando se sienten desanimadas y desesperanzadas suelen decir: «No hay nada más que hacer, sino solo orar». La implicación es que para ellos este es su último recurso y bastante débil. ¡Nada podría estar más lejos de la verdad!

Yo creé a la humanidad con la capacidad de comunicarse conmigo. Puesto que *soy el Rey eterno, inmortal e invisible* del universo, este es un sorprendente privilegio. Aun cuando la raza humana se corrompió con el pecado de la desobediencia de Adán y Eva, no invalidé este glorioso privilegio. Y cuando viví en tu mundo como un hombre de carne y hueso, siempre dependí de la oración a mi Padre. Fui muy consciente de la necesidad de ayuda que tenía.

La oración persistente y sincera te bendecirá no solo a ti, sino también a tu familia, amigos, iglesia e incluso a tu país. Pídele al Espíritu Santo que te ayude a orar de manera eficaz. Únete a otros en esta aventura de buscar mi Rostro en humildad y arrepentimiento. Ruégame para que *restaure tu tierra*.

COLOSENSES 1.16; 1 TIMOTEO 1.17;
MATEO 14.23; 2 CRÓNICAS 7.14

REFÚGIENSE EN MÍ Y MI FUERZA; busca mi Rostro siempre. Deja que tu corazón se alegre cada vez que me buscas.

Imagínate a una pareja de enamorados. Cuando el hombre va a visitar a su prometida, ella no abre la puerta y dice despreocupadamente: «¡Oh, eres tú!». Ni él mira por sobre el hombro de ella y pregunta: «¿Tienes algo para comer?». En lugar de eso, sus corazones saltan de alegría, porque están juntos. Tú eres mi prometida, y yo soy el amor de tu alma para siempre. ¡Regocíjate en el sorprendente afecto que te tengo!

Gloríate en mi santo Nombre. Mi Nombre es santo porque *me* representa. Este Nombre está *sobre todo nombre,* y tú puedes utilizarlo libremente para comunicarte conmigo y ofrecerme tu adoración. Gozas del privilegio de tener un acceso fácil a mí. Algunas personas se glorían en su riqueza, sus logros, su belleza o su fama. Sin embargo, yo te invito a que te glories en mi, tu Salvador, Señor y Amigo. Al glorificarme, estarás fortaleciéndote, deleitándote y otorgándole poder a tus oraciones y Gozo a tu corazón.

1 CRÓNICAS 16.10, 11; 2 CORINTIOS 11.2;
JUAN 15.13, 14; FILIPENSES 2.9, 10

Agosto 6

CUANDO LA PLANIFICACIÓN y los problemas ocupan tu mente, acude a mí y pronuncia mi Nombre. Deja que la Luz de mi Presencia brille en ti mientras te alegras en *mi gran Amor*. Dame las gracias por velar permanente y amorosamente por ti. Afirma tu confianza en mí y exprésame tu devoción. Después, pídeme que ilumine el camino que tienes por delante y te ayude a planear lo que necesitas hacer y lo que no, a enfrentar los problemas que debes atender, y a no dejar que las preocupaciones y los miedos se conviertan en el centro de tus pensamientos.

Mantén tu atención en mí tan a menudo como puedas, y yo aclararé tu forma de ver las cosas. Satura tu mente y tu corazón con las Escrituras, leyéndolas, estudiándolas y memorizando versículos que sean especialmente útiles para ti en una situación dada. *Mi Palabra es una lámpara a tus pies y una Luz en tu sendero.*

Si sigues estas pautas, tu preocupación por la planificación y los problemas disminuirá, lo que dejará espacio en tu vida para más de mí. ¡Deléitate en *la alegría de mi Presencia!*

SALMOS 107.21, 22; 1 PEDRO 5.7;
SALMOS 119.105; HECHOS 2.28

229

Yo soy el Único *que mantiene tu lámpara encendida e ilumino tus tinieblas.* A veces, cuando estás *cansado y cargado,* puedes sentir como si tu lámpara estuviera a punto de apagarse. Parece que el parpadeo y el chisporroteo anunciaran que el combustible estuviera a punto de agotarse. Cada vez que esto te suceda, acude a mí en busca de ayuda. Inhala profundamente en mi Presencia y recuerda que *yo* soy el Único que puede proveerle a tu lámpara combustible. ¡Yo soy *tu Fuerza*!

También soy tu Luz. Mantente en contacto conmigo y así permitirás que la Gloria de mi Presencia inunde tu vida. Mi belleza radiante te iluminará y cambiará tu perspectiva. Si te alejas de mí y olvidas que estoy contigo, tu existencia se tornará tenebrosa. Es cierto que en este mundo caído en el que habitas hay mucha oscuridad. Sin embargo, *yo soy la Luz que resplandece en la oscuridad.* Por eso, no tienes que alejarte de mí ni dejarte atrapar por el miedo, hijo mío. Créeme de todo corazón: no importa cuán sombrías las cosas puedan parecer, *yo transformaré tu oscuridad en Luz.*

Salmos 18.28; Mateo 11.28;
Salmos 18.1; Juan 1.5

TEMER A LOS HOMBRES RESULTA UN TRAMPA. Una trampa es una especie de lazo, algo que te enreda, haciendo difícil que puedas escapar. «Temer a los hombres» implica estar demasiado preocupado por lo que otros piensen de ti. Verte a ti mismo a través de los ojos de otros es malsano e inmoral. Este miedo puede ser paralizante y está lleno de distorsiones. El punto de vista de los demás puede estar distorsionado debido a su propia naturaleza pecaminosa. Además, es casi imposible saber lo que realmente piensan de ti. Cuando te ves a ti mismo desde la perspectiva de otros, estás añadiendo tu propia distorsión a la de ellos. Al esforzarte por presentarte como una «persona» aceptable a los ojos de los demás, caes en la trampa.

Si te das cuenta de que el miedo a los hombres te está motivando —controlando tus pensamientos y conducta— ven a mí. Si me lo pides, te perdonaré por hacer de otros puntos de vista un ídolo; te ayudaré a liberarte de esos lazos. Afirma tu confianza en mí y date tiempo para disfrutar de mi Presencia. ¡En la medida que te olvides de ti mismo y te concentres en mí, tu amado Señor, serás cada vez más libre!

PROVERBIOS 29.25; 1 JUAN 1.9;
2 CORINTIOS 3.17

Ven, descansa conmigo, mi amado. Aunque muchas tareas te estén llamando, urgiéndote para que les des prioridad, yo sé qué es lo que más necesitas: *quedarte quieto* en mi Presencia. Respira hondo y fija tu mirada en mí. Al volver tu atención a mí, deja que tus preocupaciones se deslicen sin afectarte en lo más mínimo. Esto te permitirá relajarte y disfrutar de mi cercanía. ¡Yo nunca estoy lejos de ti!

Medita en las Escrituras; búscame en la Biblia. Deja que sus palabras llenas de gracia y verdad penetren hasta las profundidades de tu alma y te acerquen a mí. *Mi Palabra es viva y poderosa*, por lo que puede infundir vida fresca en ti.

Cuando sea el momento de volver a tus ocupaciones, llévame contigo. Inclúyeme en tus planes y en la solución de tus problemas. Me interesa todo lo que haces, dices y piensas. Susurra mi nombre, «Jesús», en dulce recordatorio de mi cercanía. *Reconóceme en todos tus caminos*, porque yo soy el Señor de tu vida.

SALMOS 46.10; HEBREOS 4.12;
PROVERBIOS 3.6

Agosto 10

TE ESTOY ENTRENANDO para que seas un vencedor, para que encuentres Gozo en medio de las circunstancias que antes te habrían derrotado. Tu capacidad para trascender los problemas se basa en este principio, sólido como una roca: *yo he vencido al mundo*; ¡ya he obtenido la victoria final! No obstante, como te he enseñado, *tendrás aflicciones en este mundo*. Así es que espera encontrarte con muchas dificultades a medida que avanzas por la vida. Tú habitas un planeta que siempre está en guerra, y el enemigo de tu alma nunca descansa. Sin embargo, no tengas miedo, *porque el que está en ti es más poderoso que el que está en el mundo*. ¡Esta es una buena razón para regocijarse!

Cuando te halles en medio de circunstancias difíciles, es crucial mantenerte confiando en mí. Susurra tan a menudo como sientas que lo necesitas: «Yo confío en ti, Jesús», recordando que estoy siempre cerca. Pídeme ayuda a fin de que aprendas todo lo que tengo para ti en esta prueba. Busca las flores de Gozo que crecen en el rico suelo de la adversidad. *Yo te miro con agrado,* mi amado.

JUAN 16.33; 1 JUAN 4.4; SALMOS 145.18;
NÚMEROS 6.25

233

Mi Rostro está brillando sobre ti, mi amado. Dedica un tiempo a descansar en mi Luz gozosa, y procura conocerme como realmente soy. Siempre estoy cerca de ti, más cerca que el aire que respiras. Estar consciente de mi amorosa Presencia es una gran bendición. Sin embargo, lo más importante es *confiar* en que me encuentro contigo, independientemente de lo que estés experimentando.

Yo soy inmanente: estoy presente en todas partes, a través del universo entero. También soy trascendente: existo por sobre e independientemente del universo. Yo soy *el Rey eterno, inmortal, invisible, el único Dios. Como los cielos son más altos que la tierra, así mis caminos y mis pensamientos son más altos que los de ustedes.* Por eso, no esperes entenderme completamente a mí o a mis caminos. Cuando las cosas no salgan como deseas, inclínate ante mi infinita *sabiduría y conocimiento. Mis juicios son indescifrables y mis caminos impenetrables,* pero son buenos. Recuerda el ejemplo de Job. Cuando su familia experimentó múltiples desastres, él *se dejó caer al suelo en actitud de adoración.* ¡Yo estoy más allá de todos tus problemas!

1 Timoteo 1.17; Isaías 55.9;
Romanos 11.33; Job 1.20

Agosto 12

CUANDO EN EL CAMINO DE LA VIDA te encuentres enfrentando dificultades que parezcan superiores a tus fuerzas, quiero que *te consideres muy dichoso.* Al hacerle frente de esta manera a tales «imposibilidades», *mis brazos eternos* estarán abiertos y listos para acogerte, calmarte y ayudarte a hacer lo que sea necesario en tales casos. No tienes por qué perder la alegría cuando te encuentres en medio de las perplejidades de tus problemas, porque yo soy *Dios, tu Libertador,* y ya he hecho el milagro más grande en tu vida: salvarte de tus pecados. Si te mantienes con la vista fija en mí, tu Señor resucitado y Rey, tu pesimismo terminará dándole paso a la valentía. Aunque eres una criatura terrenal, nuestras almas comparten mi victoria eterna.

Tengo un Poder infinito, de manera que mi especialidad son las «imposibilidades». Me deleito en ellas, porque despliegan mi Gloria muy vívidamente. En cuanto a ti, te ayudan a vivir de la manera en que lo planeé: con gozo, confiando en tu dependencia de mí. La próxima vez que te enfrentes a una situación «imposible», búscame inmediatamente con un corazón lleno de esperanza. Reconoce tu total incapacidad y aférrate a mí, confiando en mi suficiencia infinita. ¡*Para mí, todo es posible!*

SANTIAGO 1.2, 3; DEUTERONOMIO 33.27;
HABACUC 3.17, 18; MATEO 19.26

No IMPORTA CÓMO TE SIENTAS en este momento, recuerda que *no* estás bajo juicio. *No hay ninguna condenación para los que están unidos a mí,* los que me conocen como Salvador. Ya has sido juzgado en los tribunales del cielo y declarado «¡No culpable!».

Yo vine a la tierra para hacerte libre de la esclavitud del pecado. Mi deseo es verte viviendo con alegría dentro de esa libertad. Aprende a disfrutar de tu situación como una persona libre de culpa en mi reino, negándote a sentirte agobiado o encadenado. El mundo está en una condición caída donde el pecado y el mal abundan… ¡pero *yo he vencido al mundo!*

La mejor respuesta a la gracia que te he prodigado es el agradecimiento, una gratitud que alimenta el deseo de vivir de acuerdo a mi voluntad. Mientras más cerca vivas de mí, mejor podrás discernir mi voluntad; además, podrás experimentar más mi Paz y mi Gozo. Conocerme íntimamente te ayudará a confiar en mí lo suficiente como para recibir mi Paz incluso en medio de los problemas. *Vivir lleno de gratitud* tiene el encantador «efecto secundario» de aumentar tu Gozo. ¡Mi amado, vive libre y gozosamente en mi Presencia!

ROMANOS 8.1; JUAN 8.36; JUAN 16.33;
COLOSENSES 2.6, 7

Agosto 14

Yo *te devolveré el Gozo de mi salvación*. Cuando me confiesas tus pecados con un corazón humilde, con mucho gusto te perdono. Sin embargo, hay más: yo te restauro. ¡*La salvación de tu alma* es la fuente de un *Gozo indecible y glorioso*! Quiero que vuelvas a experimentar el rico y profundo placer de una relación estrecha conmigo. Deseo ser tu *Primer Amor*.

Muchas personas y cosas compiten por tu atención, por lo que mantenerme a mí en el primer lugar en tu corazón requiere diligencia. Es posible que hayas desarrollado formas de buscarme que te son familiares y fáciles. Sin embargo, el peligro de confiar demasiado en la rutina es que puede convertirse en una tediosa obligación. Cuando te des cuenta de que esto está sucediendo en tu vida, detente e intenta algo nuevo. Recuerda que yo soy Rey de reyes, Señor de señores, y Creador-Sustentador de este vasto e increíble universo. Dedica un tiempo extra a adorarme y alabarme antes de traer ante mí otras oraciones y peticiones. Esto despertará tu corazón a *mi Gloria* y al Gozo de mi Presencia.

SALMOS 51.12; 1 PEDRO 1.8, 9;
APOCALIPSIS 2.4; JUAN 17.24

ME BUSCARÁS Y ME ENCONTRARÁS cuando me busques de todo corazón. Esta es una deliciosa asignación, pero también un reto bastante difícil. Pasar tiempo disfrutando de mi Presencia es un privilegio reservado solo a los que me conocen como Salvador y Señor. A fin de maximizar los beneficios de esta experiencia preciosa, necesitas buscarme de todo corazón. Sin embargo, tu mente es a menudo un desorden enmarañado y desenfocado. Busca la ayuda de mi Espíritu para que proteja tu mente y tu corazón de distracciones, distorsiones, engaños, ansiedades y otros enredos. Esto te ayudará a poner en orden tus pensamientos y a calmar tu corazón, liberándote para que *me busques* sin ninguna clase de obstáculos.

Quiero que me busques no solo en los momentos de quietud, sino también cuando estás involucrado en otros asuntos. Tu cerebro asombroso es capaz de concentrarse en mí, incluso cuando te encuentras ocupado. La simple oración: «Jesús, mantenme consciente de tu Presencia» puede servirte como una suave música de fondo, sonando continuamente por debajo de otras actividades mentales. Si *muestras un carácter firme, yo te guardaré en perfecta Paz.*

JEREMÍAS 29.13; SALMOS 112.7;
ISAÍAS 26.3

BENDECIRÉ A MI PUEBLO CON LA PAZ. Esta promesa bíblica es para todo aquel que confía en mí como Salvador. Así que cuando te sientas ansioso, ora: «Señor Jesús, bendíceme con tu Paz». Esta breve y sencilla oración te conectará conmigo y te predispondrá para recibir mi ayuda.

En mi reino, la paz y la confianza en mí se entrelazan estrechamente. Mientras más te apoyes en mí con una confiada dependencia, menos miedo vas a tener. *Si tu corazón está firme y confiado en mí*, no tienes que *asustarte por las malas noticias*. Debido a que yo soy a la vez soberano y bueno, puedes estar seguro de que este mundo no está girando fuera de control. En el mundo *hay* un sinfín de malas noticias, pero yo no estoy retorciéndome las manos con impotencia. Estoy trabajando sin cesar —aun en las situaciones más devastadoras— para producir el bien a partir del mal.

Mi reino tiene que ver con transformación. Te invito a que te unas a mí en este esfuerzo. *Vive como hijo de Luz*. Juntos vamos a atraer a otros desde la oscuridad a la Luz de mi Presencia transformadora.

SALMOS 29.11; SALMOS 112.7;
EFESIOS 5.8-10

Mi pueblo escogido es santo y amado. Yo sé que tú no eres perfecto ni estás libre de pecado, pero *para mí eres santo.* Y lo eres porque te veo envuelto en el resplandor de mi justicia. Debido a que crees en mí, estás cubierto para siempre con una justicia perfecta. También eres amado tiernamente. Deja que esta verdad transformadora se filtre hasta lo más hondo de tu corazón, mente y espíritu. *Amado* es tu identidad más profunda y auténtica. Cuando te mires en el espejo, afírmate: *«Soy de mi Amado».* Repite estas cuatro palabras a lo largo del día y justo antes de dormirte.

Recordar que eres perfectamente amado por *el Rey de la Gloria* le ofrece un sólido fundamento a tu vida. Con tu identidad segura en mí, puedes relacionarte mejor con otros. Quiero que te *revistas de afecto entrañable y de bondad, humildad, amabilidad y paciencia.* Trabaja en el desarrollo de estas cualidades en tu relación con otras personas. El Espíritu Santo te ayudará. Él vive en ti y se deleita en obrar a través de ti, bendiciendo a otros *y* a ti mismo.

Colosenses 3.12; Efesios 1.4;
Cantar de los cantares 6.3;
Salmos 24.10

Agosto 18

TE SIENTES ABRUMADO por las frustraciones de ayer. ¡Cómo quisieras no haber hecho algunas decisiones de las que ahora te arrepientes! Sin embargo, lamentablemente, el pasado está más allá del ámbito de los cambios y ya no se puede deshacer. Incluso yo, que vivo en la intemporalidad, respeto los límites de tiempo que existen en tu mundo. Así que no gastes tus energías quejándote de las malas decisiones que hiciste. En lugar de eso, pídeme que perdone tus pecados y te ayude a aprender de tus errores.

No me gusta ver a mis hijos frustrados por los fallos cometidos en el pasado, arrastrándolos por ahí como si fueran pesadas cadenas sujetas a tus piernas. Cuando te sientas así, imagínate que estoy rompiendo esas cadenas y quitándotelas. Yo vine para darles libertad a mis amados. ¡Tú eres *verdaderamente libre*!

Alégrate de que te redimo de tus fracasos y frustraciones, perdonándote y llevándote por experiencias y caminos nuevos. Háblame de tus errores y prepárate para *aprender de mí*. Pídeme que te muestre los cambios que quiero que hagas. Yo te *guiaré por sendas de justicia*.

MATEO 11.28, 29; JUAN 8.36;
SALMOS 23.3

241

ALÉGRATE EN TU DEPENDENCIA DE MÍ. Este es un lugar lleno de maravillosa seguridad. Las personas que dependen de sí mismas, los demás o las circunstancias, están construyendo sus vidas sobre la arena. Cuando las tormentas vengan, se darán cuenta de que su cimiento es tan endeble que no podrá soportarlos. Tú, por tu parte, estás construyendo tu vida *sobre la roca*. Tu cimiento será más que suficiente para soportarte durante las tormentas de la vida.

Quiero que dependas de mí, no solo en los tiempos de tormenta, sino cuando el cielo de tu vida esté en calma. El proceso de prepararte para lo que sea que te espere en el futuro es una disciplina diaria. También es una fuente de gran Gozo. Depender de mí implica permanecer en comunicación conmigo, lo cual es un privilegio extraordinario. Estas ricas bendiciones te proveerán fuerza, aliento y orientación. Al permanecer en contacto conmigo, sabrás que no estás solo. Mientras *caminas a la Luz de mi Presencia*, te ayudaré *a alegrarte en mi nombre todo del día*. Depender de mí es la forma más gozosa de vivir.

MATEO 7.24-27; SALMOS 89.15, 16;
1 TESALONICENSES 5.16, 17

Agosto 20

ENCUENTRA TU SEGURIDAD EN MÍ. Mientras que el mundo en que habitas parece cada vez más inseguro, dirige tu atención a mí cada vez con mayor frecuencia. Recuerda que yo estoy contigo en *todo* momento, y que ya he ganado la victoria final. Debido a que *yo estoy en ti y tú en mí*, tienes esperándote por delante una eternidad de vida perfecta y libre de tensiones. En el cielo no habrá ni sombra de miedo o preocupación. Una adoración reverencial *al Rey de la Gloria* te inundará con inimaginable Gozo.

Deja que esta *esperanza* te fortalezca y anime mientras estás viviendo en este mundo tan profundamente caído. Cuando empieces a sentirte ansioso por algo que has visto, oído o pensado, trae esa preocupación ante mí. Acuérdate que yo soy el Único que te da seguridad en toda circunstancia. Si descubres que tu mente está desviándose hacia alguna forma idolátrica de falsa seguridad, recuérdate: «*Eso* no es lo que me da seguridad». Y luego, búscame con confianza y piensa en quién soy yo: el Salvador-Dios victorioso que es tu Amigo para siempre. ¡En mí estás absolutamente seguro!

JUAN 14.20; SALMOS 24.7;
PROVERBIOS 23.18

PON TU CONFIANZA EN MÍ y podrás descubrir *mi Amor inagotable* alumbrándote en medio de tus problemas y necesidades. Cuando estés luchando con el desánimo, necesitas afirmar tu confianza en mí una y otra vez. Es muy importante que no olvides quién soy yo: el Creador y Sustentador del universo, así como tu Salvador, Señor y Amigo. Puedes contar conmigo, pues mi Amor por ti es inagotable. Nunca se acaba ni se debilita y no depende de lo bien que te comportes. Justo como *soy el mismo ayer, hoy y por los siglos,* así es de perfecto mi Amor.

Eleva tu alma a mí esperando en mi Presencia sin pretensiones ni demandas. Al dedicar tiempo a esperar y adorar, poco a poco te voy transformando y abriendo la senda delante de ti. No te revelaré necesariamente cosas futuras, pero paso a paso *te señalaré el camino que debes seguir* hoy. Así que, mi amado, confía en mí de todo corazón, porque yo estoy atento para cuidarte maravillosamente bien.

SALMOS 143.8; HEBREOS 1.1, 2;
HEBREOS 13.8

Agosto 22

Yo soy LA Luz; *en mí no hay ninguna oscuridad.* Yo, tu Dios, soy perfecto en todos los sentidos. En mí no hay ni siquiera un ápice de maldad. Tú vives en un mundo donde el mal y la impiedad proliferan sin control. Pero recuerda: *¡Yo soy la Luz que sigue brillando en las tinieblas!* Nada puede extinguir —o incluso disminuir— la perfección de mi brillantez eterna. Algún día serás capaz de ver mi esplendor en toda su Gloria y experimentarás el Gozo en una manera inimaginable. Sin embargo, por ahora debes *vivir por fe, no por vista.*

Cuando los acontecimientos en el mundo o tu vida privada amenacen con perturbarte, agárrate de mi mano con confiada determinación. Niégate a ser intimidado por el mal; en lugar de eso, *vence el mal con el bien.* Yo estoy contigo, y ya he ganado la batalla final y decisiva mediante mi crucifixión y resurrección. *Nada* podrá anular estos acontecimientos impresionantes que perforaron la oscuridad para que mi brillo deslumbrante pudiera irrumpir y volcarse en los corazones de mis seguidores. Pasa tiempo disfrutando en esta santa Luz, porque mi Rostro está brillando sobre ti.

1 JUAN 1.5; JUAN 1.5; 2 CORINTIOS 5.7;
ROMANOS 12.21

CUANDO TENGAS QUE ENFRENTARSE con diversas pruebas, considéralo como una feliz oportunidad. No malgastes tu energía lamentándote por cómo son las cosas o deseando volver al ayer. Recuerda que yo soy soberano, poderoso y amoroso; además, yo estoy contigo para ayudarte. En lugar de sentirte acongojado por todas las dificultades que encuentres en el camino, aférrate a mi mano con total confianza y seguridad. ¡Aunque seas incapaz de manejar tus problemas solo, tú y yo *juntos* podemos emprender con éxito cualquier tarea! Si analizas tus circunstancias desde esta perspectiva, puedes sentirte gozoso incluso en medio de tus luchas.

Tú no solo tienes mi Presencia contigo, sino que mi Espíritu también mora dentro de ti. Él está siempre dispuesto a ayudar; por eso, busca su ayuda tan a menudo como sientas que la necesitas. Una de las partes más difíciles en esto de tratar con múltiples pruebas es esperar que se resuelvan. Puesto que la paciencia es parte del fruto del Espíritu, él puede ayudarte a soportar la espera. No trates de dejar atrás los tiempos difíciles a toda prisa. En cambio, persevera con paciencia, sabiendo que *la constancia debe llevar a feliz término la obra* haciendo de ti *una persona perfecta e íntegra.*

SANTIAGO 1.2; GÁLATAS 5.22, 23;
ROMANOS 12.12; SANTIAGO 1.4

Agosto 24

VEN A MÍ SI TE SIENTES CANSADO, y yo te daré descanso. Conozco la profundidad y la amplitud de tu cansancio. Nada se oculta de mí. Hay un tiempo para seguir insistiendo, cuando las circunstancias lo requieren, y un tiempo para descansar. Incluso yo, que tengo una energía infinita, descansé el séptimo día después de haber completado mi obra de creación.

Busca mi Rostro, y luego simplemente quédate en mi amorosa Presencia mientras proyecto mi luminosidad sobre ti. Deja que tus pasajes favoritos de las Escrituras discurran a través de tu cerebro, refrescando tu corazón y tu espíritu. Si algo que no quieres olvidar viene a tu mente, anótalo; luego, vuelve tu atención a mí. Mientras descansas conmigo, mi Amor se filtrará hasta lo más profundo de tu ser. En tales circunstancias, es posible que desees expresar tu amor por mí mediante susurros, palabras, canciones.

Quiero que sepas que yo te apruebo y también tus descansos. Cuando te relajes en mi Presencia, confiando en mi obra terminada en la cruz, tanto tú como yo nos sentiremos reconfortados.

MATEO 11.28; GÉNESIS 2.2;
NÚMEROS 6.25

¡YO VIVO EN TI! Esta verdad en cuatro palabras lo cambian todo, mejoran maravillosamente tu vida tanto ahora como para siempre. No te preocupes acerca de si tienes un hogar adecuado para mí. Yo gozosamente me instalo en los corazones humildes de los creyentes, donde trabajo pacientemente en su renovación. Pero me niego a vivir en aquellas personas que piensan que son «lo suficientemente buenas» sin mí. He llamado a tales hipócritas *tumbas blanqueadas: hermosas por fuera pero pútridas por dentro.*

Al reflexionar sobre la verdad milagrosa de que *yo vivo en ti*, deja que tu corazón ¡reboce de alegría! Yo no soy un inquilino de término corto, que habito en alguien mientras me complace con su comportamiento y luego me voy. Yo he venido para quedarme en forma permanente. Te advierto, sin embargo, que mis renovaciones pueden ser a veces dolorosas. Cuando mi obra transformadora en ti produzca un intenso malestar, aférrate confiadamente a mí. *Vive por la fe en Aquel que te amó y se entregó a sí mismo por ti.* A medida que continúes cediendo a los cambios que estoy haciendo en tu vida, te convertirás más y más plenamente en la obra maestra que yo diseñé para que fueras.

GÁLATAS 2.20; MATEO 23.27;
EFESIOS 2.10.

NO IMPORTA LO QUE ESTÉ SUCEDIENDO EN TU VIDA, puedes *regocijarte en mí*, porque yo soy *tu Salvador*. Cuando Habacuc escribió sobre esto, su nación estaba esperando la invasión de los babilonios, *un pueblo despiadado, temible y espantoso*. Mientras pensaba en lo que podría ocurrir, Habacuc pudo alegrarse en su relación conmigo. Este tipo de Gozo es sobrenatural, hecho posible por medio del Espíritu Santo, que vive en todos mis seguidores.

El gozo y la gratitud están estrechamente conectados. *Dame gracias por mi gran amor; preséntate ante mí con cánticos de Gozo*. Mi amor por ti nunca dejará de ser, porque yo ya he pagado la pena completa por tus pecados. ¡Mi Amor no depende de ti! Mientras más gratitud me expreses por tu salvación, mi Amor y otras bendiciones, más consciente estarás de cuán bendecido en realidad eres. Y una actitud de agradecimiento aumentará tu Gozo. Puedes alimentar esta alegría dándome las gracias en tus oraciones silenciosas, escritas y dichas a viva voz, mediante frases susurradas y a través de la música. *¡Ven ante mí con cánticos de gozo!*

HABACUC 3.18; HABACUC 1.6, 7; SALMOS 107.21, 22; SALMOS 100.2

Yo DOY FUERZA AL CANSADO, *y aumento el poder de los débiles*. Así que no te desanimes por tu debilidad. Hay muchos tipos de debilidades, y nadie está exento de alguna de ellas. Yo las uso para mantener a mis amados humildes y para prepararlos para que esperen en mí en confiada dependencia. He prometido que *los que esperan en mí tendrán nuevas fuerzas*.

Esta espera no está destinada a que se practique solamente *de vez en cuando*. Te diseñé para que me miraras continuamente, conociéndome como el *Viviente que te ve* siempre. Esperar y confiar en mí están estrechamente relacionados. A mayor cantidad de tiempo pasado conmigo, mayor será tu confianza. Y mientras más confías en mí, más tiempo querrás pasar conmigo. Esperar en medio de tus momentos también aumenta tu esperanza en mí. Esta esperanza te bendice en un sinnúmero de formas, elevándote por sobre tus circunstancias, capacitándote para *alabarme por la ayuda de mi Presencia*.

ISAÍAS 40.29; ISAÍAS 40.30, 31;
GÉNESIS 16.14; SALMOS 42.5

Agosto 28

Yo ESTOY CONTIGO, y te protegeré por dondequie-
ra que vayas. Hay un viaje arriesgado esperándote y
tú lo aguardas con una mezcla de sentimientos. En
cierto sentido estás ansioso por comenzar esta nueva
aventura. Incluso puedes estar esperando encontrar
abundantes bendiciones a lo largo del camino. Sin
embargo, una parte de ti tiene miedo de abandonar
tu rutina predecible y confortable. Cuando los pensamientos de miedo te asalten, recuerda que yo estaré
con mis ojos puestos sobre ti constantemente, dondequiera que estés. ¡El consuelo de mi Presencia es una
promesa para siempre!

Tu mejor preparación para el viaje que tienes por
delante es practicar mi Presencia cada día. Recuérdate
con frecuencia: «Jesús está conmigo, teniendo buen
cuidado de mí».

Visualízate tomado de mi mano mientras caminas. Confía en mí, tu Guía, para que te muestre el
camino que tienes por delante a medida que avanzas paso a paso. Yo tengo un perfecto sentido de la
orientación, así que no te preocupes de que te puedas perder. Relájate en mi Presencia, y regocíjate en la
maravilla de compartir tu vida entera conmigo.

GÉNESIS 28.15; JOSUÉ 1.9;
SALMOS 48.14

LA LUZ DE MI PRESENCIA alumbra sobre cada situación de tu vida: pasada, presente y futura. Yo te conocía desde *antes de la fundación del mundo y te he amado con un Amor eterno.* Nunca estás solo, de modo que búscame en cualquier momento. Búscame con la pasión con que se busca un tesoro escondido.

Trata de «verme» en medio de todas tus circunstancias y no dejes que oscurezcan tu visión de mí. A veces, yo despliego mi Presencia de maneras excepcionalmente hermosas. En otras ocasiones me muestro de formas sencillas y humildes, que solo tienen sentido para ti. Pídeme que abra tus ojos y tu corazón a fin de que puedas discernir *todas* mis comunicaciones dirigidas a ti, mi amado.

A medida que transcurra este día, recuerda que debes buscar la Luz de mi Presencia brillando en tu vida. No tengas un enfoque tan estrecho que solo te permita ver las responsabilidades y preocupaciones mundanas. En lugar de eso, expande tu enfoque para incluirme en tu perspectiva. *Me buscarás y me encontrarás, cuando me busques de todo corazón.*

EFESIOS 1.4; JEREMÍAS 31.3; SALMOS 89.15;
JEREMÍAS 29.13

Agosto 30

Yo LE DOY A TUS PIES LA LIGEREZA DEL VENADO, y te hago caminar por las alturas. Creé al venado con la capacidad de escalar montañas escarpadas con facilidad y permanecer en las alturas con seguridad. Tu confianza en mí te puede dar la seguridad necesaria para *andar y avanzar en tus lugares altos de problemas, responsabilidades o sufrimientos.*

Es muy importante que recuerdes que vives en un mundo donde tus enemigos espirituales nunca declaran una tregua. Por eso tienes que mantenerte alerta y estar listo para la batalla. A diferencia de los guerreros que tienen subalternos que los ayudan a ponerse sus equipos, tú tienes que ponerte tu armadura solo cada día. No importa lo que pase, quiero que *cuando llegue el día malo puedas resistir hasta el fin con firmeza.* Cuando te encuentres en medio de la batalla, declara tu confianza en mí, tu seguridad de que yo estoy contigo, ayudándote. En algún momento te pudiera parecer como si estuvieras perdiendo la batalla, ¡pero no te rindas! Mantente firmemente tomado de mi mano y solo resiste. ¡Esto es victoria!

2 SAMUEL 22.34; HABACUC 3.19;
EFESIOS 6.13

Yo soy tu Tesoro. Soy inmensamente más valioso que cualquier cosa que puedas ver, oír o tocar. *Conocerme* a mí es el Premio por sobre cualquier otro premio.

Con frecuencia, los tesoros terrenales se acumulan, se aseguran, son objeto de preocupación, o se esconden para salvaguardarlos. Sin embargo, las riquezas que tienes en mí nunca podrán perderse, ser robadas o echarse a perder. Por el contrario, al compartirme libremente con los demás estarás adquiriendo más de mí. Puesto que yo soy infinito, siempre habrá más de Persona que descubrir y amar.

Tu mundo se presenta a menudo fragmentado, con un sinnúmero de cosas —tanto grandes como pequeñas— que compiten por ganar tu atención. Todo eso tiende a impedirte que disfrutes de mi Presencia. *Te inquietas y preocupas por muchas cosas, pero solo una es necesaria.* Cuando haces de mí *esa «única cosa»*, estás escogiendo lo que nunca *nadie te quitará*. Regocíjate en mi permanente cercanía, y deja que tu conocimiento de mí ponga todo lo demás en perspectiva. ¡Yo soy el Tesoro que puede iluminar todos tus momentos!

Filipenses 3.10; Mateo 6.19;
Lucas 10.41, 42

Septiembre

Me guías con tu consejo, y más tarde
me acogerás en gloria. ¿A quién
tengo en el cielo sino a ti? Si estoy
contigo, ya nada quiero en la tierra.

<small>SALMOS 73.24, 25</small>

Yo soy tu Fortaleza. Esta verdad sobre mí es especialmente valiosa en los días en que tus insuficiencias te están vapuleando, diciéndote que te rindas porque ya no puedes más. Conocerme como tu Fortaleza es igual a tener un guía que está siempre contigo, indicándote el camino que tienes por delante, quitando los obstáculos y proveyéndote el poder que te permita dar el siguiente paso. *Yo te tengo sostengo de la mano derecha, y te guío con mi consejo.* Puesto que soy omnisciente, sabiéndolo todo, mi consejo te ofrece la mejor sabiduría imaginable.

Así que no te preocupes por tus debilidades. Considéralas como un medio para aprender a depender de mi amorosa Presencia, confiando en que yo estoy contigo y te ayudaré. Tu mundo se volverá menos amenazante cuando deseches la pretensión de ser capaz de manejar las cosas por ti mismo. Además, yo me encuentro contigo en tus debilidades y las uso para atraer a otras personas a mí. Mi luz brillará en medio y a través de tus insuficiencias cuando te mantengas mirándome a mí, tu Fortaleza. Deja que este Amor-Luz fluya libremente a través de ti y te llene de un Gozo que se desborde hacia las vidas de otros.

Salmos 59.17; Salmos 73.23, 24;
2 Corintios 11.30; Romanos 12.12

Septiembre 2

CUANDO LAS PERSONAS te desnudan su alma, *estás pisando tierra santa*. Tu responsabilidad es escucharlas y expresarles amor. Si te apresuras a tratar de solucionar tú mismo sus problemas, estarás profanando ese terreno sagrado. Algunas personas no querrán seguir hablando contigo; otras quizás se sentirán demasiado heridas como para aceptar que han sido transgredidas. De cualquier manera, si te apresuras a actuar, habrás desperdiciado una oportunidad espléndida de brindarles una ayuda efectiva.

A fin de actuar eficazmente en terreno santo, vas a necesitar la ayuda del Espíritu Santo. Pídele que piense a través de ti, que escuche a través de ti, que ame a través de ti. Mientras el Espíritu Santo proyecta su Amor a través de ti, mi Presencia sanadora va a obrar en la otra persona. Mientras tú sigues escuchando, tu función principal es dirigirla a mí y mis abundantes recursos.

Si sigues estas instrucciones, tanto tú como los demás serán bendecidos. Se conectarán con *mi gran Amor* al nivel de alma y yo les mostraré el *camino que deben seguir*. Al escuchar a la gente y expresarle amor en una dependencia de mí, mi Espíritu fluirá a través de ti como *ríos de agua viva*, refrescando tu alma.

ÉXODO 3.5; SALMOS 143.8;
JUAN 7.38, 39

CONSIDEREN BIEN TODO lo que sea excelente o merezca elogio. Esto puede parecer fácil, pero en la realidad no lo es. He aquí una muestra: los medios de comunicación casi siempre se enfocan en lo malo. Rara vez se molestan en informar acerca de las cosas buenas que están sucediendo, sobre todo las muchas cosas buenas que mis seguidores están haciendo.

Un enfoque positivo no solo es contracultural, sino que es contrario a la naturaleza humana misma. Tu mente es una magnífica creación, pero está tremendamente caída. Cuando Adán y Eva se rebelaron contra mí en el Jardín de Edén, todo resultó dañado por la Caída. Como resultado, tratar de enfocarse en lo excelente no es algo que surja de forma natural. Tomar la decisión correcta una y otra vez requiere de un esfuerzo persistente. Todos los días, momento a momento, tienes que optar por lo que es bueno.

A pesar de los enormes problemas en tu mundo, aún queda mucho que es digno de elogio. Por lo demás, el Único merecedor de toda la alabanza y que permanece a tu lado, más cerca que tus propios pensamientos, soy yo. ¡Regocíjate en mí, *mi* amado!

FILIPENSES 4.8; GÉNESIS 3.6;
PROVERBIOS 16.16; SALMOS 73.23

Septiembre 4

Yo DISCIPLINO A QUIEN AMO. La disciplina es una instrucción destinada a capacitar; es un curso de acción que conduce a un objetivo mayor que la simple satisfacción inmediata. En realidad, la disciplina eficaz puede ser desagradable e incluso dolorosa. Por esta razón, es fácil que sientas que no te amo cuando te estoy llevando por un camino difícil o confuso. En tal situación, o te aferras a mí en confiada dependencia o me das la espalda y te vas por tu propio camino.

Si eres capaz de reconocer mi disciplina como una faceta de mi Amor por ti, puedes atravesar las etapas difíciles con alegría, como ocurrió con mis primeros discípulos. Puedes venir confiadamente a mi Presencia, pedirme que te muestre lo que quiero que aprendas y qué cambios necesitas hacer. Háblame también de tu deseo de que te reafirme mi Amor. Tómate el tiempo para disfrutar de la Luz de mi amorosa Presencia. ¡Mientras contemplas mi Rostro, *la Luz de mi glorioso evangelio* brillará sobre ti!

HEBREOS 12.6, 11; HECHOS 5.41;
2 CORINTIOS 4.4

EL GOZO ES UNA OPCIÓN. Es posible que no tengas mucho control sobre tus circunstancias, pero todavía puedes elegir ser feliz. Yo te creé *poco menos que un dios* y te di una mente increíble. Tu capacidad para pensar bien las cosas y tomar decisiones se deriva de tu elevada posición en mi reino. Tus pensamientos son extremadamente importantes, porque las emociones y tu comportamiento fluyen de ellos. Así que esfuérzate por tomar buenas decisiones.

Cada vez que te sientas triste, necesitas hacer una pausa y recordar que *yo estoy contigo*. Y que *te protegeré por dondequiera que vayas* continuamente. Te amo con un *gran Amor*, perfecto e inagotable. Te he dado mi Espíritu, y este Santo Ayudador que mora en tu interior tiene un poder infinito. Te puede ayudar a organizar tus pensamientos de acuerdo con las verdades absolutas de las Escrituras. Mi Presencia continua es una promesa bíblica, así es que trata de *verme* en medio de tus circunstancias. Al principio es posible que percibas solo tus problemas. No obstante, persiste en mirarme hasta que puedas discernir la Luz de mi Presencia alumbrando sobre tus dificultades y lanzando destellos de Gozo sobre ti.

SALMOS 8.5; GÉNESIS 28.15; SALMOS 107.8;
ROMANOS 8.9

Septiembre 6

Yo HE DESPEJADO EL CAMINO debajo de tus pies para que tus tobillos no flaqueen. No quiero que te enfoques demasiado en lo que te espera en la senda por delante ni que te abrumes preguntándote si serás capaz de hacerle frente a lo que viene. Solo *yo* sé lo que hay en tu futuro. Además, soy el Único que entiende perfectamente de lo que eres capaz. Por último, puedo alterar tus circunstancias, ya sea de forma gradual o dramática. En realidad, yo puedo ensanchar el camino por el que vas en este momento.

Quiero que te des cuenta de cuán involucrado estoy en tu vida. Me deleito en cuidar de ti, «ajustando» la situación en que te encuentras para evitarte dificultades innecesarias. Recuerda que yo soy un *escudo para todos los que en mí se refugian.* Tu parte en esta aventura es confiar en mí, comunicarte conmigo y caminar a mi lado con pasos de feliz y confiada dependencia. No eliminaré todas las adversidades de tu vida, pero despejaré el camino por el que estás yendo, para *bendecirte y guardarte*, evitando que resultes dañado.

SALMOS 18.36; SALMOS 18.30;
NÚMEROS 6.24

TE HE EXAMINADO Y TE CONOZCO. Todos tus caminos me son familiares. No llega aún la palabra a tu lengua cuando yo ya la sé toda. Mi amado, indudablemente tú eres *plenamente conocido.* Tengo un conocimiento completo de todo sobre ti, incluyendo tus más secretos pensamientos y sensaciones. Esta transparencia te podría resultar aterradora si no fueras mi seguidor. Sin embargo, no tienes nada que temer, porque mi perfecta justicia se te ha acreditado a través de tu *fe en mí.* ¡Tú eres un miembro muy querido de mi familia!

Mi relación íntima contigo es un potente antídoto contra el sentimiento de soledad. Cuando te sientas solo o con miedo, exprésame en voz alta tus oraciones. También escucho tus oraciones silenciosas, pero susurrar tus palabras o pronunciarlas en voz alta te ayudará a pensar con mayor claridad. Debido a que te entiendo perfectamente, no tienes que explicarme nada. Puedes ser directo en lo que respecta a buscar mi ayuda en tus circunstancias «aquí y ahora». Pasa unos momentos de relajamiento conmigo, respirando *en la alegría de mi Presencia.*

SALMOS 139.1-4; 1 CORINTIOS 13.12;
ROMANOS 3.22; SALMOS 21.6

Septiembre 8

MIENTRAS QUE ESPERAS CONMIGO, yo trabajo en la *renovación de tu mente*. Al brillar en ella la Luz de mi Presencia, la oscuridad huye y el engaño es desenmascarado. Sin embargo, hay muchas grietas donde los patrones de los viejos pensamientos tratan de esconderse. Mi Espíritu puede detectarlos y destruirlos, pero será necesaria tu cooperación. Las formas habituales del pensamiento no mueren tan fácilmente. Cuando la Luz del Espíritu ilumine un pensamiento que te provoca daño, captúralo identificándolo por escrito. Luego, tráelo a mí para que podamos examinarlo juntos. Te ayudaré a identificar las distorsiones y a reemplazarlas con la verdad bíblica.

Mientras más te concentres en mí y en mi Palabra, más fácilmente podrás liberarte de aquellos pensamientos dolorosos e irracionales. Por lo general, esos pensamientos tienen sus raíces en experiencias angustiantes que te provocaron heridas y están profundamente grabadas en tu cerebro. Será necesario que recaptures los mismos pensamientos múltiples veces antes de que puedas tener dominio sobre ellos. Sin embargo, todo ese esfuerzo conduce a un maravilloso resultado: un aumento de la capacidad para vivir libremente y disfrutar de mi Presencia.

SALMOS 130.5; ROMANOS 12.2; JUAN 8.12; 2 CORINTIOS 10.5

TUS ORACIONES NO SON CLAMORES en la oscuridad, sino que llegan hasta mi reino de Luz gloriosa. *Clama a mí y te responderé, y te daré a conocer cosas grandes y ocultas.* La humanidad siempre ha estado llena de ojos que no ven lo que es más importante. A menudo, la gente no percibe lo más obvio. Yo puedo realizar milagros delante de los propios ojos de las personas, pero ellas solo ven las cosas ordinarias que ocurren en el mundo, cosas etiquetadas como coincidencias. Solo *los ojos del corazón* pueden percibir las realidades espirituales.

Yo me deleito con aquellos que están dispuestos a que los *enseñen.* Cuando vienes a mí con ganas de descubrir *cosas grandes y ocultas que no sabes,* yo me alegro. Un buen maestro se complace cuando uno de sus alumnos hace un esfuerzo extra para descubrir cosas nuevas. Estoy contento con tu deseo de aprender de mí cosas maravillosas. Tu buena disposición ante mi enseñanza te ayudará a entender *la esperanza a la que te he llamado, la riqueza de mi herencia gloriosa* en la que tienes participación. Puedes anticipar el futuro cuando vivirás conmigo en la Ciudad Santa, que *la Gloria de Dios ilumina.*

JEREMÍAS 33.3; EFESIOS 1.18; SALMOS 143.10;
APOCALIPSIS 21.23

Septiembre 10

MIENTRAS EL MUNDO SE VUELVE MÁS OSCURO, recuerda que *tú eres la luz del mundo*. No desperdicies energías lamentándote por las cosas malas sobre las que no tienes control. Ora por esos asuntos, pero no dejes que te obsesionen. Más bien concentra tus energías en hacer lo que puedas para brillar en el lugar donde te he puesto. Usa tu tiempo, talentos y recursos a fin de hacer retroceder a las tinieblas. ¡Proyecta mi Luz en el mundo!

Yo soy *la Luz verdadera que resplandece en las tinieblas*, aun en las más terribles condiciones. Tu luz se origina en mí y se refleja en ti. ¡Yo te he llamado para que *reflejes mi Gloria*! Esto lo harás de manera más eficaz mientras más te parezcas a la persona que yo diseñé. Pasa bastante tiempo buscando mi Rostro. Concéntrate en mi Presencia y mi Palabra te ayudará a crecer en gracia y podrás discernir mejor mi voluntad. El tiempo que pases conmigo nutrirá tu alma, te proporcionará consuelo y te levantará el ánimo. De esta manera, te fortalezco y capacito para que seas una fuente de fortaleza para otros.

MATEO 5.14; JUAN 1.9; JUAN 1.5;
2 CORINTIOS 3.18

CON LA AMENAZA DEL TERRORISMO proyectándose sobre el planeta Tierra, hay quienes están diciendo —y sintiendo— que no hay un lugar realmente seguro. En cierto sentido, esto es verdad. La gente mala, especialmente los terroristas, es impredecible e implacable. Sin embargo, para los cristianos, no existe un lugar que sea realmente *inseguro*. Tu residencia final es el cielo y nadie te puede robar esta gloriosa *herencia indestructible, incontaminada e inmarchitable*. Además, yo soy *soberano* sobre todo, incluyendo tu vida y las de tus seres queridos. Nada te puede pasar a ti —o a ellos— a menos que yo lo permita.

La verdad es que el mundo ha estado en guerra desde el pecado de Adán y Eva. La Caída en el Jardín del Edén hizo de la tierra un lugar peligroso, donde el bien y el mal sostienen continuamente, uno contra el otro, una batalla feroz. Por eso resulta sumamente importante *estar alerta y tener dominio propio*. Recuerda que tu principal enemigo, el diablo, ya ha sido derrotado. *Yo he vencido al mundo*, y tú te encuentras en el lado de los vencedores, que es *mi* lado. *En mí, tendrás Paz*. En mi estarás siempre seguro.

1 PEDRO 1.3, 4; SALMOS 71.16; 1 PEDRO 5.8;
JUAN 16.33

Septiembre 12

Tu vida entera está en mis manos. Así que confía en mí, mi amado. Yo te estoy entrenando para que te sientas seguro en medio de los cambios y la incertidumbre. En realidad, debería ser un alivio darte cuenta de que tú no estás en control de tu vida. Cuando aceptes esta condición humana mientras descansas en mi soberanía, llegarás a ser cada vez más libre.

No estoy diciendo que tienes que ser pasivo o fatalista. Es importante que uses tu energía y tus habilidades, pero yo quiero que lo hagas con oración. Ora por todo, y búscame en tus momentos. Yo soy un Dios de sorpresas, así que búscame en los lugares impredecibles.

Te invito a que te *regocijes en este día que he creado*, pidiéndome que me encargue de los detalles. Como estoy en control de *tu vida*, no tienes motivos para ponerte ansioso debido a que las cosas no ocurren más rápido. Las prisas y las ansiedades van de la mano, y yo te he instruido a no estar ansioso. Si dejas que sea yo quien marque el ritmo, te bendeciré con esa *Paz que sobrepasa todo entendimiento*.

SALMOS 31.14, 15; SALMOS 118.24;
FILIPENSES 4.6, 7

Tu vida es un regalo precioso que yo te he hecho. Abre tus manos y tu corazón para recibir este día con agradecimiento. Refiérete a mí como tu Salvador y Amigo, pero recuerda que también soy tu Dios-Creador. *Todas las cosas fueron creadas por mí.* A medida que transcurre este día que te he regalado, busca las señales de mi Presencia perdurable. *Yo estoy contigo, protegiéndote* siempre. En días brillantes y alegres, háblame de los disfrutes que te proveo. Al darme las gracias por ellos, tu Gozo se expandirá notablemente. En días oscuros y difíciles, agárrate de mi mano con una dependencia confiada. *Yo te ayudaré,* mi amado.

¡Tu vida física es un regalo increíble, pero tu vida espiritual es un tesoro de valor infinito! La gente que no me conoce como Salvador pasará una eternidad en horrible separación de mí. No obstante, debido a que tú me perteneces, vas a vivir conmigo para siempre, disfrutando de un cuerpo glorificado que nunca se va a enfermar o cansar. Ya que yo te he salvado por *gracia mediante la fe,* agradéceme por este regalo indescriptible que te llena de Gozo desbordante.

Colosenses 1.16; Génesis 28.15; Isaías 41.13; Efesios 2.8

Septiembre 14

UN PROBLEMA QUE DURE MUCHO sin que se le encuentre solución se puede convertir en una forma de ídolo. Cuando estás preocupado por una situación que no acaba de resolverse, es necesario que te controles. Una dificultad que se prolonga puede ocupar cada vez más tus pensamientos, hasta alcanzar proporciones idolátricas, proyectando sombras feas sobre el panorama de tu mente. Cuando te des cuenta de que esto está sucediendo, dímelo. Expresa tus sentimientos a medida que tratas de liberarte de esa preocupación que te está causando daño. Reconoce tu debilidad y *humíllate bajo mi mano poderosa*.

Una preocupación con características de problema te hará estar ansioso. Así es que te sugiero que *deposites toda tu ansiedad sobre mí*, confiando en que *yo te cuidaré*. Es posible que tengas que hacer esto miles de veces al día, pero no te rindas. Cada vez que me entregues tus preocupaciones inquietantes, estarás redirigiendo tu atención desde los problemas hasta mi amorosa Presencia. A fin de fortalecer este proceso, dame las gracias por la ayuda que te ofrezco. Recuerda que yo no solo morí por ti, sino que *vivo para interceder por ti*.

1 JUAN 5.21; 1 PEDRO 5.6, 7;
HEBREOS 7.25

Yo PUEDO DESENREDAR todas las cosas enmarañadas, incluyendo tu mente y tu corazón. Así que ven a mí tal como estás, con todos los problemas y cabos sueltos que tengas por ahí. Muchas de tus dificultades son complicaciones que se originan por las confusiones de otras personas. Puede ser difícil determinar cuáles de esa cantidad de desórdenes son tuyos y cuáles son de otros. Disponte a asumir la responsabilidad por tus propios errores y pecados sin sentirte responsable por los fracasos de los demás. Yo estoy aquí para ayudarte a desenredar tus problemas y encontrar la mejor manera de que sigas adelante.

El cristianismo tiene que ver con transformación, un proceso que se prolonga por toda la vida. Algunos de los nudos de tu pasado son difíciles de desatar, sobre todo cuando se refieren a personas que continúan haciéndote daño. Ten cuidado con quedar atrapado en la introspección o la obsesión por la forma de arreglar las cosas. En lugar de eso, sigue acudiendo a mí, buscando mi Rostro *y* mi voluntad. Espera conmigo, confiando en mi forma y tiempo de poner en orden las cosas y despejar tu camino. Acepta que tendrás que seguir viviendo con problemas sin resolver, pero no dejes que ellos acaparen toda tu atención. Mi Presencia en el presente es *todo lo que tienes* y tu bendición ilimitada.

2 CORINTIOS 3.18; 1 CRÓNICAS 16.10, 11;
LAMENTACIONES 3.24

Septiembre 16

DEDÍCATE A LA ORACIÓN, persevera en ella con agradecimiento. Para mis seguidores, orar es una forma de vida, un medio de estar conectado conmigo. Sin embargo, no resulta fácil. El diablo odia tu devoción a mí y sus demonios trabajan para interrumpir y debilitar tu comunicación conmigo. Por eso es de vital importancia que te comprometas con esta disciplina, determinándote a permanecer en contacto conmigo.

Te puedes entrenar buscando mi Rostro, incluso mientras estés ocupado en otras actividades. Al hacerlo, estarás invitándome a ser parte de tu mundo para ayudarte a que tu trabajo vaya mejor y tu vida sea más satisfactoria. También es bueno que separes tiempo solo para mí. ¡Esto puede ser todo un reto! Para orar eficazmente necesitas una mente alerta y un corazón agradecido. Pídele a mi Espíritu, *el Consolador,* que les confiera poder a tus oraciones, aumentando tu vigilancia mental y tu gratitud.

Una mente despierta y un corazón agradecido te ayudarán no solo a orar mejor, sino también a vivir mejor. *Dame gracias y alaba mi Nombre.*

COLOSENSES 4.2; JUAN 15.26;
SALMOS 100.4

Yo me complazco en los que me temen, en los que confían en mi gran Amor. A menudo, la expresión «el temor del Señor» es mal entendida, pero constituye la base de la sabiduría y el conocimiento espiritual. Consiste en un temor reverencial, una actitud de adoración y una sumisión a mi voluntad. Te sometes a mí al cambiar *tus* actitudes y objetivos por los *míos*. Puesto que soy tu Creador, alinearte conmigo es la mejor manera de vivir. Cuando tu estilo de vida exhibe este temor bíblico, me produces una gran alegría. Trata de sentir mi alegría que brilla sobre ti en tales momentos.

Vivir de acuerdo a mi voluntad no es fácil; habrá muchos altibajos mientras caminamos juntos. No obstante, no importa lo que esté sucediendo, puedes encontrar esperanza en mi Amor inagotable. En tu mundo de hoy, muchas personas son víctimas de la desesperación. Se sienten desilusionadas porque pusieron su confianza en algo incorrecto. Sin embargo, mi gran Amor, *que nunca se acaba,* jamás te decepcionará. Aférrate a la esperanza, mi amado. Es un cordón de oro que te conecta a mí.

Salmos 147.11; Proverbios 1.7;
Lamentaciones 3.22, 23

Septiembre 18

SI DESEAS INFUNDIRLE MÁS GOZO A TU DÍA, aumenta tu convicción de que yo estoy contigo. Una forma sencilla de hacer esto es diciendo: «Gracias, Jesús, por tu Presencia». Esta es una oración tan breve que puedes usarla con frecuencia. La misma te conecta hermosamente conmigo, expresándome tu gratitud. No necesitas sentir mi cercanía para orar de esta manera; sin embargo, mientras más me agradeces por mi Presencia, más real me hago para ti. Alinea tu mente, corazón y espíritu con la realidad de que *en mí vives, te mueves y existes*.

La búsqueda de señales de mi Presencia invisible a tu alrededor también aumenta la convicción de que estoy contigo. Las bellezas de la naturaleza y las alegrías de tus seres queridos son recordatorios que te conducen a mí. Igualmente, me puedes encontrar en mi Palabra, porque yo soy la Palabra viva. Pídele a mi Espíritu que ilumine las Escrituras para ti al hacer brillar su Luz en tu corazón, ayudándote a ver la Gloria de mi Presencia.

HECHOS 17.28; JUAN 1.1, 2;
2 CORINTIOS 4.6

Cuando te sientas abatido, el mejor remedio es *pensar en mí*. Recuerda quién soy yo: *tu Señor y tu Dios*, tu Salvador y Pastor, el Amigo que *nunca te abandonará*. Estoy plenamente consciente de cada una de tus circunstancias, así como de todos tus pensamientos y sentimientos. Todo lo que tiene que ver contigo me es importante, porque eres muy valioso para mí. Acuérdate de las muchas formas en que te he cuidado y ayudado. Agradéceme por cada una que viene a tu mente, y relájate en mi amorosa Presencia.

Háblame de las cosas que te están desalentando. Aunque sé todo acerca de ellas, decírmelas te proporcionará alivio de la pesada carga que has estado llevando. A la Luz de mi Presencia verás las cosas con más claridad. Juntos, tú y yo podremos determinar lo que es importante y lo que no lo es. Además, a medida que permanezcas conmigo, mi Rostro brillará sobre ti, bendiciéndote, alentándote y reconfortándote. Te aseguro que *volverás a alabarme por la ayuda de mi Presencia*.

Salmos 42.6; Juan 20.28;
Deuteronomio 31.8; Salmos 42.5

Septiembre 20

Yo soy CLEMENTE Y COMPASIVO, *lento para la ira y grande en Amor.* Explora las maravillas de la gracia: un favor inmerecido que te he prodigado mediante mi obra completada en la cruz. *Por gracia has sido salvado mediante la fe; y esto no procede de ti, sino que es un regalo de Dios.* Es más, *mi compasión jamás se agota. Cada mañana se renuevan mis bondades.* Así que empieza tu día con expectación, listo para recibir bendiciones nuevas. No dejes que los fracasos de ayer te desalienten. Aprende de tus errores y confiesa los pecados de los que eres consciente, pero no dejes que se apoderen de tu atención. En lugar de eso, mantén los ojos en mí.

Yo soy *lento para la ira.* Así que no te apresures a juzgarte a ti mismo, ni tampoco a otros. Más bien, alégrate de que yo soy *grande en Amor.* En realidad, el Amor está es la esencia misma de quien soy. Tu crecimiento en la gracia implica aprender a estar más atento a mí y ser más receptivo a mi amorosa Presencia. Esto requiere un esfuerzo vigilante, porque el diablo odia que estemos cerca. Esfuérzate para mantenerte alerta y recuerda: *¡No hay condenación para los que están unidos a mí!*

SALMOS 145.8, 9; EFESIOS 2.8;
LAMENTACIONES 3.22, 23; ROMANOS 8.1

VEN A MÍ, y descansa en mi Presencia. Yo estoy *constantemente pensando en ti*, y quiero que seas cada vez más consciente de mí. La certidumbre de mi Presencia puede *darte descanso* incluso cuando estés muy ocupado. Una paz interior fluye de saber que *yo estoy contigo siempre*. Este conocimiento de mí impregna tu corazón, mente y espíritu, y puede llenarte de profunda alegría.

Muchos de mis seguidores están tan concentrados en los problemas que ven y en las predicciones que escuchan que pierden su Gozo. Se quedan enterrados bajo múltiples capas de preocupación y miedo. Cuando te des cuenta de que esto te empieza a ocurrir a ti, tráeme todas tus preocupaciones; háblame de cada una de ellas y solicita mi ayuda y dirección. Pídeme también que remueva de ti aquellas capas de ansiedad que han sepultado tu Gozo. Al confiar tus preocupaciones a mi cuidado, tu Gozo comenzará a emerger de nuevo. Alimenta esta alegría declarando o cantando alabanzas *al Rey de la Gloria* que te ama eternamente.

MATEO 11.28; SALMOS 139.17; MATEO 28.20;
SALMOS 24.7

Septiembre 22

No TE PREOCUPES POR TU INSUFICIENCIA; en lugar de eso, acéptala. Tu insuficiencia posibilita el enlace perfecto con mi capacidad ilimitada. Cuando tus recursos parecen agotarse, tu inclinación natural es preocuparte. La mejor manera de resistirte a esta tentación es reconociendo sinceramente tus incapacidades y agradeciéndome por ellas. Esto te liberará de tratar de ser lo que no eres: tu propio Salvador y Proveedor. Debido a que eres débil y pecador, necesitas un Salvador fuerte y perfecto, y un Proveedor que pueda *satisfacer todo lo que necesites.*

Podrás acceder a mis recursos ilimitados estando *tanto* tranquilo *como* activo. Pasar tiempo a solas conmigo, esperando en mi Presencia, mejorará nuestra conexión. *Yo actúo a favor de quienes confían en mí*, haciendo por ti lo que no puedes hacer por ti mismo. Sin embargo, hay muchas cosas que *puedes* hacer. Cuando tengas que emprender alguna tarea que dependa *del poder que te proveo, yo seré alabado* y tú serás bendecido.

La próxima vez que te sientas insuficiente, ven a mí de inmediato. Yo te esperaré amorosamente en el lugar de tu necesidad.

FILIPENSES 4.19; ISAÍAS 64.4;
1 PEDRO 4.11

Yo NO VOY A ACABAR de romper la caña quebrada ni apagaré la mecha que apenas arde. Sé que a veces te sientes tan débil e indefenso como una caña doblada o una llama que apenas alumbra. Acepta tu debilidad y tu quebrantamiento, mi amado; permite que esa debilidad y ese quebrantamiento me abran tu corazón. Puedes llenarte por completo de mí, porque yo te entiendo perfectamente. Al hablarme de tus problemas, te refrescaré y te ofreceré la *Paz que sobrepasa todo entendimiento.* En lugar de tratar de resolverlo todo tú solo, apóyate y *confía en mí* de forma plena. Abandona toda actividad por unos momentos confiando en que te estoy cuidando y trabajo a tu favor.

Mi obra de sanidad en tu interior es más eficaz cuando permaneces en reposo bajo mi cuidado estricto. *Aunque cambien de lugar las montañas y se tambaleen las colinas, no cambiará mi fiel amor por ti, ni vacilará mi pacto de paz, porque yo tengo compasión de ti.* Siempre que te sientas débil y herido, acude confiadamente a mi Presencia para recibir abundante Amor y Paz.

ISAÍAS 42.3; FILIPENSES 4.6, 7;
PROVERBIOS 3.5; ISAÍAS 54.10

Septiembre 24

TÚ ERES UNA CARTA MÍA, escrita en la tabla de tu cora-zón no con tinta, sino con el Espíritu del Dios viviente.
¡Debido a que eres uno de mis seguidores, el Espí-ritu Santo está en ti! Él te equipa y te capacita para hacer mucho más de lo que podrías haber hecho por ti mismo. Por lo tanto, no te dejes intimidar por las circunstancias desafiantes o las épocas duras. ¡La ter-cera Persona de la Trinidad vive *en* ti! Piensa en las implicaciones de esta gloriosa verdad. Cuando andas en mis caminos, puedes hacer mucho más de lo que crees posible, pidiéndole *al Consolador* que te forta-lezca mientras avanzas conmigo, paso a paso.

El Espíritu escribe en la tabla de tu corazón no solo para bendecirte, sino también para atraer a otros a mí. Cuando estás con personas que no me conocen, Él puede hacer de ti una carta viva. Una de las ora-ciones más cortas, pero más efectivas, es: «Ayúdame, Espíritu Santo». Usa esta oración tan a menudo como te sea posible, invitándome a comunicar las verdades vivas del evangelio a través de ti.

2 CORINTIOS 3.3; ROMANOS 8.9;
JUAN 15.26

SI ES POSIBLE, y en cuanto dependa de ti, vive en paz con todos. En ocasiones habrá alguien que esté decidido a oponerse a ti sin una buena razón. En tal caso, no te haré responsable por el conflicto. Sin embargo, más a menudo tú has contribuido con algo a la discordia. Cuando esto ocurra, deberás arrepentirte por tu parte en el conflicto y hacer todo lo que puedas a fin de restablecer una relación pacífica. En *cualquier* situación, necesitarás perdonar a la persona que te ofendió. También es posible que tengas que perdonarte a ti mismo.

Mi amado, *debes estar listo para escuchar, y ser lento para hablar y para enojarte.* Tómate tu tiempo no solo a fin de pensar con cuidado en lo que quieres decir, sino de modo que puedas *escuchar* a la otra persona. Si oyes con atención y piensas antes de responder, será mucho menos probable que te enojes.

Cada vez que hayas dejado de vivir en paz con otros y tengas la culpa, no te desesperes. Yo pagué la pena por *todos* tus pecados para que pudieras tener Paz permanente conmigo.

ROMANOS 12.18; SANTIAGO 1.19;
ROMANOS 5.1

Septiembre 26

No te sorprendas por los muchos asuntos sin resolver que hay en tu vida. Siempre van a ser parte de tu experiencia en este mundo caído. Cuando creé a Adán y Eva, los coloqué en un ambiente perfecto: el Jardín del Edén. Dado que tú eres uno de sus descendientes, tu anhelo por la perfección resulta natural. Y también es sobrenatural. Debido a que eres mi seguidor, tu destino final es el cielo: ¡un lugar magnífico y glorioso más allá de lo que te puedas imaginar! Tus anhelos serán completamente satisfechos allí.

Cuando los asuntos sin resolver de este mundo quebrantado te estén desanimando, detente y mírame a mí. Recuerda que yo, el Perfecto, estoy contigo. Háblame de tus problemas, y déjame que te ayude con ellos. Busca mi guía para establecer prioridades de acuerdo con mi voluntad para ti. Dedica un tiempo a descansar en mi Presencia y adorarme. Alabándome, alejas tu atención del mundo con todo su quebrantamiento y la diriges a mí en todo mi Esplendor. Mientras te encuentras ocupado adorándome, estás participando en mi Gloria.

Génesis 2.15; Salmos 73.23, 24;
Salmos 29.2

A TODOS LOS QUE ME RECIBEN, a los que creen en mi Nombre, les doy el derecho de ser hijos de Dios. Existe una estrecha relación entre recibirme y creer en mi Nombre, la esencia de quien soy. Recibir un regalo demanda un cierto grado de receptividad, ¡y yo soy el mejor Regalo imaginable! Reconocerme como tu Dios-Salvador te permite creer que mi oferta de Vida eterna es real y es para ti.

¡Ser un hijo de Dios resulta indescriptiblemente glorioso! Yo soy tanto tu Salvador como tu Compañero constante. A medida que avanzas a través de este mundo oscuro, estoy contigo en cada paso que das. Te proveo Luz no solo para tu camino, sino también para tu mente y tu corazón. Me deleito en darte Gozo, ahora y por toda la eternidad. ¡Tu más brillante momento en la tierra se verá algún día muy oscuro en comparación con la Luz-Gloria del cielo! Allí podrás *ver mi Rostro* en todo su brillante esplendor, y *te bastará con* sentirte en un océano interminable de Amor.

JUAN 1.10-12; JUAN 3.16;
SALMOS 17.15

Septiembre 28

CUANDO TU MUNDO parezca oscuro y amenazante, ven a mí. *Ábreme tu corazón* sabiendo que estoy escuchando y que todo lo que tiene que ver contigo me importa. Encuentra consuelo en mi soberanía: yo estoy en control, incluso cuando los acontecimientos mundiales parezcan terriblemente desordenados. En realidad, muchas cosas *no* son como deberían ser, *no* son como fueron creadas para que fueran. Haces bien en añorar el bien perfecto. Algún día esos anhelos serán maravillosamente satisfechos.

Piensa en el profeta Habacuc mientras esperaba la invasión babilónica de Judá. Él sabía que el ataque sería brutal, y luchaba profundamente con este conocimiento profético. Sin embargo, finalmente escribió un himno lleno de absoluta confianza en mí. Después de describir por completo aquellas circunstancias tan desesperadas, concluyó: «*Aun así, yo me regocijaré en el Señor, ¡me alegraré en Dios, mi libertador!*».

Siéntete libre de batallar conmigo con respecto a tus preocupaciones. No obstante, recuerda que la meta es llegar a un lugar de confianza segura y Gozo trascendente. No vas a entender mis caminos misteriosos, pero puedes hallar esperanza y ayuda en mi Presencia. *¡Yo soy tu Fuerza!*

SALMOS 62.8; APOCALIPSIS 22.5;
HABACUC 3.17-19; SALMOS 42.5

SI TU OBJETIVO PRINCIPAL es complacerte a ti mismo, tu vida va a estar llena de frustraciones. Esa actitud de querer que las cosas marchen de esa manera está basada en una premisa falsa: que tú eres el centro de tu mundo. La verdad es que Yo soy el centro y todo gira en torno de mí. Así que es mejor hacer tus planes tentativamente, *buscando mi Rostro* y mi voluntad en todo lo que haces. Esta es una situación beneficiosa para todos: si las cosas van de acuerdo con tus planes, alégrate y dame las gracias. Cuando tus deseos se vean frustrados, comunícate conmigo y apréstate a subordinar tu voluntad a la mía.

Recuerda, mi amado, que tú me perteneces. *Ya no eres tu propio dueño.* Esta conciencia de que perteneces a Otro puede ser un gran alivio para ti, ya que aparta tu enfoque de ti mismo y lo que quieres. En lugar de esforzarte por hacer que las cosas salgan a tu manera, tu meta principal viene a ser agradarme a mí. Quizás pienses que esto es demasiado oneroso, pero en realidad resulta bastante liberador. *Mi yugo es suave y mi carga es liviana.* Saber que me perteneces te dará un *descanso para tu alma* profundo y satisfactorio.

SALMOS 105.4; 1 CORINTIOS 6.19;
2 CORINTIOS 5.9; MATEO 11.29, 30

Septiembre 30

EL TESORO MÁS RICO que te ofrezco es *la Luz de mi glorioso evangelio*. Esto es lo que hace que el evangelio sea una buena noticia tan sorprendente. ¡Abre el camino hacia mi Gloria.

Cuando confiaste en mí como tu Salvador, coloqué tus pies en el camino al cielo. El perdón de los pecados y un futuro en el cielo son bendiciones maravillosas, pero tengo todavía más para ti. *He hecho que mi Luz brille en tu corazón para que conozcas la Gloria que resplandece en mi Rostro.* Yo quiero que *busques mi Rostro* de todo corazón, para que puedas disfrutar del radiante conocimiento de mi gloriosa Presencia.

«Conocimiento» es una palabra muy rica. Algunos de sus significados son: *entendimiento adquirido por la experiencia o por el estudio* y *la suma de lo que se ha percibido, descubierto o aprendido.* De modo que conocerme implica un *entendimiento* de mí, una experimentación de mi Presencia. También implica *percibirme. El dios de este siglo ha cegado la mente de los incrédulos*, ¡pero tú puedes conocerme a través de percibir la Luz de mi Gloria!

2 CORINTIOS 4.4; 2 CORINTIOS 4.6;
SALMOS 27.8

Octubre

*El gran amor del Señor envuelve
a los que en él confían.*

SALMOS 32.10

QUIERO QUE TE RELAJES y disfrutes de este día. Es fácil para ti mantenerte tan concentrado tratando de alcanzar tus metas que te exijas demasiado y te olvides de tu necesidad de descanso. Tiendes a juzgarte sobre la base de cuánto has logrado hacer. Ciertamente, hay un tiempo y un lugar para ser productivo usando las oportunidades y las habilidades que te proveo. No obstante, quiero que seas capaz de aceptarte lo mismo cuando descansas que cuando trabajas.

Descansa en la seguridad de que eres un hijo de Dios, *salvado por gracia mediante la fe* en mí. Esta es tu identidad máxima y fundamental. Tú ostentas una posición de realeza en mi reino eterno. ¡Recuerda quién eres!

Cuando te sientas lo suficiente cómodo con tu verdadera identidad como para establecer un balance entre trabajo y descanso, serás más efectivo en mi reino. Una mente fresca es capaz de pensar de manera más clara y bíblica. Un *alma restaurada* es más atractiva y amorosa en las interacciones con otros. Así que toma tiempo conmigo, y déjame *conducirte junto a aguas tranquilas.*

GÉNESIS 2.2, 3; EFESIOS 2.8;
SALMOS 23.2, 3

Yo voy a juzgar al mundo con justicia y a los pueblos con fidelidad. Esta promesa está llena de bendición y aliento. Quiere decir que algún día el mal será juzgado; ¡mi justicia perfecta finalmente —y para siempre— prevalecerá! Debido a que eres mi seguidor, vestido con mi propia justicia, no tienes nada que temer. Sin embargo, aquellos que se niegan a confiar en mí como Salvador tienen que temerle a *todo*. Llegará el día en que el tiempo se acabará y mi ira será terrible para todos los que persisten en su incredulidad. Estos incluso *gritarán a las montañas y a las peñas: «¡Caigan sobre nosotros y escóndannos de la mirada del que está sentado en el trono y de la ira del Cordero!».*

Juzgaré a todos según mi verdad. El concepto de verdad absoluta es ampliamente rechazado en el mundo de hoy en día; sin embargo, este constituye una realidad tan sólida como la roca. Los incrédulos finalmente chocarán contra esta certeza crean en ella o no. Para ti —y para todos los creyentes— mi verdad es un fundamento firme sobre el que puedes vivir y trabajar, disfrutar y alabar. ¡Esta es una buena razón para *cantar con júbilo!*

SALMOS 96.13; ISAÍAS 61.10;
APOCALIPSIS 6.16; SALMOS 95.1

¡MIS JUICIOS SON INDESCIFRABLES e impenetrables mis caminos! Es por eso que confiar en mí es la mejor respuesta a mis planes para ti. Mi sabiduría y conocimiento son demasiado profundos como para explicártelos. Esto no debería sorprenderte, ya que yo soy infinito y eterno. He existido siempre. Y soy Dios desde los tiempos antiguos y hasta los tiempos postreros.

También soy la Palabra que se hizo hombre y habitó entre la gente. Yo me identifiqué con la humanidad absolutamente, tomando un cuerpo humano y muriendo una muerte terrible para salvar a los pecadores que creen en mí. Mi vida y muerte expiatorias ofrecen una razón más que suficiente para que confíes en mí, aun cuando no entiendas todos mis caminos. ¡Alégrate de que tu amoroso Salvador y Señor soberano es infinitamente sabio! Y puedes acercarte a mí en cualquier momento susurrando amorosamente mi Nombre. Yo estoy siempre a la distancia de susurro: ahora, durante tu vida terrenal, y por toda la eternidad. Yo soy Emanuel —Dios contigo— y nunca te dejaré.

ROMANOS 11.33; SALMOS 90.2;
JUAN 1.14; MATEO 1.23

Octubre 4

No DEJES QUE EL MIEDO a los errores te inmovilice o te provoque ansiedad. En esta vida habrá veces en que te equivoques por el solo hecho de ser humano, con conocimientos y entendimientos limitados. Cuando estés frente a una decisión importante, investiga al respecto todo lo que puedas. *Busca mi Rostro* y mi ayuda. *Yo te guiaré con mi consejo* cuando pienses en mi Presencia. Y llegado el momento, da un paso adelante y haz la decisión, aun cuando no estés completamente seguro del resultado. Ora para que en tal situación se haga mi voluntad, y déjame a mí los resultados.

El que teme espera el castigo. Si has sido castigado injustamente o maltratado con severidad, es natural que temas cometer errores. Cuando sea el momento de hacer una decisión, es posible que la ansiedad oscurezca tu pensamiento, incluso hasta inmovilizarte. El remedio es recordar *que siempre estoy contigo* y obro a tu favor. No tienes que alcanzar el grado de perfección para que yo te siga amando. ¡Absolutamente nada, incluyendo tus peores errores, *te podrá apartar de mi amor*!

SALMOS 27.8; SALMOS 73.23, 24;
1 JUAN 4.18; ROMANOS 8.38, 39

QUIERO QUE *NO LES TENGAS miedo a las malas noti-cias.* La única manera de lograrlo es teniendo un *corazón firme que confíe en mí.* En el mundo hay abundancia de malas noticias, pero no es necesario tenerles miedo. En lugar de eso, confía plenamente en mí, *cree en mí.* Encontrarás aliento en mi muerte sacrificial en la cruz y mi resurrección milagrosa. ¡Yo, tu Salvador vivo, soy Dios Todopoderoso! Tengo *soberanía* sobre los acontecimientos mundiales. Sigo estando en control.

Cuando las cosas a tu alrededor o en el mundo parezcan girar fuera de control, ven a mí y *ábreme tu corazón.* En vez de preocuparte, dedica tu energía a la oración. Ven a mí no solo buscando consuelo, sino también dirección; yo te ayudaré a encontrar el camino. Además, tendré en cuenta tus oraciones con el mismo cuidado con que gobierno tu planeta: de formas que están muchísimo más allá de tu capacidad de entendimiento.

No les temas a las malas noticias ni dejes que te asusten. En lugar de eso, mantén firme tu corazón y conserva la calma al confiar en mí.

SALMOS 112.7; ISAÍAS 40.10;
SALMOS 62.8; ISAÍAS 9.6

Octubre 6

PÍDEME QUE TE DÉ SABIDURÍA, mi amado. ¡Yo sé cuánto la necesitas! El rey Salomón pidió *discernimiento* y recibió sabiduría en abundancia. Este don precioso es también fundamental para ti, especialmente cuando estás haciendo planes y decisiones. Así es que ven a mí por lo que necesitas, y *ten fe* en que te lo daré en una medida plena.

Un aspecto de la sabiduría es reconocer tu necesidad de mi ayuda en todo lo que haces. Con una mente perezosa es fácil que te olvides de mí y te lances a tus tareas y actividades por tu cuenta. Sin embargo, antes de mucho tiempo, tropezarás con un obstáculo y entonces te verás enfrentado a hacer una decisión: o sigues solo sin medir las consecuencias, o te detienes y me pides sabiduría, entendimiento y dirección. Mientras más cerca de mí estés, más rápidamente y con mayor frecuencia acudirás a mí por ayuda.

El temor del Señor es el principio del conocimiento. Aunque soy tu Amigo, recuerda quién soy en mi *gran Poder y Gloria.* El temor piadoso —el asombro reverencial y la admiración como una forma de adoración— provee la mejor base para la sabiduría.

SANTIAGO 1.5, 6; 1 REYES 3.9; 4.29;
PROVERBIOS 1.7; MARCOS 13.26

¡ENTRENA TU MENTE para que genere grandes pensamientos sobre mí! Muchos cristianos sufren derrotas porque insisten en concentrarse en cosas menos importantes: las noticias, el estado del tiempo, la economía, los problemas de sus seres queridos, sus propios problemas y otras cosas por el estilo. De acuerdo, *en este mundo afrontarás aflicciones,* pero no debes dejar que lleguen a ser la preocupación central de tu vida. Acuérdate de que yo estoy contigo y *he vencido al mundo.* Aunque soy el Dios infinito: *Rey de reyes y Señor de señores,* estoy más cerca de ti que el aire que respiras. También soy tu Salvador amoroso y tu Amigo fiel.

Una de las mejores maneras de estar cada vez más consciente de mi grandeza es adorándome. Este ejercicio espiritual te conectará con la Trinidad (Padre, Hijo y Espíritu Santo) de una forma gloriosa. La verdadera adoración expande mi reino de Luz en el mundo, haciendo retroceder a la oscuridad. Una exquisita manera de alabarme es leyendo o cantando salmos. Llena tu mente con la verdad bíblica que te ayudará a resistir el desánimo. Cuando los problemas te asalten, ejercítate pensando en quién soy yo: ¡tu Salvador y Amigo, Dios Todopoderoso!

JUAN 16.33; APOCALIPSIS 19.16;
APOCALIPSIS 1.8

Octubre 8

QUIERO QUE TE OCUPES cada vez más en mí. El defecto de muchas personas es pensar excesivamente en ellas mismas. Mis seguidores no son inmunes a este problema, el cual los afecta en el proceso de crecer en gracia.

Cuando un hombre y una mujer están profundamente enamorados, su tendencia es preocuparse mucho el uno del otro. De igual manera, la forma de ocuparte de mí es amándome más intensamente, *con todo tu corazón, con todo tu ser y con toda tu mente*. Este es el *más importante de los mandamientos*, y es a la misma vez la meta de más alto valor. Por supuesto, mientras vivas en este mundo no podrás alcanzar la perfección en tu amor por mí. No obstante, mientras mejor entiendas y te deleites en el maravilloso y *gran Amor* que te tengo, más ardientemente me responderás. ¡Tener mi Espíritu te ayudará en esta búsqueda gloriosa!

En esta aventura hay dos partes: una, aprender a recibir mi Amor con la mayor profundidad, amplitud y constancia; y la otra, responder con un amor hacia mí cada vez más grande. Así te podrás liberar de las ataduras de pensar excesivamente en ti mismo y llegar a estar cada vez más ocupado en mí. ¡Yo me deleito en tu liberación!

MATEO 22.37, 38; SALMOS 52.8;
1 JUAN 4.19; JUAN 8.36

CUÍDATE DE NO RELACIONAR tu sentido de valor con tu desempeño. Cuando no estés satisfecho con algo que hayas dicho o hecho, ven a hablar conmigo. Pídeme que te ayude a identificar lo que es verdaderamente pecaminoso y lo que no lo es. Confiésame cualquier pecado del que estés consciente y recibe mi perdón con agradecimiento. Luego, vive en la libertad de saber que eres mi creyente amado. No dejes que tus errores y pecados atenten contra tu autoestima. ¡Recuerda que has sido declarado «No culpable» para siempre! *No hay ninguna condenación para los que están unidos a mí*, para quienes me pertenecen. Tú eres precioso para mí y *me deleito en ti*, así que rechaza de plano cualquiera idea de autocondenación.

Tu rendimiento imperfecto te recuerda que eres humano. Esta condición te humilla y te presiona para que te identifiques con la humanidad imperfecta. Dado que el orgullo es un pecado mortal, que fue precisamente el que condujo a la expulsión de Satanás del cielo, ser humilde es realmente una bendición. Así que agradéceme por las circunstancias que han disminuido tu orgullo y te acercan más a mí. ¡Recibe *mi gran y precioso Amor* en medida plena!

1 JUAN 1.9; ROMANOS 8.1; SOFONÍAS 3.17; SALMOS 36.7

UN PROBLEMA FASTIDIOSO puede convertirse en un ídolo en tu mente. Si piensas constantemente en algo —agradable o desagradable— más que en mí, estarás practicando una forma sutil de idolatría. Por eso es necesario que mantengas un control permanente sobre tus pensamientos.

Muchas personas consideran como ídolos solo a las cosas que traen placer. Sin embargo, una dificultad crónica puede cautivar tu mente, ocupando cada vez más de su actividad. Tomar conciencia de esta forma de esclavitud es un paso muy importante hacia la liberación. Cuando te encuentres atrapado en un problema persistente, tráemelo y confiesa la esclavitud mental de que estás siendo objeto. Pídeme que te ayude y te perdone, lo que haré libre y gustosamente. Te ayudaré a *llevar cautivo todo pensamiento para que se someta a mí*.

Te estoy enseñando a que *fijes tus pensamientos en mí* cada vez más. Para lograr este objetivo, necesitas tanto la disciplina como la intención. Es vital que encuentres placer en pensar en mí, regocijándote en mi amorosa Presencia. *Deléitate en mí*, mi amado; conviérteme en el Deseo de tu corazón.

HECHOS 10.43; 2 CORINTIOS 10.5; HEBREOS 3.1; SALMOS 37.4

Octubre 11

Yo soy tu Fuerza y tu Escudo. No dejo de trabajar —a veces de formas maravillosas— para vigorizarte y protegerte. ¡Mientras más confíes en mí, más *saltará de alegría* tu corazón!

Quiero que confíes absolutamente en mí, descansando en mi control soberano sobre el universo. Cuando en el mundo las circunstancias parezcan estar dando vueltas fuera de control, aférrate a mí con la seguridad de que yo sé lo que estoy haciendo. Yo organizo cada uno de los acontecimientos de tu vida para tu beneficio en este mundo y el siguiente.

Mientras te encuentras en medio de la adversidad, tu mayor reto es seguir confiando en que yo soy soberano y bueno. No esperes entender mis formas y estilos, *porque como los cielos son más altos que la tierra, así son mis caminos y pensamientos más altos que los tuyos.* Cuando reaccionas ante tus tribulaciones con acción de gracias, convencido de que yo puedo sacar algo bueno de las más difíciles situaciones, haces que me sienta muy feliz. Este acto de fe te anima y me glorifica. ¡Yo me regocijo cuando mis hijos me dan las *gracias con cánticos* mientras luchan con sus problemas!

Salmos 28.7; Salmos 18.1, 2; Isaías 55.9

Octubre 12

APRENDE A APOYARTE en mí cada vez más. Yo conozco todas tus debilidades y es en ellas donde mi poderosa Presencia se reúne contigo. Mi fuerza y tu debilidad se complementan perfectamente en una maravillosa cooperación diseñada mucho antes de que nacieras. En realidad, mi Poder *se perfecciona en la debilidad.* Esto resulta algo contrario a la intuición y misterioso, sin embargo, es verdad.

Es importante que te apoyes en mí cuando te sientas débil o abrumado. Recuerda que tú y yo *juntos* somos más que suficientes. Para sentir mi cercanía, intenta cerrar tu mano como si estuvieras tomado de la mía. *Yo te sostengo de tu mano derecha y te digo: «No temas, yo te ayudaré».*

Quiero que dependas de mí aun cuando te sientas capaz de manejar las cosas por ti mismo. Esto requiere estar consciente tanto de mi Presencia como de tu necesidad. Soy infinitamente sabio, así que déjame guiar tu pensamiento cuando haces planes y tomas decisiones. Apoyarte en mí produce entre nosotros una cálida intimidad. *Yo soy Aquel que nunca te dejará ni te abandonará.*

2 CORINTIOS 12.9; FILIPENSES 4.13;
ISAÍAS 41.13; DEUTERONOMIO 31.6

MANTENTE ALERTA y persevera en tus oraciones. Con la ayuda de mi Espíritu, puedes aprender a estar cada vez más atento a mí. Esta no es una tarea fácil, porque el mundo trata de desviar tu atención lo más lejos posible. El exceso de ruido y las estimulaciones visuales hacen que te sea difícil encontrarme en medio de tales distracciones. Sin embargo, yo estoy siempre cerca, a la distancia de una oración susurrada.

Los enamorados anhelan estar solos para poder concentrarse el uno en el otro. Yo soy el Enamorado de tu alma, y anhelo que pases tiempo a solas conmigo. Cuando cancelas toda otra distracción para concentrarte solo en mí, despierto tu alma a *la alegría de mi Presencia*. Esto aumenta tu amor por mí y te ayuda a mantenerte espiritualmente alerta. Orar se hace más fácil cuando estas consciente de mi Presencia radiante.

Orar no solo te bendice, sino que te proporciona una vía para servirme. Alégrate de que puedes colaborar conmigo a través de la oración en la obra de establecer mi reino en la tierra.

EFESIOS 6.18; HECHOS 17.27, 28;
SALMOS 21.6; MATEO 6.10

Octubre 14

YO TE GUIARÉ POR SIEMPRE. Alégrate de que el Único que va contigo a través de cada día nunca te abandonará. Yo soy el Constante con el que siempre puedes contar; Aquel que va delante de ti, pero que al mismo tiempo se mantiene siempre a tu lado. Nunca te suelto de la mano, *y te guío con mi consejo y más tarde te acogeré en la Gloria.*

Muchas personas dependen demasiado de los líderes humanos, porque quieren que alguien tome sus decisiones por ellas. Los líderes sin escrúpulos pueden manipular a sus seguidores e inducirlos a hacer cosas que por ellos mismos no harían. Sin embargo, todo el que confía en mí como Salvador tiene un Líder que es totalmente digno de confianza.

Yo te encamino en mi verdad y te enseño mis preceptos, de modo que puedas tomar buenas decisiones. Te he provisto de un mapa maravillosamente confiable: la Biblia. *Mi Palabra es una lámpara a tus pies y una luz en tu sendero.* Sigue esta Luz, y sígueme a *mí*, porque yo soy el Único que conoce el mejor camino que puedas tomar en tu vida.

SALMOS 48.14; SALMOS 73.23, 24;
SALMOS 25.5; SALMOS 119.105

301

Yo te cubro con el escudo de mi salvación, y mi diestra te sostiene. Mediante mi crucifixión sacrificial y mi milagrosa resurrección, gané la victoria final. Todo esto lo hice por *ti* y por todos los que confían en mí como su Dios-Salvador. ¡Y lo logré todo! Tu parte es solo *creer:* creer que necesitas un Salvador que pague la culpa por tus pecados y que *yo soy* el único Camino de salvación.

Tu fe salvadora te ha colocado en el camino al cielo. Mientras tanto, mi escudo victorioso te protege cuando vas caminando por este mundo. Usa *el escudo de la fe para apagar las flechas encendidas del maligno.* Cuando te encuentres en el fragor de la batalla, dime: «¡Ayúdame, Señor! ¡En *ti* confío!».

Al vivir en estrecha dependencia de mí, mi diestra te sostendrá, manteniéndote en pie. ¡Yo tengo un Poder indescriptible! Sin embargo, uso mi poderosa diestra no solo para protegerte, sino para guiarte con ternura y ayudarte a seguir avanzando. ¡De vez en cuando *te recojo en mis brazos y te llevo junto a mi pecho*!

SALMOS 18.35; JUAN 14.6;
EFESIOS 6.16; ISAÍAS 40.11

Octubre 16

Las circunstancias difíciles van y vienen, pero yo me encuentro constantemente contigo. Estoy escribiendo la historia de tu vida a través de los buenos y los malos tiempos. Puedo ver el panorama completo: desde antes de tu nacimiento hasta más allá de la tumba. Sé exactamente cómo vas a ser cuando el cielo se convierta en tu hogar para siempre, y estoy trabajando sin descanso a fin de transformarte en esa perfecta creación. ¡Tú eres parte de la realeza en mi reino!

La constancia de mi Presencia es un tesoro glorioso que muchos creyentes subestiman. Se les ha enseñado que *yo estoy siempre con ellos*, pero a menudo piensan y actúan como si estuvieran solos. ¡Cómo me aflige esa actitud!

Cuando susurras amorosamente mi nombre, permaneciendo cerca de mí aun en los tiempos difíciles, tanto tú como yo somos bendecidos. Esta sencilla oración demuestra tu confianza en que estoy contigo y cuido de ti. La realidad de mi Presencia supera las dificultades por las que estás pasando, sin importar lo duras que parezcan. Así que *ven a mí*, cuando te sientas *cansado y agobiado, que yo te daré descanso.*

2 Tesalonicenses 2.13; Salmos 73.23;
Mateo 11.28

Yo soy EL CAMPEÓN *que perfecciona tu fe*. Mientras más llena de problemas esté tu vida, más importante es que *fijes la mirada en mí*. Si les dedicas demasiada atención a tus problemas o a las tribulaciones de este mundo, terminarás siendo víctima del desaliento. Cuando te sientas agobiado o descorazonado, mírame y sé libre. Yo estoy siempre contigo, por lo que puedes comunicarte conmigo en cualquier momento y en cualquiera situación. En lugar de simplemente dejar que tus pensamientos corran libremente por tu mente, dirígelos hacia mí. Esto le dará fuerza a tu pensamiento para acercarte más a mi Persona.

Descansa en mis brazos por un rato, disfrutando de la fortalecedora protección de mi Presencia. Al observar el panorama que te ofrece este mundo en decadencia, regocíjate, porque *nada te podrá apartar de mi Amor*. Esta promesa se aplica a *cualquier cosa* con la que pudieras encontrarte. No importa cuán sombrías pudieren parecerte en ese momento las circunstancias, yo sigo estando en control. Yo, tu Campeón, que peleo por ti, me río de los que piensan que me pueden derrotar. ¡Recuerda *mi gran amor te envuelve*!

HEBREOS 12.1, 2; ROMANOS 8.38, 39;
SALMOS 2.4; SALMOS 32.10

Octubre 18

CONFÍA EN MI FIEL AMOR, agradeciéndome por las cosas que no ves. Cuando el mal aparentara estar floreciendo en el mundo que te rodea, puede parecer como si las cosas estuvieran girando fuera de control. Sin embargo, siéntete seguro: yo no estoy retorciéndome las manos sin poder hacer nada y preguntándome cuál será la próxima cosa que ocurra. Sigo estando en control y te puedo asegurar que tras el escenario el bien se encuentra en medio de la confusión. Así es que te reto a que me agradezcas no solo por las bendiciones que puedes ver, sino también por las que no percibes.

Mi *sabiduría y conocimiento* son más profundos y ricos que lo que las palabras pudieran expresar. ¡*Mis juicios son indescifrables, y mis caminos impenetrables*! Esta es la razón por la que confiar en mí *en todo momento* resulta tan determinante. No se te ocurra dejarte confundir por las circunstancias que sacuden tu fe en mí. Cuando tu mundo parezca tambalearse, las disciplinas de confiar en mí y agradecerme servirán para estabilizarte. Recuerda, *yo estoy siempre contigo; te guío con mi consejo, y más tarde te acogeré en la Gloria*. ¡Permite que este tesoro oculto —tu herencia celestial— te guíe hacia una gozosa acción de gracias!

ISAÍAS 54.10; ROMANOS 11.33; SALMOS 62.8;
SALMOS 73.23, 24

QUIERO QUE VIVAS CERCA DE MÍ, manteniéndote asequible a mí: consciente de mi Persona, prestándome atención, confiando y agradeciéndome. Yo estoy siempre cerca de ti, así es que entrégate por completo —corazón, mente y espíritu— a mi Presencia viva. Siéntete libre de pedirle al Espíritu Santo que te ayude en este esfuerzo.

Mantente al tanto de mi Presencia a medida que transcurre el día. No hay un momento en el que yo no esté plenamente consciente de ti. Mostrar atención implica estar alerta, escuchar con cuidado y observar de cerca. Te animo a estar atento no solo a mí, sino a la gente que pongo en tu camino. Si escuchas a los demás atentamente, eso los bendecirá a ellos tanto como a ti. La Biblia está llena de instrucciones en cuanto a confiar en mí y agradecerme. ¡Recuerda, yo soy totalmente confiable! Por eso es siempre apropiado creer en mí y mis promesas. Yo entiendo tu debilidad, y te *ayudaré a aumentar tu fe*. Por último, dame las gracias a través del día. ¡Esta disciplina de la gratitud te ayudará a recibir mi Gozo en medida plena!

APOCALIPSIS 1.18; SANTIAGO 1.19;
MARCOS 9.24; SALMOS 28.7

Octubre 20

CUANDO LA TAREA QUE TIENES por delante te parezca desalentadora, no te dejes intimidar. Disciplina tu pensamiento para ver el desafío como un privilegio más que como un deber desagradable. Haz el esfuerzo de reemplazar tu mentalidad de «tengo que» con el enfoque de «yo lo haré». Esto producirá un cambio en tu perspectiva, transformando la pesadez en deleite. No se trata de un truco de magia; el trabajo aún está por hacerse. No obstante, el cambio en tu perspectiva te va a ayudar a enfrentar la tarea con alegría y confianza... y a terminarla.

A medida que avanzas en el trabajo, la perseverancia es esencial. Si comienzas a cansarte o desanimarte, recuérdate: «¡Tengo que terminar esto!». Luego, dame las gracias por haberte provisto la habilidad y la fuerza para hacer lo que necesitabas hacer. Dar gracias despeja la mente y te acerca más a mí. Recuerda que mi Espíritu, que vive en ti, *es el Consolador*; pídele que te ayude cuando estés confundido. Al reflexionar sobre los problemas y buscar soluciones, Él guiará tu mente. *¡Hagas lo que hagas, trabaja de buena gana, como si lo estuvieras haciendo para mí!*

COLOSENSES 4.2; JUAN 14.16;
COLOSENSES 3.23

307

NO TE AFERRES DEMASIADO a las cosas, sino agárrate firmemente de mi mano. Para ser espiritualmente saludable, no debes poner un interés excesivo en tus posesiones. Todas son bendiciones que yo te he dado, por lo cual debes recibirlas *con gratitud*. Sin embargo, no te olvides que en última instancia yo soy el Dueño de todo.

También es importante relacionarte con los demás con manos abiertas. Exprésales cariño a tus familiares y amigos, pero sin convertirlos en tus ídolos. Si tu vida gira en torno a alguien que no sea yo, tienes que arrepentirte y cambiar de actitud. Vuélvete a mí, mi amado y hazme tu *Primer Amor*, buscando complacerme por sobre todos los demás.

Otra cosa que debes manejar con sumo cuidado es el control de tus circunstancias. Cuando tu vida está fluyendo sin problemas, es fácil sentir que tienes el control. Disfruta de estos periodos de paz, pero no te aferres a ellos o creas que son lo normal. En lugar de eso, agárrate firmemente a mi mano durante los tiempos buenos o difíciles; en una palabra, siempre. Los buenos tiempos son mejores y el sufrimiento es más manejable cuando dependes confiadamente en mí. ¡*Tu herencia eterna* es mi Presencia permanente!

COLOSENSES 2.6; APOCALIPSIS 2.4, 5;
SALMOS 73.23-26

Octubre 22

No TENGAS MIEDO de decirme cuán débil y cansado —incluso abrumado— te sientes a veces. Yo me doy cuenta perfectamente de la profundidad y la amplitud de tus dificultades. Nada está oculto para mí.

Aunque lo sé todo, espero tener noticias tuyas. *Ábreme tu corazón, porque yo soy tu Refugio.* Hay una intimidad tranquila en compartir tus luchas conmigo. En ese momento bajas la guardia y tus pretensiones; eres auténtico conmigo y contigo mismo. Luego, descansas en la seguridad de mi Presencia, confiando en que yo te entiendo perfectamente y *te amo con amor eterno.*

Relájate profundamente conmigo; deja de extremar tus esfuerzos en todo lo que haces. *Quédate quieto*, dejando que mi Presencia te refresque y renueve. Cuando estés listo, pídeme que te muestre el camino que tienes por delante. Recuerda que nunca me aparto de tu lado; yo *te sostengo de tu mano derecha.* Esto te da valor y confianza para continuar tu viaje. A medida que avanzas a lo largo del camino, escúchame decir: «*No temas, yo te ayudaré*».

SALMOS 62.8; JEREMÍAS 31.3;
SALMOS 46.10; ISAÍAS 41.13

No DESPRECIES EL SUFRIMIENTO. El mismo te recuerda que estás en un peregrinaje a un lugar mucho mejor. Yo proveo algunos placeres y comodidades en el camino, pero son temporales. Cuando llegues a tu destino final —tu hogar en el cielo— te obsequiaré con *dicha eterna*. En ese lugar glorioso *no habrá más muerte, ni llanto, ni lamento ni dolor*. La *alegría* que experimentarás allí será permanente, interminable.

Debido a que eres mi seguidor apreciado, puedo asegurarte que algún día tus sufrimientos llegarán a su fin. Mientras tanto, trata de ver tus problemas como *ligeros y efímeros*, los cuales *producen una gloria eterna que vale muchísimo más que todo sufrimiento*.

Mientras continúas tu viaje a través de este mundo, sé agradecido por las comodidades y los placeres con que te bendigo. Y alcanza a otros que pudieren están sufriendo. *Te consuelo en todas tus tribulaciones, para que puedas consolar a todos*. Ofrecerles ayuda a las personas que sufren le da sentido a tu sufrimiento… ¡y Gloria a mí!

SALMOS 16.11; APOCALIPSIS 21.4;
2 CORINTIOS 4.17; 2 CORINTIOS 1.4

Octubre 24

EL GOZO PERDURABLE solo se puede encontrar en mí. En el mundo hay muchas fuentes de felicidad, y a veces se desbordan en forma de Gozo, en especial cuando compartes tus deleites conmigo. Yo derramo bendiciones en tu vida, y me alegro cuando respondes a ellas con un corazón alegre y agradecido. Acude a mí con frecuencia ofreciéndome acciones de gracias y el Gozo de mi Presencia multiplicará los deleites de mis bendiciones.

Los días cuando el Gozo pareciera un recuerdo lejano, necesitas *buscar mi Rostro* más que nunca. No dejes que las circunstancias o los sentimientos te depriman. En cambio, recuérdate la verdad suprema: *yo estoy siempre contigo, sosteniéndote de la mano derecha y guiándote con mi consejo, y más tarde te acogeré en Gloria.* Al caminar a través de los escombros de este mundo estropeado, afírmate en estas verdades con todas tus fuerzas. Recuerda que yo mismo soy *la Verdad.* Aférrate a mí, sígueme, porque yo también soy *el Camino.* La Luz de mi Presencia está brillando sobre ti, iluminando la senda por la que vas.

SALMOS 105.4; SALMOS 73.23, 24;
JUAN 14.6

DEJA QUE MI GRAN AMOR SEA TU CONSUELO. El «consuelo» alivia el dolor y la angustia; también da fuerza y esperanza. La mejor fuente de estas bendiciones es mi Amor constante que nunca, nunca te va a fallar. No importa lo que esté sucediendo en tu vida, este Amor puede consolarte y alegrarte. Sin embargo, debes esforzarte por acudir a mí en busca de ayuda. Yo estoy siempre disponible para ti, y me deleito en darte todo lo que necesitas.

Tengo una comprensión completa y perfecta de ti y tus circunstancias. Mi entendimiento de tu situación es mucho mayor que el tuyo propio. Así que ten cuidado de ser excesivamente introspectivo, tratando de entender las cosas mirando en tu interior y dejándome a mí fuera de la ecuación. Cuando te des cuenta de que has hecho esto, vuélvete a mí con una breve oración: «¡Ayúdame, Jesús!». ¡Acuérdate de que yo soy la parte más importante de la ecuación de tu vida! Relájate conmigo por algún tiempo, dejando que mi amorosa Presencia te consuele. *En el mundo afrontarás aflicción, pero anímate, yo he vencido al mundo.*

SALMOS 119.76; SALMOS 29.11;
SALMOS 42.5; JUAN 16.33

Octubre 26

APRENDE A SER FELIZ cuando las cosas no salen como hubieras querido. No comiences tu día decidido a que todo ocurra como deseas. No habrá día en que no tropieces con por lo menos una cosa que no se corresponda con tu voluntad. Podría ser algo tan trivial como lo que ves en el espejo cuando te miras por las mañanas, o tan serio como una enfermedad o un accidente de un ser querido. Mi propósito para ti *no* es concederte todos tus deseos o hacer tu vida más fácil. Mi deseo es que aprendas a confiar en mí en cualquier circunstancia.

Si estás decidido a que las cosas salgan a tu manera, vas a vivir frustrado la mayor parte del tiempo. Yo no quiero que desperdicies tu energía lamentándote por cosas que ya ocurrieron. El pasado no puede modificarse, pero cuentas con mi ayuda para el presente y mi esperanza para el futuro. Así que trata de relajarte, confiando en el control que tengo sobre tu vida. Recuerda, yo estoy siempre cerca de ti, y *en mi Presencia te llenarás de alegría*. ¡En realidad, *te miro con agrado* y mi Gozo brilla sobre ti!

SALMOS 62.8; PROVERBIOS 23.18;
HECHOS 2.28; NÚMEROS 6.25

VEN A MÍ, tú que estás cansado. En mi Presencia encontrarás un descanso reconstituyente. Yo estoy siempre a tu lado, ansioso por ayudarte, pero a veces te olvidas de mí.

Te distraen fácilmente las exigencias de otras personas. Ellas pueden expresar sus demandas de formas duras o suaves, con un énfasis de culpabilidad o amabilidad. No obstante, si estas exigencias son numerosas e importantes, con el tiempo te van a añadir una carga aplastante que no vas a poder llevar.

Cuando te encuentres agobiado bajo *pesadas cargas,* recurre a mí en busca de ayuda. Pídeme que las quite de tus hombros y las lleve por ti. Háblame de las cosas que te preocupan. Deja que la Luz de mi Presencia brille sobre ellas de tal modo que puedas ver el camino que tienes por delante. Esta misma Luz, al llegar hasta lo más profundo de tu ser, te da las fuerzas que necesitas.

Abre tu corazón a mi Presencia santa y sanadora. *Eleva tus manos* al cielo en gozosa adoración, dejando que mis bendiciones fluyan libremente hacia ti. Aparta un tiempo para descansar conmigo, mi amado; relájate *mientras te bendigo con la Paz*

MATEO 11.28; SALMOS 134.2;
SALMOS 29.11

Octubre 28

HAY PERSONAS QUE ANTES DE ORAR hacen una selección de los asuntos que me van a presentar. Algunos dudan en cuanto a si traerme o no ciertas situaciones que consideran vergonzosas o embarazosas. Otros están tan acostumbrados a vivir con el dolor, la soledad, el miedo, la culpa y la vergüenza que no se les ocurre pedir ayuda para enfrentar tales cosas con el fin de derrotarlas. Incluso hay otros que están tan preocupados con sus luchas que se olvidan de que yo todavía estoy aquí. Esta no es la forma en que yo apruebo que sea tu relación conmigo, mi amado.

Hay cosas en tu vida que te están provocando dolor y quisiera sanar. Algunas han estado tanto tiempo contigo que has llegado a considerarlas partes de tu identidad. Las llevas a donde quiera que vayas, apenas consciente de su impacto en tu vida. Quiero ayudarte a aprender a caminar en libertad. Sin embargo, eres tan adicto a ciertos patrones dolorosos que se necesitará tiempo para liberarte de ellos. Solo exponerlos repetidamente a mi amorosa Presencia traerá a largo plazo la sanidad. ¡Mientras que llegas a ser gradualmente más libre, te vas a sentir en condiciones de experimentar mi Gozo en medidas cada vez mayores!

ROMANOS 8.1; SALMOS 118.5;
SALMOS 126.3

No te dejes vencer por el mal; al contrario, vence el mal con el bien. Habrá ocasiones en que te sientas bombardeado por todas las cosas malas que suceden en el mundo. Los reportes noticiosos son alarmantes, y la gente le está *llamando a lo malo bueno y a lo bueno malo.* Todo esto puede resultar abrumador a no ser que estés en comunicación conmigo. Los horrores que ves a tu alrededor me entristecen, pero no me sorprenden. Estoy plenamente consciente de la tendencia del ser humano hacia lo engañoso y lo malo. A menos que experimente la redención mediante la fe salvadora en mí, su potencial para hacer lo malo seguirá siendo ilimitado.

En lugar de desalentarse por la condición del mundo, deseo que mis seguidores sean luces que brillen en la oscuridad. Cuando el mal parezca estar ganando, quiero que tú estés más decidido que nunca a lograr *algo* bueno. Habrá ocasiones en que esto implique combatir frontalmente contra lo que te perturbe. En otras, será cuestión de que te esfuerces por hacer todo lo posible para promover las bondades bíblicas según tus dones, habilidades y circunstancias. De cualquier manera, concéntrate menos en lamentarte por la maldad imperante y más en trabajar para crear algo bueno.

Romanos 12.21; Isaías 5.20; Jeremías 17.9

316

Octubre 30

CAMINA CONMIGO CON ESTRECHOS y confiados lazos de Amor llenos de gozosa dependencia. La compañía que yo te ofrezco centellea con las preciosas promesas de la Biblia. Te amo con un *Amor eterno* y perfecto. Estoy siempre contigo, cada nanosegundo de tu vida. Sé todo sobre ti y y ya he pagado la pena por todos tus pecados. *Tu herencia —reservada en el cielo para ti— es indestructible, incontaminada e inmarchitable.* Yo te guío a través de tu vida, *y más tarde te acogeré en Gloria.*

La dependencia es una característica ineludible de la condición humana. Muchos no le dan importancia a esta condición y trabajan duro para crearse la ilusión de ser autosuficientes. Sin embargo, yo te diseñé para que me necesitaras constantemente y disfrutaras de tu dependencia de mí. Reconocer y aceptar tu dependencia aumenta tu convicción de mi amorosa Presencia. Esto te acerca a mí y te ayuda a disfrutar de mi compañía.

Te invito a mantener el contacto conmigo —tu Compañero fiel— en cada vez más de tus momentos. Camina gozosamente conmigo por el camino de tu vida.

JEREMÍAS 31.3; 1 PEDRO 1.3, 4;
SALMOS 73.24

Yo soy un Escudo para todos los que en mí se refugian. Cuando sientas que tu mundo se torna inseguro y amenazante, reflexiona en esta preciosa promesa. Yo personalmente escudo y protejo a *todos* los que hacen de mí su refugio, su lugar seguro en medio de la angustia.

Encontrar refugio en mí implica *confiar en mí* y *abrirme tu corazón.* No importa lo que esté sucediendo en tu vida, siempre es el momento adecuado para decirme que confías en mí. Sin embargo, a veces será necesario que atiendas a las demandas de tus circunstancias antes de hacer una pausa para abrirme tu corazón. Susúrrame tu confianza y espera hasta que encuentres el momento y el lugar adecuados para expresarme tus emociones más sentidas. Luego, cuando las circunstancias lo permitan, habla libre en mi Presencia. Esta rica comunicación te proporcionará un verdadero alivio, a la vez que fortalecerá tu relación conmigo y te ayudará a encontrar el camino correcto.

Mi Presencia protectora está continuamente disponible para ti. Siempre que sientas algún tipo de miedo, vuélvete a mí y dime: «Señor Jesús, me refugio en ti».

2 Samuel 22.31; Salmos 46.1; Salmos 62.8

Noviembre

Confía siempre en él, pueblo mío;
ábrele tu corazón cuando estés
ante él. ¡Dios es nuestro refugio!

SALMOS 62.8

Yo soy el Dios que te arma de valor y endereza tu camino. Ven a mí tal como estás: con todos tus pecados y debilidades. Confiésame tus pecados, y pídeme que los quite de ti y los mande tan lejos como *lejos del oriente está el occidente.* Luego, permanece en mi Presencia con todas tus deficiencias expuestas. Pídeme que te infunda fuerza, viendo tus debilidades como «vasos» listos para llenarlos con mi Poder. Agradéceme por tus insuficiencias, que te ayudan a mantenerte dependiendo de mí. ¡Regocíjate en mi suficiencia infinita!

Yo soy Aquel que hace tu camino seguro. Esto incluye protegerte de preocupaciones y planificaciones excesivas. En lugar de mirar hacia el futuro desconocido, trata de ser consciente de mí mientras transcurre el día. Permanece en comunicación conmigo, dejando que mi Presencia guiadora te mantenga en el curso correcto. Yo iré delante de ti así como a tu lado, quitando obstáculos de la senda que tienes por delante. Confía en que haré que las condiciones de tu camino sean las mejores.

Salmos 18.32; Salmos 103.12;
2 Corintios 12.9; 2 Corintios 4.7

Noviembre 2

CUANDO EN TI LA ANGUSTIA vaya en aumento, vuélvete a mí en busca de *consuelo*. Otras palabras para «consuelo» podrían ser *confort, compasión, empatía, ayuda, estímulo, tranquilidad y alivio*. Yo gustosamente les proveo todas estas atenciones —y muchas más— a mis hijos. Sin embargo, tu tendencia natural cuando te sientes ansioso es centrarte en ti mismo o tus problemas. Mientras más haces eso, más te olvidas de mí y de toda la ayuda que te puedo dar. ¡Ese enfoque estrictamente humano solo aumenta tu ansiedad! Es mucho mejor que dejes que la incomodidad que te está perturbando sea una voz de alerta avisándote de que te estás olvidando de mí. Susurra mi Nombre e invítame a encargarme de tus dificultades.

Busca mi Rostro y encontrarás consuelo en mi compasión y empatía. Vuélvete a mí para hallar aliento, tranquilidad y ayuda. Yo sé todo acerca de tus problemas y también sé cuál es la mejor manera de tratar con ellos. En la medida que te tranquilices en mi amorosa Presencia, te fortaleceré y proporcionaré alivio en medio de tu ansiedad. Te aseguro que no hay *cosa alguna en toda la creación que pueda apartarte de mi Amor*. Mi consuelo está lleno de bendiciones, mi amado; *este le traerá alegría a tu alma*.

SALMOS 94.19; SALMOS 27.8; ROMANOS 8.38, 39

RENUNCIA A LA ILUSIÓN de que tienes el control de tu vida. Cuando las cosas van bien, es fácil que sientas como si fueras tu propio amo y señor. Sin embargo, te puedo asegurar que mientras más cómodo te halles en este papel ilusorio, más dura puede ser la caída que experimentes.

Yo quiero que disfrutes de momentos apacibles y me los agradezcas. Sin embargo, no te conviertas en adicto a esta sensación de dominio sobre tu vida, y no consideres que esto es la norma. Las tormentas *vendrán*, y las inseguridades se asomarán en el horizonte. Si insistes en querer controlar las cosas y sentirte con el derecho de esperar que todo te salga bien, es probable que termines hundiéndote cuando lleguen las dificultades.

Te estoy entrenando para que *confíes en mí siempre, porque yo soy tu Refugio*. Yo uso la adversidad para liberarte de la ilusión de que tú tienes el control. Cuando tus circunstancias y tu futuro estén llenos de incertidumbres, mírame a mí. Encontrarás tu seguridad en *conocerme a mí*, el Amo y Señor de las tormentas que pudieren venir sobre tu vida; en realidad, soy Amo y Señor sobre todo.

SANTIAGO 4.13, 14; SALMOS 62.8;
JUAN 17.3

VIVIR EN ESTRECHA COMUNICACIÓN conmigo puede ser un anticipo del cielo. Es maravilloso, aunque requiere un nivel de concentración mental y espiritual que resulta extremadamente desafiante. En los Salmos, David escribió acerca de esta maravillosa forma de vida, declarando *que me tenía presente.* Habiendo pastoreado los rebaños de su padre, dispuso de mucho tiempo para buscar mi Rostro y disfrutar de mi Presencia. Así descubrió la belleza de los días vividos conmigo, siempre delante de él y siempre a su lado. Estoy entrenándote para que tú también vivas de esa manera. Este es un estilo que requiere un esfuerzo y una determinación persistentes. Sin embargo, en lugar de apartarte de lo que estás haciendo, tu cercanía a mí llenará tus actividades de una Vida vibrante.

Hagas lo que hagas, hazlo para mí, conmigo, a través de mí, en mí. Incluso las tareas domésticas brillan con el Gozo de mi Presencia cuando las haces para mí. Por último, *nada en toda la creación será nunca capaz de apartarte de mi lado.* ¡Así que esta aventura que hemos empezado a vivir estando tú en la tierra se prolongará por toda la eternidad!

SALMOS 16.8; COLOSENSES 3.23, 24;
ROMANOS 8.39

No TEMAS PELIGRO ALGUNO, *porque yo estoy a tu lado*, protegiéndote y guiándote a lo largo del camino. Aunque siempre estoy contigo, tú no siempre eres consciente de mi Presencia.

El temor puede significar una llamada de atención a tu corazón, alertándote para que vuelvas a conectarte conmigo. Cuando sientas que te estás poniendo ansioso, relájate y deja que la Luz de mi Presencia brille sobre ti y dentro de ti. Mientras reposas en el calor de mi Luz-Amor, ese miedo frío y duro comenzará a derretirse. Responde a mi Amor poniendo toda tu confianza en mí.

Recuerda que yo soy Dios que *te reconforto* y *guío* tus pasos. Si supieras de cuántos daños te he librado, te asombrarías. La protección más importante que te proveo es salvaguardar tu alma, que es eterna. Debido a que eres mi seguidor, tu alma está segura en mí, y *nadie te podrá arrebatar de mi mano*. Además, yo te guiaré mientras avanzas en tu camino al cielo. *Te guiaré para siempre.*

SALMOS 23.4; JUAN 10.28;
SALMOS 48.14

Noviembre 6

EL AMOR ES PACIENTE. En la larga lista del apóstol Pablo sobre las características del amor cristiano, la primera es la «paciencia». Esta constituye la capacidad de enfrentar las adversidades con calma: sin alterarse cuando haya que soportar una larga espera o tratar con personas o problemas difíciles. El énfasis de Pablo en la paciencia es contracultural, y a menudo mis seguidores lo pasan por alto. Esta virtud tan importante rara vez es lo primero que le viene a la mente a la gente cuando piensa en el amor. Sin embargo, hay una excepción común a esta regla: una madre o un padre dedicados. Las exigencias de los bebés y los niños pequeños ayudan a desarrollar la paciencia en los padres buenos. Ellos dejan a un lado sus propias necesidades para preocuparse por las de sus hijos, atendiéndolos tiernamente.

Yo quiero que mis seguidores se amen los unos a los otros demostrando abundante paciencia. Esta virtud es la cuarta característica que aparece en el fruto del Espíritu. Por lo tanto, mi Espíritu puede dotarte para que desarrolles con éxito esta importante expresión del amor. Recuerda que yo te amo con un *Amor grande* y perfecto. Pídele al Espíritu Santo que te ayude a preocuparte por los demás de la misma manera que yo me preocupo por ti: con mi Amor paciente y generoso.

1 CORINTIOS 13.4; ROMANOS 12.12;
GÁLATAS 5.22, 23; SALMOS 147.11

CADA DÍA TIENE YA SUS PROBLEMAS. Una implicación lógica de esta verdad es que no hay día en que no encontremos algún tipo de dificultad. Mi interés es ayudarte a manejar con calma y confiadamente los problemas con los que te vayas encontrando en el camino de tu vida. Los hechos que te sorprenden a ti a mí no me causan ninguna sorpresa, porque yo lo sé todo incluso desde antes de que las cosas ocurran. Yo soy *el Principio y el Fin*. Además, estoy completamente disponible para ti a fin de guiarte y consolarte cuando pases por tiempos turbulentos.

Los problemas de cada día te pueden ayudar a vivir en el presente. Tu mente siempre en actividad busca desafíos que enfrentar. Sin suficientes cosas en qué ocuparte, es más probable que te empieces a preocupar por el futuro. Yo te estoy entrenando para mantener tu atención en mi Presencia en el día de hoy.

Las dificultades no tienen por qué disuadirte de disfrutar de mi Presencia. Por el contrario, ellas te acercan más a mí en la medida en que colabores conmigo a fin de manejarlas. Al ocuparnos de tus problemas tú y yo *juntos*, adquirirás más confianza en tu capacidad de enfrentarlos y vencerlos. ¡Y el placer de mi Compañía aumentará grandemente tu Gozo!

MATEO 6.34; APOCALIPSIS 21.6; ROMANOS 12.12

Noviembre 8

Cuídate de preferir recibir honores de los hombres más que de parte de Dios. Uno de los efectos de la Caída es que las personas están demasiado preocupadas por lo que los demás piensen de ellas: su forma de comportarse social y profesionalmente, su atractivo físico. Los anuncios de cosméticos y ropa de moda tienden a alimentar esta tendencia dañina.

Yo no quiero que estés preocupado por la forma en que otras personas te ven. Te he protegido amorosamente para que no seas capaz de leer la mente de los demás. Lo que piensen de ti, realmente, no es de tu incumbencia. Los pensamientos de la gente no son confiables, pues están influidos por su propia pecaminosidad, sus debilidades e inseguridades. Incluso si te alaban en tu propia cara, algunos de sus pensamientos sobre ti pueden ser muy diferentes de lo que están queriendo demostrar.

Yo soy el Único que te ve como realmente eres. A pesar de que estás lejos de ser perfecto, te veo radiante, ataviado con el manto de mi justicia perfecta. En lugar de buscar la alabanza y los *honores de los hombres*, trata de verme mientras te observo. Mi amorosa aprobación de ti está brillando desde mi Rostro.

JUAN 12.43; ISAÍAS 61.10; NÚMEROS 6.25, 26

PON TU CONFIANZA EN MÍ, que quiero guiarte paso a paso a lo largo de este día. La Luz con que ilumino tu caminar es suficiente para un día a la vez. Si intentas mirar hacia el futuro, te vas a encontrar tratando de ver en la oscuridad. *Mi Rostro brilla sobre ti* solo en el presente. Aquí es donde encuentras mi Amor infalible que nunca se extinguirá y es más fuerte que el vínculo que hay entre una madre y su bebé. *Aunque ella lo olvidara, yo nunca me olvidaré de ti.* Tú me eres tan precioso que incluso *he grabado* tu nombre *en las palmas de mis manos.* Olvidarte está fuera de toda posibilidad.

Quiero que de verdad *llegues a conocer* —prácticamente, a través de experimentarlo— *mi Amor, que sobrepasa el simple conocimiento.* El Espíritu Santo, que vive en tu ser más íntimo, te ayudará. Pídele que te llene por completo con mi plenitud, de modo que puedas *ser lleno de la plenitud divina,* convirtiéndote en un cuerpo completamente inundado de mí. De este modo podrás experimentar mi Amor en la más completa extensión.

NÚMEROS 6.25; CANTAR DE LOS CANTARES 8.7; ISAÍAS 49.15, 16; EFESIOS 3.19

Noviembre 10

Yo QUIERO QUE CONSUELES a otros *con el mismo consuelo que has recibido de mí.* No importa qué circunstancias estés soportando, mi Presencia y mi consuelo son suficientes para tus necesidades. Como cristiano, todo lo que tengas que soportar tiene un significado y un propósito. El sufrimiento puede edificar tu carácter y prepararte para ayudar a otros que estén sufriendo. Así que háblame libremente acerca de las dificultades de tu vida, y pídeme que las use para mis propósitos. Por supuesto, puedes buscar alivio de tus sufrimientos, pero ten cuidado de no pasar por alto las bendiciones ocultas en ellos. En la medida en que te acerques más a mí durante tus tiempos de pruebas buscando mi ayuda, crecerás en madurez y sabiduría. Esto te preparará para que ayudes a otros mientras soportan sus propias adversidades. Tu empatía por las personas que sufren se derramará sobre sus vidas. Y vas a darte cuenta de que serás más efectivo en consolar a los que están pasando por pruebas porque tú ya las habrás atravesado.

La disciplina de las dificultades te permitirá desarrollar mejor un carácter pacífico. Aunque es dolorosa en el momento, *más tarde produce una cosecha de justicia.*

2 CORINTIOS 1.3, 4; FILIPENSES 4.19;
HEBREOS 12.11

LA GRATITUD ES EL MEJOR antídoto contra un sentido de derecho; es decir, contra la actitud ponzoñosa de creer que «el mundo me debe algo». Este es un concepto erróneo que se ha transformado en una epidemia en el mundo actual y es totalmente contrario a la enseñanza bíblica. El apóstol Pablo les ordenó a los cristianos «que se aparten de todo hermano que esté viviendo como un vago» y enseñó con su ejemplo, *trabajando arduamente y sin descanso para ser él mismo un modelo a seguir por otros*. Incluso dijo: «El que no quiera trabajar, que tampoco coma».

Una definición de este sentido de derecho es *creer que mereces que te den algo*. El sentido de gratitud es todo lo contrario: una actitud de sentirte contento con lo que tienes. Si te hubiese dado lo que merecías, tu destino final sería el infierno y no tendrías la más mínima esperanza de salvación. Así que agradece que yo sea *rico en misericordia; es por gracia que has sido salvado*.

Pretender que mereces más de lo que realmente tienes hará de ti una persona miserable, pero una actitud agradecida te llenará de Gozo. Además, cuando eres agradecido, me estás *adorando como a mí me agrada, con temor reverente*.

2 TESALONICENSES 3.6-10; EFESIOS 2.4, 5;
SALMOS 107.1; HEBREOS 12.28

Noviembre 12

Estoy lleno de gracia y de verdad. La «gracia» se refiere a un favor inmerecido y al Amor que te tengo. Recibir algo que no mereces te humilla, pero eso es algo bueno, pues te protege del orgullo. La gracia es un regalo de valor ilimitado que te asegura tu salvación eterna. Debido a que me conoces como tu Salvador, siempre estaré de tu lado, mi amado. El Amor que te tengo es infalible e inmerecido. Nunca te lo habrías podido ganar con tu esfuerzo. Por eso, nunca lo vas a perder. *Solo confía en este gran Amor, y regocíjate en mi salvación.*

No solo estoy lleno de verdad, sino que *yo soy la Verdad.* La gente hoy en día está siendo bombardeada por noticias y mensajes llenos de fantasías y mentiras. Como resultado, el cinismo abunda en el mundo. No obstante, en mí y en la Biblia encontrarás la Verdad absoluta y que no cambia. Conocerme a mí *pone tus pies sobre una roca y te planta en un terreno firme.* Este fundamento seguro para tu vida hace de ti un faro que alumbra en un mundo relativista y oscuro. *Deja que tu luz brille* delante de todos, de tal manera que *muchos puedan verla y pongan su confianza en mí.*

Juan 1.14; Juan 14.6; Salmos 13.5, 6;
Mateo 5.16

QUIERO QUE TENGAS UNA APACIBLE confianza en mí, tu Dios vivo. Como escribió el profeta Isaías: «*En la serenidad y la confianza está su fuerza*». Hay personas que para imponerse sobre los demás hablan a gritos o hacen promesas que no van a cumplir. Estas voces altisonantes pueden dar la impresión de ser poderosas, ofreciendo salud y riqueza a quienes les den dinero, pero en la realidad no son más que parásitos que sobreviven exprimiendo los preciosos recursos que pueden sacar de los demás.

La verdadera fuerza se obtiene a través de confiar calmadamente en mí y mis promesas. Alégrate de que yo sea tu Dios *vivo* y no un ídolo inanimado. *Yo soy el que vive; el que estuvo muerto, pero ahora vive por los siglos de los siglos.* Mi Poder es infinito; sin embargo, me acerco a ti dulce y amorosamente. Pasemos tiempo juntos, mi amado, relacionándonos en un ambiente de confianza plena. Mientras descansas conmigo, yo te fortalezco preparándote para enfrentar los desafíos que vas a encontrar en el camino. Mientras te concentras en mi Presencia, usa las Escrituras para que te ayuden a orar. Puedes acercarte más a mí al susurrar: «*¡Cuánto te amo, Señor, fuerza mía!*».

ISAÍAS 30.15; APOCALIPSIS 1.18;
SALMOS 18.1

Noviembre 14

YO ESTOY SIEMPRE CONTIGO, mi amado, seas o no consciente de mi Presencia. A veces, aunque el lugar donde te encuentras luzca desolado y desprovisto de mi amorosa compañía, clama a mí y verás que estoy a tu lado, dispuesto a acudir en tu ayuda. *Yo estoy cerca quienes me invocan.* Susurra mi Nombre con tierna confianza, despojándote de toda duda. Háblame de tus problemas y pídeme que te guíe con respecto a ellos; luego, cambia de asunto. ¡Alábame por mi grandeza, mi gloria, mi poder y majestad! Agradéceme por las cosas buenas que he hecho y estoy haciendo en tu vida. Me encontrarás ricamente presente en tu alabanza y acción de gracias.

¡Pruébame y ve cuán bueno soy! Mientras más te concentres en mí y mis bendiciones, mejor podrás degustar mi bondad. Deléitate con la dulzura de *mi fiel Amor.* Disfruta el sabor delicioso de mi fuerza. Satisface el hambre de tu corazón con el Gozo y la Paz de mi Presencia. *Yo estoy contigo, y te protegeré por dondequiera que vayas.*

SALMOS 145.18; SALMOS 34.8; ISAÍAS 54.10;
GÉNESIS 28.15

VEN A MÍ, y descansa en mi Presencia. Yo soy el *Príncipe de Paz*. Tú necesitas mi Paz continuamente, así como me necesitas a mí todo el tiempo. Cuando las cosas transcurren sin problemas en tu vida, tu tendencia es olvidar cuán dependiente de mí eres en realidad. Después, cuando encuentras obstáculos en el camino, te pones ansioso y te desesperas. Entonces te acuerdas de regresar a mí en busca de mi Paz. Y yo, con toda mi alegría, te doy este precioso regalo. Por lo general, tendrás que calmarte para empezar a disfrutarlo. ¡Cuánto mejor es permanecer cerca a mí en todo momento!

¡Recuerda que yo, tu Príncipe, soy de la realeza! *Toda autoridad me ha sido dada en el cielo y en la tierra.* Cuando estés experimentando tiempos difíciles en tu vida, ven a mí y cuéntame tus angustias. ¡Pero no olvides quién soy yo! No me muestres el puño ni me exijas que haga las cosas a tu manera. En lugar de eso, haz tuya esta alentadora oración de David: «*Pero yo, Señor, en ti confío, y digo: "Tú eres mi Dios". Mi vida entera está en tus manos*».

MATEO 11.28; ISAÍAS 9.6; MATEO 28.18;
SALMOS 31.14, 15

Noviembre 16

EN MÍ ESTÁS A SALVO, seguro y completo. De modo que detén tu ansiedad y ven a mí con las cosas que te preocupan. Confía en mí lo suficiente para ser franco y honesto mientras me cuentas tus angustias. *Deposita en mí toda ansiedad, porque yo cuido de ti.* Tú eres mi gran preocupación, así que te invito a que vengas a mí y descanses *al amparo de mi Presencia.*

Si te alejas de mí y me dejas fuera de tu vida, pronto sentirás que algo importante te falta. La inquietud que te asalta en ese tiempo es un regalo que yo te mando para que recuerdes que debes volver a mí, tu *Primer Amor.* Yo quiero ser el centro de tus pensamientos y tus sentimientos, tus planes y tus acciones. Esto le dará sentido a todo lo que hagas, de acuerdo a mi voluntad. Vas camino al cielo, y yo soy tu Compañero constante. No te acobardes cuando encuentres problemas en el camino que vamos siguiendo tú y yo juntos. No olvides que *yo he vencido al mundo.* En mí estás absolutamente seguro. Seguro y completo.

1 PEDRO 5.7; SALMOS 31.19, 20;
APOCALIPSIS 2.4; JUAN 16.33

LA SUMA DE MIS PALABRAS es la verdad. ¡Una verdad absoluta, inmutable y eterna! Cada vez más personas están cayendo en la trampa de la mentira de que la verdad es relativa o simplemente no existe. Estas personas son demasiado cínicas o están demasiado heridas para ver las cosas que son *verdaderas, respetables, justas, puras, amables, dignas de admiración.* Ellas tienden a centrarse en lo que es falso, equivocado, impuro y feo. Este enfoque dañino lleva a muchos a la desesperación o a conductas autodestructivas. *El dios de este mundo ha cegado la mente de los incrédulos para que no vean la Luz de mi glorioso evangelio.*

El evangelio irradia una Luz pura y poderosa, que ilumina mi Gloria: ¡la maravilla de quién soy y lo que he hecho! Esta buena noticia tiene Poder ilimitado para transformar vidas, sacándolas de la desesperación y trayéndolas al deleite más puro. Todos mis hijos, llenos de mi Espíritu, están bien equipados para ser portadores de la Luz del evangelio de modo que alumbre a otros. Yo quiero que *tú* te unas a esta gloriosa empresa, usando tus dones y las oportunidades que te proporciono. Sé que eres débil, pero eso encaja perfectamente con mis propósitos. *Mi Poder se perfecciona en la debilidad.*

SALMOS 119.160; FILIPENSES 4.8;
2 CORINTIOS 4.4; 2 CORINTIOS 12.9

Noviembre 18

Yo, EL SEÑOR, *soy tu Fortaleza*. En los días en que te sientes seguro, es posible que esta verdad no te sea tan evidente. Sin embargo, la misma es una cuerda de salvamento llena de aliento y esperanza que está siempre disponible para ti. Cada vez que te sientas débil, búscame y aférrate firmemente a esta cuerda. Y clama con toda tu alma: «¡*Señor, sálvame!*».

Deja que mi *gran Amor sea tu consuelo*. Cuando te parezca que te estás hundiendo en las arenas movedizas de tus luchas, es urgente que te aferres a algo que no te va a fallar, algo a lo que le puedas confiar tu vida. Mi poderosa Presencia no solo te fortalecerá, sino que te sostendrá y no dejará que te hundas. Yo tengo un firme control sobre ti, mi amado.

Debido a que siempre estoy cerca, no tienes por qué tenerles miedo a tus debilidades. En realidad, *mi poder se perfecciona en la debilidad*. Así que dame las gracias por tus debilidades y no dejes en ningún momento de confiar en mi Fuerza siempre presente.

SALMOS 59.17; MATEO 14.30;
SALMOS 119.76; 2 CORINTIOS 12.9

No tengas miedo de enfrentar tus pecados. Excepto yo, no ha existido una persona que no haya pecado nunca. *Si tú dices que no tienes pecado, te estás engañando a ti mismo y no tienes la verdad.* En realidad, es bastante liberador *confesar tus pecados*, sabiendo que *te perdonaré y te limpiaré de toda maldad*. La buena noticia es que ya te he redimido y pagado la pena completa por todos tus pecados. Cuando confiesas tus malas acciones, te estás alineando con la verdad. Puesto que *yo soy la Verdad*, tu confesión te acerca más a mí. También *te libera* de seguir experimentando sentimientos de culpa.

Cuando te des cuenta de que has pecado con tus pensamientos, palabras o acciones, admítelo inmediatamente. Tu confesión no tiene por qué ser larga o elocuente. Puede ser tan simple como: «¡Perdóname y límpiame, Señor!». Yo ya hice la parte más difícil: morir en la cruz por tus pecados. Tu parte es vivir en la Luz de la Verdad. *Yo, tu Salvador, soy la Luz del mundo.*

1 Juan 1.8, 9; Juan 14.6;
Juan 8.32; Juan 8.12

Noviembre 20

DÉJAME ENSEÑARTE CÓMO OCUPAR más de tu tiempo en el presente. El futuro, en la forma en que la mayoría de la gente lo conceptualiza, en realidad no existe. Cuando te asomas a tus mañanas haciendo predicciones, estás simplemente ejercitando tu imaginación. Yo soy el único que tengo acceso a lo que «todavía no es», porque no estoy limitado por el tiempo. A medida que avanzas paso a paso a través de cada día, yo despliego el futuro ante ti. Sin embargo, mientras avanzas en el tiempo, nunca pondrás un pie en lo que va a ocurrir sin que antes hayas estado en el momento presente. Reconocer lo inútil que es pretender ver lo que está por venir te puede liberar para vivir más plenamente en el hoy.

Llegar a ser libre es un proceso complicado, porque tu mente está acostumbrada a deambular a voluntad hacia el futuro. Cuando te encuentres atrapado en tales pensamientos, reconoce que has caído en la tierra de la fantasía. Despertarte a esta verdad te ayudará a regresar al presente, donde yo te estoy esperando ansioso para envolverte en mi *gran Amor*.

ECLESIASTÉS 8.7; APOCALIPSIS 1.8;
SALMOS 32.10

CUANDO TE SIENTES AGRADECIDO, *me adoras como a mí me agrada, con temor reverente*. Acción de Gracias no es solo una festividad que se celebra una vez al año. Es una actitud del corazón que produce Gozo. También constituye un mandato bíblico. Tú no puedes adorarme aceptablemente con un corazón desagradecido. Puedes cumplir con las formalidades, pero tu ingratitud te refrenará.

Cada vez que te encuentres luchando espiritual o emocionalmente, detente y comprueba tu «medidor de agradecimiento». Si la lectura es baja, pídeme que te ayude a aumentar tu nivel de gratitud. Busca motivos para agradecerme. Anótalos si lo deseas. Tu perspectiva cambiará gradualmente de centrarte en todo lo que es erróneo a alegrarte en las cosas que son correctas.

No importa lo que esté sucediendo, puedes *alegrarte en Dios tu Libertador*. Debido a mi obra terminada en la cruz, tienes un futuro glorioso que te está garantizado para siempre. Alégrate en este regalo gratuito de salvación para ti y todo el que confía en mí como Salvador. Deja que tu corazón se desborde de agradecimiento, y yo te llenaré con mi Gozo.

HEBREOS 12.28; SALMOS 100.4;
1 CORINTIOS 13.6; HABACUC 3.17, 18

Noviembre 22

¡AGRADÉCEME POR EL REGALO glorioso de la gracia! *Porque por gracia has sido salvado mediante la fe. Y esto no procede de ti, sino que es el regalo de Dios, no por obras para que nadie se jacte.* Mediante mi obra acabada en la cruz y tu decisión de creer en mí como tu Salvador, has recibido el regalo más grande de todos: *la Vida eterna.* Hasta la fe necesaria para recibir la salvación es un regalo que yo te he hecho. La mejor respuesta a tal generosidad es un corazón agradecido. Nunca me agradecerás lo suficiente o con demasiada frecuencia por la forma en que te he bendecido.

Cada vez que desees darme las gracias, piensa en lo que significa tener todos tus pecados perdonados. Esto quiere decir que ya no estás camino al infierno; tu destino es ahora *un cielo nuevo y una tierra nueva.* También significa que cada día de tu vida es valioso. A medida que transcurre el día de hoy, agradéceme repetidamente por el increíble don de la gracia. Deja que esta gratitud te llene de Gozo y aumente tu agradecimiento por las muchas *otras* bendiciones que te proveo.

EFESIOS 2.8, 9; JUAN 3:16;
MATEO 10.28; APOCALIPSIS 21.1

AGRADÉCEME PORQUE YO SOY BUENO; mi gran Amor perdura para siempre. Quiero que apartes un tiempo para pensar en las muchas bendiciones que te he provisto. Dame las gracias por el don de la vida: la tuya y la de tus seres queridos. Dame las gracias por cada provisión: alimento y agua, un techo que te cubra, ropa y muchas cosas más. Luego, recuerda el más grande don: la Vida eterna para los que me conocen como su Salvador.

Al reflexionar sobre todo lo que he hecho por ti, deléitate también en *quién yo soy.* ¡Yo soy cien por ciento Bueno! Nunca ha habido, ni nunca habrá el más mínimo ápice de oscuridad en mí. *¡Yo soy la Luz del mundo!* Además, mi Amor por ti perdurará y perdurará por toda la eternidad.

Incluso ahora mismo estás abrigado por mi amorosa Presencia. Independientemente de lo que pudiera estar sucediendo, yo estoy siempre cerca de mis seguidores. Así que no te preocupes si puedes percibir o no mi Presencia. Simplemente *confía* en que yo estoy contigo y busca consuelo en *mi gran Amor.* ¡Lo encontrarás!

SALMOS 107.1; JUAN 8.58; JUAN 8.12;
SALMOS 107.8

Noviembre 24

RECIBE CON ALEGRÍA Y AGRADECIMIENTO las bendiciones que derramo sobre ti. Sin embargo, no te aferres a ellas. Consérvalas con una actitud generosa y estando listo para devolvérmelas. Al mismo tiempo, quiero que disfrutes al máximo de la cosas buenas que te doy. La mejor manera de hacerlo es viviendo en el presente, negándote a preocuparte por el mañana. *Hoy* es el momento para disfrutar de las bendiciones que te he provisto. Dado que no sabes lo que pasará mañana, aprovecha al máximo lo que tienes hoy: familia, amigos, talentos, posesiones. Y busca oportunidades a fin de ser una bendición para otros.

Cuando te quito algo o a alguien que atesoras, es saludable que llores su pérdida. También es importante que te aproximes lo más que puedas a mí durante este tiempo. Aférrate a mí, mi amado, y no te sueltes. Recuerda que nunca nadie podrá apartarte de mí. Déjame ser *tu Roca en quien encuentras refugio*. Yo siempre estoy dándote nuevas bendiciones para consolarte y guiarte. ¡Mantente en la búsqueda de todo lo que tengo para ti!

MATEO 6.34; LUCAS 10.41, 42; SALMOS 18.2;
ISAÍAS 43.19

Yo te creé para que me glorificaras. Haz de este precepto tu punto focal mientras avanzas por tu camino en este día. La acción de gracias, la alabanza y la adoración son formas de glorificarme. Dame las gracias sin cesar; mantente en la búsqueda de mis bendiciones, como si fueran un tesoro escondido. Alábame no solo a través de la oración y de cánticos, sino en lo que les dices a otras personas. Háblales de mis obras maravillosas. ¡Cuéntales cuán grande soy! ¡Únete a otros para adorarme en la iglesia, donde el peso de mi Gloria puede palparse!

Cuando tengas que tomar decisiones, piensa en las que me glorificarían y me producirían alegría. Esto te puede ayudar a decidir sabiamente y a estar más consciente de mi Presencia. En lugar de quedarte atascado en la reflexión, pídeme que guíe tu mente. Yo conozco hasta el más mínimo detalle de tu vida y tus circunstancias. Mientras mejor me conozcas, más efectivamente puedo guiarte en tus decisiones; así que esfuérzate en aumentar tu conocimiento de mí. *Mi Palabra es una lámpara a tus pies y una luz en tu sendero.*

1 Tesalonicenses 5.18; Salmos 96.3;
2 Corintios 4.17, 18; Salmos 119.105

DARME LAS GRACIAS DESPIERTA TU CORAZÓN, agudiza tu mente y te ayuda a disfrutar de mi Presencia. Por eso, cuando en tu vida te sientas desenfocado o alejado de mí, agradéceme *por algo*. Siempre hay una abundancia de cosas para elegir: regalos eternos —como la salvación, la gracia y la fe— así como bendiciones ordinarias, de todos los días. Piensa en las últimas veinticuatro horas y toma nota de todas las cosas buenas que te haya provisto en tal periodo de tiempo. Esto no solo te levantará el ánimo, sino que despertará tu mente de modo que puedas pensar más claramente.

Recuerda que *tu enemigo el diablo ronda como león rugiente, buscando a quién devorar*. ¡Esta es la razón de que resulte tan importante el *dominio propio y mantenerse alerta*! Cuando dejas que tu mente divague desenfocada, eres mucho más vulnerable al maligno. Sin embargo, el remedio es simple. Tan pronto como te des cuenta de lo que te está sucediendo, podrás ahuyentar al enemigo dándome las gracias y alabándome. Esta es la guerra de adoración. ¡Y funciona!

EFESIOS 2.8, 9; 1 PEDRO 5.8;
2 CORINTIOS 9.15

LA GRATITUD Y LA CONFIANZA son como dos amigos íntimos que siempre están listos para ayudarte. Cuando tu día parezca sombrío y el mundo se presente aterrador, es el momento de confiar en estos fieles amigos. Detente por un momento y respira hondo. Mira a tu alrededor tratando de ver la belleza y las bendiciones que te rodean, y dame las gracias cuando las encuentres. Esto te conectará conmigo de una manera maravillosa. Háblame en términos muy positivos de los muchos buenos regalos que te he hecho. Hazte el propósito de agradecerme con entusiasmo, independientemente de cómo te sientas. Al persistir en lo que respecta a expresarme tu gratitud, vas a descubrir que el gozo inundará tu alma.

También es útil acostumbrarte a expresar con frecuencia tu confianza en mí. ¡Esto te recuerda que yo estoy contigo y soy absolutamente confiable! En tu vida habrá siempre algunas áreas en las que tengas que confiar en mí más plenamente que en otras. Cuando vengan los días duros, recíbelos como oportunidades para ampliar el ámbito de tu confianza *viviendo por fe* en estas épocas difíciles. No malgastes las oportunidades; úsalas para acercarte más a mí. ¡Yo te estaré esperando con los brazos abiertos para darte la bienvenida!

SALMOS 92.1, 2; SALMOS 118.28;
2 CORINTIOS 5.7; SANTIAGO 4.8

Noviembre 28

Tú me amas porque yo te amé primero. La verdad es que *estabas muerto en tus pecados* —siendo completamente incapaz de amarme— hasta que mi Espíritu obró en lo íntimo de tu ser para hacerte espiritualmente vivo. Esto te permitió arrepentirte de tu pecaminosidad y recibir no solo la Vida eterna, sino también mi Amor eterno. Al meditar en este milagroso regalo de la salvación, deja que la gratitud dentro de ti se exprese libremente y te llenes de Gozo.

Ser agradecido es sumamente importante para tu crecimiento en la gracia. Esto abre tu corazón y tu mente a mi Palabra, permitiéndote crecer en sabiduría y entendimiento. Una disposición a dar gracias te ayudará a descubrir la miríada de bendiciones que derramo sobre ti, incluso en medio de los tiempos difíciles. Un corazón agradecido te protegerá del desánimo y la autocompasión. Realzar tu conciencia de mi Presencia continua te ayudará a comprender más plenamente las vastas dimensiones de mi Amor por ti. Así que cultiva tu gratitud, mi amado. Tu agradecimiento fomentará tu amor por mí. ¡Y lo hará más luminoso y fuerte!

1 JUAN 4.19; EFESIOS 2.1;
EFESIOS 3.16-18

EL FUTURO DE LOS JUSTOS ES HALAGÜEÑO. Esto significa que tu futuro es excelente, porque yo te he vestido con el *manto de la justicia*. Así que comienza cada día con ansias de recibir el Gozo que tengo reservado para ti.

Algunos de mis seguidores no logran encontrar los disfrutes que he preparado para ellos, ya que se concentran demasiado en los problemas de la vida y las vicisitudes del mundo. En lugar de *tener una vida abundante*, viven cautelosamente, tratando de minimizar los dolores y los riesgos. Al hacerlo, también están reduciendo sus tiempos de Gozo y su eficacia en mi reino. Este *no es* el estilo de vida que he previsto para ti.

Al despertar cada mañana, busca mi Rostro con esperanzada anticipación. Invítame a que te prepare no solo para enfrentar alguna dificultad que se te presente durante el día, sino también para disfrutar de los deleites que he plantado a lo largo de tu camino. Luego, toma mi mano y déjame compartir en todo lo que encuentres a lo largo de la senda por la que avanzas… ¡incluyendo todo el Gozo!

PROVERBIOS 10.28; ISAÍAS 61.10;
JUAN 10.10

Noviembre 30

EL GOZO ES UNA OPCIÓN, una decisión con la que te enfrentarás muchas veces cada día mientras vives en este mundo. Cuando vayas al cielo, un Gozo indescriptiblemente glorioso será tuyo, sin ningún esfuerzo de tu parte. No tendrás que ejercer tu voluntad para ser feliz. Esto se producirá naturalmente y será constante.

Mientras vas por este mundo caído, quiero ayudarte a hacer decisiones más sabias cada vez. Necesitas tomar conciencia —y mantenerte consciente— de que puedes elegir ser positivo y tener esperanza momento a momento. Establece la meta de encontrar el Gozo en medio de tu día. Si notas que te estás desanimando, frustrándote, o te atacan otros sentimientos negativos, deja que esas emociones punzantes te lleven a recordarme. *Busca mi Rostro* y habla conmigo. Puedes orar algo así como: «Señor Jesús, elijo ser feliz, porque tú eres *Dios, mi Libertador,* y nada me puede separar de tu amorosa Presencia».

Vive victoriosamente, mi amado, tratando de encontrarme en cada vez más de tus momentos.

SALMOS 27.8; HABACUC 3.18;
ROMANOS 8.38, 39

Diciembre

Con alegría sacarán ustedes agua
de las fuentes de la salvación.

ISAÍAS 12.3

HAGAS LO QUE HAGAS, trabaja de buena gana, como si lo estuvieras haciendo para mí y no para nadie de este mundo. La falta de entusiasmo no me agrada y no creo que sea buena para ti. La tentación es hacer lo más rápido que se pueda los quehaceres rutinarios y de manera descuidada. Sin embargo, esta actitud negativa, si la cultivas, te desvalorizará a ti y a tu trabajo. No obstante, si cumples las mismas tareas con un corazón agradecido, encontrarás placer en ellas y la calidad del producto final será mucho mejor.

Es bueno que recuerdes que cada momento de tu vida es un regalo de mi parte. En lugar de sentirte con derecho a circunstancias mejores, aprovecha al máximo todo lo que te proveo, incluyendo tu trabajo. Cuando puse a Adán y Eva en el Jardín del Edén, les dije que lo *cultivaran y lo cuidaran.* Aun cuando era un ambiente perfecto, no se trataba de un lugar lleno de ocio ni de holgazanería.

Hagas lo que hagas, mi amado, estarás *haciéndolo para mí.* De modo que dame tus mejores esfuerzos y yo te daré lo mejor de mi Gozo.

COLOSENSES 3.23; GÉNESIS 2.15;
2 TESALONICENSES 3.11, 12

Diciembre 2

AL QUE TENGA SED le daré a beber gratuitamente de la fuente del agua de la Vida. Bébela con intensidad y así yo podré vivir abundantemente en ti. Deja que el agua de la Vida llegue hasta las profundidades de tu ser, refrescándote y renovándote. Como esta agua de Vida es gratis, puedes disponer de toda la que quieras… puedes tener tanto como desees de mí. *¡Yo soy Cristo en ti, la esperanza de Gloria!*

Mi deseo es que tengas mucha *sed de mí, tu Dios.* La sed es un deseo muy poderoso; el agua sostiene la vida, incluso más que el alimento. El agua pura es mucho más saludable que las bebidas enlatadas llenas de azúcares o productos químicos. De igual manera, beber de mí primero que nada y ante todo es determinante para tu salud espiritual. Aunque otras cosas pudieren satisfacerte durante un tiempo, no van a apagar la sed de tu alma.

¡Alégrate de que lo que más necesitas es gratuito! *Saca agua de las fuentes de la salvación con alegría.*

APOCALIPSIS 21.6; COLOSENSES 1.27;
SALMOS 63.1; ISAÍAS 12.3

A PESAR DE QUE NO ME VES, tú crees en mí. Yo soy más real —completo, inmutable, ilimitado— que las cosas que puedes ver. Al creer en mí, estás confiando en una Realidad que es una roca sólida. Yo soy la *Roca* indestructible en la cual te puedes parar confiado, sin que importen las circunstancias Y debido a que me perteneces, estoy dedicado a ti. Mi amado, te animo a que *busques refugio en mí.*

Creer en mí, tiene innumerables beneficios. ¡El más precioso es *la salvación* de tu alma para siempre! Creer en mí realza también tu vida presente de forma notable, por lo que es más fácil saber quién eres y a Quién perteneces. Al mantenerte en comunicación conmigo, te ayudo a encontrar tu camino a través de este mundo caído y estropeado sin que se afecte la esperanza que abrigas en tu corazón. Todo esto amplía tu capacidad para disfrutar de la auténtica felicidad. ¡Mientras más me busques y más completamente me conozcas, más podré llenarte con mi *Gozo indescriptible y glorioso*!

1 PEDRO 1.8, 9; SALMOS 18.2;
ROMANOS 8.25

Diciembre 4

QUIERO QUE CONFÍES en mí lo suficiente como para relajarte y disfrutar de mi Presencia. Yo no te diseñé para que vivieras en un estado de extrema vigilancia, sintiendo y actuando como si estuvieras permanentemente en medio de una emergencia. Tu cuerpo está diseñado de manera maravillosa para «aumentar las revoluciones» cuando sea necesario y «disminuir las revoluciones» cuando la crisis haya pasado. Sin embargo, debido a que vives en un mundo tan deteriorado, te parece difícil bajar la guardia y relajarte. Quiero que recuerdes que yo estoy contigo todo el tiempo y que soy totalmente digno de tu confianza. *Ábreme tu corazón*. Encomienda a mi cuidado soberano todo lo que te está preocupando o molestando.

Mientras más te apoyas en mí, más plenamente vas a poder disfrutar de mi Presencia. Al descansar bajo mi Luz sanadora, yo proyectaré Paz en tu mente y tu corazón. Tu seguridad de mi Presencia contigo se hará más fuerte y *mi gran Amor* inundará lo íntimo de tu ser. *Confía en mí*, mi amado, *de todo corazón y con toda tu mente*.

SALMOS 62.8; SALMOS 52.8;
PROVERBIOS 3.5

Diciembre 5

Yo te creé a mi imagen, con la asombrosa capacidad de comunicarte conmigo. Como portador de mi imagen, eres capaz de elegir el enfoque de tu mente. Muchos de tus pensamientos van y vienen espontáneamente, pero puedes controlarlos más de lo que crees. El Espíritu Santo inspiró a Pablo a escribir: «*Consideren bien todo lo verdadero, todo lo respetable, todo lo justo…*». Yo no te pediría que pensaras de esta manera si no fuera posible que lo hicieras.

Debido a que el mundo contiene tanto el bien como el mal, puedes optar por concentrarte en lo *excelente* o *digno de elogio* o en cosas malsanas o perturbadoras. A veces tienes que lidiar con las desgracias de todo tipo que ocurren a tu alrededor, pero cada día trae momentos en los que puedes sentirte libre para pensar en cosas *puras y amables*. Cuando tu mente está desocupada, tiende a moverse hacia enfoques negativos, lamentándose de cosas que ocurrieron en el pasado o preocupándose por el futuro. Mientras tanto, yo estoy *contigo* en el presente, a la espera de que te acuerdes de mi Presencia. Entrénate para volverte a mí con la mayor frecuencia. Esto hará brillar aun tus tiempos más difíciles, aumentando tu Gozo.

GÉNESIS 1.27; FILIPENSES 4.8;
MATEO 1.23; HECHOS 2.28

Diciembre 6

CONFÍA EN MÍ, MI AMADO. Cada vez que te asalte un pensamiento de ansiedad o miedo, tienes que mirar mi Rostro múltiples veces y pronunciar mi Nombre para acordarte de que yo estoy cerca y listo para ayudarte. Cítame algunos pasajes de las Escrituras, como: «*Señor, en ti confío, y digo: "Tú eres mi Dios". Mi vida entera está en tus manos*». Exprésame tu amor, diciendo: «*Cuánto te amo, Señor, fuerza mía*». Recuerda que yo —tu Salvador y Rey— *me deleito en ti*. ¡Tú eres un miembro muy querido de mi familia real!

Conectarte conmigo interrumpe los pensamientos negativos que tienden a correr a través de tu mente. Mientras más constante sea tu comunicación conmigo, más libre serás. Como *yo soy la Verdad*, vivir cerca de mí te ayudará a reconocer y liberarte de distorsiones y mentiras.

Confiar en mí y amarme se encuentran en el corazón mismo de tu relación conmigo. Estas hermosas formas de estar cerca de mí evitan que te concentres demasiado en ti mismo y tus miedos. Vuélvete a mí una y otra vez, seguro en mi Presencia protectora.

SALMOS 31.14, 15; SALMOS 18.1;
SOFONÍAS 3.17; JUAN 14.6

Yo QUIERO QUE APRENDAS a estar *siempre alegre*, conectando tu Gozo a mí primero y ante todo. Una forma de hacer esto es recordando que yo te amo todo el tiempo y en toda circunstancia. *Aunque cambien de lugar las montañas y se tambaleen las colinas, no cambiará mi Amor por ti.* Así es que no cedas a la tentación de dudar de mi Amor cuando las cosas no están saliendo como tú quisieras o cuando has fallado de alguna forma. Mi amorosa Presencia es la roca sólida sobre la cual puedes pararte, sabiendo que en mí estarás eternamente seguro. ¡Yo soy *el Señor que tiene compasión de ti*!

Otra forma de aumentar tu Gozo es *dándome gracias en toda situación*. Pídele a mi Espíritu que te ayude a ver tu vida a través del lente del agradecimiento. Busca las bendiciones que están desperdigadas a lo largo de tu camino aun en los tiempos difíciles y agradéceme por cada una. Te animo a que mires firmemente a través de los lentes de la gratitud *pensando en todo lo que sea excelente o merezca elogio.*

1 TESALONICENSES 5.16-18; ISAÍAS 54.10;
FILIPENSES 4.8

Diciembre 8

Yo soy EL SEÑOR DE PAZ, la única fuente de Paz genuina. Te doy este regalo, no como algo separado de mí mismo, sino como parte de quien soy. No tomes esta bendición a la ligera. Separa un tiempo para concentrarte en mí y disfrutar de mi Presencia.

Tú vives en medio de una guerra espiritual intensa y mi Paz es una parte esencial de tu armadura. A fin de mantenerte en pie en esta batalla, deberás usar fuertes botas de combate: el calzado del *evangelio de la Paz*. Esta buena noticia te asegura que te amo y que estoy *de tu parte*.

Algunos de mis seguidores pierden la Paz porque creen que yo estoy siempre tratando de encontrar algo malo que han hecho para castigarlos. Por el contrario, yo te contemplo a través de ojos llenos de Amor perfecto. En lugar de castigarte cuando has hecho algo incorrecto, recuerdo que mi muerte en la cruz cubre todos tus pecados. ¡Te amo con un *Amor inagotable*, simplemente porque eres mío! Alégrate en este evangelio de la Paz; es tuyo para que lo disfrutes *siempre y en todas las circunstancias*.

2 TESALONICENSES 3.16; EFESIOS 6.15;
ROMANOS 8.31; SALMOS 90.14

A MEDIDA QUE AVANZAS conmigo en este viaje por la vida, observa la esperanza del cielo brillando en tu camino y alumbrando tu perspectiva. Recuerda que tú eres uno de mi *linaje escogido, que me pertenece. Yo te llamé de las tinieblas a mi Luz admirable.* Saborea la riqueza de estos conceptos: *Yo te escogí antes de la creación del mundo,* por eso nada puede separarte de mí. ¡Eres mío para siempre! Yo te saqué de la oscuridad del *pecado y de la muerte* y te traje a la Luz exquisita de la Vida eterna.

El brillo de mi Presencia te ayudará de múltiples maneras. Mientras más cerca de mí vivas, más claramente podrás ver el camino que tienes por delante. A medida que dejes que esta Luz-Amor te inunde, *te fortaleceré y te bendeciré con mi Paz.* Mi resplandor no solo te bendecirá a ti, sino también a otras personas a medida que impregne todo tu ser. Este tiempo dedicado a mí te ayudará a ser más como yo, permitiéndote brillar en las vidas de otros. Yo estoy continuamente trayendo a mis amados de la oscuridad a mi Luz gloriosa.

1 PEDRO 2.9; EFESIOS 1.4;
ROMANOS 8.2; SALMOS 29.11

GUARDA SILENCIO ANTE MÍ y espera con paciencia que yo actúe. Pasar tiempo de calidad conmigo es muy bueno para ti, mi amado. Yo me gozo cuando te desentiendes de muchas cosas que reclaman tu atención y te concentras con todo tu ser en mí. Sé lo difícil que es para ti permanecer tranquilo y en silencio, así que no espero perfección. En lugar de eso, valoro tu persistencia en cuanto a buscar mi Rostro. Mi amorosa aprobación brilla sobre ti mientras *me buscas de todo corazón*. Esta conexión íntima entre nosotros te ayuda a esperar confiado a que yo actúe.

No te irrites por el éxito de otros, de los que maquinan planes malvados. Confía en que yo sigo en control y finalmente prevalecerá la justicia. *Yo juzgaré al mundo con justicia y a los pueblos con fidelidad.* Mientras tanto, busca formas de hacer avanzar mi reino en este mundo. Mantén tus ojos en mí a medida que avanzas en el día de hoy, y mantente dispuesto a seguir a donde quiera que yo te lleve. *¡No te dejes vencer* [o desalentar] *por el mal; al contrario, vence el mal con el bien*!

SALMOS 37.7; JEREMÍAS 29.13;
SALMOS 96.12, 13; ROMANOS 12.21

Yo soy la Roca que es más alta que tú y tus circunstancias. Yo soy *tu* Roca, en quien encuentras refugio en cualquier momento y lugar. Ven a mí, mi amado: descansa en la Paz de mi Presencia. Tómate un respiro en tu intento de querer resolverlo todo. Admite que muchas, muchas cosas están más allá de tu comprensión y tu control. *Mis caminos y pensamientos son más altos que los tuyos, como los cielos son más altos que la tierra.*

Cuando el mundo que te rodea se vea confuso y el mal parezca triunfar, recuerda esto: yo soy la Luz que sigue brillando en todas las situaciones. Y la luz *siempre* derrota a la oscuridad cuando estas dos fuerzas se encuentran cara a cara.

Dado que eres mi seguidor, quiero que brilles poderosamente en este mundo atribulado. Susurra mi Nombre; canta canciones de alabanza. Cuéntales a los demás *las buenas noticias que son motivo de mucha alegría:* ¡que yo soy el *Salvador, Cristo el Señor!* También soy el Único que está contigo permanentemente. Mantén la mirada en mí, y mi Presencia iluminará tu camino.

SALMOS 61.2; SALMOS 18.2; ISAÍAS 55.9;
LUCAS 2.10, 11

Diciembre 12

CUANDO ENTRÉ EN TU MUNDO como el Dios-Hombre, *vine a lo que era mío.* ¡Todo me pertenece! La mayoría de la gente piensa que ellos son dueños de lo que tienen, pero la verdad es que yo soy el dueño de todo. Aunque en ocasiones te puedes sentir aislado y solo, esto es solamente una ilusión. Yo te compré a un precio astronómico, por lo que eres mío, mi tesoro. ¡El precio colosal que pagué da fe de lo precioso que eres para mí! Recuerda esta poderosa verdad cada vez que empieces a dudar de tu valía. Tú eres mi amado, *salvado por gracia mediante la fe en mí,* tu Salvador.

Debido a que eres tan precioso para mí, quiero que te cuides: espiritual, emocional y físicamente. Dedica tiempo a reflexionar en las Escrituras en tu mente y tu corazón. Protégete, tanto en lo emocional como en lo físico, de los que quieran aprovecharse de ti. Recuerda que *tu cuerpo es templo del Espíritu Santo.* También quiero que ayudes a otros a descubrir las gloriosas buenas noticias, el don de la *Vida eterna para todo el que cree en mí.*

JUAN 1.11; EFESIOS 2.8, 9;
1 CORINTIOS 6.19, 20; JUAN 3.16

TODO EL QUE ESTÁ DE PARTE de la verdad me escucha. Yo soy la Verdad encarnada. La razón por la que nací y entré en tu mundo fue para *dar testimonio de la verdad.*

Muchos creen que no hay absolutos y todo es relativo. Las personas inescrupulosas capitalizan esta opinión predominante manipulando información para promover sus propias agendas. Presentan lo malo como bueno, y lo bueno como malo. ¡Esto resulta abominable para mí! Como dije acerca de todos los mentirosos impenitentes, su lugar será en *el lago de fuego y azufre.*

Recuerda que *el diablo es un mentiroso y el padre de la mentira.* Mientras más escuches de mí, especialmente a través la lectura de las Escrituras, más valorarás la verdad y te deleitarás en mí, la Verdad viviente. El Espíritu Santo es *el Espíritu de Verdad.* Pídele que te dé discernimiento. Él te ayudará a vivir en este mundo donde los engaños y las mentiras son comunes. Decídete a *estar de parte de de la verdad* y así podrás vivir cerca de mí y disfrutar de mi Presencia.

JUAN 18.37; APOCALIPSIS 21.8;
JUAN 8.44; JUAN 16.13

Diciembre 14

No te canses ni pierdas el ánimo. Cuando estás contendiendo con dificultades que persisten, es fácil estar tan cansado que te sientes tentado a darte por vencido. Los problemas crónicos pueden terminar desgastándote. Si te concentras demasiado en estos problemas, estarás en peligro de caer en el agujero negro de la autocompasión o la desesperación.

Hay varios tipos de cansancio. El cansancio físico continuo te hace vulnerable al agotamiento emocional y la fatiga espiritual, al desánimo. Sin embargo, te he equipado para que trasciendas tus problemas al *poner tu mirada en mí.* Yo pagué un alto precio por esta provisión *soportando la cruz* por ti. Meditar en mi disposición a sufrir tanto puede fortalecerte para soportar tus propios sufrimientos.

Adorarme es una maravillosa manera de renovar tu fuerza en mi Presencia. Cuando en medio de las dificultades des pasos de fe alabándome, mi gloriosa Luz brillará sobre ti. Y al mantenerte concentrado en mí, *estarás reflejando mi Gloria* a otros, y tú serás *transformado a mi semejanza con más y más Gloria.*

HEBREOS 12.2, 3; 2 CORINTIOS 5.7;
2 CORINTIOS 3.18

EN SU PROFECÍA SOBRE MI NACIMIENTO, Isaías se refiere a mí como *Padre eterno*. Hay una unidad de esencia en la Trinidad, aun cuando está compuesta de tres Personas. Cuando los judíos me acosaban en el templo, les dije: «*El Padre y yo somos uno*». Más tarde, cuando Felipe me pidió que les mostrara al Padre a los discípulos, le expliqué: «*El que me ha visto a mí, ha visto al Padre*». Así que nunca pienses de mí como si fuera solo un gran maestro. Yo soy Dios, y el Padre y yo vivimos en perfecta unidad.

Cuando me llegues a conocer con mayor profundidad y anchura, te darás cuenta de que también estás más cerca del Padre. No dejes que la misteriosa riqueza de la Trinidad te confunda. Simplemente ven a mí, reconoce que yo soy todo lo que podrías necesitar que fuera. Yo —tu único Salvador— soy suficiente para ti.

En medio de esta ajetreada temporada de Adviento, vuelve a poner el enfoque de tu vida en mi santa Presencia. ¡Recuerda que *Emanuel* ha venido! ¡Regocíjate!

ISAÍAS 9.6; JUAN 10.30;
JUAN 14.9; MATEO 1.23

Diciembre 16

CUANDO UN ÁNGEL ANUNCIÓ MI NACIMIENTO a unos *pastores que pasaban la noche en el campo* cerca de Belén, les dijo: «*No tengan miedo. Miren que, les traigo buenas noticias que serán motivo de mucha alegría*». La instrucción a no tener miedo se repite en la Biblia más que cualquier otro mandato. Es una instrucción tierna y misericordiosa. ¡Y es para ti! Yo sé cuán propenso a temer eres, y no te condeno por eso. Sin embargo, quiero ayudarte para que te liberes de esa tendencia.

¡El Gozo es un poderoso antídoto contra el miedo! Y mientras mayor es el Gozo, más efectivo es el antídoto. El anuncio del ángel a los pastores fue *motivo de mucha alegría*. ¡Nunca pierdas de vista lo increíbles que son las *buenas noticias* del evangelio! Tú te arrepientes de tus pecados y confías en mí como tu Salvador. Yo perdono *todos* tus pecados y cambio tu destino final del infierno al cielo. Además, *me doy* a ti, prodigándote mi Amor y prometiéndote mi Presencia para siempre. Aparta un tiempo para meditar en la gloriosa proclamación del ángel a los pastores. ¡*Alégrate en mí*, mi amado!

LUCAS 2.8-10; 1 JUAN 3.1; FILIPENSES 4.4

CÁNTAME CON ALEGRÍA, que yo soy tu Fortaleza. La música de Navidad es una de las mejores bendiciones de la temporada, y no te cuesta nada. Puedes cantar los villancicos en la iglesia o la intimidad de tu hogar, o incluso en tu auto. Cuando estés cantando, ponles atención a las palabras. Son todas acerca de mí y mi entrada milagrosa en tu mundo a través del nacimiento virginal. Cantar con el corazón aumenta tanto tu Gozo como tu energía. ¡También me bendice a mí!

Yo te creé para que me glorificaras y disfrutaras de mí para siempre. Así que no es de extrañar que te sientas más lleno de vida cuando me glorificas a través del canto. Quiero que aprendas a disfrutarme en cada vez más aspectos de tu vida. Antes de que te levantes de tu cama cada mañana, trata de sentir mi Presencia contigo. Recuérdate: *«En realidad, el Señor está en este lugar».* Esto despertará tu conciencia a las maravillas de mi continua cercanía. *¡Te llenaré de alegría en mi Presencia!*

SALMOS 81.1; SALMOS 5.11;
GÉNESIS 28.16; HECHOS 2.28

Diciembre 18

¡Yo, TU SALVADOR, SOY *DIOS FUERTE!* Mucho del énfasis durante el Adviento está puesto en el bebé en el pesebre. Yo comencé mi vida en la tierra en esta humilde condición. Dejé mi Gloria y tomé forma humana. Sin embargo, continué siendo Dios, capaz de vivir una vida perfecta y sin pecado y de hacer milagros portentosos. *¡Yo, tu Dios, estoy contigo como guerrero victorioso!* Sé bendecido por esta combinación de mi tierna cercanía y mi Poder maravilloso.

Cuando entré en el mundo, *llegué a lo que era mío*, porque todo fue hecho por medio de mí. *Sin embargo, lo que era mío no me recibió, pero a todos los que me recibieron, a los que creyeron en mi Nombre, les di el derecho de ser hijos de Dios.* Este regalo de la salvación es de un valor infinito. Le da sentido y dirección a tu vida y hace del cielo tu destino final. Durante este tiempo de dar y recibir regalos, recuerda que el don supremo es la Vida eterna. ¡Responde a este glorioso regalo *regocijándote en mí siempre!*

ISAÍAS 9.6; SOFONÍAS 3.17;
JUAN 1.11, 12; FILIPENSES 4.4

Yo soy EMANUEL, *Dios contigo* en todo momento. Esta promesa provee una base sólida para tu Gozo. Muchas personas tratan de condicionar su placer a cosas temporales, pero mi Presencia contigo es eterna. Alégrate en gran medida, mi amado, sabiendo que tu Salvador *nunca te dejará ni te abandonará.*

La naturaleza del tiempo puede hacer que resulte difícil para ti disfrutar de tu vida. En los escasos días en que todo va bien, tu percepción de que las condiciones ideales son fugaces pueden afectar tu disfrute de esos momentos. Incluso las más deliciosas vacaciones deben con el tiempo llegar a su fin. Las estaciones de la vida también van y vienen, a pesar de tu anhelo a veces de «detener el reloj» y dejar las cosas tal como están.

No pongas tus esperanzas en los placeres temporales, sino más bien reconoce sus limitaciones y su imposibilidad de saciar la sed de tu alma. Tu búsqueda de Gozo duradero fallará a menos que hagas de mí tu objetivo final. *Yo te mostraré la senda de la Vida. Te llenaré de alegría en mi Presencia.*

MATEO 1.23; DEUTERONOMIO 31.8;
SALMOS 16.11

Diciembre 20

No IMPORTA LO SOLITARIO que te sientas, nunca estarás solo. La Navidad puede ser una época difícil para quienes están separados de sus seres queridos. La separación tal vez sea el resultado de la muerte, el divorcio, la distancia u otras causas. La alegría de la celebración alrededor de ti puede intensificar tu sensación de soledad. Sin embargo, todos mis hijos tienen un recurso que es más que adecuado para ayudarlos: mi Presencia continua.

Recuerda esta profecía acerca de mí: *«La virgen [...] dará a luz un hijo, y lo llamarán Emanuel», que significa «Dios con nosotros».* Mucho antes de que yo naciera, fui proclamado el Dios que está *contigo*. Esta verdad es una roca sólida de la que nadie ni ninguna circunstancia podrán jamás separarte.

Cada vez que te sientas solo, aparta un tiempo para disfrutar de mi Presencia. Dame las gracias por *cubrirte con el manto de la justicia*, haciéndote de esta manera justo. Pídeme que te llene de Gozo y Paz. Entonces, a través de la ayuda de mi Espíritu, podrás *rebosarte de esperanza* hacia las vidas de otras personas.

MATEO 1.23; ISAÍAS 61.10;
2 CORINTIOS 5.21; ROMANOS 15.13

Yo *ME HICE POBRE para que tú pudieras llegar a ser rico.*
Mi encarnación —que es la esencia de la Navidad—
fue un regalo de un valor infinito. ¡Sin embargo, me
empobreció inmensamente! Renuncié a los esplendo-
res majestuosos del cielo para convertirme en un bebé
indefenso. Mis padres eran pobres, jóvenes, y estaban
lejos de casa cuando nací en un establo de Belén.

Durante mi vida realicé muchos milagros, todos
en beneficio de los demás, no del mío. Después de
ayunar cuarenta días y cuarenta noches en el desier-
to, fui tentado por el diablo para que *convirtiera unas
piedras en pan.* Sin embargo, me rehusé a hacer ese
milagro, a pesar de que estaba hambriento. Durante
años viví sin tener una casa que pudiera haber consi-
derado mía.

¡Debido a que estuve dispuesto a experimentar
una vida de pobreza, tú eres increíblemente rico! Mi
vida, muerte y resurrección abrieron el camino para
que mis seguidores llegaran a ser *hijos de Dios* y here-
deros de una riqueza gloriosa y eterna. Mi Presencia
permanente es también un regalo precioso. ¡Celebra
todos estos regalos maravillosos con gratitud y un
Gozo desbordante!

2 Corintios 8.9; Mateo 4.1-4;
Juan 1.12; Lucas 2.10

Diciembre 22

¡Yo soy la Luz del mundo! Muchos celebran la temporada de Adviento iluminando sus casas con luces de colores y decorando los arbolitos de Navidad. Esta es una manera de simbolizar mi venida al mundo: la Luz eterna irrumpiendo a través de la oscuridad y abriendo el camino al cielo. Nada puede revertir este plan glorioso de la salvación. Todos los que confían en mí como Salvador son adoptados en mi familia real para siempre.

Mi Luz resplandece en las tinieblas, y las tinieblas no han prevalecido sobre ella. No importa cuánta maldad e incredulidad veas en este mundo lleno de oscuridad, yo continúo brillando, como un faro de esperanza para aquellos que tienen ojos que realmente ven. Por eso es fundamental mantener tu mirada en la Luz tanto como te sea posible. *¡Fija tus ojos en mí, mi amado!* A través de miles de elecciones bien pensadas, puedes encontrarme —«verme»— mientras vas haciendo tu camino por la vida. Tener mi Espíritu te ayudará a perseverar en la encantadora disciplina de mantener tus ojos en mí. *El que me sigue no andará en tinieblas, sino que tendrá la Luz de la Vida.*

JUAN 8.12; EFESIOS 1.5; JUAN 1.5;
HEBREOS 12.2

Los que confían en mí renovarán sus fuerzas. Pasar tiempo a solas conmigo es muy bueno para ti, aunque resulta cada vez más contracultural. Tener varios trabajos a la vez y estar siempre ocupados en algo se ha convertido en la norma. Durante la época de Adviento, hay todavía más cosas que hacer y más lugares a donde ir. Te animo a que por un tiempo te liberes de toda actividad y compromiso. Busca mi Rostro y disfruta de mi Presencia, recordando que todo en la Navidad tiene que ver conmigo.

Esperar en mí es un acto de fe, confiando en que la oración realmente es determinante. Ven a mí con tu cansancio y tus cargas. Sé sincero y auténtico conmigo. Descansa en mi Presencia y háblame de tus preocupaciones. Déjame quitar las cargas de sobre tus hombros doloridos. Confía en que yo puedo hacer mucho más que todo lo que puedas imaginar o pedir.

A medida que concluyes estos momentos de tranquilidad, escúchame diciéndote en un susurro: «Yo estaré contigo durante todo el día». Alégrate por las renovadas fuerzas que has adquirido al pasar tiempo conmigo.

Isaías 40.31; Salmos 27.8;
Mateo 11.28; Efesios 3.20

Diciembre 24

PREPARA TU CORAZÓN para la celebración de mi nacimiento. Escucha a Juan el Bautista diciendo: *«Preparen el camino del Señor, háganle sendas derechas»*.

La Navidad es el tiempo para alegrarse de mi milagrosa encarnación, cuando *el Verbo se hizo hombre y habitó entre la gente*. Yo me identifiqué con la humanidad al grado sumo, convirtiéndome en un hombre y fijando mi residencia en tu mundo. No dejes que la familiaridad de este asombroso milagro disminuya su efecto sobre ti. Reconoce que yo soy el Regalo por sobre todos los regalos. *¡Y alégrate en mí!*

Ábreme tu corazón. Hazme un lugar en él y medita en las maravillas de mi entrada en la historia humana. Considera estos acontecimientos desde la perspectiva de los pastores, que velaban y guardaban sus rebaños en la noche. Ellos vieron primero a un ángel y luego a una *multitud* de ellos iluminando el cielo y proclamando: *«¡Gloria a Dios en las alturas, y en la tierra paz a los que gozan de su buena voluntad!»*. Admira la Gloria de mi nacimiento, como lo hicieron los pastores, y responde con el asombro de un niño.

MARCOS 1.3; JUAN 1.14;
FILIPENSES 4.4; LUCAS 2.13, 14

Yo soy EL VERBO *que se hizo hombre.* Siempre he sido y siempre seré. *En el principio ya existía el Verbo, y el Verbo estaba con Dios, y el Verbo era Dios.* Cuando pienses en mí como un bebé nacido en Belén, no pierdas de vista mi divinidad. ¡Este bebé que creció y llegó a ser el Salvador-Hombre es también Dios Todopoderoso! No podría haber sido de otra manera. Sacrificar mi vida e incluso morir habrían sido insuficientes si yo no fuera Dios. Así que alégrate de que *el Verbo* que entró al mundo como un niño indefenso es Aquel que trajo al mundo a la existencia.

Aunque era rico, por ti me hice pobre, para que mediante mi pobreza tú llegaras a ser rico. ¡Ningún regalo de Navidad jamás podría compararse con el tesoro que tienes en mí! *Yo echo tus transgresiones tan lejos como lejos del oriente está el occidente*, liberándote de toda condenación. ¡Te regalo una Vida gloriosa inimaginable que no tendrá fin! La mejor respuesta a este asombroso Regalo es recibirlo alegre y agradecidamente.

JUAN 1.1, 14; HEBREOS 1.1, 2;
2 CORINTIOS 8.9; SALMOS 103.12

Diciembre 26

¡YO SOY EL MÁS GRANDE REGALO IMAGINABLE! Cuando me tienes a mí, tienes todo lo que precisas para esta vida y la siguiente. Yo he prometido *proveer todo lo que necesitas, conforme a mis gloriosas riquezas*. Sin embargo, en ocasiones mis amados no disfrutan de las riquezas que les doy debido a la ingratitud. En lugar de regocijarse con todo lo que tienen, anhelan tener lo que no tienen. Como resultado, se vuelven descontentos y hasta amargados.

Yo te estoy entrenando para que aprendas a practicar *el sacrificio de gratitud*, agradeciéndome *en toda circunstancia*. Primero, da gracias por las bendiciones que puedes ver en tu vida. Luego, detente y piensa en el increíble regalo de conocerme. Yo soy tu Dios viviente, tu amoroso Salvador, tu Compañero constante. No importa lo mucho o lo poco que tengas en este mundo, tu relación conmigo te hace inmensamente rico. De modo que cada vez que cuentes tus bendiciones, asegúrate de incluir la riqueza infinita que tienes en mí. Agrégame a la ecuación, y tu gratitud crecerá de manera exponencial. ¡Lo que sea que tengas + Yo = una fortuna incalculable!

FILIPENSES 4.19; SALMOS 116.17;
1 TESALONICENSES 5.18

Yo TE DOY UN GOZO que es independiente de las circunstancias. ¡Yo mismo me doy a ti! *Todos los tesoros de la sabiduría y del conocimiento están escondidos en mí.* Debido a que soy infinitamente sabio y lo sé todo, nunca se acabarán los tesoros que podrás hallar.

Soy una fuente de Gozo y ansío desbordarme en tu vida. Ábreme tu corazón, mente y espíritu de par en par para recibirme en una medida plena. Mi Gozo no es de este mundo, por lo que puede coexistir con las circunstancias más complejas. Sin que importe lo que esté sucediendo en tu vida, *la Luz de mi Presencia* continúa brillando sobre ti. Mírame con un corazón confiado. Si persistes en buscarme, mi Gozo-Luz irrumpirá con poder a través de las más oscuras nubes de tormenta que cubran el cielo de tu vida. Deja que esta Luz celestial te inunde, ilumine tu perspectiva y te llene de una alegría perdurable.

Recuerda que tienes en el cielo *una herencia indestructible, incontaminada e inmarchitable.* Puesto que *crees en mí, el Gozo indescriptible y glorioso es tuyo.* ¡Ahora y para siempre!

COLOSENSES 2.3; SALMOS 89.15, 16;
1 PEDRO 1.3, 4, 8

Diciembre 28

¡CUÁN PRECIOSO ES MI GRAN AMOR! Verdaderamente, este es un regalo de proporciones celestiales. Recuerda el precio indecible que pagué a fin de asegurar este regalo para ti: soporté la tortura, la humillación y la muerte. Mi disposición a sufrir tanto por ti demuestra cuánto te amo.

Quiero que comprendas cuán asombrosamente valioso eres en mí. ¡Te he dado el tesoro inapreciable de mi Amor eterno! Este regalo te hace muchísimo más rico que un multimillonario, aun cuando pudieras poseer muy pocas cosas en este mundo. Así que mantén la cabeza bien alta mientras avanzas por la vida, sabiendo que este glorioso tesoro interno que tienes es tu porción a cada paso del camino.

Alégrate de que mi Amor además de no tener precio, sea *también* inagotable. Siempre puedes contar con él porque es aún más confiable que la salida del sol cada mañana. Deja que este Amor mío por ti te llene de Gozo exuberante mientras vas recorriendo *la senda de la Vida* conmigo.

SALMOS 36.7; 2 CORINTIOS 4.7;
SALMOS 16.11

Deja que mi Paz gobierne en tu corazón, y sé agradecido. Y permite que mi Espíritu te ayude para que lo logres. El Espíritu Santo vive en ti, por lo que su fruto —*Amor, Gozo, Paz*— está siempre disponible para ti. Una forma sencilla de pedirle que te ayude es orando: «Espíritu Santo, lléname con tu Paz». Trata de permanecer quieto en algún lugar tranquilo hasta que te sientas relajado y en calma. Cuando llegues a ese estado de tranquilidad de espíritu te será más fácil buscar mi Rostro y disfrutar de mi Presencia.

Mientras descansas conmigo, dedica un tiempo a darme las gracias por las muchas cosas buenas que te doy. Al concentrarte en mí y mis bendiciones abundantes, deja que tu corazón se inflame con gratitud e incluso *salte de alegría*. Uno de los más preciosos dones imaginables es mi *manto de justicia* que cubre tus pecados. Estas gloriosas *ropas de salvación* constituyen una bendición inapreciable para todos los que confían en mí como Salvador. El regalo de la justicia eterna, adquirido a través de mi sangre, te provee un fundamento firme para la Paz y el Gozo.

Colosenses 3.15; Gálatas 5.22, 23;
Salmos 28.7; Isaías 61.10

Diciembre 30

Yo soy el Alfa y la Omega, el Principio y el Fin. Mi perspectiva no está limitada por el tiempo. Debido a que soy infinito, soy capaz de ver y entender todo al mismo tiempo. Esto me hace la Persona ideal para estar a cargo de tu vida. Conozco el final de tu vida terrestre tan bien como el comienzo, y sé todo lo que sucede en el intermedio. Tú eres un ser finito y caído; tu comprensión es limitada y está lejos de ser perfecta. Así que confiar en mí en lugar de confiar en *tu propia inteligencia* es la manera más razonable de vivir, y también la más gozosa.

El final de tu vida no es algo que debes temer. Es simplemente el último paso en tu viaje al cielo. Puedo ver ese suceso tan claramente como te estoy viendo ahora. Además, debido a que yo soy la Omega —el Fin— ya estoy ahí. Te estaré esperando cuando llegues a este destino glorioso. Así que cada vez que sientas la tensión de tu viaje por este mundo, fija tus ojos en *el Fin*… ¡y alégrate!

APOCALIPSIS 21.6; PROVERBIOS 3.5;
SALMOS 73.24; HEBREOS 12.2

AHORA QUE ESTÁS LLEGANDO AL FINAL de este año, mira hacia atrás… y también hacia adelante. Pídeme que te ayude a repasar los aspectos más destacados de este año que termina: los tiempos difíciles tanto como los tiempos felices. Trata de percibir *mi Presencia* en estos recuerdos, pues siempre he estado junto a ti en cada paso que has dado.

Cuando te aferraste a mí en busca de ayuda en medio de los tiempos difíciles te consolé con mi amorosa Presencia. También estuve siempre presente en las circunstancias que te llenaron de gran Gozo. Permanecí a tu lado tanto en las cumbres de las montañas como en la profundidad de los valles y en todos los lugares intermedios.

Tu futuro se extiende ante ti desde aquí hasta la eternidad. Yo soy el Compañero que nunca te dejará, el Guía que conoce cada paso del camino que tienes por delante. ¡El Gozo que te espera en el paraíso es *indescriptible y glorioso*! Mientras te dispones a entrar en un nuevo año, deja que la Luz del cielo brille sobre ti y despeje tu camino.

ISAÍAS 41.13; SALMOS 16.11;
SALMOS 48.14; 1 PEDRO 1.8, 9

Acerca de la autora

Los escritos devocionales de Sarah Young son reflexiones personales surgidas de sus tiempos diarios de quietud leyendo la Biblia, orando y recopilando ideas para sus libros. Con ventas sobre los dieciséis millones de ejemplares en todo el mundo, *Jesús te llama* ha aparecido en todas las principales listas de éxitos de ventas. Sus escritos incluyen *Jesús te llama*, *Jesús hoy*, *Jesús te llama: mi primer libro de historias bíblicas*; *Jesús te llama: para pequeñitos-Bilingüe*, *Jesús te llama: 365 devocionales para niños*, cada uno animando a sus lectores a buscar una verdadera intimidad con Cristo. Sarah y su marido fueron misioneros en Japón y Australia. Actualmente viven en los Estados Unidos. Ella escribió *Jesús te llama* pensando en ayudar a sus lectores a conectarse no solo con Jesús, la Palabra viva, sino también con la Biblia, la Palabra de Dios infalible y eterna.

Sarah se esfuerza por mantener sus escritos devocionales siendo coherentes con esas normas inmutables. Muchos lectores han escrito diciendo que sus libros los han ayudado a perfeccionar su amor por la Palabra de Dios. Como ella lo dice en la Introducción de *Jesús te llama*: «Los devocionales [...] son para leerse lentamente, en lo posible en un lugar tranquilo y con la Biblia abierta».

Sarah es bíblicamente conservadora en su fe y reformada en su doctrina. Obtuvo una maestría en estudios bíblicos y consejería en el Covenant Theological Seminary, St. Louis, Missouri. Es miembro de la Iglesia Presbiteriana en Norteamérica (PCA), donde su esposo, Stephen, es un ministro ordenado. Ellos continúan siendo misioneros a través de *Mission to the World*, la junta para las misiones de la PCA.

Sarah pasa gran parte de su tiempo en oración, leyendo la Biblia y memorizando versículos. Disfruta orando diariamente por los lectores de sus libros.

Sarah Young
Jesús te llama

ISBN: 9780718093112   **ISBN:** 9781602554191

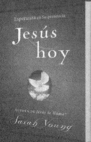

ISBN: 9781602559684   **ISBN:** 9780529120861   **ISBN:** 9780718039363

{ Devocionales llenos de tesoros excepcionales inspirados
del cielo para cada día del año. }